Praise for FALLEN GODS:

Beneath the fantasy and horror, a simmering love story brews. One that left me uneasy and completely unsure how to feel. Not because Ms. Simper failed, but because she succeeded so very, very well.
-Evie Drae, award-winning author of Beauregard and the Beast

Simper has created a brilliant combination of gruesomely dark fantasy and scorching romance. The protagonists are both so flawed, you are at once drawn to and repelled by them. Simper takes the idea of grey morality and writes it to perfection.
-The Lesbian Review

The Sting of Victory tugged on the darker parts of my soul-- the parts easily tempted. In addition to a fascinating fantasy world and gripping plot, Simper offers the ultimate dark fantasy: a selfish but beautiful love story that grabs you and refuses to let go. Many of us secretly long to be loved selfishly, with an all-consuming passion, no matter the consequences. Simper captures that feeling exquisitely and, in the process, makes horror seem beautiful.
-Rae D. Magdon, award-winning author of Lucky 7

Praise for SEA AND STARS:

"If you like your fantasy with an extra dark twist, exceptional world building and deeply complex characters then reel this book in fast. You'll be hooked."
-The Lesbian Review

"The Fate of Stars, the first book in the Sea and Stars trilogy, is delightfully dark and sexy, full of lush imagery, vibrant characterization, and enough adrenaline to keep me up way past my bedtime."
-Anna Burke, award-winning author of Thorn

"The Fate of Stars is an irresistible, seductive fantasy that'll have you swooning over the beautiful mermaid, Tallora, and the badass princess, Dauriel! A five-star read that'll bring all fans of enemies-to-lovers to their knees!"
-Michele Quirke, author of The Fires of Treason

Other books by S D Simper:

The Sting of Victory (Fallen Gods 1)
Among Gods and Monsters (Fallen Gods 2)
Blood of the Moon (Fallen Gods 3)
Tear the World Apart (Fallen Gods 4)
Eve of Endless Night (Fallen Gods 5)
Chaos Undone (Fallen Gods 6)

The Moon, the Stars, and the Desert Below
(Patreon Exclusive)

Carmilla and Laura

Beneath the Dark Moon (Sea and Star Prequel)
The Fate of Stars (Sea and Stars 1)
Heart of Silver Flame (Sea and Stars 2)
Death's Abyss (Sea and Stars 3)

Beneath the Loch

Forthcoming books:

Fallen Gods: Series 2

CHAOS UNDONE

S D SIMPER

© 2024 Endless Night Publications

Fallen Gods 6: Chaos Undone

Copyright © 2024 Endless Night Publications

All rights reserved. Except as permitted under the U.S. Copyright Act of 1976, no part of this publication may be reproduced, stored in a retrieval system, or transmitted in any form or by any means electronic, mechanical, photocopying, recording, or otherwise without the written permission of the publisher. For information regarding permissions, send a query to admin@sdsimper.com.

Cover art by Jade Merien

Cover design by Jerah Moss

Maps by Marshall Simper

Interior Art by Cynthia Inesta

ISBN (Paperback): 978-1-952349-23-2

Visit the author at www.sdsimper.com

Facebook: sdsimper
Twitter: @sdsimper
Instagram: sdsimper
TikTok: @sdsimper

For Anna

Publisher's Note: Chaos Undone is a fantasy horror novel intended for adults and may contain material upsetting to some readers. Please visit sdsimper.com to view a list of spoiler-free content warnings.

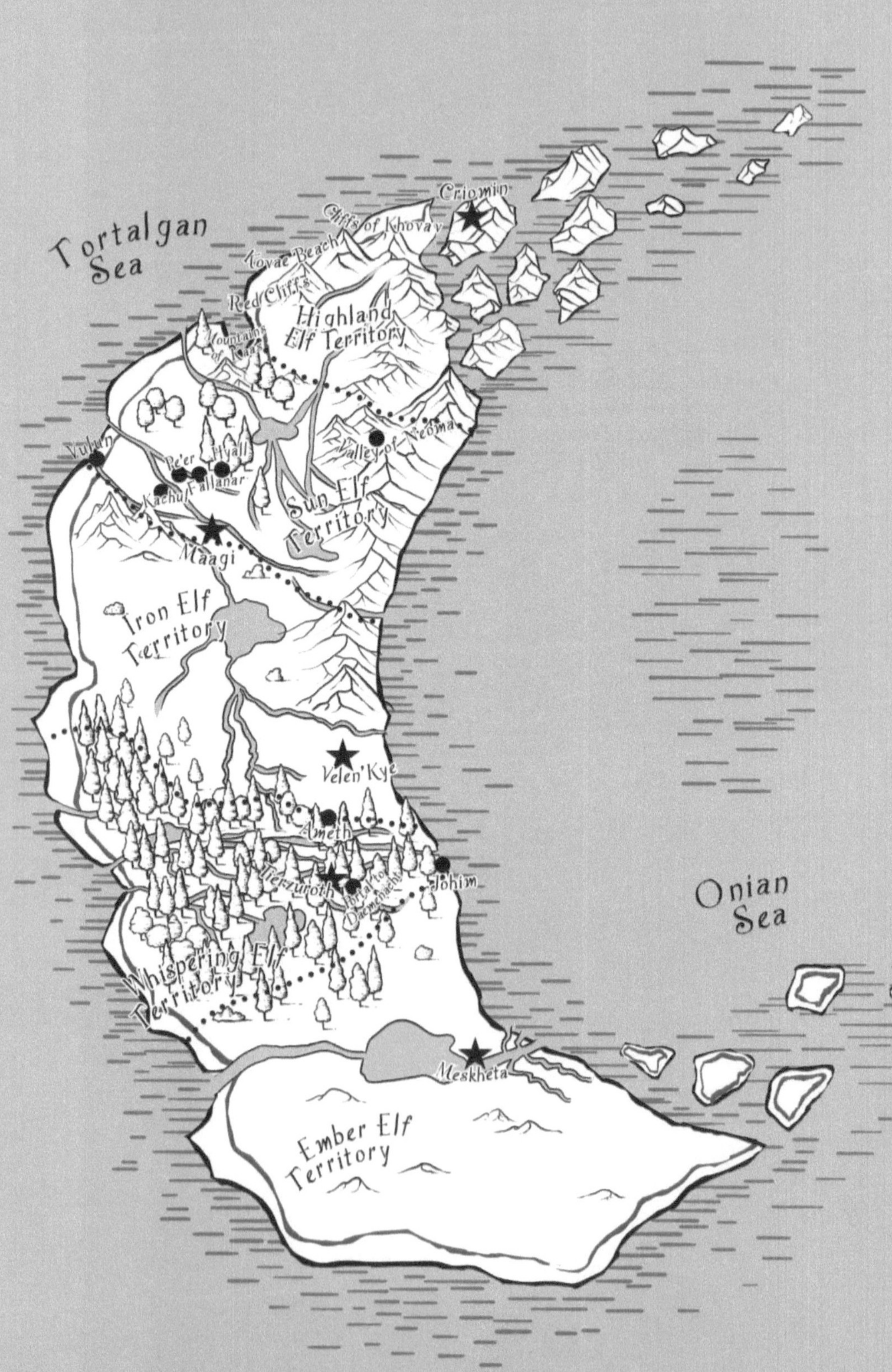

Tortalgan Sea
Criomin
Cliffs of Khovay
Kovae Beach
Red Cliffs
Highland Elf Territory
Mountains of Raaz
Valley of Neoma
Vulun
Pe'er
Hyall
Kachul
Fallanar
Sun Elf Territory
Maagi
Iron Elf Territory
Velen'Kye
Ameth
Tierzuroth
Portal for
Daemonahu
Johim
Onian Sea
Whispering Elf Territory
Meskheta
Ember Elf Territory

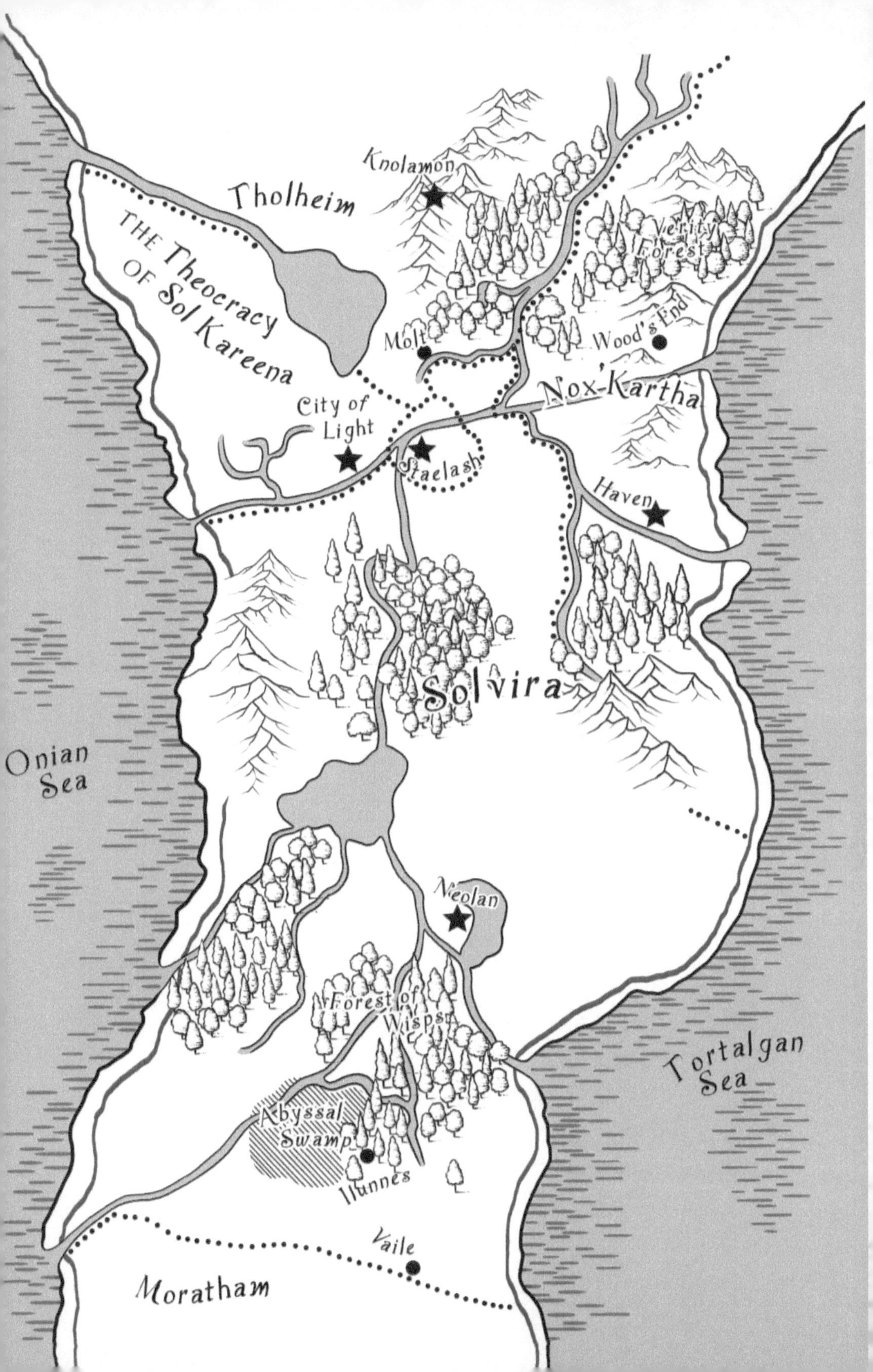

Tholheim
Knolamon
Verity Forest
THE Theocracy OF Sol Kareena
Molt
Wood's End
City of Light
Nox-Kartha
Staelash
Haven
Onian Sea
Solvira
Neolan
Forest of Wisps
Tortalgan Sea
Abyssal Swamp
Ilunnes
Vaile
Moratham

NAMES

THE COUNCIL OF NOX'KARTHA
Casvir – Kas-**veer**
Murishani – Mur-eh-**shah**-nee

THE ROYAL COUNCIL OF SOLVIRA
Etolié – Eh-**toh**-lee-ey
Zoldar—**Zohl**-dar

THE COUNCIL OF STAELASH
Marielle Vors – **Mair**-ee-el **Vohrs**
Zorlaeus Vors – Zor-**ley**-uhs

OTHER PLAYERS
Flowridia Darkleaf – Floh-**rid**-ee-uh **Dahrk**-leef
Ayla Darkleaf – **Ai**-luh **Dahrk**-leef
Sora Makosa – **Sohr**-ruh Muh-**koh**-sah'
Khastra – **Kas**-truh
Kah'Sheen – Kuh-**sheen**
Uluron – **Oo**-luh-ron
Soliel – Suh-**lil**
Dira - **Dir**-uh

GODS OF CELESTIÉRE

Sol Kareena – Sohl Kuh-**ree**-nuh

Eionei – **Eye**-uhn-eye

Staella – **Stey**-luh

Alystra – Ah-**lees**-truh

Morathma – Moh-**roth**-muh

Ilune – Eye-**loon**

GODS OF SHA'DEMONI

Ku'Shya – Koo-**shy**-uh

Onias – Uhn-**eye**-uhs

Izthuni – Iz-**thoon**-eye

THOSE WHO HAVE PASSED

Demitri – Dih-**mee**-tree

Thalmus—**Thah**-muhs

Odessa—Oh-**des**-uh

Alauriel Solviraes—Ah-**law**-ree-ehl Sohl-**veer**-es

Mereen Fireborn – Mer-**een Fire**-bohrn

Tazel Fireborn – **Taa**-zuhl **Fire**-bohrn

Sarai Fireborn – Suh-**rye Fire**-bohrn

Neoma – Ney-**oh**-muh

PROLOGUE

One year after the end of the world . . .

At the cusp of midnight, Etolié stared, disgusted, upon a dilapidated structure in the Mountains of Kaas.

Her golden wings illuminated the shadows around her, yet the prevailing sound of silence unnerved her most of all. Not unnatural, no, but the sort of quiet that settled only in the presence of a predator. The hair rose on the back of her neck. The chances of her dying were inordinately higher than usual, and dying would be deeply unpleasant due to the fine print of her contract with Imperator Casvir.

Twenty-two years to go, and he would gladly drag her spirit back to complete her servitude.

She whispered a soft prayer: "Goddess Momma, stay near."

A gentle presence within her stirred, filling her soul with warmth.

The building had once been grand, a place of nightmares made manifest, but now it was little more than a hollow shell filled with ash. Etolié had only heard of the fire, but now saw the results, wondering if it had purged the evil that reigned within or simply enhanced it.

The porch had collapsed, as had half the door. Etolié ducked inside, her wings casting light upon the ruined structure within.

The remains of charred bones lay shattered upon the floor—an unnatural amount, far more spines than one might expect. What little décor remained on the walls had burned, now covered in soot or bearing fragile black edges. Her steps did not have to be loud to sound like gunshots, the stillness of this place only fueling her rising fear.

Because she wasn't alone. That was simply fact.

Amidst unnatural shifting shadows, Etolié loudly said, "Ayla?"

The name echoed across the floors and stone walls.

"Ayla Darkleaf! It's Starspawn!"

It's not that she liked the 'pet' name, though she was neutral at worst, but hopefully it conveyed that this was no trap, no illusion.

"I know you're here! The locals said they hear wailing some nights. Superstitious folk, but wailing is difficult to dismiss. And it's too damn evil for anyone else to be here."

She swore the temperature of the room fell.

"Ayla?"

From around the corner appeared a wraith of a woman, gaunter than Etolié's memory recollected, pale enough to reflect the golden light. Ayla had never looked healthy, but her skin had become paper, dried and withered, her hair brittle and matted against her scalp. Her silver eyes—forever unnerving—were dull, yet her clothes looked deceptively clean, as though hastily put on.

A mere echo of the legendary monster, The Endless Night. Last Etolié had seen her, she had been screaming, covered in Flowridia's blood. Etolié did not have to like her to be haunted by the memory of Ayla cradling her dead wife's corpse.

And all to the backdrop of an infant's cries. Ayla had not even looked at it.

Ayla spoke with a dusty voice. It cracked at the seams. "What do you want?"

"Straight to the point. I always liked that about you—which is saying something because I don't actually like you."

"And you have not lost your charm," Ayla replied, her dead eyes rolling. "Get to the point."

"Casvir's war is escalating. The Ember Elves are dead. Small pockets of Iron Elves are hanging on, but it's a fool's hope. He's talking about returning to Tholheim, or even marching on Moratham. Things are moving fast, and I'm fucking terrified."

"I do not see how any of that is my problem."

"I know. And I didn't come here to convince you to join the war, as invaluable as you would be."

Ayla's exhaustion was alarming to see, and while Etolié had no love for her, she recognized that vacant stare. She saw it in the mirror some days, when the loneliness rose to choke her.

"I don't want to hurt you," Etolié continued, her empathy rising, even for this evil creature. "Please know that as much as anyone can possibly understand what you've been through this past year . . . I'm there. Not trying to undermine it, but I know how it feels to lose your reason to live. And it's a struggle, some days, to not give in to the urge to lie in bed until I rot. When Khastra was killed—"

"I'm not a priestess. Do not unburden yourself to me."

"I'm sorry. I know." Etolié had thought she was prepared, had a whole speech at the tip of her tongue, but all of that fell apart to consider who Ayla had left behind. "It's been a year, like I said.

Which means she's just turned one. She hasn't quite grasped words yet, but she's shockingly light on her feet. Charming little speck of light—and fuck me, but she looks exactly like you."

Etolié's breath hitched, the rising sensation of danger filling her as Ayla's dead eyes sharpened. "Don't," the vampire spat, and Etolié held up defensive hands, even as Ayla took an imposing step forward.

"Casvir is molding her to become the weapon he wants, but you and I both know . . ." Etolié's words faltered. "She can't stay there."

A sardonic grin tugged on Ayla's cracked lips, splitting and healing the skin. "I'm sure you're doing a grand job steering her toward the light."

"Listen, I have a plan. My momma has agreed to take her in. All I need is a reason for him to not look for her, and you're the perfect alibi. We fake her death."

Ayla raised an eyebrow. "You want to fake a toddler's death?"

"Ayla Darkleaf returns in a fit of jealous rage and kills her own flesh and blood? He wouldn't question it. You have illusion magic, and I'll make certain Murishani isn't around to witness it."

"And what's to stop me from actually tearing her head off?"

Etolié had feared this, and she spoke the cruelest words she could. "Because that's not what Flowers would have wanted."

Ayla's sneer twisted her entire face. "Don't say that name."

"Why haven't you killed her already? Clearly you don't give a shit enough for that. So what do you have to lose? Just imagine how fucking furious Casvir would be."

"Admittedly a compelling point."

"My momma will take her. Even if Casvir does eventually catch hints that she's still alive, you tricked him, and she's safe in Celestière. He can't navigate the mists."

Ayla said nothing, stiffening as she looked to the ground. Etolié prided herself on reading people—except that damn monster spawn. A closed book, and Etolié feared her reasons hadn't resonated after all.

"Fine," Ayla whispered. "I shall assist in faking her death. Tell me when, and I shall put on a show."

"Swear on Flowers' grave you won't actually rip the kid's head off."

Ayla glared—not the most pleasant thing to be on the receiving end of. "I swear."

"Excellent. Let's discuss a plan. Doesn't have to be complicated. And I promise—Flowers would want this."

"Don't manipulate me. I already agreed."

"But I mean it—"

"Shut up," Ayla said, seething. "I will not discuss plans with you. Tomorrow at sundown, make certain Murishani is nowhere near the . . . the child."

She spat the word, the derision lingering like poisoned air. "That works. Once you've done it, wait with her in Sha'Demoni. I'll find you as soon as I can."

"Good. Now get out. I have much to prepare."

"Nice talk," Etolié said, unnerved by it all.

But she wasn't slain as she left the ruins, heard nothing as she traipsed back into the mountainous arena. *Goddess Momma, everything is in motion.*

Fear not. All will be well, Etolié.

Etolié spared a glance for the ruins behind her, the ash unsettled by her presence. She hadn't wished to unearth Ayla from the depths of despair, but there simply was no other alibi, no one unhinged enough to murder the imperator's protégé in his own home.

Etolié summoned her focus, then meditated upon her home in Solvira.

When her body vanished, it left not a trace.

Etolié stepped into a broken world, nerves alight from the residual anger she'd witnessed. "Fucking hell, Darkleaf," she muttered, surveying the misty, monochrome land, "you'd better not have actually killed her."

Etolié hadn't been there. She had been distracting Murishani, the one risk factor. But Casvir certainly believed it, and if the fist-sized hole in the door was any indicator, he had never been more unhinged.

Sha'Demoni spread before her, the details of the landscape lost in the endless fog. She sent a sparkle of light high into the sky, hoping to catch the attention of one of its most fearsome residents.

In the distance came a small burst of silver flame.

Etolié ran, her wings signifying her as an interloper. In the distance, yellow eyes peered upon her, some curious, others hungry. Etolié ignored them, prepared to scream the Goddess of War's name in their faces if necessary, and slowed when she reached a quiet haven.

There sat Ayla beneath the boughs of a shadowy tree, a statue cradling a bundle of infinite worth. She had washed up, her hair luxurious instead of matted, apparently keen to be put together when Casvir saw her again. The baby slept, and that was no easy feat, for she was fitful and wild and vivacious. A legend in the making, which was a secret only they knew.

And Sora, though the half-elf hadn't been seen in years.

It seemed Ayla held a magician's touch, however, for Etolié had never seen the child so still—not in the arms of a stranger. In the moments before she noticed Etolié's light, Ayla gazed upon the sleeping baby's face with something . . . different upon her oft fierce countenance.

Etolié bounded forward, to which Ayla responded by glaring. She placed a finger to her lips, keeping her protective hold upon the baby.

When Etolié was a mere step away, Ayla finally whispered, "She is asleep."

"For the best," Etolié replied, nearly inaudibly, but Ayla was a creature known for heightened senses. "We don't want to attract attention."

"The demons won't talk."

"We shouldn't stay any longer than necessary." Etolié knelt beside Ayla and the cradled child, the small reveal of pudgy cheeks and dark eyelashes a relief after the wailing in the castle. "Casvir bought it. They all did. He's fucking furious, so you'd better hide."

"Easy."

"Well, Celestière awaits."

In a normal interaction, the statement would reasonably trigger someone to offer the baby—at least, Etolié assumed. But Ayla remained still, the barest hitch to her breath, despite not needing to breathe.

Hesitation slowed Ayla's actions, though she did finally offer the sleeping, swaddled bundle.

But Etolié did not move to accept her, instead speaking soft words—words she prayed she would not regret. "If you have reservations, I don't have to take her."

Taken aback, Ayla pulled the infant back to her chest. "I beg your pardon?"

"I'm not saying you're exactly 'mother of the year' material, but I would never keep a baby away from her momma. Not if her momma wanted to keep her."

Dangerous words, and Etolié remained silent as Ayla visibly wrestled within herself, her shock fading to something softer as her gaze fell upon the baby once more. She stroked a tender line across the baby's face, pushing the blanket away to reveal more of her precious countenance, her wispy black hair thin but growing, her precious ears ending in rounded points. She was ashen, yes, but not pale, her skin a smooth olive instead.

If she opened her eyes, there would be precious silver. If she smiled, there would be fangs.

"I should not," Ayla whispered, but the words were unsure.

"I won't force you, but my momma would understand."

"It would not be safer."

"I don't doubt you would protect her."

"She deserves a finer life."

"Then give her one. Be something other than a fucking wraith in the ruins. You're a powerful person. So be fucking powerful."

Ayla kept her stare upon the baby's sleeping face. The shadow of a smile flickered upon the woman's mournful countenance. "I don't see me at all in her visage. We share a few features, but by god—she's Flowra."

And with that name, Etolié knew the baby's fate was sealed.

Ayla faced her, determination on her sharp features. "Fine. She is mine."

"She *is* yours. I won't argue." Etolié stood up, dusting dirt from her illusionary dress. "If you need anything at all, find me in Solvira, or send me a message. I'm happy to assist with her Silver Fire outbursts, but you're better equipped, honestly. My momma knows a few things about raising a baby with the Silver Fire, so don't be shy. That said . . ."

Against all odds, against every fact and terrible truth Etolié knew of this awful woman, in seeing the protective hold Ayla had upon her baby girl, hell itself would not move her. Certainly not Casvir.

". . . I believe in you, Darkleaf. Raise her in love."

PART ONE

CHAOS

 CHAPTER 1

Current era . . .

In the darkest moments of the night, it always began with dissonance.

Ayla did not sleep. She sat on the floor beside her bed, seeking to be invisible, lest she cause a scare. And all was well this night, until those gentle, lulling breaths—Flowridia's sweet, precious breaths—stopped. Ayla heard it like a break in an orchestra, the pause before the crescendo.

The crashing of cymbals was violent and harsh, the sudden catch in the cadence of her sleeping breaths. A gasp; a cry; her wailing filled the night. Ayla split her palm with her nail to keep quiet, though she longed with all her heart to soothe her.

Flowridia thrashed about, caught in her bedsheets. But to restrain her would only make it worse. Ayla sat aside, helpless, tears rising in her throat as her wife screamed to shatter the silent night.

What visions of horror did she see? Surely bloodstains in an underground dungeon, knives and gore, memories of tearful pleas for mercy falling upon a monster's deaf ears . . .

Or perhaps those were only Ayla's visions.

Eventually Flowridia sat up, her frail body heaving from her panicked cries. Ayla peeked as Flowridia's fingers smoothed across her face, her treasured locks of hair—restored by magic, and thank the wretched Celestial for that—and finally caught her breath when she met Ayla's eyes. Flowridia's fear spiked anew. Ayla smelled it like her cold sweat and ineffably floral aura.

"It's all right, Flowra," Ayla whispered, for her name was the best way to coax her home. "It's over. You're safe."

When Flowridia reached, Ayla crawled to her side. In the falling action of the orchestral cacophony, Flowridia clung to her like the edge of a cliff, weeping, heart racing as her mind settled back into reality. Ayla held her tight, whispering tender affirmations as sweetly as she could muster. "Breathe, Flowra. Breathe. I love you."

"I'm sorry, Ayla."

Gods, her anguish was too much. "Never say that."

Every night, they played this song, and Ayla could hum the finale herself. Flowridia would drift back to sleep, hopefully resting until morning and not repeat this discordant melody of nightmares and panicked pleas.

And when Flowridia had fallen back into the lull of dreams, Ayla began her own dissonant solo of guilt, weeping silently into the night.

There were more suited caretakers than Ayla. She let them lead.

Sora was a constant, and as much as Ayla despised the judgement of her presence, she could not deny her use. In the passing months, Sora had become something of a shadow at Flowridia's side, encouraging her to walk, to run, to garden as she did before. Flowridia did not speak her feelings, no, but she did laugh and allow her newfound sister to lead. Sora helped her to eat, exercise her mutilated hand, and though their interactions often contained silence, their familial bond meant they shared a few common traits—notably, their love of the outdoors and animals.

Flowridia grew in Sora's company, which was more than she did in Ayla's.

Casvir was not constant, but he was consistent, visiting when he was not busy with the war and escorting her on walks to regain strength. Ayla could not say if she imagined the judgement in his silent glances or not, but he was good for distracting Flowridia, keeping her grounded as only a father figure could do—though the word was distasteful in Ayla's mouth. But this was not the time for grudges. Ayla bit her tongue in his presence, content to leave the two alone to make puerile jests or speak of magic.

Flowridia smiled in Casvir's company, which was more than she did in Ayla's.

Etolié visited only once, but the Celestial held her own thinly veiled anguish behind a constantly leaking dam. Perhaps she hadn't realized Ayla could see past her illusions—to her unkempt hair and swollen eyes, her naked form slowly withering away. During her visit, Ayla walked past a closed door and heard her quiet sobs, a wreck since General Khastra had gone, captured by the elves Casvir fought in his endless war.

Ayla understood that all too well.

She remembered the day they took Demitri, Flowridia's anguish still an echo in her mind. Ayla's own heart had ached—a rare thing—to watch him dragged away in chains after he had nearly torn Sora's arm off. His bestial mind had won. He did not even know his name. Casvir did not crush his mind to make him compliant, and Ayla respected that. Instead, the wolf remained behind bars, so lost in his fear that he snarled at all who passed— even at Flowra, who had wept all through the night and struggled to eat for days.

Not Ayla, though, her vampiric aura alluring to creatures such as he. When her mind became loud, she danced into the shadows of his cage and stroked his soft head, soothing him into compliance. "Somewhere in your head is the boy she adores. Please, hold on. She's lost without you."

Every day, Flowridia flinched when her left hand had to lift on its own, her pain chronic and silent—for she wouldn't speak of it. Not to Ayla, at least.

Sora knitted her a glove to fit the mangled limb and keep it warm on difficult days. Casvir provided braces for her comfort and doctors for its stability.

"The doctor said it might benefit from, um, massaging," Flowridia had said one day. "To help the blood flow. Is that something you know anything about?"

Ayla had fallen silent at the offer. Of course she was capable, but behind each blink she saw the tender, exposed tendons, each bone skillfully split and restored . . . "I am not the right person to do that for you."

Flowridia hadn't asked again.

Flowridia winced any time she passed a mirror, those auburn curls restored through magic, but within them lived the memory of shears and anguished cries, thick locks of hair in a bundle idly discarded.

Ayla was cursed to have it be her memory too, and she played it on a loop in the darker times of night. Somehow, the sickening sound of metal and hair cut deeper than the torture and blood, the betrayal the deepest of all—

"*. . . strap you to the table and fuck you anyway—*"

No. There was a worse one.

But in two months, Flowra gained enough weight to no longer be in danger, had regained her feminine curves, filled in her hollow cheeks, bled her monthlies and had a proper appetite again, no longer having to be stopped from gorging herself at mealtimes.

At first, she struggled to bathe, and so Sora had assisted. But once, Ayla had stood nigh instead, witnessing the gruesome mass of scarring on her back, the nightmarish cross upon her chest. Flowridia had hunched in the tub to hide her body beneath the cover of soap. The question remained of whether she was this demure about her body in front of her sister or if it was Ayla she sought to hide from.

Ayla remembered each and every incision. She returned the responsibility of Flowridia's care to her sister, unworthy of seeing her so vulnerable.

Flowra did speak to one person—at Casvir's insistence, a Priestess of Staella was called to coax the truth from her lips and unburden her soul. Priestesses of the Goddess of Mercy specialized in healing emotional wounds, and Ayla hid herself in the shadows of their sessions, listening to the terrible truths Flowridia wouldn't say.

"It would be easier if Demitri had simply died. Then, I could mourn and move on, but instead I'm kept heartbroken because he's—"

"It's so stupid and petty to care so much about my hair, but it was always my favorite part of me growing up and for her to—"

"I can barely grasp anything with my left hand without it shooting pain—"

And sometimes, she would speak of Ayla.

"Just hearing her voice would cause me to panic. I'm still struggling. She can't ever know—"

"Just because she didn't want to do it, doesn't mean it didn't happen. She didn't rape me, but I was raped—

"I had never felt so helpless. Not even when I lived with my mother. Watching Mereen rip Ayla apart, over and over . . . I can't forget her screams—"

Once, a single refrain haunted her for days, spoken in tearful, guilty tones.

"Everyone is so worried for me, but no one worries for her. They broke open my body, but they broke open her mind. She should be sitting here, but she won't. She won't talk.

She's pulling away from me."

Hearing that, Ayla had sunk deeper into the shadows and wept.

In the darker moments of her self-loathing, Ayla went to her ruined cathedral.

A graveyard of ambition, all was ash and stone. The great walls were stained from smoke, the floor around it littered with charred leather, sooty remains of wood and bone, and with each step she took, the stagnant ash gained life, clinging to her skirts like the victims who once begged at her feet for mercy. Once, there was a statue here; all that remained were a few scorched gems amid the desiccated pile of leather and soot. Once, this had been magnificent. Once, she had been magnificent. Both had gone up in flame.

Though she had burned it down in the aftermath of Flowridia's torture in the Mountains of Kaas, it remained infested with ghosts who wailed in Ayla's memory. So many lives had been cut short within these haunted walls. So many screams echoed off the stone.

Once a sanctuary; now merely a monument to horror and shame. So many regrets, but burning it was not one of them.

Flowra didn't know. Flowra didn't know a great many things.

"This is my second monthly in a row," Flowra said one morning, apprehension in her gaze as she lingered in the washroom doorway. "Which means we can reopen the conversation of . . . you know."

The words did not come easily, trapped behind iron to which Ayla held no key. "The full moon is three weeks away."

And Flowra . . . smiled? So soft, so tentative, and Ayla shied beneath it. "All right. Three weeks."

Ayla managed to nod. Nothing more, and Flowra left her alone to contemplate.

Since she had first presented it, Ayla had studied Goddess Staella's Scroll, usually as Flowra slept in her rare instances of serenity. It was as much a curse as a blessing, but it offered the element of 'choice.'

To idly stand by as a man fucked her wife was not a choice at all. Not for either of them.

Someday, she would stuff Casvir's cock down his own throat, let him choke before she finally tore his head off. But the truth remained that she had no lead on his phylactery, Flowra's mortality ticked by, and Demitri's sanity slipped further away.

Ayla held resentment miles long—toward Flowridia for selling something Ayla equally held the right to, to Casvir, to Empress Alauriel . . . But reality held no moral lens, and Goddess Staella offered a bitter compromise; the chance to use the Silver Fire to complete the bargain themselves.

To create life.

A baby.

Sold to the highest bidder.

And so Ayla studied the scroll in quiet moments, the simplicity of the spell a part of its genius: a few tender words, a few tender touches, and an intimate act Ayla prayed they could perform.

Soon, Flowra no longer flinched in mirrors, sometimes she slept through the night without fear, and Ayla realized she was making progress. To contemplate all that her wife had lost—her familiar, a father figure, a grandmother, a mother, even Ayla herself, and so much more—meant to realize Flowridia was far more resilient than Ayla ever gave her credit for. Humans were, by nature, but Flowra especially.

Ayla could not shake the feeling that perhaps she herself was weak.

One night, as she watched Flowra's gentle breaths, Ayla wondered when the idea of touching her began bringing such visceral fear. Behind her eyelids, she relived the memory of splitting flesh beneath her knives, the ripping of skin from sinew, screams and sobs and glistening organs exposed for her study and play

"Say my name . . ."

Ayla wrenched her gaze away, lightheaded as her nails tore grounding lines across her skin, her exposed flesh pulsing relief through her stagnant blood. She bit back a scream, bombarded by Flowra's bloody face, stained with tears and dirt, the anguish in her beautiful eyes, her naked body carved with scars, the taste of blood, the feeling of plunging her fingers into flesh, into *her* and fucking her amidst the blood and dirt and darkness, her sobs, her screams, her cries—

Ayla grabbed a pillow and screamed, finding no relief in release. She tore from the bed, falling into a shadow before tearing skin from flesh and flesh from bone, silver flame rising to consume a vampiric skeleton.

She returned before morning, rebuilt, reborn, but not restored.

"It's the full moon tonight."

"Yes."

"I'll tell Casvir we'll be gone for the night," Flowridia said, her countenance lit by the gentle sunrise. So soft in her bed, but Ayla was not worthy of softness. "Then he won't worry if anyone comes to find us."

Ayla had not felt nauseous since death, but the feeling did not fade. "Are you not . . ."

Flowridia watched with earnest intent. Ayla understood. It was more than she had spoken in days.

". . . are you afraid?"

"Of pregnancy?"

"No." Ayla bit back her words, regretting poking that tender wound. But Flowridia waited. She could not be denied. ". . . of intimacy."

Flowridia's hands settled in her lap, small as she rubbed her left, coaxing feeling into the mutilated limb. "I don't know. But I feel ready to find out."

Ayla nodded.

"I've done some, um, exploration of myself alone. At the priestess' behest. It's helped."

Again, Ayla nodded, refusing to dwell on it.

"I trust you. I want to try."

Ayla said nothing at all.

Flowridia spoke so tepidly. "If you're worried, we could . . ." Her hand fell upon Ayla's upper thigh, the implication left unspoken, but that hardly mattered. The tender stroking of her fingers sounded louder than gunfire.

Thank every god, Ayla had no need to breathe. She would have no hope of keeping it steady. "We should wait for tonight."

Flowridia's hand fell away. Ayla pretended not to notice her misty gaze. "I should get breakfast anyway."

Flowridia left. Alone, Ayla's sobs came violently.

Five months had passed since their rescue, and when the sun set and the moon rose to fill the space, Ayla led Flowridia through the Shadow Realm.

Their old home awaited, but Ayla mulled over a thousand unknowns, mind racing. No breath to convey her fear, thank the gods, but surely Flowra sensed something. Surely she knew, but neither spoke a word.

Soon they emerged into a dream long forgotten, to a time when bliss was their default state of mind.

In the large estate, a layer of dust covered the floors and furniture. Flowridia beckoned her to the parlor room, then grabbed a broom from the closet and swept. "You said you needed to draw a few runes, right? I think this room will do nicely."

Lost, Ayla simply watched, fixated on the handle trembling against her love's left hand. It hurt her today, but she wouldn't say it, resilient in ways Ayla coveted. Only when Ayla was handed a piece of chalk did her mind settle upon the task at hand instead of her beloved's frail form.

"Goddess Staella won't mind if I grab a pillow, right?" Flowridia teased, genuine joy in her eye. Oh, why was it so jarring? Ayla only managed to shake her head, hiding her rising panic until Flowridia disappeared from the room.

Something far stronger than uncertainty threatened to drown her resolve. Ayla swallowed her anxiety, coping by drawing, copying in perfect lines the circles and runes drawn upon the scroll by the Goddess of Stars' hand. Perhaps this was wrong. By every god, there were so many unknowns, so many dangers. Dhampirs were wretched creatures, assuming that's even what this would be. Most women died by their fetus' teeth and claws, but most women didn't have Ayla Darkleaf to supervise a risky pregnancy.

Already, Ayla hated this awful creature, yet with that turbulent emotion came a plethora of worry, of fear, of wondering whether this baby signified the beginning or the end.

Flowridia's footsteps drew her from her tempestuous inner world. Ayla glanced back to see her holding the promised pillow, but also her exposed form. A gorgeous gown covered her body, alluring in ways Flowridia typically shied from, clearly meant for conveying intentions. Yet her stance was demure, the pillow covering the vicious scarring between her breasts.

"I-Is this all right?" Flowridia asked, timid as she shut the door. Moonlight caressed her as she stepped into the window's silver glow, the same light cast upon the emblems written onto the floor. "I thought . . . Well, it's been so long. I thought this dress might be something you'd like."

"You look beautiful," Ayla said, and though she meant it, the final word choked her. She tried to sit up and be enticing, yet something stopped her. Perhaps it was that awful scar along Flowridia's sternum, a shadow of screams and blood and desperate pleas—

Instead, Flowra came to her side, her smile nervous yet kind, kinder than Ayla deserved. "What's wrong?"

In the ensuing silence, a thousand different things bombarded Ayla's mind, apprehension freezing her tongue as she tried to force a comforting lie. Yet there came nothing, nothing at all, so when Flowra knelt before her, Ayla did what she hadn't done in five long, painful months—offer a kiss.

Oh, what tentative joy, what pleasure came from the innocent gesture. They kissed like besotted children, shy and serene. Ayla deftly parted her lips, timid in ways she hadn't felt since undeath stole her nearly two thousand years ago, but the sensation of Flowra's tongue was worth it.

"Go slow, please," came Flowra's sweet plea, and Ayla remained still, simply reacting as her love placed kiss after kiss upon her mouth. All was well, until her wife came closer—too close—and straddled her lap, coaxed Ayla to touch her, grope her, and when those beautiful, buoyant breasts filled Ayla's hands, with it came Flowra's precious moan.

Ayla's thumb caressed the mottled scar upon Flowridia's sternum and behind her eyelids came visions of blood and ecstasy, the rising pleasure of breaking her ribcage and tearing her open, revealing every beautiful, secret thing.

"Oh, Ayla . . . Oh, please say my name—"

Ayla pushed her off, the vision disappearing, replaced with Flowridia's wide eyes and broken heart. Scrambling back, she froze in the shadow. *Run away*, screamed her wicked mind. *You know it's inevitable. You can't stay.*

Upon the ritual drawing, Flowra shrunk in upon herself. "Ayla?"

Oh gods—her heartbreak.

"Is . . . Is it me?"

The panic in Ayla's stomach faded, replaced with something far more viscerally gutting. Though frozen, her mind screamed.

"I know I'm not . . ." Tears filled her beloved wife's eyes. Flowra's mutilated hand trembled as it rested on her sternum, the scar forever a reminder of pain. "You have, um, illusion magic. I-If you need to use it, I understand."

Ayla slowly thawed her useless limbs, managed to shuffle half an inch forward, but Flowra kept talking.

"You've barely touched me since . . . a-and I was worried that . . ." She swallowed. Her tears slowly fell. "I understand. I know I'm not beautiful anymore."

"No," Ayla said, and she finally shuffled forward on hands and knees, a supplicant before her wife. "I don't care about scars. I have always been weak to your radiant light, and nothing has changed. You are my wife, and you are beautiful—your heart and body both. But . . ." Anguish rose to choke her, but this time she did not bend. "Every time I think of touching you, I . . ."

A wail tore from her throat, leaving her weak and weeping. Flowridia's arms came around her, holding her tight as she sobbed and sputtered her horrible words—that she was tormented with visions of violence and pain, that to close her eyes in Flowridia's presence meant to see her covered in blood and dirt, strapped to a table or sprawled on the floor. Ayla screamed and sobbed, revealing the hateful words in her head, the fingers digging into her skull, and how she wept alone at night, afraid and vulnerable.

"I'm sorry," she managed to blubber, a rise of self-loathing evoked at the awful phrase. "I shouldn't . . . I shouldn't be . . . Not to you. I hurt you—"

"Ayla, no." Flowridia's words were stained with tears. "All this time, you've been silent. And I felt that you were hurting, but I didn't know how to . . . I never want to push you to talk, but you must. Otherwise, you'll never heal."

Ayla remained secure in her arms, heaving her sobs.

"Will you let me take you to bed?"

Ayla managed to meet her eyes. "What about the ritual?"

"You're not ready. And that's all right."

The world slowly repaired. Ayla hadn't realized how shattered her life had become.

After a tear-filled night, Flowridia held her hand as they walked through the hallways—and the grey world Ayla had lived in filled with color. She hadn't known it was missing, yet now the saturation returned in vibrant hues. They hadn't held hands in months. There was joy in touching her, the innocence something she had never truly explored.

There was merit in seducing young, flower-laden diplomats, but there was something unbearably precious in courting her anew, no intention in her gestures.

They kissed before bed—chaste and sweet. Flowridia's nightmares remained, shattering Ayla's heart. But when Flowridia awoke, she clung to Ayla with new urgency, a silent bid for her to stay.

In the following days, Ayla contemplated Sarai.

Her world spun rapidly: her life filled with a tangle of sweetness and healing and sorrow, yet within her, down in the deepest, tenderest parts of her soul, something new had sparked to life. She thought of Sarai's confession, their reunion, their parting—not with anguish or longing, but with finality.

Amidst the storm of guilt and anguish and healing . . . the eye held peace.

And what did it mean, for a creature of darkness to feel peace?

After a week, Flowridia, her wife, her dearest and beloved, asked a vulnerable question: "Do you swear I don't revolt you?"

Ayla kissed her deeply then, even dared to skim her waist, and when she was met with no resistance held her close and tenderly. "I promise, darling. I find you beautiful beyond compare."

The words were true and precious. They might have remained innocent as well, except Flowridia pressed her against the wall, unabashed as she kissed Ayla's neck. "Will you touch me? Will you try?"

Ayla carried her to bed and kissed her, savoring the sensation, touched her chastely, then amorously, her hands skimming Flowra's intimate parts, yet . . .

Ayla's touch faltered, her rising fear choking her resolve. "I'm sorry."

Flowridia held her, patient and kinder than Ayla deserved. Ayla forced her mouth shut, forced her tears to dry, shame filling her to think she couldn't show the love of her life that she meant it, when Flowra asked, "Might I try instead?"

Ayla met her gaze, lip trembling. "What do you mean?"

"Let me make love to you," Flowra said, the purity of what she asked far more than a creature of darkness deserved. "We've both gone through hell, but I know you're holding guilt. I know you hate yourself. You don't deserve that. It was not your fault."

The words broke something within Ayla. Fresh tears rose, and with it the innate desire to fight, to run. All her shame came crashing down, content to destroy her utterly, to ruin what minimal progress she had made.

"It was not your fault," Flowra whispered amidst the raging storm, louder than even the thunderous bashing of Ayla's calamitous thoughts. "Ayla, I love you. I love you so much."

For a brief and brilliant moment, the storm clouds parted, and Ayla believed her.

They did not make love that night. Instead, they resumed their chaste and innocent life, and Ayla contemplated Sarai once more.

Sarai, who had courted her properly and built her up with no thought of reward. When they'd made love for the first time, Ayla had felt reborn, cherished and adored, no twisting dread in her stomach, no sanguine lies with the whisper of, *"Little dove . . ."*

And she wondered, for the first time in all her years, who she might've become if Izthuni had not betrayed her. Would it have truly been a quiet, blessed life? Or would she have succumbed to her base urges again and broken Sarai's heart?

Ayla's own heart said it would have been bliss.

One night, during the waxing moon, Ayla left Flowridia's bed to stare beyond the window, upon the stars and brilliant celestial body . . . and wept.

Bittersweet tears streamed down her face as she said a final goodbye to the life she didn't live, to the chance she'd never had, to the child who had been twisted and molded and manipulated from her earliest years. Ayla cried for her, for the little elven girl with no mother. Ayla cried for Sarai, who had done the wrong thing for all the right reasons.

Yet with the shedding of sorrow came the beautiful truth—that Flowridia was not a consolation prize, but a second chance in every magnificent way. She adored an empty, unlovable creature, cherished her despite her wicked deeds, loved her unconditionally, it seemed. Though Ayla felt unworthy of that pure love, she accepted it, basked in it, and had . . . grown.

Such a strange and painful, wonderful thing, to grow. Flowridia was everything.

Sarai was gone, and Ayla hoped she found rest in the Beyond. But still she wondered . . . who she might've been in that other life.

What was a monster without monstrosities?

A strange shift in Flowridia and Ayla's roles occurred. Now, Flowridia doted upon her, asking of her health, of her feelings, and while her night terrors continued, she had become so much stronger in her day-to-day life.

Flowridia still spoke to the priestess but held Ayla's hand with no hesitation. She still shed tears for her lost magic but did not fall to pieces to hear Demitri's name.

She did visit him, standing apart with the bars between them. The undead wolf had grown docile after months of captivity, largely unresponsive to guests—unless that guest was Ayla, who slipped into his cage with Flowridia watching and coaxed him to show her his golden eye, to see her when she waved and spoke sweetly to him. He didn't understand. Ayla knew that, but she caressed his fur, nevertheless, letting Flowra speak. It was what she needed.

A part of Ayla wished Flowridia would simply accept a new familiar, for her safety and sanity, yet Ayla could not deny the bond her wife and Demitri had shared. Flowridia was better with him in her life.

The full moon neared, and so did the chance for her and Demitri to reconcile, if Ayla could act.

That evening, with the waxing moon beyond, Ayla kissed her dearest wife a moment longer before they fell into bed, lingering, silently willing her to act—and Flowra did, so tentative as she tested the waters between them. So much damage had been done, but Flowridia's touch rebuilt the bridges Mereen had tried so hard to burn. When she pulled her into bed, Flowridia kissed her neck, her breasts, brought healing with every glowing, golden touch.

There were scattered pieces still screaming cruel words in Ayla's head, decrying her love, shaming her for what she'd done, content to whisper all the while that she was unworthy of anything soft and kind. Yet Ayla forgot them all when Flowridia moved inside her, sealed to her wife by more than mere promises and idle words.

Against all odds, Flowridia loved her. Loved her still.

When Ayla finished, she wept. She held her greatest love and wept.

That night, they bonded as newlyweds might, joyfully rediscovering the other. After six months apart, their bodies were sensitive, parched with lust, and Ayla touched her wife with no shame or fear. When the sun rose, they bathed and giggled like children, brazenly groping the other until Flowridia neared collapse from exhaustion.

To hold her nude form as she slept brought boundless peace to Ayla's healing heart.

Flowridia had grown, resilient above all else, shown in part by her increasingly infrequent visits to the priestess of Staella.

"I informed Casvir I no longer wish for pain management. My hand is tolerable if I'm careful."

"I miss my magic, but I'm starting to find my other hobbies again."

"I'm frustrated by how useless I feel, but every time I see Demitri, I have hope it might be different someday."

But what touched Ayla the most was what was said about her.

"We finally had sex, and I don't wish to say too much, but it was so beautiful."

"She's quiet, still, but she's getting there."

"I'm starting to recognize my wife again."

The full moon came, and they hadn't spoken of it. Yet it remained like a taut string between them, and when Flowridia informed Casvir that she would be out that night, Ayla knew it was time.

She studied the scroll in her moments alone, as Flowridia gardened with Sora or spoke to the priestess for emotional healing.

For the Creation of New Life:

The joining of the Silver Fire and your beloved's womb . . .

The idea petrified her, all the various unknowns. But a few more months, and they would be free. Half-elf pregnancies held a fluctuating timeline, but it would be less than nine months. A blink in eternity. Flowridia would be made immortal. A creature of darkness like Ayla herself, but *truly* like Ayla, free to dance in the sun. With both of them undead, Demitri would be restored as Flowridia's familiar. They could leave Nox'Kartha and be free.

Truly free—from Casvir, from Izthuni, from hatred and grudges and pain . . . She would set aside her quest to destroy the phylactery if it meant never seeing Casvir again. A foreign exhaustion had settled somewhere deep inside her. She was tired of fighting. She had fought for so long. What would it mean, to rest?

What would it mean, to live a peaceful life?

That night, they held hands through Sha'Demoni, anticipation brewing between them. Flowridia's smile held hope, and Ayla prayed she could see it every day until the sun burned out.

In their little forgotten cottage, Ayla's chalk drawings remained, still pristine. Flowridia released her, shyly tip-toeing to the center of the circle. "What's my role in this? You've been cryptic, love."

"Go grab that pillow," Ayla said, unbearable feelings of softness welling within her. "You'll be laying down for a while."

Flowridia skipped off and obeyed, and Ayla wondered if she felt the same building sensation of freedom. Oh, she was pure light, and Ayla laughed when she returned with *only* a pillow, apparently having misplaced her clothes. They'd touched each other every night since that first impassioned reunion, creating fresh memories both sweet and profane. Some nights didn't end in sex. When Flowridia's mind was loud or Ayla's haunted by grief, they simply held the other chastely, sometimes with tears, but always with love.

Pain meant growth. Each day, they were trying.

"And you're certain this is what you want to do?" Ayla asked, helpless as she knelt before her. "I know you've feared this bargain. We can still walk away."

A small whisper inside her prayed Flowridia did.

Instead, something soft fell upon Flowridia's visage as her hand touched her womb. "I told you once that I'd given up any dreams of having my own children when I realized I could only love women. But to have one with you? I don't fear that. In fact, I . . ." She bit her lip, her eyes glistening with sudden tears. Ayla feared until she smiled. "Yes, I want this."

"Lay down this way," Ayla instructed, directing her to the center, positioning her between runes of power. "I need to warm you up first, darling. Tell me if you need to stop."

After a quick peck on her wife's lips, she immediately kissed between her legs, making love with her tongue, reveling in Flowridia's cries and taste, nearly forgetting her task. Ayla did not use her fingers—not yet—instead gleefully bringing her to climax with her mouth.

Flowridia's delightful laughter put Ayla back on course—for her quest, in the end, was to preserve her darling's joy for all her life and afterlife. "Now that you're properly wet," she cooed, her own lust apparent in her voice. Oh, how she adored Flowridia's submissive gaze, "we begin the spell. It won't take long."

Ayla had recited the words a hundred times to herself, both before last month's full moon and then today. She did not need the scroll for the rest. Instead, she knelt between Flowridia's thighs, focusing on the brewing power within her.

Gods protect them both. The magic here was unlike any other.

Glowing silver light sparked at Ayla's fingertip. Flowridia watched it like a moth to flame as Ayla dipped it down to Flowridia's forehead, touching it to the center. She repeated the action at her scarred sternum, above her heart, and then upon her womb, where she lingered. "Let your mind, your heart, and your womb be unified. Let their intentions be aligned."

The next step scared her so, imagining all the horrid ways it might go wrong, but she hadn't voiced that. Flowridia needed to be relaxed. Her vulnerable stare offered trust, and Ayla refused to break it.

Silver flame rose upon her hand, engulfing it to her wrist. Ayla's eyes conveyed a question, one Flowridia gave a soft smile to answer. "We'll go slow," Ayla said, praying her voice did not tremble. "If you feel any pain at all, or if something feels wrong, tell me immediately. We can stop."

Flowridia nodded, eyes wide and wanting as Ayla dipped her hand low and rubbed along the wetness dripping from her vulva. At Flowridia's pleasured sigh, she sought her entrance, carefully slipping two burning fingers inside.

She didn't miss the sudden expansion of Flowridia's pupils, but her moan was like any other spot of pleasure in her life. Ayla gently thrust—slowly, as promised—needing to prolong this for a moment more. First two fingers, then a third, and Flowridia's fists clenched as magic burned within her. A fourth, and Ayla was glad now for their sexual escapades. Otherwise she'd be in pain, but as it was, Flowridia's pleasured countenance held a delirious half-smile. Ayla wished she could savor the warmth of her cunt, caress and tease those wonderful ridges inside her, but instead she slowly spread her burning fingers and stretched the tender, sensitive skin.

All the while she watched, focusing her power, mindful of Flowridia's pain and pleasure threshold. "Are you ready for the rest?" she asked, and her wife slowly nodded, likely few thoughts in her head for where her blood had pooled.

Ayla withdrew, then carefully positioned her fingers outside her wanting entrance. Her palm burned silver, the power steady but maintained, and she pushed her whole hand inside, genuine pain crossing Flowridia's features as Ayla's thumb joined the rest.

Ayla stayed perfectly still, her hand forming a fist. "Look at me," she whispered, and Flowridia opened her eyes, vulnerable and small, perhaps even scared for what was to come. "Are you ready?"

Flowridia breathed, first in then out, her body relaxing around Ayla, though the space remained tight. "I'm ready," Flowridia managed, and oh, the trust in those beautiful eyes.

Something new rose within Ayla, waiting at this crux of a new and terrifying world. Tears welled in her eyes, yet depthless love bound them as they held the other's gaze. "Brace yourself," she said, and she channeled her power anew. Within Flowridia's most sacred part, the Silver Fire burned.

It showed in Flowridia's face—not pain but shock as power pulsed through her. Something akin to panic twisted her visage, and Ayla instinctively took her wife's hand with her free one, letting her grasp it tight. "I love you," Ayla said, more a plea than a comfort. "Just a moment more. Just hold on. You'll know when it's time."

The spell had not said how long, only that the one receiving the power would know. Flowridia held her gaze, her eyes now rimmed in red. She broke eye contact and looked to her womb—which showed no sign of change, yet suddenly she smiled and squeezed Ayla's hand, tears falling from her eyes. A beautiful sound left her lips, some blending of a laugh and sob and when she met Ayla's gaze, Ayla swore something new bound them.

Her heart swelled to look upon the woman she loved and see radiance shining back, the moment binding and eternal. Ayla's power pulsed all the while, until Flowridia nodded and said, "That's enough."

The fire extinguished. With care, Ayla withdrew her fist, Flowridia's slight gasp as precious as gold. Surely her love ached, so Ayla came down to hold her, mindful of her soiled hand as they embraced. "How do you feel?" Ayla whispered, both of them crying, tears mingling.

"Different," Flowridia said, a hint of laughter in her voice. "Did it work?"

"I suppose only time will say." Ayla kissed her sweetly, exhausted in ways her undead body simply shouldn't be.

Ayla bid her to stay as she left to wash her hand, catching a glimpse of Flowridia cradling her womb, heart yearning for how sweet and soft she looked, a new sort of happiness shining in her wife's countenance as she looked upon where Flowridia's hands had settled.

Something new, and Ayla felt . . . different.

Disconcertingly different.

All of this was a bargain to fulfill, the plan a perfect compromise to the unthinkable, for Flowridia to birth a man's child and hand it to Casvir and walk away. Let it be Ayla's instead. She could not care less, nor care less for it. The spawn would be born—a weak little aberration, as all dhampirs were. They would be free, and Casvir would receive an abysmal prize.

She lingered in the shadows as Flowridia tenderly embraced herself, unable to name this new, rising apprehension.

Only that Ayla knew, like she knew the weight of her knives, the bliss of her muscles when she danced, and the tender machinations of her beloved's mind, that her world would never be the same.

CHAPTER 2

The end of the world . . .

"Yes," Flowridia said, yet forgot what for, instantly.

The dark mists surrounding her faded into nothing. Her eyes fell upon an abyss; not even darkness; merely a void. She tried to look at her hands, yet there was nothing. She was nothing.

Within that abyss sounded a voice she ought to know but did not: *"Witness the world without you. See what will be lost."*

She fell. The abyss swallowed her whole.

Memories Flowridia once had fell like sand through her fingers, final remnants of the hourglass of her life emptying. Twenty-two years of life swept clean as waves upon the beach, and no matter how hard she tried to hold them, it all ebbed away.

Three years of marriage—a tapestry woven by love, by thoughtless devotion, by pain, and by heartbreak—unraveled at the seams, vanishing from thought.

Kingdoms that had fallen from her legacy—succumbing to flame, to tyranny, to demons in the darkness—nothing but shadows, then gone for all time.

All the souls she'd extinguished, lives lost to the powers she commanded—undead, necrotic magic, even the monsters she held on a leash—gone and forgotten, as well as the guilt they brought.

What was good and cruel in her world—the family she'd forged and found, the family she'd murdered, the lives she'd saved, and those she'd led to ruin—sank into the void. Gone.

In the absence of identity, Flowridia ceased to be. Flowridia was Flowridia—but who was Flowridia?

Not a person. Barely a soul.

Until . . . Flowridia was no more.

Yet time moved forward. As matter formed and darkness returned, she settled into substance. No longer floating. A mortal shell embraced her, and all the memories with it.

But . . . they were not her own.

Some memories were little more than dust. But the value of dust was in its composition. Even dust could be valued like diamonds and gold.

"It is not much. But we will be safe for the night."

Already the words were swept away in the wind—for they meant nothing. Merely dust. But the words roused the soul from sleep. The world was warm. The voice was kind and . . . familiar. She tried to move, but her arms and legs were bound by blankets and . . . perhaps even an embrace.

She opened her eyes to see a face that was not familiar, but it smiled. Every motion of that countenance held her utterly enthralled. Each blink. Each flickering shadow upon her loose hair. Warm hues illuminated an alabaster face, sharp yet tender in its smile. This person was a stranger, yet she knew the person's smell like instinct—shared blood, shared magic, shared undeath.

Oh, the soul burst with something, some joyous emotion that screeched from her mouth as pure elation.

Such tenderness in the person's laughter. "Well, look at that. Etolié did not bluff. You are glowing, dear one."

Merely dust; the words swirled away. But the soul loved the way they made her feel.

"Who is it you smile like? Not Flowridia. Not me. Not quite. Perhaps you simply smile like yourself. Little . . . *Kedira*."

Oh! That was a word she knew! It meant something. It meant . . . her. But why was it said so unkindly?

"Oh, sweet Flowra, letting sentiment ruin practicality. Kedira— what unfortunate connotations the name brings."

Why was the face so angry? The soul couldn't smile anymore.

"Perhaps . . ." The face came near, and when cool lips touched her, she found she could smile again. "Dira. A respectable elven name and near enough to honor your late mother and her wishes."

And so she was . . . *Dira*. Dira remembered so little, all of it glittering dust in the breeze. She could hardly move yet felt pure joy, swaddled in softness. She was warm, and there above her was a smiling face.

"My darling Dira . . ." The face twisted, but it was not angry, no. It smiled, yet moisture rimmed argent eyes. "Gods, I have missed so much, haven't I? Only one year old, yet Etolié says you can walk. She says you breathe fire when you scream. You are pure magic, and I . . . I did not expect this to hurt. I did not expect to love you at first sight."

Waxen fingers caressed her cheek, their ice startling. Yet they soothed her eyelids to shut, for the world was tiring and the embrace was soft and kind. "You are all that is left of Flowridia," the voice continued. "She is who you deserve. Not me. And I am far from deserving of you. I have already abandoned you once, and I hope you can forgive me someday. I hope you can understand. I hope . . . No, it is not a hope. It is a vow. You will have everything I never did, and that includes a mother who will never abandon you. Never again. You will be protected, dear one. You will be loved."

All was dust, yet Dira remembered how it felt to be safe—for the first time in all her days.

"My darling Dira—what a wonder to think you could ever love me, too."

Current era . . .

One month of waiting. One month of Flowridia's mind buzzing in anticipation. On the evening of the next full moon, she hid her impatience behind layers of dirt, but though the world inside her brought hope, the world beyond cruelly turned.

Flowridia held the trowel in her good hand, digging small holes for the moist seeds. Autumn filled the world with warm shades and cool breezes, but some flowers thrived in the waning months. Today, she planted pansies.

Her left was wrapped today, the compressing fabric said to stimulate blood flow. It did reduce the pain, yet the tingling never quite seemed to fully fade. She kept it to her chest, the steps added by having only one good hand wearing her patience thin.

"Let me help with that," came Sora's voice. Sora had filled the shadow Demitri left behind, at Flowridia's side if Ayla was not. Rarely when she was, but Flowridia did not besmirch Sora that.

They knelt in the Nox'Karthan Gardens, which Flowridia had avoided until recently. Sora took the trowel, leaving Flowridia to wrangle only the seeds, but she nudged Sora away. "I'm fine."

To prove it, Flowridia set the trowel into her wrapped hand, willing it to grip—and it did, sending sharp shooting pain through her forearm. She recoiled. The trowel dropped as she steadied her breath. She bit back rage at her own inept body. Sora didn't need to see that. Sora didn't need to know how much it hurt.

"I know you're fine," Sora said. Bless her for ignoring that overt display of weakness, even if Flowridia hated to be pandered to. "I just don't want you to get frustrated and leave the gardens again. It's good for you."

Flowridia lifted the trowel with her good hand, resuming digging small holes. "I love being outside. But it's . . . difficult. I can't feel it like I used to."

Her magic was gone, and with it, the sensation of the world. Of course she could feel the cool earth, smell the floral delights, taste the fresh air after a rainstorm, but once the plants had sung to her. Once, she had felt their lives as delicately as her own. Once, she had all but spoken to them, and once she *had* spoken to animals in a way, learning to coax them to trust her. Once, she could heal all things.

Nothing. The world was empty now.

"Have you considered taking medication for the pain again?" Sora asked.

No, because Flowridia had stopped at the cusp of the ritual. There would be no risk to the potential life inside her. "It's not bad enough for that."

"You're a terrible liar."

Sora didn't know what she was talking about, but only because Flowridia hadn't told her of her bargain with Casvir.

"You've been quiet," Sora said. "Are you feeling all right?"

Flowridia resisted the urge to touch her stomach, which still showed no signs of change, but a hope had sparked. She prayed it ignited into flame. "Emotionally, I'm actually feeling good. I'm finally starting to feel free. Which isn't to say the memories are gone. I'm afraid of sleeping, and not just because of nightmares." Her mood did fall at that, for her next words broke her heart. "I worry about Ayla disappearing in the night. I think her willingness to be intimate with me again is a sign she's finally on the path to forgiving herself. She spoke of it once, and I'm grateful for it."

She held tight to her final words, praying that to speak them would not validate this final fear. "But there's more she hasn't told me. I fear this has affected her more than it even affected me."

For if nothing else haunted Flowridia's sleep, it was Ayla's plea that she shut her eyes as they lay upon the cursed dungeon floor, tortured by Mereen's own hand: *"You don't need to remember this part."*

In errant moments, the memory rose to choke her.

"Hold on," Sora whispered, and Flowridia stilled as her sister crouched and crept along the garden's path. She moved as if stalking prey, her ensuing pounce into the bushes validating the thought.

Sora emerged holding a little toad in her hands. "Would you look at that?"

Flowridia laughed as Sora set it into her lap, the creature startled but still.

Since the discovery of their shared blood, Sora had plunged into sisterhood head first—no hesitation or fear. Flowridia savored the moments where they found common ground. Sora knew nearly as much about plants as she, could identify just as many, could catch insects and animals for Flowridia to fawn over. They'd spoken of family, of life in southern Solvira, of their very different experiences in Staelash—and it was not always seamless, but Sora was trying and so was she.

When the toad hopped away, Flowridia allowed it, watching until it disappeared back into the moist underbrush.

"It's in Ayla's hands," Sora said, coaxing Flowridia's attention back. "All you can do is be there when she's ready to talk."

Flowridia nodded, but when she returned to her work, she could no longer see her hands. The sun lingered on the horizon, but the moon rose beside it, a portent of night. "I've done what I can. I'll wash up and meet you at dinner."

"I'll accompany you."

Explaining that she really needed to be alone with Ayla shouldn't have been suspicious, but everything felt suspicious when you had a secret to hold. "I'll be fine. I was actually hoping to find Ayla first."

Sora compromised by escorting her inside.

Flowridia washed her hands and arms in a washroom on the first floor, taking extra care with her infirmed hand. The damaged nerves tingled as she removed the wrapping. At least she could move the digits now, though it had taken months of stretching, of working the destroyed muscles. Three fingers remained, scarred up their centers where the monster had split them in twain, her palm and wrist a mess of shining scars. Most of the bones had been repaired, but Casvir had said there was metal in her wrist replacing the carpals, which had been shattered into dust.

The warm water irritated it, the feeling of static rising when Flowridia gently rinsed it of soap. The pain was far less than it had been, the nerves healing in small degrees, but still it radiated, constant and cruel. Sometimes she tuned out the sensation, but to even glance at it brought both reminders of pain and of the monster's artistic, sadistic mind.

But if they used Izthuni's dagger to make her like Ayla, her hand would be whole again. All of her would be whole, her scars a memory instead of cruel writing on her skin. Ayla was porcelain, flawless in her complexion. Flowridia longed to be as immaculate.

Was it vanity to erase them? Was it vanity to finally rid herself of pitying looks from strangers? If so, she would chase the sin.

Flowridia rewrapped her hand, wincing at the flashes of cold shooting up her forearm. In the meantime, she was disabled.

To Ayla's old bedroom; her wife awaited, and joy could fill her for that. A jaunt up the stairs, past countless doors—

"Flowridia, good evening."

The voice held ocean's depths, deeper than the core of the earth. Flowridia stopped at Imperator Casvir's approach, the clang of his armor a signature of his steps. Perhaps he was fearsome, but she was used to his presence—his massive, curved horns, the corpse-blue of his skin. He towered above her, his muscular bulk nearly as wide as she was tall, and those red eyes were a memory seared in her mind, for long ago, a demon in the woods had stalked her, granting her a familiar and a second chance.

A lifetime ago. And though her resentment ran deep, she could not deny the friendship they shared. "Good evening. I'm due to meet Ayla."

"Then I will escort you. We need to talk."

Not stern, no, but the innate knowledge remained that arguing would be met with resistance. She nodded and followed at his side—more his equal than any, by far, even with no title.

A strange truth to consider.

"I have not pried, but the priestesses of Staella claim you are making progress," he said. "I have witnessed it for myself, as well. You have been laughing freely in my presence recently, and I had not realized I missed it."

Oh, it was unbearably sweet. Flowridia could not help but smile. "I still have a long journey, but I'm feeling hopeful."

"A long journey is to be expected, but it has been seven months. Do not mistake my next statement for impatience. I am happy you are here. But I think it is appropriate to ask of your goals."

The statement would be ludicrous, had he known the truth. But she did not even know if Ayla's spell had worked. Now was not the time to mention it. "My goal is to heal, and to help Ayla heal too."

"Noble, but you are more stable now. I wished to ask of Demitri."

The name struck like a knife to her stomach—or perhaps a bullet to her head. "What of him?"

"He remains in his cage, a mindless beast. I wished to know what steps you have taken toward changing that."

His tact was as laughable as the irony, given she was potentially well ahead of schedule. But Flowridia's composure held by a thread. "I fail to see how it's your business."

"Every part of this is my business, but I will not press if it distresses you—for now."

Her rage simmered behind pursed lips. "How *charitable* of you, though I seem to recall you saying I would be protected for as long as it took."

"I did, but there has been no progress toward accomplishing your bargain. And in the interim, I wonder if you would consider repaying my so-called charity in other ways, given your good health."

Ah, yes. Her bargain. Selling her firstborn child to pay for the freedom of Alauriel Solviraes' soul: a contract signed under duress to save a woman she could have loved, while wondering if her wife was dead. Thank every god that Ayla's room approached. Flowridia's blood boiled. "Such as? I'm not exactly of much use anymore."

To her surprise, he gave a small frown. "I disagree. My court would make great use of your skill set, magic or no magic."

Flowridia stilled at the door, the words unexpectedly alluring. "I . . ." Within her, a desire sparked, little more than a candle seeking to light the whole sea. "I will consider it."

She entered Ayla's room without a goodbye.

Her residual rage faded to see Ayla herself seated upon the bed.

Ayla's room had once held a shrine to Flowridia—strange, perhaps unhealthy, but flattering—though the trinkets had been moved from center stage, relegated to a single corner of the room after Flowridia had admitted it felt strange to make love surrounded by pictures of herself.

So the drawings had been carefully stacked and placed in a drawer, and many of the glass globes housing stolen trinkets had been set aside. But a few remained in places of honor, emitting gentle light. The one nearest Ayla herself was a yellow flower from a lifetime ago, that Flowridia had worn to a ball where they had not met—Ayla hadn't even noticed her, she had eventually admitted—but still marked their first encounter, for Flowridia remembered it well.

To watch Ayla dance . . . to watch her flicker in and out of shadow like a candle . . . In her young years, it was the first time Flowridia had ever *craved*.

Ayla wore simple clothes, her black dress modest compared to the audacious gowns in the wardrobe. Her hair fell luxuriously down her back, her pale skin glowing in the odd light. She held a clear vial, filled with opaque, grey liquid, bearing a glimmering sheen. At Flowridia's entrance, Ayla's sharp features softened. "Hello, darling."

Flowridia sat beside her, warmed when Ayla placed a protective arm around her waist. "That's it?"

"It is. As requested, I was disguised all the while. No one will know." Ayla offered the vial for inspection.

Flowridia assumed it was magical, but how blind she felt, even months later, to feel nothing of the world around them.

"The witch said to place a drop of your blood into the mixture. If it turns the color of blood, you are not pregnant. If it becomes gold, you are."

Flowridia could hardly contain herself as she attempted to uncork the vial—an attempt which failed when her ruined hand failed to grip the stopper. Instead, a sharp sting ripped through the tingling appendage. She flinched, swallowing rage.

"Allow me," Ayla said, but Flowridia brought the vial to her mouth instead, managing to grip it with her teeth and tug the cork out. The elixir emanated the sweet aroma of magic, as well as a biting edge.

She offered Ayla her wrist. "Would you like to do the honor?"

Ayla chuckled, and act which had come easier lately. And thank every god for that. There were few better indicators of healing than laughter.

Yet, joyful or not, Ayla became a monstrous vision at the anticipation of blood, her fangs elongating in her mouth. Flowridia stiffened to face those black eyes.

"Flowra?"

Yet tangled with the potent fear was *lust*. "It's nothing. Carry on."

Perhaps when Flowridia could face the predator without fear once more, she would be truly healed. Perhaps, too, when those moments were not so elusive and rare, Ayla would be herself once again.

They had come so far. They both had leagues to go.

Ayla brought the offered wrist to her mouth, careful to not touch the hand itself. There were times Flowridia asked for aid massaging the brutalized appendage, but today she preferred to not think about it.

She did not even feel the sting, though blood welled from the tiny prick. Flowridia wiped the droplet against the side of the vial, all the world fading as she watched it slowly slide down the glass and mix with the dark elixir.

In the stillness before the storm, Ayla took her in her arms, stroking tender lines against the thin fabric of her dress. The liquid transformed . . . and like lead to gold, the elixir conveyed a clear message.

Emotion welled fast, and Flowridia cried out for joy, her scream falling rapidly into tears. Ayla took the vial as Flowridia's face fell into her hands, her joy effervescent.

"Congratulations, Flowra," Ayla cooed, her voice a sensual pull. "It seems we've succeeded."

Flowridia hugged her torso, for within her was impossible life, delicate life—*her* baby, the one she had dismissed from tender years.

Not simply her baby. Ayla's baby.

She turned to Ayla, stealing her mouth in a fierce kiss. "Thank you," she managed, her tears smearing onto Ayla's cheek, but her wife didn't mind. She never had.

Ayla smiled softly, but it sent no tingles down Flowridia's spine, no stirring of fear and lust between her legs. "The countdown begins," Ayla said. "The timeline varies for half-elves, perhaps six more months, but then Demitri will be yours to love. Your magic will be returned. Your bargain will be fulfilled, and we can be free."

And somehow . . . at that final phrase, Flowridia's joy dimmed.

Free . . .

But she hid behind impassioned kisses, bidding Ayla to touch her. Her wife complied, the blessing of her intimacy all the more valuable when it had been lost for so long. Ayla kissed her, groped her, soft prayers of worship in her sighs, and Flowridia saw only the ritual scene, wherein they had created beautiful life. When their bodies conjoined into one, Flowridia held her silver gaze, enthralled by the touch deep inside.

Her thrusts were tortuously tender. Ayla's lips came near, brushing against Flowridia's mouth, her cheek, her ear. "I love you, Flowra."

The affirmation soothed her heart, spiked passion in her blood. Flowridia craved closeness, an old desire aching deep inside. "Ayla, would you . . ." Flowridia presented her neck, pressing Ayla's face against it. "Taste me, please. Just . . . Just a little bit."

Yet Flowridia did not feel teeth against her throat. The rhythmic thrusting never faltered, but Ayla's words were faint. "A-Are you certain?"

Gods, Flowridia burned. "Yes, oh yes, *please* . . ."

There came a kiss upon the curve of her neck, evoking a sigh, a moan. Flowridia felt teeth scrape against the sensitive flesh, then gasped at the slight prick of pain. Cold seeped through her limbs, yet pleasure bound them. Oh, how she'd missed this. Oh, how she'd craved feeling the monster again—

Only for Ayla to become stone.

In motions far too deliberate, Ayla withdrew her hand, leaving Flowridia aching inside, then revealed her monstrous visage, evoked by the presence of blood: hardly a ring of silver around those blown pupils, her fangs jutting unnaturally from her mouth, and blood—so much blood—dripped from her lips.

Flowridia froze, uncertain of what sensation bound them. "Ayla?"

Ayla's hitched breath evoked memories of a dungeon far away: where once her beloved had screamed; where she'd pled to her tormentors to, "*Stop it! Stop!*"

Flowridia's stomach clenched, her pulse rising to dampen all sound, but when Ayla's fingers drove into her own skull, Flowridia all but launched herself to grab her, heart shattering to hear her screams, an echo of her torture months ago. "Ayla, don't. You're here with me. You're safe."

Ayla's shriek devolved into sobbing. When Flowridia guided her hands away, gaping holes were revealed around her ears. Flowridia brushed aside her precious locks of hair as the bone and skin repaired before her very eyes. All the while Ayla clung to her and wept.

"I love you, Ayla," Flowridia said, but it was not enough, for love was healing, but it did not heal. Ayla was healing, but she was not healed.

Ayla screamed. Flowridia wept. Gone were all memories of joy, but one quiet truth remained to quell Flowridia's battered heart: Ayla was still here. She had not run.

Today, it would be enough.

Amid the torturous cycles of healing and pain, something new had come to brighten Flowridia's world. It was a private time, and while Flowridia knew it would not remain quiet forever, how beautiful it was to have this small and precious secret growing inside her.

Still, she burst at the seams to tell a select few, but Ayla bid her to wait.

"Darling, I don't know how Silver Fire will impact this, but miscarriage is more common than birth with dhampirs. And while that is typically a blessing to the mother, that does not a bargain fulfill. Please save yourself heartache, just in case, and wait a few months more."

They agreed upon four-and-one-half months, precisely—the half being important, Ayla insisted, proclaiming it a safety marker for miscarriage among elves.

And though it was beautiful to have a small and precious secret, the reality remained that pregnancy had a few distasteful aspects. The nausea began at month two.

Despite Flowridia's efforts to remain discreet, when Sora walked in on her vomiting for the third day in a row, her half-sister would not let it go. "You need to see the healers."

"I don't. It must be a flu."

To which Sora responded by placing a hand on Flowridia's forehead. "You don't have a flu."

"I suppose I must've eaten something."

"You haven't been eating."

Also true. Any food that wasn't plain bread evoked the nausea anew.

Flowridia longed to explain, and Ayla would understand, yes, but the secret remained behind gritted teeth. "I'll ask Ayla. She might be the best doctor in the castle."

"You're technically not wrong."

The words held an edge, but Sora had let the issue go.

Despite the temptation, Flowridia treasured this secret and pondered it only in her heart—except to one other. One who could not speak it.

On one such sleepless night, Flowridia held a lantern as she stepped barefooted through moist grass, the dew luminous beneath the silver moonlight. A splendid night, the silence marred by the buzz of insects, of nocturnal creatures beyond the castle walls. She passed a hooded figure, who did not speak, merely watched, and made her way to a private place.

Secluded behind stone walls, Flowridia took her personal key and unlocked a worn door, covered in ivy and moss. The wood creaked as she entered, and she shut it right away.

A stone prison lay before her, the metal bars revealing a docile monster. Demitri did not stir at her approach, the lantern's flame casting his dark fur in warm hues. He did not sleep. He merely lay as a corpse, one eye open, the other . . . gone.

The giant wolf blinked; the only sign of sentience.

Flowridia sat before the metal bars and set the lantern to the side. How she yearned for his embrace, for his humor, his comfort. He was just a boy, a child, his life cut short by a bullet.

Sora had told Flowridia the story of Mereen's final end. Flowridia only wished the death had been prolonged, though it would still be but a fraction of her own pain.

"Hello, Demitri."

The wolf did not react.

Like a fool, she dared to reach within the bounds of the cage, her heart seizing when her fingertips touched coarse fur. When he growled, she pulled her arm back, lest he strike.

Demitri had first been banished to the outdoors when he became aggressive with servants. And then, one day, he had nearly ripped off Sora's arm.

He did not know them anymore.

But he faced her now, and Flowridia imagined that golden eye holding light. "Something wonderful has happened," she whispered, for even the walls had ears. She placed a hand upon her stomach, for though there was no bump, there was a presence. "I'm going to have a baby. You're going to have a . . ."

. . . no. He wasn't. It wasn't meant for her.

"It's Ayla's baby too," she continued, "and it's a magic I'll explain when you're ready. But once the baby comes, you can be mine again."

In the hidden recesses of Ayla's treasures, Izthuni's knife waited. She did not fear its blade. It was hope. Ayla would drive it through her throat, and Flowridia would awaken like her: immortal, nigh unkillable, and free—from the pain in her hand, from the scars on her body, from Casvir's shadow . . . Freedom was but a few months away.

"We're so close, Demitri. This is for you, and you're worth it. I love you."

Demitri perked up, and for a moment Flowridia's heart leapt.

Soft footsteps filled the space. Ayla approached, the wolf's eye upon her instead. She said nothing, merely slipped through the bars of the cage and offered a gentle hand to the undead creature—for more than that, wolves loved vampires by instinct. Loved them by scent.

And so when Ayla sat by his side, he set his head in her lap.

Warmth filled Flowridia, some amalgamation of jealousy and love. At least he could love someone.

"There is a spirit still inside him," Ayla said. "Otherwise, he would not care about me. Hold onto hope, Flowra. He is worth waiting for."

If there was any aspect of Ayla Flowridia loved most, her quiet affection for Demitri certainly contended for the crown. "And all can be as it was," Flowridia said. "You and me. And Demitri."

Yet while the statement had once encapsulated every part of her heart . . . a hole remained now. But no, no—she would soon have Demitri to fill it.

"And thank every god," Ayla replied, her smile delicate and soft, so foreign to what Flowridia had once known. Nearly a stranger. "Do you want to return to our home in the woods?"

"It seems like an appropriate first step, at least while I acclimate to vampirism."

"For all my centuries, I have done little travel on this continent. When you are ready, we can explore the frozen north, if you would like. Or perhaps south of Moratham. Gods, we could visit the sea, and not from Onias' Realm . . ." Such radiant joy in Ayla's gaze, her eyes sparkling with light. "There is a whole world out there to see. I shall revel in walking through Nox'Kartha's gates a final time. Can you imagine it? We can be anything. Be anyone. Eternity awaits us, Flowra. I cannot imagine a happier ending."

Flowridia actually laughed, so endearing it was. "You only wish to travel?"

"For a time, at least. I don't know where we will be a century from now, but how beautiful it is to think we will have that time. What would you like to do, Flowra?"

The question truly gave her pause. For so long, Flowridia had dreamt of the house in the woods with Ayla and Demitri—and that dream had come true, a blissful year spent together, though shadowed by the search for the phylactery and by Ayla's restless nature.

But now . . .

"I don't know. But I'm not worried. I suspect my purpose will come to me when I'm immortal."

That odd, light smile remained on Ayla's lips, her oft severe face . . . serene. She stroked the fine hairs of Demitri's head, lost in thought as she stared through the bars to the stars. "Soon, you will have all the time in the world to decide."

"Just a few more months." Unbidden, Flowridia set her hand upon her womb, the spark inside it promising a perfect future.

. . . A spark with no place in their future.

Again, Flowridia shoved that aside, refusing to falter so close to the end. All she had worked for, all she had earned, every bargain she had made . . . All would come to fruition with the birth of this child.

Flowridia had vowed to live a life of no regrets, to purge what weaknesses still lurked inside to torture her. Perhaps that meant purging her conscience, too.

Whatever it took to set that innocent baby in Casvir's arms and walk away.

CHAPTER 3

Three years after the end of the world . . .

"Mind your volume, Starspawn. She has just fallen asleep."

Mother's voice roused Dira from tentative sleep, where she was met with only darkness and the subtle shadows shifting within it. But shadows were safety. Shadows kept the world away.

Yet with each blink into wakefulness, more images appeared: outlines of her small dresser, a table, bookshelves filled with her favorite stories, and a couch where Mother often lounged, reading by candlelight.

Golden light filtered gently through the door's seams. But Mother never used lights when alone. Mother could see in the dark far better than her.

"Yeah, yeah—I know how babies work."

"She's three. Not a baby."

"They're all babies until adulthood as far as I'm concerned. And even then."

Dira knew that voice. But why was Etolié here so late?

Mother told her to always use light steps, to make no noise, to never make the floorboards creak. She brought a blanket from the bed, the chill of winter leaving her shivering without protection. There were warmer lands, Mother said. But warmer lands were not safe.

She set her ear to the door. Mother said to always study her surroundings in secret.

"What are you doing here?"

"Is it so bad to make a social call?"

"It is never so simple."

Dira peeked through the luminous space between the door and the wall, catching a glimpse of glowing wings. And so that was the light. Dira fought to suppress her excitement, lest she reveal herself and lose this game of stealth.

What was the first lesson? To survey her surroundings. Were there any traps that might spring?

"While I do want to see the kid, I'm here to warn you that this house might not be a haven much longer. There's been unrest in Tholheim, and Casvir is planning on sending troops."

"Damn him."

Dira did not know the name, only that it caused the hair on her arms to raise. Still, her heart sank—did this mean they had to move again?

"Look, I've said it before—"

"No."

"You don't have to be in hiding."

"She does."

"That's not the same thing. The elves are hanging on, but just barely—"

"You would ask me to leave her all alone?"

"If you're looking for nannies, I can offer a few candidates—"

"I cannot risk it. I'm done with the war."

"So you'll hide forever? What about when she's not a baby anymore?"

"Then she will be old enough to understand."

Dira didn't understand, only knew that her stomach felt twisty and her palms felt cold. Mother always said it was what fear felt like—and Dira didn't like it at all. Unbidden, tears welled in her eyes. Oh, she tried to be quiet, but she was so afraid.

"Lying to her isn't going to help."

"I am not lying. I'm protecting her."

Dira's tears fell faster. She cut off her snivel, but it was too late. The voices faded.

Mother made no footsteps, unless Dira strained to listen—and she stumbled back when the door swung open, revealing Mother's form, backlit by golden light. "Darling, what's wrong?"

Dira whimpered as she held up her arms, unable to articulate the fears hurting her heart. But Mother's cool touch soothed her instantly, the tight grip around her body as she lifted her up setting her soul free.

Within Dira, something warm brewed, silver light shining faintly from the pores of her skin. The tighter she clung, the brighter it shone.

A kiss touched Dira's brow. "Sweet darling, there is nothing to fear. Not when I am here. Now, won't you come say hello?"

Current era . . .

Content with her plate of various meats, Sora sat in a small dining hall, the space decorated for guests to appear at a moment's notice. Today, it was simply for a lone half-elf's indulgence. Sora couldn't even regret the bit of extra weight that had formed around her stomach—ten months of eating like royalty in a castle was a treat, especially after a year of traveling in the wilds.

Though truthfully, she had eaten well on the road, but dwelling on Odessa's cooking meant dwelling on Odessa, and some memories still cut like a knife.

Instead, Sora savored the sweet grease of bacon on her fingertips, indulging each bite with joy. The door opened, but she paid it no mind—not until the De'Sindai servant stopped directly in front of her. "Sora Makosa, there's a messenger at the gates for you."

Sora stopped in the middle of licking her fingers. "Me? From who?"

"He did not say where the letter was from, only that it was for you—well, for your Fireborn name."

"How can . . ." Sora's stomach still gurgled from the delectable scents, but the matter seemed pressing. Should she be suspicious? Nobody sought her. Nobody knew she was in Nox'Kartha. "Have someone bring my food to my room, please."

Sora scooped Leelan up from his pile of birdseed and made her way through the carpeted halls. The palace's first floor held more living servants, and so she preferred to spend her time here. Still, the occasional undead guard stood at its station, following her gait with hollow eye sockets. Their presence sickened her, but she was well used to being sick. The inescapable aura of death sang discordant to the magic within her, but Leelan had, at least, not sickened.

As the servant had said, a human man waited just beyond the gate, staring warily upon the undead guards at the doors. He perked up at her approach. "Sora Fireborn, I presume? You match the description."

"Who's asking?"

"I don't know precisely, but this letter has come a long way."

He offered a crumpled letter, dirtied at the edges, even showing signs of water damage—but intact it was, and it bore a seal she knew.

This was from Falar'Sol. Sun Elven lands.

"Thank you," Sora muttered. She tore open the envelope and quickly skimmed its contents:

From the office of Magistrate Autumnvale of Star Tree . . . in light of the late Mereen Fireborn . . . invited to claim your inheritance and estate . .

.

Sora's hunger disappeared.

Though she had forsaken her Fireborn name and claimed Makosa instead, she was still the final member of the elven half of her bloodline. Mereen Fireborn, the late Dark Slayer, had left no will, the letter explained. Legally, the wealth fell to Sora should she come to claim it.

Sora looked to Leelan, her precious golden bird. "What do you think? Do we take a trip?"

Leelan tweeted in approval.

But to leave meant to leave behind a sister—albeit a sister who was doing much better.

Her sister oft spoke of nightmares. Sora did not speak of her own, lest it diminish the horrors Flowridia had experienced. But the memory of her sister's screams was a relentless torture, and though she had accepted the offer of speaking to a priestess of Staella, it had assuaged the guilt but not the memories.

Could she leave Flowridia behind? It would not be forever. If she could implore a particular friend with teleportation magic for aid, it would be less than a week.

"Famous last words," she muttered. Perhaps it was a mistake.

Sora smoked as she packed a bag, still not committed either way. But best to prepare. The estate would be sold, lest the memories taint her. The money would mean she had a future beyond the imperator's good graces—the same imperator who had destroyed the country she had technically been fated to inherit.

The thought came to pray, the instinct well-ingrained, but Sora swallowed it back, the film of unworthiness lingering. Days had become weeks, then months . . . Sora loved her goddess, but what news was there to tell her? That Sora lived under the roof of the tyrant who had destroyed her people? That Sora tended to the wife of a monster Sol Kareena herself had once slain?

Sol Kareena had better champions than Sora.

Leelan chirped from his perch in her room—a suite suited for politicians and other esteemed guests. It held no personal touches. An extra bag, and she could leave without a trace, save the lingering scent of Spore in the curtains.

Flowridia would not stay here forever. And whether Flowridia would choose to keep her in her life once she left Nox'Kartha was a question Sora hadn't dared to ask.

A knock interrupted her musing. "Enter," Sora said, and there appeared the sister in question.

Flowridia's smile evoked nostalgic joy within Sora, who now understood its worth. Their shared father lived anew in her visage, and Sora clung to that. Her loose dress was new. Surely gifted; Ayla was too meticulous a seamstress.

To Sora's surprise, Ayla entered as well, though she lurked like a wraith in the doorframe. She did a fine job feigning disinterest, but something was assuredly interesting, if the fingers twisting in her skirt were any indicator. Ayla only fidgeted when nervous.

However, Flowridia's words stole Sora's focus. "Sora, there's something I need to tell—" But that cherished smile faded when her eyes landed on Sora's suitcase. "Where are you going?"

"Truthfully, I'm not committed yet." Sora offered the letter to Flowridia, whose eyes widened as they scanned the text. "I wanted to talk to you first."

"You should definitely go." Her expression fell fully, brow furrowing. "But it takes months to cross the sea, yes? You could be gone for . . . for six months, at the *minimum*."

"I was going to ask Etolié if she could help speed that along. There's a permanent portal set between Nox'Kartha and Solvira, so I'll have an answer today."

Relief flooded Flowridia's visage, and while Sora was flattered to be loved, something was different. "Oh, that's fine."

Sora was struck by the memory of Odessa—who had also behaved a particular way when she had a wry sort of secret. "Did you say you needed to tell me something?"

"Well, yes, but it's not important."

"You're normally better at lying."

"Yes, but if I tell you, you won't go to Falar'Sol. And you should. My news can wait." Yet Flowridia's smile practically glowed, radiant excitement behind it.

"Are you sure?" Sora asked.

"I'm sure."

"You have me worried, kid."

Flowridia considered that, her lapse in words hardly noticeable. "Casvir occasionally uses bonded mirrors to communicate with his subjects far away. I'll borrow a set and give you one. How about that?"

Sora supposed it fair and nodded.

When Flowridia offered an embrace, Sora accepted, the gesture still a little strange despite ten months spent in each other's company—and slightly daunting, given Ayla's looming storm cloud. But Flowridia hugged like their father, holding tight with all her strength.

While Sora would never critique, something about this hug was different. Flowridia had gained weight. Not much, but Sora was oddly aware of her breasts.

When they parted, there shone familial affection in her sister's countenance. "Be safe."

"I'll be back in no time," Sora replied, and when Flowridia stepped back, she resumed her packing.

Perhaps it was instinct, a subconscious skip to Flowridia's step, but Sora whirled around just in time to watch her sister stumble—

Sora surged to steady her, dancing perfectly in time with Ayla, whose cold touch nearly caused Sora to falter. She noted the grimace upon Flowridia's face, though it vanished beneath a forced smile.

"Clumsy me," Flowridia said.

"Are you sick?"

"I might be."

"Will you finally see a healer?"

"Ayla says I'm well."

Sora bit back her objection because Ayla was *technically* qualified to be a doctor. She looked to the 'doctor' in question, unnerved to meet her gaze. Not from intimidation, no. Ayla hardly carried herself tall enough to deliver that anymore. "Is she full of it?"

"If she were," Ayla muttered, "why would I tell you?"

The words were bait. Sora let it go. To Flowridia, she said, "If you're still like this when I get back, I'm carrying you to the healers myself."

"And I will consent—once you're home."

Home. Sora was going home, but it would be cold and vacant. There was warmth here. Home was with family.

Flowridia left, but Sora could not shake the unease inside herself. Ayla followed like a shadow, but before she could vanish, Sora gathered her courage. "Ayla, a moment?"

Ayla gripped the doorframe with tense fingers, her pale skin thin enough to see the outline of each bone and tendon. But Ayla's gaze was no longer intimidating, no. Instead, to face her evoked memories of soulless eyes in a dungeon across the sea. The carnage had ended. The trauma might never fade, but for all the rage Sora had once felt toward this monster . . . there was no fire now. "I didn't mean to offend you."

Ayla twitched, clearly itching to leave. "You did not."

"If you're certain—"

"Is that all?"

It had to be, yet this was the first time they'd been alone since coming to Nox'Kartha. Sora had rehearsed a hundred different statements to deliver to her unwilling sister-in-law, faltering just as many times. Hatred was Sora's inheritance, the feud between them spanning generations, made personal by her own blood spilled upon a cathedral floor years ago. This woman was wickedness incarnate, and of course Sora despised her, yet when faced with the opportunity to end her forever, Sora had orchestrated her rescue.

She still struggled with what that meant in the eyes of her goddess. She struggled with what it meant for the world. Against all odds, however, her conscience was clear, though what that meant for herself had yet to unfold.

Perhaps that was the message she wished to convey, but Sora's tongue remained frozen beneath Ayla's icy gaze. She managed a nod.

Ayla left, the chill following after.

"I can and will stand here all night!"

Sweat pooled upon Etolié's brow, the jungle atmosphere humid and heavy. Sunset neared, and she stood before what technically wasn't an impenetrable gate—if she could be teleported this far, she could theoretically be teleported closer—but self-preservation said teleporting inside the walls of the enemy's capital city could easily lead to a war crime.

Once again, an exasperated elven guard peeked his head over the expansive stone wall guarding Tierzuroth, his faintly lavender skin reflective in the waning light. "I told you—Executor Faeborn will see no one. Certainly not messengers from Solvira."

The advantage of Etolié's illusionary magic was that she could often be a one-woman show. Disguised as a Celestial noble, there was simply no use in trying to capture her and hold her for ransom.

They might try to kill her, but she could handle that.

She made a show of huffing, playing the part of a pompous noble messenger. The more harmlessly floozy she sounded, the less likely they were to shoot her on sight. "Empress Etolié of Solvira, Daughter of Stars, Granddaughter of Eionei, Savior of Slaves and former Magister of Staelash has a generous offer."

Fucking hell, she was starting to sound like Casvir with those ludicrous titles.

"Though if Executor Faeborn would be more comfortable sending a diplomat," Etolié continued, rather enjoying her grandiose accent, "the empress wouldn't be insulted."

"If you don't leave, I will be forced to shoot."

Etolié didn't see a crossbow—or worse, a fucking gun—but that didn't mean he didn't have one hiding below the wall. "The empress wouldn't be happy about that."

"Need I remind you we are already at war?"

Alas, he wasn't entirely wrong. "The empress does not condone Nox'Kartha's actions, and in addition to payment would be willing to negotiate with Goddess Ku'Shya and have it written that she not break through the veil between worlds and level your entire country."

A beat of silence, and then the guard said, "One moment, please."

There was little Etolié loved more than dropping that cursed, beautiful name. From what Flowers had said, Executor Faeborn had only lived through the massacre in Velen'Kye because of their healthy fear of the Goddess of War. When Kah'Sheen had appeared, the Whispering Elf envoy had fled before the bloodshed had time to begin.

Was it a bluff? Yes, to a degree. Goddess Ku'Shya couldn't emerge onto the mortal realm without a host—they would have far worse problems if she could, though also no God of Order to contend with—and the only host capable of not burning out within seconds was Khastra. Etolié also couldn't guarantee that Ku'Shya actually gave two shits about what she wanted, but the demon was apparently under the impression that she was Etolié's mother-in-law. News of her relationship to the goddess' daughter had spread far and wide, the nature of it exaggerated here and there, but Etolié was a fan of lying by omission.

But it was precisely because of Khastra that Etolié stood in a humid jungle, disguised as a diplomat, pleading to exchange a few words with the executor. A prisoner of war Khastra remained, and Etolié had always coped with depression with political action.

The quiet grew increasingly daunting. High above, torches were lit one by one on the wall. The thick jungle behind Etolié steadily hummed to fill the void of sound, countless insects and worse emerging for their nightly habits. When something zipped past Etolié's ear, she swatted it. The buzzing lingered.

The sun fully set, and then a silhouette appeared upon the wall. "Executor Faeborn will see no one," came the familiar guard's voice. "In fact, they would like to send a warning."

Etolié swallowed her disappointment. "I'm listening."

"Inform Empress Etolié and Imperator Casvir that the Four Kingdoms will negotiate a treaty soon. Should Imperator Casvir not comply, he shall be subjected to the wrath of our Goddess."

Intriguing, but full of hot fucking air. "I speak for Empress Etolié when I ask why you aren't subjecting them to your Goddess now. You worship her. Pray harder."

"She will personally come to deliver our vengeance."

According to Uluron, it was theoretically not completely insane, and the notion prickled uncomfortably against the back of Etolié's neck. "Can you cite your source on that?"

"That is all I will say to an envoy from our enemy," the guard replied. "Now go. This is your final warning."

"What if I get it into a contract that the Bringer of War won't be brought out to fight—"

His crossbow appeared. Etolié held up her hands and stepped away, defeat rising bitterly within her. "I understand."

She faced the gate as she backed into the jungle's depths, disappearing from sight.

Once beyond the wall's eyes, Etolié's illusion faded. The jungle filled with golden light, her wings luminous in the dark night.

It was not the first time she'd begged for an audience at the base of those walls. It would not be the last. But Etolié swallowed tears as she shut her eyes and silently prayed. *Send me home, Momma. Today wasn't my day.*

A warm presence filled her, enveloping her in a godly embrace. Though far away across the veil of worlds, Staella was always near.

Etolié blinked, and the world shifted, first becoming a sea of magnificent stars. She stared upon the space between the realms. Weightless, she wondered what it might be like to simply step into the void. Would she cease to exist? Was there more to find?

These weren't questions with answers. The world returned to what she knew, and Etolié stood upon dark wood, surrounded by shelves and shelves of books.

Her library in Solvira did not hold the same memories as her old one in the manor in Staelash. But her first haven of books and scrolls was long gone, buried in the aftermath of the Earth Orb's power, and travelling there for nostalgia's sake precluded she was willing to see Marielle, and Etolié didn't trust she wouldn't throttle that betraying harpy.

And so Etolié settled into a nest that had no skylight to light it. Instead, windows cast streams of sunlight across the many scrolls, books, and shelves. Strange, to move across the continent and experience sunset and sunrise in a few short moments, but it was a new day here. Etolié pulled her familiar flask from her inter-dimensional stash and drank, willing the noxious liquid to steal her quickly.

It never would though. There were few brews strong enough to defeat the granddaughter of the Drinking God, and Etolié wasn't willing to negotiate with Casvir for the powerful stuff. Instead, she chugged the whole flask, then let it clatter onto the ground.

Ten months. No news, except the knowledge that Khastra hadn't been destroyed—in theory. Her very soul ached from loneliness, and on the worst days, she went to Celestière, her momma's company at least warm.

Etolié, half-buried beneath a pile of blankets and scarves, stared at the cluttered space. With a snap of her fingers, a large figment appeared beside the shelves, and if Etolié shut off every bit of common sense she had, she could embrace and believe it.

"It is daytime, Etolié," Khastra said, her broad stature familiar, the silver tattoos upon her deep blue skin a marvel of art and magic. Her hair was long, for that was how Etolié remembered it best, the lavender locks braided back, reaching her digitigrate knees. Her horns bespoke her demonic heritage, but just as much of her was mortal. "You should be awake."

"You know I'm nocturnal, asshole."

Khastra chuckled, the sound soothing. "Have you eaten today?"

"Not quite."

"Not quite? Etolié, you must keep up your strength."

Unbeknownst to her personal demon, Etolié set her fingers around her bony wrist, cursing its frailty.

"May I join you?" Khastra asked. "I have some time before I must train the soldiers."

"Always, ya big lug." Etolié rolled aside, leaving space for her companion.

Her beloved figment settled beside her, even disrupting the blankets. The touch on Etolié's face was not quite warm, but it was rough from her callused fingers, a sensation Etolié knew well enough to imagine.

If they embraced, it would end. Etolié could not recreate the weight of her arms, nor the sensation of magic as those tattoos illuminated. But she shoved that aside, savoring the moment of insanity. "I love you."

"I love you, Etolié. I think of you every day."

Tears welled in Etolié's eyes, and behind her misty sight, the illusion of glowing eyes and sweeping horns faded away. The touch on her cheek was the last to go, for Etolié clung to it with all her might. She shut her eyes, and it lingered . . . lingered . . .

Gone. Etolié opened her eyes, the first of her tears spilling onto her blanket. "I miss you, Khastra."

The words filled the lonely space, becoming her only companion.

Zoldar, her loyal bug, was also partially nocturnal, surely snoozing somewhere among the rafters, so Etolié rolled over, willing sleep to steal her quickly.

Except dainty footsteps approached, and Etolié rolled her eyes as she sat up.

"Hi, knock knock," came Murishani's unwelcome presence, making a show of knocking on the nearest bookshelf as he peeked around the shelves. Ever the dandy, everything about him wafted insincerity. "Hope I didn't disturb you!"

He had, and he knew he had. No point in illusioning away her tears. Silver Fire bastard here could see through them. "What do you want?"

He was her neighbor now, living in a mansion next to her humbler estate—which was a little gross, given half of Neolan had been leveled. Repairs continued, and his audacious setup felt supremely unnecessary. "You have a visitor. Sora Fire— uh, *Makosa* is waiting in the foyer."

Sora's presence was innocuous. Something in his tone had Etolié sitting up and fuming. "You came all the way to my fucking house just to tell me I had a visitor?"

Murishani's smile remained adorable, perfectly pleasant as he said, "Yes, because I'm invigorated by witnessing your tears."

"I'm not exactly friendly with Ayla, but I can and will ask her to cauterize your tear ducts. Now get the hell out."

Ten months of being this bitch's neighbor had made her lose all charm.

Murishani gave a creepy little wave with his fingers, leaving Etolié with the inescapable need to shower. But thank Alystra's Ass—he was gone. Etolié dabbed at her eyes with her scarves in the ensuing quiet, composing herself as Sora's light footsteps approached.

Sora could be silent when necessary, but this was not necessary. Frankly, Etolié appreciated the warning, though the faint scent of Spore would have given her away. Her half-elf friend had a pack over her shoulder, her blonde locs tied back in their usual tail. The bird—LeeLoo or something—sat obediently on Sora's shoulder, his beady little eyes not particularly intelligent.

The recent permanent portal between Nox'Kartha and Solvira was a convenient little feature, as well as *finally*, albeit accidentally, solving the damn mystery of how Casvir had access to teleportation powers. The portal, being permanent, required a power source—in this instance in the form of a clear crystal, housing specific power.

"You mean to say Murishani can siphon his own portal magic into little rocks for you to use at your leisure?"

Casvir hadn't even granted her the respect of a spoken reply, only an infuriating nod. Suffice it to say, he always had a teleportation crystal on his person.

"It's been a while," Etolié said to her approaching friend. "How's the wayward sister?"

Not that Etolié particularly cared, but in a show of good faith, she had let Sora use her as a confidant for some of her nastier feelings—and had learned quite a bit more about the Mountains of Kaas than she'd wanted to.

But it was only fair. Etolié had once cried for an entire week about her sex life to a hostage Sora trapped in a carriage.

"She's under the weather," Sora replied, "but she's stubborn and won't see a healer. She's hiding something from me."

"A wasting disease would be an ironic end, given everything."

"She and Ayla are closer though. I think things are mending between them."

"I'll admit, I don't give a shit about their marriage."

"Whatever my opinion on that, I do give a shit about Flowridia." Sora entered fully, seating herself on the floorboards beside the makeshift bed. "I'm sorry to come by just to start asking for things, but I was wondering if I could ask you or your mother for a favor."

"Any favor encompassing the two of us means a portal. Where to?"

"I received a letter regarding inheriting the Fireborn Estate. I need to go, but that's three months on a ship."

"Cruel and unusual. I'll ask Momma."

Scrutiny furrowed Sora's face. "Are you all right?"

Instead of cry or rage or scream . . . Etolié opted to laugh. Hysterical cackling wracked her body, echoing the darkest recesses of her mind. Sora wasn't exactly a stranger, and Etolié wiped her eyes of fresh tears, struggling to quell this new insanity. "Sora, you're a fucking idiot."

"It seemed more polite than saying you look like shit."

"At least you'd be honest though." As Etolié collected herself, she cast her illusion anew—of pristine hair and a washed body, halfway to looking alive. "I'm taking each day as it comes."

"Are you allowed to take some time away? What if you stayed with me at the estate for a few days? I think you'd love exploring it."

Rather than rebuke her on principle, Etolié shut her mouth and let her damn brain actually mull it over. This place was awfully stuffy. The idea of exploring whatever the hell an elven estate looked like did sound . . . at least not boring. "I should bathe first and delegate a few tasks. But that sounds all right. I'll leave a note for Imperator First and Last so he doesn't fucking freak."

Look, despite a disconcertingly pleasant stint in the woods, she and Casvir weren't friends. Etolié had more than a few reasons to throttle the bastard—committing genocide on the City of Light while she hid underground with Sora, the archbishop, and a bunch of orphans, for example. Or being the reason she was in the golden shackles of empresshood.

However, stealing Staff Seraph deDieula was the most current of the list, followed by the fact that she was under a very strict soul contract to say absolutely nothing about said staff to anyone ever. Highly unfortunate, given the threat it likely posed in handing a necromancer like Casvir the power to control *all* undead, including vampires and other liches. But he would have an aneurysm if she disappeared.

"We should wait anyway," Sora said, setting her pack aside. Just a satchel, which meant she had definitely assumed the answer to her request would be a yes. "It's night in Falar'Sol. Can't really get into the record's hall at midnight."

"An oversight, honestly." Etolié extracted herself from the enticing blankets. Was she tired? No. She was depressed, and the oblivion of sleep meant she didn't have to feel.

In her darkest moments, she wondered if it would be better for Khastra to simply be gone instead of being haunted by hope. Then again, Khastra *had* actually died once, and that hadn't exactly been great for Etolié's psyche either.

Travelling would be good. Etolié marched herself upstairs to the washroom, seeking to look more like the unwilling empress she was.

Teleportation wasn't comfortable, though the last time Sora had traveled through Goddess Staella's power, she had eaten hallucinogenic mushrooms.

Star Tree was one of the oldest cities in Sun Elf lands, one of very few to not be decimated in The Endless Night's onslaught a thousand years ago. It held less grandeur than Velen'Kye, buildings of stone spread wide instead of built to the stars. Sunrise cast its brilliant light, and Leelan chirped happily, content to welcome the morning no matter what time it was at home.

The peace of the moment was interrupted by sudden dry heaving. Etolié hurled into the grass, though there was little more than bile. "Goddamn teleportation."

Sora left her to her grumbling, content to savor the sunrise. When Etolié finally rose, the Celestial gulped from her flask as she followed Sora along.

"Are you going to hide your wings?" Sora asked.

"Who cares if they recognize me? I'm not at war with these people."

"If you're sure."

"I'm not sure," Etolié said, her words utterly flat. "What I am is depressed, which means I'm apathetic as fuck."

There was no point in reasoning with Etolié.

Star Tree had no gate, though guards did patrol the perimeter, their double take at the stumbling Celestial nearly comical. Sora approached one. "Excuse me, sir. Can you direct me to the records hall?"

The man surveyed her, the gun at his hip evoking distant memories of Mereen's crimes. "Town square. You can follow the path straight there."

She thanked him and went on her way, though slowed for Etolié to keep up.

In a city filled with Sol Kareena worshippers, it made sense for it to be bustling even at sunrise. Temple services were most common in the early morning, meant to greet the returning sun, and those not attending busied themselves with errands and work. Still, Sora shied when they passed a fanciful building bearing Sol Kareena's symbol—the sun and a spear—and kept her eyes averted.

Years ago, in Staelash, she had led those same worship services. Not anymore.

Sora felt eyes, her appearance unique in this city of pure-blooded elves, but while the Sun Elves held their prejudices, they understood oppression in ways the other kingdoms simply couldn't. While dismissive, Sora felt no overt hostility regarding her heritage.

The records hall was easily found, a distinguished brick building set near the road. The interior held the silence of a library, where even a whisper would shatter the unnatural peace.

However, Sora was forced to announce herself and do just that, discomforted at the many eyes diverting to her at the mention of her surname. "I'm Sora Fireborn, daughter of Mariam Fireborn, distant granddaughter of Mereen Fireborn, the Dark Slayer. I don't quite know how I can prove it aside from showing you this." Sora presented the letter to the clerk.

Before the man had a chance to speak, Etolié coughed. "Hi, I'm Empress Etolié of Solvira, yada yada titles, and I'll vouch for her. If I'm lying, sue the treasury."

The clerk said the letter was enough. Given Etolié's slight slurring, Sora suspected the Celestial's claim of royalty was far less believable than even a half-elven Fireborn.

Soon, Sora held the deed to the Fireborn Estate, a claim check for the bank, and an iron key. After quick instructions from the clerk on how to get there—it had been many years—Sora and Etolié stood outside once more. "The money can wait. Did you still want to see the estate?"

"My gut says you're asking for another magic trip."

"Star Tree is only a short ride."

"I don't ride." But instead of resuming what Sora had come to recognize as Etolié's prayer pose—consisting of her holding up one hand to shush anyone who might interrupt her while she shut her eyes and scowled—she merely settled upon the scowling. "How well do you remember the estate?"

"Decently well."

"Well enough to not get us spliced if I try to use your memories to teleport us there?"

"You can do that?"

"Yes, but it's only in the last . . . month-ish that I managed to get anywhere except Momma's house."

"And never spliced, right?"

"Momma hasn't had to sew me back together yet."

Sora couldn't say she liked the sound of any of that, but trusting Etolié was inexplicably the best plan most of the time. "I can picture the estate clearly, if that's what you're needing."

"All right, hold my hands."

Sora tucked her things away, then obeyed.

"Picture it clearly. No distractions. You're going to feel a bit tingly."

Sora obeyed, shutting her eyes as she crystalized the image in her mind. An enormous mansion built of white stone, decorated with climbing vines and a gorgeous garden path . . .

Her stomach twisted. Her body became weightless, the world becoming a void—but just as quickly, the weather changed. When

Sora opened her eyes, she stood beneath a cover of clouds and faced the place of her mother's murder.

The grounds were overgrown, the bushes tangling together, trees covering the stone walls around it. Between iron bars, Sora saw a glimpse of the estate itself, the climbing vines overrunning the pillars. But though the gate protested, with some effort the ancient gears shifted with Sora's key, creaking open to reveal the expansive, overgrown grounds—and a venerable fortress ahead.

The dirt path became stone, and Etolié said, "I should have guessed this when you said 'estate,' but you didn't bother to mention your family was fucking loaded."

Etolié's levity was appreciated. Sora chuckled. "The Fireborns were very influential, even before Mereen. She used this as a base for over a thousand years as a vampire, and before that, it'd been in my family for many generations."

"And it's still standing?"

"Money is often more powerful than magic."

"Well, it could obviously use a bit of love and care, but I like it. Does it have a library, by chance?"

"It does. Take anything you want."

"Oh, fuck yes. You've made this worth my while."

Haunting, the silence of this place, though thankfully dispersed by the occasional chirping bird. Sora was wrenched back nearly sixteen years, shaken at how it had changed. But with Mereen on the road, she had likely not wished to pay for its upkeep. Sora passed a mossy fountain, the green water smelling of mildew. Many of the vines had become briars upon the stone, needing to be cleared away, but some greenery still climbed up the aged rock. Behind each blink, Sora saw the estate anew, the fountain becoming pure and clear, with babbling water joined by birdsong, topiaries cut into all manner of geometric shapes, and of course roses upon the climbing vines, hiding the austere building behind a mask of beauty.

But one thing had not changed. The cold chill down her spine was a staple of this derelict place. Sora had not felt welcomed then, and she couldn't say she felt particularly welcome now.

Sora suppressed a shiver and used the same key on the grand double doors, the creak of old wood preceding a spray of dust.

A gorgeous entryway spread vast before them, leading to a staircase and a legion of doors. Daunting, to think it all belonged to her—the money, the home, even the forest beyond. The statues held images of elven heroes, the paintings fine and holding golden frames. Mereen had amassed a fortune even greater than her progenitors.

And what a delicious irony, that the one Mereen had disowned would be the only one left.

Still, waves of loneliness bombarded Sora, to stand within the empty entry hall. Last she'd been here, Sora had crawled into her ailing mother's bed, her own fever causing delirium. She had awoken drenched in sweat . . . in a cold, stiff embrace.

The light from Etolié's wings was a friendly comfort, at least. Perhaps the memories could be rewritten.

Something so large should not house only one person though. Would Flowridia come here? Doubtful, for it seemed so wrong to bring Ayla. Even aside from Sora's own conflicted self, bringing the woman back to the land of the people she had murdered was not something she could justify.

The ghosts of dreadful memories lingered. Perhaps selling it was the better option, let some lucky soul live out their days in this splendid place.

"You, uh . . . you all right?"

Etolié's voice echoed across the spacious walls, pulling Sora from her contemplation. "Even the most beautiful places can be marred by shit memories," Sora replied. "My mom died here."

"Fuck. I didn't realize."

"It was a long time ago," Sora said, for this wasn't something she wished to speak of. Not here. Not when she needed a level head. "The library is through there. I'm going to assess the damage, if you want to meet up later."

"I'm here to get drunk on knowledge, but if you need to get drunk in other ways, just let me know." Etolié's swaying steps suggested she was nearly there herself, but Sora had come to expect that as a constant.

Sora set about exploring the estate alone, first investigating the abandoned parlor room. She gripped dusty sheets, coughing at the spray of dust as she ripped them away to reveal beautiful furniture, far older than she, perhaps older than her mother. A fireplace lay dormant before it, the ancient ashes coated in dust. On her first night here, at the tender age of fifteen, she had sat here with her mom, the warmth of the fire cutting through even the chill ambiance.

When Sora sat upon the embroidered cushions, she recalled that sweet embrace, though the moment had been stained by tears.

"But if Papa is alive, how will he find us here?"

Even now, Sora recalled with perfect clarity the heartbreak in her mom's gaze. *"It's a fool's hope, Sora. It's best that we try to move forward."*

A fool's hope, indeed. Sora withdrew her beloved locket from her tunic and opened it to reveal the smiling faces of Papa and Mom, forever memorialized in joy. Papa was dead—a truth she had yet to reconcile the details of—but the blessing of seeing her papa's face in her sister's still touched her.

Sora had spent only a few months in this place, but Mom had lived centuries. Perhaps there was a legacy here to preserve. Mereen was only one person. Mariam Fireborn had lived here and loved it too.

Sora shut the locket and stood, only then noticing a distinctive shape behind a covered emblem hung above the fireplace. She brought her tunic up to cover her mouth as she tossed it aside, revealing a gilded carving of Sol Kareena's symbol bearing down upon her.

Leelan's little feet shifted upon her shoulder, giving a sweet chirp. But Sora turned away, stomach twisting to be faced with further reminders of what she'd left behind.

Sora resumed her exploration, deciding to head upstairs and avoid Etolié for the moment. The windows were in good repair, the wallpaper not new but fine enough—little damage overall, simply neglect, and the funds Sora had been given would more than pay for a professional cleaning. She certainly could not maintain this place herself.

But what if she did keep it? What if she someday began her own family? Would she regret not leaving something so fine for her children? What if Flowridia ever adopted a child? Was the curse of this place ingrained in its very foundation, or could those memories be written anew?

There were too many hypotheticals in that statement to say.

She merely glanced inside most bedrooms, few bearing any personal touches anymore, but stilled before a door barely ajar, spotting discarded clothing on a bed that was covered only in dust, but not sheets. Sora peeked inside, heart stopping to see a child-sized rapier hung on the wall, displayed with love. So many small inventions lay littered about, gears and metal scraps, all as forsaken as the rest of the space—but a lump rose in Sora's throat.

This had been Tazel's room. Her cousin. Her fallen hero.

All these little forgotten dreams, a man who had only wanted to be an inventor, a scholar, as destroyed as the rest of them by Mereen's toxic influence. Sora's night terrors were less dramatic than Flowridia's, but often she saw his ghostly final image, the gruesome burns covering his body, felt the cut of his weapon on her cheek. Tazel had cursed himself in his final moments, Flowridia had explained—and Sora had undermined it by saving Flowridia's life.

Perhaps that meant he had moved on. Was it selfish to hope he was judged by his legacy instead of his cruel final days?

It would mean there might be hope for her, too.

What also came was the memory of birdsong and holy light infusing her body, allowing her to escape the burning mansion . . . and it had been the last time she'd felt Sol Kareena's light.

Mist filled her vision as she blinked, breath hitching as she left the room, quietly shutting the door behind her.

If that was Tazel's room, she knew what waited next door. Sora held her breath as she peeked inside—finding her mother's room sparse, void of any personality at all.

Mariam Fireborn had died in here and then been blotted from the family tree.

Sora slammed the door shut. By the Light, this place was stifling. Perhaps she would take Etolié up on her offer of alcohol after all.

Rather than cry, Sora returned outside, her hand skimming the knife at her hips. Animals ran wild in the woods beyond, and the chance of a wildcat or bear having made residence in her absence was probable. But she could finally *breathe*, no longer suffocated by ancient dust and memories of the dead. The haunted atmosphere still brought fresh air, and already her spirit lifted.

The estate's walls expanded wide, but the woods behind were part of the property as well. Rather than go around, Sora scaled the stone wall, finding the physical labor gratifying after so long cooped up in a castle. She ran, keeping a steady pace as her body adapted to the increased rate of her heart. Exhilaration filled her, the burning in her blood a welcomed sensation. Perhaps she would sell the estate and keep the woods for herself, build a cabin and have a quiet place to retreat to.

When she finally slowed, she inhaled the crisp morning air, savoring each sensation.

Except...there were no sounds. No birdsong. No insects. Silence, save for the crunching of Sora's boots.

As a little girl, Sora's first experience with true danger came at her father's side. All night, they had stalked a deer, finally encroaching upon it in a meadow—when the stag darted off anew. Sora had tried to run. Her father's hand had stopped her.

"Listen."

"I don't hear anything."

"Precisely."

Little did she know of the wildcat lurking in the trees. The deer had known, but Sora was not a prey animal—merely an interloper who had to be taught what prey innately knew.

Something lurked.

Sora drew her knife. At her shoulder Leelan remained still, further proof that a predator was nearby—and what predator wouldn't want to prowl the rich hunting grounds? People didn't trespass onto lands known for vampires. There was plenty of game here.

As Sora wandered through the thick trees, she swore the clouds darkened, the shade nearly mimicking night. Storms were commonplace here, but the air held no moisture, no distant smell of rain. Odd, but then she caught a glimpse of something enormous and . . . white?

She slowed, creeping forward, only darting when she found the next tree to skulk behind. If Sora prided herself in nothing else, it was her father's teachings of how to be the hunter and not the hunted.

"Face them like the powerful force you are."

However, as Sora realized what lay in the clearing in the private woods, she knew no one could be more powerful than this.

For there before her, curled like a resting cat, a massive skeleton dragon was fast asleep. The undead dragon did not breathe, merely remained a statue, the purple glow of her eyes extinguished.

There was only one creature in all the realms like this. Uluron cast a mighty presence, even in rest.

Sora froze. Intellectually, she knew she had nothing to fear, but instinct screamed to run—and then the dragon stirred.

Light appeared in Uluron's eyes as she spread to her full length and stretched her bones, claws curling like a feline. In a cavity in her spine rested the Dark Orb, and a green light shone from one claw, revealing the Earth Orb. The dragon stared at her. Sora did not move an inch.

To her surprise, the dragon extended a claw and then one digit. Sora recalled Etolié's interaction with the beast all those years ago and touched it gingerly.

You are familiar.

Sora resisted the urge to stumble at the gentle whisper in her mind. Not sound, no—the wise, feminine voice was as natural as her own thoughts.

Have we met before? You have not run, so I would assume so.

"Y-Yes," Sora replied. The woods remained silent. The undead dragon was answer enough to that mystery. "I was there when the Theocracy of Sol Kareena was destroyed. You flew a group of us to Staelash."

I do recall. Are you a friend of Etolié?

"I am. My name is Sora."

Sora could not decipher draconic expressions—especially when there was naught but a skull to read—but intrigue washed across her like a rolling fog. *Sora Makosa?*

The name caused Sora's pulse to race. "Nobody knows that surname."

I apologize. I have not meant to startle you. Like the Daughter of Stars, yours is a name I have heard before. Your presence is a good omen.

"That's . . . good," Sora said, because what else did one say when an ancient dragon knew your name?

I have napped a long while, so this place must be safer than most. Has Etolié spoken to you? Do you know of my woes?

"Soliel is hunting you. Etolié mentioned that much. These woods belong to my family—no one comes here."

What a marvelous coincidence. My Father has not come in many months, and I have finally found proper rest. Though I ought to move back to my Mother's grave. But it has been wonderful to find sanctuary in your woods, Sora. Thank you.

"Etolié is at the house, if you want to see her before you go."

I would. Would you like a ride?

Sora's mind still had not caught up to the reality of there being a dragon in her forest, but when Uluron placed her clawed hand—paw?—onto the ground, Sora nimbly stepped upon it, stomach lurching when it rose. Uluron did not fly, no, simply slinked gracefully through the woods, despite being taller than most trees. What had been a jog for Sora was but a few steps for the enormous beast, yet her agility meant she hardly parted the trees.

When the estate was in sight, Sora was unsurprised to hear profanity: *"What the actual fuck—Kitty?!"*

So it is the Daughter of Stars, whispered Uluron, and Sora felt affection flow from the dragon like waves upon sand.

Etolié's wings spread wide when they neared. She shot into the air, level with Uluron's face and Sora. "I have questions."

Uluron offered her opposite hand to Etolié, the silence suggesting she spoke to the Celestial now instead.

"Soliel left you alone? That's . . . different." Etolié's frown suggested a conspiracy deeper than Sora could guess. "Not to jump straight into business—glad you're doing well, Kitty—but the Whispering Elves were talking about sending their Goddess to attack Nox'Kartha. Any, uh, basis to that theory?"

Sora did not hear the dragon's response, but she felt confusion as though it were her own.

"I was told that literally hours ago," Etolié continued. "If there's any truth to it, perhaps that's where Dragon Daddy is."

Sora mentally added *Dragon Daddy* to the list of Etolié-isms she'd rather never hear again.

"I guess that would be a big deal, huh."

Uluron stood taller, peering upon the southern horizon.

"If you're setting sail, you wouldn't mind putting in a word for little ol' Etolié with the executor, would you?"

Sora balked at that. "I beg your pardon?"

"Uluron's going to Tierzuroth to see if her mom's there. She thinks she—uh, the Goddess of Chaos—might've killed Soliel, which . . . would be anti-climactic but ideal. And I'm thinking the presence of a dragon might actually convince Executor Faeborn to fucking see Empress Etolié."

A prudent plan, but there was a glaring hole. "Uluron is going to bring the orbs to where Soliel might be?"

"She seems to think everything will be fine."

Sora considered the estate and the task ahead—and then Etolié and her stubborn grit. If Soliel were dead . . . was the quest done? Was the world simply saved? No aplomb, but Sora would accept that to save her goddess' world.

And Etolié could rest without the guilt of Lara's quest hanging above her head. Lara had died trying to stop the God of Order—but was he already dead? Etolié deserved to know. "If you're going, I'm going."

"I would expect nothing less from you," Etolié replied. "It's just a small detour."

Small detour. Sora sensed irony coming their way.

CHAPTER 4

Four years after the end of the world . . .

At the cusp of springtime, Dira stood as a statue in the shadow of a tree, watching a bird gather sticks for a nest.

Over and over, the little mother bird flew down to the forest floor to scavenge for the perfect twig.

"She will repeat until she has enough to complete her nest," Mother whispered, her arm around Dira's body, holding her tight. Mother's head was level to Dira's when she crouched. "She has only a limited window of time before her eggs are laid. She must be ready."

"How does she know how to build it?"

"It is pure instinct, my darling. Every mother has it in some way—even birds."

Dira suppressed a grin, her lips pursing instead as she spoke an impish thought. "Do you know how to build a house?"

Mother stared the way she might survey a stain on the ground, but then she chuckled. "Of course you have a sense of humor. Just like your sweet mom."

Dira laughed when Mother kissed her cheek, only to gasp when it startled the bird away. "Oh no!"

"She's fine, my love."

"But what about her babies?"

"She will come back to finish her nest."

Dira's eyes watered, nevertheless. "But what if she doesn't finish in time?"

"My sensitive little girl." Mother released Dira, then rose and took her hand instead. "Your soft heart is a gift. What if you found some sticks for her? You can leave them in a pile for her to look through."

Dira's heart leapt, her sorrow forgotten. "I could help?"

"Of course. Just remember to avoid the sunlight."

Dira set about foraging upon the forest floor, gathering her pile in her hands. Mother's shadow remained near, occasionally offering approval or encouraging her away from the spiky ones. *"You don't like getting thorns in your hands, right? Neither do birds."*

Spots of sunlight did occasionally kiss her skin, and though Dira loved the sensation, it burned her quickly. "Why does it have to hurt?"

Mother always avoided the sun. "Why does what hurt?"

"The sunshine."

"There is little to do about it without magical intervention—though I can certainly do some investigation into that if it would soothe you. But I have explained how I am a vampire, and your dearest mom was a mortal. And so you are a child of two worlds, and one of those worlds fears the sun." Mother knelt before her, tenderly taking one of her hands. With skin paler than moonlight, Mother shone in monochrome hues. Dira had always struggled to know what color she was, her own warm hues countered by shades of grey. "It was how you were made, my darling girl. Do you see well at night instead?"

Dira nodded.

"Do you have magic?"

Again, Dira nodded.

Mischief twisted Mother's smile, filling Dira with radiant joy. "Perhaps you could remind me."

Dira squeezed her eyes tight. Mother said it was fine to do, if it helped her focus. She lifted clumsy hands and tried to breathe as Etolié had taught and Mother too, but no warmth came with it. Silver Fire tickled like a feather, though Mother said to use it with care, but as much as she wished it, she remained distracted by the speckled sunlight and the tweeting birds and rustling grass in the breeze and screaming—

Dira lurched when Mother suddenly ripped her from her stance. Before she could even cry, Mother knelt in the dark shadow of a tree, setting a finger to her lips. Dira fought against tears, against fear, only to hear the scream once more.

"AYLA!"

Dira's body remained cold, but the voice sparked recognition. "Mother, that's—"

Mother pressed her finger hard against Dira's lips, so much so that it hurt—but Dira dared not whimper. Panic filled Mother's eyes, yet her voice remained serene and soft. "You will stay here. You will not move. You will shut your eyes and hug yourself as tight as you can and pretend it's me, all right? Count down from one hundred. I will return before then. Promise me."

Dira nodded, even as tears prickled in her eyes.

"I love you, my darling." Mother stood, the flicker of her form barely perceptible—but Dira saw it, saw her vanish into the darkness.

She had made a promise, and so Dira squeezed her eyes shut and hugged herself so tight her arms burned. "One-hundred," she whispered. "Ninety-nine, ninety-eight . . ."

But why was Etolié here? Why was she screaming for Mother?

"Eighty-six, eighty-five . . ."

At *sixty-four*, Dira realized there was no more birdsong. There were no sounds at all, save for her whispers.

Her tears fell fast, a small sob escaping her throat. "Sixty-three, sixty-two, sixty-one . . ."

Far, far away, she heard . . . something. It was not a sound she recognized, nor one she could try to name—like wailing, but a beast. Screaming, but guttural. Broken. And not one, no—many.

"Fifty-nine, fifty-eight . . ."

As faint as the breeze, she smelled . . . fire.

"Forty-five, forty-four . . ."

More screaming. More wails. Was Mother among them? Was Mother all right? Dira's nails dug into her side, bunching into the fabric of her dress. "Forty, thirty-nine, t-thirty-eight . . ."

With her breath came a sob. Fear clung far tighter than she ever could. Dira dropped to the ground and curled into a ball. Weeping, Dira clung to the idea of darkness, wishing she could disappear as Mother had, but instead she wailed unbidden. *"Mother!"*

The smell rose; the screams in tandem. Dira kept her eyes shut and sobbed in her little ball, pleading for salvation. *"Mother!"*

Her sob cut off as *something* yanked her backwards—and Dira was enveloped in cold and bombarded by the stench of smoke.

But she knew Mother's touch. She knew Mother's gentle *"Shh,"* as it caressed her ear, and when Dira finally opened her eyes, there she was, holding her tight in her lap.

The world had changed, from bright colors to strange darkness, everything around them black and grey. But though Mother smelled of fire, it was assuredly her presence, her touch on Dira's face. "Darling, darling, it's all right. You're safe."

But though relief flooded her, Dira could not quell her tears, instead clinging tight to Mother, sobbing into her embrace.

"Dira, love, I'm so sorry."

Current era . . .

Uluron flew much faster than an airship.

Sora watched boundless terrain flash by beneath her, mountains passing from her peripheral within minutes. Chilled from the high altitude, Sora clung to blankets from the estate, encouraged to bundle up at Etolié's insistence.

"Pretty sure I just about lost Sheen Bean to the cold last time I rode a dragon. Just trust me."

Etolié hadn't grabbed her own, content to study the world through the cage of Uluron's claws. "So Uluron knows you, too?"

"She called me Makosa," Sora said. "I don't understand."

"Well, get used to being left in the dark. She won't explain."

"She said I was a good omen."

"And she said my service to her mother would be invaluable. Both make no sense without context."

At dusk, the Celestial verbalized her less-than-stoic thoughts. "Explain to me why I get airsick on fucking flying horses but not dragons."

Sora glanced up from her cocoon of blankets. "The fact that you've ridden either of those things, much less both, is really what you should be asking the universe to explain."

"Good point."

Cupped safely in her hands, Leelan napped, and Sora soon followed, safer than she had been in years with a dragon to protect her.

Sunrise awoke her, blinding as it reflected off the clouds.

She knew not where they were, only that the ground below showed dense foliage, an endless sea of green.

"Morning, sleepy."

Sora roused herself, unprepared for the rush of cold assaulting her when her blankets fell. She gripped them once more, clinging to the warmth. "Did you sleep at all?"

"Sleep means thinking about Beefcake. I just spoke to my momma."

Ah, you are awake, came a gentle voice. *Are you rested?*

Sora's stomach fell as Uluron brought her high, matching her and Etolié with her skull. "I am!" Sora cried, seeking to be heard over the wind.

We are near the city. I have already asked Etolié to advocate for me. But I would appreciate it greatly if your word could stand beside hers and mine. If my father is not dead, I cannot anticipate what my mother thinks.

"Of course."

Sora's stomach lurched once more as Uluron began a rapid descent. Amid the trees, she spotted small signs of something more—towers that soared above even the highest branches, specks of light from below the thick leaves.

This will be difficult. Bear with me.

In Uluron's other claw, the Earth Orb flashed, and a section of ground wiped away like spreading butter, the trees clumping as thick as trees could. But soon a dragon-sized section of cleared land awaited. And though the earth rumbled like an earthquake, Uluron landed as daintily as a bird. *I can only communicate to those I've touched. Tell them I must see my mother.*

Sora stepped down from Uluron's claw, grateful for the stable ground. Though an affirmation sat at the tip of her tongue, her words faded at the sight before her.

So this was Tierzuroth, capital of the Whispering Elves—stone walls had been built between thick trees, the massive plants incorporated into the structures themselves. The trees stood perhaps a hundred feet high, surpassing even Uluron, and Sora took unsteady steps toward a wooden gate seamlessly attached to the stone structure. The harmony of nature and technology resulted in a strange sort of beauty, ancient stone hiding the iron fragments connecting it to the world. Though daytime, the dense leaves hid most of the sun, leaving the ground moist and the ambiance dark. Instead, massive torches were lit beside the walls, casting flickering light.

Etolié floated down, her appearance changing to that of a Whispering Elf—with their near translucent skin and sharp features. Her hair and eyes remained the same, for silver and purple were common enough. Most importantly, her wings vanished from sight. "Do you want a disguise?"

"Unlike you, I'm not worth capturing for collateral. No need."

"I've been trying to get an audience with the leader here for months, and all it's gonna take is a fucking dragon."

"I'm guessing you didn't realize the leader was answering to a literal Goddess."

"No, but that's not exactly special to me."

Sora occasionally forgot the weight of Etolié's mother's title.

Upon the wall, elven guards studied the ancient dragon with some amalgamation of respect and fear. When Sora waved at them, they gave heed as she cried, "The dragon, Uluron, requests a meeting with the Goddess of Chaos!"

The massive gate swung inward, and out came a single runner. Clear confusion filled his face as he looked from the dragon to Sora's party. "You both speak for the dragon?" he said, disbelief in the words.

"We both arrived with her, didn't we?" Etolié replied.

"You are a worshipper of Goddess Chaos?"

"Sure."

The runner turned his skepticism upon Sora alone. "Do *you* worship Goddess Chaos?"

"I am a Sun Elf," Sora replied, because there was no use in denying it, "but I am also a friend to Uluron. I'm here with my companion to deliver her request to meet with the Goddess of Chaos."

At the reiteration of their quest, the man's sneer faded as he looked again upon the gargantuan dragon looming in the background. "Come with me," he said. "You may deliver the message yourself."

Sora glanced at Uluron, whose purple eyes conveyed curiosity. "We'll be back!" Sora cried, and the dragon settled on her haunches.

Past the gates, the city spread extravagantly before them. The Whispering Elves lived simpler lives than many of their counterparts, their culture more focused on music and art and other luxurious pursuits rather than technology. But it meant there was beauty in every sight, everything from the carved buildings to the streetlamps saturated in splendor. The elves here were pale, paler than even their Iron Elf counterparts, their translucent skin bearing hints of purple and blue. To insinuate that demon blood ran within them was blasphemy, but rare elves with inborn magic did occasionally make a name for themselves. These elves were born in darkness, the thick trees of their homeland casting eternal shade, and many died in the same state, never truly seeing the sun.

Such a strange way to live, Sora thought, for she savored the sensation of sunshine upon her skin, content to bask in her goddess' domain. But they did not worship Sol Kareena here—a fact further proved by the grand statue before her.

Standing fifteen feet tall at least, the statue was of a woman, arms spread wide in welcome. Flame poured eternally from inlets set into the statue, creating a mesmerizing vision of their Goddess engulfed in fire. Behind her stood what Sora presumed was a castle of sorts, built into the trees yet made of stone. Though Sora would have loved to see more, the runner did not slow before the statue. She followed him to the arch leading inside.

In the entry hall, massive tree roots grew within the walls, providing a foundation as well as design. A wooden door, carved with an image of the same Goddess beyond, stood before them. The runner, however, stopped Sora. "You will bow before her, Worshipper of Sol Kareena." Derision came with the name, practically spitting upon the ground. "No one cares for your false goddess here."

"I will bow before her," Sora said.

"If you do not, it will not matter who brought you here. You will be struck down for insolence."

Sora nodded, uncertain of how to further agree.

The door opened from within. Sora stepped into a magnificent throne room, bearing finery unmatched. Tapestries depicting the Goddess in various poses adorned the walls, the torches emitting blue light. Sora's eyes fell first upon Soliel, unmistakable with his golden armor and aura, glowing in the dim light. Near stood an elf who she suspected was Executor Faeborn, their robes bearing beauty appropriate for their station.

The path led to a decorated throne upon which sat . . . Her.

She so precisely matched the corresponding artwork, this being of fire. The Goddess of Chaos emitted silver light, a silhouette covered in flame. The throne she sat upon did not catch any sparks, nor did the rug as she rose. Such grace in her motions, beauty in the sway of her hips, her figure oddly distinctive beneath the radiant . . . magic? Fire? Despite it, however, Sora had a clear image of glowing orbs where eyes should be—one silver, one gold—and when the Goddess smiled, her expression was as clear as day, filled with mischief . . . and joy. "Sora! Etolié!"

Her rich voice echoed through the room, and Sora stood frozen.

She remained so even as the Goddess practically danced down carpeted steps, her excitement surely infectious, were Sora not reeling from the name. Her grand stature shrank with each step, until she stood as tall as a normal elf—a few inches shorter than Sora, even. But it did nothing to impede her imposing figure, for she carried herself as high as the sky, and it was not until she was near enough to touch that Sora remembered the threat—and promptly fell to one knee.

Luxurious laughter filled the space. "No need for that. Stand tall, Sora Makosa."

Sora obeyed, her quest forgotten as she stared upon the Goddess' visage.

Etolié, it seemed, had not recovered from the startling use of her name. "You must have me mistaken—"

"I would recognize you in any time or on any world, Etolié. My friends won't hurt you."

Etolié's smile remained painfully forced as her illusion faded.

Sora dared to speak. "How do you know my name?"

For Chaos did not simply know her given name. She knew her chosen one.

"Oh, please," the Goddess teased. "You're the Champion of Sol Kareena. How could I not know you?"

Sora had nothing to say to that, stunned by Chaos' grandiose words.

"How are you? Tell me of you. Both of you!"

If there were any obvious tell that Etolié was about to piss herself from anxiety, it was her ensuing nervous laughter. "Are we friends, uh, ma'am?"

"Oh, yes! Well, no. In a way, but also not yet. You are one of my dearest!"

Again came that paralyzed chuckle. "Well, I'm doing just dandy," Etolié replied. "Thought I was signing up for a weekend vacation, and now I'm meeting another Old God."

Sora's jaw remained slack. She collected herself as best she could, seeking a reply that made any coherent amount of sense. "I-

I'm well. I came to Zauleen to collect an inheritance. Before that, I was in Nox'Kartha, caring for my sister. S-She's recovering from an accident. Soliel knows. He witnessed part of it."

Only then did Sora match Soliel's gaze, noting the murderous glare upon his handsome features. Uluron had presumed Chaos would kill him. Perhaps Chaos knew nothing of his crimes.

But his smile came when he spoke, Chaos' attention diverting to him alone. "Indeed. And you are a kind sister to assist her."

There remained a warning in his gaze, narrowing when Chaos looked once more to Sora. "I am so happy to see you. I insist we throw a feast in your honor."

The words struck Sora like a slap to the face. "What?"

"Executor," Chaos said, whirling around on graceful feet, "tonight we shall treat our guests to fine food. They are my friends, and you shall proclaim that to all of Tierzuroth."

"Of course," Executor Faeborn said, their confusion thinly veiled. No mention of the fact that a monarch they were technically at war with had invaded their capital city.

"I'm sorry," Sora said softly—for only Chaos to hear, "but are we also, um, friends?"

"Yes, in a way. Not yet, but soon. I love you dearly, Sora. By gods, it has been so long."

At those words, something shifted in Chaos' countenance, her stance becoming . . . different as she came a step too close. The hair rose on the back of Sora's neck, for she had stared upon predators before—and she could not dismiss how the Goddess' heterochromatic eyes faded into black pits. Sora faced hunger. She faced . . . *hatred.*

Chaos' voice became a whisper. "You'll be lucky if I don't tear you limb from limb first." Chaos lingered far too near, and Sora swore something akin to a guttural *growl* escaped her throat. "But that's an old grudge. It can wait."

She stepped back, her charm returning, but Sora remained off balance. Her heart pulsed in her ears even as Chaos barked out orders about what food to serve. Sora looked to Etolié, whose many years as a politician were clearly failing her, given her manic eyes.

Elsewhere, Soliel's attention remained fixed upon Chaos, and Sora could not shake the feeling that he was just as nervous as she felt.

"Etolié! Sora!"

The name pulled Sora from her accidental meditation.

"Accommodations are being set for you," Chaos said. "Only the finest, obviously. You are both royalty, after all."

"I . . . I suppose, technically—"

"Rightful Archbishop of the Theocracy is what you are, Sora, and you shall be treated as such. And for the Empress of Solvira, there shall be a splendid selection of wines. But, but, you have not come by accident, and somehow I doubt it was to see me—so what is your quest? What brings you to the beautiful city of Tierzuroth?"

Sora supposed she shouldn't be surprised that a Goddess with presumably the same time-warping habits as her God of Order counterpart had some level of omnipotence, but it did not make her continuous stream of reveals any less daunting. With her gaze set warily upon Soliel, Sora listened as Etolié said, "We came with Uluron. She's waiting outside the gates."

Immediate joy sparked from the Goddess' smile. "She is here?"

"That's what I said—"

"Soliel, come on!" Chaos sprinted from the room, far faster than any mortal could follow—but Soliel was no mere mortal. Sora noted his panic, wondered if it fueled his steps, and watched as guards ran to follow.

Sora did not move again until Etolié ushered her on. "Sora, I have opinions, but I'll withhold them for the sake of the executor in the room."

"I don't know what I think, but I definitely have questions."

"I don't feel any kind of enchantment, but I'm not discounting the possibility."

They reached the doors and ran.

By the time they came upon the city gates, Chaos' delight echoed across the thick jungle, her laughter radiant. Sora came upon a heartwarming sight—the great dragon gathering her mother into her claws and curling around her like a cat. Though mythical, Uluron was still a creature, and Sora knew animal body language enough to recognize happiness.

Sora stood nigh with Etolié, unwilling to interrupt this reunion of mother and daughter. To think of how long this dragon had been alone . . . Sora supposed she could relate at least a little, for not a day passed when she did not miss her own mother.

But the joyous mood faded at pacing metallic footsteps. Uluron immediately uncurled from her mother, bristling though she had no fur. Sora stumbled away lest she cross Soliel's path. The hated God held his hands up in defense, his words purposefully kind. "Uluron, my—"

A vicious roar interrupted the words, purple flame filling Uluron's mouth. Fear surged through Sora, for while Uluron was a friend, she suspected they would all be sacrificed if it meant slaying the dragon's father.

Chaos stood between them, her fire not receding as she stroked Uluron's jaw. "Ulu, no. I understand the impulse, but listen— Listen!"

Some silent interaction occurred, only seconds long, yet Sora felt a frenzied change in the wind—and perhaps it was literal, given Soliel wielded four orbs, each spinning behind his back.

"Oh, I know what he did. I've always known." Her laughter filled the empty space, though it held a strange edge, malevolent in ways Sora suspected she should fear. "Soliel, my *love*, it seems you've really fucked a few things up."

No kindness in the title; only malice and mockery. "She disagrees with the plan to separate the realms," Soliel replied.

"Ulu, dear one, won't you give the orbs to me? Your duty is fulfilled. I don't have time to explain now, but I will soon."

Sora felt radiant waves of confusion emanate from the great dragon, yet her gut twisted as Uluron withdrew the Dark Orb from her spine, presenting it and the Earth Orb.

Chaos did not pick them up, but they lifted nevertheless, floating around her in the manner they did Soliel. "I know you're apprehensive— I know, I know. Will you trust me, please? I promise to explain."

Chaos came forward, and Sora felt the rise in power as the six orbs neared, the greatest magics in the realms reunited. Was this the end? Sora's hand graced the dagger at her hip, wondering if tackling a Goddess to save the realms would work or be suicide.

"This is a grand moment," Soliel said, coming near. The power grew stronger between them, tension rising in the air. "If we wish to make an announcement of the separation of the realms, we have the time, but there is something to do first—"

His words were stolen by Chaos' gentle *tsk tsk*. She came near, so near that the orbs circled in unison around them both as she placed a glowing hand upon his armored chest. So much smaller than him, yet her presence remained indomitable, and he was the smaller force. "If you keep your damn mouth shut, perhaps one of our friends will *help*."

Sora glanced at Uluron, noting the dragon's restless panic, how she pawed the ground. This was not at all the plan—not that there had been one—and Sora saw only one course of action. She matched eyes with Etolié, recognizing that same insanity reflected in her.

She muttered, "We need to—"

Etolié nodded. "Wait for my cue," she whispered back, "then grab the orbs."

Soliel spoke, again, to Chaos. "Only if you can keep your threats to yourself."

"You were never the sharpest tool in the—"

Then appeared a second dragon.

Sora had only heard of Valeuron and his gruesome end, the undead dragon a slave in death until freed by being burned on Solvira's battlefield. The undead beast bore signs of rot, gargantuan staples sealing his head to his neck. No question of what this was— and there was only one person who could have caused this.

The beast roared. Soliel drew his sword, followed by the elven guards. Chaos shrieked. Amid the confusion, Sora bolted toward the Goddess of Chaos and—

Ran straight through her.

Sora's body reeled at the wash of cold, losing all stamina as she tumbled to the ground.

"Don't give me a reason, Sora!"

Sora blinked and faced a wrathful creature, a virulent shadow leering above.

"How dare you use my son against me! *How dare you!?"*

Rough hands grabbed her—though not the Goddess. Guards had swarmed her, predictably. Sora struggled. If she could just grab a knife from her sleeve—

The dragon vanished with Etolié's sudden scream. The ground opened, swallowing the Celestial whole—save for her head, which peeked from a crevice.

"Stop it! Stop it!" Chaos screamed, her fire rising as she confronted Soliel. *"Don't hurt her, stupid boy!"*

"Stand down!" Soliel cried, and never, in all her years, had Sora heard something so . . . *unnatural* as the God of Order losing his temper. "She's not hurt!"

Chaos seethed but said nothing as Soliel stepped around her. He held six orbs, and with it came the power to separate literal planes of existence and thus the ability to manipulate the very fabric of space. Might was his aura, his Godhood never so apparent. He marched to Etolié, helpless in the ground—who for all her power was nothing in his shadow. "A worthy attempt. But some of us know your tricks."

Etolié tried to spit, but the pitiful spittle barely made it past her lips.

"Take Sora!" Soliel commanded. "Bring me the maldectine shackles!"

To the sound of obscenities vile enough for only Etolié to concoct, Sora was dragged away.

When Etolié tried to spit out a stream of fire, a bubble of ice surrounded her head.

Her heart beat in her throat as her panic rose, the ground encasing her entire figure. Her wings prickled from the sensation of dirt, and each gasping breath became shallower—was there enough air in this pocket of ice?

At least she would suffocate before she died of hypothermia. Etolié momentarily debated the merit of praying to Momma for help and abandoning Sora—

The ice melted, a significant amount falling straight into her throat. Etolié choked even as the earth ejected her. Upon the moist ground, she heaved, sick as she coughed the icy water from her lungs.

One little *click* around her wrists, and all her awareness of the world faded. She recognized that shade of green in her shackles.

Fucking dammit.

Soliel yanked her up by the arm, though he kept his distance. "Someone fetch this woman a robe!"

Right. Maldectine meant no illusionary clothes—and so, tits out. "So half-drowning a lady is fine, but gods forbid we let someone see her cooch?"

"It is basic decency."

"Soliel, cousin, you're hours away from murdering literally a billion fucking people, so I appreciate the thought, but I'm thinking you should reconsider your definition of decency." Etolié wrenched herself around. There sat Uluron, whose capacity to emote was likely half the reason Etolié wanted to rip off her skin from anxiety. "Kitty, I'm second guessing everything."

Uluron didn't speak, but her tail thumped the ground like a cat, if a cat's tail were capable of shaking an entire fortress.

"You could help an angel out if you wanted to."

Uluron remained agitated but said nothing. Etolié looked to Chaos, who was oddly silent as she sat in a far too mortal way upon the ground, head in her hands. "Any updates on that feast, ghostie?"

In meticulous motions, as though stepping around shattered glass, Chaos rose anew, her candor far more subdued. "Ulu is quite agitated. Soliel has six orbs, and she has none," Chaos said, her sobriety frankly making Etolié ill. "There remains the threat that all of us could be struck by lightning in an instant—and without the Dark Orb's protection, it would shatter her bones. Do not hold her inaction against her."

"Kinda shitty that you put her in that position." Etolié gritted her teeth as she suppressed her rising rage. They were fucked on a technicality, and with Soliel mere inches away, she had nothing but her words. Her voice rose. "I'm not saying if the worlds get separated that it's your fault, Kitty, but I am saying you're the only one in a position to stop it."

"Etolié, riddle me this." Chaos seethed, yet those glowing pits weren't focused on Etolié—but upon Soliel. "If there were a way to end this madness without the death of billions, you would endorse it, right?"

"Are we still talking millions?"

"One."

Etolié feared whiplash for how rapidly she reeled back. "Well, shit—sacrifice me at the altar."

Chaos said nothing. Instead, Etolié was offered a robe by an approaching guard. After an awkward shuffle and unlatching one shackle, Etolié's skin prickled from the itchy canvas. "Look, I appreciate the thought, but I'd much rather be nude." She was ignored, of course, instead dragged back into the city. "So are we burning me at the stake?"

"No," came Soliel's rather grumpy reply.

"So much for being friends."

To her surprise, Chaos spoke up. "I never said I canceled the feast."

Chaos was talking bullshit again.

As they dragged her back into the city, Etolié debated the merit of trying to shut off the maldectine now or later. Soliel had six orbs, and she had teleportation powers and a momma capable of backing her up—so perhaps waiting for him to fucking leave was best.

Even with the maldectine, she could still host Eionei. It would hurt like a bitch, but she'd done it before. Perhaps he could help her rescue Sora.

Numerous elves watched from the streets—some looking to her, others trying to catch a glimpse of the massive dragon beyond the walls. However, Etolié's attention drifted to the grand sight before them.

The image was well known in learned circles—the Goddess of Chaos carved from stone, arms spread wide in something that wasn't quite welcome. More . . . a challenge.

Soliel's armor bore heat from their skirmish, the metal embellishments bruising her skin as he pressed her close. They breeched a stone arch beneath the statue and took a sharp turn underground. Torches burned in their sconces. Stone steps led down into flickering darkness.

Yet more daunting was a subtle, secondary film that enveloped her mind—not nearly so invasive as maldectine, but something was assuredly wrong. "What is this place?"

"The Temple of Chaos," said Soliel.

Etolié could only see forward, caged by Soliel's oversized arms, but metallic steps meant they were far from alone. "Why do I feel weird here?"

Fucking hell, she hated his chuckle. Etolié figured that would be the end of it, trying to be subtle as she brought her wrists closer, touching the unmistakable rocks embedded into the shackles.

No one needed to know she could turn this shit off. But the moment had to be right, and this tiny-ass hallway wasn't it.

Ominous silver light followed, starkly contrasting with the torch's flame. The Goddess of Chaos appeared in her peripheral, her stare shockingly demoralizing for someone with no facial features.

To Etolié's surprise, the Goddess spoke up. "This place is older than the Convergence. The magic that lingers is and has always been mine. You cannot pray here. You cannot summon any of your angels—or demons. The New Gods have no power in these places."

Etolié didn't like that one fucking bit. The urgency of turning off the damn shackles just went up. "Well, that's just lovely."

"We would not normally use this for prisoners, but there are special exceptions."

"It's damn clever, but I'm still hung up on that whole 'killing one instead of a billion' thing, so I'd love if you'd elaborate. I have recommendations if you won't accept me. "

She was ignored.

The stairs ended, leading to a large antechamber. Rough stone made up the walls, carved into the very earth, and numerous halls branched away, creating a labyrinth. How large, Etolié couldn't guess, but Soliel released her, keeping only a hand on her shoulder.

When Chaos drifted away from their party, Etolié shifted to keep her distance. A quick glance back—six guards. And then Soliel. Not the best odds.

Fuck it. Etolié narrowed her focus, grasping onto the maldectine's aura. Long ago, she had practiced over and over in a library to the chorus of Flowers' berating. If she could focus through that, she could ignore a God breathing down her neck.

Like snuffing a match, the aura muted.

One chance. Best to make it count.

An illusion to all but her. Etolié burst into flame.

Heat seared even Etolié's skin, her belief in her own lies honed over the years. The stone walls should not have ignited, yet the fire rose rapidly. The guards cried out, weapons readied, some scattering to the stairs. Etolié slipped with ease from Soliel's startled grip. She unlatched the shackles, her most trivial talent, and tossed them to the floor.

Invisibility was a bitch to maintain, so instead Etolié became the Goddess of Chaos—but met the hated Goddess' gaze. Her illusion threatened to flicker when Chaos made a show of snapping her fingers.

The flames rose, and it wasn't Etolié's doing. The guards screamed as it burst toward them, driving them away from the stairs. Soliel neared, but the path to freedom had cleared.

Chaos made a slight flick with her head, directing Etolié to the stairs.

Well, there was no way Etolié was doing that anymore. She ran into the labyrinth, opting to take her chances—and hopefully circle back when that crazy bitch was out of sight.

Her focus waned, and she kept her wits for the winding stone maze instead.

Soliel's voice echoed through the halls. *"How did she escape?"*

"She can mute maldectine, stupid."

Chaos sounded oddly bored.

Etolié passed open arches, occasionally diving through them. No doors, but she ran through a small chapel, sparing no attention for what was surely gorgeous décor. But no, no—history could wait.

Should she hide? Etolié slowed at the chapel's exit, diving beneath the deep altar instead.

Old wood met her nose, joining with dust and ancient rock. Her wings disappeared at her will, her body camouflaging to match the altar. Heavy footsteps neared, soon pounding into the room.

"Do you feel her?" Soliel asked.

Etolié debated turning the maldectine back on and risking the glow, because if Chaos had Silver Fire, she could sense magic.

"No, but there's some bad shit she could find down here. Don't stop."

What?

Etolié held her breath until Soliel and his counterpart were a memory. She focused her thoughts and sent a silent prayer to Celestière. *Goddess Momma?*

Nothing. Chaos hadn't bluffed.

Chaos did have illusion powers, however—or elemental fire. Etolié shouldn't have been surprised, but the reminder that this new threat had a smorgasbord of unknown magical powers was far from comforting.

She glanced out from her hiding place, still tucked tight beneath the hollow altar. An ancient tapestry depicted the ancient Deity. Not covered in flame this time, no, but simply a dark silhouette with glowing eyes. One silver; one gold.

More footsteps approached. Etolié shut her eyes as lighter steps passed through—guards, surely. At their exit, she gathered her courage and crept out, letting her natural color return. Her wings remained invisible—safer to avoid the glow—and she ran the way she'd come.

A new issue arose, however. Etolié glanced down the hall and realized she was lost.

"Well, fuck me," she muttered, then took her chances and bolted one way, hoping the dusty footsteps on the ground were her own. She had no fear of elven guards. Just Soliel and maybe that Goddess Bitch.

What the hell kind of game was she playing?

Etolié illusioned away even her pattering footsteps, the eerie silence causing her skin to crawl. Etolié slowed at corners, illusioning a mirror to peek around them before sprinting to the next turn. Was this familiar? Was she lying to herself when she said she might've recognized the indents in the rock walls? More than likely.

There came a point when Etolié knew she'd taken more turns than the way she'd come. Creeping panic set her nerves on edge, along with the realization that Soliel could just cave the labyrinth in if he were truly desperate to keep her. The fuse was lit, and she only had so much time to escape the blast.

She barreled ahead, kept checking corners with her mirror, until, amid the daunting silence, she heard the rustling of heavy chains—

And a faint, metallic groan.

Something about it froze Etolié's burning blood. She stopped, for her spirit knew even if her mind did not. Her heel pivoted toward the noise. Down into a dark tunnel, not lit by torches at all.

Etolié's wings returned, illuminating the space. Breathless, she ran, heat rising as the path sloped downward once more. Her hands shook, losing feeling as her mind finally grasped what horrible thing this was—confirmed as she entered a massive antechamber deep underground.

Khastra was unmistakable, though bars stood strong between them. She was naked, her blue skin greyed from dust, her tattoos muted beneath layers of grime. Chains were set around her hooves, with old blood caked around the shackles. Her arms spread wide, hands encased in metal boxes attached to chains bolted to the walls. Iron encased her head, creating a torturous helmet covering her entire face. Surely a suffocating sensory hell, its own chain attaching to the ceiling—so while she slumped, she could not sit, forced to stand.

Again came that horrible moan, muted by metal around her face.

"Khastra?"

No reaction.

Etolié couldn't breathe, but she searched for a door. The bars had been welded from floor to ceiling, no entrance—and so no locks. Perhaps she could slip through instead.

What's that light? Check the prisoner!

Etolié wrenched her shoulder through the bars, stopped by her own damn tits. "Khastra!"

Khastra shifted—and not in a random way.

Heavy footsteps fell upon her, Soliel's speed deceptive for his size. Strong arms wrenched Etolié back. "Khastra!"

More arms grabbed her. The vague thought of fire flittered through her head, but—

Pain struck her head, her vision going white. Her head spun as her legs lost strength. She swore she heard chains, but more pressing were the grimy hands forcing her mouth to open. She bit down—only for her teeth to strike metal.

"Force it down her throat!"

Etolié choked as what felt like grains of sand filled her mouth, followed by the sharp taste of wine. She swallowed, lest she drown—

And all her awareness, her connection to magic—gone.

She managed merely a groaned, "Khastra?"

"I will take her."

Etolié forced her eyes to open, cursed to see Soliel's hated face. She fought his grip as he dragged her away. She sought fire, sought sparkles, sought any damn illusion she could—

Oh gods, the sand. Was it maldectine?

Chains shook behind her. Khastra struggled with her bonds. Etolié clawed desperately at Soliel's armored body, heaved away unwillingly. *"Khastra!"*

"Someone hand me a gag."

"Khastra—"

Her screaming mouth was muted by cloth.

Etolié struggled and shrieked, blinded by tears as she blinked. Khastra was here. Khastra was trapped underground where Ku'Shya could not be. Where even Etolié's own momma could not be. How long had she suffered here? Had she been here all along?

Etolié did not cease her fighting, but Soliel's strength far surpassed hers. When he threw her into a cell, she collapsed. The lock clicked.

"I will discuss with Executor Faeborn if they think it is worth using you for leverage against Nox'Kartha," came Soliel's voice—but she refused to face him, instead watching as her own tears dotted the earth beneath her. "Though given the gravity of what you witnessed, I cannot promise you will be released."

Etolié's tears fell fast. She tried to focus on the maldectine inside her, but where the hell was it? She couldn't fucking feel it.

His heavy footsteps faded away. Through sobs, Etolié caught sight of the Goddess of Chaos following behind her hated counterpart.

She ripped out her gag. "Is Khastra your fucking sacrifice?! Just tell me what you mean! *Tell me what I have to do!*"

Chaos did not even spare her a parting glance.

One final hope—Etolié forced herself to stand, stumbling against the barred door.

The lock did not click. Her magic had truly gone.

Etolié collapsed against the vertical bars, weeping against her will.

Seated in a simple prison cell of wood and metal bars, Sora finished her silent count of her remaining knives.

Seven. Fewer than she preferred, but the guards had taken all the ones they could find. Luck still followed her, however. The small one tucked into her vambrace could double as a letter opener. Perfect for slipping into mechanical locks.

Sora rose, feigning a stretch as she reached for the ceiling. No windows. Only a lantern on a desk beyond. The sole guard remained impassive in his chair, attention fully invested in whatever novel he kept hidden under his desk. She might have been amused, but he'd confiscated both her matches *and* her Spore when she'd tried to light her pipe. Would she have burned down the prison? Only as a last resort, given Sora had already escaped more burning buildings than preferable.

At least he'd let her keep the pipe.

Instead, Sora remained alert and restless, shifting between casually inspecting her small prison and pacing. Leelan stood peacefully on Sora's shoulder, and she debated the risk of letting him fly through the bars before stuffing him carefully into her shirt, letting only his little head peek out from the collar of her tunic. Seven knives. With the right aim, she could hit the guard, but the chance of killing him in one blow was slim. Even then, he was simply a man doing his job. Whatever Sora's prior sins, murdering innocents was not an option.

Elsewhere a door creaked open, heavy steps approaching. When the guard slipped his book back under his chair, Sora smoothly sat back on the splintered floorboards, only to stiffen at the approaching God.

In the dim lighting of the prison, Soliel's inner radiance added to his angelic illusion, his halo out of place in so dank an environment. The only piece that fit in was the adventure-worn pack hanging from his forearm, and if the subtle glow was any indicator, those were the Convergence Orbs. Nearby, a silver hue followed—the flame-engulfed Chaos, his unfortunate shadow.

The guard stood to bow, then left them alone—Sora and these two ancient titans. "Good afternoon, Sora Makosa," Soliel began, the chosen surname feeling grimy spoken by his hated tongue. "I wished to inform you that I am in talks with Executor Faeborn to secure your release."

Highly suspicious, but Sora had gotten far in life by being underestimated. She kept her stance small, mimicking the squirrels she'd spent countless hours studying in her youth. "Why?"

"You are no threat on your own."

That didn't feel right, but Sora had no rebuttal. Her gaze shifted to the entity of what could only be Silver Fire beside Soliel, something akin to eyes glowing in its depths, flickering as virulently as her fire.

"However," Soliel continued, his voice far gentler than the omen of his presence should have allowed, "I must inquire: Where is your sister?"

Sora wouldn't say she had any overt talent for reading people or predicting the flow of conversation, but every statement from Soliel's mouth was increasingly strange. "Would you like to first explain how you know I have a sister? You didn't seem surprised at all when I mentioned it."

Chaos replied, and Sora waited for the threat, to feel her skin crawl as she became prey—but it did not come. "Just because something is kept quiet now does not mean it always will be. Besides, did I not say I loved you? It would be safe to assume I know nearly everything about you."

That was in no way comforting. Sora mulled over her words, wary of the dynamics at hand. But while Sora was no politician, this seemed far too simple. "So what you're telling me is if I tell you where Flowridia is, you'll let me go."

"Correct."

"It's clearly very important to you, then. I'll be keeping my mouth shut, thank you."

To Sora's horror, Chaos cackled—bloodcurdling, malevolent, yet it was not toward Sora—but at Soliel. "What did I tell you, *stupid* boy? She won't say anything. Not if it comes from you."

Sora's gut twisted from some pang of familiarity, yet she could not place it.

Chaos' attention fell upon her, and though a mere silhouette, Sora shrank before that vindictive smile. "Don't listen to him. Say nothing, or I'll rip your tongue out."

The nostalgic nature of the threat delayed her a moment, leaving Sora blinking. No point in giving the Goddess any ideas, though. "Then I suppose we agree."

"Keep that lip, and I'll rip it out anyway—" Chaos flinched, stumbling back with an eerie grace. Yet Soliel followed in perfect sync, a dance they'd performed before it seemed, but remained helpless as his hands merely hovered around her, never touching.

Sora was once against struck by the ineffable presence of a predatory creature. When Chaos stared from behind the shield of her hands, the world became silent save for the beat of Sora's heart.

Chaos' eyes shut. "I would never," the Goddess muttered into her hands. "I would never hurt you. I am so sorry."

"Why do you care about my sister?" Sora asked, though the words held no backbone at all, hardly more than air.

Chaos neared, passing through the cell bars without so much as a flicker. There emanated no heat from Chaos' fiery silhouette. Instead, seeping cold. Sora's hand slipped to her sleeve, gripping a knife as the Goddess came near enough to reveal the outline of a humanoid figure beneath the flickering flame—and the unmistakable glow of heterochromatic eyes.

"He wants to save her life," Chaos said, mockery in the words. "He's proved it time and time again, you see. Except when he hasn't."

A faint, guttural rumbling raised the hair on the back of Sora's neck. She had her knife, but would it do anything? Were Chaos more than a silhouette, she'd be baring her teeth. "I could kill you anyway. Sooner than it's supposed to happen, but I don't give a fuck. Should I describe your death? You know all about mine—"

"Dira, stop."

The air remained stale even as Chaos whirled back, her mercurial mood fixed upon Soliel. "You think I'm Dira?"

Soliel remained stalwart, even as she grew to match his height. "I know who you are, and you're out of control. We will come back later."

"But I'm having so much fun—"

But Soliel was already marching out, his light disappearing as he rounded the corner.

Left alone, Chaos seemed to struggle, visibly straining against some invisible force. As if dragged, her body drifted through the metal bars. Though horrified, Sora didn't dare to move, her only protection having literally walked away.

"One of us is lying," Chaos muttered. Even covered in fire, Sora felt that gaze sear straight down to her soul. "It isn't me."

Sora reeled at the statement, seeking a trick, any explanation at all.

Chaos' attention never wavered as her hand passed through the mechanical lock, the faint *click* louder than a gunshot in the quiet. She came no nearer, instead stumbling back until she made a graceful turn—and followed where Soliel had left.

Sora gasped for breath the moment the Goddess disappeared, every nerve alight. Absently, she felt for Leelan's little head in her shirt, making certain he hadn't died of fright.

As she rubbed feeling back into her arms, her mind replayed the exchange, left with far more questions than answers. Was this a trap? Sora gripped the wall to help her stand, managing to ward off the rush of blood to her head.

Sora removed her boot, careful not to upset the knives hidden in their sheaths. Arm outstretched, she touched the firm leather to the door—and watched it swing open, its lock disabled.

What did it mean?

The guard had not returned, and Sora slipped her boot back in its place. Silent, she crept through the open door, awaiting a trap, yet nothing stopped her. Nothing attacked her. Sora kept her back to the wall as she peered around the corner.

The ancient floorboards groaned beneath her light steps. Sora ducked as she entered a larger foyer, immediately barreling toward a vacant desk. The front door was ajar, letting in a cooling breeze. No guards in sight.

What had Chaos done?

Sora held her breath and crept out, anticipating a trap. Yet spots of sunlight soon blessed her. Sora increased her pace but stayed low, sequestering herself behind barrels by the prison's back door.

But now what? She could run, yes. She would likely succeed. She could forage in the jungle and make her way north—surely the Whispering Elves would arrest her on sight, but perhaps the Iron Elves wouldn't receive the message. And if so, farther north still, to the Sun Elves, then secure a boat across the sea, return to Nox'Kartha—

That would take months.

Where was Etolié? Would Goddess Staella help her if it were in service of her daughter? Any service Sora had known her to provide involved portals, which would only take Sora farther away. Could Sora even reach the Goddess of Stars anyway?

But all that paled in comparison to the greater issue at hand: Soliel had six orbs. What was the use of Sora escaping if Soliel separated the worlds tonight? There would be no Goddess Staella to help.

Soliel had the orbs with him, but hadn't Mereen managed to steal one? He was a God, but if Sora had learned anything on her journey of disillusionment, it was that Gods were little more than ascended mortals. Anyone could be tricked—why not him?

There were causes worth dying for. Sora couldn't imagine a greater one.

Executor Faeborn had made mention of a room for Soliel. Sora made her way toward the executor's hall once again.

Presumably, Sora's arrest wasn't common knowledge, but she bore the curse of being unique looking among elves. She stuck to the backstreets, the paths dirt instead of stone. She ducked behind barrels whenever someone passed, wishing she had a hood to hide her hair, but no one was looking, and so no one saw.

Yet the weight of her task fell upon her, all the panic she had felt in Chaos' presence returning tenfold. She heard nothing except her throbbing heart, but her anxiety quelled when soft feathers rubbed against her sternum.

The wall surrounding the executor's hall was rough stone stacked in layers. Sora had little trouble clinging to its natural ledges, surprised to find it minimally guarded when she peeked her head over the top. A few elves chatted before the entrance, but the melding of tree and building meant there were plenty of crevices to duck into.

But first, she had to get down.

Sora skirted along the top of the wall, ducking to be as small as she could, until she found a corner less occupied. She gathered her bearings, recalling years of leaping from trees with her mother in the woods—and jumped.

Bless the soft foliage—when Sora rolled, she had little more than grass stains upon her clothes.

She had expected more security, due to the Godly presences, or perhaps it explained why the home was so vacant. What protection could a mere mortal possibly provide an Old God? Still, Sora kept her ears keen as she spotted an open window on the second floor and a clear path of roots climbing around it.

Sora gripped the firm bark, heaving herself up and over the window frame.

She landed in a sitting room, thankfully empty. Bookshelves lined the walls, along with couches too fanciful for her dusty clothes and a cold fireplace.

One room down, and countless more to go. Sora reached into her tunic to pet Leelan, his chirp reassuring. "If they send me to the gallows, I'll make a case for them to spare you."

Leelan said nothing, but he did rub against her finger.

Sora set her ear to the exit and hand to the ground. No footsteps. With any luck, appearing nonchalant was her best course, assuming she didn't run into Executor Faeborn. Or Soliel. Or that damn Goddess. Or any of the guards involved in her arrest.

Perhaps it wouldn't be so simple.

Sora slipped through the door, calculating where one would house a God. Surely not the first floor—or perhaps assuredly, to spare them the extra steps. Or perhaps the top floor for safety, but again, what use was protection to a God?

Sora did what she did best and set her ear to the next door, heard nothing, then peeked inside—finding a closet of brooms and mops.

They wouldn't put a pair of Gods near where servants kept supplies. But servants knew where a pair of Gods would be. Sora continued forward, alert for any chatting. She willed her heart to steady, fearful it would beat louder than her footsteps.

The hallway ended in a door, but when Sora peeked through the seam, she recognized the throne room's ceiling. Deftly, she opened it, realizing she was on a balcony skirting the edges—and ducked upon hearing familiar voices below.

". . . must understand what it would mean for my people should the empress spread the news of the Bringer of War's location."

"Executor Faeborn, that precludes she escapes." Soliel's soothing tones merely served to boil Sora's blood. "She has no means to contact anyone in the Celestial Realm from her prison."

Sora peered through the natural balcony, grown from the tree encompassing the massive building. There stood Executor Faeborn facing the Old Gods, their terse words only barely controlled. "And so I will keep the Empress of Solvira as a hostage until the end of my days? With all possible respect, God of Order, this pit grows ever deeper. I have expressed time and time again my disapproval of keeping the Bringer of War hostage in the first place, much less with my people. I would have withdrawn my support of the war if not for your assurance of my people's safety—and again, with all possible respect, you have me questioning the validity of that promise."

"Do you truly fear Ku'Shya more than me?"

"I assuredly do, God of Order. For ten thousand years, my people have done what we must to appease the monster lurking in *Daemenacht*—sacrifices, rituals, gifts, *anything* to stop her from unleashing her might upon us. She sent another messenger asking for updates just this morning. I can only lie for so long. The fact that she has been this patient suggests there is some respect between us—and how dare you put me in a position to lose it all. And not only me—my people will be slaughtered should she find out what we've kept from her."

Sora nearly forgot her quest, so enthralled she was by what she witnessed.

"You have my solid vow, Executor," Soliel said. "Your sacrifices for the war and for the world may never be known to the public, but you hold my favor and hers."

Silence settled. Sora strained to hear any whispers, but then—

"Executor, if my counterpart has given his word, believe him," Chaos said, yet her words held a strange edge. "However, I would never approve of the slaughter of my own people for any cause. The other elven kingdoms only know of Ku'Shya's power—you and yours have bravely borne witness to it for ten thousand years, as you said. And you are braver still, to speak your mind so freely. Six Convergence Orbs against the might of the Goddess of War might be enough, but perhaps we should convene again when our tempers are quelled and discuss what it is you, the elected leader, truly want."

All anger faded from Executor Faeborn's tone. "That would be ideal, Goddess Chaos. Thank you."

"In the meantime, there remains the matter of what to do with Empress Etolié. We shall discuss it privately."

They all moved to part. Sora watched their exit carefully, then dashed along the balcony to the adjoining door a floor above.

By the Light . . . what had she just witnessed? The Bringer of War was here? Ku'Shya personally sought her?

There were more pressing matters, but it would not be forgotten.

Sora slipped through the adjacent door, walking briskly as she navigated the fanciful hallway. One glance into an open door revealed a plain bedchamber—so perhaps she was in the right place after all.

Sora peeked inside every open room she could, finding nothing lived in, but finding no servants, either. Emboldened by the silence, she peered between the door and floorboards, finding this one empty too, only to enter a parlor room.

Over and over, she checked each door, frustration rising in tandem with paranoia. Each passing second meant ... well, something bad, surely.

Footsteps sounded. Without bothering to check, Sora slipped inside the next room—only to lose her breath.

The oversized bed confirmed her suspicions, the empty armor rack further evidence. Though rich in décor, there was nothing personal about it. The paintings could have been in any upscale inn, the washroom was pretty but strange for a warrior, and were it not for the clothing hung in the half-open wardrobe, Sora would have assumed it vacant.

The doorknob twisted. Sora dove beneath the bed, mindful of Leelan pressed against her chest as she scuffled under the heavy wood. Not quite cramped, but certainly uncomfortable. One startle, and she'd bang her head, but at least she could crawl on her elbows.

The armored boots were familiar, but as soon as the door shut, the entity of silver flame . . . changed.

Sora only saw as high as her ankles, yet the fire dissipated and revealed dainty elven feet—in shades of eerie blue. Her toes left the ground, floating inches high.

Chaos . . . was a ghost?

"Soliel, I am sorry. I told you."

"I know."

"It was my mistake. We never should have asked Sora—"

"Yet you mocked me for approaching it peacefully."

"It was not—"

"Is it Dira now?"

In the lapse of silence, Sora swore time slowed when a worn pack was placed carefully on the floor before her, faintly glowing from within.

"Yes."

The bed creaked above Sora. She glanced back, watching thick fingers fumble with bootstraps. With agonizing slowness, she scooted herself forward.

"Soliel . . ." Chaos' voice came gently now, entirely foreign to what Sora had witnessed before. "I know where Flowridia is, and if you would only listen—"

"You know the trouble I've gone through to keep her alive."

"And I'm here to tell you it was a mistake."

"Dira—"

"Were you planning on living on after you tore the worlds apart?"

"I don't know."

Above, the buckles and singing of metal and fabric meant he was likely removing that golden armor. Sora hardly dared to breathe, because the end of the world could literally be minutes away, and she was the one trapped with two genocidal Deities and the Convergence Orbs, which meant this might be the culmination of her entire purpose on this realm. She reached. Her fingers brushed against old leather.

But one slip-up . . .

"Then why does it matter if she dies?" Chaos asked.

The silence stretched on, tension rising in the void. Sora froze.

Soliel's words came tersely. "I won't agree to this."

Sora's nail touched metal rings and paused, fearful of alerting the Gods.

"I have had ten thousand years to contemplate it—"

"Dira, no. The orbs are foolproof. Your plan is barbaric."

"Barbaric?!" All softness disappeared from Chaos, her cackling laughter returning full force. "In what way is it barbaric to kill one to save a billion?"

Sora managed to grab the bag, the slight rustling lost behind Chaos' mania. Not for the first time, she cursed her progenitors for never teaching her how to slip into Sha'Demoni.

"I won't do it. Dira—"

"Why the orbs, Soliel? Is it so you can justify murdering my son?"

"The greater good says—"

"The greater good is defeating Casvir, and we both know who could have done it."

Sora managed to drag the bag a little closer, but was now faced with a new dilemma—escaping.

And while she was concerned about the casual discussion of her sister's death, that would only be a problem if she managed to steal the orbs. Sora's finger slipped inside, seeking to secure her grip, and brushed against something—

Dark.

Sora bit back a shriek at the massive influx—and immediate withdrawal—of power. By the Light, it was caustic, her own power recoiling, her very soul disgusted.

. . . had she made noise? Sora remained deathly still. How could no one have felt that?

"Your plan hinges on assumption," Soliel said. "Mine takes away Casvir's path to power. It cannot fail."

Could Sora use any of the orbs? Perhaps the Light Orb, but a slip-up with unfamiliar magic would condemn the world.

"Fine, use the damn orbs. Do it tonight."

Sora didn't often swear, but this was definitely the time for a well-placed, *shit*.

"I know what you're trying to do," Soliel said, his gentle tone returning, "and I think you're missing the full implications of what I am working toward. I have thought about you all along."

"Soliel, don't—"

"There need not be moonlilies in this new world."

"Shut up."

"I have done it all for you."

A beat of silence ensued, and Sora did not dare breathe.

"Do not pretend you're selfless," Chaos whispered, and a shiver teased Sora's spine at the icy phrase. "It's the one thing he and I agree on."

"Dira—"

The ensuing gasp and smacking of lips stirred odd questions, and Sora, confused, witnessed the first flickering of flame returning to cover Chaos' elven feet.

If Silver Fire could touch ghosts and souls when wielded by mortals, did the same principle apply the other way? Given the sensuous, feminine sigh, the answer was yes.

Sora had wanted a distraction. Next time she would be more specific, but the sardonic part of her knew it wasn't worse than walking in on Tazel and Mereen.

Sora had nightmares from the Mountains of Kaas, and to admit aloud that the memory of Tazel and Mereen's debauchery appeared in dreams as often as her sister's torturous screams undermined Flowridia's suffering, made a mockery of it, really. Which was why she didn't mention it. But while both memories made her want to scrub her skin until it bled, only one made her want to puke.

"Oh, Soliel . . ."

Sora moved just a little faster.

She released the pack as she scooted forward on her elbows, ears unfortunately peeled to the growing intimacy above her. But nothing broke rhythm, and soon Sora, though still on the ground, was freed from the bed's confines. The door was shut, but potentially unlocked—the window would be too obvious.

Soliel faced away from the door, not wearing his tunic, which was the end of Sora's study of *that,* but as she tentatively slipped the pack over her shoulder—

She made stark eye contact with the flame-covered Goddess and became stone.

"I think you can be wearing even less," Chaos said, nudging her head toward the door.

"Dira—"

Chaos stole his lips, still staring at Sora.

She crept to the door, quite confident she was about to die—but better to die on her feet.

"Let me help you with those," Chaos said, her words syncing with the twist of metal. "Just because I can't feel it doesn't mean you can't."

And that's when Sora successfully slipped away, six orbs in tow.

The door shut. The decorated hallway stretched on either side. Sora remained numb, uncertain of when she had released the knob. The soft glow of magic from her stolen pack drew her eye, the awareness of holding literal godly power—godly power she would surely blow herself up with if she tried to wield—finally settling.

Now what?

Sora remained perfectly still, until approaching footsteps from down the hall struck a match to her adrenaline. With light steps, Sora sprinted as fast as she was able without rattling the Convergence Orbs. A door half-ajar drew her attention. Sora slowed and peeked inside, finding a vacant study room—and more importantly, a window.

The afternoon sun cast brilliant beams upon the beautiful city, removing any hope for natural cover. Backstreets it would be again. But as she pried open the window, coughing at the rise of dust, there came a damning inquiry—what next?

She would reach the city's gates and . . . continue to run? Uluron had shown her loyalties. She would be no help. So what was Sora to do? Study the water orb as she made her way to the sea and walk across the ocean? Was escape even feasible? Where *did* she go?

Could she leave Etolié behind?

The idea caught in Sora's throat, but there was a whole city to search, and Etolié would happily die for the cause of saving the world. Sora knew that with certainty.

She offered no prayer, simply a whispered, *"I'm sorry, friend."*

Sora checked the security of her pack and made a careful descent from the second floor, gripping the gnarled knots and natural indents until she could make a safe leap to the foliage below.

Sora crept through thick leaves, the lush jungle infiltrating the city's main sector. How she wished she knew more of this city's layout—surely there was a backdoor, but instead Sora would have to sprint for the only one she knew.

She kept her head low as she wove through foreign plants, creating a makeshift path to the city's alleyways. Not much security here, and Sora wondered again if things were lax *because* of the Deities' presences.

The disconcerting fact remained that Sora had exactly as much time to escape as Chaos could keep Soliel busy. She stepped a little faster, praying her sacrifice of stealth for speed didn't damn her prematurely.

But what in the world had she overheard? Chaos was a ghost. Chaos wanted her sister dead. Casvir was marching—did she not mean the war? And by Sol Kareena's Light, Chaos had helped her escape. Twice, even.

And *Dira* . . . was that the true name of the ancient Goddess?

Gods, she wished Etolié was here to either explain it all or deliver a drunken rant to soothe Sora's nerves. As it was, she kept her head low as she passed the occasional citizen, though her golden locs did little to help her remain inconspicuous. If she escaped—*when*, she corrected—she would contact Flowridia. In the absence of Etolié, there was one other truly insane force in her life, willing or not, who might be able to think of a temporary haven for these orbs. Ayla was as clever as she was wicked.

Ayla and Flowridia could likely teach her how to use them, now that she thought about it.

Instinct said she neared the gate, and so Sora breached the seclusion of the narrow buildings, peering into the main street. The Whispering Elves paid her no heed, though many spoke excitedly of the dragon beyond the gates.

Yet another obstacle. But the city's entrance neared, wide open today—because of Uluron's presence, Sora supposed.

Or Chaos' orders. The idea caused her breath to fail, her feet to slow. How much of this had Chaos orchestrated?

The animated energy only escalated when bells rang throughout the city. Yet with it came cries of, *"Shut the doors! The orbs are missing!"*

"Shit." No time for hesitation. Sora sprinted for the gate.

"All citizens return to your homes!"

Sora ran, even as thick braids of rope fell from the top of the doors. Numerous guards took their stations and tugged, the creak of primeval wood spurring Sora onward.

"You there! Stop!"

Sora gripped the comforting leather hilt of a knife. Guards pursued, and the first *bang* of a revolver spelled doom. The whirring bullet whizzed past her ear. Sora grabbed Leelan from his hiding spot, all but throwing him into the air. Gods forbid the bullet struck her—Leelan would be crushed with her fall.

His wings caught air, making an easy escape over the walls.

Another *bang*. The sharp scent of gunpowder filled her lungs. Sora glanced back, eyes level with a cocked gun behind—

Only to ram full force into a wooden door.

She collapsed. Sora's vision went white.

"Search her bag!"

Sora blinked, sight spinning but filling with color. Instinct fueled her, not thoughts—she yanked the pack to her chest, rolling to protect it with her body.

Rough hands grabbed her, but Sora had become a stone, refusing to rise. Then came the cock of a revolver.

No thoughts at all, except the knowledge that she would die by bullet or by orb. Sora thrust her hand inside the pack and grabbed the first orb she touched.

Sora had some familiarity with magic, but two years was nothing to a lifetime of practice. So when heat burned through her, a more skilled priestess might've been able to yank the strings of magic, bid them to still.

Sora merely became a conduit, bursting with flame.

Screams sounded. The smell of burning meat filled the air. Sora could hardly see from fire and smoke, uncertain if she were truly burning or merely emanating fire through her pores. But she managed to rise, the pack intact against all odds.

The orb's power infiltrated every cell of her body, its language foreign and virulent, like speaking Demoni. Through shades of red, Sora saw seared bodies all around, some still, some attempting to rise as they sobbed. The gate burned, but not quickly enough. She stumbled forward, wondering if she appeared as Chaos or as simply a ball of fire.

Bang!

Instinct took control. Sora whipped her arm around, arcing flame following—and deflected the oncoming bullet.

She stumbled back, the force more than her dizzy mind could counter. Surely concussed; she'd heal herself once she had a moment to breathe. But to breathe, she had to escape.

"Sora Makosa, drop the orbs or Etolié dies!"

Unquestionable, Soliel's voice. With perfect clarity, Sora saw the Old God approach with a collection of guards and his Goddess counterpart—who glared but remained silent. Soliel wore no armor, but he did hold a limp Etolié in his arms.

Sora had resolved to let Etolié die for the cause, but oh gods, to actually see her . . .

"Drop them!" Soliel cried, and Sora halfway obeyed, the fire orb clattering against its fellows as it fell from her hand. The retraction of power left her gasping, coughing, her throat half choked by smoke. Soliel kept his hands on Etolié's chin and shoulder, prepared to snap her neck. Though clearly disoriented, Etolié appeared to be conscious, her muttering lips a tell.

Sora glanced back to the burning gate, wondering how stupid it would be to try again—not too stupid with the Fire Orb, but then Etolié would die. Nearby, Chaos didn't look at Sora or Etolié. She stared daggers at Soliel.

One final, impossible hope. Sora reached her hand halfway into the bag, prepared to grab an orb and run. "Goddess of Chaos," she said, though she struggled to project, voice ragged from inhaling smoke, "I don't know what to ask for, but—"

A blast of light came from Soliel, sending him and the rest flying back.

Except it was not from Soliel, no. Nor was it Etolié, despite coming from her body. Eionei's infectious laughter filled the scene, his fractal wings sending him soaring into the air. He whipped out his rapier, pointing it at the errant Old God. "Well, well! Just when I think it's the last time, you always find your way back to me. Fate seems to have it out for us. But look at you—so handsome without that damn helmet. Handsome without any armor at all, by the Suns! Well, if honor says I must also remove my clothing, so be it. We can wrestle it out, man to man."

From the same mouth yelled a rather irate, *"Don't you fucking dare!"*

"We would take it to Celestière, Starshine. No need to subject you to that—"

Bang! Eionei shot higher into the sky. "Not this time!"

He dove down, rapier in hand, and began his clash with the masses. Soliel had brought a sword but nothing more, vulnerable when Eionei's blade sliced across his chest. "Offer still stands," Eionei said, and Sora didn't have to see his wink to feel it.

"For fuck's sake, Grandpa!"

"I'm just having a little fun! Though I wouldn't say no if—"

Bang! Eionei released what could best be described as a yelp. "Fucking dammit!" he cried, reminiscent of his granddaughter.

He continued his fight. Apparently it hadn't hit anywhere vital. Eionei fighting an orb-less God and several guards might've been decent odds were he not in a weakened mortal body.

Intelligence said to run with the orbs and leave Etolié to sacrifice herself for the world. Common sense said that Soliel needed six orbs to destroy the world and risking one was well worth it.

Sora grabbed the first orb she touched—immediately imbued with radiant, crackling energy. No time to experience it. "Eionei!" she cried, and she heaved the blue and yellow orb into the crowd, triumphant when Eionei rose into the air to catch it.

The Drinking God gave a hearty laugh as lightning danced across his glowing skin. "Marvelous!"

And with no warning or even clouds—a bolt of lightning struck the ground.

Even Sora fell back at the blast, the rest no better. As she scrambled to her feet, she heard a victorious, *"That's fucking payback, bitch!"* in Etolié's voice.

Sora's hair stood on end, and only some of the guards rose, Soliel among them. Chaos, however, studied from the sidelines, her posture bored.

Eionei fell back into the crowd, his sword crackling with virulent energy—but Sora ran when Soliel bombarded her.

No time to even scream for help before the massive God tackled her to the ground. Though strong, Sora was no match for an over-sized Deity, failing to shove him off. He wrenched the bag away, dragging her with it. The leather scraped her hands, but Sora clung on, managing a kick to Soliel's hip, her foot catching on something attached to his belt.

He would win. But he needed six orbs. Sora shoved her hand inside, wasting no time in seeing which she grabbed, and released.

In the moment Soliel lost balance, Sora slipped through his arms like butter, knowing innately she'd grabbed the Light Orb, and ran full speed to the gate. Not exactly appealing, the idea of running through a burning gate, but she'd done worse.

Bang came the bullets, and Sora stumbled when her leg spiked with pain. Adrenaline kept her moving, but she slowed, cursing her own mortal shell. She hated to curse her own branch of magic, but the Light Orb was useless for combat.

The choice was taken away when a great shadow covered her. Uluron had returned.

The massive dragon landed behind Sora, the earth shaking. Weakened by her bleeding leg, Sora toppled, resisting tears at her sudden failure.

Gentle claws scooped her up. Leelan sat perched in Uluron's paw. *You're safe now. We're leaving.*

Shock filled her at this twist. "G-Grab Etolié!" Sora managed, and Uluron hardly had to turn to obey, snatching Eionei with ease out of the air.

Fire rose, blasting Uluron. The dragon roared and launched, evading a second blast of the Fire Orb's power.

Sora's body radiated adrenaline, yet her head spun from her concussion, and her leg burned from the bullet. "Stay awake," said a kind voice, and beside her, Eionei pulled her into his lap. "Etolié says you hit your head. Stay awake."

Sora settled into a strange embrace, wiry and strong from the godly interloper, yet still bearing evidence of Etolié's waifish figure. "Just talk to me," she said, and Eionei did what he did best—tell stories.

CHAPTER 5

Four years after the end of the world . . .

"Well, you really pissed him off—"

"Keep your voice down, Starspawn."

Dira stirred, a soothing weight falling upon her arm. With it came the faint smell of dust and old books, overpowered by the smoke clinging to Mother's gown.

"Dira Darling? Are you awake?"

At the words, Dira blinked into wakefulness, confused that her pillow was Mother's leg instead of Dira's own bed. Around her were unfamiliar walls, covered in books and scrolls, but above her was Mother's face, her concern fading into a smile.

"You might as well say hello to Etolié."

Etolié's golden glow was familiar, casting golden light onto the comfortable space around them. Sequestered by bookshelves, flickering light from behind the shelves suggested that a fireplace warmed the scene, but it was Etolié who truly lit the world. Her appearances were always a portent of gifts—but instead of the jovial friend Dira loved, she faced a somber figure. Even so, Etolié sat beside them on what Dira realized was the floor and offered a hand.

Unlike Mother, Etolié didn't like hugs. Etolié liked to hold hands, and so Dira squeezed hers tight.

"You have a good grip, kid." Yet ire filled her gaze when she faced Mother again. "You could pretend to be grateful. I didn't have to put my ass on the line."

"Consider our company." Mother seethed, and Dira shied at her tone.

"And consider whose basement you're in, bitch."

"You would do well to stop disrespecting me in front of my child. I can be grateful and still ask you to shut your damn mouth."

Dira shrank, becoming a ball—and it seemed Mother sensed it, instead coaxing her to relax. "Darling, try to sleep. Etolié and I have grown-up things to discuss, all right? Nothing to worry about."

Dira shut her eyes, but she could not sleep—she could only remember Mother carrying her through the demon world, eventually lulled into sleep by her steps . . .

Mother still smelled of smoke.

"You pissed him off, like I said," Etolié whispered. "All this does is prove that I'm right."

"And how?"

"You're the only one with any power to slow him down. Sure, you burned your house down, but you stopped an entire battalion of you-know-whats in its tracks. You don't give a shit, but the town? They evacuated. They had time."

"You have some audacity implying I'm a hero."

"No, I have some audacity implying you should use your evil for the greater good."

Evil? Dira tried to sleep, but her mind clung to every word.

"We have discussed this time and time again—"

"Ayla, do you really think this will be the last time?"

Mother said nothing.

"He's marching. You're not safe. She isn't either."

"Take care how you speak."

"I'm being kid-friendly, so shut the fuck up."

Safe? Dira clung to Mother's dress, soothed when she placed a hand on her back.

"You've been a nomad for almost four years," Etolié continued. "She'll be five soon—doesn't she deserve some stability?"

"If you're implying I can stop him before her fifth birthday—"

"No, I'm implying that you could give her a home that fuckface won't force you to burn down."

Again, Mother said nothing.

"Sora's kept the house in good repair—"

"Stop. Just . . ." The weight against Dira's back increased, Mother's tension apparent. "Let me think. Alone. We will reconvene when she is actually asleep."

"Do you want me to sit with her? You smell like death, no offense."

"She will not be leaving my sight for as long as we are in Solvira."

Beside them, Etolié shuffled and stood. "I'll come back in an hour. Zoldar will get suspicious if I keep him out for too long, just a warning. I told him the shit I need transcribed can only be read under moonlight, but he'll figure out eventually that means fucking nothing with his maldectine amulet."

Dira peeked at the first sound of footsteps, verifying that Etolié had, indeed, walked away. But the hand on her back soon left, stroking her thick hair instead. "Sleep, darling."

Despite the heartbreak in Mother's words, Dira was soothed by the emergence of song from her lips. Mother hummed a somber tune, and Dira let it fill the fearful spaces in her mind, easing her body into sleep.

Current era . . .

There was putrid work ahead. Etolié hated gore much more than she ever admitted aloud.

"Hand me one of those knives, Sora—yeah, I know you have some left. We're getting that fucking bullet out of your leg."

Sora said nothing, merely bit the leather strap of her small pack. A thousand or so feet in the air, held up by a dragon, Etolié and Eionei managed to remove the intrusive bullet. Flecks of blood stained the dragon's white bones, but it was not a lengthy operation, nor a particularly invasive one, though Sora did become increasingly tense.

She's not a screamer at all, said Eionei inside Etolié's head, as Sora lay reeling from impromptu surgery. *I wonder what could fix that.*

For fuck's sake, Grandpa, I will puke on you.

Sorry, sorry. She's very pretty."

Etolié wondered what she'd done to deserve this concoction of curses—a perverse grandpa and a helluva bad time awaiting as soon as he left her immortal coil. If she puked enough, would the maldectine eject itself? How fucked was she?

Sora glowed faintly from within, clutching that little bird of hers as the wound on her leg patched itself together. The bruises on her face and head vanished as well. Sora sat taller—and then shivered. "Any way I could get another blanket?"

"They made me eat maldectine. I have strictly Eionei's magic, and even then, it's a struggle."

Horror fell upon Sora's countenance, as it fucking should. "Are you going to be all right?"

"I don't know yet."

"The most obvious solution to me," came Eionei's voice, "would be to bring you to your mother. She has teas to help you shit your organs out, nasty rocks and all. We can't have her teleport you, but there are natural entrances to Celestière, and we do have a dragon who seems willing to help."

"Go to Celestière?" Sora said, bewildered—as any mortal would be.

"Why not? I can even introduce you to some friends of mine. I hear you're a fan of Sol Kee."

Sora stared as though Eionei had sprouted wings. Well, more wings. "Y-Yes."

"Delightful. I'll arrange a meeting. In the meantime, I have questions. The dragon is one of them."

Sora told her story, and inside Etolié, grandpa's admiration grew. *She can really take a pounding, can't she.*

Grandpa, I swear to mom.

"... and that's when you appeared." Sora narrowed her gaze. "Is it true you saw Khastra?"

Etolié's mind hadn't settled after what she'd witnessed. She nodded. "She doesn't look good." Tears filled her eyes, though a comforting warmth embraced her from within. Grandpa's presence was good for something. "I don't know what to do."

"Tell Ku'Shya," Sora said, "though ... I worry about what would happen to the elves."

"It will be incredibly uncomfortable if you pray while hosting me," came Eionei's voice, "given she thinks I'm squishy and edible. That's assuming you can reach her anyway, given your, uh, condition."

"Momma can tell her—" Etolié's gaze narrowed on something caught on the half-elf's boot. "What the fuck is that?"

Sora grabbed where Etolié pointed, revealing a small leather pouch tangled around her shoe. With care, she extracted it, and Etolié's stomach lurched when Uluron lifted them up.

Sora spoke up. "Uluron is trying to talk to you, but she says she can't feel you."

Dammit. "It's the fucking maldectine. Her words are magic."

Sora pulled the strings and dumped the glittering contents onto her hand, revealing long prongs of metal refracting the light in shades of gold, and an antique ring that had clearly seen better days. A bit of tarnish marred an indent at the end of each prong, reminding Etolié of a broken brooch. "What is that?"

Sora looked up at Uluron. "She says the pouch is her mother's. Apparently Chaos kept it with her. She doesn't know what it means."

"It's filled with garbage."

Sora stuffed the gold prongs back inside the pouch but frowned as she studied the damaged ring. She said nothing of it, though the look lingered as she dropped it with the odd prongs. "Soliel had this with him, I think. It must have caught on my boot when we had our scuffle."

Etolié's stomach lurched again, and not from the dragon's flight. Eionei clutched tighter. "What the fuck do we do? Now we have two Old Gods to contend with, and you said Chaos fucking helped you escape?"

"She did. Twice."

The audacity of it all. Etolié groaned and looked to Uluron. "I need to land. I need to puke. And I need to think."

"Near a town, if possible," Sora added. "I need food."

Uluron obeyed, shifting her course. All the while, Etolié's brain played through a thousand different things, struggling even to latch onto the memory of Khastra's torture—the extent of which she couldn't even consider while Eionei was near.

She'd have her breakdown later.

Her minimal stomach contents heaved when the dragon swooped downward, finding a clearing at the outskirts of a forest. The ground shook, though not as much as it conceivably ought to given Uluron's size. Hardly midday, and already this was looking to make the list of Etolié's top ten worst days.

Uluron set her paw upon the ground. Sora wasted no time stumbling off, kneeling as if to praise the grass, and Etolié followed, letting Eionei pull the strings. "All right. Celestière, you said? How do we get there?"

"The Valley of Neoma is north of here," Eionei said. "We can walk right in, though we should probably leave the orbs with your dragon friend . . ."

Eionei's words faded as a subtle shift of energy permeated the air. When Uluron recoiled, Sora scrambled to her feet, dagger readied.

"Well, well—a spectacular show," a spectral voice emanated, cast as a fog through the air. "I applaud your escape."

Skeletal claws fell around them, protective as a familiar ghostly figure rose from the ground before them. The Goddess of Chaos held up placating hands, though the inherent threat of her fire minimized the effect.

Etolié clutched the orbs to her chest. "I am fully prepared to die to protect these from you."

"No need for that," Chaos said, suspiciously sweetly. "But it seems you accidentally took my pouch."

From her pocket, Sora withdrew the leather pouch. "This?"

"What the fuck is it?" Etolié asked, but Sora spoke up instead.

"Uluron says it must be her anchor to the world." At which point Sora stared daggers at the Old Goddess. "You're a ghost! I saw you change!"

Chaos gave a small, soundless applause. Her silver coloring faded to blue, revealing her true, ghostly hue. "You were always observant, Sora."

Etolié glanced to the pouch, finding it innocuous. "So we're throwing that thing in the ocean and leaving, right?"

"You helped me," Sora said to the ghost, ignoring the frankly brilliant solution. "You're the reason I escaped. Why?"

When Chaos did not immediately speak up, Etolié did so instead. "Because she doesn't want Soliel to separate the worlds. She said there's another way."

"No, there's not!" Chaos snapped, and Etolié flinched at the unnatural twitch in her neck. "I lied!"

Goddess of Chaos, huh? Is she all right?

Eionei's question was too stupid to warrant an answer. Instead, Etolié asked, "Who are we sacrificing on the altar, Goddess Ghostie?"

"No one! Throw it in the ocean. Be done with us—" Chaos reeled, stumbling back. She did an odd thing for a ghost—she sat herself on the ground and placed her head in her hands. "Go away."

"No," Etolié replied, wary of the odd display.

Chaos rose anew, something gentler in her stance. Though she floated, she appeared smaller, the worried lines of her face apparent even shrouded by flame. "What must I do for you to return me to Tierzuroth and not throw me into the ocean?"

"Forgive me for interrupting," Eionei said, though the ghost didn't shirk at the change in voice, "but ignoring the fact that you only just asked us to throw it into the ocean, why do you want to go back? You don't endorse our shiny man's plan. Why not help us stop him?"

Internally, Etolié reeled, but then Eionei's voice came softer inside. *Trust me, Starshine.*

Chaos appeared forlorn as she looked up to Uluron, who brought a tentative paw down beside her. Her hand flashed true silver as she touched the dragon's bones, affectionate as she stroked soft lines across them. "I admire your trusting nature, Eionei."

"Are you also Eionei's best friend?" Etolié asked, unable to quite squelch that one down.

Chaos chuckled, her fondness far from here. "No. Though I have no quarrel with him."

"Dira," came Sora's tentative voice, and the ghost turned immediately. "That's your name, isn't it? Dira?"

Chaos stilled in her motions, her focus set nowhere. "Dearest Dira. Dira Darling. My mother hated my name, and so I was Dira. Sometimes, I am still Dira."

"May I call you that now?"

Within Etolié stirred the question of if appeasing psychopaths was a familial trait. As it was, Chaos sobered at the question, taking soft steps forward. "Yes, though if I ever resist, call me Chaos. It is what I am."

Etolié wouldn't say her bullshit senses were tingling, but the weirdness kept getting more and more layered. "Care to explain what the hell that means?"

Chaos stared upon her, each second increasingly daunting. Something . . . shifted, in her stance, in her stare. To Etolié's horror, her words came laced with tears. "I've missed you."

"Lady, we just met."

"No, no—but we have! You just don't know." And just as quickly, that teary gaze became menacing as it turned upon Sora.

Sora's arms came up in defense, her useless knife readied. "Dira—"

Horrible laughter sounded from Chaos, a perfect summation of her erratic self. "If only I could hold that knife to your throat—" She cut herself off, again holding her head as though in pain.

Etolié nudged Eionei toward Sora, who carefully tugged her back from the mercurial ghost. But Sora and her big mouth just couldn't stay quiet. "We want to help you—"

"I don't," Etolié offered.

"—but I can't let go of what you said about my sister. Why do you want her dead?"

Chaos shook, scratching at her form. Were she corporeal, she'd be leaving marks. As it was, she passed harmlessly through herself. "I don't! So throw me in the ocean and save her!"

"But you said to Soliel—"

"Oh, fuck Soliel! I should have *ripped him limb from limb when I had the chance!*" Chaos gripped what might've been hair, were she not on fire, heaving as though she could breathe. "Damn this form," she whispered.

"I won't argue with the motive," Etolié said, still gripping Sora's arm, "but care to explain?"

But Chaos didn't seem to hear, instead wrenching herself to the side, screaming into the sky. "A thousand times, I *knew this was coming*! I told you! I told you!"

Etolié couldn't feel Uluron's emoting anymore, but it didn't take magic to know the dragon was agitated. "Ask Kitty if this is normal, would you?"

Sora shared a look with the dragon. "Uluron says no."

At that, Eionei took control, taking careful steps toward the sobbing ghostly Goddess. Through flame, her silhouette had never been so apparent—not frail, though not large, a slight softness to the edges of her face. "Goddess of Chaos," he said, "you're a lovely person, you know? How can we help you?"

"*It's so loud,*" she wept, and even Etolié felt a pang of pity.

"And how can we help it become not so loud?"

"It was never like this before the explosion." She heaved a stabilizing breath—odd for a ghost—and finally matched Etolié's eyes. "Never this loud."

Something tells me 'explosion' means 'Convergence,' Etolié whispered internally, to which she felt a spark from Eionei. *Which means it was all her fault.*

"Do you mean your death, Dira?" Eionei asked. "Did you die in an explosion?"

The pitiful ghost nodded, still trembling from sobs.

"I don't have much experience with ghosts, admittedly," Eionei said, but he stilled at Sora's approach, who walked with defensive hands up.

"We could get her a body," Sora said, but before she could qualify that statement, Etolié bit back a scream.

"You mean like Odessa?!" Etolié clamped her mouth shut, lest she agitate the ghost. "Remember how Odessa was crippled and then she wasn't? Because she had a fucking body? Perhaps not the best fucking plan for a crazy Goddess ghost. Also, need I remind you how Odessa said to acquire the body? Nearly dead? Seems a little dark for you."

"While I won't speak for her sanity," Eionei said, "I think Dira here has at least proved she wants to stop Soliel. Perhaps if we get her the means to think properly, she can be of help. Who better?"

"Anyone, Gramps. Literally anyone."

"You were always the skeptic, Etolié," came Chaos' miserable voice, a pained chuckle to punctuate it. "No, no—not always. Etolié fought for freedom. She was filled with hope and light."

"I have no patience for cryptic bullshit," Etolié said. Sora held the pouch in her hand. When Etolié tried to swipe it, the half-elf dodged. "Ocean. Now."

"Perhaps if we get her a body," Sora said, "she'll be less cryptic."

"*Or* we restore some of her power prematurely. You see why that's bad, don't you?"

"I'm voting with Sora," Eionei said.

You just think she's pretty.

I also agree with her.

"I know it seems to be triggering," Sora gently said, her attention on Chaos, "but can you swear to me that you won't kill Flowridia if we help you?"

"Don't listen; don't listen," Chaos muttered. "I told you one of us lies— *Stop it!*"

Her sudden shriek sent Etolié stumbling. Thank god for Eionei, lest her headache be unbearable. "See? Straight from the crazy's mouth. She'll kill Flowers if you . . ." A very obvious couple of pieces fell together in Etolié's head. "So Flowers is the one who has to be burned at the stake to save a billion people."

"No," snapped Chaos, but Etolié wasn't falling for it.

"This fucking sucks because I already vowed I wouldn't kill her. Though if Flowers would volunteer—"

"Etolié, we're not going to get a straight answer out of her unless we get her a body!" Sora was quite tall—tall enough to typically get into Etolié's face, but today, with Etolié being worn like a puppet, Sora had to peer up to have a chance at looking her in the eye. "We can destroy the body if we have to. But all we're doing is tormenting her!"

I want to help the ghost, Etolié.

"Forgive me, but what about me?" Etolié said, petulance the least virulent of her emotions. "Etolié, here, is just dying from having eaten maldectine, but fine—go half-kill some poor sucker and let the crazy ghost possess them."

"Well, hold on," Eionei interrupted, and his placating tone returned. "Dira, you're a Goddess, which tells me you have a bit more power than the average ghost. Does the body need to be alive for you possess it? Or are you made of stronger stuff?"

"I . . ." The ghost trembled, holding to a fetal position in the air. "I do not know."

"Oh, so now we're grave robbers," Etolié said.

Sora spoke up. "Does it have to be humanoid?"

Etolié paused at that, grasping onto this compromise. "I insist it not be. Find something tiny and squishable. A squirrel or something."

To her surprise, Sora obeyed, traipsing off into the woods.

I really fucking hate this, Etolié said internally.

I can't promise I can stay in your body forever, but Dira seems the least reactive toward me. At least let me help get the situation stable.

Meanwhile, Chaos simply held still.

This would be a great time to have calming song magic.

We'll get you to your mother soon.

I don't want to take this fucking ghost to Celestière, Grandpa.

Eionei fell silent at that, contemplative within her. *How comfortable are you leaving Sora with the ghost? The dragon can come back for her.*

Sora is who the ghost is angriest toward.

Then let's see how the ghost reacts to a body.

Soon, Sora returned carrying a bloated rabbit corpse. "The best I could do."

"It's small enough to hog-tie if she acts up," Etolié muttered, simmering as Sora presented the corpse—and backed away.

A strange shift appeared in Chaos' countenance as she noticed the rabbit, eerily still as she studied. "I won't fight this one," she whispered, which was hardly a soothing phrase, assuming it fucking meant anything. The ghost who was Chaos reached to touch the dead mammal, seeping inside like fog and vanishing.

The rabbit's eyes glowed—silver and gold.

Nausea rose anew as Etolié watched the nasty thing right itself into standing, the pungent smell of its rot wafting anew. But as it inspected itself, the lacerated skin sealed up and a few wiggling maggots popped out from raw patches of skin.

It gave a small hop toward Etolié as new fur grew to fill the spaces. Oddly endearing, though Etolié wasn't falling for it. "All right. Now talk."

The rabbit who was Chaos gave a small whine as it took another hop toward her. To her horror, it pawed at her clothing—Eionei's clothing, technically—further disturbing her when Eionei picked it up.

It settled like a kitten in her arms, even going so far as to faintly *purr*.

"Oh, by Alystra's Plump Ass—you are really fucking pushing it," Etolié said.

"I don't think she can talk in this state," Sora replied.

The rabbit behaved as though asleep, though dead rabbits couldn't sleep.

"I feel like it's inappropriate to pet her," came Eionei's voice, "but the urge is strong."

"You're both bastards," Etolié grumbled. "Sora, we have a terrible plan, but hear us out."

And she explained it—the notion of abandoning Sora with a ghost in a forest. "And then Uluron comes back to get you," Etolié concluded.

Disappointment settled upon Sora's face, though Etolié was too agitated to give a shit. "What then?"

"That . . . is a good question. You still have Spore, right?"

Sora shook her head. "They confiscated it."

"Bastards. All right, so Momma can't talk to you unless you can get that back. I doubt Uluron would take you to Nox'Kartha, but if you go to Solvira, I'll meet you there. Just avoid Murishani, though he'll accept that you've adopted a weird rabbit. But if Ghostie pulls anything—dump her. Protect yourself first."

"How long will you be gone?"

Etolié looked to the dragon, who looked to Sora, who proceeded to answer the question. "Uluron says she's familiar with the Valley of Neoma and can be back tomorrow morning to get me."

"Excellent. So stay here."

The rabbit truly might've been asleep, given how floppy it had become. With the care a living rabbit would have needed, Etolié gently set the creature into Sora's arms. "Remember—your safety is the most important. I want to see you again, all right?"

"I'm good at surviving," Sora replied, the sentiment as soothing as anything else. The rabbit stirred but did not protest, its little paws content to cling to Sora's arms.

Nearly cute. Only nearly. "I'll see you soon."

She prayed the words were true.

Cradling a suspicious rabbit, Sora waited until the dragon was long out of sight before she roused it.

This plan was, by all accounts, terrible, but Etolié was suffering—and thus not thinking entirely straight. Yes, longing had filled her to consider going to Celestière—but perhaps there was a higher calling here.

Sora held the rabbit up, mindful to support its back, and stared into those heterochromatic eyes. "I know you helped me. Angrily or not, you did. You're not what Etolié thinks."

The rabbit twitched its whiskers, the only sign of death its chill touch.

"Can you really not talk in this state?"

A useless question, really, given the rabbit could lie—in fact, Chaos had made that quite clear.

"You know something about my sister," Sora muttered, the pieces impossible to assemble. "You said something about a sacrifice. So my sister must die?"

Again, the rabbit only stared, docile in Sora's grip.

"I need to know what you know."

So without further ado, Sora marched her way toward the nearby town, resolving to find a mausoleum—and some breakfast.

It was not a long way, and Sora kept her head down as she entered what appeared to be an Iron Elf town. The architecture was reminiscent of Ameth, bringing memories of a vivacious woman seeking mushrooms while Tazel and Mereen had done their own dirty work.

Sora still did not know how to mourn, only that she did. But that was a secret meant only for her.

She kept to the outskirts, knowing a graveyard would be kept away from the city square. The money on her person was Sun Elven, but a pitying merchant accepted it for a small loaf of bread, even if they definitely overcharged.

She managed to cradle the rabbit as she ate, stepping from alley to alley, avoiding detection as well as she could. Word would spread of a half-elf who had stolen the Goddess of Chaos. Whatever differences the kingdoms of elves had, they shared in their worship. Protecting their goddess superseded all other loyalty. Running from the law wasn't ideal, but she'd done it before.

The graveyard was not difficult to find, though at midday, mourners walked the grounds. A funeral had brought a small flock of people, and Sora kept her distance, seeking the crypts in the back. "How close do you have to be to a body to possess it?" she whispered to her docile companion.

The rabbit stared with glowing eyes, then gave a small twitch with its whiskers.

"I'm praying this didn't ruin your intelligence."

When she had confirmed there were no wandering eyes, Sora set the rabbit Goddess down, then slipped a knife from her vambrace, making swift work of the iron lock protecting a mossy mausoleum. Dirt fell with the *click,* the ancient iron protesting but coming apart. Bless the elves and their non-magic. After a brief inspection, Sora pushed open the iron door, assured of no tricks.

The rabbit had stayed put—proof there must be something in her head. Sora lifted it with care, mindful of how delicate her spine might be. Though did it matter at all in her undead state? Better to be safe.

With one arm, she shut the massive door, plunging them into darkness. Tucking the undead creature away, Sora summoned a spark of holy light, revealing a tunnel.

Bodies were laid to rest within insets in the wall, varying in their stages of decomposition. The front revealed the freshest of the lot, though the older the better, technically, if Chaos could restore the body with magic—less likely to be missed.

A few coffins lay in the back, and Sora kicked the lock of a particularly dusty one, coughing at the wafting dust as she lifted the lid.

Terribly old, nothing more than bones. "Is this enough, or do you need something newer?"

For the first time, the Chaos Rabbit struggled. Sora set her down, then kept her free hand to the hilt of her knife.

A familiar shade of purple emanated from the rabbit, and with it emerged the glowing specter, illuminating the room in blue. Sora's light extinguished, though the spell lay waiting within her, should the ghost become violent. "Well?"

Chaos remained eerily silent, her inspection of the crypt raising the hair on Sora's arms. "You are not a trusting person by nature. Is it something about me? Does our bond transcend even time?"

Well, no. But Sora feared what reaction a reply would evoke. "I will happily answer that once you've gotten your body."

Chaos reached for the body—then froze. Her hand flexed, visible even through the pulsing flame. "Sora, you stupid, *stupid* girl. She'll do it. She told you."

Sora readied her knife—a habit, though useless today. Chaos stared upon her, the predator returning. "What will she do?"

"She lies— Stop it!" Chaos clutched her head, the flame rising around her body. Sora stumbled back, fearful of the cold energy as holy light burst from her hand once more.

Chaos flailed about, fighting whatever impulse resisted within her. Her spectral hands plunged within herself, fighting nothing. In a desperate maneuver, the ghost dove toward Sora—

Only to be forcefully diverted to the corpse in the coffin by her own self.

The only sound became Sora's rapid breaths. Blue light shone from the coffin. A horror arose—a skeleton worn as a shell, the ghostly figment clear inside it. But its motions were smooth, perfectly balanced as it stepped from the coffin. Sora might've found it amusing, how it proceeded to inspect itself, but her heartbeat refused to steady.

The skeletal Goddess embraced herself, and from her emerged gruesome magic. Sinew spread across the bones, muscle too, complex organs growing from nothing within her abdomen. Blood vessels slithered as snakes. Skin followed, slathering in layers upon the exposed innards. Not pale, no, but ashen and grey, yet gentle signs of life appeared in her rosy cheeks, in the translucent veins in her wrist. The glow within her skull became silver and gold—and then not a glow at all, but mesmerizing eyes.

Naked, she bore the figure of a warrior, lean despite her musculature. Perpetual youth shone in her round cheeks and bright gaze. Despite that, the subtle elegance of age showed in her laughter lines and the greying temples within her thick, black hair; not young at all; older than Sora. Those large eyes fell upon her, a new clarity within them.

The light had faded with the disappearance of her ghostly form, leaving only Sora's glimmer of holy light. Chaos touched her own cheek, inspected her hand—and smiled.

And daunting above all, behind those full lips lay . . . fangs?

Chaos' gaze fell upon her, nothing wicked here. "So strange, to see you young," Chaos said, genuine warmth in the words. "Oh, so many memories. So much love. I would hug you, but I'm naked. That would be uncomfortable for both of us. Although . . ."

A snap of her fingers, and clothing wrapped around the newly formed Goddess. Sora's eyesight was limited in the dark, but Chaos was at least no longer exposed.

"Much better, though I will want real clothing for travel. We can make our purchases here."

"Forgive me," Sora said, her paranoia on high alert, "but you keep using the word 'love.' You don't mean . . . like . . ."

Chaos' chuckle held whispers of malevolence. "No, not like that."

"I have more questions, but I'd prefer to ask them outside so I stop inhaling crypt dust."

"What kind of promise do I have to make to get you to put that knife away?"

Sora contemplated that, unsure if she could trust any promise this woman made. "I'm not putting it away."

"You do not trust me at all."

"I think you're more trustworthy than you want me to believe, but just because I'm stupid enough to give you a body doesn't mean I'm stupid enough to risk you killing me."

By the Light, her impish grin clawed at Sora's memory, struggling to break free.

When they emerged, the sunlight revealed more of the ancient Deity—the simplicity of her costume, for one, the shades of deep blue meant for adventuring. But her hair evoked something from Sora's very heart, its familiarity bearing instant connection.

For they were locs, just like her own, though let free instead of bound.

There was nothing 'pure' in her blood at all, for the light revealed her ears as well, their point softened by heritage. Surely this was not her true form. This Goddess could be anything with this sort of necromancy. "Is this what you look like? Or what the body you took was?"

Chaos hummed to match the breeze. "It is mostly me."

"While you enjoy the sun, I have a few more questions—"

"And you shall have all day to ask those questions, once I've purchased supplies in this town." Chaos began marching away.

Sora kept pace, determined to appear nonchalant. "Tell me about my sister."

"Which one?"

The question punched like a blow to the stomach, leaving Sora shocked—until Chaos cruelly laughed. "Oh, you are too easy. No, it is only you and her. But did you not claim it yourself? One of us lies?" Chaos humor never relented. "But perhaps I meant Soliel."

"You claimed it. Not me." Sora gracefully stopped before her, but Chaos sidestepped with just as much fluidity. "And I don't think you meant Soliel."

A strange dance they choreographed. Chaos whirled around without a care. Sora filled the space before her, blocking her path once more.

"You wished to talk about Flowridia," Chaos said.

"I'm suspicious about your intentions, but if I'm following your implications—killing Flowridia means not needing to separate the worlds. Why?"

"I'm not going to tell you, Sora."

Again, Chaos tried to dance around her. Sora matched her fluidity. "Why? What if you convince me to help you?"

"We both know that would never happen."

It seemed Chaos hadn't bluffed about knowing her.

Sora brought her knife up to Chaos' neck. If the Goddess moved, it would cut skin. "So you will try to kill her?"

"You are attracting attention."

The mourners watched from their gravesite. Sora remained still. "Convince me to care."

"They will throw you in prison if I summon my fire. Or kill you on sight. Let us not play that guessing game. And then I shall steal my anchor from your pocket and run to wherever I please—which I could, in fact, do anyway, so it is a testament to my liking you that I haven't."

Sora glowered as she lowered her dagger. It seemed she didn't quite wield the control she'd gambled on, but admitting her fear meant admitting defeat.

"A few truths for you," Chaos continued. "One: I do not want to kill your sister. Two: I cannot kill your sister. Three: if your sister were to die, it would save the realms."

Sora stepped back, baffled by the statements. "I have questions about all of that."

"And *you* will get no answers—yet. I will speak to Etolié. You may be present. If she agrees Flowridia should not die once I have laid out my truth, then I will be convinced."

Etolié was many things—a wildcard among them. She would throw herself upon the pyre for the greater good, but would she throw another? Potentially. "But if Etolié agrees, you're going to make Etolié do it. Since you can't do it yourself, supposedly."

"She will certainly be in the best position to accomplish it."

"Then we can resume this conversation with her." Though frustrated, Sora tucked her knife away, uncertain if this was a triumph or not. "But left alone—will Flowridia die?"

"Left alone? Surely not."

Only an idiot wouldn't be skeptical at that. Sora began her own march. "Let's buy those supplies."

To her surprise, Chaos stumbled forward as a supplicant, reminding her of a cat trying to garner favors. "Nothing about me is malicious—"

"I can cite exact quotes that disprove that."

"And I apologize for them. I was not myself."

Sora couldn't shake the idea that the phrase was literal. "Are you Dira?"

Chaos' tentative sanity remained startling, her smile nearly cute as she said, "Yes. It is not a name I would like you to share with others who know my true identity, but I would love for someone other than Soliel to call me that."

Graceful steps became Chaos' signature, bearing the poise of both a dancer and a warrior. Sora couldn't shake the memory of Tazel, stunned at the likeness, truly.

The potential for this to be a terrible mistake remained, but she trusted Chaos in one singular thing:

Soliel would not be long for this world if he appeared.

The longer a god lingered inside you, the more . . . *goopy* your insides became.

Hang on a little longer, Starshine.

Her arms around herself were as warm as any true embrace.

But a truly miserable few hours passed with Eionei occasionally singing in her head to distract her. The sun sank low into the sky before Uluron lifted her paw . . . and then lowered it.

They couldn't talk, dammit.

Clouds gathered, blocking the sun. Memories of Soliel and his lightning set her on edge, but she held the Lightning Orb. Nothing could hurt her from the sky. Uluron rose high in the air—high enough for even Etolié to be aware of the chill, though far more aware of the gargantuan mountain range before them. When Uluron finally soared above the clouds, Etolié was embraced by her momma's domain—millions of glittering stars above, swirling galaxies beyond.

Before she could admire the sight and experience a single good feeling in this miserable existence, Etolié's stomach lurched when Uluron dove straight down.

She was ashamed to say she did puke a little on the dragon's claw, thankfully having the foresight to angle her head, lest it backsplash onto her face. Tiny specks of glowing green melded with the bile, but when Etolié tried to touch her magic, she felt nothing at all.

More puking would be necessary.

The clouds broke. Drenched from the condensation, they descended into a sprawling valley, lush with green. The details crystalized as they neared—a brook, a cottage, trees dotting the sides. A quaint little home, and the truth of it struck Etolié like a bullet. She had been here before. "Neoma's Valley."

Uluron landed with grace, her presence oddly at ease within the magical realm. Here, the seams of the world were thin, melded in places. A well-placed step, and one would fall right into Celestière, not unlike stepping into shadows.

"It's beautiful," Etolié said, which was the last coherent thing she said as the slimy sensation of a god exiting their host coated her insides.

Immediately, the noise of the world bombarded her, even in this sacred place. Etolié stumbled into her glowing grandpa's arms—who remained, for gods could dwell here. Again, her stomach heaved, only for nothing to emerge. Her head split from pain. Heat pulsed in her veins, rising to her skin—which itched like fire from the goddamn robe. "I hurt everywhere."

She so rarely saw her grandpa's true face—handsome and topaz, his sharp angles were her inheritance. He lifted her with ease, cradling her as he had in her youth. "Just a short journey more. Sleep if you can."

"I might puke on you."

"Nothing you haven't done before."

Damn, he actually made it sound sweet.

Her grandpa's voice came again, though not directed at her. "Best of luck, Uluron. Etolié is safe in my care. Tell Sora she can pray to me if anything is amiss. If she can find one of my temples, I can speak to her." A pause; Etolié felt his dumbass mind turning. "In fact, encourage it. I'd love to see her."

"Grandpa, I swear to—"

"Yes, yes, fine. But I can think what I want now. You're not there to hear it."

She groaned and all the world became white.

"Keep your eyes shut, Starshine."

The transition into Celestière did alleviate her headache, at least. A thousand times, she had contemplated if she were simply not meant for the mortal realm, her angelic blood too potent. Angels could not walk the realm, but Etolié managed to on a technicality—a quarter of her blood was human, but it did not mean it was comfortable.

She was never drunk enough to cope.

Her fever rose, her body reeling from hosting her godly grandpa for so long. But all would be well. She clung to the hope of her momma's aid with each torturous step through the mist, obeying her grandpa's request to shut her eyes.

It was an undeniable shift when they emerged into her momma's valley. Soothing darkness overtook the blinding light. Etolié blinked, met with the image of stars and her grandpa's countenance.

Yet when she blinked again, soft hands soothed her silver hair. The voice wasn't Eionei's. *"Can you drink this? Are you able?"*

Momma?

Another blink, and she lay in a warm place, wrapped in blankets. Her momma's presence remained, but she struggled to grasp it.

"She won't die in her sleep, don't worry. Tell me what happened."

When Etolié blinked anew, she was alone.

Her limbs had feeling, though her connection to magic remained severed. This was her bedroom—her childhood room. Old sweat coated her, but she did not feel warm. Instead, she detangled herself from her blankets.

Though her head spun, she managed to grasp the doorknob for stability, already hearing voices beyond. Out she stumbled, keeping close to the wall lest she relax.

In Staella's sitting room, the goddess herself sat upon a cozy couch, her magnificent wings the main source of light. Etolié's mirror and not; her silver hair and lavender eyes were shared, but her short stature and curves were all Staella. Eionei sat nigh, immediately perking up at her appearance.

Staella rose to meet her, taking her hand in an affectionate gesture. "Eionei says you fainted in the mists. How are you feeling now?"

"Less like I'll faint."

"My magic is useless until we help your stomach. Eionei explained everything. The tea I made is a bit cold, but that doesn't affect its potency. Not magic at all—just something to, uh, speed up what's already happening inside you."

Etolié groaned as Momma led her to the couch. "So I'm gonna shit myself."

"I have the chamber pot all set up," Staella said, far too brightly for someone discussing diarrhea. "I even put books around it—and a second pot in case you puke."

With a motherly smile, Staella handed her the tea. Etolié pouted but accepted it. It smelled of lavender—potent enough to be masquerading whatever nastiness was laced beneath.

No sense in waiting. Sora was babysitting a rabbit ghost, and despite being as capable a woman as Etolié had ever met, the half-elf was both mortal and prone to stupidity. Etolié downed the bitter brew gulp by gulp, only breathing when the teacup was empty. "How long?"

"Not too long, but long enough for me to ask you—Eionei said you mentioned Khastra."

The memory made her sicker than the tea, though her stomach gurgled. "Momma, she's in Tierzuroth, beneath the Temple of Chaos. I had no connection to anyone in Celestière. Soliel said the New Gods have no power there. But she's . . . Momma, it was awful."

Again, Staella took her hand, the comfort lessened by the lack of magic, though her motherly aura remained. "I'll take care of it, Starshine. Don't you worry."

Safe in her momma's home, free from her grandpa's inner presence and the threat of a Godly ghost, her tears rose anew, fresh anguish with them. For ten months, she had lived in agony, knowing nothing. For nine months, she had waited for news of her beloved demon's demise.

To know Khastra was still in the realm was nearly worse. Her hope sparked within darkness, but the smallest breath would kill it.

"I felt so helpless," Etolié said amid her tears. "I couldn't save her."

Staella's own eyes mirrored them, glistening as she stroked Etolié's hand. "No one could have."

"If I hadn't let Soliel grab me—"

"There is no sense in 'what ifs.' They will only drive you mad. First, you must help yourself. And then, we will walk this path together. If there is a way to save Khastra, it will be found."

Etolié's stomach grumbled once more, the ineffable warning of imminent bodily functions driving her to stand. "And so it begins."

"Good luck!" Eionei said, to which Etolié showed him her middle finger.

Escorting Chaos through town was odd.

The Goddess gushed over dresses and slowed to savor smells, all the while keeping near Sora—who kept her anchor nearer. Coins appeared as Chaos needed them, sparing no expense as she purchased adventuring garb and gowns, even offering to pay for Sora.

"I'm happy with what I have," Sora said simply, to which Chaos laughed.

"So practical. I admire that. I may simply be overexcited to have a body again."

The statement did nothing to curb her spending, and the fact that all the clothing mysteriously fit inside a single satchel made Sora question the limits of Chaos' powers in her current state. Yet it was Odessa all over again, the way she inspected the gowns and jested with the merchants.

And that was it. That was her laughter—maniacal and malevolent, even in its most joyful. Sora could not decide how she felt about it.

At sunset, Chaos left the town wearing one of her new purchases, clearly reveling in her red ensemble. Her haughty gait rubbed uncomfortably at Sora's memory, reminiscent of a particular arrogant vampire she had tangential loyalty to—for better or worse.

Yet the sunset highlighted an odd truth. "You have no shadow," Sora said.

Chaos' laughter remained unnerving. "Ghosts don't have shadows, silly."

Odessa had definitely had a shadow, but Sora bit her tongue.

"What a lovely day," Chaos said as they traversed back to the woods. "Thank you for joining me. I know you didn't have the best time, but I do appreciate your company, all the same."

Sora went to work removing brambles from the clearing. "I've accepted that I'll be living in confusion for the foreseeable future."

"Oh, me too, Sora. Me too. I have no memory of this era at all. I'm quite disoriented."

Sora paused. "Do you live in this timeline? What does that mean?"

Chaos continued her pacing, her graceful steps never upsetting her rhythm. "It is difficult to encapsulate into words. I know I am frustrating, and I apologize."

"Frustrating isn't the word."

"Perhaps not. But it is quiet here—quieter than even before the explosion. I feel free—but no, you asked a question. I have no memory because I was not here. Though I struggle, even now, to recall what is and isn't yet, what has and hasn't. And so I seek to err with caution and say as little as possible, lest it be too much. But you saying things about yourself helps me to know—such as you having a sister!"

Sora bit back her first response, then gave in anyway as she resumed clearing a space for camp. "The one you think should die."

"I would think that whether you knew she was your sister or not. Hardly personal."

"You don't have siblings, do you?"

Chaos stilled at the statement, contemplative. "I do, in a way. I would wring his neck if I could."

"How charming," Sora muttered, finding she might've preferred the rabbit.

Chaos said nothing, perhaps sensing her derision.

Sora soon lit a campfire, content to shiver behind it for warmth, but Chaos sat across from her, disturbing her tentative peace. "Do you have a tent?"

"No."

With a mere wave of Chaos' hand, a modest tent appeared beside them. "Yes, you do. And you have me to keep watch."

"How do I know you won't steal your anchor and run in my sleep?"

"Where would I go?"

"If your antics in the graveyard are anything to go by, you would orchestrate a plan to kill my sister."

"Only if Etolié agrees. And . . . A-And listen, Sora. I am contemplative of my future now. The fact remains that I was caught rather unwillingly with Soliel. As a ghost and he a paladin, there was a stark power imbalance between us. And so I played his game, though I protested."

"Is that why you helped me? So I could thwart his plan?"

Chaos' smile held those wicked undertones once more, leaving Sora unsettled. "It was a calculated risk—had Etolié escaped like I'd hoped, she would have been the better candidate, but both of you are prone to bullheaded heroism. You played your part even better than I had hoped. And, yes, you left with as many orbs as you went in with, but you have to admit—my plan could have worked."

"But why in the world would you risk giving him all six in the first place?"

"Because I knew he wouldn't act yet."

Sora's gut twisted at the memory of the jail cell. "Because he wants to 'save Flowridia' or something."

Chaos nodded emphatically. "He has good intentions. He is simply naïve, is he not?"

"Actually, you called him stupid several times. And look—I'd kill him in a heartbeat given the opportunity. And while I am a little softer on genocidal maniacs in recent months, I'm increasingly skeptical that you have loyalty to anyone."

Chaos said nothing, no longer meeting her gaze.

Sora's annoyance rose. "I can't help but feel like you're just toying with all of us."

"I have not lied to you, Sora. You are dear to me, and I wanted you safe."

Sora stared blankly at that. "You're the one who said you were lying in the first place."

To her surprise, Chaos seemed to shrink at that. "You rightfully hate me."

"I don't, actually. But you were adamant that you hate me. Is that a lie or not?"

Chaos rose, and Sora did not know what to do with her obvious hurt. "It is quieter now. I'm sorry. I do love you. I would take a bullet to save you—"

She lurched, her grimace sneering into hatred. "Don't jest. Don't jest. You *know* what that feels like. Don't waste it on her."

The acrimony faded, replaced with sorrow. Instead of speaking again, Chaos stalked off into the darkness, her silhouette clear within the line of trees.

Sora resolved to keep a knife in her hand as she slept.

The sun fully set. Sora's agitated mind craved the comfort of Spore, and she cursed her lost stash in Tierzuroth. Instead, she soothed herself with deep breathing, willing her racing heart to steady.

Soon, with firelight enough to see, Sora withdrew her gifted mirror and tapped. How did one even begin to explain?

It was morning in Nox'Kartha, and Flowridia rose early each day. Her cheery face appeared, flush with freckles, lit by gentle sun. "Hello."

"Hi, Flowridia. I don't know where to begin."

"Is everything all right?"

"Is Ayla with you?"

Flowridia turned away, beckoning to a distant figure. A glimpse of raven hair appeared, though nothing else. "She is."

Far away, Chaos had taken a meditative pose. If she overheard, it did not matter. "I'll condense this as well as I can."

At the first mention of Uluron, Flowridia frowned. Her expression did not soften at any point.

"So in conclusion," Sora said, "I disobeyed Etolié. And now the Goddess of Chaos and I are camping until Uluron arrives to take us to Solvira. Though I'm having doubts about that."

Yet the truth froze on her tongue—Flowridia did not need to worry about cryptic goddesses and their plots, not with her health being fragile as of late. That was a conversation to have in person, at the very least.

"Why?"

"I don't know if I trust her," Sora said, and there was no lie in that. "But I do trust that she would murder Soliel, given the chance."

"Interesting," Flowridia said, though she didn't elaborate on that—Ayla took the mirror.

Though the vampire was sleepless, something ragged was etched into her countenance. "So because you disobeyed Etolié, the ancient and unhinged Deity, who you knew without question was unhinged, is now more powerful than we can fathom. What a lovely mess you have made. Good luck."

"I also know she's the reason I was able to escape," Sora said, pride bruised at the mockery. But she wasn't about to worry Ayla with potential news of her wife's death. "I . . . I had my reasons."

Ayla said nothing. The mirror returned to Flowridia. "Forgive me if this is trivial, but do you know when you'll be back? Not specifically, but do you think it'll be months? Days?"

"I truly don't know," Sora replied. "How are you? Are you feeling better?"

How shy, Flowridia's smile, yet her joy was undeniable. "I wanted to wait until you were home to tell you, but I also want you to be the first to know, and I can't keep it a secret much longer."

Worry furrowed Sora's brow, joy or not. "Are you all right?"

"Sora, I'm pregnant."

The statement was merely words. Meaningless, until the distant Deity rose in her peripheral. And then the glass shattered in Sora's mind, for approaching in the darkness was a half-elf of vampiric origin with hair far too reminiscent of Sora's, who claimed to love her dearly, who inherited Odessa's laughter and smile—

"Sora?"

By the Light, every part of Dira was a puzzle, and Sora now understood the familiar pieces.

Though she had questions, rather than burst with this new and impossible theory, Sora tapped the mirror's lens. Flowridia's face disappeared.

"You did not have to stop for my sake," Chaos said, but Sora could not relinquish the clear mirror of her face to a mother—

. . . she was plotting to kill?

"I have been contemplating what it is I want, as I said," said Chaos, whose hair was her heritage—but how? "There is conflict inside me, but there is one clear path I cannot deny, and it is that I do not want Soliel to separate the worlds. I do not want Valeuron to be a martyr—he was murdered. And I do not believe in murdering the very people I sacrificed everything to save."

Sora nodded, hardly hearing it. Gods, she had Flowridia's face. She had Odessa's face.

"But I do not currently have the power. I fear I will not even upon my true rebirth. And Soliel will not be dissuaded by talk— believe me, I have tried."

How far along was Flowridia? The countdown had begun.

"I have four nations of people who worship me, but Soliel has his own, and he has the orbs. He has inspired fear, and most believe I am dead. I don't precisely know what to do, but if my vow means anything at all, it is that whatever power I gain will be used to kill Soliel and stop him from separating the worlds."

Sora still reeled at the impossibility of it all—because every part of her that was not Flowridia was Ayla, from that withering stare to the pride in her stance, even in humility. That was not possible, yet Chaos wielded Silver Fire.

Did she tell Chaos? Would it lose her any ground?

. . . Oh gods, Dira was her blood. Her admission of love was true.

"You have four nations," Sora said, her wariness receding, "but what if we found more? Power comes through worship. How many more pledges would it take for you to surpass him?"

"To counter the orbs? Who can say. But who would listen?"

"You have Silver Fire. Perhaps Solvira could be convinced to care? O-Or the Sun Elves? Obviously we've deviated from your worship, but we share common ancestors."

Chaos scoffed. "Both of those scenarios involve convincing worshipers of Sol Kareena to waver in their ideology, and you would know better than most what a lost cause that is."

And as Sora considered the statement, a small chirp from Leelan sparked a thought beyond sanity. "Then . . . what if we went straight to the source? Can Sol Kareena pledge her power to a God?"

Chaos became still. Sora could not unsee it, the clever twist of her lip, the fluidity of her motions. She danced because she was Ayla's daughter. But how? "You are brilliant. And why stop there? Celestière only houses the angelic gods. We can go to Sha'Demoni too. We must speak to *all* the New Gods."

Sora reeled at the statement. "We?"

"Would you accompany me, Sora? Who better to have as a companion on this quest than the woman who successfully stole six orbs?"

"And lost most of them, but . . ." Sora considered the weight of the quest, the weight of the knowledge of Dira's parentage . . . One thread of doubt remained. "I will on one condition. If I help you, will you swear to not harm Flowridia?" *Your own mother*, Sora did not add. She still struggled with what to say.

Chaos fell silent. Thoughtful, like Flowridia inspecting floral rot, and soon Chaos' frown came to match. "I already gave you my compromise, Sora. But if we can defeat Soliel, there would be no need for Flowridia's death."

What a fool Sora was, but Dira was her family. Dira was her *niece*. Sora stepped around the fire, near enough to touch, and offered a hand. "I will turn on you if you try to hurt my sister, Goddess or not. But Dira, whatever else . . ." A chasm filled the space, her stomach hollow, head dizzy. Flowridia was pregnant, and it was somehow Ayla's child. ". . . in this, I'm going to choose to trust you."

Chaos accepted the hand, but instead of shaking, she gave a small curtsy, despite her trousers. "It warms my heart to hear it."

Whatever mysterious insanity lurked within her, Dira, when herself, was someone Sora would someday love. And though she faced an older iteration, Sora supposed she understood why.

PART TWO

CELESTIÈRE

CHAPTER 6

Within dark woods, Dira clung to a beloved lifeline—one hand in Mother's, the other grasping her skirt, seeking to hide within its folds.

Dira shivered as they walked, the chill of the forest heightened by the many sounds of night: insects and owls, howling creatures beyond. Foxes screamed. At least, Mother had said they were foxes and not little girls being snatched by monsters, but still Dira wanted to weep. The darkness was supposed to be safe, but Mother had said to stay near. Fearful, Dira pressed her face against Mother's thigh, cushioned by the thick layers of her dress, seeking to dampen the horrible sounds.

"I see a light ahead. We are almost there."

She loved Mother's voice, for it was familiar, something stable to cling to. She dared to peek. In the breaks between trees shone distant light. But this was not a simple cottage. This was something far larger.

The ground changed. No longer did Dira hear crunching leaves and pine needles but the tapping of shoes upon stone. Here upon more solid ground, Dira kept her feet as light as Mother had taught, hardly a sound between the two of them.

Eventually, Mother slowed. Dira gasped when Mother tugged the dress from her face, revealing her countenance to the world. She faced a great iron gate, lit by moonlight and revealed by her own keen eyes. Beyond, a single source of light shone on the second floor of a massive building. Mother had said it was someone's home.

Before Dira could react, Mother gripped her by her armpits, lifting her smoothly into her arms. Courage filled Dira, for she was taller now, and Mother would protect her; Mother always did. From demons, from shadows, from predators in the woods—Mother was there.

With one hand, Mother swung the gate open, the metal well-oiled, for it hardly made a squeak. Though dark, Dira studied an extensive courtyard, the greenery lush though overgrown.

It was only when they reached the massive double doors that Mother tensed.

Faster than lightning, Mother whipped around and grabbed the blade of a dagger.

Yet the dagger's wielder looked to have seen a ghost, for when Mother casually released the weapon, it clattered to the stone ground.

"Surprised to see me?" Mother laughed, though colder than Dira had ever heard. Yet it set her at ease, for though Dira's stomach cramped, Mother was not afraid.

"Not you," the attacker said, a woman with amber skin and blonde hair styled into strands thicker than Dira had ever seen.

Mother stroked Dira's hair, even as she tucked her face into Mother's shoulder. "I am remiss to admit it, but I need your help."

"Anything."

"Dira Darling, won't you say hello?" Mother coaxed her to face this new woman, though Dira shied beneath her scrutiny. "This is your Aunt Sora."

Dira so rarely met anyone, only knowing Mother and Etolié by name. But at Mother's beckoning, she waved a hand, even felt a smile come unbidden when 'Aunt Sora' waved back, the happiness in her smile unquestionable.

She smelled of earth and sweet things, her coloring a tree in autumn with a sunrise peeking over, and she stood far taller than Mother. But behind her thick hair was a familiar sight that caused Dira to perk up. Sora's pointed ears were . . . rounded? Like Dira's!

"Dira Darling, Sora is someone very special. Do you remember how you had another momma?"

Dira nodded, the concept strange.

"This is her sister."

Dira studied this 'Sora,' her family by blood. When she sat up, there shone undeniable affection in Sora's smile, and when she squirmed, Mother set her down. Sora met her there, crouching to match her in height.

"It's really wonderful to see you—meet you," Sora said, and she offered a hand, just as Etolié did. Dira took it and squeezed.

Current era . . .

In Nox'Kartha, Flowridia tapped her mirror for a fifth time, anxiety rising when the light extinguished, leaving her own image in its place.

"What a bastard," came a grumble beside her.

Tucked into bed, Flowridia set her hand to her stomach, still flat by all accounts, though she liked to imagine the life inside. Again, she tapped, despite her waning hope. "Do you think something happened?"

"I truly don't know, Flowra." Ayla clad in a lush robe and nothing else, set an arm around Flowridia. "She *is* travelling with an unpredictable Goddess of unfathomable power. We cannot dismiss that. But she may also simply be processing this news away from you."

"But it's joyous news."

"I suppose, yes, but consider the most plausible explanation, which is you stepped out on your dearest wife and got left with a bastard."

That . . . had not occurred to her. "I could have said it better."

"No, *she* could have waited a second longer and let you explain, but it is what it is. I am not actually concerned."

"She thinks I cheated. I'm concerned."

"And she will speak to you in time. Sooner rather than later, assuredly, with stories of rogue Goddesses and perhaps having saved the world." Ayla's hand stroked up her thigh, her hips, and Flowridia hoped she would stop at her womb—but no, she caressed the side of Flowridia's swollen breast instead. "How are you feeling?"

Flowridia blushed at the attention, her body parched for intimacy. Vomiting daily was an excellent way to ruin one's sexual appetite, but it had been a few days since her last nauseous spell. "Like I want you to continue."

Ayla made no effort to hide her ogling. "You need breakfast first, but if you would consent, I am immensely enjoying what pregnancy is doing to your body."

"My stomach will catch up to them soon enough," Flowridia teased, bringing Ayla's hand to grope her. Even separated by her nightgown, she savored the touch, though it was strange for her breast to be spilling from Ayla's hand—strange and wonderful.

"And you will be beautiful still, my love. Though I will have to be gentler with you." Ayla placed a teasing kiss upon her clothed breast, then released. She opened her mouth as if to speak, yet a frown stole her words. "Your cheeks are sallow. Are you certain you're well?"

Flowridia briefly recalled her dizzy spell during her goodbye with Sora, but that was nothing. A fluke. "More than well enough for this."

"I will take your word for it. Go eat, lest I eat you first."

Her wink left Flowridia blushing.

She dressed and went on her way, knowing Ayla cherished time alone as much as Flowridia did. Except . . . it was strange to be alone, when she considered it.

Demitri had always been her shadow. Then Sora, when Ayla did not fill the role.

But was she truly alone? Flowridia had a new companion growing in her womb. She stilled in the hallway, seeking any bump at all through her dress. Yes, it was best that her small weight gain was more evenly distributed, lest rumors fly prematurely, lest she cradle her stomach and thus the little life inside, and grow attached . . .

The less thought she gave it, the better.

As she passed the door to Casvir's office, the door was open. "Flowridia, step inside."

Casvir's office was as utilitarian as his personality would suggest, with shelves filled with books, stone walls, and no decorations. His desk was large, suited for a man of his stature even wearing his black armor. Still, she wondered if it were paranoia or a sign of an eccentric ego for him to wear it always. Piles of paperwork surrounded him, for he trusted no one else but himself to give his signature, but there had been more than usual lately. Murishani had once read documents for him. However, Murishani was out of the castle, temporarily banished for her comfort and safety.

"Good morning," Casvir said, though his oft stoic face held a frown. "Are you well? You seem pallid."

"I'm fine. Simply hungry." She took the wooden seat before his desk, which she suspected was specifically designed to be uncomfortable.

"Flowridia, I am becoming a broken record, so I will be plain. I am frustrated with you."

The creeping heat of shame filled her. Her arms fell around herself. "W-Why?"

"It has been ten months since you came under my roof, and I am glad you have made progress in your healing journey. You seem well, and you spend your days gardening or with your wife. Those are not poor habits, but you are stagnant."

"If you're referring to my indecision about Demitri—"

"I am."

Flowridia did not fill the silence, fighting to suppress her rising anger. She held the key to send him slinking away with his tail tucked, but perhaps he didn't deserve to know.

"You are sentimental, and so I shall use a sentimental argument. It is cruel to keep him here. It is not a betrayal to allow his spirit to move on, but instead he is trapped inside a body without an intelligent mind. We have watched his mental capacity deteriorate over the months. Worse, he is a danger to you and others."

Anger pulsed as heat in Flowridia's blood. She cursed her welling tears. The explanation was so simple, but her mouth remained shut.

"Accept a new familiar, and let him go. I value your trust enough to not release him without your consent, but your refusal to mourn and accept his loss is stagnating your healing and your development as a witch. Your power is a gift, yet you have thrown it aside."

Flowridia stood, surprised at the rush of blood. Her vision blurred, but she blinked it away, refusing to show weakness. "Ana held a personality."

"Ana was not a familiar. Her intelligence and memories were not magical."

"Well, if you were a better necromancer, perhaps that wouldn't be a barrier."

Gods, his anger was delicious. His red gaze narrowed, the insult striking a rare blow. "Leave my office."

She took a step toward the door—and collapsed.

The wall caught her fall, striking her arm instead of her head. Burning rose within her womb. Her vision blurred as though plunged in dark waters, the ground her only stability.

A large hand touched her back, cool and familiar. "Flowridia, can you move?"

She managed to meet his gaze, or at least the fuzzy assembly of features suggesting his countenance. But her panic rose, even as the fire inside her evoked a sob. Desperate, she clutched her stomach, tears falling fast. "Please, no."

"I am taking you to the healer—"

"I need Ayla."

His metallic embrace surrounded her, lifting her with ease. "I will send for Ayla, and she will meet you in the healing ward."

Flowridia managed no reply, uncaring of the world beyond— merely the fragile life within. The pain spiked, and so she wept. But the bone-deep ache was but a droplet in the storm of her terror. *Please stay,* she pled, as though the soul could listen. Her head spun, dizzy even in Casvir's arms.

"I will not leave," came Casvir's rumbling reply.

He barked out orders, called for servants to prepare a bed, to alert her wife, but Flowridia barely heard it, praying the pain meant life. She sought to clutch her womb, the sharp stabbing in her maimed hand merely noise amidst her anguish.

In the healing ward, her vision cleared. Ayla rushed in mere seconds after they did. "What happened?!"

"She collapsed in my office," Casvir said, calm despite the tense mood. He set her atop an unfamiliar bed with care. Flowridia breathed, and with her exhale, the pain subsided.

A weight fell beside her, but Flowridia barely heard her wife's panic. She felt nothing; merely weakness. But nothing meant death, did it not? She rolled to her side, holding her womb, praying, praying . . .

"*Imperator Casvir,*" came a foreign voice, "*please give us your account.*"

As they spoke, Ayla filled the space between them, her hand falling beside Flowridia's. "Are you in pain?"

"Not anymore," Flowridia whimpered. Gods, her heart ached, yet she had never felt so numb. "Is it dead?"

Beneath the covers, Ayla slipped her hand up Flowridia's gown, her cold hand soothing against the lingering heat within. In Ayla's silence, Flowridia heard nothing—not the healer, not Casvir, not even her own pounding heart.

Ayla's lips came near to her ear. "Breathe easy. There is life."

Fresh sobs overtook Flowridia, this time driven by relief.

Flowridia consented to a physical examination by the De'Sindan physician, caught in the turmoil of her shifting emotions. Clothed, she sat still as the woman checked her mouth, shined lights in her eyes, cast a spell to check her heart, but Flowridia paid it no mind, lost in her own head. The baby was alive, but was it hurt? Was she hurt? What did this mean?

"Imperator Casvir," the woman said, "with all possible respect, would you step out while I finish my examination?"

Casvir did agree, the implication of her modesty made clear.

But to Flowridia's surprise, the physician looked to Ayla, though struggled to meet her gaze, more so than even Casvir's. "Lady Darkleaf, I must ask you to step out as well—"

"I beg your pardon?" Ayla's forced smile showed teeth.

"There is news that is meant for my patient's ears alone."

Flowridia recognized the predatory rise within her wife and took her hand. "I promise, whatever it is, you may speak in front of her. I think we may already know."

"So you are aware you are pregnant?"

The word evoked a smile, despite the grim mood. "Yes, we know. We've chosen to keep the news private for now."

"If the imperator asks, I know nothing," the physician said, yet her sober countenance remained. "Unfortunately, that is all I know with any certainty. If you have miscarried—"

"She did not." Ayla's voice struck like a chill breeze. Flowridia nearly shivered.

"It is possible you are simply dizzy from pregnancy."

"I felt burning," Flowridia said, the memory veiled by a fog of pain. "Literally, as though a fire had been lit inside me."

"I have never heard of such a thing. It is possible you are sick tangential to the pregnancy. I would recommend you stay here for monitoring. Will you be telling the imperator?"

"In my own time, yes."

"Doctor," came Ayla's seething voice, "kindly leave us, would you? I would like a moment alone with my wife."

The doctor gave a short bow and left through a different door.

Ayla's menace immediately fell away, worry etched upon her countenance instead. "Tell him."

Flowridia reeled at the words. "I'm not ready for that."

"Flowra, Nox'Kartha has nigh the most advanced medicine in the world, even aside from the expertise of its magical healers. If he knows, he can help."

"And you would accept his help?" The words were said in disbelief, but to her surprise, Ayla nodded.

"I want you alive." Ayla stroked sweaty locks of hair from Flowridia's face, her hands fidgeting at her hairline. "I know pitifully little of Silver Fire pregnancies, and now I see my error. I will do what research I can, but there are no Solviraes left to ask for aid. I don't have to hold any liking for Casvir to know with certainty that he has the means to help."

"Ayla, it was a fluke," Flowridia said, but the word felt shallow even as she said it. "Do the research, yes, but if it's something we can manage on our own, I would prefer that. I don't want any fuss over me."

Ayla pursed her thin lips, her touch becoming stiff. "A compromise, then. You will stay here and be monitored while I conduct my research."

"Fine."

"But explain to me why you won't tell him."

Flowridia's words caught in her throat, too tangled for her to understand them herself. She had been ecstatic mere months ago, bursting to tell the world about her baby . . .

. . . and as soon as she told Casvir, it would be his baby instead.

"Once the secret is out, it can't be caged," Flowridia said, praying it was not a lie. "It's all the more precious when it's only our family who knows."

Ayla's tension rose. "You know it is not a part of our family, right?"

Though the words were a slap in the face, Flowridia swallowed the urge to wince. "I'm well aware."

A brutal reminder, but necessary in these moments of weakness.

The doctor knocked from her distant door. At Flowridia's word, she returned. "Shall I inform the imperator of your status?"

"Only that I live and will be monitored for the time being."

Though tension lay in the healer's throat, she nodded. "I shall prepare a more permanent suite for you."

When she left, Ayla curled around Flowridia, her embrace protective and stiff. "I wish we had a firmer timeline."

Despite the dour mood, Flowridia managed a teasing smile. "You mean no one knows the gestation of a half-elf dhampir?"

"I am not convinced there has ever been one before."

Casvir returned, his concern foreign on his oft stoic face. "The healer says your condition is a mystery."

"For now," Flowridia said, forcibly bright.

"Unfortunate. How are you feeling?"

"Relieved to not be in pain."

Their small talk remained awkward. When he left, Flowridia finally breathed.

She sunk into the examination bed, the mattress thin. Exhaustion fell upon her in crushing waves, the need to drown in her blankets greater than that for food and water. But before sleep could take her, she squeezed her beloved's hand, soothed when her love squeezed back.

CHAPTER 7

Current era . . .

Sora awoke to an earthquake.

She tore away blankets, readied her knives, threw aside the canvas—

It was not Soliel. Uluron had landed.

When Sora emerged, the tent vanished. Chaos ran to her dragon daughter, laughter spilling from her lips. Even in joy, it never lost that malevolent edge. "Ulu, my dearest, look what Sora has done!"

Chaos twirled, showing her new body from every clothed angle. Sora struggled to not think it adorable, but perhaps that was not wrong. Dira was her niece, and that warmed her heart.

It struck her that she hadn't spoken to Flowridia since. Surely her sister was reeling.

Chaos spoke rapid words, conveying their new plan to Uluron. Meanwhile, Sora dug rations from her pack, wondering if she could justify a moment alone with the mirror.

"Are you ready, Sora?"

With half a cracker in her mouth, Sora shook her head. "I need to relieve myself. I'll just be a moment."

She hurried into the woods, knowing time was of the essence.

Thick trees enveloped her, the sounds of birds hopefully loud enough to muffle conversation. When she deemed herself truly alone, Sora withdrew the mirror and tapped the surface.

It glowed . . . and faded.

Again, Sora tapped it. Her heart raced, muttering silent prayers to no one—simply the ether—when a shrouded face appeared at the other end. Silver moonlight cast deep shadows across Ayla Darkleaf's face, her annoyance clear. "Flowra is asleep. It is best she stays that way. What do you want?"

Caught under pressure, Sora realized she didn't know. "Well, I disappeared awfully quickly after her news, and uh—"

"She didn't step out on me."

"Good to know," Sora replied, uncertain how to explain that she already knew. Did she mention her theory? That seemed like the sort of news to deliver in person. "How is she?"

"Fine," Ayla snapped, which Sora took to mean she perhaps was not. "But she is currently under medical observation, so I cannot say she is well."

Sora's heart sank, anxiety rising beneath her skin. She couldn't return—or could she? Flowridia needed her, but so did the world . . .

So did her niece. But if she had a niece, surely Flowridia would be fine. Chaos had said as much . . . though Chaos wasn't always the most lucid. "I'll come back as soon as I can."

"Kindly leave the mercurial ghost behind."

"I absolutely will."

"The news is not public. Tell no one."

"Got it."

"Next time you reach out, take heed of what time it is."

"Fair enough—"

But Ayla's face had already disappeared, leaving only Sora's own.

She returned to camp to find a quaint sight: Chaos tucked into Uluron's paw, her whispered words too soft for Sora to decipher. The Goddess perked up at her arrival. "I took the liberty of praying to Eionei to let him know we were coming. Are you ready?"

Oh, Etolié might never forgive her. Hopefully she at least shut up long enough for Sora to explain. Sora braced herself and nodded.

Uluron lowered a massive, bony paw. Not looking forward to the chill, Sora sat herself firmly in the center, with Chaos following behind, her satchel of clothes in tow. The Goddess placed a hand on Uluron's claw, stroking affectionately. "Bring us there safely, Ulu."

The dragon launched into the air, and Sora immediately brought her arms around herself, the wind cutting through her traveling clothes.

"Shivering already?" Chaos said, her laughter far louder than the wind.

A blanket appeared around Sora, who did not question its existence. You spent enough time around Etolié, and nothing felt impossible. "Thank you."

Chaos had no fear, standing as she peered between Uluron's claws upon the world below. Serenity softened her visage, her full lips pulling into a smile.

How much like Flowridia she looked. Yet elements of Ayla remained, ineffable as they might be.

Safe in her blanket, Sora reached into her pocket to grab the mirror, only to brush against Chaos' pouch instead. She withdrew it, staring at the glittering contents within. "Dira, are you still attached to this?"

Chaos glanced at the bag, then her. "I feel its pull, so I would say yes. If you killed this body, I wouldn't be banished."

With care to watch Chaos' reaction, Sora withdrew one of the broken prongs. "What is this?"

"An heirloom from my mother, originally."

Sora couldn't say she recognized it. She set it back in the pouch. "Did it break in the Convergence?"

Chaos shook her head. "No, otherwise the pieces would be long scattered and destroyed. I already carried them in my pouch."

"I'm sorry it broke."

"I'm the one who broke it. For a cause, of course."

Sora next withdrew the damaged ring. "What about this?"

Chaos' easy smile faltered. "Another heirloom. Be careful with that one."

Sora glared at the ring once more, desperate to place its familiarity—when the truth struck her like a slap to the face.

She had once held this very ring, or something like it. This was Flowridia's. Her wedding ring—perhaps ruined by the ravages of time. It was a clear enough explanation for the damage, but still Sora wondered.

Sora tucked the ring and pouch safely away in her pocket, then withdrew a locket of infinite worth. Would it mean anything to Chaos? Surely. They were her family too. "My father died away from home, and my mother sold all we had to move across the sea. All I have left of them is this."

Chaos came to sit by her side, her smile filled with the mischief of her maternal grandma—not her grandpa. "A treasure. Would you tell me about them?"

Sora did, wondering what this Goddess—her niece—already knew or didn't. She claimed to love Sora, so why did some instinct inside also hate Sora? "I'm still processing the knowledge that my father was heir to the Theocracy. I doubt I'll ever fully reconcile it. I can't speak to him. But I'm grateful I could at least know Lunestra, even if we didn't know what we were to each other."

"Family is precious and irreplaceable."

Sora contemplated that, finding it difficult to agree anymore. "Sometimes there are reasons to leave them behind. But I have my sister now." Was there any reason to withhold her truth? Sora considered Flowridia, far away and pregnant against all odds. "She's pregnant."

Chaos remained impassive, her smile benign. "Congratulations, Auntie."

"I was hoping you could explain how."

That passive smile became false. Sora remained silent, waiting.

Chaos' attention drifted toward the horizon, appearing with each pump of Uluron's wings. Nothing but the wind to fill the space between them, and Sora feared she would remain quiet until they landed.

"The Silver Fire is complicated," came Chaos' whisper, though the wind did nothing to dampen it. "Just as Staella birthed Ilune, Flowridia birthed me."

With the dissolution of Sora's doubt flooded those thousand questions anew, and one answer among them. "If Flowridia dies, it means you die too."

"Perhaps that was the point all along."

Still, Chaos did not face her. Shame shone starkly on her lovely face, and Sora did not understand yet grasped her implications. "Why, though?"

"I fucking told you. We're seeing Etolié."

Sora froze at the shift in tone, at the sneer upon Chaos' lip. She faced the sun, her bestial growl causing Sora's hair to stand on her arms, her neck. "Dira . . ?"

Only then did there come an eerie twist to Chaos' neck, the angle far from natural. The face remained the same, but there was nothing resembling Dira in that predatory stare. At the raise of her lip, there shone her fangs, a mark of her dhampir heritage.

Sora had faced lions, bears—even dragons. They held more humanity than that soulless glare. At least a lion held no glee as it tore you apart. When Chaos grinned, the instinct to run outshone the fear of falling to her doom from a dragon's paw.

"So you're not Dira," Sora said, praying Uluron might save her if she had to jump.

The Goddess who was not Dira kept her empty stare. "I wasn't there when *you* died, but I was told you screamed all the while— ripped apart by tooth and claw by mindless dead. They said it was noble. I only care that it was painful."

Sora had nothing to say to that, merely fought the icy dread filling her limbs.

But as she contemplated the merit of screaming for Uluron, Chaos seized, face contorting with rage—before she breathed it out. Her attention fell to her hands, listless upon her lap. "I'm sorry."

Though wary, Sora dared to speak. "If that's not Dira, who is it?"

But Chaos frantically shook her head. "Names have power. Names summon things we don't want taking control. Call me Chaos—Dira is Chaos, but Chaos is not always Dira. Gods, I have missed being Dira."

Her face fell into her hands, her body becoming like stone.

Though her trust remained tentative, Sora scooted closer, daring to set a hand on Chaos' shoulder, who did not even twitch. "Who is Dira, then? Tell me about her."

Chaos' voice came as a whimper. "Dira is your niece. You opened your heart to her and loved her until your dying breath. You were a rock for her—for *me*—even at the end of the world. You don't regret your death. There is no doubt in my mind that you would choose it in every life if it meant you saved mine."

And Sora, who had many times nearly died for a cause, did not doubt it either. "We're family. Even now. Even if I haven't met you yet. And even if some part of you seems to want me dead."

Chaos' laughter came pained, laced with sorrow. She did not cry—Sora suspected she lacked the capacity in her dead body—but her anguish showed in those large eyes, familiar and not.

"You're trying to prevent that future, though," Sora pressed, for within her burned that distant yearning. Dira would someday hold a piece of her heart, yet Chaos would erase herself.

"When we see Etolié again, I will tell you the full truth. As I said, we will let her decide. She leads with her heart but understands the greater good. I think I would be soothed by her judgement. But the future is a painful thing. I don't wish to dwell. Will you tell me of the past instead?"

They had a long flight. Sora kept the blanket snug around her as she spoke of herself and Etolié, beginning with the longest carriage ride of Sora's life.

And all the while, Chaos smiled.

As the journey progressed, Sora snacked on boring crackers, longing for something proper.

It evoked an odd question. "They have food in Celestière, right?"

"They do," Chaos replied, her amusement clear. "There are predominantly Celestials there now, and they need something to supplement the light. Full-blooded angels are rare."

"Do angels not need to eat?"

"With proper light, they do not. But the Convergence extinguished their Triple Suns, so magic is necessary to aid in that. They can eat mortal food, however. It also helps supplement what they've lost.

"Though it is worth mentioning that there were and are rare angels sustained by starlight instead," Chaos continued. "They did not suffer as the rest did. Goddess Staella is a notable example."

"So Etolié isn't lying when she says she can subsist off starlight?"

"She is lying when she says it's *all* she needs, but it provides a foundation for her."

"Good to know, especially if Khastra never comes back." Sora glanced up, hoping to glean a reaction to that, but Chaos remained stoic.

"Etolié is prone to letting outside forces dictate her health."

And that was that.

Night had fully fallen by the time Uluron informed them that they neared. The dragon clutched them to her ribs, the winds growing fierce as she flew higher and higher, above spacious mountains . . .

And dove below the clouds. Sora clung to her blanket and touched Leelan for reassurance, who remained snug in her tunic.

But just when nausea threatened to rise, the clouds broke. The wind faded. And Sora beheld a magnificent sight.

The Valley of Neoma—said to be a magical place where there was no veil between worlds.

Uluron landed, hardly a lurch as her massive claws touched the meadow. Sora stumbled into the lush grass, collapsing with joy into the cool meadow. Magic radiated from the very earth. The gentle stirring of a brook invigorated her senses. She resisted the urge to speak her relief at touching the ground—lest she offend Uluron—but Chaos practically danced from her dragon daughter's paw, arms spread wide to embrace the beautiful night.

Yet her peace faded as she made graceful steps toward a meadow flower—a moonlily, Sora knew. The Goddess knelt to pluck it, holding it near to her heart. "My visits to this place are rare, in my future," she said, her olive hues luminous beneath the moon's silver light, "and what a terrible oversight. I would build myself a home here if it were not so, well, politically complex. This is something of a sacred place to the angels now, the home of their former savior."

"Neoma?"

Chaos nodded, and as she rose, she let the flower flutter down into the grass. "Few would dare to visit, assuming they know how to find it at all. The mountains are nearly unsurpassable to mortals. The winds would rip apart any elven airships, hence why a dragon is ideal for travel."

Sora finally sat up, releasing Leelan from the safety of her tunic. "Do you know how to get to Vanir Sol?"

It felt blasphemous to ask, yet the reality of it struck her like the blunt end of a blade—that Sora would go to the realm of gods and goddesses.

"I do," Chaos replied, "though it has been a long time . . ." Her attention turned to a distant light.

Sora leapt into action, alert at the approaching interloper—only to recognize those fractal wings.

"No need for alarm!" came a gallant voice. "Just me, your friend Eionei."

Sora removed her hand from her dagger's sheath, struck at how different the angelic man looked without Etolié to host.

Pure topaz, shining from within, with wings to match as they shifted with each step. Yet he remained nearly human in all the important ways, from his bold stance to his charming smile. Sora had never beheld a true angel, struck by how humanoid his form was. Clear resemblance to Etolié showed in his cheekbones, his lithe physique, even those bright, mischievous eyes, but he was his own person.

"Something is different about you," Eionei said to the Goddess of Chaos, "and that something is everything. I had wondered how you prayed, but you're not a rabbit anymore."

Chaos' wink held the teasing nature of her fallen witch progenitor. "Sora thought I deserved a voice."

"Etolié won't be happy, but she doesn't need to know yet." He turned to Sora, something of intrigue shifting into his friendly demeanor. "You look much stronger. Are you well?"

"Better than before," Sora replied, uncertain of his sudden attention. "How's Etolié?"

"Currently shitting her brains out, but she'll get better. I didn't want to assume you knew where to go, so I thought I'd come to collect you. Kareena— *Sol* Kareena has been informed of your intention to speak with her and awaits."

Dread rose within Sora—for even under good circumstances, to stand before her goddess felt overwhelming. But now? After Sora had evaded her for months? Had committed crimes she'd overtly hidden?

"You look a bit ill," Eionei said, coming nearer. "You sure you're all right?"

Sora nodded, forcing her smile. "A bit daunting to, um, face Sol Kareena."

"Nonsense. She's just a woman doing her best, like you or me." He offered an arm, as the elven nobles might. Sora wrapped her own around it. She would be in denial to say he did not remind her of Tazel—his coloring, his wiry frame—but his smile shone to rival the sun, setting her at ease.

But instead of follow, Chaos reached out a hand to Uluron, who met her with a claw. "Stay safe, my love. Protect the orbs. We'll be back before you know it."

Uluron gave some silent retort, then turned her attention to Sora. *Once we have completed this quest, I will take you across the sea. Good luck, Sora.*

With that, Eionei offered a hand to Chaos, and the trio stepped past an invisible veil.

Hardly a blink. Gone was the Valley of Neoma, replaced with blinding, white mist. Sora flinched, her eyes struggling to adjust to the vast nothing. "Just follow along," came Eionei's reassuring voice, and Sora shut her eyes and followed, trusting the god to lead them to safety.

"If memory serves, it is not far," Chaos said. "Merely requires precise steps."

"Correct," Eionei replied. "And may I just say you seem significantly more stable than before."

"Having a body helps solidify one's mind. I remain a little disoriented, but my thoughts are less fluid."

"I'm intrigued. Say more."

"That's really the end of it," Chaos said, though Sora knew that was partly a lie. It was not simple madness that lurked inside her. Sora knew not what to name it at all.

In fact, Chaos had implored her not to.

"What stories you must have," Eionei said. "Any tips for us unversed in the future?"

Chaos remained quiet a moment, perhaps truly contemplating the teasing question. "Songs are a beautiful memorial. When I was the Goddess of this world, in the era before the Convergence, I sang your songs to my children. Your work is never forgotten."

Sora dared to open her eyes for that, noting the surprise on the Drinking God's face. "That may be the kindest thing I've ever been told, and I've been told many kind things, so don't dismiss it. Certainly the highest compliment. I . . . thank you."

"We all strive to leave a legacy," Chaos replied. "All gods have an advantage in that, but songs are unity. Songs bring hope amid darkness. Songs are passed down through generations, never fading the way memorials might. So that is what I would leave with you— to sing, even as the realm falls apart."

"Very touching, truly. And I appreciate it, but I do want to say that final bit was ominous."

"Do we not face the end of the world? The God of Order is getting desperate, and I have no doubt my apparent kidnapping and the stolen orbs have only spurred him onward."

"Fair enough," Eionei said, though Sora couldn't say it settled her own nerves.

But all that faded as the mists parted, revealing a beautiful, alien world.

Buildings of white stone appeared, bearing no roofs, some no doors. Yet touches of mortal life remained, of plants native to Sora's home, of building materials that surely did not come from here. As a child, she had always envisioned clouds as pillows, and beneath her feet, the mist became just as pliant.

At the edges were more ominous hints of the mist, the scene fading out as a storybook might. But the Celestials gave it no heed, going about their day with joy as they greeted their neighbors.

Sora kept her hold on Eionei's arm as he escorted them, amused at how the Celestial populace waved to greet him. No bows; he wasn't the type. But his popularity was undeniable, and Sora noted a few confused glances sent her way.

Few gave Chaos any heed, unaware of the titan in their midst. Chaos herself softly smiled as she gazed upon Vanir Sol, quiet as she followed.

Eionei, however, pointed out every new thing. "We're about to step into the market district. Stay close. But if you look up ahead, you'll see Sol Kee's palace— Sol Kareena, sorry."

Sora followed his gesture, startled at the distant staircase rising to what appeared to be a cloud. Yet pillars made up a magnificent structure, gleaming in white and gold. "It's beautiful," Sora said, yet discomfort rose once more within her, her limbs threatening to numb.

She had fallen by the wayside, but a former high priestess would not simply be forgotten. By the Light, she felt like a child awaiting reprimand, for she would stand before her beloved goddess in her own home.

She clung to Eionei's words, though hardly heard them. Absently, she reached up and stroked Leelan's feathered head, her heart soothed when he chirped by her ear. Yet the ambiance faded to the deafening beat of her heart, unable to savor the sights any longer.

For a year, Sora had stood by Mereen as she hunted The Endless Night, and *gods*, it should have been a worthy quest. But Sora had not slain The Endless Night, no. She had stood nigh as her sister was nearly tortured to death.

The memory turned Sora's fingers to ice.

They reached the cusp of the palace. Innumerable steps led up to Sol Kareena's domain. But Sora didn't feel her burning thighs. Her whole body had become numb.

Eionei said, "Don't be alarmed. She has been unwell. The destruction of the Theocracy left her . . . unwell, as I said."

Guilt weighed upon Sora, the thought of the goddess' heartbreak unfathomable. Surely her crimes were hardly a blip in the goddess' memory. Perhaps. She hoped. But it did not change that Sora had freed her goddess' antithesis, saved her from a fate well-earned but cruel, so cruel—

"Sora?"

The memory of a broken supplicant before her tortured spouse appeared with Sora's blink. Sora released Eionei, nearly falling down the stairs. "I can't—" Her breathing came in painful, panicked gasps. Vision swimming, she sank to her knees.

Here she would face Sol Kareena, be judged for both her horrendous crimes and for failing to execute them. Here she would say aloud that she had not killed The Endless Night, that she had run away instead, lest she lose her soul.

Her tears fell fast. "You have to go without me," Sora managed through her cries. "I . . . I'm a liability. She can't trust my word."

How many nights had she cried over this? How many nights had she bitten back prayers to the goddess that had once been her whole world?

Amid her tears, she felt a cool touch against her back. A dhampir appeared in the slits between her fingers. "Sora, breathe," Chaos whispered. "Setting aside my undead limitations, can you breathe with me?"

Chaos mimicked the sound of inhaled air. Sora followed, though she trembled and shook. When Chaos released her false breath, Sora followed in sync.

Eionei had vanished, but Sora couldn't spare him any mind. She focused on breathing, on purging the horrible images inside her head, of Flowridia who had wept in the corner of a cold, dark dungeon—

Breathe in . . . and out.

When her body finally ceased to shake, Chaos directed Sora's tear-stained face to match hers. "I need you, Sora."

"I can't see Sol Kareena. What I've done . . . and what I didn't do . . ."

"She is a merciful goddess—"

"I nearly tortured a woman to *death!*" Sora's body heaved from quiet sobs. "M-My own sister," she continued, forcing her voice into submission. "I chose to save her, and so I chose to save The Endless Night." Sora buried her face back into her hands, her tongue growing stiff.

"Do you regret it?"

No, but to admit it upon her goddess' steps would be the final nail in her betrayal.

But then a voice spoke. "Sora Makosa?"

Sora's gaze shot up, for behind Chaos' ethereal form stood Sol Kareena, serene atop the stairs.

Eionei was a clear support, his arm at her waist, her body half-leaning upon him. It was as he had said, that her hollowed cheeks sunk deep, her angelic glow faint and marred by the dark rings beneath her eyes. But her face looked cut from marble, elegance in her bold features—as magnificent as any statue, with flowing locks of gold hair and wings spanning the width of the palace itself.

Yet while artwork depicted her as a stoic figure, Sol Kareena smiled like the Sun she embodied.

Eionei led her those few remaining steps. In careful motions, Sol Kareena knelt before Sora and offered a hand.

Sora merely stared, too horrified to speak, too broken to stanch the flow of her tears. Instead, Sol Kareena gently parted the locs covering Sora's disheveled face. "I've missed you so much."

The words shattered the floodgate already cracked. Sora sobbed anew and fell into her goddess' arms, who held her tenderly. Like hugging a burning star, but not painful, no—soothing; pure light shining through to her broken soul, healing her shattered spirit. "I'm sorry," Sora whispered. "I-I thought . . . I'm supposed to be your champion, but I . . ."

"There is nothing for me to forgive, Sora," Sol Kareena said, and the words fluttered into Sora's heart. "Given impossible odds, you did what was *right* in favor of what was righteous. I would never condemn you for that."

When Sora felt her tears finally slow, she pulled away, daring to gaze into the goddess' kind visage. Sol Kareena placed a single kiss upon her forehead. "I want you here. Please come inside."

With Eionei's assistance, Sol Kareena stood, and when she offered her hand, this time Sora accepted. The goddess' touch illuminated the lines of Sora's work-worn hands, and when Sora had steadied, Sol Kareena led her up the stairs.

Sora passed Celestials clad in armor, all of whom nodded in respect at their goddess' approach. Chaos trailed quietly behind, her heterochromatic eyes glossing over every detail. There were no walls. The pillars created a welcoming barrier, leading to a magnificent throne.

They passed it by, led behind a partition decorated in gold. Within waited a private space, signs of living apparent.

A massive bed—round, like Etolié's nest—and shelves filled with scrolls, books, and artifacts of priceless worth. Gorgeous tapestries were hung to block the outside world, though natural light filtered in through the open ceiling. The glory of the sun lay apparent in nearly all the artwork, though a few tapestries were in homage to the moon instead.

Nearly lost among the décor, a cradle sat beside the bed—and in it, Sora caught a glimpse of golden hair.

Sol Kareena's touch released, and Eionei led the goddess to a large chair, laden with pillows. She slumped, clear pain in her face as she settled. "Please, sit."

Sora obeyed, sitting across upon a comfortable couch of mortal design. Chaos, however, remained standing. Eionei did as well, behind the goddess' chair.

Sol Kareena's wings floated limply, casting far less light than Eionei's. "I hate to dismiss further pleasantries, but I must be mindful of my own weaknesses."

Sora studied the pitiful image of the once-magnificent goddess, a thousand questions welling with it. "If you don't mind me asking for clarification, Eionei said the destruction of the Theocracy did this to you. How can that be?"

Instead of replying, the goddess looked to Eionei, who said, "When the followers of gods or goddesses pass away, they lose the power those followers granted. Twice now, Kareena's followers have been victims of genocide, though the first was slower. But when it happens as rapidly as it did in the Theocracy's destruction, it takes a physical toll. Far less time has passed here than on the mortal realm, and even answering prayers drains her."

"Regretfully, I am only able to answer a few directly," Sol Kareena said, though her anguish far surpassed the monotone words. "But I am able to watch a few more, through my animal servants."

Sol Kareena's smile held a fair bit of mischief—and Sora realized she looked not to her but at the little bird peeking from her tunic. "Wait . . ."

"I proclaimed you my champion, Sora. Of course I did what I could to help you—even indirectly."

All those moments of Leelan's cleverness, his warnings, his influence . . . Perhaps the little bird was just that—an animal, but his eyes served his goddess. Sora's tears had barely quelled, yet new ones threatened to well. "You've been watching."

"It becomes more difficult the less you pray, I'll admit. But while it is no longer my way to interfere directly, there are times where action is more powerful than influence. I helped you when I could."

"So my bursts in power were . . . you."

"You were a conduit, yes. I couldn't have you die just as you took a turn to make things right."

Sora could hardly breathe, and so Sol Kareena continued.

"We can speak more of it later, if you wish. In the meantime, Eionei told me what he witnessed on the mortal realm." Sol Kareena's attention fell to Chaos. "He believes you have good intentions, and given you have not struck me down, I am inclined to believe him."

"I do not endorse the God of Order's quest to separate the realms," Chaos said, vitriol in the title. "I would stop him at all costs."

"And what would you ask of me?"

"I need power. He has worshippers. He has orbs—I, too, have worshippers, but I fear it will not be enough. He has swayed the elves toward his quest by wielding my name. So, I seek pledges of worship from the New Gods—both of Celestière and Sha'Demoni. Currently, I am but a ghost haunting a shell, but my full power will be attained when my infant self is born. I have until then to gather enough strength to stop him for good. If you were to grant me the honor of pledging, the rest of the angelic gods would follow."

"Most," Sol Kareena replied. "Not all, but most." With clear reticence, Sol Kareena reached up to pat Eionei's hand. "Eionei, would you please leave?"

The Drinking God frowned as he stepped aside. "If you wish it."

"There is a private matter I would speak to this Goddess of."

Eionei obeyed, drifting beyond the bounds of the screen.

Sol Kareena held no magnificence as she looked away, staring upon a beaded tapestry of a silver doppelganger basking beneath the moon's light—Neoma. "You wield the Silver Fire?"

In response, Chaos presented her hand, a silver spark catching in her palm.

Again, Sol Kareena remained contemplative, her sorrow thinly veiled. "And is it true that I would call you my daughter-in-law?"

So she did know of her son's fate.

"We never married," Chaos whispered, "but your sentiment is correct."

"Yet there is more to you." Sol Kareena's golden glow shifted, her stare tearing away from her sister's image, returning to the ancient Goddess. "I fear I know your face. But that cannot be."

Chaos closed her hand, the silver flame extinguishing. "Forgive me if the name is tender, but Ilune should not have been conceived either."

"By the Suns . . ."

"And before you ask—yes, I am my mother's child. I do not disavow her, which means I know there boils a blood feud between us, but rest assured that I will do anything to save your realm, Sha'Demoni, and my own."

There remained a studious aura around Sol Kareena, as though Chaos was a scroll to be deciphered. "You have two mothers, Goddess of Chaos. The other is an heir to the ruins of my kingdom, second only to the woman seated beside you." Her attention shifted to Sora. "Her heritage is no surprise to you."

"I figured out the truth."

"Do you trust her?"

"I trust that she wishes to defeat Soliel and stop him from ripping the worlds apart."

Beside her, Chaos held the ghost of a smile.

Sol Kareena returned her focus to Chaos, sorrow marring her beautiful face. "I have contemplated countless times whether my son's death would save this world."

"No," Chaos said, and the Sun Goddess noticeably relaxed.

"Instead, we must kill his elder self."

Chaos nodded. "But in doing so, perhaps it will spare this infant his fate. The future is not set."

"Then swear to me you will not harm him."

As if summoned by her words, there came a small stirring from the cradle.

Sol Kareena stood. Perhaps her son's cry gave her strength. From the cradle, a red-faced child sat up, remnants of sleep clear on his pudgy face. Nearly human, yet an unmistakable glow radiated from his figure, notably around his head. When Sol Kareena neared, he held up his arms, settling his sleepy self against her as she held him.

"Swear to me," Sol Kareena said, "and I will deliver the terms of my pledge."

Yet something shifted in Chaos' countenance as she stared upon the small boy, perhaps a year old in Celestière time. Sora's gut knew, her hand sweeping out her knife as she leapt before the Goddess—who was certainly not Dira; not with that sneer.

"Don't," Sora said, her dagger level to Chaos' throat. "Don't ruin this."

"Ripping his—"

"Don't say it. Don't say a damn thing."

Empty eyes; silver and gold. With a mere flick, Chaos' bestial stare fell upon Sol Kareena instead. "But if it saved the world, would you do it?"

Sora did not dare look back as she spoke. "It won't stop the God of Order from using the orbs."

Despite her words, Chaos did not face her—merely stared unblinking upon the Sun Goddess. "I'm not talking about the orbs. There's something worse on the horizon. Over and over the cycle repeats."

"What is it?" came Sol Kareena's small voice.

Sora kept her stance readied, prepared to tackle Chaos if necessary. But she made no move forward, merely flashed that predatory smile—far too reminiscent of Ayla, yet not. "Envision the genocide of your kingdom. The Theocracy fell in a bloodstained night. It's only the beginning. The rest of the world follows. Celestière falls. Sha'Demoni after. But the carnage doesn't end at the end of these worlds—there are limitless others. They bow or are destroyed."

Sora could not breathe. "Do you mean . . ?"

"Casvir," Sol Kareena whispered.

Sora kept her dagger to Chaos' throat yet trembled despite her training. "Is this why Soliel is trying to separate the worlds? To prevent Casvir from marching?"

Only then did Chaos' attention return to her, that hatred fading to cold calculation. "It is. Sacrificing billions to save infinite." And back to Sol Kareena. "Casvir's so-called benevolence fades as his power grows. His conquests aren't lucky like Nox'Kartha, but soon Nox'Kartha isn't lucky. Casvir seeks power for power's sake. He does what he does because he *can*. You can't stop him. I couldn't stop him. Neither could Soliel. But I blame Soliel for the death of the one who could have—"

Chaos reeled back, but Sora recognized the shift and slipped her dagger away. Sora turned to her goddess—whose wings were held at the ready, prepared to burst into the sky despite her disability. "She's all right now."

Sol Kareena clutched her son close, staring at Chaos—who sank to her knees.

"Not true, not true," Chaos muttered, unquestionably Dira's own anguish. "It was not Soliel."

"Dira doesn't think Soliel is to blame?" Sora asked.

"Dira does not." Chaos remained a supplicant as she gazed beyond Sora. "Sol Kareena, I am so sorry. I wish I could swear to not hurt your son, but there are parts of me I cannot control. I will escort myself out of your castle for this breach of trust. Do not blame Sora. She does not understand."

Chaos rose, but Sol Kareena said, "Wait."

Chaos froze at the cusp of the screen's bounds.

"Goddess of Chaos, there is a strong part of me that wishes to trust you and wishes to believe your intentions are pure." Sol Kareena stared upon nothing, the distance in her gaze suggesting whatever she saw, it was in memory alone. "But I was there when the Convergence shattered my home. My parents were killed, my brother—nearly everyone I loved died in a cataclysm with no explanation, except that you were the cause." Tears filled the golden goddess' eyes, lip trembling as she soothed the boy on her hip. "Celestière was lucky to have any pieces left. Sha'Demoni too. We witnessed entire worlds blown apart by Silver Fire. I cannot even fathom the death toll—surely billions, *trillions*. I assumed you must be a monster—yet to meet you here and now, I don't see a monster. I sense you are sincere. So explain it, please."

Sora only knew the legend in passing—that the Goddess of Chaos caused the Convergence that smashed the three realms together. Sol Kareena had witnessed it. Sol Kareena had lived to recount it.

Yet Sora's heart sank to witness Chaos' lost breath, her broken stance. "Soliel—my Soliel—claimed to have seen that as well. Upon our reunion, we wept of so many things, among which was his plea at my feet to understand why I would destroy the legacy we had built. I told him my truth, and I shall tell you as well—that I did not cause any Convergence of Planes."

Sora accepted it in stride, for legends were ancient, fickle things, but the hitch in Sol Kareena's breath suggested this was not so idle a statement.

"I don't expect you to believe me," Chaos continued. "Soliel certainly did not. I had been taught the very same thing, even before knowing I would become the very Goddess of legend. But I was slain in the same explosion, and all I recall is being blinded by light—and awaking as a ghost in a cave deep underground."

Sol Kareena's scrutiny held no ire—simply unshed tears. "Sora, take my son to Eionei. I would speak to Chaos alone."

Disappointment filled Sora, but it was its own honor to hold her goddess' son, amused to find him as floppy as any other young child. Soliel immediately rested his head upon her shoulder, his thumb finding his mouth.

Sol Kareena joined Chaos upon the floor. "What is this part you can't control?" she asked, but it was the last Sora heard as she left the duo alone.

Eionei waited several paces beyond the barrier, alert at Sora's approach. "How did it go?"

"I genuinely don't know. Sol Kareena wants to talk to Dira—*Chaos*—alone."

"Oh, I already heard, and I won't tell. I'm a God of Secrets. Do you know how long they'll be?"

Sora shook her head.

"We should assume hours, then. How about I take you out? Give you a tour of Vanir Sol?"

His wording was highly suspect, yet her own want surprised her. "I would love to see the city, but I can't abandon Chaos."

"Perhaps a tour of the palace instead?"

"I think that would be all right." When he beckoned, Sora offered the small boy to Eionei, whose reputation in no way suggested he would have any interest or skill with children. Yet this man had been pivotal in Etolié's upbringing, and the way Soliel melted into his arms suggested this was nowhere near the first time. "He really likes you."

"Oh, this little lad? We're fine friends until he wets himself. Then he's the nanny's problem. But he can stay for now, if we're to be in the palace."

Eionei had a kind smile, the sort that sparkled with boyish delight with the slightest provocation. He was terribly endearing—though also, in Etolié's words, a whore. Sora couldn't guess angelic standards of beauty, but by her own, he was handsome in his alien way.

"Does he know his father?" Sora asked. Did anyone know? She certainly didn't.

"Nobody knows his father."

Eionei led her deeper into the palace's recesses, the tapestries and art illuminated through the open ceiling and walls. But Sora mulled over that odd admittance—that Soliel had a father but nobody knew whom. "What do you mean 'nobody knows'?"

"Now we're getting into scandalous territory," Eionei said, his wink only causing her to frown. "I'd be a piss poor God of Secrets if I told them all."

Sora swallowed her questions, which was made easier when they entered a room filled with ancient art.

"I would never call Sol Kareena a hoarder," Eionei said. "Not like Staella, bless her, but Kareena does have a habit of holding onto treasures. She's a sentimental woman, even when it hurts. Just take a look at this one."

Eionei gestured to a dagger displayed half drawn from its sheath, bearing the moon and numerous stars embossed into the fine leather. "Her wedding gift to Neoma," Eionei continued. "Half her home is a tribute to her sister."

As though to punctuate his point, he stilled in front of a beaded tapestry depicting a woman bearing Sol Kareena's face, but the similarities ended there, her stance one of power and steel, her silver hues emanating from deep inside. She wielded a great sword, the tip set into the ground, and stared as though facing an army—and held the confidence to win. The Moon Goddess had been dead for a thousand mortal years, but all the world knew her name. "So this is Neoma," Sora said.

"It is, yes. Many art pieces were taken to Vanir Sol from Solvira after the Solviran Civil War. Neoma . . ." Eionei's enthusiasm fell by small degrees. "Well, Neoma was dear to us all. Staella suffered a great loss, but it can't be forgotten that Kareena lost a sister."

Yet more lay unspoken. Sora gently pressed. "What about you?"

"Neoma was one of my oldest friends, though she'd never admit aloud that we were." His chuckle held sorrow, held depth millennia old. "Never has there been anyone born on this realm with such an unwavering sense of justice. When the Convergence crashed the worlds together, Celestière was in shambles. She rose up to lead us and saved our whole world. She was a hero like no other, and I know I don't only speak for myself when I say I don't know if Celestière has fully found its way since she passed."

Sora knew enough of Solviran history to know the barest emblems of the story—that during its civil war, Solvira had been split in twain between Neoma and Ilune, the God of Death, each fighting for their own interpretation of justice.

It had ended in a battle that had bathed the whole world in silver light—and left the Moon Goddess dead.

Yet beside the tapestry, upon a shelf filled with trinkets and smaller art pieces, was a large quartz cut smoothly in twain—and painted on it was a quaint scene, of Sol Kareena holding a baby. But it was not Soliel, no, nor was it Etolié—the baby had hair like midnight and wings in dual hues of gold and silver.

Sol Kareena was Etolié's aunt—but Etolié had not been the first to make her an aunt. "And how does Sol Kareena view Ilune?"

Eionei's reticence lingered like fog. "Neoma had one blind spot in her justice—and it was Ilune. History says facts, but it does not tell of how much Neoma adored and treasured her. The rest of us saw Ilune as she was—a self-serving, diabolical psychopath. Even Staella saw it and tried to temper those selfish instincts. Kareena certainly recognized her darkness. Ilune wielded the power of her antithesis, and as much as Kareena loved her as family, they grew apart. Kareena told Neoma countless times that her leash on Ilune was too long—and when Neoma was murdered, something in Kareena changed. The stories will tell you that Ilune was spared execution because Staella begged for her life at the trial, but between you and me, it was only because no one knows where her phylactery is, forcing them to imprison her instead. Kareena was more than willing to do it herself."

Despite the somber mood, Sora couldn't help her wry retort. "It's something not even a God of Secrets knows?"

"There are some secrets too dangerous for even me to hold onto. Her phylactery isn't for us mere immortals to trifle with."

"I was told once that only Ku'Shya and Sol Kareena know where her prison is."

"That's certainly more information than any other mortal I've met has," Eionei said, amusement clear in his tone.

"I was told that by an immortal," Sora replied, though she withheld specifically who. Common sense said that Kah'Sheen probably shouldn't have mentioned that little tidbit.

"Well, you're correct that they're the only two who know. Staella wasn't trusted with the knowledge. Neither was I, before you ask. I'm a disgrace of a God of Secrets."

His wink lightened the fog around them, yet Sora's curious mind still spun. "You said Sol Kareena . . . changed?"

"Oh, I've teased Sol Kee countless times about becoming just as much of a hard-ass as her sister. She was left with large shoes to fill. She does the best she can, but I know it's difficult for her."

"A hard-ass, you say?"

Soliel stirred at the new voice. Sora jumped at the quiet tease, the fear of disrespecting her beloved goddess causing her to bow instead. Sol Kareena used a gilded cane as she walked side by side with Chaos, her tone gentle and chiding. "Sora, there's no need for that."

Sora rose, her spirit warmed to simply hear her goddess' voice. Yet Chaos, too, held an aura of peace. "Sol Kareena has agreed to call a council of angels and gods. I will make my case before them."

"That's good enough reason for me." Eionei bowed, sweeping and gallant—and humorous, given he was still holding a baby. "I already liked you though." In his bow, he took the Goddess' hand. "I pledge my power and loyalty to you, Goddess of Chaos. May the worlds not be destroyed."

A strange thing happened, an odd dimming in Eionei's wings— and a glow in Chaos' eyes. A mere moment, a flicker, but Eionei's pledge had been received, the first of the angels to give it. He kissed her knuckles, then released.

"Thank you," Chaos said. "Your faith in me truly is appreciated."

"I will still be attending the meeting, of course. Not to brag, but as the oldest surviving angel, I do hold a little bit of sway here and there."

The words took Sora aback. Of course he was ancient, but to say it in that way . . . how lonely.

"The meeting will take place tomorrow," Sol Kareena said. "I will send messengers to inform the rest of my godly counterparts. In the meantime, there are things I still wish to discuss with you, Goddess of Chaos. Eionei, could you show Sora to the guest chambers? She is welcome to bathe and rest."

"Anything for you, Sol Kee." Eionei offered Soliel back to his mother, who set the infant upon her hip.

Sora watched the pair fondly, unwilling to be hopeful just yet.

"Your stress is radiant," Eionei said. "What do you say about that tour now?"

"I'd like to clean up first, but . . ." Sora tore her gaze away from the exiting duo, her duty fulfilled—for now. Mild agitation filled her, but the lack of Spore could explain that. "That sounds fun. Forgive my query, but do angels, uh, smoke?"

Only after asking did she recall what a stupid question that was, given Etolié's scum of a father had literally made his name in hallucinogens, but thankfully Eionei's chuckle permeated the palace as he led her along. "We do anything we like! I would be happy to introduce you to Celestière's finest."

"Please," Sora said, already relieved at the prospect.

After hours of unmentionable happenings done in the lavatory, Etolié finally felt a spark ignite inside her.

As gentle as a crackling fireplace, it warmed her within, bringing assurance and awareness of the world. A snap of her fingers, and there came a puff of glitter.

The torture was over. Etolié set about cleaning up.

Staella's bathtub had more in common with a luxurious pond, decorated with rocks and plants, bearing an open skylight to the eternal night. Etolié's wings lit the scene, and she felt she could finally breathe after too long underwater. To celebrate, she conjured a wineglass, filling it with merely her will, and drank until her vision tilted.

After a soak in the bath and some time spent drying herself, Etolié emerged with an illusioned gown and wet hair. Staella's messy home was a welcome sight, and bustling from the kitchen suggested her angelic momma was making it messier. "Momma?"

Staella peeked her head around, beaming as she came to greet Etolié. She offered a hand. Etolié accepted the stand-in hug. "How are you feeling?"

Etolié snapped her fingers, revealing a puff of glitter. "I'm as good as new."

"Oh, wonderful! Let me get you some water. That can't have been easy on your poor insides."

Sweet Momma, always practical. Etolié settled herself on the cozy couch as Momma went away, returning in time with . . . tea. Well, the spirit of the law said Staella hadn't lied, and Etolié took a sip, the refreshing sensation not natural at all. "Where's Eionei?"

Staella's kind smile faltered. "I don't know how you're going to feel about this, but he went to the Valley of Neoma to meet Sora. And, um, Chaos."

Etolié blockaded her tirade of curses behind pursed lips. "They're in Celestière?"

"That's correct."

"The unhinged, world-ending Deity? And Sora?"

Staella nodded.

"You don't happen to know any recipes for half-elves, do you? Because I'll be skinning one alive." Etolié gulped the rest of her tea, uncaring for her scalded throat. "Any idea why?"

"Given a messenger came by to invite me to a *very important* council meeting in Vanir Sol, it surely has something to do with that." The emphasis on *very important* suggested skepticism, which Momma wasn't generally prone to. "I don't know the details."

Panic twisted Etolié's gut. "Please don't go. What if it's a trap?"

"I don't have to be convinced, don't worry. I only told the man I would think about it."

"They're in Vanir Sol then, right?"

"If they didn't come straight here, I presume so."

Etolié set the teacup onto the table, smoothing her false gown as she stood. "I swear I'm gonna drag Sora back to the mortal realm by those mostly pointy ears of hers. If you need me, I'll be in Vanir Sol."

"Do you need me to come with you?"

"Nope. Stay here in case it all goes down in flames."

"Good luck. Remember to disguise yourself."

It struck Etolié then that she was potentially being rather rude to her momma, who by all accounts had saved her ass. Etolié stilled, feigning calm with her curt sigh. "Thank you for your help, by the way. That was, uh, kinda traumatic."

There came Staella's sympathetic smile. Etolié supposed she'd done right. "Of course, Starshine. Are you hiding your pain behind action, or is this really worth the fuss?"

Damn Momma, cutting right to the heart of it. "Yes and yes. Chaos is batshit, but I did, in fact, spend most of the time shitting my brains out worried about Khastra." The timeline struck her, then. "Wait, you said you'd take care of it. What . . . What happened?"

Staella had a very particular stance and tone when she hedged a dangerous question, something impish in the way she shrugged. "Hopefully not an awful thing."

"Momma, please don't fuck around about this. Is Khastra all right?"

"I don't know. But you have to understand my position—which is if I tell Ku'Shya, she'll eat an entire country, and that still wouldn't necessarily get Khastra back, if I'm understanding the intricacies of her prison correctly. So instead of speak to Ku'Shya, I . . . sent a dream *as* Ku'Shya."

Staella still looked guilty. "Momma, what does that mean?"

"It means I visited Executor Faeborn in their sleep and gave them potentially the worst nightmare of their life. That isn't to say I won't take a harsher approach if that doesn't work, but I think I at least made an impression. Just reminding them what would happen if Ku'Shya found out from the wrong people where her daughter truly was. Hopefully they do the right thing."

Etolié merely blinked. "And what will that do?"

"I don't know. But telling Ku'Shya directly will get an entire country eaten, as I said." Staella grimaced, her false airs fading away. "Etolié, I hate this. And of course I'm going to do everything in my power to save Khastra. But Ku'Shya isn't a diplomat. She's a battering ram. If it were only the executor standing in the way, I wouldn't hesitate, but it's a city filled with children and mothers and fathers who don't deserve to be killed for their leader's folly."

Visions of the City of Light haunted Etolié in rare moments of sleep, the stench of death and blood, the screams of innocents slaughtered for a tyrant's dark ambitions. Fucking hell, she wanted to scream, but Momma was right. "I understand. But Ku'Shya can't leave her realm, right?"

"No, but there is a portal leftover from the Convergence barely a hike from Tierzuroth leading to *Daemenacht*. Ku'Shya can send her army, and she can still do severe damage even as a shadow on the realm."

Etolié cursed her tears, swallowing them back as she said, "I hate this."

"I know. I hate it, too."

"Just . . . let me know what happens. I'm gonna go hide my pain behind action now. Yell at a dumbass priestess. Kill a ghost. Healthy stuff."

Staella simply nodded. "I love you, Starshine."

"Love you, Momma—" But the word was cut off by Etolié herself rolling the door shut behind her, determined to keep composure even in the face of torment.

Khastra had been within arm's reach, yet Etolié had failed.

Etolié sank to her knees on the doorstep, *finally* able to feel. Khastra was underground, trapped in a prison too fucking cruel for even Etolié's imagination, and she had fucking failed. She bit back a sob, anger surging along with grief. She pressed her palms to her eyes, but it didn't stop the flood of tears.

Somewhere in her head, Etolié heard the door open behind her. When Staella knelt beside her, Etolié leaned into the touch on her back, offering her broken heart to the Goddess of Mercy and Comfort.

"It's going to be all right," Staella whispered, but over ten months of waiting had left Etolié weak.

The words broke the dam. Etolié wept in her mother's arms. "I'm just so tired."

"Then stay and rest. The world can wait a little longer. You've already done so much."

Etolié sought to protest, but as she cried, a plot brewed in her addled mind. The stupidity of it was liable to get her killed, but Chaos would be at that meeting, no doubt about that. Etolié's impression of her momma had gotten pretty damn good throughout the years.

No need to worry Staella, however. It could all wait.

For now, Etolié let herself feel.

Eionei hadn't exaggerated the variety of Celestière's smoke offerings.

Though the exterior of the Temple of Eionei was built of the same marbled stone as most of the rest of Vanir Sol, the interior could have been a particularly opulent Solviran tavern. The only truly alien feature was the lack of roof over the main area, letting the pervasive light illuminate the jolly space. Though gaudy, the fountains pouring different colors of drink were quite impressive, surely sustained by Eionei's magic. Revelers were about, and all greeted Eionei at his entrance. Sora remained shy, uncertain of standing so close to the spotlight.

Eionei beckoned to one. "You there!" A Celestial man met him with particular enthusiasm. "Could you part with a pinch of Spore for my friend here?"

For all the charms of the day, the relief of breathing Spore once more neared the top. Sora savored the pleasurable calm washing over her. "Thank you."

"But of course! I'm more inclined toward liquid courage, but that doesn't mean I don't indulge in different pleasures from time to time." He offered his arm. "Shall we continue on?"

Perhaps it was the Spore. Perhaps it was Eionei's charisma finally chipping a crack into her wall of reservations. Or perhaps she was simply excited to explore this strange new world. But Sora took his arm with gusto, ready for any adventure.

What beautiful temples there were to see! Eionei led her through rich holy districts, pointing out temples to all the gods and goddesses who resided in Vanir Sol itself. The grandeur surpassed even Neolan in its heyday, and while it was not as large as Haven, even Casvir would envy the collection of statues and other artistic pieces. For all of it was art—every bench carved with love and care, the paving stones aligned with precision, artwork painting most every wall.

Sora absorbed it all with wonder, reminded of the first time she had visited Neolan and its beautiful glass palace.

After a walk through the market district, Sora asked a pressing query. "Do angels sleep?"

"We are capable, though we gods need it less."

"How do you sleep in eternal daylight?"

"Practice," the unflappable god said, but even beyond the haze of smoke in her mind, Sora saw distant sadness in his gaze. "But there are pockets of night in Celestière, and I think our night skies may even rival yours." Conspiracy raised his eyebrow. "Would you like to see for yourself?"

Intrigued, Sora offered a nod. When he offered a hand, she took his arm instead, and let him lead her back through the streets—and to the edge of mist.

How strange, the thrill it shot through her. Sora's cheeks flared, even as her mind wandered back to Chaos in Sol Kareena's place. Surely fine, yes. But farther, still, Flowridia was pregnant in Nox'Kartha. Urgency rose inside Sora. Flowridia needed her; Chaos needed her; here was Sora, fraternizing with a *god*.

"Brace yourself," Eionei said, drawing Sora back into the moment. "You already did it once, but traveling through the mist is always daunting, even for me."

With that warning, he led her through the curtain of white.

Again, Sora shut her eyes, the mists making her head spin. "How do you navigate this?"

"I hate to say 'practice,' but after a few thousand years, you sort of passively count your steps. It's rare that anyone gets lost anymore."

The idea of getting lost in this endless landscape of nothing sent a chill through her blood. "Only rare?"

"Well, we've mapped out what we can. We can sometimes find people who wander a bit too far. However, children are taught very young to keep their distance from the mists' walls. I've made up more than a few stories about monsters lurking in the white for parents to pass along. But I assure you, there's nothing here. Which is somehow more frightening than there being something, don't you think?"

If Eionei were trying to reassure her, he was doing a questionable job. "I hate to say it, but it's nigh impossible to prove a negative. There's nothing here because no one has found anything—yet."

To her surprise, Eionei sounded merely amused. "Well, there's a terrifying idea, Sora Makosa. Perhaps you're a storyteller yourself."

"Be that as it may, I think I'd rather face nothing. I'm far too used to monsters lurking in the dark."

"A worthy priority, given what I know of your Fireborn family name. Which isn't much, but word of vampire hunters reaches even my ears. But setting that aside, keep your eyes shut for just a few more steps."

The pervasive light shining behind her eyelids vanished, leaving only darkness.

Sora opened her eyes, gasping at the sights before her.

A boundless field cast in darkness, but more incredible still were the billions of stars above their heads. Sora had seen incredible sights upon the mortal realm, admired the night sky from the sea, from mountain tops, from the darkest recesses of the woods—but there was nothing at all to detract from the beauty above her, no trees, no buildings, not even a moon. Simply she, Eionei, and a vast sea of celestial lights.

What startled her most, however, was that the constellations were familiar. "My papa taught me how to navigate using the stars," Sora said, idly stepping forward. She released Eionei's arm, but his light followed close behind. "I know these patterns. How can they be the same as in the mortal realm?"

"We occupy the same space, don't forget," Eionei said, his wings and innate glow the only other source of light. "The ground might converge differently, but we share the same sky."

"There's no moon, though."

Eionei shook his head. "There never was one here."

Sora supposed that was another difference. There was no silver light to join the stars. "It's beautiful."

"It is, though I never truly appreciated it until I had to travel to see it." Eionei's smile remained splendid, but that distant sorrow returned. "The stars truly are a perfect sight."

The statement settled discomfortingly inside Sora, drawing her back to the reality of her situation—that she stood here with a god, the grandfather of one of her closest friends, no less, and said friend had alluded more than once that the Drinking God might favor the Stars. To think of Staella meant to think of Etolié, which meant to think of her quest, of Chaos, of Flowridia, her pregnancy . . .

"Drink?" Eionei conjured a wineglass from thin air, dark liquid filling it just as smoothly. He offered it, then conjured his own.

Sora accepted the glass, even matched the *clink* of his toast, and sipped the wine. Sweeter than any she had tasted before, hardly a bitter trace upon her tongue, and while Sora generally preferred smoke over drinks, this far surpassed any mortal concoctions.

She gazed back upon the sky, calculating just where in the mortal realm she would be with these stars as her guide. She knew these ones intimately, which meant somewhere in or near Solvira. Did that mean Flowridia looked upon the same sky? Was she safe?

Mischief twisted Eionei's charming smile. "Who are you thinking about?"

Sora glowered, taken aback by the implication. "It's not what you think. My sister is pregnant. I just wish the world could be saved so I could go back and care for her."

"Congratulations, Auntie," Eionei replied, and the title left Sora grinning. It was a lovely thing. "No, it wasn't what I thought, but I do accept it. I had wondered why you seemed so distracted."

"Not from any spurned lovers, no," Sora said, and though the words were technically conveying an assumption, Eionei's wink suggested she had spoken true of his intentions. She sipped the wine, noting that it never seemed to empty.

"Have you ever been in love, Sora?"

The question took her aback, Eionei's intrigue not what she expected at all. "No."

"No? I'm shocked, truly."

"Love isn't something I take lightly."

"Whereas I fall in love with every new person I see, but I suspect you're wiser than me." Eionei chuckled, perhaps to convey his tease—or, at least, Sora prayed it was teasing.

"Feelings are what they are, but loyalty and commitment are what truly matter. My papa always said that once you've found the one to let nothing shake that foundation. Let nothing be more important than them. That's what love is to me. I'm holding out for that."

Eionei placed a dramatic hand over his heart. "Just warning: this is how the mightiest fall. Love isn't meant to be logical. I look forward to the day the enigmatic and gorgeous Sora Makosa falls prey to the insanity of love."

Sora's cheeks flared hot, but the spike of annoyance was far more potent. "That's awfully presumptuous."

Eionei's laughter held all the charm of his songs, music in every note. "Oh, sorry, sorry. What I should say is that it's sweet you have them to emulate. Keep your family close."

"Sadly, my parents did both pass away. But I have my sister."

Eionei's impish attitude faded. "Keep her close. I lost my sister thousands of years ago. I lost everyone. I understand the pain."

Sensing the shift in mood, Sora withdrew her precious locket from her tunic. She offered it to Eionei as she opened it up, revealing the smiling faces of Mariam Fireborn and Zanoram Makosa. "I keep them close to my heart, you might say."

To her surprise, Eionei said nothing of the jest, instead studying the locket with care. "Treat that like the treasure it is. I forgot my parents' faces long ago."

Of all the ways the tour could go, feeling heartbreak for the oft riotous drinking god was never on the agenda. Emboldened by wine, Sora returned the locket to its place and set a hand on his shoulder, though kept her distance from his wings. It seemed too intimate. "I can't even imagine what that feels like. But I have no doubt they'd be proud of what you've become."

Such mischief turned his lip, though his eyes remained distant. "My sister would, perhaps. What about you? Is your sister proud of all you've done?"

Sora joined Eionei in gazing up at the stars, her hand leaving his shoulder. Shame rose, and Sora knew she didn't wish to unburden the darker parts of her and Flowridia's pasts onto this near stranger. "Recent things, yes. We have a difficult history, but we're trying to overcome it. We want to be in each other's lives, and I'm doing what I can to atone for . . . for how I hurt her."

With the deafening *boom* of a gun had come Flowridia's doom, though her life was not the one forfeit. Sora hadn't pulled the trigger. Some days, she felt it didn't matter. And with memories of guns came screams in dark dungeons, blood-soaked ballgowns, derelict mansions in forsaken mountains . . .

One strange memory surfaced, one of the many that played in her mind on sleepless nights. Not a nightmare, no. But an anomaly. Odessa's words haunted her. *"I see right through you, you poor, lonely child."*

"Thinking about your sister again?" Eionei asked.

"Yes," Sora lied, for now she dwelled upon a friend she never should have had, upon a woman who by all accounts was the worst sort of monster, yet had done nothing but build Sora up. Flowridia didn't know. It seemed as grand a betrayal as Demitri's death, to think Sora considered her vile progenitor a friend. All families kept secrets.

"I am doing an exceptional job at botching this seduction attempt," Eionei said, and Sora quite adamantly did not join him in his laughter, though her amusement was certainly high.

"It wasn't going to happen tonight."

Eionei made a show of stabbing a make-believe knife through his heart, though he held a smile all the while. "You can't blame a man for trying. You're quite beautiful. I can't believe you have no suitors."

"I've been busy." What an understatement. The past two years had been all about family, for better and worse. "And it's not always easy when you have ears like mine."

"What?! Your ears are adorable. But mortals do have their prejudices, now don't they? I remember when angels used to, but then Neoma was a lesbian and our savior, and all the biases slowly unraveled from there." Conspiracy twisted his grin, his wink oddly sweet. "Perhaps *you* prefer the fairer sex."

"I have no preference."

"So you're saying I have a chance."

"You already know my terms."

Eionei gave a mock sigh, then laid back into the cool grass. "Well, respectfully, I have a piss poor track record of commitment."

"I know. I'm friends with Etolié."

"Yet you came on my tour anyway. You're awfully brave to be alone with a strange man in a strange world."

Sora raised an eyebrow, admittedly amused by his antics. With any other tone, it might've been a threat; Eionei's good nature shined despite it.

"God or not," Sora replied, "I'm sure a well-placed fist to your nose would break it just like anyone else's."

Eionei's chuckle validated the notion. "I like your spark, Sora. I'm a terrible monogamist, but I do make a half-decent friend. I have references—Kareena will vouch for me. What do you say?"

The sweetness of it nearly made her reconsider. But best not to take back her reservations after this turn. "I'd like that. You're . . . not what I expected."

"No?"

"You've lived through so much."

Eionei shrugged, his gaze kept to the stars. "You don't become the oldest angel without surviving a few unpleasant things."

This enigmatic fellow—full of laughter and smiles, charismatic and beloved among the angels and Celestials alike, yet holding depthless sorrow. "I can't even fathom that."

"No need to try. I am hardly that deep."

"I think there's more to you than you think."

Eionei's chuckle conveyed reticence. "This is why we're more suited to be friends, Sora. Typically, I try to *convince* the women I sleep with that I have any depth at all. You have the gall to claim it. Apparently, I need to act more the fool."

Sora shrugged as she joined him in gazing up at the stars. She was hardly suited for boosting egos, men or women alike. "Tell me about your sister."

"I will if you tell me about yours."

Yet Sora's heart sank. "If I tell you about my sister, I have to tell you about my sister-in-law."

"Wait, I think I know this one. Is that the monster girl? The vampire? Staella and Etolié have mentioned it."

Sora nodded.

He was always a breath away from laughter. Eionei did so even now as he rose. "Could be worse. Your nephew could be Morathma. That's Sol Kee's plight."

Sora chuckled, though was remiss to admit how little she knew about Morathma. His country bought and sold slaves—anyone familiar with Etolié knew that—but that hardly scratched the surface.

Blessedly, Eionei did not push, instead speaking lightly of Old Celestière and the sister he had lost thousands of years ago.

CHAPTER 8

Four years after the end of the world . . .

"What do you think of your room, darling?"

Mother extracted Dira from the folds of her dress, tugging the fabric from her hands. Dira stood exposed in a room far too large, far too warm. The fireplace burned bright, casting flickering shades of orange and red across the lush space, highlighting the colors of the embroidered bedspread, the floral arrangements, and the collection of toys in the corner. She took a tentative step toward them, then quickly turned back to Mother, wary of the dark corners. "It's too big."

Mother knelt, and Dira glowed beneath the sparkle in her eyes. "Dira, my love, let's explore it together, shall we?"

When Mother offered her hand, Dira gripped it with all her strength, resisting the draw of hiding in her dress. Mother walked her first to the empty bookshelf. "We can put anything you want in there."

"Not only books?"

"We can put as many books as you would like, but if you have any toys you want to display, or drawings, you can do that too. It is your decision."

"But all my drawings are at our house."

Oh, why did Mother's face fall? Had she said something wrong? Even so, Mother spoke gentle words. "This is our home now. We can make new drawings—together."

Mother led her to the chest filled with toys, withdrawing a pretty elven doll. "What if you learned to make dresses for her? She could be your twin."

Dira beamed as she accepted the doll, squeezing it tight. "Is she for me?"

"Everything in here is for you."

There was suddenly so much more to see.

"I know you expressed dismay regarding the size, but look." Mother released her, evading when Dira tried to snatch her hand back. Instead, Mother posed in the center of the floor, touching nothing even with her arms spread. She gave a graceful twirl, the fabric of her dress fluttering like wings. "If there's room enough for me to dance, there's more than enough for you."

At Mother's beckoning, Dira accepted her outstretched hand, becoming her partner in a waltz. The steps were well-practiced, moving decidedly in threes, and when Mother gave her a twirl, she spun until the room spun faster. Laughter took her, and when Mother lifted her up, Dira giggled in her arms.

"But look at this! The bed is perfect. Not too big at all."

Mother laid her down upon the blankets, having to hunch to fit in beside her. Dira curled into Mother's arms, savoring the safety of her embrace.

"And if you truly despise it, I can work with Sora to create something new, but I would appreciate it if you gave it a chance. It would make her happy if you did."

Dira nodded against her chest.

"This is a safe place, my love." Mother's fingers stroked lines across Dira's scalp, the thick curls parting for her touch. "Aunt Sora has graciously agreed to let us live in her home and has even offered to help care for you. As remiss as I am to say it, you would benefit from guidance from more than only me."

"She's going to be my mom, too?"

Dira did not know what to make of Mother's chuckle, nor her gentle chide. "Darling, she will be your aunt. That is a wonderful title in and of itself. But she can tell you more of the mom you lost. And . . ." Mother's hesitation set Dira on edge, but her firm embrace remained. ". . . There will be times when I leave. Just for a few hours. Sora will watch you then, too."

Something in the words froze Dira's blood. "You're leaving?"

"Dira . . ." In that moment, Mother shifted to be small as she curled around her. How it frightened Dira to feel Mother be small. "My beautiful girl, it will not be for long. But there are some things I must do."

Dira clung tight to Mother. Silver glowed beneath her skin in tandem with her welling tears. "I don't want you to go."

"You will hardly notice my absence."

"Why do you have to go?"

"Dira Darling, I cannot tell you. But I can swear upon your sweet mom's grave that I will return. Sora is someone I trust, and these grounds and these woods are safe for little girls. There are no monsters here."

Mother often spoke of monsters. "Are you going to fight a monster?"

"I am, but you need not worry. Everything I do, I do for you."

Current era . . .

Flowridia's suite was far more extravagant than a medical ward would typically be.

Lush in its décor, with embroidered comforters and pillows, a cozy desk, even a fireplace and couches. Flowridia suspected it had been created specifically for her, given the floral arrangements. Little plants in pots sat on the large windowsill, with all she could ever need to tend to them at a station nearby.

But it was not a suite meant for guests. Hints of its true purpose remained—metal dishes stacked under the bed, endless piles of towels, and exploration had led Flowridia to discover a stash of surgical knives and medicine in a drawer.

Below it, Ayla had placed Izthuni's knife, locked in a box lined with maldectine. *"Just in case."*

Not exactly comforting.

Despite its beauty, Flowridia found the space a prison. Multiple times a day, the physician examined her, took her temperature, cast a few charms, only to begrudgingly state she was stable, then whisper that the baby seemed well.

And that was fine and good, except she was berated whenever she tried to leave—by the physician, the nurses, even Casvir.

"I feel so . . . so useless!" Flowridia paced between the bed and the set of couches, willing her body to not betray her this day. She ached, the permanent pinching in her back inexcusable given her lack of baby bump, but she vowed to stay on her feet. "At least I had the garden before. Now they won't even let me breathe fresh fucking air."

In her tirade, she marched to her bedside table and tapped her mirror, which glowed and revealed . . . nothing.

She had stopped bothering to voice her concerns. Ayla said Sora was fine, because Etolié would have told them if she wasn't. Still, Flowridia's anxiety grew each day. Sora's disappearance was far from comforting.

Breakfast had been delivered. Flowridia bitterly grabbed a slice of bread, only to flinch and withdraw her mutilated hand. "Dammit."

"Flowra?"

"It's nothing. Just . . . nothing." Flowridia swallowed the pain and grasped the slice as lightly as she might touch a butterfly's wing. Her hand prickled in warning, but it was better than feeling stabbed by knives. She forced down a bite, though her stomach protested.

"I do see their point," Ayla said gently, despite Flowridia's glower. Ayla sat on one of the couches, contemplative with a sketchpad in her hands. "I am willing to negotiate with them if you'll consent to letting me follow you."

"Of course."

"I do hope it is not too much for you, though. I know you cherish time alone. If I am ever annoying, will you tell me?"

Flowridia's anger faltered at the vulnerable phrase. She set aside her breakfast bread, instead examining her precious wife. Ayla had been doting, even more than usual, but Flowridia would never call her annoying. "You're the rare sort to let me be alone even when we're together, if that makes sense."

Ayla's smile was directed at her drawing, but Flowridia knew it was for her. "I am attempting to make the best of this. Just a blink in eternity." She turned the sketchpad around, and Flowridia's hand flew to her face. "I visited Demitri last night."

A stunning piece, her lost wolf's image so clearly conveyed. Ayla herself sat beside him, her face pressed to his head. And though Demitri remained dead, something glimmered in his eye, a light Flowridia had not seen in months.

Tears welled in her eyes as she accepted the drawing, heart warmed and broken all at once. "It's beautiful. Thank you."

"You are welcome, my darling. I am trying to find my old hobbies again and thought Demitri might spark some creativity within me. I was right."

Little reminders remained of Ayla's trauma by Mereen's hands. Lapses of silence too long to be natural, hesitation in her kisses, and more than once Flowridia had awoken to find her beloved softly weeping beside her . . .

This was progress. Flowridia set the drawing onto the table, then came to sit beside her. When they kissed, there was no hesitation, no fear. Flowridia gently coaxed her wife's hands to touch her, melting at the anticipation of pleasure.

"Are you certain?" Ayla whispered.

The question was . . . oddly irritating. "Shall I explain in visceral detail precisely where I want your mouth—?"

The door burst open—and in marched a face she had not seen in years.

Marielle Vors, the former Queen of Staelash, now Governor of the Nox'Karthan-claimed territory, wore a dress of Nox'Karthan design, ample amounts of her cleavage shown in the plunging neckline, the skirts longer than her legs. Her red hair held an elegant bun, her eyes darkened with rouge. She wore less makeup than Flowridia's memory recalled, perhaps finding equilibrium as a proper adult.

Marielle screamed to see her. Flowridia managed to part from her wife, confused above all else as she stood—only to be crushed in a hug. She struggled to breathe, far closer to Marielle's nearly bare breasts than she preferred. "Flowridia, you beautiful little witch! You're all grown up!"

Not the reaction Flowridia expected, given Marielle theoretically had been told that Flowridia had killed her cousin, but if the rumors were true, Marielle also let Murishani whisper in her ear. "It's lovely to see you too," Flowridia said, struggling with the onslaught of Marielle's enthusiasm.

She nearly didn't notice Zorlaeus slumped in the doorframe, the De'Sindai made small by his stance. With red hues, maroon hair, and horns solidifying his demonic heritage, he offered a wave and a soft, "Hello, Lady Flowridia. And, uh, Lady Ayla."

Ayla had once described Zorlaeus as a 'pet'—a pet who had run away from his master in favor of Marielle. Not a friend, certainly not a lover, but a pawn she'd loved to toy with. Ayla spoke in monotone. "Hello, Lae Lae. Marielle."

"And Ayla, how wonderful to see you too!" Marielle came to Ayla's side, though thankfully forewent offering a hug. Ayla did not quite exude murder, but there were certainly storm clouds surrounding her. "I had been considering coming to Nox'Kartha for a while on business, but when news came of Flowridia's condition, of course I had to visit!"

Seated on the couch, Ayla's smile held only dead eyes. "Flowridia's health has been precarious for months, yet only now is it pertinent?"

"The day to day of Staelash has been busy on my own. News slips in one ear and right out the other!" She laughed as a politician would, and Flowridia kept her expression neutral when Marielle returned her attention to her. "It's so good to see you. You really do look stunning, if a bit pale. What happened? Word spread that you had a fall."

Flowridia did not wish to accuse a supposed 'old friend' of ill intentions, especially given their last encounter had been at Flowridia's own wedding—and it had been delightful. But she didn't have to hold even an ounce of emotional intelligence to know Marielle was acting like a buffoon. "It's exactly that. A week ago, I fell while in the imperator's office. The healers are baffled, so I'm under observation here."

"That's awful. I'm so sorry. It must be frightening."

"I trust Nox'Kartha's medical experts." Flowridia took Marielle's hand, channeling all her own experience as a charming public figure—which far paled to Marielle's, yet the former queen's words held cracks. "I desperately want to catch up, but you caught me right as we were on our way out. We have a meeting scheduled with Cas—Imperator Casvir. Can't keep him waiting. But come see me this evening, if you have the time."

"Of course!" Marielle offered a softer hug, even a polite kiss on the cheek. "If my schedule allows, I'll make it my first priority."

She whirled away, leaving only her perfume behind.

Zorlaeus lingered, downcast eyes glancing down the hall where Marielle had gone. "I hope you feel better soon, Lady Flowridia."

Zorlaeus was either a master political stooge, or he was sincere. Flowridia suspected the latter. "Thank you, Zorlaeus. Forgive me— is it 'consort'?"

"No. I'm 'Lord,' by my own choice. You don't have to refer to me as anything but my name."

Odd, but Flowridia did not inquire further.

The De'Sindai man turned to Ayla, whose demeanor remained ice. "W-We did know your wife had suffered an accident. Almost a year ago, right? Perhaps less. But Viceroy Murishani encouraged us to give her space."

"You must know that Murishani has only ill-intentions for my wife, don't you?"

Zorlaeus said nothing, instead glancing once more up and down the hallway, before giving a small and subtle nod. He left.

Flowridia shut the door, finally releasing her breath. "Well, that's suspicious."

"Don't drink anything she hands you."

"Noted. I would like to see Casvir, in case they come back. Or at least not be here."

By the doorframe, Flowridia offered a hand, the invitation extended . . . and rejected by Ayla's grimace. "I would rather not see Casvir, but I will escort you. I have a pile of books awaiting my attention." Ayla spoke clinically, no emotion at all. "I have yet to find anything promising in my study of Silver Fire pregnancies, aside from confirming that there is a danger."

"You're unhappy."

"I was rudely interrupted from making love to my wife by a cunt whose grating voice I had finally managed to purge from my memory, and now my wife has to leave in case the aforementioned cunt returns."

"Oh, Ayla . . ." Flowridia came behind her, leaning down to impishly press her swollen breasts to her wife's head. "I really don't have to go. Not yet. If Marielle comes back, we'll say we were finishing up business. We wouldn't even be lying."

Ayla held a rejection on her lip, which faltered as Flowridia slipped her nightgown over her head, revealing her bare breasts and less-than-alluring oversized bloomers. But before Flowridia could step out of them, Ayla was on her knees on the couch, stealing a taut nipple with her mouth.

"I'm rather fond of these new tits," Flowridia teased, then gasped when Ayla bit her. "Let me come around—"

The door opened. "Lady Flowridia, it is time for—" The nurse gasped as Flowridia dove for her nightgown, holding it up to preserve her modesty. "I'm so—"

"Is it too much to ask for a fucking lock on the door?!" Ayla cried.

The nurse kept her gaze to the ground. "We can't risk—"

"Then get me a sign to hang on the knob so the world can know when I'm fucking my wife!"

The nurse backed out, silence settling with the *click* of the door.

Ayla released a seething breath, shaking her head when Flowridia revealed her bare form once more. "I'm too angry."

"You can always take it out on me." Flowridia winked, but her laughter faltered as Ayla shook her head, replaced by disappointment.

Ayla shrunk as she returned to the couch, both in pride and stance. "I won't risk that. Not in your current state."

"I've been fine for days—"

"Flowra, even if I were in a mindset to perform, you are *pregnant*. Too much trauma *will* cause your body to miscarry."

She was tragically right, though something in her words left Flowridia uneasy. As she returned to the couch, Flowridia slipped her nightgown back on, then took her wife's hand in her own. "What do you mean by 'mindset'?"

Ayla's hesitation confirmed her worry, that this was deeper than her current bout of rage. "Do I need to elaborate on why the idea of beating you for pleasure makes me ill?"

"No," Flowridia whispered. Yet, the idea did not make her ill, no . . . Simply left her curious if she actually could. "But I do think you should speak to someone."

Ayla raised a scathing eyebrow.

"I know you're uncomfortable talking to the priestess, but what if she could help?"

"What would a Priestess of Staella possibly know about torturing your partner for sexual ritual?"

"It's not the act itself. It's the idea of reclaiming something you once enjoyed."

But Ayla shook her head, her attention far too focused on the fibers of the couch.

Flowridia gently cupped Ayla's cheek, coaxing their lips to meet. Chaste and slow, simply a comfort—a comfort returned when Ayla matched the gesture, her small lips a pleasure to feel.

When they parted, Ayla curled up beside her. "I am contemplating a great many things," Ayla whispered. "And I am working to find my words. Perhaps then I can find a priestess to pour my heart out to."

Flowridia kissed Ayla's hair, supposing this was progress. "Whenever you're ready."

"You should go see Casvir."

"I don't want to leave you alone in this state."

To Flowridia's surprise, Ayla gave a sweet smile. "I am not so fragile as you think, don't worry."

And though Flowridia sensed nothing but honest intent in her wife's words, she clutched Ayla tight, nevertheless. "It's as you said— we can tell Marielle we had unfinished business."

Ayla did not argue, instead melting into the touch, filling every crevice between them. Peace settled, and Flowridia savored the moment.

For in these moments, she knew everything would be all right.

Flowridia did eventually emerge to find Casvir, even allowed to walk alone.

"Scream if you collapse. I'll make excuses for your absence."

Flowridia paused to laugh at the sign on her suite's door: *Knock First. Do Not Disturb.* Classier than *I'm fucking my wife. Go away.*

She and Casvir had not discussed their bitter exchange. Flowridia felt no need to, and she knew enough of his character to know he would not mention it until her health had returned.

When she knocked on his office door, there came a stern, *"Enter."*

Casvir's demeanor softened at her entrance, his pile of paperwork never seeming to shrink. "Good morning, Flowridia. Did the physician clear you for visiting?"

Flowridia resisted the urge to roll her eyes, his concern sweet, she supposed, but stifling. "If by 'physician,' you mean Ayla, then yes."

"I will admit she is qualified."

Flowridia sat herself in that uncomfortable chair, acutely aware of where she had fallen. Her voice lowered, conspiracy in her grin. "I'm actually here because I used you as an excuse to get out of talking to Marielle. I assume you're aware she and Zorlaeus are here."

"I am aware." His lips twisted in a rare smile. "She is not the most subtle. I suspect Murishani wants information."

"There isn't much for him to know."

"No, but that will not stop him from trying." Casvir withdrew folded parchment from one pile and slid it forward, revealing a map of tunnels connecting the various elven kingdoms. "Since you are here, I would ask for your thoughts on a matter concerning the elven war. Did they ever make any mention of the underground tunnels between the Highland Elves and Iron Elves?"

Flowridia considered the past, to the time before her life had fallen into ruin. "Y-Yes, actually. It was in a meeting they held the night before the masquerade—before everything, well..." The memories were forever raw, even months later. "In any case, they were discussed at length."

"Would they be capable of evacuating an entire populace?"

"They were sturdy enough to transport machinery, so I would assume so. They were also deep enough to avoid Sun Elven interference. It's really an incredible feat of architecture when you consider it. My point is, they would have to move quickly, but I think it would be feasible."

"Did they ever mention the location of the entrance?"

"No."

"Unfortunate. Their behavior is baffling," Casvir remarked, stealing the parchment back. "The Highland Elves are all but defeated. Their capital city was evacuated before my troops were able to invade, so the casualties were minimal. Yet they refuse to wave the white flag, and they behave as though they are no longer engaged in war. Only Executor Faeborn will even correspond, and they are just as cryptic."

Flowridia knew precisely why, the realization striking like a slap. "Casvir, let me apologize first, because I didn't withhold this maliciously. I learned this the same day I had my fall."

He straightened his stance, intrigued.

"The Goddess of Chaos is in Zauleen."

Casvir sat back, perhaps even startled. "Is she now?"

Flowridia conveyed what Sora had said—of the ghost, of Sora and Etolié's capture and escape, and Etolié's subsequent trip to Celestière.

"This explains why the empress has apparently disappeared," Casvir said, clearly unamused, "and certainly explains the change in the elves' behavior. If they await her rebirth, they are stalling for time. But you say your sister is with this ghost?"

"I think so." Anxiety brewed, for Sora had vanished off the face of the realm. "Ayla spoke to her briefly once after she told us, but I've heard nothing since."

"If you are using the mirror, it cannot communicate between realms. Is it possible she joined Etolié in Celestière?"

Comforting, actually. Especially given what Flowridia knew of the time dilation between worlds. "That would make sense."

"The presence of their Goddess is disconcerting," Casvir said, though his tone conveyed no true fear. "Yet she does not support them, if your sister's account is correct. Perhaps this is why Executor Faeborn has been particularly frustrating."

"I presume you have offered a treaty?"

"I have, but they have shut down any attempts to negotiate from myself, Murishani, and even Empress Etolié."

An idea welled, curiosity driving it just as much as practicality. "What if Ayla tried?"

To her surprise, Casvir did not dismiss it. "Would she be willing?"

"I can ask. Executor Faeborn respects her, and they were the least hostile of the executors toward me. Perhaps her reappearance would spark something."

Casvir slid forward a pen and blank parchment. "Her name carries weight, as does yours. Though if she refuses, I will not be surprised."

"If nothing comes of it, then we lose nothing anyway." Flowridia stood, thankfully not crumbling into a heap this time. She took the offered supplies. "If she agrees, I'll make certain you have your reply written by tomorrow."

"I look forward to it."

"I don't appreciate being volunteered."

Flowridia waited until evening to approach the topic with Ayla, instead enjoying time alone in the library. But now she had returned to the medical ward, and Ayla glared petulantly from the bed.

Flowridia supposed the rejection was not surprising. "I understand." She set the writing material upon a desk, thoughts of the elven war far away. Here she was, cooped up in a castle across the sea, disengaged from the world beyond. Her only worry was the world within herself, and the growing life she held.

"Where do we stand with the elves?" Flowridia asked, for the last time she had seen them, there had been a massacre in a ballroom. "Would we ever go back?"

"No. They were cruel enough to you when they only *thought* you were pregnant and vulnerable. Now you actually are, and I won't risk your safety."

"I can't disagree." Flowridia's attention returned to the desk and upon the potential of the blank parchment. Flowridia struggled with illustrious speeches, but her writing was far more fluid. "What if I wrote the treaty proposal? Would you sign it?"

Ayla remained unreadable, which meant she did not want Flowridia to read her. "If it would make you happy, I will put my name behind your words."

"It wouldn't, because it would make you unhappy."

"Flowra, I am confused. Whose side of this war do you want to be on? We cannot forget what we were told in the woods. Soliel marches with the elves, but Casvir . . . He will march well beyond their reaches."

"I don't know," Flowridia admitted. She slumped into the desk's seat, idly stroking the pattern on the padded chair. "I am neutral, I suppose—" It was not outlandish to presume she would be spending more time in this castle. Conspiracy struck her, the prospect of adventure with it. Her voice lowered. "Ayla, when I was travelling with Soliel, we spoke about Casvir's phylactery."

Intrigue raised Ayla's brow. "Did you?"

"He never found it, as he said. But he told me everywhere it wasn't or couldn't be. Not in Sha'Demoni, because the demons would have sensed its magic. Not in Celestière, because losing it in the mist means it's lost forever. Wherever it is, he had to have placed the protections himself, because he trusts no one. It has to be easily accessible to him. Ayla . . ." She whispered; Ayla would hear it even far away. "I think it's in this castle. Somewhere in its depths. And we're in a prime position to look for it."

But Ayla did not share her enthusiasm, it seemed. "To what end?"

"What do you mean? We can end this. It was part of why we joined with the elves in the first place."

"You're pregnant. Why does it matter? Would you abort if we succeeded? The bargain will be fulfilled, so why risk your safety further?"

Ayla spoke as though lost in a swamp, her aura just as heavy. Flowridia stood from the desk, taking tentative steps toward her. "Well, the greater good also stands, though I know you don't care. I'm worried, though, if the thought of killing Casvir doesn't invigorate you. Worried about you."

When Flowridia sat beside her, Ayla kept herself small, arms wrapped around her knees. "My depression waxes and wanes."

Flowridia set her good hand upon Ayla's back, acutely aware of her spine, her ribs. Ayla was dead, but the sensation evoked sympathy, all the same.

"I am tired of grudges," Ayla whispered, mist filling her eyes. "I have been a being of rage since birth, but after everything Sarai said, I feel . . . extinguished. Of course I despise Casvir. I despise that no matter what game I play, he will be victorious. But more than I would like to win, I don't wish to play at all. I am tired. I want this baby to be born so we can leave and be done with him."

The first of Ayla's tears fell. Behind her cutting cheekbones, behind those engrossing eyes, her vulnerability shone bright. Flowridia rubbed a soothing hand across the fabric of her dress.

"I will help you," Ayla said, all the weight of her thousand and more years in the phrase, "but if we don't succeed before the baby is born, I want to let it go."

Flowridia nodded, yet already something within her shifted uncomfortably at the notion.

"Why do you want this?" Ayla asked. "I thought you cared for him."

"I do, but . . ."

Her words faded. Ayla was right. Why did she want this?

". . . habit, I suppose."

Ayla's lip trembled. "How was your hand today?"

"Not giving me too much grief. It's a neutral day."

"What about this morning?"

Flowridia bit back a retort, shocked at her own compulsion to tell her wife to *shove off*. "It's fine if I don't try to use it for anything useful."

"Oh, darling. May I?" Ayla offered a hand, in which Flowridia gingerly set her own. Though her tender massaging brought tingles, her touch did not bring any pain. "You have refused pain management since getting pregnant."

"Can you fault me?"

Ayla shook her head, though she said nothing more.

Flowridia kept her soothing gestures while Ayla worked, stroking her wife's silken, black hair. "I'm proud of you for drawing today."

Ayla's expression softened.

"What else have you done for yourself lately? What about embroidery? Or, uh, *science*?" Flowridia's laugh came nervously, the word hardly innocent. "You still have your laboratory. I don't doubt Casvir has a prisoner to spare. Shall I propose it?"

Ayla's hesitation showed in the twitch in her lip, the sudden vacancy in her eyes. "I need smaller steps to return to normalcy. Art will do for now."

"Would you embroider something for me?"

"I can do that." Ayla shifted beneath her touch, releasing her hand as she stood from the bed. "I have supplies in my old room. Give me just a moment."

She disappeared into the shadow of the bedframe.

Marielle's promise to return *if she had time* lingered like smoke in the air, but Flowridia had her doubts. She returned to the desk, worry soothed for now. There lay the parchment.

Executor Faeborn, I write to you on behalf of Imperator Casvir . . .

A short proposal to meet, polite and efficient. Yet a chasm waited at the bottom, seeking to be filled. No, her wife had no desire for this.

-Flowridia Darkleaf, wife to The Endless Night

A spark of pride flared somewhere deep inside.

CHAPTER 9

Five years after the end of the world . . .

"Come on, kid. Just a little more 'oomph.' I know you have it in you."

Etolié's golden wings lit the world at twilight, the overgrown courtyard of the Fireborn Estate ethereal beneath their light. But try as Dira might, she could not summon a silver glow to match.

"You used to sneeze fire out as a baby," Etolié teased, and in her hand appeared a feather. "Do we need drastic measures?"

Indignant, Dira crossed her arms, no longer wishing to appease Etolié. "I can still sneeze fire."

"Prove it. Or, better yet, scream one out. Your mom was a menace with magic when she was pissed."

Dira kept her scowl, not feeling a spark at all.

"Look at you! Let's funnel that rage. Scream at me! Give me all you have."

Dira did not scream, but she did her best to roar. She summoned all the energy of a wolf, a lion, all the animals she and Mother had studied. But . . . nothing. If anything, her inner glow had dimmed.

"Are you hungry? Thirsty? You don't normally have this much trouble."

Sora appeared from inside, steps hurried as she joined them. "Is everything all right?"

"Yeah, yeah, kiddo and I were just practicing her Silver Fire. She's having trouble coaxing it out. But I know those Solviraes always spewed it when they were pissed, as did Flowers with her necromancy."

Dira swallowed the urge to cry, her frustration slowly rising even as Sora lowered her voice. "She's been having a difficult time since Ayla started going out. Try to be patient."

Mother's name brought the first of Dira's tears.

"Oh, kiddo." Etolié was now beside her, kneeling to match her height. But Dira refused to take her hand, simply clutching herself, pretending it was Mother's embrace. "Your mother is out there doing important adult things for me, so you have every reason to be angry at me. And I'm encouraging you to let it out."

But Dira fought her tears, squeezing her eyes shut as she shook her head. Everything hurt; everything tensed. She wanted the fire, but it wouldn't burn.

"Respectfully, I don't know if you have the magic touch with children," she heard Sora say.

"Bitch, I basically raised Lara. I mean, Khastra helped, and Lara had a very loving father, but let's not discount Auntie Etolié." Etolié muttered the rest. "Khastra did have *the* magic touch with babies though. She'd have loved this kid."

Sora's touch appeared on Dira's shoulder. She refused to let it break her. "Let's go inside. Dinner's almost ready."

"Not until—"

"Etolié, she needs time." Sora tried to coax Dira's arms open, but she was much too frustrated to move. "Dira, are you angry about the Silver Fire or about something else?"

Tears seeped from Dira's eyes, hot and angry. "I just want to be done!"

"Then we'll be done—"

"I want my mother!"

Dira's sobs came swiftly, crying out into Sora's shoulder when her aunt embraced her. "I promise she'll be home soon. Do you want to do something nice to welcome her? What if you drew her a picture?"

But Dira said nothing, barely hearing Sora's words at all.

"Fucking hell, she's clingy," came Etolié's muttering. Dira knew swear words were bad, but she always seemed to hear them best anyway.

"Don't make me comment on your relationship with Staella."

"Touché, bitch."

Dira tried to fight it, but everything hurt—her heart, her body, her head . . .

"Dira, look!"

Dira followed where Etolié pointed, gasping to see Mother emerging from the dark shadow of a tree.

Dira tore from Sora's embrace and ran into Mother's arms, her happiness bursting. When Mother caught her, she spun her around, and within Dira something burned—not hot, but energetic.

Mother's smile wavered as she wiped a tear from Dira's eye. "Darling, what is wrong?"

"I missed you," Dira said, but no more tears fell.

"Hey, kid!" she heard Etolié say. "Try giving me that fire one more time, would you?"

And though content in Mother's arms, soothed by a kiss on her forehead, Dira lifted a hand away from their faces and let her energy soar—and with it came a spark of flame.

"Oh, that is sickeningly sweet. I'm gonna puke."

Current era . . .

With Staella's gentle hands to help find the pieces, Etolié collected herself and spent a few hours anxiously awaiting any news regarding Khastra.

Of course, no news came.

At a time she hoped wasn't suspiciously close to the time of the meeting, Etolié bid farewell to Staella and traversed through the mists of Celestière.

Never had she done this alone, but as her capacity to teleport increased, so did her innate sense of direction even in endless voids. Between the magical pull inside her and her own distant memory, Etolié soon emerged into the bustling city of Vanir Sol.

Well, nothing was on fire, which meant there was no reason to hurry. Etolié was allergic to sweat and exercise, so instead she illusioned her momma's height and physique. Her own angular features became soft and sweet, and she stepped through Vanir Sol as a whole new person.

Still, she kept her head down, paying more attention to the ground and her feet. No, she had no idea why Sora would bring that fucking ghost here, but Sol Kareena didn't just call a meeting of gods for nothing.

After what Etolié had hoped had been nonchalant prodding, Staella had revealed the meeting's location—in the Amphitheater of Romanth, the largest and oldest meeting hall in Vanir Sol.

Among the familiar bustling sights of the ancient city, Etolié saw a haunting beacon in the distance—Sol Kareena's palace in the sky.

There, her beloved auntie had . . . thrown her away, it felt like. Tossed her into the mortal realm, too passive to question laws older than the Convergence. Etolié had been fourteen, too young and filled with guilt and grime to comprehend that perhaps Sol Kareena was not the core of all wisdom. Back then, she had been petrified.

Worse, however, was that Etolié had learned the merit of forgiving and letting go. She wasn't nearly as angry about it as she'd prefer to be. As it was, to say she felt empty was a lie, but naming this . . . *something* was impossible.

Well, there was no need to interact. Etolié swallowed those bitter feelings and went on her way.

Thank Morathma's Whore Mother that Staella was an anti-social hermit. As Etolié neared the amphitheater, she recognized a few godly faces but felt no pressure to impersonate her momma any further. For all the angels she passively recognized, so many more she didn't—both gods, demi-gods, and full-blooded angels of no power, though their influence in Celestière might as well have granted it.

Except shit, fuck, there at the entrance was Alystra in conversation with Tortalga, God of the Sea—and no one had a better bullshit detector than Alystra. She was also the least likely person to reveal Etolié's subterfuge, but better safe than sorry.

Surely there was a back entrance. Staella, Goddess of Stars, was something of a big deal, so it wasn't as though she would get in trouble if she were spotted in the wrong place. Etolié kept her wings tucked in as tight as she could manage as she stepped nonchalantly around the circular stone structure, looking as spacey as possible whenever anyone passed her by, lest they think about talking to her. Plenty of surprised looks, for certain, but while a few people bowed at her passing, no one tried to get too friendly.

And there was her quarry—an open archway on the opposite side with a few armed Celestials standing around it. At her approach, those present bowed. One spoke. "Goddess Staella, forgive me for asking, but are you lost?"

Etolié had learned to manipulate sound from a young age, so while she could do a damn fine Staella impression even without it, throwing her voice with a bit of magic was well within her repertoire. She rounded her words, raised her pitch, and forced a smile big enough to make her cheeks hurt. "Always. Is it all right if I come in this way?"

"Of course," the Celestial said. "There is a seat assigned to you, but I have no doubt God Eionei or one of the others can direct you."

Dammit. "Oh, I'll most likely plop myself in the overflow seating, but thanks for the thought."

She entered the archway, the echo of countless voices already prickling at her senses. But where to find a wayward, idiot half-elf? Chaos could look like anything, be it rabbit, ghost, or something else, but Sora lacked both the ability to shape-shift and common sense.

A gathering of gods—what the fuck was she thinking? If Chaos had an evil plan, this was a stellar way to enact it. Etolié stood beneath a massive stone sector, keeping her head down as she passed the occasional attending Celestial. No gods here. Apparently the back entrance wasn't often used. Open arches led toward the massive amphitheater in the center, but each glance revealed nothing.

The issue remained that she sought Sora but really needed to avoid—

"And who has granted us the honor of her elusive presence but the Goddess of Stars herself!"

Shit. Damn. NO. Etolié forced her most Staella-like smile at Eionei's approach—and who was with him, but Sora-fucking-Makosa.

Those two looked awfully chummy, if Etolié were being honest. Sora, who had apparently learned nothing, bowed.

"Oh, no need for that," Etolié continued, praying her Staella impersonation held up in front of someone her momma had known for literally thousands of years. "Well, I couldn't disappoint Sol Kee—areena by turning down her invitation to the very important meeting, now could I?"

"We've all done our fair share of disappointing sweet Kareena," Eionei replied, "but I suspect she would have forgiven you eventually. Forgive me, though, but I'm surprised you're here. Is Etolié doing all right?"

"She's much better. She's just resting. I actually came to talk to Sora on her behalf. Would you mind giving us a moment alone?"

Nothing suspicious crossed Eionei's countenance, and the man was typically an open book. He stepped aside. "Of course. I'll be center stage, preparing things for our Goddess friend. Find me when you're done."

It took every ounce of willpower Etolié held to not snap at the egregious misuse of the word 'friend.' Instead, she kept her smile until Eionei had skipped far enough away, at which point she grabbed Sora's arm and dragged her toward the wall. "What the fuck were you thinking, bringing the fucking Goddess of Chaos here?!"

Yes, she whispered. But emotionally, she screamed.

Sora, though taller, stared like a child being reprimanded by a drunk aunt. "G-Goddess Staella, I—"

"Oh, for fuck's sake—it's me, Sora." Etolié waved her hand in front of her face, briefly revealing her true self, before whisking it back, resuming her Staella disguise. "Where is Chaos?"

"Last I saw, she was with Sol Kareena."

"You left her alone with the maniacal ghost?!"

"It's not the first time."

It was a damn good thing Staella had a reputation for being kind and not prone to losing her temper in public. It was the only thing curtailing Etolié's rant. "And now you're bringing all these nice, unsuspecting gods and goddesses to, what? Bask in her glorious presence? What the fuck is going on?"

"We're seeking pledges from gods so she can gain the power from their followers—"

"Are you fucking stupid—?!" Etolié slapped her hand over her lips, lest she scream. She forced a calm breath, resisting the urge to illusion fire to punctuate it. "And Eionei supports this too?"

Sora nodded, looking a bit too much like a deer prepared to sprint away.

"So, you've all lost your minds. Great."

"Etolié, listen."

Etolié seethed, but she did manage to shut the fuck up.

"Whatever Chaos' flaws, she wants to stop Soliel," Sora continued, her pacifying tone all the more rage-inducing. "I think it's better that she explains it herself, but—"

"So we're just going to deny what we witnessed in Tierzuroth?"

"I'm not. And I won't pretend to understand everything, but she's on our side."

"She wants to kill your baby sister, Sora."

"She wants to talk to us both about that, though I'm definitely keeping her out of Nox'Kartha."

No, her glower was terribly un-Staella-like, but they were mostly alone, only the occasional passing Celestial guard nearby to pay them any heed. "If she blows up Celestière, don't say I didn't warn you."

"She won't—"

"Goddess Staella?"

They both turned at the approaching Celestial—not armed, but bearing gold and white robes. Etolié reinforced her smile. "Yes, dear?"

"Forgive the interruption, but Goddess Sol Kareena has asked if you might spare a moment to assist her. I can escort you."

Well, shit, damn, and fuck, indeed. What would Staella do? "Oh, of course!"

Etolié's gut squirmed as she followed the attendant, though not without risking it all to shoot a glare and angry middle finger at Sora.

Yet only once they had left Sora behind, did Etolié realize what daunting reality now faced her.

She had come to confront Sora and Chaos. The reality that she would be in close proximity to Sol Kareena hadn't occurred to her in so many words. Now she was about to face her directly.

Etolié's heart threatened to hammer out of her chest as she debated the merit of faking an emergency—illusion magic meant anything was possible, like spontaneous dismemberment—but they turned a corner, and there she was.

Last Etolié had seen her, Sol Kareena had worn Meira's body. Here, she sat alone on a bench in a vacant hallway, a figure of gold and sorrow, her wings lacking the magnificence Etolié had known in her youth. In her arms, she held a fitful baby Soliel, the baby's fussiness threatening to devolve into cries at any moment.

Etolié met her gaze with a surge of convoluted emotions. Sorrow, yes, and joy. Bitterness, even, but all of it paled to the nostalgic comfort of standing in her aunt's presence, even in disguise.

"Thank goodness," Sol Kareena said, wearing no mantle of godhood in this private space. No, no—instead, she was a bedraggled mother, exhaustion etched into her face like cracks in stone. "I'm so sorry to put this on you, but Soliel won't take his nap, and I can't have him crying while I'm trying to lead a meeting. Is there any way you could help me soothe him?"

A simple request, even for a fake Staella. Etolié willed her impression to hold. "Of course." She sat beside Sol Kareena, shy to let her illusionary robe touch her aunt's real one, only for her breath to hitch when their skin brushed. Sol Kareena set Soliel in her arms, and Etolié held herself together by rapidly fraying threads.

What sort of song would Momma sing? Not any of Eionei's lullabies. Frantic, Etolié dug deep into her memory and recalled one Momma herself had sung decades ago. The magic flowed with each word, and Soliel's eyelids slowly drooped . . .

Sweet little angel, you've come from so far,
So be soothed by my song and the light from my stars.
I loved you before you were even a thought.
Sleep, little angel—you're a piece of my heart.

At the song's conclusion, the baby lay silent in Etolié's arms. The gentle mood lingered, and Etolié's soul was swept up in longing—all those bitter feelings in tandem with yearning. Sol Kareena was someone she so dearly loved.

Sol Kareena was someone she had never thought she'd see again.

"Thank you," her aunt whispered. "I'm surprised you came at all, if I'm honest."

"I do feel a little cooped up every now and again," Etolié replied, already plotting her exit. She couldn't stay here. Any moment now, Sol Kareena would see straight through her. "Might as well see what all the fuss is about. I can't promise to stay for any after-parties, though."

"I meant more in regards to your, um, guest."

Etolié's gut clenched, the statement far too pointed to be coincidence. Fucking hell—what could she say? Did Sol Kareena even know she and Momma were talking again? Was this news? Surely she knew something, given the state of Solvira, but . . .

Fuck.

As it was, Sol Kareena looked like she faced the gallows with that statement. Etolié didn't know what to make of that at all. "I figured you wouldn't call unless it was important."

Sol Kareena's smile conveyed only pain. "If you need to be somewhere else, I understand."

And there it was—Etolié's exit from this blundering interaction. She carefully moved to set the sleeping Soliel into his mother's arms, then illusioned a far more sincere smile. "Perhaps you're right. Send me the transcripts, won't you?"

Sol Kareena kept her gaze to Soliel, hesitation in her trembling lip. "How is she?"

Fuck. Etolié hadn't even stood up yet, dragged back down into a conversation she really didn't want to be having. "Her poor stomach finally settled. She's just resting."

"I'm glad to hear that."

Etolié rose, yet her own stupid feelings kept her shackled. She stilled, casting her gaze down onto her estranged aunt—an aunt who didn't even know she was there. "Is there any message you'd like me to deliver to my 'guest'?"

There again came that hesitation. "I doubt she'd want to hear from me."

"I can be the judge of that. Depends on what you'd like to say."

"You know there is so much I wish had gone differently," Sol Kareena whispered, as though too ashamed to actually be heard. "I wish I could explain. I don't wish to burden you with that conversation again, however."

Etolié shrugged, doing her damnedest to appear nonchalant. "You're talking like there are things I don't know." The statement was a longshot, but Etolié was validated by the sudden trembling of Sol Kareena's lip.

"What do you want me to say? How precarious her safety was if she wouldn't speak out? Expecting a victim to lay out her whole heart is cruel, but subjecting her to the judgement of the elder angels wasn't any better. I did what I thought was the only solution, but I wish I had insisted more or fought against their prejudices."

Momma hadn't mentioned that, which meant either Momma was withholding the truth—doubtful—or this was genuinely new information—plausible, given the fraught relationship between Staella and her sister-in-law. "What prejudices?"

Sol Kareena hugged Soliel a little tighter. "It's not something you'll like hearing, Staella. I don't wish to fight with you."

Etolié's gut clenched to speak, but oh gods she wished to know. "I'm offering diplomatic immunity."

"Surely you see the connection between what Etolié did to Camdral and what Ilune did to Neoma. What do you think they saw when another daughter of Staella murdered her progenitor? I know the situation is different, and most of Celestière agreed. But there were those in the shadows who did not. Even if she had spoken, I don't know how welcome she would have been. By refusing to do so, she unknowingly signed a death sentence."

And with those words, Etolié understood a thousand things she thought she had before—but no, no. Etolié fought tears. "Yes, you should have done more," she said, that simmering rage rising, years old, "but perhaps politics are fucked up no matter where you go."

Sol Kareena met her gaze, clearly startled, and probably not only because 'Staella' had used the word 'fuck.'

"All of it was wrong," Etolié continued, her Staella impression holding on by mere strings. "We're all villains here. I've told Etolié I hold more fault than anyone else, except for Camdral himself, but you really swooped in during the finale to blow it all apart. It's not just you though. Celestière's politics have been fucked sideways since Neoma died, haven't they? Etolié was strong enough to survive it, but it doesn't mean she should've had to."

No, it truly didn't make it right. Etolié's tears rose. "It's fucked up, what you did. I get it, but it's fucked up. I— Etolié is better for being in the mortal realm, all the ensuing, fucked up trauma aside. Eionei's probably the only reason she survived, and he still fucked it all up anyway. All of you— All of *us* really fucking failed her, didn't we? All of it makes sense, why we did it. But it isn't fucking right. She didn't deserve a damn bit of it."

Etolié cried. Staella's illusion didn't, but Sol Kareena certainly did, too. Quiet tears, wiped away before they could disturb her infant son. "You're absolutely right," Sol Kareena whispered.

"But you know what else?" Etolié forced her voice to steady, catharsis but a few words away. "Because of what she went through, she's strong enough to forgive the ones who deserve it. You could come visit her. I . . . I think she might be ready to give that to you, if you're willing to tell her what you told me."

It wasn't quite the same, that yearning still lurking inside her. But Etolié felt peace to admit it aloud.

Sol Kareena gave a small nod. "If you'll let me, I would love to see her."

"Come on over after the meeting." Etolié choked back a sob, instead forcing her final words to steady. "She still loves you."

Something ineffable shifted in her aunt's countenance; something akin to peace. "I love her, too."

Etolié gave no farewell, forced to flee lest she become a sobbing mess on the floor. She charged through the expansive hall, half-heartedly waving to the guards at the door she'd entered through, and illusioned herself away entirely.

Sight. Sound. Everything.

Etolié wept in a quiet place in Celestière, old scars torn open, bleeding anew.

But finally—*finally*—they could heal.

There was a time and place to be reprimanded by a furious Etolié, and at the cusp of the most important moment of Sora's life thus far, this was not it. As soon as Etolié left with the guard, Sora returned to the amphitheater's stage.

Celestière was a world of eternal day, yet with countless glowing wings so closely gathered, Sora was nearly blinded. It reminded Sora of a sports colosseum, where chariots raced or gladiators fought to first blood or death. Nox'Kartha's capital hosted one such place, the inherent dangers of participating accepted and signed by a waiver.

This one gleamed, built of something related to marble. Circular, yes, but many buildings in Celestière were, she had noted. Seats were built into the rising rows, expanding wider with each ring, though situated farther apart than might be normal in the mortal realm—and the cause was clear. Some angels had wings as wide as the span of their arms, but others spread vastly wider, magnificent in their own unique ways. Most were shades of gold, yellow, a few reds, blues, and greens.

Perhaps power showed in the expanse of their wings. Sol Kareena's certainly made an impression, even in a sickly state. Staella's wings were magnificent.

There were only a few in the crowd one could truly call gods, but demi-gods with smaller followings were common enough among the angels. Demons consolidated all their power among only three. Angelic worship was more diverse, aside from those made great directly after the Convergence and a select few exceptions.

"Sora!"

Sora was drawn from her musing by a familiar tenor. Eionei approached gallantly, his charming smile admittedly well received. He was an exception, she realized. His wings were the most striking of them all, fractal instead of whole and not nearly so large as his power might suggest—instead, an assembly of a whole, unremarkable until you saw all the pieces as one. Eionei was not the grandest, but he was the oldest. He was known throughout every realm.

"Is Etolié all right?" he asked.

Sora recalled then that she had been accosted. "She's fine. Staella said she's feeling much better." It wasn't a lie, if they were referring to her physical state.

"That's good to hear. I assume Staella wouldn't come otherwise, but it's best to never assume. Assumptions have gotten me into mighty bits of trouble over the years." He chuckled, but Sora didn't have to be intuitive to sense nerves behind it. "Where did Staella go?"

"Sol Kareena called for her, actually." It was then that Sora realized interfering might've been useful, given Etolié was clearly trying to uphold a ruse. But Etolié was a capable idiot. She would be fine. "I'm not sure when she'll be back." Or *if*, but, again, the ruse.

"Well, your Goddess friend is feeling a bit out of sorts. Let's cheer her up, shall we?"

Led to the center of the amphitheater, Sora glowed, illuminated by the angelic light. Even if she did recognize anyone in the crowd, their features were lost amid the sea of glowing bodies.

In the center was a circular stone platform with stairs far less worn than the rest of the ground. Celestial guards stood around the perimeter, revealed by their lack of wings, and there in the center, Chaos sat hunched on a bench, mostly hidden from the crowd. Sol Kareena had bid her to hide her Silver Fire for now. The angels would recognize it immediately, and once she revealed herself, the questions would not cease. So she wore her half-elf face, yet her emotions were as veiled as though behind a mask of flame.

"Are you nervous?" Sora asked.

Chaos shrugged. "I have faced them before. Hopefully things work in my favor this time."

"This time?"

"Ask me later. Though I fear I may be at an even greater disadvantage. Last I was here, in what is your future, I did not know of my destiny as Goddess Chaos, nor did they. They trusted the Silver Fire. But I am not exactly a beloved figure in their history. Sol Kareena spoke the truth, and I doubt they will be as receptive to my own."

"Regarding the Convergence?"

Chaos gave a grave nod. "I wish I had answers, truly."

"Sol Kareena may have told me a little bit of what you said," Eionei began, his usual mischief replaced by wonder. "For what it's worth, I'm choosing to believe you. However, as someone who witnessed and lived through the Convergence . . ." Hesitation stilled his words. ". . . I would swear we all saw you."

"Saw me?"

"It was awe-inspiring, if horrifying," Eionei said, his subdued tone utterly sobering. "Massive rips in space appeared, bursting with what I now guess was, somehow, Silver Fire. Through those portals, we saw other worlds going through the same apocalypse. But through one such portal . . . and I swear I've corroborated this with those few others who lived . . . I would swear I saw you."

Chaos' face revealed nothing.

"A woman coated by silver flame—and not just any woman. She looked like . . ." He struggled, then settled on waving his hand before Chaos. "Well, as much as anyone covered in fire can look like another person. She glowed like one of our extinguished suns before she exploded like everything else. But it was so strange. I don't believe she was in pain. She stood like she was at peace." Eionei shook his head, as though banishing the memory. "But if you say it wasn't you, it wasn't you. I am willing to look like a fool to trust in the greater good."

"That's kind of you," Chaos whispered, though with thoughts a thousand miles away.

"When you live through the end of the world, you're left with two choices—to become jaded or to hold to hope. I made peace with the latter in time."

For all she'd seen of Eionei, Sora felt this was the truest glimpse into his soul she'd ever had. His roguery returned, but Sora felt unbearably young beside him. The oldest survivor of the old world, the oldest of the gods, his soul forever young but his heart eternally lonely.

It wasn't a void Sora could fill, nor was it a responsibility she felt tasked for. But her heart broke just a little bit for Eionei, who had lost everything yet moved on.

"Ah, look who's come to join us!" Eionei gestured grandly toward Sol Kareena in a decorated chair that floated above the ground. It moved neither quick nor slow, and perhaps that was purposeful, given the sleeping infant in her arms.

"Everyone has gathered," Sol Kareena said as she neared. "I'm sure you understand why I couldn't invite Morathma, but all the rest have gathered. I will give my piece, but they will want to hear from you, too."

For the first time, unease settled into Sora's stomach. "I would assume if you spoke on Chaos' behalf, they would listen."

"Mortals hold a high opinion of me." Sol Kareena's hesitation showed in the hitch of her breath, the sudden twitch in her lip. "Celestière has never forgotten that I'm not my sister."

The cognitive dissonance was too much. Sora merely stared. Sol Kareena was the greatest among the angels ... Was she not?

"Shall I call them to order?" Eionei asked.

"I'm ready when she is."

And though Chaos looked anything but, she nodded her affirmation.

Surely it was magic, for when Eionei next spoke, it rang out to every ear. "Angels, gods, and those who aspire to be—welcome! Please take your seats!"

Some semblance of order slowly descended. Sora realized there were only a hundred in the crowd, perhaps even less. But by the Light, each and every one cast a mighty presence, the weight of her own comparative insignificance daunting. At least the Celestial guards held angelic blood. She was a mere mortal, pulled from her comfort by fate.

Or was that true at all? Sora glanced at Chaos, her niece, looking ill on her bench.

No, Sora had chosen to be here.

"It has been far too long since we last gathered together," Eionei continued, a natural in drawing every focus. "Many of you I am blessed to see often, but just as many I haven't seen in years. I hope you're well, truly. I'm hosting a party in my temple after, so please, come have a drink and forget. However, work before play. No doubt you're all curious why our beloved Sun Goddess called you here today. All good things, I assure you. I hope you will keep an open mind and heart as you hear her words. I would echo each and every one."

When he gestured to their golden leader, applause erupted from the crowd. Sol Kareena stood from her chair, covering Soliel's exposed ear with her hand. But whatever spell enraptured him held strong. The infant breathed in peace.

"Angels of Celestière," Sol Kareena began, a new mantle upon her shoulders, "time is short, and I will not mince words. There is a threat to our world that has gone overlooked for too long. The destruction of my people left a grave wound on my soul, but I can stay in the shadows no longer. Surely you have heard from your people—the God of Order has returned to the mortal realm, and he seeks to separate us from them forever."

Gone was the vulnerable deity in the palace. Whatever energy Sol Kareena could spare infused her speech. No, she was not a natural, though Sora would never say it. But Sol Kareena was earnest and true.

"We would be destroyed, the disaster finishing what the Convergence did all those thousands of years ago. The God of Order has four Convergence Orbs. Per my sources, he held all six for a few dire minutes, but due to the action of a few brave heroes, he has been thwarted in the interim. The threat remains, but a new weapon has come to fight on our behalf—the Goddess of Chaos."

Murmuring rose through the crowd at the title, and with it, Chaos herself, Silver Fire coating her figure as she came beside Sol Kareena.

"I have spoken to this Goddess of the Old World," Sol Kareena continued. "I trust her when she says she stands against what her counterpart seeks to bring upon our worlds. However, with his four orbs and his followers, she does not hold the power to stop him.

"She comes seeking pledges from gods. With our support and the support of our people by proxy, she can put a stop to this monster now and forever. Eionei has already pledged his support. I will pledge to her now."

The crowd held an eerie silence as Sol Kareena offered the baby to Eionei and knelt with the support of her guards. "I pledge my power and strength to you, Goddess of Chaos," Sol Kareena said, her reverence the sort reserved for worship. "Please, save Celestière."

And Sora swore, once more, that Chaos glimmered just a little brighter.

Her hope rose as one ruby figure stood among the crowd. Her sensuous figure pinged as familiar in Sora's memory, and Eionei's sudden interest confirmed it—this was Alystra, Goddess of Beauty. "That is a bold leap of faith," Alystra said, loud enough for the masses to hear, "and an even bolder assumption that we would follow blindly. Give us a reason to believe this apparent Goddess won't use our power to betray us."

"There is little more I have than my word," Chaos said. The crowd's energy rose, but Sora feared it was not for the better. "Perhaps the ominous musing of wondering what other choice you have, but I do not wish to threaten you."

"Oh, but you just have," Alystra replied.

A being of sapphire rose next. "I am inclined to believe you," the man said, his emblems bearing signs of the sea. Perhaps this was Tortalga, who ruled the oceans. "I wish to know on what grounds Sol Kareena believes in you."

"The word of her champion bears weight," Chaos replied, and Sora's anxiety suddenly surpassed the clouds. "I come with Champion Sora Makosa, the heir to the fallen Theocracy of Sol Kareena."

Sora definitively did *not* like the feeling of so many eyes upon her.

"Champion is a prestigious title among mortals," another one said—a deity with flowing wings of emerald. Sora did not know him. "Far less so among us angels, however. What is important to a mortal might be but a blink in our lifespans. What threat is this Old God truly? What damage has he actually done?"

"Having faced him down personally," Eionei said, "I can attest that he's nothing to scoff at. He is responsible for the death of Solvira's late Emperor Malakh."

And Empress Alauriel, Sora thought, but that was not common knowledge. Etolié had confided the bitter truth to her.

"And for the murder of Archbishop Xoran," Eionei continued, "which I personally bore witness to."

As had Sora, though Etolié was . . . oddly hedgy on that one.

"So he has killed mortal monarchs," the emerald one continued. "Mortals are frail. This threat seems overblown."

Sora's words choked in her throat, her courage managing to surpass her fear of speaking out. "He also murdered Valeuron, a dragon." Oh, she wasn't keen on all those eyes on her, but the worlds depended on this. Chaos depended on this. "He's shown he'll stop at nothing to accomplish his goal. The God of Order is who you inherited this world from, and he'll take it away."

"I can accept that he's a threat," Alystra said, "but, again, why is the Goddess of Chaos the answer? Why could we not rally ourselves and defeat him?"

"Then do so," Chaos replied. "I welcome it. Yet I somehow doubt your own political scuffles will allow it. Is it not better to consolidate that power into one?"

"Oh, assuredly not," came a whisper on the wind. Sora's breath faltered.

Descending from the stairs came 'Goddess Staella,' everything about her entirely correct to form—except the death glare she directed at Sora.

"The God of Order is undoubtedly a terrible threat to the realms," the doppelganger Star Goddess continued, "and something we really ought to take a little more seriously. But if my contacts in the mortal realm are of any credibility—and they assuredly are— the Goddess of Chaos is not someone we have any business trusting. The fact that she has manipulated the most prestigious of us into falling for her tricks should tell you enough. She is unpredictable, unstable, and entirely untrustworthy in her loyalties. We would all be fools to offer our power to her."

Damn Etolié. Damn her to Onias' Hell.

"Staella's word is good enough for me," Alystra said, and if the crowd's murmuring was any indication, she wasn't alone.

Chaos' glowing eye twitched. "Perhaps I might speak to Goddess Staella and plead my case directly."

"Oh, why not," 'Staella' replied. "Perhaps a short recess?"

"Y-Yes, perhaps that would be wise," Eionei said, his shock apparent.

Sol Kareena said nothing, merely looked as startled as Eionei.

A few gods rose, talking amongst themselves as Staella made the final steps to the center. "I stand by every word."

"I forgot how belligerent you are," Chaos spat.

Staella sneered right back. "A little bird told me you wanted to speak to Sora and I—"

Eionei came forward. "Staella, I'm confused."

"And I'm terribly curious to hear what this woman said to persuade you that she's anything less than diabolical."

Truthfully, Etolié's Staella impression was quite impressive, though Sora was reluctant to admit it.

A Celestial guard came from the outskirts and quickly approached Sol Kareena. "Goddess Sol Kareena, a word?"

"Do you realize what damage you have just done?" Chaos seethed, but the fake Staella merely shrugged.

"Well, one of us has a history of exploding worlds and the other doesn't, so may-fucking-haps—"

"All of you, stop."

They did, all turning to face the now tense Sol Kareena.

The Sun Goddess held her son near to her chest, voice lowering. "The God of Order is in the Valley of Neoma."

"What of Uluron?" Chaos asked.

"My sentries reported nothing about a dragon."

"Is there any threat to us?" asked Eionei.

"Only if he leaves his orbs behind. They can't leave the mortal realm." With Sol Kareena's hitch in breath came a lapse in the supreme goddess' mantle, her gaze falling upon the infant in her arms—an innocent Soliel, not yet burdened by Godhood. "Tell me truly, Goddess of Chaos. What good would a mother's plea do for my son?"

Sora's blood ran cold to consider it, for Sol Kareena was magnificent but frail, so utterly frail. Soliel killed with impunity, yet had shown mercy, too . . .

Chaos fell silent. Her words, when they came, were soft. "What would you ask of him?"

"I would tell him that you've told me all the future has to bring and offer whatever aid we in Celestière can to stop it in any other way. Of course my priority must be saving Celestière, but my heart breaks to consider what must be done to stop . . . him." Mist filled Sol Kareena's eyes—no longer a goddess, but a mother first. "Children are so precious and rare among the angels. Surely you understand why I would beg for a peaceful end to this madness. Would he listen to me?"

Chaos gave a kind smile, a gesture far too out of character for Sora to feel any ease. "If there is anyone who can sway him, it is you, Goddess Sol Kareena."

Sora took some vindictive pleasure in watching 'Staella' sputter and fail to find any excuse to get out of babysitting Soliel. The pseudo-Goddess of Stars eventually took the baby, agreeing to bring him to her home for protection.

The rest of them left the assembly of angels, followed by a battalion of Celestial guards. Sora wondered if they truly would return triumphant. Chaos had spoken of hope.

Sora's stomach remained sick.

When they came to the mists, Chaos' fiery figure disappeared, replaced with her half-elven façade. All were silent and somber. Even Eionei.

When they breached the Valley of Neoma, there he stood—an errant beacon of gold in a meadow of silver.

No sign of Uluron. No sign of violence at all. Soliel stood peacefully with four orbs orbiting behind him, their ominous presence stirring. His hardened expression softened as it fell upon them—upon Chaos, whose stance remained strong.

Sora stilled when Chaos held her arm out, making the final approach alone. "Hello, Soliel."

"Dira, you . . ." He smiled, conveying light and laughter. "How is it possible?"

"I could ask you the same thing. How are you here?"

"The Earth Orb's power led me through the mountains. But you . . ." Affection showed in his gaze, some semblance of genuine love. ". . . you are beautiful."

"You say that as though this is my authentic form."

"No, but it is the one I first fell in love with."

Sora felt their wordplay, but what it meant, she could not say. At her side, Eionei kept one hand upon the hilt of his rapier.

"Uluron fled at my appearance," Soliel continued, daring to come forward. Chaos stood her ground. "Am I correct in assuming your kidnapping was a misunderstanding?"

"An accident, yes. But I have no intention of returning with you." When he stood at arm's reach, she held her ground, yet bristled at his proximity. "Soliel, your mother wishes to speak to you."

"My—"

At the word, Sol Kareena and her armed envoy stepped from the veil.

Her steps were deliberate though slow, her expression hardened despite the delicate nature of her quest. Sora kept her hand upon the hilt of a dagger, uncertain if the danger was assumed or not.

Some misgiving stiffened Soliel's form as he stared with a false vacancy. "Goddess Sol Kareena, this is unexpected."

Sol Kareena studied the man, her ice melting into grief. "Soliel . . . By the Suns, this is surreal."

What was the relationship between them? Mother and son, yes, but family was just as often fraught as it was friendly. Sora could not guess; only saw that Soliel remained wary.

Muted, Soliel spoke once more. "What are you doing?"

"I am here to say your counterpart has told me everything," Sol Kareena replied, her weakness increasingly apparent. Yet behind her back, attached to a belt, a knife waited. "And that I'm heartbroken for you. For all you have had to go through. What else is a mother to feel? Even aged, you are my son."

Soliel glanced to her envoy—a small battalion—then to Chaos, who nodded to validate the words. "Then you understand the weight of my quest."

"I have come to beg you to stop. I fear for Celestière, I fear for the little boy I've held in my arms, and for you. For your soul."

There came a subtle sneer to Chaos' lip, and Sora understood, struggled not to mirror it. Soliel had slain so many—Empress Alauriel and her father, and the dragon Chaos called *son*.

"If you are so worried," Soliel said, "evacuate your people here. This valley will likely remain in the aftermath of what I must do. But I will not debate with you, Mother."

Mother came after a beat, and Sora could not fathom its meaning.

"Let us help you," Sol Kareena pled. "My powers have waned in my sickness, but—"

"All the more proof you have nothing to offer. If she's told you everything, then you know precisely what power defeated your people and what power you have turned away from as it grew more and more powerful beneath your nose."

"You judge me as though I have the gift of foresight—"

"Have necromancers not been your bane before? You have no excuse." Soliel looked to Chaos, then grabbed her hand. "Where is your anchor?"

Chaos glared at where he touched her. "Why?"

"So I can bring you to safety. The elves fear for you."

Chaos wrenched her hand away. "I told you. I am not leaving." When she stepped back, he snatched her by the arm. "Soliel—"

"And what will you do instead? Use these people to complete your own selfish wants?"

"I want to save the realms, Soliel. The only one being selfish is you. Content to slay billions to save one? You are a sentimental fool."

Soliel's glower fell upon Sora, who kept her hand firmly around the hilt of her knife. "Her desires are far more self-serving than you know, Sora Makosa. You are in danger."

Sora forced herself to stand tall. Sol Kareena was near. She could be brave for her. "I trust that we both want to stop you. That's good enough."

"No, it is not. And she will stab a knife through your back the moment she reveals herself."

"You have some audacity, speaking for me so boldly," Chaos said, yet Sora could not deny the hurt in the words. "Uluron is not here, so there's nothing for you. If you have any respect for me, you will go back to Tierzuroth and leave me alone."

"You are not in your right mind. Does Sora have your pouch?"

Absently, Sora tucked the pouch from her belt to her pocket, but unfortunately made eye contact with the God of Order.

Soliel, with his magnificent armor, his glittering sword, released Chaos, making rapid strides toward Sora. "I will not hesitate to behead you—"

His words cut off as the envoy drew their swords. Eionei stepped in front of Sora, his own weapon set.

"If there must be violence, so be it," Soliel said. Next he readied his shield—and charged.

Reflex took over. Sora darted out of reach, far nimbler than he. But he never arrived, instead meeting a Celestial's sword. He bashed with his shield, slamming the woman to the ground. Another took her place.

The ground shifted. Sora stumbled back, panic rising. "Watch out—!"

The earth crumbled beneath them all. Screams arose as Celestials sank into the ruined valley, Eionei among them. Sora's feet slipped on sinking rocks, her own balance failing—

Until a glowing figure wrapped her in a tight embrace. Sora's feet left the ground. "Hold on, Sora."

Sol Kareena did not fly as a bird, no, but floated as gently as a feather. High in the air, Sora watched in horror as Soliel wrenched Chaos by the arm into his own, the orbs glowing anew. "Dira!"

At the words, Sol Kareena began her descent toward the Godly duo. "Are you confident you can stop him?"

"I can't just let him take her—"

A sheet of ice swept across the scene, encasing the trapped Celestials. The chill touched even Sora high above, and around her Sol Kareena became stiff.

"This calls for something greater. Sora, my champion . . ."

Time slowed in Sol Kareena's hesitation, for down below Soliel dragged Chaos farther away.

". . . never forget your calling."

Sora's stomach lurched as their descent escalated, yet around her, Sol Kareena . . . expanded.

In a blink, Sora was set upon the ground at the distant perimeter of the valley, far from the frigid cage of Celestials. Yet she stood at the feet of a giant, Sol Kareena's figure rapidly growing to rival the mountains surrounding them, the destroyed palace in Solvira. Her wings stretched as far as the valley's barrier, her magnitude unfathomable—yet when she stepped, Sora barely felt its vibrations.

An avenging angel, Sol Kareena slammed her great spear to the ground, causing the valley to tremble. "I regret this, my son."

Soliel, a distant figure of light, turned to face her.

". . . but there is no denying the monster you have become."

With the precision of thousands upon thousands of years of practice, Sol Kareena took her stance and launched her spear toward the fleeing God.

He was not impaled. He was crushed, the spear's tip larger than even his massive stature.

Stillness settled upon the valley, despite the struggling Celestials in their morass of ice and sand. The spear's holy glow faded. Sora saw nothing of Soliel, nothing of Chaos . . .

Was Chaos struck as well? Did the holy light . . . ?

Sora sprinted toward Soliel's supposed corpse, panic rising to steal all else. Perhaps it was over, but if Chaos were dead—

"Sora, wait—"

The ground burst.

Sora tumbled into the dirt, gasping as a monumental . . . *thing* emerged from the earth. Humanoid in shape, yes, and it grew with every step, this . . . this golem of earth. Within the cracks shone fire, shone ice, shone . . . *death.*

Sol Kareena ran for her spear, surging into the air to avoid a blow by this monster's fist. She landed beside it, withdrawing her weapon as a barrage of ice spread to coat her feet. When she could not step, she bashed the monster's head—only for fire to rain from the sky, singeing even her holy aura.

Sora dodged a few stray beams, but the bulk of it rained upon the goddess' figure. Sol Kareena's cry of pain was merely a portent to her weapon's blow. When she impaled the creature, it merely tore the spear away, sending chunks of earth and fire flying to the ground.

Within Sora sounded a warning, as clear as a whisper in her ear: *Run.*

From the monster pulsed darkness.

More cloying than the elemental rain, it caused Sora's very soul to lurch as she obeyed the warning and sprinted for the edge of the valley. The aim was to survive, it seemed, but when she turned, that same darkness spread across Sol Kareena, thickening to dampen even her light.

The goddess was stalled, and so the monster grabbed her shoulder, her chin—

And with cracking bone and spraying blood, the monster ripped Sol Kareena's head from her shoulders.

Sora screamed, but she did not hear it. The earth trembled, but she did not stumble. Sora breathed, yet took no air. The goddess' severed head tumbled to the ground, it and her gruesome, bloodied figure shrinking to their natural size.

The golem crumbled, an avalanche of fire and ice and death, revealing, at its center, a heaving God of Order.

He fell to his knees. He puked on the valley's desecrated ground.

Sora rose, but she was a mere puppet to her will. She felt nothing at all, save the worn leather of her dagger's hilt.

She ran for the broken God of Order, vision red and blurred by tears. Around her, a graveyard of ice and earth ravaged the once-sacred grounds, a few struggling angel limbs still seeking their escape. But Sora had but one target, her will invigorated as she passed the dismembered corpse of the goddess she loved.

Soliel rose. Sora leapt, only to be smacked to the ground.

She tumbled and rolled, quickly back on her feet. Again, she flew toward him with a cry, dagger drawn. Just as aimlessly, he shoved her away, his size his greatest asset.

As she righted herself, he stumbled forward. A flash of green, and the earth parted—revealing Chaos, limp but groaning.

Sora ran for her, this time grounded by a kick to her stomach. Pain distracted her from her brutal landing. Sora's vision spun as she fought to sit. When she coughed, flecks of blood splattered the ground.

"Mourn your goddess," Soliel said, exhaustion weighing his words. "And leave us alone. I grow tired of sparing your life."

Sora tried to stand, only for a sharp pinch to send her back to the ground.

Soliel knelt beside her and ripped the pouch from its place at her belt, stuffing it into his pocket instead. He then forced Chaos to rise, shoving her forward as they walked to the edge of the valley—and vanished.

CHAPTER 10

Current era . . .

Not one single fucking bit of this had gone as expected, and Etolié was fully prepared to punt Sora into the same ocean she would drop Chaos' anchor in.

But of course Goddess Staella had no business in a potential war zone. Neither did any of the rest of them, and Etolié had had a few nasty words to say to that.

In the end, here she was, bringing a slowly rousing Soliel to the real Staella.

Thankfully, the sleepy child had only tugged her hair once on the journey, which ended with her unceremoniously setting him onto Momma's couch—who quickly took over, far better equipped to care for a baby than she.

"I don't know everything," Etolié said. "I just know that the God of Order is in the Valley of Neoma and Sol Kareena wanted him brought here."

Staella kept her cooing tone as she asked, "Why do you look like me?"

Dammit. The illusion dispelled. And then, Etolié trauma dumped all the rest, though found her tears had stalled. "Maybe I did the wrong thing, Momma. I don't know anymore. But I'm hurting because Sol Kareena still fucking loves me and I'm supposed to actually talk to her, and Sora is a fucking idiot, and—"

Eionei burst into the room, his light dim, his face spelling shock. "I can't stay long. I . . ." He leaned against the doorframe, strength failing him as even his wings went limp.

Sora stumbled in after, eyes swollen, face glistening with tears. She collapsed to her knees. "She's gone."

Etolié spoke up. "Crazy ghost is gone?"

"T-That too. But Sol Kareena, she . . ."

Sora didn't have to say the rest. She fell into fresh tears, yet Etolié felt nothing at all.

"Sol Kareena was killed in the Valley of Neoma," Eionei said, his breath heaving and labored. "She was murdered by the God of Order."

Soliel, the tiny boy, didn't understand, and so chose that moment to let out a riotous giggle with no cause. It shattered Etolié's heart.

Her tears came slowly, the news incomprehensible—yet they wouldn't lie. Why would they lie? Sol Kareena . . . Dead? "What does this mean for . . . for Celestière?"

"I-I don't know," Eionei said. "I need to go back to Vanir Sol, but I . . ." His words caught, the light of his wings dimming. "But I'm not a leader, nor am I composed." His eyes glistened, a wet sheen surfacing.

With Etolié's blink came mist, for she was uncertain of what to feel at all. Momma's voice was calm. "There is a time for tears, but news will spread quickly, and it must come from someone of angelic influence, Eionei. If not you, I will go, but I wasn't there to witness it. If we don't control the narrative, someone else will—and that someone is Morathma."

Eionei nodded, his voice collected despite his falling tears. "Soliel needs to stay here, for now. He might be one of the few uncontested heirs, when he comes of age, and Morathma may come for him."

"There is no doubt in my mind he will do what he can to seize the moment," Staella replied. "He will also mourn, for he and Kareena were family. But Celestière is assuredly in crisis, and with no leadership, it's vulnerable."

Morathma was a passive evil in Etolié's mind, though she had never met him. Simply knew his politics—which weren't particularly kind to women, among others—and how he had treated her momma when she had been by his side—badly.

"Etolié, there's more," Sora cried, and when Staella offered a handkerchief, she wept into that. "Soliel stole Dira—Chaos. I couldn't protect her." Her cries came louder, apparently the news of the insane Goddess being kidnapped at the same level of her aunt's death.

"Like I give two shits about—"

"You already ruined everything, so will you just *shut the fuck up?!*"

Oh, damn. Sora had a spine today.

"We risked everything to set up that meeting, and you had to go and ruin it instead of just talking to me!" Sora's tears spilled faster, but oh it did nothing to slow her ire. "Has it ever occurred to you that you're not the fucking be all end all of the universe?! That for once in your goddamn life you could shut up and listen?!"

Oh, the fucking *nerve*— "What the fuck am I supposed to be listening to?!"

"The fact that Eionei and Sol Kareena thought she was worth trusting should mean something to you, but you had to blow everything up by masquerading as the one other person Celestière might've listened to because you knew your opinion would have meant fucking nothing—because maybe it does, Etolié! Maybe it does—"

"SO WHAT DO THEY KNOW THAT I DON'T?!"

"All right, let's not turn on each other just yet," Eionei said gently.

Etolié seethed, too angry to even illusion smoke for emphasis. "I know what I saw. I know she's an unhinged monster who—"

"Shut up! Just shut up, and—" Sora visibly bit back a scream. "Come outside."

Etolié followed, already rolling up her illusionary sleeves. "I know you're gonna break my jaw, but that's worth it to fucking deck you right now."

Sora rolled the door shut behind them, tension in her clenched fists, face stained with tears. "Etolié—"

"So how do we start this—"

"Chaos is Flowridia and Ayla's child."

Etolié's fists dropped. She blinked, the order of words not making any damn sense until— "Oh."

The scroll. The scroll from Momma; specifically, the scroll from Momma that taught how to make babies from Silver Fire. Momma's scroll. Etolié slowly sat down in the dirt, struggling to find air.

"There really are things you don't know," Sora said softly. "Eionei doesn't know that, but Sol Kareena did."

What . . . What did it mean? What did it *change*? Etolié could hardly breathe much less think. But Chaos . . . that mercurial bastard . . .

"And somehow we trust her because of that?" Etolié managed, brain frazzled at the implications—none of which were falling together, if she was being honest. "Explain this like I'm a child."

"Chaos—Dira—is the daughter of Flowridia and Ayla. She's not just some mindless evil Deity. She's my niece."

"Being the daughter of Flowridia and Ayla isn't a reason to trust someone. Kinda the opposite."

"I'm choosing to trust her."

"Your choice and your funeral—" Etolié choked on a realization. Oh gods, oh gods . . . "Sora, she doesn't want to kill Flowridia. She wants to kill herself. She wants to stop herself from being born." What *did* it mean? "I guess there is a little something more to her. I—"

The door rolled open. From within the warm home, Staella peeked out. "Oh, good. You haven't come to blows. I've made some calming tea, and I insist you both drink it."

Numbly, Etolié accepted Momma's aid to stand, her motions stilted, automatic as she returned inside. A teacup was all but shoved into her hands, magically not spilling all over her arms.

Soliel was held in Eionei's arms, her grandpa hardly aware if his vacant expression were any indicator.

"There are a lot of high emotions swirling about," Staella said, as she forced tea upon Sora as well. "Now isn't the time for blame."

Etolié forced herself to nod, the ache inside her warped by expanding, putrid anxiety.

"One of Kareena's final acts was to pledge," Eionei said, "but with her death, that power is lost. I . . . I will see what I can do to sway the others. Perhaps they'll be convinced the God of Order is a proper threat now. If I can succeed, that would mean all the angelic gods have pledged. Everyone except Morathma."

"And me," Staella added—her final words before she disappeared into the kitchen.

Soliel managed to wrangle his way out of Eionei's embrace. He toddled his way over to Etolié, placing his pudgy little hands on her skirt. "Da!"

"How very astute," Etolié replied, the cruel reality inescapable—that this innocent baby would become someone capable of slaying his own mother.

Again came the thought of killing him, the question of if it would even matter, but she wouldn't act in front of Momma.

"So, uh, where is Kitty in all of this?" Etolié asked.

"She flew away before we got there." Sora wiped her eyes, swollen and red. "I don't know what she knows."

"Does she still have the orbs?"

Sora nodded.

Etolié raised her voice. "Momma, remember that one time we used a Convergence Orb to find Uluron?"

From the kitchen came a melodic reply. *"Yes, Starshine."*

"Could we do that to find Soliel?"

"I don't see why not."

Etolié braced herself for a bad idea as she looked back to Sora. "Let's say I agree to help you save her. First of all, does she actually need saving?"

"Dira can't fight him," Sora whimpered. "She's a ghost. He wields holy light."

"Once you're calm and rested, we'll go to the Valley of Neoma with Momma. Hopefully Uluron is there. If so, Momma uses an orb to find Soliel's location and teleports us there."

Again, came a still, small voice. *"I can't teleport a dragon, sweetheart."*

"But you could teleport us, and then the dragon could fly to us, right?"

"That's up to the dragon."

Generally headaches didn't follow her in Celestière, but this Goddess' parentage was just too much. What the hell sort of game was Chaos playing? Did this change anything? "And you're abso-fucking-lutely sure it's worth risking our lives for . . . her?"

"It's worth risking mine. You can stay."

Etolié groaned, pained and furious. "You *know* I'm going to come with you though."

"I can be on standby if you need me, Starshine," Eionei said. "My sword is at your command."

"And I appreciate that."

"Solvira needs me," Etolié muttered, the reality still floating around her, refusing to settle. "They're . . . They're not going to take the news well."

Staella returned with a steaming teacup and saucer, which she offered to Eionei. "Do you need to go?" she asked.

"No, I need to help my friend Sora save the world, apparently. But then I'll have to go home."

Momma took her hand, squeezing lightly. "All will be well, Starshine. I can make an appearance in the temple if that would alleviate your burden. I can answer any questions the priestesses have, and they can tell the masses."

"That would help a lot, actually."

"Then I'm happy to do it," Staella said. "But I think it would be healthy to center ourselves first—even you."

Momma's eyes filled with tears, but Etolié shook her head. "I'm not ready for that yet."

And to her surprise, Momma simply nodded. "Sometimes thinking is unbearable. I understand."

Of course she did, and the reminder cut Etolié deep.

"Dammit, where's . . ." Sora frantically dug in her pockets. "M-My mirror, it's—" Her breath hitched, trembling as she withdrew her familiar from her tunic.

The bird appeared . . . like a bird, but if Sora's panicked eyes were any indication, Etolié was missing something. "What's wrong with Leeloo?"

"Leelan's cold." Sora hugged him to her chest, for despite the condemning word choice . . . the bird didn't appear to be dead. "H-He's not moving."

"Do you still have magic?"

Sora snapped her fingers, and a flicker of holy light appeared.

Etolié turned to the obvious source of hope. "Momma, can you heal birds?"

With gentleness in every motion, Staella knelt before the despondent Sora. "May I hold him?" When Sora set the bird into her hands, Staella stroked his feathers, softly prodded at his beak, peered into his eyes . . . only to frown. "He's alive. There's nothing to heal, as far as I can feel. But it doesn't take a goddess to see that something is different. Keep an eye on him. Hopefully, he's only in shock after the death of your patron." Staella set Leelan back into Sora's arms, an apology in the gesture. "Starshine? Would you mind coming with me to the kitchen?"

Etolié followed numbly, mind still reeling over all she'd heard. She felt no compulsion to cry, calloused as that was, but her tears most often came when the battle was done, when she was alone or surrounded by strong, tattooed arms . . .

"Perhaps this isn't the time, but I'm quite cross with you."

Staella's whisper jarred Etolié back into the present, her mother's terse, tearful visage setting her on edge.

"For you to use my image like that was entirely inappropriate," Staella continued, her quiet anger utterly unfamiliar. "You had no right to speak for me that way. I don't know who's right or wrong out there, but it is my right to decide for myself—and how dare you take away my voice like that."

Damn, there came Momma for her throat. Shock and guilt rose to choke her. "I'm sorry."

"Is it true that you're the reason they failed?"

Etolié shrugged, genuine in her uncertainty.

Conflict brewed in Staella's features, eventually settling into a sigh. Etolié wasn't prepared for Momma to take her hand and squeeze. "I forgive you, but please be careful."

"Momma, I really don't trust Chaos, but . . ." Etolié spared a glance for the other room, where Sora and Eionei kept their tears at bay by entertaining baby Soliel. "Look, Sora told me something I really shouldn't repeat, but it's left me questioning everything and . . . a-and perhaps there's more depth to that Goddess bitch than I thought. I don't know what to do."

"What does your gut say?"

"My gut says everything I thought about her is now suspect, both the good and the bad."

"And what about your heart? What does it say?"

Etolié forced her mouth to shut. Introspection was a bitch she most often shut up. Quiet meant feeling. Quiet meant to hurt. "My heart says the world needs saving. My heart says what we're doing now isn't working. No matter what, Sol— the God of Order just keeps moving forward like a fucking lava flow. He killed Lara. He nearly killed Khastra. What chance do any of us have? We need something bigger than even them." Gods, it hurt, releasing control. But Etolié wouldn't be the one to save the world, would she? "Perhaps this Goddess of Chaos is the answer."

Etolié released Staella's hand, cursing her rising tears. "Dammit, I have to fix this. Not to sound like I'm justifying what I did, because I get that what I did was bad, but I can't exactly show up in Celestière as myself though."

Staella wiped her tears on her sleeve. "Technically, there's no one to enforce the rules anymore."

"I told you, Momma—they think I'm like Ilune."

Such hardness in Staella's gaze; such resolve. "Then perhaps it's time to prove to them that you're not."

The words lit a fire in Etolié's heart.

"Calm down, Sora. I'm practically tasting your damn stress."

That was disregarding Etolié's own, but she wasn't fixating on that right now. They stood before the amphitheater—and once again, Etolié wore Staella's face and body. This time, Momma had approved of her plan, and Etolié clung to the comfort of this mask for a little longer, knowing she would have to shed it before the end.

"I'm just worried about—"

"And we're gonna get to that," Etolié said. "But Momma's doing her thing in the Valley of Neoma. With any luck, she'll find Uluron and figure out the other orbs' location."

Celestière was in quiet uproar, confusion swirling above all else. The world was wrong, changed, different, but so few knew why.

"Are you certain about this, Starshine?" Eionei asked.

"Not even one bit, but if this doesn't sway these bitches, nothing will."

Etolié marched forward, the fact that she couldn't feel her legs irrelevant to the task at hand.

Of course guards parted at her passing—for she was Goddess Staella, accompanied by Eionei. They entered the arena.

There was no peace here. Deities from every walk of life were talking, yelling, some deathly silent. Who stood in the center of the platform but Alystra, whose disdain for leadership really was a crime. She was certainly suited for it.

"No one leaves until we have answers!" Etolié's de facto ex-grandma cried. Alystra then noticed their approach. "See? Here is Eionei and Staella! Now sit down and *listen!*"

Alystra stood apart from Eionei, the slight narrowing of her eyes suggesting she was well and truly *not* over their semi-recent breakup. Etolié stood in the center of the platform, throwing her voice across the arena. "Sol Kareena is dead!"

That shut them up.

Silence brewed. To speak the words only forced Etolié to feel— but no, no. Here she wore her Momma's face, determined to do her proud. "And I'm not Staella. In fact, I disrespected her when I came and told the Goddess of Chaos off. That was my fuckup, and I'm here to fix that."

Etolié's illusion dispelled. A few gasps of recognition sparked from the expansive crowd, but the majority seemed—blessedly—confused. "I am Empress Etolié of Solvira, Daughter of Staella, and some of you might not remember, but I was banished from Celestière by Sol Kareena when I was fourteen years old. And that's a whole fucking conundrum, but now isn't the time. What matters is I've spent a lifetime living on the mortal realm, and I shouldn't have to tell you the danger of the damn God of Order, but here we fucking are! It's like they said before: the God of Order murdered Emperor Malakh of Solvira and Empress Alauriel, thus ending Neoma's line forever." Let them chew on that bit of trivia—the mortal realm still thought Lara had died in the explosion of her palace. "He murdered Archbishop Xoran of the Theocracy of Sol Kareena, thus crippling Sol Kareena's kingdom." A lie, but the world didn't need to know that truth. "He murdered the dragon, Valeuron. He's the reason the Bringer of War fell. And now, despite all of the warning signs, the God of Order had to murder Sol Kareena herself for you to actually pay attention to my fucking words. And I will be completely fucking honest—I don't know if the Goddess of Chaos is trustworthy. But I do know she's opposed to the God of Order, and with everything he's done, I've changed my stance. I'm willing to take that risk and place the hope of the realms with her.

"Some of you don't trust me," Etolié continued, her nerves rising to even breach the topic. "Some of you look confused, and honestly that's ideal. But I've spent the last thirty-six years living in the mortal realm, and I've seen what damage the God of Order has done in just the last three. Sol Kareena's last act was to put her faith in the Goddess of Chaos—and you know what? Fuck it. That'll be my next act in her honor." Etolié clasped her hands together, focusing on the image of Chaos.

Goddammit, she prayed she didn't regret this. "Goddess Chaos," she said aloud, "I pledge my life and loyalty to thee."

She nearly pissed herself in the ensuing silence, her nerves painful and alight. But to her shock, Alystra, the skeptic, gave Etolié an approving nod and followed Etolié's lead. First a few, and then many. Every angel and Celestial deity followed. Hands clasped within the array of seats. Muttered prayers filled the space.

Etolié swayed, breathless beneath the display.

When the last angel had spoken, Eionei came forward. He set his arm around Etolié, and in his countenance was more sobriety than Etolié had ever seen in her grandpa. "May I just say shame on all of you?"

Etolié stared in surprise. One could have heard a pin drop.

"And not every single one of you, but you know who you are," Eionei said, his voice trembling, somber. "Bless Sol Kareena, for she was my closest friend, but it was ultimately her word that sent Etolié away. I have spent Etolié's banishment watching over her, and she did more good in the mortal realm as a mere child than most of you lounging in your seats have ever even conceived of. Celestière's folly is inaction. Sol Kareena is dead because of that inaction. But Etolié is all action, and she has not stopped since the day she set foot into the mortal realm.

"Listening to her today was a step in the right direction," Eionei continued, and Etolié swallowed rising tears, "but each and every one of us should be groveling at her feet for forgiveness."

No one spoke. Etolié nearly jumped at the soft touch on her hand, but it was only Alystra, who held it softly and squeezed.

Eionei, however, removed his arm from around Etolié's shoulders and stepped aside, looking lost until he moved to leave the arena.

Etolié watched him go, the awkwardness between them diminished but not gone. Etolié felt the eyes of the crowd and broke away anyway, leaving Alystra's touch.

She ran from the amphitheater to the halls beneath. "Grandpa, wait."

Eionei did still, his sobriety hurting her heart.

"You have a lot to be sorry for, sure, but we've talked about that," Etolié said, feeling like a child again, back when Eionei was a beacon of hope and love. "You've said you're sorry, and you meant it. But the fact of the matter is you were there at my side. You've always answered when I called, without question. You've always taken action, for better or worse. You don't let things fester like the rest of the gods. You ..." Etolié's lip trembled, the weight of the day finally too much. "You've always been there for me, on my side, even when no one else was. I can't ever thank you enough for that."

Eionei cried, his silent tears so unlike him. He offered a hand. "Perhaps we could start over?"

Etolié took his hand and held tight.

CHAPTER 11

Some nights, Dira could not sleep. And so, she elected to wander.

The Fireborn Estate reminded her of storybook castles. She couldn't imagine something bigger. Two entire floors, and a tower with a third on one end, and of course the expansive grounds. Mother even said she could go into the woods with an escort, but bid her to only stay inside at night.

As Dira passed a window, she peered upon the beautiful courtyard, lit by silver moonlight. Over the past year, it had slowly been cleaned up and set to order, the fountains no longer filled with moss, the vining plants controlled instead of wild. Dira loved helping Sora trim the plants, though wished, on days when outside help came to clean the grounds, that she could say hello.

Mother said it was not safe. The outside world was dangerous. No one could know they were there. Instead, they would sit in Dira's room and draw, making a game of it. Mother would draw whatever she asked, assuming Dira made her own attempt first, resulting in a massive stack of animal portraits stashed beneath her bed. As much as Dira wished to meet the visitors, nothing compared to quiet time with Mother.

Even so, her seventh birthday was tomorrow, and sometimes she read books about children with friends and . . . yearned.

Down the stairs she went, wondering if Sora had gone to bed already. Was Mother here? She often left at night to go . . . somewhere. To fight monsters, or so she had been told.

Mother disappeared in shadows, and as Dira climbed the steps back up, mindful to avoid the creaky ones, she wished she could, too. Apparently it was dangerous. Apparently demons lived in shadows, and Dira would do well to avoid them. But how much quieter could she be if she could disappear entirely?

When she entered the kitchen, she traversed down into the cellar without fear, the cold soothing in Mother's absence. From the icebox, she withdrew a pitcher of orange juice and poured herself a glass, cringing at the tiny *ping* as glass touched glass, and again at the unavoidable stirring of liquid.

But there was no sign of Sora, and so Dira drank her juice and hid the dirtied cup. It was not a crime to be awake this hour, but it was a game she loved to win.

As she left the kitchen, faint sounds of conversation pulled her focus. On silent steps, as she'd been taught, Dira crept to the parlor room, finding the fire stoked and the door slightly ajar.

". . . only one person. I can only be in so many places. Casvir burns entire cities to the ground while I burn his troops on the other side of the continent. He is privy to my games now. Something needs to change."

Dira dared not even breathe. Who was Casvir? What games involved burning cities? Was it played with matches, or did Mother use her silver flame?

"I don't like it either," came Sora's voice, *"but your intentions are good. Do you think they would listen to you?"*

"Assuredly. They know my actions this past year. I would only need to whisper in the right ears to gain a title. But there are only two kingdoms left. I worry it is not enough."

"Three, if you count the Sun Elves."

"That is a joke. Their memory runs deep, as it should, nor has Casvir attacked them yet."

"Would you ever consider asking . . . Gods, I can't believe I'm saying this, but would The Endless Night make a difference?"

Dira hadn't heard the words before, but something in Sora's tone suggested it was best to not repeat them. Still, her curiosity remained piqued.

"I would rather be a politician again than consort with Izthuni. Besides, I think he holds a grudge given I never actually delivered what was promised in exchange for that pledge."

The name chilled her blood, for that was a demon god. Mother did not speak of demon gods, but Etolié did in passing. Sometimes she made jokes and told Dira to never repeat them.

"I'm sorry I can't be more helpful," Sora said.

"You are helpful. There is no one else I trust more with my Dira. You give me peace of mind, and that is not something I have been afforded much in my life."

"You're welcome, then. She's a wonderful child."

"She is."

"But regarding the situation at hand . . ." Sora's pause drew Dira closer. *"You really think the elves might be the key?"*

Dira pressed her ear to the doorframe, lest she miss Mother's whisper. *"Truthfully, the idea of playing that part again makes me ill, and I have not been ill in many centuries. I was miserable in the political arena.*

I hated the scum I was forced to pander to, but not so terribly as I hated myself. I can look back and see that it was self-harm, to put myself in those positions over and over. Alas . . . I was good at it, though I have gained self-respect enough to hopefully not descend so low as I used to. Even so, if that is the price of Dira's safety, nothing is too steep to pay. I have everything to lose, and so I will not fail."

That twisty sensation came to Dira's stomach. What safety was there to pay for? And why . . . why would Mother hate herself?

"I understand. Just don't forget why you're doing it. You've come a long way. I would hate to see that undone."

"If I do this, I will invariably be gone for longer bouts of time. Are you all right with that? Dira will be in your charge."

"Of course. She's never a burden."

"No, but you have already put your life on hold for us. I worry about imposing any more than I already am."

Hesitation hitched Sora's breath. *"She's all I have left too."*

Dira's stomach ached. Her heartbeat rose. She wanted to listen, but she did not understand, not one little thing—and so she softly knocked on the door.

Mother was there in a blink, her expression soft. "Darling, what is wrong?"

Words felt impossible. What would she even ask? Instead of speak, Dira raised her arms with a silent plea, to which Mother responded by lifting her into her arms.

"Come sit by the fire for a while. Perhaps you can ask Auntie Sora for some tea."

Current era . . .

Flowridia awoke, yet the sun had dimmed.

Ayla lay in stasis beside her, so Flowridia stared undisturbed upon the window. Did she imagine the change? As sure as the freckles on her cheeks, she witnessed a dull sunrise. What omen was this?

Her lips moved to whisper the precious name, *Kedira,* yet she paused, fearing what it would mean to bless a cursed sun.

Instead, she gently jostled her serene wife. "Ayla, something's wrong."

Alert, Ayla placed her hand to Flowridia's forehead. "What's happening?"

"Not me. Outside. Something . . . Something is amiss."

Ayla stood and followed her stare, wandering curiously toward the window. "There is an odd feeling."

"Can you investigate?"

Ayla gave a swift nod and vanished into the curtain's shadow.

Flowridia rose, deciding to dress in the meantime, though she grimaced at the ache in her back. Her hips protested as she stood, but Flowridia forced herself forward. She had only stripped by the time Ayla's cold presence returned. Instead of muted sorrow, Ayla held an odd smile. "What a strange day indeed, Flowra. Haven is in a riot. Goddess Sol Kareena is dead."

Flowridia hardly comprehended the words, stunned into silence.

"The prevailing rumor is it was the God of Order. Beheaded her."

Flowridia's most recent memory of Sol Kareena was a literal nightmare, a trick by Izthuni, but it did not change that she had stood before the goddess more than most, had once received a warning: *Child of Odessa . . .*

She felt nothing at all. "What does this mean?"

"I have no doubt Celestière is in turmoil. A void in leadership rarely leads to good things. Perhaps it will come to blows."

"The angels would go to war?"

"That is speculation. But they have lives just as you and I do."

Flowridia recalled then that she was nude and resumed gathering her clothing. Mindful of her hand, she managed to slip into her dress without aid. If it weren't for the pain in her abdomen and hips, this would nearly be a good day. "I don't know what to feel."

"Feel nothing. She was not your goddess."

"No, but she did *kill* you."

Ayla grinned—and oh gods, how long had it been since Flowridia had last seen that? It pulled a blush to her cheeks. "A pity for her," Ayla cooed. "I can die a thousand times, but she can only fall once. Perhaps I should bake Soliel a cake."

"Did you hear anything at all about Sora?"

"There were some whispers of the Goddess of Chaos. I know not where she is."

Flowridia smoothed her skirt, deeming herself pretty enough as she moved to manage her hair. "I don't know what will happen today, but it won't be boring." From the desk, she withdrew her magical mirror, praying she might finally see her sister's face.

It glowed . . . and faded.

"What if Sora is hurt?"

"Most likely she is disoriented and mourning."

Flowridia nodded, though she despised her own helplessness.

Gentle fingers touched her, caressing soft lines along her back. "Darling, she will contact you when she is ready. I have no doubt of it. I was able to clarify the situation, so at least she knows you weren't unfaithful."

A small mercy, Flowridia supposed. She set the mirror aside. "Did I tell you I dreamt of Sol Kareena when I was dying from fever?"

"No, though I'm curious now."

"It was a trap by Izthuni, I suspect just to torment me further. She claimed that if I abandoned you and returned to her light, I would be rescued, but when I saw the fallacies in her speech, she was revealed to be Izthuni, who, well, tried to eat me." To speak the words made her grow cold, yet a weight lifted with each one. Speaking of pain helped it ebb. "Every memory I have of her, false or not, is a nightmare—ironic, isn't it?"

"I suppose I could say the same. It is all right to feel conflicted."

"I'm not conflicted. I think I might even be happy. Not that I can admit that to anyone else, but . . ."

Was it relief? Was it freedom? Surely Sol Kareena had lost faith in her, but now there was truly no turning back. Salvation had been beheaded.

"No, there are plenty in this kingdom you can admit that to," Ayla said. "Your sister is the only one to be mindful of. However, if I may press, you have me curious. Had it truly been Sol Kareena in that dream, would you have done it?"

Flowridia frowned, the question surely a trap, yet Ayla held no judgment upon her impassive features. "For all the same reasons I didn't stab you, I would have said no. Even if I had an ounce of trust in her intentions, I would have stayed."

"I am trying to decide if you are a saint or a fool. Perhaps a little of both."

Flowridia shook her head, cautious as she cupped Ayla's precious face, lest she scare the broken woman away. For Ayla was, assuredly, shards of the woman she had been. "There is nothing in this world I would not sacrifice to save you. Call me a fool if you wish, but that includes myself. I cannot stand to think of how helpless I was in that dungeon, but the one power I could cling to, the one thing I could spite Mereen with, was holding to my devotion to you. I knew all along that you were in there, somewhere. And look at us now, Ayla. Every day, we're healing." Flowridia kissed her cheek, desperate to convey the innocent affection Ayla so dearly deserved and craved. Though Ayla could not blush, her smile was sweet enough to match. "Every day, I see more and more of the woman I married. After everything I've done, do you really think I would let you go?"

A knock stole her words. Though annoyed, Flowridia looked to Ayla for validation, who gave a small nod. "Come in."

Casvir entered, every motion precise as he shut the door and took a chair at her bedside, an odd vacancy to his expression. He held an opened envelope. "Good morning. Perhaps you have already heard the day's strange news."

"That Sol Kareena is dead?"

Such an odd twist to his smile, nearly cruel. So rare to see. "I am uncertain of my feelings, except to say that they are positive."

"I think it's safe to say that everyone in this room has been personally victimized by Sol Kareena," Flowridia said, her own impish smile appearing.

Yet Ayla's glower dampened the already dark sun. "Speak for yourself."

"I . . . I apologize." Flowridia bit back clarification, confused at her animosity, but bickering in front of Casvir was the last thing she wanted.

"Be that as it may," Casvir said, "it is not why I came." He offered the envelope, and Flowridia noted the broken seal of the Whispering Elves. "Executor Faeborn has accepted your request for a meeting."

Flowridia hastened withdrawing the letter, startled by the news.

"Their only stipulation," Casvir continued, "is you, Lady Flowridia Darkleaf, must be present."

Ayla's tone held ice. "I don't like that."

"It is not your decision."

"They want you to bring a vulnerable woman to a political summit."

"Every precaution will be taken."

"Then send Etolié in disguise. Do not endanger her."

Flowridia failed to tune them out, yet absorbed the contents of the letter, nevertheless. "They think I work for you."

"And you don't, so you owe them nothing," Ayla snapped.

"I don't think they know if you're alive," Flowridia muttered, and she offered the letter back.

"What if there is an incident? Flowra, you collapsed—"

"And there has been no incident since." She faced Casvir, surprised at how she yearned to say . . . *yes*. "I will think on it. You'll have an answer by tonight."

"Should you agree, I will personally guarantee your protection." He stood, his business conveyed, and Flowridia knew he would say little else. "I will leave you alone to prepare for the day. Tonight, I will return for your answer."

The moment he left, Ayla said, "I will say this calmly once. Please do not speak of my history in front of Casvir. Do not hint. Give him nothing."

"Given you have a meat statue of Sol Kareena in your cathedral, I don't think it's much of a stretch to assume you have a grudge." Flowridia laughed to convey her tease, but Ayla remained deathly quiet. Her joy faded. "I'm sorry. I'll remember."

"Flowra, you cannot possibly be considering this."

Ayla had clearly made up her mind. Flowridia spoke with care. "It might be beneficial—"

"To *who*?! Casvir? Do I need to remind you that we're—" Ayla cut off her words, then lowered her voice. *"That we're actively plotting his death?"*

"It's nothing to do with the war, it's—" Yet the truth startled her, so much so that she lost her words, praying Ayla might interrupt her as an excuse.

But no. Ayla remained silent as she waited, fire burning at her tongue like a lash.

". . . I want to know why," Flowridia admitted, uncertain of this rising want within her. "Executor Faeborn has no reason to respect me, yet they've agreed to a meeting with Casvir after months of hedging, if I'll attend."

"All the more reason to be suspicious."

"Would you accompany us?"

Again came Ayla's glare, though Flowridia struggled to understand the cause. "I am not a member of Casvir's council. I do not work for him, nor will I ever again. I have no investment in this war, except for an outlandish hope that it ends in his destruction. Furthermore, I have no investment or care toward Executor Faeborn, nor do I wish to explain why I've apparently switched sides after offering perfectly compelling reasons to hate Casvir. I would say to consider your reputation, but you've already gone and told them you're here and apparently speaking for Nox'Kartha. Gods forbid they find out you're expecting again. Rumors that you're carrying a little De'Sindai heir will be circulating within days."

"You and I both know the truth," Flowridia said, though the sting of her words remained. "It won't matter in a few months."

"So why would you invest yourself into this war? Are you bored? I understand this room is stifling, but don't go out and endanger yourself because of it."

Flowridia sat back against the headboard, feigning interest in the patterned comforter to avoid Ayla's scathing stare. Her fingers traced the embroidered patterns, seeking answers in the nonsensical art. "I told you I feel . . . *useless.*"

In hesitant motions, Ayla came beside her, her acrimony fading into something soft. "Please don't do this. I am not trying to manipulate you with guilt. I am simply begging you as your wife to decline. Not only for your safety, though that is the prevailing factor, but because Casvir will slowly entangle you into his fold. He's called you once, and he will call you again, until you're so wrapped up in the war that even once the baby is born, you will have no choice but to stay. And I—" Ayla's visage twisted with grief. Horror filled Flowridia to see her tears. ". . . I cannot stay here, Flowra."

With her good hand, Flowridia reached to cup her wife's cheek, wiping the first of her falling tears. "Casvir isn't manipulative. In fact, he's been entirely upfront in the past about his desire for me to join his council, but he's never fought me when I've said no. I . . . I'll turn him down."

Before regret could seize her, Ayla fell into her arms, clutching tight enough to risk puncturing the nightgown's fabric. "Thank you."

"You're my wife," Flowridia said, the sacred truth a constant, a comfort. "I made a vow, and my first duty is to you, always and forever."

Peace did fill her, surpassing the regret threatening to bubble to the surface. She had made a vow against regret, but the war would not last forever.

Ayla, however, was eternity.

When they entered the Valley of Neoma, visions of violence fell upon Sora once more.

The meadow had been churned like tilled earth, the once beautiful place destroyed in a moment of violence. The dead had been moved, but signs remained of pieces of armor, cloth, and blood—so much blood saturated the earth.

Death did not discriminate between mortals and gods. Angels bled like any other.

A gentle hand fell upon her back. Eionei's presence had become familiar, and Sora leaned into the affection. It was a rare thing to find in the world.

The earth rumbled, and Sora feared the God of Order's return, but it was only Uluron, who she had not noticed amid the carnage.

Sora? came the dragon's voice.

Sora looked up.

Staella has explained all. I am so sorry for your loss.

Sora gave a nod, determined to withhold her tears. All the while, she massaged her bird, willing him to wake—for she could not pray.

There was no goddess to pray to.

But the fact remains that we must find my Mother.

"Yes," Sora choked, and it felt like a failure. By the Light, was she a fool to see herself as a protector? She had vowed to help, but here she wept.

No, not a fool. Dira was her niece. Age was merely a number. Sora was still her aunt.

And she had failed.

"Did my momma tell you the plan, Kitty?" Etolié asked.

Some conversation took place. Sora worked to silence her fresh tears. She kept her attention to Leelan, placing kisses and tender affirmations both. "Please live."

The bird lay limp, somehow alive.

The silent meadow evoked peace, despite the evidence of violence around them. She didn't notice Staella until she approached with the Lightning Orb, held lovingly in her hands. "It's strange," Staella whispered. "I don't actually feel them."

"What do you mean?" Etolié asked. "What do you feel?"

"I simply don't. There are no orbs to feel. Perhaps he found something to block it."

Uluron shifted. Etolié interpreted. "Kitty says she can feel the orbs, though he's far away."

"Can the dragon take you to him instead?"

"Yes, but now I'm suspicious . . ." Etolié looked to the dragon, conspiracy in her pursed lips. "Kitty, riddle me this: when I was trapped in the Temple of Chaos, I was told the New Gods had no power there. I couldn't pray to Momma. If Soliel and his orbs were in a Temple of Chaos, would you be able to feel it while my momma couldn't?"

Etolié turned to Staella. "Kitty says that sounds plausible."

"So Soliel is in a Temple of Chaos," Staella affirmed. "All the way back with the Whispering Elves?"

"He wouldn't take her there immediately," Sora interjected, recalling their many exchanges. "If she speaks out against him, the elves would turn on him. He knows where she stands now. He can't risk losing elven support."

"That assumes we fucking trust her word, but that's apparently beside the point. Are there any other Temples to Chaos?" Etolié asked, and after a moment, she turned to Staella. "Kitty says there are, and she suspects she knows which one based on his location."

Staella offered back the orb and kept her hand extended toward the dragon. "Do you mind telling me? Then I can paint a picture in my head."

Whatever silent exchange followed, Etolié turned to Sora and Eionei. "What if he just puts her anchor down and leaves?"

"She can grab it now," Sora said, but then a nasty truth struck her, "unless he completely destroys her body. Or banishes her. Or hurts her in some other way."

"Should we bring a rabbit corpse just in case?"

"You joke, but it's not a bad plan."

Staella approached. "I'm confident in the location. Are you certain you don't want Uluron to take you?"

"Time is of the essence," Sora said. "I don't quite know what he'll do, but the sooner we can rescue her, the better."

"Uluron did confirm it would be a few hours away. She is going to wait here, however, until Etolié confirms that you are, in fact, in the right place and don't immediately need me to pull you back. Then she will come to you."

"Perfect." Sora accepted Etolié's hand.

Sora hadn't ever minded the feeling of teleportation, though she could count on one hand the number of times she had done it. With the shift from ground to air came the sensation of sailing on calm seas, and she savored the glimpse of the space between worlds, wondering if the stars she witnessed were the same in her sky, or another entirely.

Her feet landed on cold earth.

Etolié's wings cut through the dark night, casting light upon the ruins before them. A dilapidated archway, ravaged stairs, the remains of a statue—this was not a grand temple, but a graveyard. All around, remains of ancient stone structures lingered, overgrown with weeds and the occasional moonlily, but before Sora could ask, Etolié fell to her knees. She dry heaved, visibly sweating.

"Etolié?"

"It's nothing. It's normal." Etolié coughed, though nothing emerged, finally standing with a small sway to her steps. "By Eionei's Asshole, I fucking hate that."

"Do you have to swear on your grandfather's asshole?"

"I do, in fact."

Sora took tentative steps to the temple, mindful of Leelan, who she tucked into her tunic. "I don't have a plan, except stay quiet."

"If you want, I can illusion away our footsteps and make us look suspiciously like part of the walls. How about that?"

Sora nodded, supposing that would be good enough.

It was confusing, navigating down a dilapidated tunnel when you couldn't recognize your own feet, much less an entire person next to you. But Sora forged cautiously down the dark steps, not even wings to light their way. Slow work, but when Sora's foot touched flat ground, there came hints of light beyond.

In the minimal illumination, Sora recognized antiquated elven characters, speaking a language she only passively understood. This was old elven, not the language of her peers, or even of Mereen's era. No one living could speak this, save the Old Gods themselves, but Sora did pause to study the occasional image. Ancient artwork, all depicting the Old Goddess—

And all depicted only half a face. Sora stopped to study one, wondering if it was simply age, but no—too deliberate, the perfect line of her face, cutting it in twain. One side was fire, and the other . . .

A skull? But not quite, no. Something was wrong about it.

A tug on Sora's arm spurred her onward.

The hallway branched out as they crept onward, following the glow of light. There came a distant voice. ". . . don't understand you,

Dira. You trusted me in ages past. I am praying for you to listen once more."

Unquestionably Soliel. The sound boiled Sora's blood.

Whatever response came too faintly for Sora to decipher, yet was assuredly stained with tears. Etolié floated to silence her feet. Sora crept like the shadows themselves, trained by those who walked among them.

They rounded the corner and came upon a harrowing scene.

A grand antechamber revealed a massive space, filled with ancient ruins of statues and writing on the walls. The light from Soliel and his orbs cast a rainbow of color across the sacred space, revealing an altar and seating. This had once been a place of ritual. There knelt Chaos, with bonds of simple rope around her ankles and wrists. Soliel stood above her, his expression pure steel.

"You cry without tears."

"I cannot cry in this body, Soliel," Chaos replied, anguish in each word. "I meant no harm, I swear it. Please don't leave me buried."

Sora grasped the knife at her hilt, but Etolié's touch nearly caused her to jump. The Celestial put a hand to her lips, then mouthed, *Wait*.

"After everything you have done, those are bold words."

"I have done what I must to survive. It's what I have always done." Chaos released a sob, so human it shook Sora to her very core. "When have I ever betrayed you?"

"Shall I order the list by date or severity?"

"That was *him*, not me."

There came a crack in Soliel's armor, his own sorrow shining through. "Many times, I have questioned how loudly he actually speaks."

"Fine, then. Bury me. Leave me to be shredded when you tear the worlds apart. Is that what you want?"

That crack became a chasm. Soliel said nothing at all, simply took the light orb in his hands and studied its perfect sphere.

"I love you, Soliel," came that small voice, yet something in it rang wrong within Sora, for it was counter to everything Dira had said before. "I have always trusted you. I need you to trust me too."

Soliel knelt before the despondent Goddess, unable to meet her eye. "I want to."

Yet in the span of silence following his breath, Sora felt a thousand unspoken questions.

With illimitable gentleness, Soliel cupped Chaos' cheek. She did not turn away. "Help me right this. Uluron will come, so implore her to give up the orbs once more. She will listen. We can save the elves. We can save Haven. We can save the mortal realm and destroy every threat to come, once and for all."

Cold rose to envelop Sora's limbs. But though she twitched to act, Etolié's hand gripped her arm, causing her to falter.

"And I can save you, too," he continued. "I can give you the life you always deserved—both of you. Think of the girl who grew up in her gilded tower. She could be free and loved unconditionally, raised by the family she deserved and always dreamed of."

Chaos turned into the touch, her lips grazing his palm. "Perhaps that would be beautiful after all. Sora heavily implied she's in Nox'Kartha—so go there. Use the orbs. Find her. But don't leave me, Soliel. I-I should not be there, but . . . I will stand aside while you find my mom."

And though Soliel rose calmly, he swiftly took a fighter's stance. He unsheathed his sword—and set the tip to her neck. "You are not Dira."

"Soliel—"

"Don't."

In the space of silence, Sora did not dare to breathe. Tension rose. Chaos' grin held bestial malevolence. "She's scared of you, you stupid boy! You think she wants to talk to you?! *Stupid!*"

There it was. The shift. These new words were quick. Terse. Nothing like the opulent Dira.

"Couldn't even keep me captive. *Useless*," Chaos continued. "Should've let my friend go. What happens now? Gonna return without me? Faeborn doesn't trust you. You abandoned them."

"I have done no such thing."

"Do you really not know? Stupid, stupid boy."

Sora crept back out of sight, her own body reappearing as Etolié joined her.

"You think I have not studied history?" Soliel spat. "You think I do not know the cataclysm we've set in motion? Fine, spare the worlds from the orbs. Let the mortal realm be turned to rubble instead. Is that what you want?"

"There is no we! Dira told the executor to fix it! Rubble and grime. Ruins and dirt. That's what Tierzuroth is now, *stupid*. And that's only the start."

"You had no business orchestrating the death of the one goddess who might've stopped it, yet you threw Sol Kareena at my feet, nevertheless."

Chaos' gave not a chuckle, but a growl. "I don't tell lies. That was Dira."

Sora's stomach dropped.

"Perhaps we are both slaves to our futures," Soliel continued. "The fuse is lit. Will you help me extinguish it? As you've said, Executor Faeborn does not trust me, so will you return to help me save them?"

"What'll that do? Make her love you? Not likely."

There it came—another chink in his armor, revealing the heartbreak beneath. "Perhaps it would spare me the burden."

"So self-sacrificing," Chaos snapped. "Blame me. Blame her. You didn't have to kill your mother. You didn't have to kill our son. You didn't have to find us. You could leave the orbs, but you're too pigheaded to see another way."

"Name the way."

"Kill her."

It took all Sora's extensive years of stealth training to not gasp when Etolié jabbed her in the side. Illuminated words appeared in the air: *What the fuck?*

Sora did not know what to think, only that tears prickled in her eyes.

New words appeared. *We can just leave them here.*

Sora wrapped her hand around the hilt of her knife as her attention returned to the scene.

"Oh, but you won't," came Chaos' vicious tone. "You won't! So just bury me, *stupid boy*. Bury me alive. Buy yourself time. Do it. I fucking dare you."

And to Sora's surprise and horror, the earth rumbled like thunder.

Etolié screamed as the walls crumbled around them. Sora grabbed her, yet already the light had vanished, save for the glow of her wings cutting through the earth. She coughed as dirt threatened to clog her throat, the weight of the earth threatening to crush her. "Etolié!"

Etolié was limp. Sora felt warm blood trickle down her hand.

As though underwater, muffled voices cut through the slog of dirt. *"Damn you, damn you, damn you, Soliel! What did you do!?"*

"I did not know—"

"I'LL EAT YOU ALIVE IF SHE'S DEAD."

There sounded a roar. Far from human. Barely beast. Sora clung to the limp Etolié, vision sharp despite the putrid, dusty air as the pulse of adrenaline kept her alert. Etolié's wings glowed. She was not dead. The earth and rocks shifted beyond as *something* tried to dig them out, yet Sora could not shake the feeling of terror.

When Etolié faintly groaned, Sora squeezed the skin of her back—which was suddenly bare of clothing, but Sora had far greater things to worry about. "Etolié, wake up!"

Etolié slurred like a night of drinking gone wrong. "Serra, wha the fuh?"

"Etolié, you need to call your mother now. We have to get out of here."

"I . . . try."

"Focus."

"Can't if you don shu it."

Sora gasped as their prison of rocks and dirt shook—and from a crevice came a blast of silver light. "Etolié—"

The wall tore away, but it was not Chaos who faced them. Not the Chaos Sora knew.

This was no human, but a beast set aflame. Silver Fire coated its hunched figure. Sora couldn't breathe, struck by the memory of the Bringer of War tearing down the walls in the City of Light. But this monster was lithe, skeletal claws silhouetted beneath its magical coating as it grabbed Etolié and yanked her away—dragging Sora with it.

She fell, face stinging where she landed. The beast held Etolié, staring at her with eyes that glowed silver and gold. It was surely not all skeletal. Something of substance lay within, yet only in patches. Sora could not make out the shape of its head, only that it was animal and skeleton both. It towered above them, and when Sora scrambled to her feet, she had to look up to face it.

Sora whipped out her knife and charged—only to be launched back, the wind knocked out of her as her sternum met the monster's foot.

Sora barely felt the cave floor, only struggled to breathe after.

The beast cradled Etolié, flashing gold. With it came the return of her vibrant glow, no longer dimmed.

"WHAT THE FUCK!?"

Etolié was fine.

The beast set her down, then spoke in a voice far from Dira's—and unlike any Sora had heard before. *"Get out."*

The voice was not bestial. It was . . . small.

It launched itself at the looming God of Order. His sword clanged as though meeting steel to land a blow to her arm, and the beast wasted no time ripping its claws across Soliel's face. Before Sora's eyes, the wounds sealed, but terror showed in the God of Order's eyes. The red orb flashed. His sword burst into flame.

Etolié grabbed Sora's arm, wrenching her up. "We're getting the fuck out of here."

"But Chaos—"

"ARE YOU FUCKING SERIOUS!?"

Sora's stomach rose in suspension, the sensation before imminent teleportation. In those final seconds, she watched as Chaos literally threw the mighty God across the amphitheater.

Their eyes met. Sora stood paralyzed beneath the weight of the monster's hatred.

The ground disappeared from beneath her, and Sora flew among a sea of stars.

CHAPTER 12

Eight years after the end of the world . . .

Dira scowled with each tug on her hair. "Auntie, do we have to do this every time?"

Dira didn't know how long they had been sitting in her bedroom. She only knew that the sun had been up, they had taken a break for dinner, and now the sun had set.

Sora's chuckle held hints of a chide. "It wouldn't take so long if you weren't so wiggly. But, no. Though these will take time to set."

Dira groaned as Sora sat beside her with a mirror. Over and over they'd sectioned her hair, twisted her hair, tugged on her hair, oiled her hair . . . Everything was sore—her head from being fussed over and her body from sitting still. "How much time?"

"With your hair texture, I would guess a year."

"Auntie, you told me that. I mean tonight."

"Not much longer."

It would help if she could see, but instead Dira pouted as she kept as still as her wiggly body would allow. But she could play with the rug, right? That didn't count as wiggling. Dira tugged on the fabric loops, grateful for something to do with her hands.

"Did my mom have locs?"

"No. I told you we didn't grow up together. If we had, I suspect she would have."

Dira knew in so many words that her late mom and Sora hadn't met until later, but the depth of that absence finally struck her. "Why didn't you grow up together?"

"To tell you the truth, I didn't meet her until we were adults. I didn't know I had a sister, but that's a story you'll need to ask your mother's permission to hear."

Sora never lied. At worst, she said, *Ask your mother.* However, today the statement irked her. "But why not?"

"Because your mother and I didn't always get along, and I don't want to poke any old wounds."

Dira frowned to hear it. "Why weren't you friends?"

"How about we change the subject, kid?"

Dira crossed her arms, her scowl extra deep for Sora's benefit. "You never tell me anything."

Sora remained quiet as she resumed the tugging motions upon Dira's scalp. Tension lingered, until Sora softly said, "I think your mom loved plants more than people."

"Mother said that," Dira grumbled. "She loved plants and animals and tried to always be kind."

"What else has Ayla—sorry, your mother—said?"

"She hasn't said much. She gets sad if you ask her too many questions. But she did say mom loved me even when I was just a spark."

Sora chuckled, grounding Dira in the warm space. "No doubt about that."

"And she said mom loved her too, even when she didn't feel like she deserved it."

Sora's hands stilled, her silence indicative of her contemplative mind. Sora always became quiet when she said something she wasn't supposed to. "Your mom was an uncommonly kind person in many ways."

"But you won't tell me anything else?" Dira grasped this conflict tight, praying Sora would answer. Every day, she discovered more and more secrets with no answer, or whose answer was a stern, *Ask me when you're older, Darling.*

"You knew she was a necromancer, right?"

"Yes."

Sora became quiet once again. "I had magic, once. I had a familiar—a bird named Leelan. He made me a priestess to a goddess who granted holy light to her followers. But necromancy is the opposite of that. It's death magic."

A chill shot down Dira's spine, yet with it came intrigue. "Like Mother? Vampires are dead."

"Very much like that, yes. She could raise the dead. My goddess taught that necromancy is evil, and so that's what I thought, too. Your mom helped to soften that belief, but not before we had some friction. But once we learned we were family, we were able to see past our magic and instead see who we were inside. We were a lot alike, we discovered. I got to know her during a vulnerable time in her life. She had been . . ."

Dira held her breath at Sora's hesitation.

". . . in an accident, and I helped her recover. It was a special time for both of us, and I came to love her like the sister she was."

Oh, how she wanted more. Mother was her whole heart. To think she had a second mom could only mean joy, right? "Mother says I'm a lot like her."

"You're a lot like how Flowridia was when we met. She was eighteen, but she was still just a kid to me. She had the wryest sense of humor—like you. She was very sweet—like you. She always looked out for others—like you. You have so much in common."

"So what happened? Why did she die?"

Dira had come to anticipate a rejection from a question just a step too far—from Sora, there would come a hitch in her breath, a grimace, a groan . . .

And then . . . "You should ask your mother about that. But in the meantime, you're done. Are you ready for your first look?"

Relief escaped in Dira's sigh. She forced herself to rise and absently accepted the mirror—only to squeal unbidden at the face she saw. She laughed as she touched the twisted strands. "I look just like you!"

Dira was eight years old—the age Mother had deemed was appropriate to make long-term decisions regarding her hair. So of course she wanted to be like Sora, even if her locs were short and twisted for now. But someday, Sora had assured her. Someday, they would be long and thick.

"Can we show Mother now?!"

Sora nimbly rose and offered a hand. "She's going to love it."

Dira all but tugged Sora through the hall to Mother's room, excitement radiating from her figure. So much so, that she forgot to knock, simply flung the doors open and ran inside. "Look! Look!"

Mother glanced up from her desk, exhaustion apparent in her eyes, but Dira loved to watch the light fill them and know it was because of her. "Oh, Dira Darling, you look so beautiful!"

Dira hopped up and down, enjoying the weighted strands against her head. "It took *so long* but Sora says it's done now."

"It's done *for* now," Sora said from the doorway.

Mother pulled her into her arms, then whispered, "Did you tell Auntie Sora thank you?"

Stark horror filled Dira. "I forgot."

"Don't leave her waiting."

Dira ran to Sora and clung tight around her waist, still bouncing on her toes. "Thank you, Auntie!"

Sora's arms came around her—or, as well as they could with her leaning down. "You're welcome. I really enjoyed this."

"Because of your papa?"

Sora had said her papa had loved his locs, had helped Sora care for her own, and Dira loved to think she had a grandfather at all, much less one she could emulate.

"That's part of it," Sora replied. "He would have absolutely adored you. But I also love spending time with you."

Current era . . .

"And then she turned into some kind of monster animal thing. Sora confirmed I didn't hallucinate that part."

Back in Solvira—and thank the remaining gods for that—Etolié regaled the tale to an enraptured audience of two.

"A monster?" Zorlaeus asked, but Zoldar then signed the more important part.

"Animal thing?"

"It kind of had claws—well, nasty, gnarly skeleton claws. Look, I was a little roughed up from having a cave collapse on me. She technically saved my ass, and I'm processing that."

They sat in Etolié's library, secluded underground. Zorlaeus gripped a pillow tight enough to tear its seams, while Zoldar kept interrupting with clicks and signs.

"What about Sora?"

"I'm getting to that part. After Chaos-monster healed me, Sora and I got the fuck out of dodge. But Sora chose to stay with Uluron and find her again. I couldn't talk her out of it. Momma sent me to Solvira, and now I'm here with you two—thank Morathma's Whore Mother."

"Are you certain you're all right?" Zorlaeus asked.

"Chaos-monster healed me, remember?"

"No, no—I mean about Sol Kareena. She was your aunt, wasn't she?"

The words sunk like a stone, and Etolié slumped. "It's a lot. I'm not thinking about it right now. I'll cry at the funeral."

"And Khastra?"

"Look, I *will* cry about that, so don't bring it up. Momma says Ku'Shya hasn't said anything about it yet."

Khastra waited in an underground prison in Tierzuroth, trapped in sensory hell. Urgency screamed inside Etolié, that she should be there, not here. Not shackled by gold chains to a kingdom she had sold her soul to save.

But the people wept in the streets, according to Zorlaeus. When morning came, she would address them.

Zoldar suddenly became alert, and though his crystalline eyes technically didn't show humanoid emotion, Etolié had learned to recognize when they glinted just a little differently. He gave a few terse clicks, then crossed his spindly arms.

Etolié braced herself for annoyance.

"Hi, knock knock!" came her least favorite voice. Fucking hell, she was gonna hear that earworm on her deathbed.

Multiple footsteps approached, and of course trailing Murishani was Marielle, who Etolié resolved to be *very polite* to for the sake of Zorlaeus, but Etolié couldn't promise she wouldn't poison her tea. With non-deadly substances, of course.

Though bearing a very Nox'Karthan-esque collar, her dress was layered like a cake, while Murishani was the decorated cupcake beside her—his robes more formfitting though no less opulent. "Rumor is you had quite the adventure," Murishani proclaimed. "I assure you everything was perfectly boring while you were gone, aside from the news of a certain goddess being beheaded in the Valley of Neoma."

His smile remained pleasant, but Etolié couldn't shake the violent word choice. Perhaps he was testing her. He didn't know if she *loved* Sol Kareena. Only that she knew her. "Well, nothing was boring where I went, but I'm used to that."

"I'm told you met the Goddess of Chaos."

"Yes, and she epitomizes her name. Sora likes her. I'm torn. End of story. Should we make this an official meeting where you bring me all the boring paperwork, or will you fuck off now?"

Murishani's grin conveyed no malice, merely mischief. "No paperwork, and don't be surprised. Aren't you going to ask me for news?"

"You already told me everything was boring."

He shared a conspiratorial look with Marielle, to which Etolié resisted rolling her eyes. "Don't know if you heard," he said, "but a certain mutually hated flowery witch has fallen mysteriously ill."

That would certainly explain his glee. "That's not exactly new. She's been in a bad state."

Murishani pursed his lips. "She had a fall."

Etolié looked to Marielle, oddly anxious at the escalating events. "Since Blondie won't get to the point, will you?"

"She's fine," Marielle said. "Just fallen prey to something mysterious."

"You keep using the word."

"Oh, you forgot the best part!" Murishani practically giggled in his off-putting way. "Apparently, she's getting fat."

Etolié said nothing, the word far too specific.

"I just love watching people I hate go downhill so quickly, don't you?"

A terrible suspicion welled in Etolié's stomach, her words forcibly mild. "Fat how?"

"I . . ." He looked to Marielle. "You reported it."

"Larger than I've ever known her to be," Marielle replied, her shrug as rude as the conversation itself. "I felt it when we hugged. Her stomach was particularly notable."

Etolié glanced to Zoldar. Her Skalmite friend signed behind his back. *"Should I fake an emergency?"*

"No," she signed back, caught between playing along and remembering to breathe, because while Flowers really should be gaining weight after her ordeal, for Marielle to point it out—aside from being rude as fuck—meant it was noticeable, but the causes of noticeable weight gain in so short a time were concerning, especially given the identity of a certain nutty Goddess across the sea . . .

And a certain scroll in their possession. "I have no polite segue. Bye."

Etolié marched out—and ran once she reached the stairs. Court gossip was gossip, but gossip had truths, and Flowers . . .

Flowers was an idiot. But it took two to get a lady 'fat.' Ayla was the worst, but she wasn't an idiot.

The permanent portal placed between Nox'Kartha and Solvira was set as far away from Etolié's spaces as possible. She drank before she opened the guarded door, beckoning for the guards to wait. No, she was not drunk enough, but Flowers was 'fat,' and that affected a great many things.

The room holding the permanent portal was simple wood, no decorations lest they be drawn toward the tear in the planes. Etolié held her breath as she ran through the portal, praying she could outrun her headache—

And landed at the other end, holding her stomach until she reached the waste bin specifically for this purpose.

She emerged and handed the underpaid De'Sindai guard the waste bin, who bowed despite the unsavory offering. "I promise to tip you next time," she said, then resumed her sprint.

Etolié asked every servant she passed, living or dead, for Flowers' whereabouts, and was directed to the medical ward. Yet when she asked the healer, she was informed Flowers was out with her wife, so Etolié's quest resumed.

Was she gardening? Reading? Crying? Flowers had many hobbies, but just when Etolié was contemplating the merit of waiting back in her medical suite, she felt the prickling familiarity of Silver Fire approaching. *"FLOWERS!"*

She rounded the corner, acutely aware of how her golden wings reflected off the alabaster grey of Ayla's skin. The vampire became defensive, though laden with books, while Flowers . . . looked like death.

'Fat' was not the word Etolié would have chosen, though her loose clothing did make it difficult to tell. If anything, she was nearly as sallow as when she had first returned to the castle. "Etolié?"

Etolié marched forward, the truth increasingly apparent. "Permission to touch you?"

"Yes?"

Etolié's hand shot out to her stomach, which was mostly flat but firm in the appropriately condemning way. "Rumor is you got fat."

Flowridia shoved her hand away, clutching her stomach protectively. "I beg your pardon—"

Etolié leapt as a pile of books fell onto her feet—and might've tripped were she not blessed with the ability to levitate. Not exactly pleasant, having an irate Ayla Darkleaf bare her teeth at you, but Etolié had faced worse.

"But you're not fat," Etolié said. "You picked up a parasite." She glared at Ayla, presumably equally guilty in this bullshit. "What the actual fuck?"

"Did Sora tell you?"

"No, I just have a knack for these things," she said, which was a lie much fatter than Flowers, but Sora had really only revealed it halfway. Etolié glanced back to Flowers, the news all but confirmed. "I know about the scroll."

Flowers forced her smile, keeping her hand on her occupied womb. "Let's move this conversation somewhere else, please. No one else knows except the healer."

When Ayla stooped down to collect the books, Etolié assisted, noting the odd titles. "*Nox'Karthan History: The Early Years*. Why history?"

"Do I ask you about your reading habits?" Ayla snapped, which was a far harsher reaction than the question deserved.

"No, but you could. I'm really into studying bilge pumps lately."

But Ayla didn't elaborate, and while Etolié hadn't been suspicious before, she certainly was now.

Etolié was led to the medical ward, to Flowers' private room— which was larger than most cottages. Ayla quickly set the books on a desk, then helped her wife to the bed, which might've been cute were Etolié not simmering.

Etolié shut the door. "So you're fucking pregnant."

Flowers' smile came sweetly, and Etolié's gut churned. "Yes, I am."

"You used the fucking scroll."

"We did."

And you made a fucking Goddess, but she didn't say that. Etolié clasped her hands together, struggling to convey the extent of their stupidity without being thrown out. Did she care? Oddly yes, though the reasons were far more complex than she was going to figure out standing there and now. The world wasn't ready for fucking Darkleaf-Spawn—

Except . . . Chaos wanted herself dead. She was the one to burn on the pyre to save the world. Or, at least, Chaos thought so. But why?

"Do you know anything about Silver Fire pregnancies?" Etolié finally managed to spit out.

Ayla immediately perked up. "Do you?"

"Of course I fucking do. I practically raised Lara, didn't I? You wanna know why? I watched her mother fucking waste away and die."

The mood shifted, Ayla's tension radiant. But Flowers merely frowned. "Go on."

"I met Empress Ralaena when she was five months along, and she looked at least as bad as you do." Etolié reeled at the memory of the frail woman, cursed to carry a child she never should have, cursed to never meet the absolute angel of a girl she died to birth. "She was a human with no magic—kinda like you are right now. She wasn't supposed to ever be pregnant, because Emperor Malakh wasn't supposed to take the throne. But his brother died, he got his crown, and they were expected to provide an heir. But babies with Silver Fire have no control, and the fetus slowly fed on her life, sometimes bursting and burning her inside."

Flowers' gaze fell to the bed, but Ayla's snapped to meet Etolié's. It seemed they already knew.

"I watched her die," Etolié continued, steadying her voice. "Not the precise moment, but it was a slow and awful death. She collapsed at eight months in the hallway. The baby had eaten her soul, so there was simply nothing. Lara had to be cut from her womb."

Flowers' voice came muted. Not once did her hand leave her womb. "Lara confided as much in me, but—"

"You knew?" Ayla asked, the accusation clear.

"I didn't know the extent of it. Just that she had consumed her mother's soul."

Etolié sensed a marital spat coming on, and that was neither her circus nor her monkeys. "Look, I don't think you realize what a fucking precarious position you're in, Flowers. And I know you're a romantic sap, but Lara was lucky she lived. I'm not going to tell you what to do. I'm just going to lay out the facts, the most important of which is that you will die."

"You have no right." Flowers seethed, her meekness a thing of the past.

"No right to what? Tell you the truth?"

"Get out."

Etolié held up defensive hands as she backed toward the door. "I've said my piece. You can choose to be a self-sacrificing dumbass if you want."

When Flowers tried to rise, Ayla set a hand on her shoulder. "I will walk her out," Ayla said, and her strut suggested imminent death.

Etolié followed anyway, prepared to teleport to Sha'Demoni—except Ayla could follow her there, shit—but the moment the door shut, Ayla's entire demeanor shifted. Gone was the protective wife, replaced with something . . . smaller. "You tend to be hyperbolic," Ayla muttered. "Is her death truly so assured?"

"I . . ." Etolié bit back her snarky words, struck by Ayla's sudden humility. This was not the Ayla she knew. "Well, people *have* survived, but it was actually one of the practical factors that led to the Solviraes being so keen toward incest. Someone with Silver Fire could birth a Silver Fire baby with little trouble. And if Flowers had her magic, I would say there was a solid chance. But she doesn't. How far along is she?"

"Not quite five months, but half-elven pregnancies have an unpredictable timeframe, not to mention the danger of fetal vampires. Full-blooded elves only gestate for six months, so she could be due in less than two months from now."

Etolié was not keen to lie, despite it being the very core of her political career. Comforting platitudes were practically part of her title, but Ayla was not one who wanted to be lied to.

Ayla would not have come to her for comforting platitudes.

"Whether or not the baby lives is up to chance," Etolié finally said, determined to be unbiased. "Flowers living to meet the baby, though? I don't see how that's possible without serious intervention."

Ayla was so often a nuisance, a megalomaniac, but here she stood defeated, and Etolié . . . wished she could help.

"Thank you for your honesty," Ayla said.

"Why, though? You're not happy about this, are you?"

After a glance to the door, Ayla whispered, "It is Flowra's business. But there are deeper reasons than you realize. She won't be easy to sway."

Sway . . . Etolié's heart panged at that, memories of a desperate youth in way over her head rising to steer her words. "I know the means—"

"So do I—"

"To make it look like an accident."

Etolié prided herself on reading humanoid nature like a book, having learned and memorized the small tics that made up a mortal when she realized she didn't understand them at all. Yet Ayla remained an enigma, blank pages throughout. Her vacant stare conveyed nothing. Her words, however, wrote a novel. "Do not tempt me."

Ayla left, the click of the door a nail in Flowers' coffin.

Flowridia seethed all the while.

Etolié wouldn't lie, but Etolié did not know the full truth. Etolié likely meant well, but Flowridia was not Ralaena. Ralaena did not have Ayla, did not have Nox'Kartha . . .

Gods, what was this dread? Flowridia cradled the small life within her, hardly a spark, but it was *her* spark.

Ayla returned, her aura indecipherable as she lingered by the door. "Flowra, I am frightened."

With only minor strain, Flowridia rose from the bed to meet her wife, embracing her tight. "Etolié doesn't know everything."

"She knows much more than anyone else we have spoken to."

"I don't want you losing hope. We had one scare. One scare doesn't lose a pregnancy."

When Ayla pulled away, she took Flowridia's hand instead, escorting her as a lady to a ball. "You do recognize the finality of having your soul consumed, right?"

All too well, the threat made clear years ago when Murishani had threatened to steal Ayla's. "I do. And I'm taking this seriously, I swear. But just a few months more, and we're free. It's as you said, we can leave Nox'Kartha and explore the world."

That hole in her heart remained, but now was not the time to consider it. Today was for Ayla, who threatened to unravel before her.

Her wife squeezed her hand. "Just a few months," Ayla echoed, though there was little weight to the words.

Ayla so rarely smiled anymore—neither sweetly nor as the predator Flowridia loved. Was it Nox'Kartha? Was it because of Mereen? Flowridia stroked a stray lock of Ayla's hair from her face, that simple affection sparking a bit of light. "My love, what if we took time away?"

That bit of joy dimmed. "Leave Nox'Kartha?"

"Perhaps not Nox'Kartha, but Haven. I've been fine, and if anything does happen, you'll bring me back."

"Flowra, no. We can't."

Flowridia frowned, the rejection far from expected. Out of character, really. "I thought you wanted to leave."

"Of course I do, but not when I'm concerned about you collapsing dead in the hallway."

Damn Etolié. Ayla's paranoia had been given a foundation. "There is no path but forward. We can be afraid when there's a reason to be."

"There are most certainly other paths," Ayla said, her biting tone boiling Flowridia's blood.

"What? Get rid of it? And lose Demitri forever?"

"You don't know with certainty that Casvir would withhold him from you if you broke your contract."

"You're the one who said it in the first place."

"If you begged—"

"I can't—" Flowridia shut her mouth, remiss to bring up the core of it, but Ayla's gaze became dangerous.

How sensuous, Ayla's words—a façade Flowridia had not seen in months. "So you would die for Lara?"

Heat burned behind Flowridia's cheeks at the name, an old shame rising to seize her heart. "I thought we had resolved the topic of Lara."

"We had, and then you sold a *baby*. Your baby. By extension, *my* baby."

Ayla had never spoken so possessively of it, yet the statement only brought grief. "Yet you agreed to get me pregnant anyway?"

"I could not care less for it. I am simply reminding you of the purpose of this transaction, since you seem to have forgotten it."

The word crept like chills across her skin. *Transaction.* "It's still a child."

Ayla's mouth snapped shut, her fury seeping in waves. Her grin became terse, cruel. "You are correct, but lest I say anything I regret, I am leaving."

Ayla turned on her heel, leaving Flowridia reeling. "Wait, you can't just—"

"Yes, I can." She threw open the door. "I am going for a walk."

"Ayla!"

Ayla slammed the door.

As though punched, all the air left Flowridia. She stared in shock at the shut door, torn between ripping it open and screaming or collapsing into bed and crying.

Instead . . . something ripped through her.

Flowridia seized, falling against the door as heat seared her insides. "*Ayla!*" she screamed, for that was her lifeline, the pain sharp as it stripped her of layers, starting within. Her strength failed. She collapsed to the ground. "*Ayla, help—!*"

The door tore open, and Ayla fell beside her, frantic as she set her hand upon Flowridia's forehead, quickly inspecting her prone figure. Elsewhere, footsteps thudded, frenzied voices approached, but she clung to the sight of Ayla, even as her vision swam.

Again, she screamed as pain tore across her abdomen, resistant when Ayla calmly rolled her onto her back. *"Get back! All of you!"* Ayla did not hesitate to touch her beneath her skirt, her cool hand paling to the burning within her womb. *"Empress Etolié is in this castle! Fetch her before she leaves!"*

Behind her misted eyes, her wife's image swirled, but Ayla gripped her shoulder hard enough to bruise, forcing her to remain in the moment. "Stay awake. Whatever else, stay awake."

Flowridia obeyed, even as darkness threatened to overtake her vision. When Ayla withdrew her hand, blood stained her pale skin.

Her eyes became black, fangs growing unbidden. "I need to remove your dress," Ayla muttered, utterly numb. "Stay with me."

Flowridia wept yet clung to the pain to keep her awake. Behind each blink, she was back on that cold dungeon floor, suffocated by screams and blood—so much blood. Fabric ripped, but she felt no cold. She swore she was burning alive. "The baby?" she managed between sobs. "What about the baby?"

"I don't know."

"Fucking hell—MOVE!"

Glowing wings. Silver hair. Flowridia knew the presence beside her, even as her vision spun.

"Oh, this is gonna hurt like a bitch. Fuck you, in advance."

Flowridia gasped as the pain abruptly ebbed. She wept, even as her head cleared, the black spots at the edge of her vision vanishing. Elsewhere, a woman cried out in pain; Ayla's touch left her; Flowridia tried to sit but failed, too dizzy to right herself.

Next to her, Etolié wailed as she clutched her stomach. Flowridia gasped for breath, body reeling at the memory of pain, but managed to take one of Etolié's hands, wincing when the Celestial crushed it.

"Thank you," Flowridia whispered, for the gravity of the Celestial's warning had never been so apparent.

"As I said, fuck you." But Etolié clung to her all the same.

Ayla warded away the doctors, though kept a wary eye on Etolié as she cried.

This was the price of her continued life. "We need to tell Casvir," Flowridia said, though her heart ached to speak it.

Ayla gave a curt nod. "Once she's recovered."

Minutes felt like hours, but Etolié did finally go limp. Her breathing came in spurts. When she tried and failed to rise, Flowridia set a hand on her head. "Don't hurry. May I play with your hair?"

Etolié managed little more than a nod, still gripping Flowridia's hand.

Flowridia looked to her wife, as helpless as she had ever seen. "Can you check? Is the baby safe?"

Only then did she realize her immodesty, her dress ripped to reveal more than she would ever show outside the bedroom. But Ayla did not hesitate to place a gentle hand on her stomach, her expression blank as she said, "There is life inside you."

Flowridia's tears welled anew—of relief. No more fear.

At the entrance to Casvir's war chamber, Flowridia lingered a moment too long.

"Flowra?" Ayla stood near, her hands desperately clasping the other.

"When we tell him," Flowridia said, "there is no going back."

"When we tell him, he will pour every resource he has into your care. And there is *always* a way back, my love. This means nothing."

Such assurance in her wife's features. Flowridia let it fuel her courage. She knocked.

Nothing.

"Just open it." Etolié was pure gloom, but Flowridia would deny her nothing today. She obeyed, shoving the heavy wood forward.

Within, Casvir stood at the head of a massive table, decorated with figurines Flowridia presumed represented troops. Around him, a variety of De'Sindai listened intently, advisors to his army. Casvir was bold, but he was not so arrogant to dismiss the input of others just as bold.

Yet the stark lack of General Khastra showed in a massive empty seat beside him, and Flowridia's heart ached for Etolié.

Casvir did not frown, but he certainly seemed surprised. "Hello, Flowridia. Ayla. Empress Etolié. I am assuming this is important."

"Not more important than—"

"You already interrupted," Etolié muttered. "Just fucking tell him."

The seconds ticked by. Casvir finally said, "Should I dismiss my lieutenants?"

Should he? Did it matter? Was it worth keeping it secret or would the whole world know?

Ayla spoke to fill the silence. "That would be preferable—"

"I asked Flowridia. Not you."

Clear darkness colored his tone, as radiant as the ice wafting from her wife. "If you would not mind," Flowridia said. "This is important."

How close had she brushed with death? Could the baby have truly stolen her soul? The room cleared at his beckoning, and Flowridia gripped Ayla's hand for stability, grateful her wife's fingers couldn't break, or could at least mend if she did manage to snap one.

Casvir alone stood at the table now, severity upon his visage. "What is so important?"

"I'm pregnant."

All displeasure faded, replaced by pure intrigue. By every god, he actually cracked a smile. "I understand now."

"What do you mean?"

"I apologize for accusing you of stagnation," Casvir replied. "Is this the reason for the sudden turn in your health?"

"It is. But . . . when this is done, Ayla and I have the means to make me immortal. If I'm undead, will you swear to return Demitri to me?"

Approval showed in his nod. "Absolutely—"

"All right, hold the fuck up," Etolié said. "What is going on?! You're not surprised? What's this about being immortal?!"

Flowridia gathered her thoughts, but before she could speak, Ayla said, "Flowridia bought Lara's soul to free it. The price was her firstborn."

Etolié stared, the gears visibly turning in her clever head. She said nothing at all, merely blinked.

"Demitri is dead," Flowridia said, the statement threatening to choke her. "But when I become undead, to be immortal, he can be my familiar again."

With far more self-control than Flowridia thought she had ever seen the Celestial exhibit, Etolié remained silent, nodding in lieu of what Flowridia suspected was screaming. When she turned, Flowridia did not stop her, watching as Etolié marched from the room and shut the door.

"Congratulations are in order," Casvir said. "Pregnancy is worth celebrating, especially after your health journey these past months. Might I ask who the father is?"

"There is no father." Flowridia gulped, debating how best to explain to Casvir she held a truly godly secret.

"The method is not important," Ayla said, and Flowridia hardly felt her fingers for how tightly she gripped, "but for the purposes of science, the father is me."

"Are you implying artificial insemination, or are you offering me a half-elf dhampir?"

"A half-breed vampire spawn, yes," Ayla replied, though the wording made Flowridia sick. "She is nearly five months along."

Casvir remained thoughtful a moment. "It has Silver Fire."

Ambivalence colored Ayla's words. "Also correct."

"The doctors need to be informed. Flowridia will require careful monitoring as the months go on."

"She collapsed minutes before we brought her here," Ayla said, though Flowridia stared in shock at the admittance. "Etolié was there to save her."

"Then Empress Etolié shall be assigned to her bedside."

Flowridia could not hide her grimace. The Celestial would have a few colorful words to say about that.

"Return to the medical ward," Casvir continued. "It is one thing to keep a pregnant woman alive and healthy, but when the child is a dhampir, there is a significant risk to both mother and child."

"I am well aware," Ayla said, menace in the words.

"Then you may join me when I meet with the top doctors in my nation, assuming you can keep your emotions in check."

With a glance to Flowridia, Ayla audibly steeled her words. "I can do that for her."

"Good. Now, go. And congratulations."

Ayla tugged just a little too hard as they left the uneasy chamber.

In Khastra's abandoned space, Etolié sobbed in a pile of oversized tunics.

There remained the faint residue of Khastra's distinctive, alien scent, warm and laden with spice. Etolié's tears marred it, yes, but there were others. Her time with them was finite, but for now she wept into their comfort, thinking not of her lost love, but of Lara.

Lara, who had deserved better than this godawful realm, who had deserved better than her cruel death. Lara, who would not have let Solvira fall to Casvir's manipulations, but instead was murdered by a rampaging God. Lara, who had been torn from her rest in the Beyond to serve as a slave to a tyrant . . .

And then Flowers, fucking Flowers, who had tangentially caused her death, had saved her. Now, Etolié knew how. "You smothered fire with tinder, you goddamn idiot," she muttered into the cloth. She was forced to be grateful, but the payment . . . fucking hell, the payment was horrendous.

And now Flowers would die to pay the debt. The baby would apparently live—Casvir would have a baby Goddess, for fuck's sake—but Flowers? There was no way.

A knock interrupted her sobs. Etolié illusioned a face that wasn't swollen and covered in snot. "Enter."

One of those frightening hooded figures floated in the doorframe, its aura ice against her soul. "Imperator Casvir requests your presence in the medical ward. The matter is urgent."

"Respectfully, no."

"Respectfully, he is insistent."

Casvir had little to hold against her—aside from the lives of every citizen in Solvira, but threatening them over this seemed beneath him. Still, she roused herself, sniffing back tears as she trudged less than magnificently upstairs.

Etolié returned to the medical ward, the memory of pain prickling at the threshold of Flowers' suite. Casvir stood at Flowridia's bedside, who had been propped up with pillows. Ayla knelt protectively beside her, her embrace far too stiff to be merely loving. No, Ayla bristled like a threatened feline, and Etolié suspected tall, blue, and gloomy was the culprit.

"Empress Etolié, I owe you my gratitude," Casvir said. "I am told you healed Flowridia at great risk to your own health."

"Something like that."

"I am rarely insistent with you, given you have duties in Solvira. But Flowridia's continued health is important to me, so I must insist that you be relocated to Nox'Kartha—"

"What?"

"—until the baby is born," he finished, ignorant to her appall. "You will be compensated for your time and for any injuries you sustain."

Etolié did not bother to illusion any sort of happy face, keeping her sneer at the surface. "You don't have any normal-ass healers for this?"

"None that would not risk harm to the dhampir baby she carries. I am told you inherited your healing powers from your mother, who does not heal with light."

With great pain, Etolié resisted the urge to puff out her wings like a bird. Immaturity would not help her cause. "Is any compensation actually worth me essentially stepping down from ruling?"

"I am willing to negotiate payment, but I will not accept a no."

Damn him. Etolié looked to Flowers, fragile behind her apologetic smile. Oh, this pregnancy was a shit idea, despite whatever so-called 'noble' intentions had led to it. Flowers wasn't quite at death's door, but the baby also wasn't capable of eating souls yet either. "Can we step outside?"

Casvir gave a curt nod.

Etolié wrestled with the stupidity of her next words as she marched out of the room. But this was about Lara just as much as it was about Flowers, and Flowers was more than likely about to lose it for both of them.

When the door clicked, she forced a smile and calm words. "So when she dies, what happens to Lara's soul?"

Casvir looked unamused, but when did he ever look any other way? "You are convinced of her death?"

"Answer the question."

"If the terms of the contract cannot be fulfilled, then the contract is voided. The late empress' soul is free for me to do with as I please. Perhaps that alone is good enough incentive to help."

"All risk. No reward. Especially given I wouldn't place any bets on Flowers living to see that baby. So, listen . . ." Etolié braced herself for stupidity. "Let's make a counter deal."

Casvir continued to look unimpressed. "You wish to also bargain for Alauriel Solviraes' soul?"

"*If*, and only if, Flowers dies, then yes." Oh, she felt sick, any contracts with this man only ever falling in his favor. She had twenty-three years left on her roster. Would he accept any more? Would she give it?

"What would you offer?"

"Well, you're not getting my womb, so don't even plot around that. I suppose my default is to offer even more years of fucking slavery, so that's on the table, I guess."

Casvir did appear to mull it over, subtle intrigue in his searing gaze. "It is tempting, but what else could you offer?"

"Can we put a pin in this and fight about it after Flowers kicks it? The price of my help is that you'll even fucking consider it."

She had never seen him look more scathing. "I find your lack of faith disturbing. Yes, we can discuss it if the time comes."

Casvir marched past her, back to the door. Etolié followed.

Back in the medical ward, Ayla remained a shield around her wife, the caustic stare shifting between Etolié and Casvir.

"We have come to an agreement, for now." Casvir looked to Flowridia, and Etolié couldn't shake the oddness of his treatment of her. He softened in ways he shouldn't have been capable of, given his fucking evil core, and Etolié couldn't say if it made her sick or not. "My duties must call me away, but I will make it my priority to return this evening. There is much to discuss."

"Thank you," Flowridia replied, and silence settled as he left the medical ward, none daring to speak until the door *clicked*.

Etolié marched forward, struggling to keep her voice calm. "If I'm going to be your nurse, you're going to listen to my instructions, the main one being that unless I'm with you, or unless I know precisely where you are, you don't leave this fucking room."

"Take care how you speak to my wife," Ayla snapped, but Etolié had no time for that tone.

"Oh, fuck off, ya leech. What's a little verbal abuse among friends? That aside, I have a quest for you, Darkleaf."

Etolié had no fear of that scathing glare. They both knew Etolié was the only one who stood a chance of keeping Flowers alive. "I decline in advance."

"That's nice, but I need an extract of scotch sorrel. It's common enough. You'll find it in town in no time."

"I'm not leaving my wife," Ayla spat, but Etolié remained nonplussed.

"We're at an impasse then, because I *will* spitefully camp at my momma's house until your wife gets torn open by little dhampir teeth."

"How dare you—"

Ayla's words cut off at Flowers' touch, her gentle hand cupping her cheek. A monster on a leash; Ayla became amiable under

Flowers' gaze, even softening. "It's all right," Flowridia said. "If Etolié says you must, I trust it's important."

"If anything happens—"

"You'll rip my tongue from my throat and force me to eat it," Etolié interrupted, waving away the threat. "I know. She'll be fine."

Ayla glanced between them, her fury fading as she settled upon Flowridia. She slipped from the bed and stepped back into the shadows, disappearing entirely.

Etolié came forward, sparing a wary glance to Ayla's exit point. "All right, Flowers, listen. Every fucking thing I said stands. If you have any chance of living, it's not about saving you. It's about delaying the inevitable until the baby is born, and we hopefully salvage what's left of you."

"There's something you should know, then," Flowridia said, voice lowering. "But you must swear to not tell."

"Lay it on me."

Flowridia scooted to the edge of the bed, then pointed at the bedside table. "Open that, please."

Etolié touched it, then frowned, feigning ignorance. "It's locked."

"And you can unlock things."

The statement jarred Etolié from any semblance of control. "Excuse me. No one knows that."

"I'm not stupid, Etolié. I worked for you for eight months."

"Well don't fucking tell anyone else," Etolié muttered, disgruntled to say the fucking least. The drawer opened without reserve, and there lay a wooden box.

Flowridia grabbed it, and when she opened it, Etolié reeled at the radiant waves of pure fucking evil. "What the actual—"

A knife, its red hilt some sort of polished stone, its blade a consuming black. Her headache screamed in its presence, and Etolié leaned away from the obviously cursed object. "I'm listening."

Flowridia shut the box. "That knife belongs to Izthuni. It creates creatures like Ayla—"

"What?!"

"Whatever state I'm in, this will make me undead. If the baby is born and I'm at the brink of death, stab me."

Etolié's smile remained plastered, because while that wasn't a bad plan in the existential sense—hell, perhaps Flowers would fucking live in a less literal sense—it was utterly and completely fucking evil. "You want me to stab you with a cursed dagger and turn you into a super-vampire?"

"Keep your voice down," Flowridia spat. "Casvir can't know about it, for reasons I don't think I have to explain."

Given Casvir already had one cursed and very evil necromancy artifact? No explanation needed. Etolié nodded. "You know,

Flowers, this isn't part of my contract, nor what I wanted to get at with this conversation."

Wordlessly, Flowridia slipped the dagger back into the drawer. The lock clicked. "What is your point then?"

"My point is that I truly believe this is stupid, but the fact remains that this is your choice. Not Casvir's, not Ayla's, and not mine. No one but yours. Imperator First and Last seems to think you'll live, though I'm not convinced he knows the risks, but if you want that baby gone, it's fucking gone, bargain or no bargain."

"And enslave Lara's soul?" Flowridia said, incredulity in the phrase.

"Let me worry about that. But, listen, if you want it gone, I'll make it look like a miscarriage."

Darkness fell upon Flowridia's visage, and Etolié, for all her trust in Ayla to not cut her face off in her sleep, oddly didn't trust Flowridia the same way. Such a shifty moral center this bitch had, and Etolié nonchalantly stood and stepped away. "That's not what I want," Flowridia said.

"You're sentimental, Flowers. Of course it isn't what you want. You say you want it, so I'll defend you. I'll stand by your side until your final breath or until the baby breathes its first. People will judge you no matter what you choose—and I'm definitely one of them, don't get me wrong—but I get it. It's not an easy choice."

"How could you possibly understand?"

The bitch's judgement radiated. Etolié took no glee in playing her trump card. "Because I didn't make the choice you did, Flowers, but I still had to make one. Not that I was facing certain death, but I was even younger than you when a bun landed in my metaphorical oven. You think, in ten years of fucking slavers to have a chance at stabbing them, that I didn't lose the roulette? Angels have famously low fertility, but I'm only mostly one."

Flowridia brought a hand to cover her mouth. "I didn't know. I'm sorry."

"No one knows, and life moves on. I don't think about what I did, and I don't regret it either."

Flowridia's fingers lightly caressed the fabric covering her stomach, clear torment on her pretty face. "Is it wrong to want this?"

Etolié sighed, prepared to regret her words. "Wrong? No. Stupid? Closer. But keep in mind that just because it's your decision, it doesn't mean other people won't be affected by it."

Flowridia held the monster's leash, so what happened if Flowridia burned?

What of the baby?

"I want this," Flowridia whispered. "I can change course later, but for now, I want to try. I want to finish my bargain. I want to walk away with no more strings."

Etolié nodded, fearing the wrath of a mercurial Goddess—but that was for her future self to sort out.

Ayla returned, petulant as she all but tossed the elixir to the floor. Thankfully, Etolié could illusion a great many things, including a pile of pillows to cushion the potion's fall. "Thank you. Not like this was important or anything." Etolié popped off the lid, took a whiff of the sharp liquid, then chugged it in one gulp.

"Excuse me?" Ayla said, liable to bite, but Etolié waved her off, savoring the noxious taste and numbing sensation as it went down.

"Oh, that was for me, to prematurely help with the inevitable headache of dealing with your bullshit. Anyway, relax and unwind while I commandeer some servants to build me a nest in your room."

Scotch sorrel invoked hallucinations in lesser folk, but for Etolié, she was merely drunk. She stumbled out of the room, more relaxed than she'd felt in days, despite the murderous vampire growling behind her.

CHAPTER 13

Nine years after the end of the world . . .

"Sir Kitty? Sir Kitty! Won't you please come down?"

Sir Kitty would not, it seemed, and Dira watched despondently as he walked along the courtyard's wall, content to ignore her pleas.

On rare occasions, cats wandered into the courtyard, appearing from thin air, as far as Dira knew. But rarer still would they actually let her pet them.

Vines grew along the wall, and Dira hoisted herself up using the stone and plant growths, determined to win Sir Kitty over. "Don't go too far! Please!"

Sir Kitty merely sauntered along the wall, sparing her a glance and nothing more.

Dira's muscles strained with each motion, but soon she reached the top, heaving herself up into sitting. "Sir Kitty!"

Sir Kitty continued his walk.

Beyond the wall was a sea of trees. Dira took a moment to admire it, even noticed a road. Was that how the gardeners came here? Was that how Sora traveled when she left and returned with food? Surely it was not how Mother traveled. She walked through shadows instead.

And then Dira remembered her quest.

With care, Dira stood atop the rocky wall, finding her bearings as she took her first step. Sir Kitty was far away now. "Come back!"

"Dira?!"

Dira froze, swaying awkwardly atop the high wall.

Sora raced to the base of the wall. Only then did Dira realize she was nearly adjacent to the manor's roof. "What are you doing?!"

"There was a cat."

"Just . . . stay right there. Sit down and don't move!"

Disappointment filled Dira as she obeyed, heartbroken as she watched Sir Kitty disappear down the other side of the wall.

Soon, Sora heaved herself up beside her, though looked far less winded than Dira felt. "You know you could fall and break your neck, right?"

"So could you."

"But I'm an adult." Sora pointed behind her. "Get on my back, kid. I'll carry us down—somehow."

But Dira could not move, suspended by sorrow. "Why didn't he want to be my friend?"

"Because cats don't tend to like people if they weren't raised around them, and I'll bet that was one of the village strays who wandered a bit too far away. Don't take it personally."

Dira forced herself to nod.

When she didn't move, Sora's hand appeared around her shoulders, pulling her close. "Talk to me."

The feelings struggled to emerge. Oh, what to name this terrible thing? "I just . . . I feel . . . lonely."

To her surprise, Sora nodded. "I see that. If you let me help you down, I promise to talk to your mother, all right?"

Something within Dira came alight. "You mean it?"

"Of course I do."

Oh, but what would that bring? Companions? Friends? A trip down the road? Dira's smile spread wide as she clung to Sora's back.

Sora, however, groaned as she slid to the wall's side. "You're lucky you're tiny."

And that evening, after Dira bathed and changed for bed, there came a knock at her door. "Come in!"

Mother peered inside, her coy smile utterly alien. "Sorry I'm a little late, Dira Darling. But I had a few friends stop me on my way."

The door swung all the way open, revealing a basket in Mother's arms, and inside—

Dira gasped and ran forward, her joy radiant to see two little kittens peering out. Her squeal came unbidden, and she laughed when they meowed right back. "Are they for me?!"

"Of course. Two new friends for my Dira."

Yet despite the love bubbling from her heart, despite the precious little kittens to love . . . Dira's heart sank.

She sat when Mother beckoned, forcing a smile when the first kitten plopped into her lap—a calico, which meant it was a lovely little girl, with eyes as green as emeralds—and despite the affection filling her, Dira sniffed back tears.

Mother held the other—a scruffy grey kitten with golden eyes—to her own chest, and Dira hated to see her worry, hated to see her disappointed. The kitten struggled, but Mother had eyes only for her. "Do you not like them?"

"I love them," Dira replied, and it was the purest truth. The kitten seemed confused as she meowed up at Dira, but when she brought a hand down to pet her, she rubbed her head against her hand. "I just . . . I thought, when Sora said she'd talk to you, that I would get an elven friend."

Mother set the kitten down next to its companion in Dira's lap, the duo immediately leaping upon each other. "Darling . . ." Mother did not breathe, and so her sighs were rare—and poignant. "I see. You need a friend your age."

"I just get a little lonely sometimes."

When Mother scooted closer, she scooped up a kitten attempting to climb Dira's thigh. "Mind their claws. You will likely get scratched here and there as they learn. They can't control themselves yet."

"Mother—"

"I know. I am thinking." Mother brought the kitten to her neck, then frowned as she stared it in the eye.

"Is it all right?"

"He is perfectly fine," Mother muttered, her voice far away. "There is a particular . . . well, *godly* friend of mine who owes me a great many favors. I wonder . . ." Mother glanced from the kitten to Dira, her smile twisting to something frightful. "Be patient with me, Dira love. I will find you a friend."

Dira took a breath to speak her excitement—only to gasp and giggle when her calico kitten leapt onto her nightgown. She didn't even mind the stinging pinpricks as she climbed. She only laughed and kissed her little head when the kitten made it to her shoulder.

"In the meantime, I am well aware you won't be going to bed on time," Mother said, her teasing apparent as she set the other kitten onto Dira's head, where it gripped her slowly forming locs. "Would you like to help me set up a sleeping area for them?"

Dira wrangled the two kittens back into her arms, heart warmed anew. "Yes, please."

Current era . . .

The exhilaration of flying never wavered. Sora gazed upon the world from new heights, tucked safely in Uluron's grasp.

"How much longer?!" she cried into the open air, her stomach lurching when those massive claws brought her up to face the great dragon.

Patience, Sora. Just a few hours more.

But Sora could not be patient, the incessant stirring within her fueled by both anxiety and a lack of Spore. Dira was gone. Dira was a monster. Dira had apparently orchestrated the death of Sol Kareena. Dira . . .

"Name the way."

"Kill her."

But kill who? Dira herself? Or had that been a lie to protect her true motive?

"One of us is lying."

Had Dira spoken any truths at all?

But Uluron had insight. *My mother told me she did not wish to be separated again, and should we be lost, to meet in Tierzuroth.*

Back to the elves.

Sora settled into a fetal position, deeming it the safest way to doze. Her hand skimmed past her locket, wishing she had not lost her mirror. Flowridia was pregnant, and Sora wished so badly to be at her side and celebrate this strange but blessed news. However, the child was unborn, and the ghost of Chaos was tangible and real. Sora's first duty remained to what was here now, but her mind would not settle.

Instead, Sora managed to smile at her parents' images in her locket, her mother's features painfully reminiscent of Tazel, of Mereen, even Sarai who she had barely met. But also her own self, and Sora felt pride to carry that bloodline, even if she had shirked the name.

And then her father, whose beaming smile her sister embodied. Not Dira, no. Dira was Odessa in ways that Sora still reeled to consider, for Odessa was something Sora had yet to put to rest. Dira's smile held mischief, her laughter carried malevolence, but Dira herself was . . .

. . . Sora wished she knew. Dira was kind and full of life, but Dira had orchestrated the death of a goddess Sora loved. But she could not deny the love in Dira's gaze in her lucid moments, the childish joy directed at Sora. So what was this monster that had taken hold of her? Dira was sometimes Dira, but who was Chaos?

The light waned when Uluron descended into the Gozrith Jungle, the capital city awaiting. Yet as Uluron gracefully broke through the canopy of trees, already Sora felt something amiss in the scenery.

Be alert. Something is different.

Uluron touched the ground. Her words might've been laughable, were it a laughing matter.

For there was nothing. There was no Tierzuroth.

Evidence of rubble, yes. Ancient trees torn apart, shredded like paper. The once-massive wall was simply flat terrain, as though rolled over by a gargantuan carriage. No statues, no homes, no hall for the executor—nothing.

Sora gripped tight to the stability of Uluron's bone finger, dazed at the cleanliness of it. For though memories of the Theocracy's downfall haunted her on sleepless nights, the screams, the blood, the bodies—there was none of that here. "Set me down."

Uluron obeyed, and Sora stumbled into the gargantuan circle of rubble, verifying her observation. Nothing dead was here.

No birds sang, but Uluron was an imposing enough presence to account for that. No lingering aura of dread and death, no unholy curse upon this land. The destruction held peace.

"What could have done this?" Sora's voice echoed across the amphitheater of trees, the sole living voice amid the debris.

My Father has the power, but it is not in his character. Nor would he have a motive.

Sora's boots scuffed against wreckage, mostly dirt and wood. No food, no supplies, no children's toys—too organized to be a traditional genocide. A new fear froze her, though it did not quite fit the puzzle. "Forgive me, but could it have been Chaos? She turned into . . . something."

I cannot fathom my Mother's motive either. Not in any form.

Sora stepped over shattered glass, seeking any explanation at all. What did it mean, for Tierzuroth to simply be gone? With eyes peeled to the destruction, lest she trip, she asked, "Your mother turned into something. A-A beast. Do you know what it was?"

I do. The 'beast,' as you called it, is not Mother. A part of Mother, yes, but not her. He is something different.

Sora stilled at that, unable to deny the course of shivers running down her spine at the idea. Dira had begged her never to name it, yet Uluron spoke of this . . . *other* with affection. "Can you explain?"

Laughter laced Uluron's elegant voice, a nostalgic sort of joy within it. *He was not a parent. A brother and a friend. He was mischief and would allow my brothers and sisters and I to miss our naps and roll in our own filth. He taught us to hunt and fight as would suit a dragon. The only uncomfortable truth to admit amid all the beautiful memories was that, unlike Mother, he despised Father.*

"So Chaos truly is two people?"

I never knew, Sora. I never thought to ask. I simply assumed everyone's mothers had multiple forms.

Sora resumed her cautious exploration, uncertain of what to make of any of it, but she forgot all that as she reached what she could only assume was the former town center.

A perfect circle had been cleared among the ruins, larger in diameter than Sora was tall. Emblazoned in the earth, fire still smoldering at the edges, was a frightful sigil, the demonic character quite clear.

Ku'Shya, Goddess of War, had been here.

The truth settled in cursed layers—that Khastra had been found here, that Etolié had surely told anyone who would listen, and that Ku'Shya . . .

"But no one is dead," Sora muttered.

What have you found?

Sora crept back from the symbol, darkness descending with each step. A spark of holy light appeared in her hand, yet there was no comfort in the gesture. The eerie peace dissolved into dread, for the entrance to *Daemenacht* was near.

"It was Goddess Ku'Shya."

Uluron's silhouette shone starkly against the night sky, the stars and celestial visions thick enough to illuminate her white figure. She came closer to meet Sora, stepping haphazardly on debris. *Will she return?*

"I don't know, but . . . I remember the executor was afraid of what would happen if she found out they had been hiding Khastra in their city. It has to be connected."

Uluron's glowing eyes surveyed the dark jungle, no peace in her sudden alertness. *Be silent.*

Sora obeyed, following Uluron's line of sight. Nothing sang among the trees; no birds, no howling creatures. Yet a glimmer of silver cut through the blackness beyond. Sora withdrew a knife.

It charged. Sora readied her weapon, even as Uluron shifted to grab her—

And gasped as the world became . . . nothing.

Sora blinked, blind save for a pool of light engulfing her. Weapon readied, she stepped forward, yet made no progress at all, trapped within this spot of light.

Thought I'd finally lost you, Sora.

It was not Uluron, though the voice pervaded the corners of her mind instead of her ears. Nor was it Dira, for it was not a woman, no . . . "Chaos?"

So you do have thoughts in that dumb head of yours.

. . . Nor was it a man. This voice held the androgyny of a child, though derision marred its innocence. "Are you Uluron's, um, friend?"

She told you?

Sora attempted another step, yet nothing changed in her magical prison. "A little bit. Is this real?"

Your brain thinks it is.

"Why am I here? What did you do?"

Dira says I have to stop my nonsense. She agreed to let us talk. Only talk. No eye for an eye. Too bad. I'd love to rip yours out.

Sora lowered her weapon, finding no sense in fighting in a mind prison. Chaos ruled this realm, whatever it was. "You're the one who keeps threatening me."

It's only fair.

"What does that mean?"

It means we'll never be even, but it helps me feel better.

Though her better judgement screamed, Sora slipped the weapon back into her wrist sheath, letting her arms fall slack. "Dira is my niece. I knew her in another life. But who are you?"

It's a secret. But Dira says you'll keep it.

Something shifted in the darkness beyond, a figure pacing beyond the comprehension of her vision. Yet Sora stiffened not at the sight but at its gait—for it did not walk, it lumbered oddly, as though . . . not a humanoid. "I swear to never share whatever you're about to show me."

I believe you, Sora. You kept mom's secrets, too.

Too personal. Too . . . direct. "Do I know you now?"

The entity paused, and Sora swore she caught a glimpse of gold. *If you don't, I'll take back my promise and eat you.*

It grew with each step; its distance farther than Sora had anticipated. Bestial, yes, and within the fraying darkness approached a creature Sora could not meet the eye of, so massive it stood. Akin to horses bred for half-giants, but this was no steed. Emerging from the blackness was a giant wolf—one eye whole, the other one glowing from an empty, shattered socket.

Sora swayed, struggling to draw her breath as she stared up at this ghost—for he was, oh he *was*, one of many who appeared in her nightmares. "Oh, gods . . ."

Chaos held threadbare sanity, spoke of voices in her head, her form mutilated not by injury but by dark, demonic magic.

And what had Odessa said of witches who consumed their familiars? They were never the same again.

Say my name.

Sora stared into death's visage, for she had watched his final breath—and his brutal, violent end facing the barrel of Mereen's gun. "Demitri."

Sora blinked, and the world reappeared.

She faced a sky of stars, the clearing left by the leveling of Tierzuroth leaving one beautiful thing. Another blink, and a face appeared—a silhouette backlit by those same celestial lights, but Sora would know Dira's shadow in any life.

And though it was Dira, her locs distinctive, moonlight illuminated a frightful truth to her countenance. A skeletal hand caressed her face, drawing their gazes to meet. Yet the bones were not human, no. A paw, yes. And Sora knew it now to be a wolf.

That frightful visage bore half of Dira's face, but the other half was bone—a wolf's skull, deformed to fit her beautiful face. One eye reflected silver; the wolf's eye glowed gold. There was beauty in her broken smile, part of her lips torn away in the macabre deformation of her face. A second glance revealed exposed neckbones disappearing beneath her tunic, culminating in the skeletal, bestial arm. Moonlight cast her shadow, no longer hidden behind what was surely magic. Not a woman, no, but an animal's shape. Watching within was the wolf himself. "Sora?"

She spoke kindly, and so it was Dira.

Yet Sora's adrenaline surged, leaping up as she whipped out one of her many knives—only to grow dizzy from the speed, stumbling until Uluron's claw righted her.

Chaos rose, hands held to placate. Around her neck, she wore the pouch containing her anchor. "Sora, I do not know precisely what you overheard in the temple, but—"

"You're a witch." Sora's memory roared with the haunting refrains from Odessa of familiars and those desperate enough to consume them. "You're a witch, and you ate your familiar. That's why you're . . . u-unstable."

Chaos' smile held amusement and cruelty both, but perhaps that was not her fault. "You can say I am insane."

"You're not, though. You're more calculating than Soliel. You have an agenda. You . . ." Sora's breath came as a gasp, her mind reeling from every new revelation. "You're Demitri."

"Sometimes, yes. He always speaks. Sometimes he manages to break through. Sometimes I allow it because it's easier to give in."

"Who granted you Demitri as a familiar?"

"Ayla."

The name rang like an omen in the silent night.

Sora rapidly shook her head, uncertain if she would cry or scream. "You killed Sol Kareena."

"That was clearly Soliel—"

"You *knew she would die!*"

Chaos faced the earth, her skeletal hand grasping her fleshy wrist. "And what a perfect rallying cry it was. I felt the godly pledges. Whatever you said afterward, kudos."

Sora's rage simmered, arm trembling as she held the knife aloft. "How dare you."

"I'm trying to thank you—"

"Shut up!" Sora took a step back, knife readied. "Don't you *dare* make me a part of this!"

"It wasn't always like this between us, you know," Chaos said. "You and I were thick as thieves. You practically raised me—"

Sora took another step. "I've killed family before."

"So you will walk away and go where? Leave me to hunt down your sister on my own—" Chaos wrenched herself to the side, anger pulling her mutilated mouth into a grimace. "You won't."

Sora warily lowered her weapon. "I want to talk to Demitri."

With the eerie twist of Chaos' head, her skeletal side facing out, Sora knew without the confirmation. "I'm speaking."

"You said, 'one of us is lying'—and you meant her. You've only ever told me the truth, as nasty as it was."

"Your point?"

"My point is that you're going to give me straighter answers than Dira. So tell me this, Demitri—who did you tell Soliel to kill?"

"Be more specific."

"In the cave, you said to 'kill her.' Was it Dira? Or was it Flowridia?"

"You're stupid. You really think I would kill Mom?"

Sora curtailed her own insults. "I see your point. In my defense, I didn't know it was you then. So . . . why?"

Chaos shifted uncomfortably, the unnatural stance revealing her bestial self. "Dira said she'd tell you when Etolié was here."

And so Etolié . . . was right. "This was never about Flowridia. Dira only wanted Flowridia dead so it would kill her unborn child."

"No. Dira would prefer to kill her too. She's just willing to compromise."

"And . . ." Sora's grip on her knife wavered, sudden emotion rising. "A-And Soliel wants to save Flowridia. Is she going to die? Will she die in childbirth?"

Chaos remained impossible to read, staring as blankly as the animal she was. "I don't know."

"You don't know, or you won't tell me?"

"Both."

Sora shoved that unnerving answer aside—for now. "I suppose that's it, then. I'll leave you two alone."

When Sora turned, a more soothing voice chilled her blood. "Really? That's awfully selfish, Sora."

Sora marched toward the distant trees, or as well as she could as she navigated the rubble.

"Yes, I orchestrated the death of your beloved goddess," Chaos shouted—and it was Dira once more. "She was always dead in my time. So was it me? Was it fate? Who can say. But we sacrificed one to gain how many pledges of power? Let me tell you a bitter truth, Sora. The angels failed us. They are passive, listless fools, too acquainted with luxury to get off their arses and save the world, much less see the threat of Casvir. In my time, Soliel and I entreated them for aid, and they said no. The demons? They joined us, and every one of them perished because they were the first to show up to the fight. Only once Sha'Demoni was a graveyard did Celestière take notice—and it was too late!"

Sora stilled in her steps, blood boiling, pounding in her ears.

"You saw it in the meeting," Chaos continued. "You saw them quarrel like chickens in a coop rather than unite against the greater threat of the God of Order. Nothing *short* of Sol Kareena's death would have gotten them to unite. But now? We have a chance."

Sora's fury festered, rejecting the truth in the words. "I'm done with you. You have Uluron. You don't need me."

"Dammit, I do need you!"

The only sound became Sora's careful steps. Slipping wouldn't do well for a confident exit.

"I always needed you, Sora!"

Sora did pause for that, hating her intrigue at the crack in Chaos' voice. She looked back, daring Chaos to speak.

Chaos stood so small, but Chaos was known to manipulate. "You did raise me. Mother was often gone, but you were there. You fed me, you taught me to read, to climb, to hunt, you tucked me in bed most nights, and I cried myself to sleep for years after your death. Demitri never liked you, but I loved you. I still do. I felt invincible when you were at my side—and I still do." Chaos' lip trembled. She could not cry in this body, or so she claimed, but her ensuing gasp so painfully masked a sob. "Gods, I am so lost."

Sora watched her warily, combating the rise of empathy inside her. "Do you feel any remorse at all for what you did?"

"For orchestrating Sol Kareena's death?" Chaos shut her eyes, face falling into her bony hand. "She was a tool to wield. Her death was for the greater good. But I hate that I broke your heart. I'm sorry."

Sora kept her glare, even as she took a tentative step back toward her despondent niece. "You betrayed me."

"I know."

"Say you're sorry for that too."

"I am sorry for betraying you."

Sora stood her ground, finding her heart still lay in pieces. Hope was gone, and there was no goddess to pray to and restore it. "I used to think I understood the greater good. But I learned I have my limits. When the monstrous acts you commit make you just as monstrous as what you came to destroy, it's gone too far. You didn't murder Sol Kareena. You just made sure she was given to the monster who would. I've done exactly that—stood by while a monster did the work I couldn't do myself. But I wasn't innocent. And I'm still paying for that sin."

Chaos remained still, gaze set to the ground. "What do you want me to pay?"

"You *can't*. No matter what's done, Sol Kareena is dead."

The statement lingered in the air like smoke. Chaos said nothing at all.

Sora's fists clenched, hating the words even before she spoke. "For the sake of the greater good, I'll rejoin you. I'll stand by your side as you gather pledges from gods. But if you *ever* use me or lie to me like this again—even a lie by omission—I'm gone. Just because you need me doesn't mean you get to use me. Do you understand?"

Chaos nodded.

"I know you—both of you—want Soliel dead. I trust that one, single thing. But once that's done, I rescind all loyalty to you. My goddess will be avenged, or I'll die trying." Sora offered a hand.

Chaos stepped forward, taking Sora's hand in her one of flesh. "Worry not. I will kill myself for you."

Given Chaos had all but stated that as her goal before, Sora believed her.

"What's next?" Chaos whispered.

"There are two angelic gods we don't have the pledges of—Morathma and Staella. And of course, there are the demon gods. The entrance to Ku'Shya's Realm is in this jungle, but she doesn't exactly like me. We would be wise to ask Etolié to advocate for us. She's waiting for us in Solvira."

"To Solvira, then?"

"To Solvira."

Part Three
STARS

CHAPTER 14

Nine years after the end of the world . . .

On a warm spring day, Dira teased her two new feline friends, Narella and Nilly, with a feather in the garden, laughing at each of their clumsy leaps.

Each were brave in their own way, friendly and affectionate too, though Nilly was more inclined to nap in Dira's arms, whereas Narella loved to guard her bed from above. Their own beds had been long abandoned.

"Dammit all! Keep him away—"

Sora's yelp echoed even as far as the garden.

Dira abandoned her feather and scooped up her kittens, running to the manor instead. Was there danger? Was Sora hurt? Was Mother here to save them?

Dira dashed through the kitchen, perched her kittens on the counter, and grabbed a knife instead. Sora had taught her to not run with knives unless the job was worth the risk. Anything that made Sora scream was surely of that caliber.

A bestial snarl pulsed adrenaline through Dira's blood. When she burst into the entry hall, she nearly ran into Sora—who narrowly ducked to avoid her blade.

But she couldn't apologize. Dira's tongue froze to witness what beast stood before them.

Mother stood beside it, unbothered as she stroked its fuzzy cheek. "What do you think of him, Dira Darling?"

Truthfully, her first thought was terror. But muzzled, the wolf did seem docile, at least. And large, though that failed to capture the scope of him. The wolf towered above any horse she had seen, his bulk surely not natural, no.

"I'm out," Sora said. "I'm not getting my arm ripped off today. Don't call me until he gets his brains back." Sora left, leaving Dira to study the wolf alone.

"What is he?" Dira asked, still clutching her knife.

"He is a dire wolf named Demitri, and he is for you."

Dira stayed warily in her corner, her confusion rising. Even in Mother's expansive entry hall, the beast seemed to fill the room. "For me?"

"I should explain. I apologize." Mother came forward. The wolf tried to follow, only for Mother to hold up a hand, the silent command apparently conveyed. "You wanted a friend. And I know he is an unconventional solution, but you are familiar with the concept of familiars, right?"

"Familiars give power to witches, like Mom."

"Precisely, darling. But what you may not realize is there is no better companion for a person to have. A familiar is a piece of your soul in physical form, the truest friend you could ask for. He will know your thoughts and feelings as though they were his own. Whether or not he will talk is unknown, but he is at least a start. What do you say, Dira? Familiars come with the gift of magic as well. Is that something you want?"

The idea was strange . . . and intriguing. "I already have magic."

"It would be more, the extent to which even I cannot predict." Mother deftly took the knife from her grip and replaced it with her hand instead. "Demitri is very special, however. A familiar must be in the same state of life as its witch, and you, being half dead, are a puzzle. And so, he is too. He was killed before your birth and brought back and tidied up with the aid of a contact I had initially thought might be your godly patron. Instead . . . I was told it could be me. In any case, I took it upon myself to add back the pieces to make him at least somewhat alive. His spirit remains through necromancy, but he is warm to the touch. His heart beats. And he has proved himself to be a fierce protector in the past. I can think of no grander legacy than to bequeath him to you, my darling."

With the reassurance of Mother's hand, Dira dared approach, curious to look into his eyes—such soothing shades of gold. "You know him?"

"He belonged to your mom. He was her whole heart, and who better to protect you, my love?"

Dira stilled at that, caught at the cusp of destiny, for this was a mantle she was shy to accept. "Is that allowed?"

"Darling, I can promise she would love nothing more than to think the little boy she loved most could have a sister."

How curious, his gaze, intelligence somewhere behind those glazed eyes. Dira carefully offered a hand, but shied when Mother shook her head. "The connection ritual has already been done. The final component is your touch. So be certain, my Dira. He will become a piece of your soul."

No hesitation; Dira stroked the fur behind his muzzle, the connection as natural as sunshine upon petals. Magic had a sensation, a song in her blood, and it rose to new heights in this binding of souls. Dira felt so much, yet so little. It was not painful at all, yet when she looked once again in his eyes, she saw not a wolf, but a mirror.

Everything in Demitri's stance shifted, his gaze darting all about the space, as though understanding for the first time—and she knew, she *knew* that he was confused, the knowledge as clear as the beat of her heart in her throat.

He looked intently to Mother. "There is so much you have missed, Demitri," Mother said, "and much I would like to discuss with you alone. But it is truly wonderful to have you back. Your mother is gone, but . . ." She gestured to Dira, which his golden gaze followed. "This is Dira, and she is our daughter. I place her in your charge."

That's a lot to take in.

Dira gasped and stumbled back, for the sound was . . . within.

How in the world did Mom and Lady Ayla make a baby?

He sounded so young, younger than even she. "I don't know. How does anyone make a baby?"

It wasn't that she didn't expect a response, but nothing could have prepared her for it. *You look a lot like Mom.* The wolf came forward. This time, Dira kept her stance. *I don't like this muzzle.*

"M-Mother, can you take off the . . ."

Mother understood and obeyed, deftly removing the strings. Demitri stretched his gargantuan jaw, capable of engulfing her entire torso. *That feels much better. Tell her thank you, please.*

"Demitri says thank you."

Mother's chuckle was so sweet, so . . . foreign. "You are very welcome."

It's nice talking to someone again. Dira giggled as Demitri's nose sniffed around her head, her locs, though it escalated into laughter when his tongue slathered across half her face. *You're just a little kid.*

"I'm not little. I'm nine—"

Demitri curled his paw around her body, pulling her close to his fur. A hug, of sorts, and Dira embraced him back, the exhilaration fading into simply . . . affection.

I have a lot of feelings. I'm not really sure what to do with them yet. But I'm happy to be here with you.

Current era . . .

"He's a little vacant, but he's still a baby boy."

Flowridia managed to chuckle at Etolié's odd choice in words, perhaps desperate for any comfort in this bittersweet prison.

The evening air chilled Flowridia's skin, stimulating after so long cooped up inside. In his cage, Demitri lay in stasis. He stared with one golden eye, the other a macabre hole, hints of his skull visible in the lingering sunset. Despite the disturbing image, Flowridia took comfort in watching his eye track their motions. No recognition, but there remained awareness, at least.

When Etolié reached through the cage's bars, Flowridia stopped her. "You shouldn't do that. He'll snap at you."

Etolié brought her hand back, calculation falling upon her pretty face. "Will he snap at *you?*"

Flowridia couldn't speak of it, lest she break her heart anew. She nodded instead.

Etolié hummed a simple tune. To Flowridia's shock, Demitri stirred. First, he merely sharpened his stare, entranced by the sound, then rose by labored degrees, as though weighed down by stone. But Demitri sat, nearly lifelike as he watched Etolié, whatever magic she emitted enchanting something inside him.

"Come here, baby boy," Etolié sang, her tune nonsensical. Flowridia gasped as he obeyed, emotion rising to choke her when he stopped at the edge. Etolié reached through without fear, running a hand across his coarse fur. She continued singing, *"He's calm. You can touch him."*

Flowridia could not slip through the bars, nor did she have the key to his cage. But she reached as far inside as she was able, managing to bring her arms around his neck with only the bar between them. Her hand tingled today, a numb sort of pain radiating if she jostled it, but she swallowed the discomfort, desperate to find the strength to hug her beloved familiar.

Of course she wept. Of course she savored his smell—warm despite the chill of death. Yet heartbreak lay in his stillness. No reciprocation. No little voice in her head teasing her for her tears or telling her he loved her.

Demitri was here yet remained far away.

When Flowridia pulled away, she wiped her tears on her sleeve, fighting to hold back a sob. Etolié's song faded, and immediately Demitri's stance shifted, becoming defensive. Hackles raised, he stumbled back, fur bristling.

"Demitri . . ." But Flowridia's plea faded. There was nothing to do.

With the setting sun came the extinguishing of hope, leaving only Etolié's golden wings for light. "If we do this a little every day, he might start to respond better."

That hope returned. Flowridia grasped it tight. "You mean that?"

"He's undead, so it'll take time. But even the undead can learn a few things. I'm not saying he'll be affectionate or even friendly, but he might not be afraid."

Flowridia couldn't help but fall into her arms, clinging tight to this woman who was her enemy and savior both. She felt Etolié's stiffness, then acceptance, her thin figure matching the grip of her hug. "You give good hugs, Flowers. I'll give you that."

Demitri's growls had quelled. He simply glared from the shadows. Flowridia offered a small wave, unsurprised when it led to nothing. "I love you, Demitri."

Perhaps somewhere, somehow, he heard. Even if he couldn't understand, he heard.

The darkness swept a chill across Flowridia's skin, her good hand rubbing instinctively against her bare arm. "Let's go back."

"You tired?"

"No, just cold."

"Good, because I'm dragging you to the library. It's the one redeeming quality in this prison."

Flowridia followed along, unwilling to argue with the flippant use of 'prison.' Nox'Kartha was not a cage to her, but pregnancy was proving to be its own sort of cell, trapped in her own body. Thus everything connected became an extension, her medical suite in particular.

The night was young, the crisp air more invigorating than discomforting. Etolié's wings provided ample light, and Flowridia, still unused to their presence, studied their undulating motions. Etolié had never been so free to show them in Staelash, constantly complaining of grabbing hands and narrow hallways, but she had fewer qualms here. They were beautiful; Etolié was beautiful, but the happiness found in her presence held a perpetual shadow. They were not friends. Etolié was here by contract and nothing more.

Flowridia knew it was deserved, but the sting of that casualty lingered.

"Ugh, my skin is crawling." Etolié twitched as she glanced about the darkness beyond her wings. "Where's Darkleaf? I keep expecting her to jump out of the shadows and . . . I don't know, tap me on the shoulder."

"She's been reading up on dhampir pregnancies today. Per her account, it's been at least six hundred years since she's done any research on it and wants to know if any new technology or magic has been discovered. She's fairly confident she'll find nothing, given how rare dhampirs are. But she's anxious and needs to feel helpful—her words." Flowridia cracked a smile. "So while I don't think your fears are unfounded, I think she's too stressed to play any pranks."

"I *will* stab her. Make sure she knows."

"I think she would expect nothing less—"

A shadow shifted. But Ayla would never be so obvious.

Flowridia froze when a knife glinted in the darkness, its wielder sprinting toward them. Masked and covered from head to toe in black fabric, Flowridia froze at the first sting of the blade against her stomach.

But when she flinched, awaiting death, it never came.

Flowridia opened her eyes, witness to a hyperventilating Etolié wielding a miniature re-creation of Khastra's crystal hammer. Flecks of blood and gore coated the edges. The assassin lay groaning on the ground, clutching his head.

Etolié shrieked. A cage fell over the man, appearing from thin air. "Help! Someone help!"

Flowridia stared in a daze upon the masked person, hardly hearing Etolié's cries, until—

"Flowers, you're bleeding!"

Caught in a fog, Flowridia brought her hand to the wound on her stomach. Shallow, yet it seeped warm blood, staining her hand in deep hues of red. Before she could think, before she could feel, a plethora of guards appeared, as though summoned like the cage. Flowridia did not fight being led away, taken from Etolié's light as the Celestial frantically rambled her story.

The world blurred as Flowridia stared at her bloodstained hand, her other falling protectively around her womb. Firm, but hardly swollen at all. None would imagine she was expecting if they saw her on the street.

But life was there. And life stained Flowridia's hands.

In the medical ward, she allowed the nurses to fuss over her, tending to the wound without magic for the baby's sake. "Once Empress Etolié returns, she can fix you up properly," the head physician said, though worry remained on her aged features. "Are you all right?"

"Am I?" Flowridia whispered, yet she did not recognize her own voice, nor her compulsion to speak.

"The wound is shallow and clean, and there is no sign of poison. Whoever did this was very precise, however. Much deeper, and it would have punctured your uterus."

Flowridia remained quiet as a nurse washed the blood from her hand, the soreness of the wound finally settling. Not so bad, but it stung when she shifted.

"And the baby is fine?" she finally asked.

"There is no reason to imagine it isn't, but I can perform a spell to check."

Flowridia nodded, uncertain of this rising heat within her. By every god, she could have died. And the baby . . .

Flowridia said nothing as the physician placed glowing hands upon her womb, avoiding the bandages. "You can breathe easy. The baby is alive."

Despite the confirmation, Flowridia felt no relief. "Thank you."

The door burst open, and in stumbled Etolié's flustered form. "Fucking hell, are you dying?!"

The most startling factor was that Etolié seemed near tears, her panic sincere as she came to Flowridia's side. "No. I'm fine. You . . . You saved my life."

"Hammer to the face is a pretty effective way to stop an assassin," Etolié stammered. "D-Do you need healing?"

Flowridia lifted her shirt, revealing the bandaged wound.

A whirlwind sprinted through a shadow.

Ayla gasped and nearly collapsed before her, fear in her large eyes as she took Flowridia's face in her hands. "They told me what happened. Who did this to you?"

"I don't know," Flowridia said, yet remained numb to it all, hardly aware of the passing of her pain to Etolié.

"Casvir has him in the dungeon," Etolié said, groaning as she curled upon the bed, waving away the nurses even as blood stained what Flowridia knew was an illusioned dress. "They want to question the bastard and figure out who sent him."

Flowridia rose, the compulsion as natural as breathing. "Then I will visit Casvir in the dungeon."

"Darling, stay here," Ayla said, coaxing her vainly to sit. A tear fell down her face, carving a trail across her stark features. "The stress isn't good for you."

"I'm not stressed." Flowridia continued her march, even as Ayla took her hand and followed.

"Flowra, please take a moment—"

Flowridia wrenched her hand away, anger spiking. "You either come with me or stay behind, but don't you dare try and stop me."

Panic had etched itself into Ayla's features, her posture shrinking as she nodded.

Flowridia marched forward, aware of graceful footsteps trailing behind.

"The assassin has been silent since his arrest," Casvir said, encroaching darkness all around.

Gone were the rich carpets and tapestries showcased in the palace's public areas. Flowridia walked upon stark stone, cold radiating from the austere walls. The occasional crystal sconce cast light, but shadows flickered as though alive. Beside her, Ayla was her own living shadow.

Flowridia felt nothing. Not even the cold.

"A witch has been sent for, to cast a Circle of Truth," Casvir continued. "Though he can choose to remain silent, it will be made certain it is not in his best interest." He spared a glance for Ayla. "There is no one better than you at non-lethal torture. Would you like the honor?"

Some simmer of a thrill jolted through Flowridia. To her surprise, however, Ayla shook her head. "Respectfully, I am too invested."

"That is understandable."

They descended a flight of stairs. Deeper underground, screams sang their elegy behind the walls. Not simply one. An amalgamation. Each closed door was a prison, and not all prison accommodations were comfortable.

There rose the visceral memory of Mereen's dungeon, but Flowridia drove her nails into her palm to shove it away. No, no— these were not her screams. This was not her prison. Ayla was here, but there was nothing monstrous in her countenance. The woman was a stranger with her vulnerable stance, but she was not a monster.

And Casvir, for all his faults, was not someone for her to fear.

The screams continued, as faint as a night breeze, and they sent a shiver down her spine just the same.

Eventually, Casvir came upon a guarded door, skeletal soldiers stepping aside at his silent command. Casvir held the door, and within Flowridia beheld a new sort of monster.

Her would-be assassin sat upon a chair in chains, placed in the center of a large, circular prison cell. Numerous armored skeletons guarded from the wall, their weapons readied in case the prisoner twitched.

It was not a simple chamber, however. Various scalpels and frightful blades dotted the walls, their purpose clear. Nothing complex. Nothing like Ayla's laboratory in the basement. Knives and needles and all manner of piercing weapons—no less effective in a creative torturer's hands.

The assassin's head wound was bandaged though not healed by any magic. His pointed ears and cutting features revealed his heritage immediately, but far more fascinating were the subtle purple hues to his skin, nearly translucent. An odd sallowness dented the Whispering Elf's cheeks, but he seemed otherwise healthy aside from his wounds.

The iron door creaked shut. "I assume you do not know this man," came Casvir's voice, its volcanic depths appropriate for the atmosphere.

"No." Flowridia left Ayla's protective presence, holding out a hand for her to stay behind. She entered the circular chamber, holding the gaze of her would-be murderer. No remorse; no fear.

The memory of pain lingered in the flecks of blood upon her gown. But something far more virulent rose to surpass the idle sting. Anger pulsed through her veins, fueling her better than adrenaline ever could. "Who was your target? Me, or the baby?"

The man said nothing, though his eyes flicked to her womb, following where her good hand rested.

Something was . . . off. "Open your mouth."

He did not, though he glared.

"Ayla, force his mouth open."

Ayla appeared at the call, selecting a knife from the wall. She did not use the blade, but the blunt end, wasting no time in jamming it against his teeth. The man cried out, but the metal pried his jaw open, revealing precisely what Flowridia feared.

The man had no tongue. It had been cut out.

"There are assassin guilds who remove the assassin's tongue before a mission," Ayla said, "and restore it upon its completion. They cannot be tortured into talking."

"How unfortunate," Flowridia muttered.

When Ayla came to her side, Flowridia slid the knife from her grip, finding its weight comforting in this horrible place. Gods, it was cold—so cold—and with that came the memory of pain, of cowering beneath a bloodied table, awaiting her torturer's return—

Instinct rose, and Flowridia tried to clench her fist. Instead, the blade punctured her skin. Blood pooled into her hand, the wound shallow but long. Minutes ago, she had been stained by her own life fluid, but death had not been intended for her. She was merely a casualty.

"You can still turn your head. You can give me a yes or no. Did Executor Faeborn send you to murder my baby?"

The man stared warily as she approached but did not shift his head either way. The first inklings of fear appeared upon his face, and Flowridia . . . smiled.

Purely instinct, yet she could not deny her glee. Her pulse pounded in her ears, stammering her speech. "I-I'm sorry. Did you already forget what you nearly did?"

She slashed the knife across his stomach, mimicking her own wound. The man cried out, the sound invigorating. Not too deep, no. It would only be deadly if infected.

And while the man did deserve death, there would be no joy in that—not yet.

Amid his cries, laughter wracked Flowridia's figure, echoing across the walls in malevolent tones. "So you remember now? How you came to murder an unborn child? A gentle baby with precious curls—"

She brought the knife to his forehead, carving a slice of skin from his hairline.

"Perhaps little dimples to kiss—"

She impaled the knife through his cheeks, one after the other.

The man gurgled his screams, blood spilling into and from his mouth. Flowridia let him flounder, her laughter never ceasing even as it quieted. The lingering echo sang louder, causing an unexpected thrill through her blood. "Ten little fingers to count—"

She impaled the first finger, an easy target with how the man was chained. He screamed and clenched his fist—so she drove it through his hand instead and yanked, slashing the digit nearly in half. It hung by threads of flesh and sinew, blood pouring onto the chains and wooden chair.

Through his choking sobs, Flowridia heard a semblance of begging, hindered by his lack of tongue. He met her eye, pain and pleas in his falling tears.

She pierced his untouched hand, severing skin down to the bone. He screamed anew, yet she hardly heard it, deafened by her own pulse. Each gristly cut evoked a sensation she knew; a sensation she had once savored.

Gods, she thought she had lost the euphoria of necromancy. Yet the high rose to even surpass her pulsing rage. Power surged through her veins, rejuvenated by his screams, by each severance of flesh with her knife.

She brought the blade to his face, breathless as she cupped his blood-soaked cheek. Fresh laughter overtook her as she slashed at the line of his lips, connecting to the hole in his cheek. His screams could not outmatch her joy, and she aligned her knife with his lip to mirror it—

"Flowridia, that is enough."

—and slashed, gasping as a warm spray of blood coated her face.

In the tense silence, she stumbled back. Her hand slackened. The knife clattered against the floor.

Her breath came in spurts as she gazed with clarity upon her victim—a mutilated mess, bleeding from masses of split flesh. He wept, a horrible gurgling sound. When she moved to tuck her hair from her face, warmth smeared across it. Blood coated her hand. It splattered her dress. She spat, the taste of metal sharp against her tongue.

A large shadow covered her, Casvir's voice familiar. "There is merit to brutality, but not at the cost of losing control."

"Sorry," she whispered, yet she did not mean it at all. "I got carried away." Ecstasy burned in her veins, and she whirled around, seeking Ayla—yet found nothing. "Where is my wife?"

To her alarm, Casvir frowned as he followed her gaze. "I do not know when she left."

Flowridia stepped in a daze toward the door, knowing full well her wife didn't need it, yet opened it nevertheless and peered into a vacant hallway.

As her pulse quelled, some semblance of sanity returned, sparking memories of *why*. "Casvir, did you send a rejection to Executor Faeborn yet?"

"I have not."

Her hand gripped the doorknob, slick from blood. Whatever game the Whispering Elf Executor played, she would accept the challenge. "Tell them I would be absolutely charmed to meet."

"ALYSTRA'S FAKE TITS—WHAT THE FUCK DID YOU DO?!"

Flowridia had forgotten she was covered in blood. "None of it's mine."

A lie, but she didn't need to mention her hand. Statistically, the majority wasn't her own.

In the medical ward, Etolié resumed her meltdown, accompanied by understandably concerned nurses muttering about bloodborne diseases. Soon, she was whisked from Casvir's presence and into a supervised bath.

Flowridia was allowed to undress herself, but a young nurse did help scrub the blood and grime from her skin.

Etolié continued her interrogation. "What do you mean the questioning got out of hand?!"

"Precisely that."

"Did you fucking shower in his blood?!"

Flowridia remained hedgy, still processing the event herself. The residual flow of power coursed through her, though the errant want to fuck her wife in the ensuing puddle of blood finally quelled, replaced by worry.

Where had Ayla gone? Did she hide in the walls? In Sha'Demoni? Was witnessing torture too much now? The thought was too strange to contemplate.

But contemplate it she did, until a warm sleeping gown covered her, and the nurses tried to coax her into bed. "I need to find my wife first," she said, her protests unheard.

"Well, she's not gonna sleep with all you people hovering around." Etolié ushered the nurses away. However, once alone, the interrogation resumed. "Where is your wife, Flowers?"

Flowridia hugged herself, uncertain if she should be scouring the castle or simply patient. "I don't know. But I'm starting to worry."

"I assume if I make you sleep, you'll either sneak out of bed later or kick my ass in the morning for employing magic?"

Flowridia paused at that. "You have sleep magic?"

"I fucking do. Now, put on your shoes—"

"No need."

Flowridia gasped at the new voice. Ayla appeared in the shadow of the mantle, the fireplace casting dark shadows wherein she could hide. She smelled faintly of smoke, hints of ash at the seams of her dress, but Flowridia clung to her with all her strength, breath catching to feel the embrace returned.

"Looks like you two have a few things to catch up on," Etolié said. "I'm gonna get drunk with the nurses. Scream if you start dying."

The Celestial disappeared with the healers.

Once alone, Flowridia kissed her dearest wife, seeking answers in the motions, fearful of what she might find. Ayla returned the gesture until Flowridia's touch became sensuous, shrinking from the pawing at her breasts. "Flowra, I—"

"No, no—I'm sorry. I should have asked." Flowridia cupped Ayla's precious face, cursing her undeath. If she had been crying, there would be no lingering sign. "Where did you go?"

Ayla remained silent a moment, hesitant to meet her gaze. The crackling fire filled the space, providing comfort amid the tension. "I . . ."

Flowridia faced a stranger, this shy creature, a doe liable to flee. How long had it been since Flowridia had truly seen her magnificent predator?

"I don't want to hurt you," Ayla finally said, increasingly withdrawn, but Flowridia latched to this small bit of insight with all her might.

"Please just speak your mind. I want to help, even if it hurts to hear."

When Ayla stepped back, Flowridia let her go, hesitant to even move. Ayla's hands clenched each other behind her back, likely ripping holes through her skin, but to reprimand that might scare her away.

Ayla spoke so softly. "It feels good, does it not? The splitting flesh beneath the knife. The spray of blood. Their pleas for mercy. But nothing compares to their fear—to see it, to smell it, to bask in it and know you're the very core. The power is euphoric."

Ayla said nothing false, yet Flowridia hesitated, trapped for reasons she could not guess. "Yes."

"It is a dark path to tread."

The statement made Flowridia stiffen, for it rang uncomfortably in her memory. "It's not the first time I've felt this way."

"It is different to feel a high from magic than to achieve godhood through torture. But that is the feeling, is it not? To be helpless, and then to steal that power back? Incredible. Nothing like it."

Again, the words were a test. Flowridia dithered, uncertain of where the words led. "What are you saying?"

"There is no peace in it, Flowra." Ayla gently took her hand, the words a plea. "I wish to say a few presumptuous things, notably that there is a void inside you, carved by your mother, though cut raw by Mereen. Filling it this way will only leave you more and more hollow, until there is nothing but the violence. I know it feels incredible now, but soon enough you'll be starving without it. It becomes a need instead of a want, lest you feel nothing at all." Tears misted Ayla's eyes, the first quickly falling. "You have a beautiful soul, and this is the surest way to bury it."

Flowridia reeled in the ensuing silence. Whatever she had expected, suspected . . . Not this.

"Ayla, it wasn't . . . You're projecting."

"Perhaps. I am a hypocrite, if nothing else."

Flowridia drew her hand away, tumultuous thoughts battering to escape her head. It had felt glorious, and he had deserved it. "He could have killed me." *And my baby*, though she did not say it. Ayla would not care.

"Yes, and he deserves death, assuredly. I would do it myself if offered the opportunity."

"Casvir did offer."

"Casvir was quite clear that he wanted the perpetrator *alive*. I do not torture for Casvir anymore."

The statement evoked guilt within Flowridia, to recall what she herself had agreed to. "I told Casvir I would meet with Executor Faeborn."

The sorrow drained from Ayla's countenance, leaving only horror. "What?"

"They sent the assassin. I want to know why, and this may be the only opportunity."

"So you would put yourself back into the line of fire?!"

"I won't be gone long. Casvir can create a portal to bring me in and out and be done with it."

Ayla stepped back, her eyes searching, searching . . . Whatever she sought, it was not found. "I explicitly asked you to not do this."

"The circumstances changed. The Whispering Elves hadn't sent an assassin after a pregnant woman when I agreed to that."

"And then what?"

Flowridia blinked at the question. "What?"

"The meeting ends. You find your answer. What then?"

"Then it's over—"

"And since you have proven your diplomatic skills, which we both know you will, Casvir invites you to the next summit with Executor Faeborn, or perhaps with Tholheim as they negotiate surrender. Perhaps Moratham, if he seeks allies or more bloodshed. Or most likely with Soliel, since you are friendly with the neighboring apocalyptic God. What then? Do you agree?"

Flowridia frowned, pride bristling at Ayla's tone. "I decline."

"And the next time he asks? And the next?"

"At some point, we leave Nox'Kartha and it becomes a non-issue."

Ayla slumped, defeat in her stance. "That is all I want, Flowra." She fell upon one of the couches, head cradled in her hand. "Forgive me. Do what you will, but please don't lose sight of the prize."

With care to not startle her, Flowridia sat by her side, tentative as she touched Ayla's back. "I haven't. I promise. A few more months, and we run away. Just you and me. And Demitri."

And not the little spark within her, though Flowridia bit back that discomfort. Now was not the time, not when Ayla finally smiled. "A perfect immortality."

They embraced, and in Ayla's grip there came silent desperation. "Forgive me. I hope you don't find me overbearing. You frightened me, and all I knew to do was run."

Flowridia kissed her hair, her cheek, returning the embrace with zeal, even if the words left her unsettled. What did it mean to frighten Ayla Darkleaf?

"Not overbearing," Flowridia said. "I . . . I trust you."

Conflict brewed within her, the expectation of guilt far surpassing any actual remorse. Nothing. Simply the memory of screams and splitting flesh, the tender breaking of bones and spirit. How intimate, his pain. More so than any she had delivered with necromancy. He had deserved her vengeance, her only regret was that she could not finish it.

Casvir had only berated her for losing control. If she kept her rage in check, would he allow her to try again?

. . . Perhaps it was a slippery slope.

She purged thoughts of violence with the sanguine scent of Ayla—her Silver Fire, her perfumes and soaps, marred only by the barest hint of smoke. They kissed by the firelight, chaste despite the lush atmosphere.

"I love you," Flowridia whispered, and blushed when Ayla returned it, forever soft for affection.

Upon the couch, she fell into the luxurious bliss of her wife's embrace, soon drifting off to sleep.

CHAPTER 15

Nine years after the end of the world . . .

In the courtyard of the manor, Dira walked her new wolfish friend with curiosity.

Demitri was undead, yet he sniffed the air with all the enthusiasm of a living animal, basked in the sun, even lapped at the water spewing from the rich fountain with his pink tongue. Mother had said Demitri was nearly living in his own way, a creature worthy of Dira's company.

Taller than her by far, Dira found shade in his shadow as she gave him a tour.

"Sora is very particular about the hedges by the outer wall," Dira said, pointing to the angular plants. "I have to stay inside when the gardeners come visit though. That's the rule."

Sora's too lazy to do it herself.

Dira reeled at the statement. "No. She just has other things to do."

Why don't you do it? Why don't you garden?

Dira blinked at the words, having never considered the notion. "I'm too short to cut the hedges."

Then get taller. Mom never let that stop her.

Dira stilled, a strange new truth occurring to her. "You knew my mom really well, right?"

Better than Lady Ayla, I bet.

"Can you tell me about—"

But a joyous scream cut off her words. She and Demitri both turned to see a riotous Etolié running through the open gates.

Demitri whined and ran for the Celestial, who immediately bombarded him with an embrace. "Baby boy!" Tears welled in her eyes, absorbed by the wolf's thick fur.

Mother appeared, stepping gracefully from Demitri's own shadow. "Oh. That was your scream."

Rage etched into Etolié's face when she pulled away from Demitri. "You could have fucking told me! I had to find out from Sora."

"Gods forbid I let my daughter bond with her familiar."

Dira ran to Mother, immediately pulled against her side. "So Demitri knows Etolié?"

"Fuck yeah, I know Demitri," Etolié replied. "I've known him since he was just a little potato." Etolié mimed cradling a baby, even as her watery gaze remained on the wolf. "How is this possible? You're not a necromancer. You're also not a god."

"Apparently I've gained power enough to mimic it, or at least grant power to one precious someone," Ayla said, her hold starting to feel too tight. When Dira tried to shift, Mother stood firm. "And don't play dumb about the necromancers in my arsenal."

Etolié frowned. "You're not implying..." Dira withered beneath Etolié's glance, quick as it was. "You didn't bring anyone here, did you?"

Mother's grip tightened, stiff from the challenge. "It would be none of your business if I had."

"It would be entirely my business if some bitch had walked through those doors and been within blast range of my silver sparkling."

Dira winced at Mother's claws, even through the fabric of her dress. "*Your* silver sparkling?"

"Well, given only one of us seems to give a shit about her safety—"

Dira gasped at Mother's sudden release, panic rising when Mother appeared from Etolié's shadow. *"Don't you EVER—"*

Demitri's snarl silenced the impromptu arena. It lingered as it lightened, a guttural warning in the air.

Etolié took a wary step back. Mother only stepped toward him. Dangerous words slid like ice down her tongue, yet it was Dira who froze solid. "I gave you new life. Learn your place, or I will take it away."

Demitri's growl faded.

To Etolié, Mother directed her ice next. "If you ever say a damn word about this again, you'll be banned from coming to this estate. Understood?"

"She blasted Kah'Sheen into the Beyond in literal pieces, and you want me to fucking say nothing?!"

"I do, because this is not your house."

Etolié said nothing, visibly seething.

"Come speak inside," Mother said. When she met Dira's eye, her gaze immediately softened. "Darling, I am so very sorry. You should not have had to see that."

Dira nodded, yet found she couldn't speak.

Mother approached, setting a soft hand upon her forehead. "You are a little warm, love. Have you been outside too long?"

Dira shook her head. "I-I feel fine."

She shied to see Mother's regret, her forced smile. But when Mother set a kiss on Dira's forehead, the ice in her soul finally melted. "I will be home all day if you need me. I love you, my Dira."

"I love you too."

Mother's anger returned the moment she stepped in time with Etolié. Dira watched, even as Demitri's shadow covered her.

You'll let me say what Etolié says, right?

"What do you mean?"

Mom said I couldn't say 'fuck.' But you can't stop me. I can say all the bad words I fucking want.

Dira giggled at the scandal, her heart already lighter.

Didn't know Kah'Sheen was dead.

"Who is that?"

Some demon girl. She saved me from getting my soul eaten. But she also helped Mereen kill me. But so did Sora, and no one cares. Apparently.

Dira balked. "*Who* killed you?"

That's a long story. Settle in.

Current era . . .

"Next round. Let's go!"

Etolié brought the stein to her lips, chugging to a small chorus of cheers. When she tasted only foam, she dropped it, wood meeting wood as it clattered upon the ground. One by one, the steins fell, and the three remaining nurses swayed as they swallowed the last of it, one hiccupping.

Another rapidly turned green. "I think . . ." She rushed from the room, sounds of retching soon echoing from the washroom.

With a swipe of Etolié's hand, new steins appeared on the table, filled to the brim with Eionei's finest. "You ready, or do you need a moment?"

One nurse held up a hand, clearly fighting to stay conscious. The second hid her drunkenness well, raising her eyebrow at her companion.

"We'll give her a moment—"

"*Etolié.*"

Etolié paused at the whisper, an undeniable sound, then realized the remaining nurses had also stilled. It was not in her head.

"*Etolié, I am hiding from Endless Night. Please come to the corner.*"

Her own name, though unmistakable, held a humorous mispronunciation—the likes of which could be attributed to only the most demon-blooded among them. Etolié followed the whisper to a dark shadow in the corner, wary as she held her hand out toward the nurses. "I think it's fine—"

She flinched when a deep blue hand reached from the shadow, as spindly as Zoldar's.

"Definitely fine. Game's on hold." Etolié took the hand, unsurprised when the world gently shifted, leaving her encircled by blurred shadows and a vast grey world.

Sha'Demoni held a unique filter, as though dust had blown into her eyes, unable to be washed out no matter how much she scrubbed. Remnants of the castle remained, as well as spots of light where the nurses surely panicked at her disappearance. Yet Etolié spared them no mind, far more curious about the impossibly tall half-demon before her.

Kah'Sheen held the frailty of death despite her immortal form, gangly in every dimension, her age indeterminate because of it. But only her top half bore any reminiscence of a humanoid, deceivably elven aside from her dark-blue coloring and four arms. Her lower half held an arachnid form, evidence of her demon progenitor. With twice the number of average eyes, pupilless and yellow, and black hair as long as she was tall, Kah'Sheen was the most interesting person Etolié had ever met—and she had met a lot of interesting folks.

Kah'Sheen kept hold of her hand. "Endless Night is near. I am taking you farther away, yes?"

Etolié nodded, following as a child would to her mother. Kah'Sheen led her through rapidly shifting hallways, their speed enhanced by Sha'Demoni's time dilation. Etolié did not know the precise mathematics of it. She only knew that weeks here could be mere days on the mortal plane.

The world shifted to reveal pure monochrome, their escape from the castle apparent even in the other world. Evidence of the city of Haven shifted in and out of clarity, Sha'Demoni's own terrain far more barren.

"Sorry to bother you," Kah'Sheen said, finally releasing her. "I am needing to ask something."

Kah'Sheen often called them sisters, and Etolié was prone to giving family far more leeway than most others. Besides, her visits were rare, and Etolié craved friendly faces. "Of course, Sheen Bean."

"You are working for Casvir, yes?"

"Yes."

"Um . . ." Kah'Sheen mulled over her words, which meant this was either a translation error or she was being especially fucking careful. "And when you are working for Casvir, you are telling him things, yes?"

"Well, sometimes."

"But there is no magic forcing you to tell him?"

"There's occasionally magic forcing me to *not* tell other people things he's told me," Etolié said, bitter at that one. That damned Staff Seraph DeDieula existed somewhere in this castle, but she'd lose her soul to even mention it. "But any compulsion to tell him shit? No."

Kah'Sheen's smile revealed shark-like teeth. "You must come to Mother's. Now, yes?"

"I mean, it's not every day you're demanded to go to the literal Goddess of War's house."

"Oh, no. No demand. Uh . . ." Kah'Sheen grimaced as she looked to the castle, then across the terrain. "I can say nothing here. We must go."

"I could potentially take us there. Are you comfortable risking getting spliced?"

"Spliced?"

"Having your soul separated from your body and existing only between realms."

Kah'Sheen actually considered it, much to Etolié's amusement. "I am trusting you."

Well, Etolié had resolved to practice. For better or worse, she took two of her half-demon sister's four hands. "I won't be able to take us there with my connection, but I can use you. I need you to think hard on a particular place in Ku'Shya's house. Whatever place you have the most connection to. No distractions."

Kah'Sheen nodded. "I am ready."

Similar to empathically healing, Etolié allowed herself to open to Kah'Sheen's presence, feeling her aura envelop her as a second skin. She felt . . . anticipation, though it was not her own, fear and wonder, anxiety for what was to come . . .

And saw with perfect clarity a room from Kah'Sheen's memory, bearing the red walls of Ku'Shya's home.

Etolié cast her spell.

Sha'Demoni vanished, replaced with darkness all around as Etolié felt skin leave muscle, muscle leave bone, all of her insides catching fire at the expulsion of power. She clung to Kah'Sheen amid the pain, muttering obscenities to keep her fucking mind in place—

Until a particularly virulent *fucking cunt shit* echoed off cave walls, the vermillion color reminiscent of the rocks in Momma's meadow.

But it was surely not Momma's meadow, the humidity immediately descending upon her. Upon the walls, floating globes emanated light. A rounded bed, not unlike a nest, sat in the center, an endless array of scrolls dotting the walls. Personal items, children's toys, and a collection of mummified heads created a comfortable space.

Kah'Sheen's clapping filled the room, her four hands creating their own small applause. "Very good, Etolié! I am grateful you are not splicing us."

Bless Kah'Sheen. Too sweet for this world. "What was it you couldn't tell me?"

"Well . . ." Kah'Sheen glanced toward a large exit, sized for a demon far bigger than her. "Come with me. I will explain."

Etolié obeyed, amused at how Kah'Sheen so clearly slowed her steps for her. The exit led to a bend in the cave's path, creating privacy without a door.

"You are involved in the war, yes?" Kah'Sheen asked. "Do you know anything of the Whispering Elves?"

Etolié's grudge with the Whispering Elves had fallen far away from any level of humor, replaced with the nightmare of Khastra's prison. "I know they're holding my favorite beefcake as a prisoner of war."

"Well, not really."

That . . . was not a logical response. "They're not really holding her hostage?"

"No, because Mother is destroying Tierzuroth. Khastra is here now."

Etolié swayed. She breathed yet caught no breath, her mind reeling from ten months of wondering, waiting, of weeping from loneliness, of craving a soul she loved more than her own. Her vision misted with her blink, but she did not feel sorrow, no. Not even joy; she could not feel at all.

"Etolié?"

Her name evoked a sob. Etolié's legs failed her, and she collapsed to the ground as the first of her tears streamed down her face. Crushing waves of relief left her faint. She did not fight as lithe arms scooped her up, Kah'Sheen's bare chest her only stability. The half-demon led her rapidly through the hallways, yet Etolié's yearning rose to new heights, the impossible truth descending that she would see . . . she would touch . . .

Kah'Sheen brought her to a dimly lit enclave, as spacious as her bedroom, and there upon the bed, Etolié's favorite demon lay sleeping.

The gentle rise and fall of her chest brought comfort to Etolié's bruised soul, her broad figure having deteriorated in captivity. Not thin, no, but lacking the supreme power Khastra had once radiated. Gashes marred her tattooed skin, burns around her wrists and neck mirroring where her awful shackles had been. Surely there were more, but a blanket covered her naked figure up to her waist. Her sallow cheeks rivaled only the hollow space beneath her eyes, but she was Khastra. She was here. She was whole.

Etolié's wings did the work of steadying her when Kah'Sheen gently placed her down, her steps stumbling as she made it to Khastra's bedside. "Can I wake her?"

"You may. Be gentle."

At Etolié's touch, Khastra's silver tattoos illuminated her skin, starkly contrasting with her deep-blue hue. Etolié traced them by habit, following the runes up her bicep, circling her substantial deltoids, and ending in a swirl around her neck.

Khastra's eyes blinked open, revealing pupilless blue orbs. She smiled upon meeting Etolié's gaze. "Beautiful."

Her voice held elegance, held depth and femininity, and though dusty, it healed Etolié's tattered soul.

Etolié wept, grasping Khastra's arms as her sobs overtook her once more. "You're a fucking sap, you big lug."

At Khastra's coaxing, Etolié crawled into bed, praying this dream did not end. But no, Etolié's illusions could not create scent, and Khastra smelled of soap, of warmth, of the ineffably alien world of her mother. Strong arms wrapped around her, their weight grounding.

Kah'Sheen left on silent, spindly legs, and Etolié cupped her demon's cheek, heart breaking at the protrusion of bone. But she was Khastra. She was here. Amid her tears, Etolié kissed her soundly, bliss filling her to feel those lips return the motions, sensuous and slow.

"I have missed you," Khastra whispered, and Etolié left her love's lips to weep into the curve of her neck.

Etolié could not even speak, simply savored her beloved's presence, her heart whole once more.

"Etolié!"

Though boisterous, the sheer volume of the voice triggered Etolié's fight response. She launched up, unprepared for the gargantuan figure approaching.

Though called 'The Great Spider,' Goddess Ku'Shya bore more resemblance to a dragon in Etolié's opinion, her exoskeleton resembling scales. Her arachnid lower half was far thicker than any spider Etolié had ever seen, her four massive legs akin to tree trunks. Forty feet tall at least, Ku'Shya stared down with four eyes and four arms each wider than Etolié was tall. Like Kah'Sheen, she had monstrous teeth, but fangs jutted from her frightful maw. Her voice struggled to articulate her Celestial words, but Etolié understood well enough. "Good to hear Imperator Casvir is not forcing you to speak."

Etolié wiped her blinding tears, perturbed to be stolen from her emotional collapse—she had damn well earned it—but there was a time and place for tantrums, and she could hold it together. "Hello, Godde— Mother."

Etolié couldn't keep up with lies, but when the most powerful deity in Sha'Demoni decided you were married to her eldest daughter, you didn't argue, and when she said to call her 'Mother,' you obeyed.

With far more dexterity than her size should have allowed, Ku'Shya nimbly tucked her legs beneath her body, not unlike a gargantuan armored cat. "Very good to see you. What is Kah'Sheen telling you?"

"I kinda had a breakdown when she said Khastra was alive, so not much."

Khastra made no attempt to sit up, simply rolled over to face her goddess mother. Strange, to consider their supposed tension. Khastra was always antagonistic at the mere mention of Ku'Shya, yet the Goddess of War seemed at ease. Today, Khastra simply rested. Etolié, however, sat at the edge of the bed, holding Khastra's hand as she settled.

"You are at war with the Four Kingdoms, yes?"

"By proxy of being under the control of Nox'Kartha, yes."

"You are hearing from Executor Faeborn?"

"No, though I heard in the rumor mill that they've finally agree to meet with Casvir."

"Yes, yes—they are returning my Khastra to me. They are telling me before that they do not have Khastra, and now they are revealing their disrespect to me. But they are returning Khastra, so I am telling Executor Faeborn that Tierzuroth has three mortal days for evacuation, and then I destroy it. That is done. There is no Tierzuroth. I am appeased."

Etolié simply blinked, rapidly trying to dissect Ku'Shya's cadence and meaning. "Tierzuroth is destroyed?"

"Correct."

"Holy shit . . ." Tierzuroth had lasted through the Convergence, had withstood countless sieges from elves, demons, from every sort of threat. Their tension with Ku'Shya had waxed and waned through the eons, but past executors had established tentative peace.

In the end, it had not mattered. Ku'Shya had wiped it away. Yet because they had returned her daughter in the final hour, she had allowed them to evacuate. Etolié didn't understand Demoni Law, but this was slightly less reprehensible than the Theocracy's destruction.

"Khastra is weak," Ku'Shya said. "She is deteriorating slower than a living prisoner, but she is also recovering slower. Kah'Sheen is saying to see you will aid in healing Khastra's spirit. I am agreeing."

Etolié squeezed her demon's hand, heart soaring to feel the sensation returned. "What then?"

Gone was Ku'Shya's jovial tone, or as much of a jovial tone as her guttural voice could convey. While Etolié could not claim to understand Demoni facial expressions, or lack thereof, an unquestionable shift occurred in her aura, her good nature fading into menace. "I am contemplating. But that is not for you to worry about. You are always welcome here, Etolié. Later, I would speak to you alone, but I will leave you now to care for my Khastra."

Ku'Shya left, not even a dust cloud in her wake.

Etolié slipped in the blankets beside Khastra, blushing at the touch of calloused fingers upon her cheek. Her illusion of clothing vanished, leaving their naked bodies touching. "You heard the woman. I'm supposed to care for you. What that means is dictated by your stamina."

Khastra's laughter evoked memories of comfort and joy. "I wish for you to tell me what has transpired in my absence. Last we spoke, you were contemplating talking to Eionei again."

"Fucking hell, that was a million years ago."

"That was ten months, Etolié."

"Listen, Flowers is pregnant with the Goddess of Chaos, Sora is Flowers' sister, Ayla is fucking depressed, Mereen is dead, Sol Kareena is dead, Demitri's still dead, Marielle's a catty bitch, Murishani has lost his goddamn mind, Casvir is Casvir, and Zoldar has learned to count cards—it's felt like a million years."

Forever unflappable, Khastra simply nodded. "I would like you to elaborate on half of those."

"Which half?"

"You may begin with the Goddess of Chaos."

Etolié blew out a dramatic breath, settling with her back to the bed as she conjured the image of the ghostly Goddess. "Buckle up, Beefcake. You're not gonna fucking believe this."

Etolié began her yarn, spinning even the most dramatic parts to make her favorite demon smile, seeking only the sound of her laughter.

Exactly as it should be.

Blessed hours were spent in Khastra's surreal presence, regaling the stories of each and every update in the world, both mundane and apocalyptic. But the half-demon ailed, and when she confessed the need to rest, Etolié sang to help her along, soothing her into a dreamless, restful state.

Though it tore her soul in twain, Etolié extracted herself from Khastra's embrace, wandering alone through the great tunnels of Ku'Shya's home.

Nearly ten mortal months had passed since she had been here, but she had seen little aside from the makeshift medical ward.

Staella's presence had soothed the transition, for Ku'Shya's home was utterly alien, but she had not stayed long.

Despite being underground, Etolié felt no claustrophobia at all, the cave's ceilings carved to accommodate a goddess who could but would not make herself smaller. When clattering footsteps sounded against the stone, Etolié backed against the wall as an arachnoid demon passed, its colors far brighter than the Goddess of War. Fifteen feet tall at least, but it paid her no mind, simply went on its way.

Etolié was welcome here, as Ku'Shya had said.

There was no urgency, for Solvira was far away. Time moved slowly in Sha'Demoni, and Flowers would be fine for a while longer. And so Etolié wandered leisurely, peeking into large rooms and larger amphitheaters. She stumbled upon a particularly enormous space, the pile of bones large enough for her to swim in, and before it was a path climbing upward—perhaps the exit.

What drew her eye were the three pedestals behind the throne of bones—a crystal bow, bearing the same amethyst color as Khastra's beloved hammer.

Speaking of . . . upon the other two pedestals were two crystalline hammers, one dustier than its twin.

Khastra had feared this all along, had spoken in ominous whispers of what mayhem could befall the mortal realm should Ku'Shya acquire her hammer again. The weapons enhanced each other, their power broken with the missing triplet. For thousands of years, Ku'Shya had held stunted power.

Here it sat. Apprehension welled in Etolié's gut.

Each weapon stood over twice her height. And though identical in design, subtle scuffs distinguished one to be Khastra's stolen hammer, repaired and polished by the half-demon's hand, but bearing scars, nevertheless.

"Etolié! I see you are wandering."

Etolié's heart skipped at the booming voice, uncertain if she were in trouble or not. Was Ku'Shya smiling? Did demons smile at all? Her countenance was rigid, frightful, but her tone bore no malice. "Hi there, Mother."

The goddess made little noise as she approached, her legs oddly nimble for their size. "I am pleased to have *Maz'Khamon* returned to me. I am claiming it from the battlefield in the north when Khastra is taken."

Etolié fought a frown, then realized she meant the hammer, which apparently had a name.

"When Khastra is strong again," Ku'Shya continued, "we will negotiate. Perhaps fight in the arena and allow the victor to lay claim. It is dishonorable of me to withhold it from her when it is not taken in honest combat."

"That's a spiffy honor code you got there," Etolié said, tracing her reflection on the crystal's surface.

"What is 'spiffy'?" Ku'Shya choked on the double 'ff,' and Etolié bit her lip to suppress laughter.

So much like her daughter. "Uh, fancy. Respectable."

"I see." Ku'Shya settled upon the pile of bones, the frankly upsetting *cracks* causing Etolié to flinch. "Khastra is saying many times you are not like Staella. Khastra is saying you are stubborn. More stubborn than my Khastra." An odd, braying chuckle escaped Ku'Shya's mouth. "It is funny to imagine someone more stubborn than Khastra."

The true oddity of this demonic small talk was in its . . . utter normalcy. Etolié gave a wary smile. "I'm flattered she thinks so highly of me."

"Yes, yes—she is thinking very highly of you. I am not understanding marriage, but I am knowing it begins when they are thinking highly of the other."

Was Ku'Shya onto the ruse? She and Khastra were very much not married, but Etolié had once been asked to play along. Surely there was an agenda, but demons weren't known for that. "Do you mean that you, personally, don't understand marriage, or do demons not get married?"

"It is not Demoni way. Khastra is explaining romance and love to me, but it is not something known to us. But it is the highest honor for mortals to make the marriage contract, and I am understanding contracts, as well as understanding holding another in high esteem. You are loyal to Khastra above all, yes?"

"I would say so, yes."

"And the marriage contract is not broken because of her death?"

No mention of Khastra 'faking her death' as she and Kah'Sheen often insisted was the truth. Perhaps Ku'Shya was indulgent to a fault, because stupidity didn't grant a goddess more power than any other in her world. Etolié shook her head.

"Good, good. I am pleased to hear." Ku'Shya's four eyes never blinked in sync, much to Etolié's irrational annoyance. Sometimes they at least moved in succession, but most often they acted on their own accord. "Etolié, I am wanting to be . . . how do you say . . . transparent? It is not to be see-through, but for my *meaning* to be see-through, yes?"

Etolié resisted the urge to grin. "Yes, that's what it means."

"Khastra is returning to the imperator when she is recovering. She is agreeing to stay while she heals, but then I cannot control her. She is not trusting me. But what are you wanting, Etolié? Do you want Khastra to return to the imperator?"

A test surely, but overt trickery violated Demoni Law. Etolié's gut twisted to speak the truth, but speak it she did. "I want her to be with me, but I don't want her to be miserable. I know she was tired of the war, and Casvir will throw her right back in as soon as she's able."

"So she is hating Casvir?"

"Oh, absolutely."

"Then I am asking you to speak to Khastra. Her body is not dead or alive, but she is infused with necromancy. Necromancy is . . . tricky. But necromancy is also about control, and there are spells to seize control. You are following, yes?"

Etolié nodded, though her limbs had fallen numb. "You're saying there are ways to steal Khastra from Casvir."

"Yes, yes—precisely. Blood magic is Demoni way. But Khastra must be convinced."

"Have you asked her?"

"No. She is not strong enough to hear it. She also is not listening to me or to Kah'Sheen. But you have the marriage contract. She is listening to you, yes?"

"In theory," Etolié muttered, yet something about it seemed off. Too simple; too easy. It could not be this easy. "You want me to convince her to let you do a blood ritual."

"I am asking you to convince her to trust me. She is infusing malice into my intentions, but I am not understanding malice. It is an elven emotion. It is not Demoni way. My place in Sha'Demoni is not upheld if I am not upholding Demoni Law. Without Law, there is no power. Were I to disobey, I would cease to be the Goddess of War. Khastra is forgetting this."

Etolié stared back into her reflection in the crystal surface, aching for it to be true. Yet she faced a vast unknown, fear her constant undercurrent. "I'll talk to her. But I doubt she'll agree to anything until she knows the terms and conditions."

"Khastra is stubborn, but I am stubborn for many years more than Khastra. It is sickening as a mother that my eldest is held in captivity. Better she is dead, but best she is free."

No, Etolié couldn't decipher Demoni faces, but years in the political arena helped a girl to know when she was hearing bullshit. Ku'Shya was many things, but she wasn't full of shit. "I'll talk to her when she's stronger. You're right, she doesn't need to be worrying about anything other than healing."

"Yes, yes—in the meantime, Khastra is not worrying for the realms beyond. I ask you to preserve that peace."

Etolié considered the future, that dark void, wishing so badly she could simply stay and forget the world. But even if she had the heart to abandon Solvira, it wouldn't change Soliel's plans. The God of Order marched, and there would be no Sha'Demoni at all if he were successful. "I can come back here again, right?"

"You are leaving?"

"Not immediately, but there's bad shit happening in the mortal realm."

"I am telling you, you are welcome here."

Etolié smiled at that, this strange new home oddly warm for being, well, filled with a small lake's worth of bones. "Good talk, Mother. You've left me with a lot to consider."

She gave a brief farewell, wandering back to where her memory said Khastra lay.

She could spare another hour. The world could wait that much longer.

CHAPTER 16

Nine years after the end of the world...

Every two weeks, Sora marched Dira to the washroom and dunked her whole head in a basin of soapy water. "You will keep those locs of yours clean, kid."

After reassuring Demitri that this wasn't corporal punishment—and sending him away for a time—Dira and Sora fulfilled their bi-monthly ritual. But after the miserable experience of washing and drying, there came the far less miserable experience of oiling.

Dira loved this part, where she and Auntie sat before the fire in their nighties and took turns oiling the other's hair. She sat between her aunt's calves, safe and secure in the little cave it created. Sora's locs reached her hips, the subtle ombre in her blonde hues where the hair had been bleached by the sun starkly apparent when viewed as a whole. Dira envied the length and color, but Sora said her color was far more typical. "My father's family all had hair that was your color, and of course your mother too. It's an heirloom. It means you're connected."

Dira did smile at that.

Her own locs reached just past her shoulders, their growth as slow as it was methodical. "Do you think my mom would have gotten locs if she didn't die?"

"I don't know. I've told you she didn't grow up in our family, but I don't think it would have been disrespectful if she'd decided to. She was still a part of us."

Dira frowned as a new realization struck. "But how could you have a sister and not know? Did your mom and dad hide her?"

She didn't have to see Sora's wince to feel it. "You see—"

"Ask your mother," Dira mocked. Oh, to never hear that damn phrase again.

"Well, no. Or yes, perhaps, but not for the reasons you'd think."

Dira shifted slightly, steadying her breath. "Mother!"

"Dira, what—"

"Mother, I have a question!"

And in no time at all, Mother stepped from the shadow of the fireplace. Confusion furrowed her brow, but she did not seem unhappy. "Am I intruding?"

"Why didn't Sora meet my mom until they were grown-ups? Did her mom and dad hide Mom? Why would someone do that?"

Dira couldn't turn to see the look Sora gave Mother, but some interaction was had. To her elation, Mother sat on the floor beside her as Sora resumed her work. "Sora and your mom had the same father but different mothers."

The idea was . . . odd. "That can happen?"

"Yes. And their shared father died before your maternal grandmother gave birth. Does that answer your question?"

None of that made any sense, truthfully. "Who was my grandma?"

"Her name was Odessa. She is also dead."

Dira slumped, frustration rising. "Why does everyone have to be dead?"

Judging by her bit lip, Mother tried to fight her chuckle but failed. "Because it is a cold and dangerous world, my lamb. Be grateful you need not be a part of that."

A part of the world . . . What would that even be like? Was death truly everywhere? "How did Odessa die?"

"That is a tale too gruesome for nine-year-old ears."

The words punctured her hope. Dira glowered. "What about Mom?"

"What about her?"

"How did she die?"

Mother always saddened at that, and Dira so hated to see it, but what if this was the moment? She cringed when Sora spoke. "Dira, that's not appropriate—"

"No, it's all right," Mother whispered. "I knew this day would come." Resignation colored Mother's sigh as she took her hand. Dira clung tight. "Darling, do you remember when we talked about what it means to be pregnant?"

Dira nodded. "It's when there's a baby inside you, and it's still growing."

"That's right. And when your dear mom was pregnant, she became very sick." How quickly Mother's eyes filled with tears. Already, her voice broke. "But she did everything she could to care for you anyway. You were just a tiny spark inside her, and she wanted to protect you."

"She died because she got sick?"

"That's right. But she clung to life long enough for you to grow to be healthy."

Dira frowned, for something wasn't right. "But didn't she have medicine?"

"Sometimes medicine is not enough."

Uncertainty filled her, a cloying sort of cold. "But you always say medicine makes you get better."

"When you are a healthy little girl, it does. But there were other factors—" Mother's voice caught, her tear-stained face hurting Dira's heart. "Your mom was a hero. She clung to life with all of her strength because she wanted to keep you safe. She loved you—loves you—so much, my Dira. And just because she can't tell you that herself does not make it any less true. That love is why you are here with me and your auntie."

Dira's lip trembled. That cold went away, replaced with warmth, expanding until it had nowhere to go but well in her eyes and fall as tears. "I wish she could be here too."

Mother released her hand, immediately pulling her into her arms. Sora's hands left her hair. Dira clung to Mother instead. "I miss her every day," Mother said. "She would be so proud of you, my darling."

Dira cried, sweeping loneliness balanced with love. When she finally pulled back, wetness stained Mother's dress. "Can you tell me more about her?"

Sora resumed her motions, her own sniffles barely stifled. For hours, they swapped stories, sharing anecdotes of a mother far away.

Current era . . .

Seated for hours on a dragon's claw, Sora's muscles ached from inactivity.

She ate, she slept, she shivered beneath blankets Chaos conjured. The first day they spent in discomforting silence, Sora's own anger the wall between them. Gods, she wished she had her mirror, her worry quiet but chronic for Flowridia, but it was as lost as any of her other hopes.

Sol Kareena was dead. The sunrise felt hollow and cold.

When night fell, the darkness of the sea became an empty void, pure blackness below. The winds whipped, but Sora never shivered. If Chaos had done nothing else, the summoned blankets did their job.

Sleep evaded her. Behind blinks, Sora saw only visions of blood and murder, the horrible crack of Sol Kareena's neck . . .

Sora winced in her nest of blankets. She forced herself to rise, claustrophobic as she fought to subdue her panic. Gods, the memory hurt, it hurt . . .

The cold lacerated her skin as she shed the blankets, but at least she was free. Nearby, Chaos sat in a meditative pose; she had for hours now. If she heard Sora struggle, she ignored it well.

Cast in celestial lights, Chaos reflected her own ethereal glow. No sign of wolfish bones; no sign of Demitri at all, save for the subtle shape of her own shadow—no longer hidden.

Chaos was a monster. Perhaps Dira was too. But she hadn't always been. And the monster she had become . . .

What if Sora had set those stones in motion too? "Demitri?" she dared to whisper.

In an eerie, languid motion, Chaos rolled her neck to face her. "I don't want to talk to you."

"Then don't talk. Just listen. Or don't, but I need to say something."

Chaos didn't move, just kept that frightful glare.

No, Sora didn't face a wolf's countenance, but there was nothing humanoid here. All beast. All rage. "I told Dira that she couldn't fix Sol Kareena's death. I told her she couldn't pay it back. But in the same breath, I told her I was trying to pay for my own sin, of watching a monster do the work while I stood nigh. And . . ." Sora hid sudden emotion behind a shiver, the chill ever-present. "And what a hypocrite I am. Because no matter what I do to help Flowridia, you're still dead, Demitri."

"You don't fucking say."

"I'm sorry." Sora swallowed a lump in her throat, too cold to cry but liable to anyway. For months, she had watched Flowridia slowly flourish anew, but Demitri was gone. Stolen by the *boom* of a firearm, the crack of a skull, and spray of blood. Gone. "It doesn't fix a damn thing, but I'm sorry, Demitri. I swear I've done everything I can to help your mom. Flowridia has been my sole focus for the last year, but nothing I can do can bring you back from the dead. I'm so sorry."

Chaos stared, void of emotion except derision. "You should be."

Then, Chaos turned away, back to meditation.

Sora sniffed, the wind cutting against the prickle of tears in her eyes. When she brought the blankets back around her, that claustrophobia remained. She dabbed her eyes, forcing her will to steady. Crying was impractical, given the current state of their rations, notably their waning water.

But all her grief, all her nightmares, rose to choke her, and despite her apology, she felt no relief.

"Why did Dira eat you?" The words tumbled clumsily out, half sobbed.

Chaos whipped around faster at that one. "Why do you care? You hate us."

"I don't hate you. Or her. I'm hurt, but I don't hate anyone."

So Ayla-like, that glare—the sort mortals could never have a hope to mimic. "The last time I fought Casvir, Dira and Soliel tried to banish him instead of kill him. It was my idea. Mom told me once that Lara tried to do that to stupid Soliel, but she exploded instead. I didn't mention Soliel. I just told Dira to not get exploded. But then Casvir almost killed me instead. Dira didn't think she had a choice. So instead of finishing her spell, she . . . *we* became one. That's when Casvir somehow twisted her spell, and he sent us to the past."

"You seem resentful."

"I hate everything and everyone. Except Uluron." Chaos punctuated the statement with a pat to her bony seat.

"I met a witch once who had eaten her familiar—"

"Just say Odessa, fuckhead."

He really had gone to the Etolié school of insults, it seemed. "All right, I got to know Odessa. I just wanted to comment that you and Dira are a little, uh, different."

"Or we're normal and Odessa is 'different.' Putting it lightly. She ate babies."

Sora could concede to all of that. Odessa had said Rulan was always silent.

Before she could slink back into her blankets and pretend to not exist, Chaos' voice spoke anew. "Dira and I never understood each other."

Sora hesitated to reply, lest she startle Demitri. He spoke instead.

"It's not like how it was with Mom. Familiars are supposed to be a piece of your soul, but I was already part of Mom's soul. I could never be part of Dira's. It was fine when we were young. Like babysitting a sister. But we fought and fought later on. I didn't care about the angels. Dira and Soliel always had big plans. Too big. I just wanted to eat Casvir's face. Apparently that was too much to ask."

"It was never that simple," Chaos replied to herself—for it was Dira once more, "and you know that."

"Because all you wanted to do was kill him, and I said we could capture him or dismember him or put him in a box underground like the God of Death or—"

"That wouldn't have stopped him—"

Chaos pounced up, looking to fight. "And killing him did any good?!"

Her stance turned aggressive, unsteady. "We were trying—"

"And failing and failing and failing and failing—"

"So did you!"

"How about," Sora gently said, cautious as she stood, "we not have a fight while precariously perched on a dragon's paw above the freezing ocean?"

Chaos' vicious glare held the perfect combination of her entwined entities—bestial and crafty, vengeful and . . . sad. Her posture slumped. Daintily, she sat, resuming her meditative pose. "You are correct. I am sorry."

From that same mouth came, "I'm not."

"And you don't have to be," Sora said. "But please refrain from violent fights until we're back on land."

"Fine."

For now, Demitri was appeased.

Another day passed. Sora felt . . . unfinished.

But the following afternoon, land appeared, and by evening they came upon Neolan.

Gone was the legendary Glass Palace, no glittering spectacle to greet them. Instead, Sora beheld a vast blight of black. Excavation of the remains was ongoing, by Etolié's orders.

Uluron landed beyond the city's gates, the land settled and overgrown with grass. Already, Sora spotted panicked guards upon the wall.

"My magnificent Uluron," Chaos said, placing a kiss upon Uluron's claw. "I will return soon to tell you our plan. The orb, please."

Uluron offered the Light Orb, keeping the Lightning Orb upon her person. Chaos gave no reaction at the touch, despite the holy light, simply tossed it nonchalantly—as one did with ancient, powerful artifacts. But her stance fell when she faced Sora, uncertainty in her words. "What do you think, Sora? Should I appear as Chaos or will they let us in as Dira?"

"The guards know me as the empress' friend. Keep a low profile for now."

It was humorous to say that a half-elf dhampir was in any way inconspicuous, but a Goddess covered in silver flame was guaranteed to draw attention.

Sora waved at the guards attending the open gate, their attention flitting on the duo before returning to Uluron far behind. "We're here to see Empress Etolié. I'm Sora Makosa, her friend."

"And the dragon . . ?"

"Nothing to worry about. She'll wait outside."

The guards remained incredulous as they shared a look, at which point Chaos spoke up. "The alternative is we bring her with us. Either way, we politely request entry into your city."

The threat was clear. The guards let them pass.

With sunset came a spectacle of light. Even without the Glass Palace, Neolan remained a beautiful beacon—the parts that remained, that was. Chaos beamed, absorbing every sight and sound, immune, it seemed, to the attention she attracted. "It has been so long. I forgot how beautiful this city was."

'Was' lingered ominously in the air between them, but if the end of the world came, Solvira was but one casualty among countless.

It struck Sora then, the depth of that loss. To envision an apocalypse seemed so . . . impersonal. What did it even mean, for the world to end? But to imagine Neolan gone? She had half experienced that already, when The Endless Night had blown it up. And she had witnessed carnage unparalleled with the Theocracy's destruction. Did Neolan fall to blood and death? Or was it instant, like the Silver Fire's might?

It was an answer she feared to know. Sora said nothing, simply watched her niece dance through the streets, her grace and poise painfully reminiscent of her undead progenitor. All this time, she had thought of Flowridia alone, but what of Ayla? What damage would a monster inflict upon someone so vibrant?

"You move like Ayla," Sora dared to say, for Chaos wasn't plotting Ayla's death.

Chaos stilled, her large eyes wide and curious. To Sora's surprise . . . she smiled. "Thank you. At least, I would assume that is a compliment."

"She's a very talented dancer," Sora affirmed, but surely Chaos knew that.

Without even a glance to see who watched, Chaos illusioned a flowing skirt to replace her trousers, twirling in the street to soundless song. She truly did embody her vampiric mother, a precision to her dance that only masters could emulate.

Sora kept a wary eye on passersby, but Solvira was a lively city. Few paid Chaos any mind, unaware of the Deity in their presence. Instead, Chaos danced all the way, carefree despite the stakes.

The gates to the empress' manor were shut, but the guard gave a knowing nod to Sora. She was 'on the list' as Etolié had put it, given blanket permission to come and go as she pleased. But the gates did not open. The guard held up a hand. "Greetings, Sora. Who is your friend?"

Chaos offered a friendly hand, which the man warily accepted. "Goddess Chaos, at your service."

The guard looked to Sora for confirmation, who could think of no reply except to nod. "Empress Etolié is currently stationed in Nox'Kartha," the guard said. "I'm afraid the imperator has her enlisted for an important project."

"What sort of project?" Sora asked.

"Truthfully, I don't know. Rumor says it's something to do with Flowridia Darkleaf's pregnancy." He spat on the ground.

At Etolié's insistence, the citizens of Solvira didn't know Sora's blood relationship to the defamed Empress Consort. Sora swallowed uncomfortably at the reminder. She forgot, at times, about her sister's crimes in Solvira. However, the fact that the pregnancy was apparently public knowledge was an interesting development. "Is there any way to send a message to—"

"Anything for you, Sora Makosa!"

Sora glowered at the approaching figure, an audacious beacon in the fading light.

Murishani clasped his hands with glee, eyes roving up and down Chaos' form. "Well, well—what an esteemed visitor you've brought. Rumors reached us that you had returned to this plane." He swept into a low bow. "It would be an honor to host the Goddess of Chaos while I send for the empress."

Sora's nerves rose, coming to recognize the subtle shift in Chaos' stance, shoulders rolling forward into a hunch. When the Goddess bared her fangs, Sora grabbed her niece's shoulder, stealing her attention away. "Don't do it. Don't ruin this."

"You wanna stop me from biting his face off?"

. . . Truthfully, no, but Sora couldn't say that aloud. "Chaos—"

She wrenched from Sora's grip, her bestial stare set on Murishani, only the gate between him and probable death. "Get out. Or I'll wear your face like a mask. I'll finish what I started years ago. I'll fucking do it, bitch."

Murishani's shock mirrored Sora's, the range of threats beyond what she'd considered the wolf capable of. "I see," the viceroy said, but before he could step back, Sora withdrew the orb from Chaos' pocket.

"Am I still good to—"

"Yes, fine," Chaos said, the lingering derision making her identity quite clear. "He's gross, but he doesn't want to blow the worlds up."

Wordlessly, Sora offered the Light Orb to Murishani, easily slipping it between the gate's bars. Shades of white and gold reflected off Murishani's startled countenance, staring at the orb like a vat of snakes. "Can you protect that?" Sora asked.

Murishani nodded, giving no reaction at all when he touched the artifact, quickly slipping it into his robe instead. "Is this the last?"

"No, Uluron has the last. But gods forbid Soliel finds us, the world won't be lost. No funny business. Etolié will know you have it soon."

"As your . . . *colorful* friend said, I don't want the worlds blown up, no. It will be hidden in a box and never discussed or looked at." He glanced to Chaos, her relentless stare causing him to sneer. "Since you're definitely not coming in here, where will you two go instead?"

"Moratham, I guess," Sora said, and Chaos' curt nod confirmed. "Etolié won't be of much help there anyway."

Murishani raised a scathing eyebrow. "You two? Good luck."

When the viceroy moved to leave, Sora pressed against the gate. "Hold on. What does that mean?"

Murishani whirled back, his hair tussling like an ocean wave. "Rumor has it you're seeking pledges from gods to boost your rude Goddess' power. But two half-elven women of your color seeking an audience with the Speaker? Much less convincing God Morathma to pledge himself to one? I'm not saying your quest is impossible, but you'll have to be cleverer than simply waltzing in and asking. I would offer a letter of recommendation, but while I do have a dick, I too often stick it in the wrong places for his taste."

"What would you recommend, then?" Sora asked.

Murishani glanced warily at the looming Goddess. "Make a spectacle. God Morathma's weakness is pride—which is highly unfortunate, given his appearance—but presenting your position in public with a proper appeal may back him into a corner. Pledging to another god—especially, and forgive me, a woman—would be a blow to his pride, so phrase it in a way suggesting that withholding aid from the Goddess of Chaos is an even greater blow to his pride."

Sora knew little of God Morathma, but she did recall her weeks in the slave camp, when she'd been taken at the border during her nomadic years searching for her father. Her fate would have veered in a very different direction had Etolié not come and freed her. Anxiety brewed inside her to consider it, and so she had avoided the subject entirely.

Perhaps that had been a mistake. "Thank you. Truly."

"I have my flaws, Sora, but I'm not a misogynist. Speaking of—" He clasped his hands together and gave an unenthused, "Goddess Chaos, I pledge to thee." Murishani spread his arms wide. "See? You threatened me, but I care more about the fate of the world than my pride. Make Morathma feel the same."

His robes fluttered as he resumed his trek into the darkness.

Sora bid a quick goodbye to the guard, then dragged Chaos away. "That was an impressively colorful threat you gave him."

"I'm friends with Etolié. Learned a few things."

Her sneer suggested Demitri still held the reins. Sora found it refreshing to not be on the receiving end of his threats. "So you failed to murder him?"

"I'm surprised you don't already know."

"We have a long walk back, if you want to tell it now."

As they began their walk, Chaos granted Sora an unquestionably wolfish grin. "Murishani tried to threaten mom using Lady Ayla's soul. This was when she was dead. He took it from Lady Ayla's body. He said mom had to sleep with him, otherwise he'd destroy it. He can take souls, did you know?"

Sora stopped dead in her tracks, utterly appalled. "What?"

"But I was there to try and bite his face off. Unfortunately, he tried to eat *my* soul. Then the spider girl stabbed him."

'Spider girl' was most likely Kah'Sheen, but Sora hadn't the time to consider that one yet. "Why in the world would he want to threaten her into sleeping with him?"

"Oh, he wanted a baby."

Perhaps it was the animalistic spirit, but Demitri was frustratingly sparse on details. "Why?"

"Because he wants to be important to Casvir."

"And he isn't already?"

"He's jealous of mom."

"Why?"

"Because Casvir likes her more than him. You ask a lot of questions. Is this why Lady Ayla says you're nosy?"

This was news to Sora. "You would know better than me, apparently."

"Yeah, I would."

Sora let the matter go.

I will keep you shaded as well as I can. But try to stay out of the sun.

After travelling all night, Uluron spoke the prophetic words at sunrise. By noon, Sora had sweat through her clothing, even in the shade.

A thousand miles of desert stood between Moratham's capital of Andiamen and the Solviran border. No greater defense from Solvira in its heyday, though Sora knew that feud had quelled in recent centuries. Everyone in Solvira knew the Moon had stolen the Stars from the Desert Sands, but when Neoma, the Moon, had perished at the hands of Ilune, her daughter, the Desert Sands had barely rumbled, had even left the Stars alone.

"Morathma was married to Staella once, wasn't he?" Sora asked her Goddess companion.

Neither had spoken much. To her surprise, the brusque cadence suggested Demitri. "Obviously not. They just were together."

"Etolié has only mentioned the stories in passing, with the expected expletives."

"Oh, yeah. He's a rapey motherfucker. That's what Etolié always says, and she means that literally."

Sora blinked at the crass phrase, never quite prepared for Etolié-isms, paraphrased or not. "What?"

"Uh, he beat her mom, Staella. And raped her. Don't you know anything? Then Neoma organized the team to rescue her—"

"No, I gathered the meaning." Sora wiped fresh beads of sweat onto her sleeve, torn between amusement and appall at what a wolf considered humor. "Tell me more about him. I've never been particularly tactful, but I'll be expected to speak." *Unfortunately,* was the unspoken final bit, because while Sora considered herself lucky to have never experienced that sort of assault, it didn't mean the idea wasn't deeply harrowing.

"I never talked to him. Ask Dira."

Sora waited a beat, surprised when Dira didn't naturally manifest. "Do you mind getting her?"

Chaos' sudden sneer revealed fangs. "Stop being a coward. Talk to her!"

Sora flinched at the outburst—but she wasn't the target.

"That's what happens when liars lie, Dira! Now fucking face her or so help me—"

Her rage evaporated, replaced with a contrite smile. "My apologies. Sometimes Demitri is dramatic."

Though clearly bullshit, Sora nodded. "I'd like to know more about Morathma."

"Everything Murishani said was true. He is not a good man, but he is also not a stupid man, and when the angels finally agree to engage with Casvir's forces, he set aside his old grudges to fight alongside them. While the grudge against Solvira has quelled, there is a deep resentment toward necromancy in Moratham's culture. Although he is an earth deity, he and his forces were highly effective against the undead."

"If I may ask . . ." Sora hesitated, any questions regarding the future taboo, but she was apparently 'nosy' anyway, so what was there to lose? "Goddess Staella is concerned that Morathma will try to take advantage of the power void in Celestière. Is there any merit in that?"

Chaos sneered as she mulled it over, biting back a few words until finally saying, "Yes, but Celestière will be in crisis for some time. He is not the only one who tries to take the throne."

"But you're not going to elaborate on that ominous statement, are you."

"No. That aside, I do believe he will pledge," Chaos continued, though she remained contemplative, "but he will need to be approached with care, as Murishani said."

"How honest should we be about the future?"

"Let me lead on that. However . . ." Chaos gazed up through the slivers of sunlight cast through Uluron's claws. "I chose honesty with Sol Kareena because I knew she would not be there."

The ache of Sol Kareena's death remained fresh and raw, stained by bitterness and grief. Sora merely nodded.

A forced smile spread across Chaos' face. "How is Leelan?"

From the safety of her satchel, Sora withdrew the ailing bird—catatonic, yet alive. She brought her waterskin to his beak, heart breaking when he did not react. "Do familiars die when their gods pass on?"

"No. That power remains." When Chaos beckoned, Sora set the bird into her hands. Chaos cradled the small creature, brushing gently along his feathered head. "I am so muted in this body. I feel something strange inside him, but I'm not strong enough to say what. Perhaps when my power is restored, I will have an answer."

"You're from the future. Do you know . . ?"

Chaos shook her head. "Truly, I do not. I sense . . ." Her shoulders slumped as she returned Leelan, words fading in tandem. "Sometimes I am gifted foresight into things I should not know. You will get your answers. I see you staring into a mirror. And . . . there is water. Lots of it. It is dark, though. That is all I can tell you."

Sora set Leelan back into his private space, praying he stayed cool enough. "Anything else I should know about Morathma?"

"Only the obvious, which is to not insult his appearance."

We are near, came Uluron's voice, and Sora shielded her eyes when the dragon uncovered them from her claw.

Andiamen held gleaming towers, glittering in the sunlight without being blinding. Its silhouette shone starkly against the horizon, one of the oldest cities on this continent, rivaling even Neolan and the fallen City of Light.

Sora's stomach lurched as Uluron began her descent, far sooner than she would have thought. "Shouldn't we get closer?"

"The Morathans won't take kindly to an undead dragon. Murishani said to make a spectacle, but we should save Ulu as a final resort."

Sora dreaded the hike, even as Uluron touched the rocky ground. She stumbled onto the scorching terrain, startled at the harshness of the landscape. Shades of orange and yellow colored the rocks, though massive mesas held a vermillion hue, reaching up to the sky. No grass, but a field of shrubs and cacti, many of which Sora did not recognize. Common sense said to not touch a plant covered in spikes, but that did not stop the birds perched inside alcoves carved inside some of the taller ones, their thick growths jutting like arms. Elements of Goddess Staella's meadow were evident, though the eternal night of her home failed to illustrate the brutality of the sun.

Movement caught Sora's eye as a banded lizard waddled lazily from one shrub to the next, its black and bright orange colors a warning that this creature held venom. Sora kept her distance, grateful for her tall boots, as Chaos gave her farewell.

"I anticipate this could take days," the Goddess said. "Don't worry for me. Stay safe, my love."

She kissed her daughter's jaw, her stature minuscule beside the great dragon.

Take care, Sora. Protect my Mother.

"I will," Sora replied, and when Chaos joined her, they began the long trek to Andiamen.

In the late afternoon, Sora drank through her third waterskin. Sweat stained her clothing, dripped from her brow, but finally they stood at the outskirts of Andiamen.

No city gates, but why would they need them? Most travelers did not have a dragon, and the desert would deter all but the most committed of villains. The roads were laid in perfect straight lines, an oddly precise grid for so ancient a city. The homes remained more modest at the outer reaches, but Sora passed mansions as they entered the city proper.

Those they passed stared at the duo of half-elves, but Sora stared right back, unnerved at both their beauty and how . . . disconcertingly similar the majority looked to each other. Gaggles of blonde children followed respectable blonde mothers, protected from the sun by bonnets and wide-brimmed hats. Fathers spoke among themselves as they worked or walked, most clean-shaven. There were outliers, yes, a few brunettes or especially tanned folks, but certainly no elves.

"Are they all Celestials?" Sora whispered to Chaos, who stood equally alert.

"Unless they're converts, they're direct descendants of Morathma, so yes. Heavily angelic-blooded compared to most people. You won't find too many slaves in the larger cities either."

The city grew upward the deeper they walked, and when Chaos took a turn, Sora followed, noting the gleaming white steeple in the distance. The main road was alarmingly wide, large enough for a stagecoach to turn around without trouble, and the flawless grid structure never wavered.

Small temples were commonplace, though symbols of worship were scarce. Sora slowed before one, for it showed a circle of four-point stars but without the crown in the center, setting it apart from what Sora knew of Morathan imagery. "Is that a temple to Staella?"

"They're rare, but they exist. The people love their Goddess Mother and await her return to Father Morathma."

Sora frowned at that, the pieces scattered far too wide to fit together. "That never happens in the future, right?"

"Gods, no. Staella has her flaws, but returning to Morathma? Never."

Chaos continued onward, less inclined to dance in these streets, instead evading carts and horses by sticking to the sidewalk.

Six towers soared to the sky upon the castle in Andiamen. Built of beautiful, white stone, Sora did not have to understand its occupants to appreciate the design. Most of the city was white, perhaps to keep it cool in the sun.

A golden statue rose atop one of the high towers, too distant to decipher the details. But Sora's attention fell from the castle to the approaching guards—not visibly armed, but Celestials held inherent magic. They did not need physical weapons to be formidable.

"How big of a spectacle are you thinking?" Sora whispered.

"The spectacle needs to be to Morathma. But I should at least assume my known form." Silver Fire engulfed her body. She grew to tower above Sora, nearly twice her height.

Now the guards came running, more appearing. Sora prepared the dagger at her wrist. "*Agents of Neoma are not allowed here!*" one guard cried, and Sora stumbled when the earth shifted beneath her, ensnaring her feet.

"I am not of Neoma," Chaos said, her voice emanating as wide as the wind. "I am the Old Goddess of this world. You may know me as Chaos. My Silver Fire was not granted by a goddess. It was infused in me by magic and the mantle of Godhood."

Sora tried and failed to yank her foot from the earth, holding back curses. The guards did still, though remained wary. "What is it you want?" one asked.

"I request an audience with the Speaker of Morathma. No doubt you have heard of my counterpart's return. Perhaps rumors of his quest to separate the planes have reached the desert as well. This is a matter of utmost importance to the New Gods, and God Morathma must speak to me or risk death."

"Wait here," the same guard said, and he stepped aside, muttering into some sort of object.

Sora tightened her core to keep from falling, the reflex of flight fully active, aggravated by her prison. Chaos remained still, floating as a specter above the ground.

Minutes passed, no peace amid the tension. From the castle emerged an elderly man, dressed in white and black. Wisps of white hair remained on his head, his face clean-shaven like the rest of his companions, though he was far spryer down the steps than his age would suggest, calm as he approached Sora and the Old Goddess.

"Greetings," the old man said, his smile either practiced or sincere. "I am Speaker Hemoni, Son of Morathma."

"A pleasure, Speaker Hemoni," Chaos said. "Perhaps your brethren informed you—I am the Goddess of Chaos, and it is of the utmost importance that I speak to God Morathma."

"I have no doubt it is very important," Hemoni said, and Sora could not help but equate his tone with a parent to a child, "but an immediate audience is impossible, unfortunately. Father Morathma has matters in Celestière he is attending to."

"With all due respect, the threat of the God of Order transcends the vacuum of power in Celestière. There will be no Celestière if he is not defeated."

"Surely so, and I encourage you to kneel in prayer and ask. But he is preparing funeral services for the late Sol Kareena. A direct audience is currently impossible."

With a final wrench, Sora managed to yank one foot from the dirt—only to collapse, given her other was still trapped.

"My apologies," the Speaker said, and with a small wave of his hand, Sora was free. "And who are you, companion of Chaos?"

Sora looked a mess, drenched in sweat and now covered in dirt. But she managed to stand tall, forcing power into her voice. "I am Sora Makosa, descended of both the Lineage of the Theocracy and the Fireborns across the sea."

"A respectable family tree on both sides—one royal and one hunters of the undead." The Speaker returned his attention to Chaos. "There will be no audience today. But I encourage you to visit his temples and pray. He will listen."

When the Speaker turned away, Sora suppressed the urge to surge forward. "When, then?"

The Speaker did still, contemplative a moment. "Time is different in the Celestial Realm. Perhaps tomorrow."

Again, he moved to leave. Sora cried, "And what accommodations will there be for the Goddess of Chaos? Would God Morathma have an Old Goddess stay at a common inn?"

The Speaker sighed in a fatherly way, causing Sora's blood to boil. "Accommodations can be made, though it would please Father Morathma if you would dampen your Silver Fire. Whatever its origin for you, it is ungodly to him."

To Sora's surprise, Chaos obeyed, the fire receding to reveal her beautiful half-elf form. When she smiled, she bore no fangs, just as she held no shadow—both illusioned away. She shrunk, but only just so, still standing taller than Sora. "Your hospitality is appreciated. Lead the way."

Sora followed at Chaos' pace, wary of every turn as they entered the castle's decorated doors. The desert heat dissipated as they passed its barrier. Within, the stone gleamed white, decorated with emblems of gold. The Speaker led them through hallways filled with fine furniture and art, the latter mostly dedicated to God Morathma. Sora focused on memorizing the turns, lest they need to escape, even counting the steps when they ascended a fine staircase and rose above even the crystal chandeliers.

They were brought to a spacious suite, filled with embroidered furniture and a magnificent chandelier. Sunlight emanated through grand windows, revealing them to be on the third floor, at least. "There is a font to bathe in through that door," the Speaker said, "and a second bedroom through there, for your companion. Do you require sustenance?"

"No, but Sora does," Chaos replied.

"Then it shall be brought at each mealtime. I must ask, as I do not know precisely how long you will be staying here, that neither of you leave the castle. The populace would be startled by the presence of someone so . . . *esteemed*. It would be preferred you stay in this room, though we would deny church services to no one. On our holy days, you are invited to join us."

"We will respect your instructions while under your roof," Chaos said, "assuming we are granted the same respect."

"There is nothing to fear from me. But ask again tomorrow, and I shall tell you if Morathma has announced his return. In the meantime, rest from your journey. Dinner will be brought soon."

The Speaker and his guards left.

"They're so polite," Sora grumbled, and she marched her way to the washroom. "Is this what you expected?"

"I cannot say what I expected." Chaos settled upon the bed, her height returning to what Sora had come to find familiar. "But I fear I botched the spectacle. In elven lands, Silver Fire is associated first and foremost with me, but across the sea, of course it would be for Neoma and her lineage."

"Well, it's like you said: the spectacle is for Morathma."

"Silver Fire may not be the right way with Morathma either. I'm questioning everything."

"We got this far." Sora stilled in the doorframe, torn between hunger and cleanliness. Sweat did dampen one's appetite, though. "Is there any merit to praying to Morathma?"

"I can try, but I fear that was simply a hollow platitude." Chaos smiled, though tension lingered in her stare. "But tomorrow for certain, right?"

"Tomorrow. Don't lose hope, Dira."

"You're right." The Goddess' shoulders finally relaxed. "Go bathe."

"Before I do . . ." Sora grimaced as she mulled over her words, choosing her next with utmost care. "This is going to be an awkward wait if you keep avoiding talking to me."

"I am not—"

"Demitri never lies. You didn't want to face me earlier, and I suppose I can see why. But we're partners in this quest, and if we can't rely on each other, we might as well part ways."

Humbled, Chaos held her gaze and nodded.

Sora left her to stew, relishing the hope of being clean.

 Chapter 17

Twelve years after the end of the world . . .

Despite her growing discontentment, Dira continued to learn—and with Demitri at her side, new magical powers began to emerge.

Though sweat settled upon her eyelashes, threatening to obscure her vision, Dira trembled as she coaxed the rose bud to open. By small degrees, as minute as the inching of a worm, the flower slowly bloomed.

When it reached maturity, Dira gasped and fell back, exhaustion leaving her dizzy.

That was all right. Just try not to faint next time, dummy.

"I still did it."

You did. And get some water before you do it again. If you die, I lose my brain again.

Dira did manage to stand, sticking out her tongue at her petulant wolf before trudging back to the manor.

Past blooming trees; past blossoming rose bushes; spring had come once more, and with it, Dira's twelfth birthday. She had asked for only one thing.

"What if I could see the beach? Like in my books."

Mother had tutted and patted her head. *"Perhaps you should be reading less exciting literature."*

For her birthday, yesterday, she had received a new knife from Sora, foreign sweets from Etolié, and seven new dresses from Mother.

Why did the walls feel so claustrophobic lately? Dira paused before standing beneath the back patio, the distant stone wall not insurmountable, but . . .

What of those monsters? The ones who stole daughters from mothers?

"You're going to lose my support if you keep up with this bullshit!"

Dira crouched as she slunk forward, drawn by the yelling through the open window.

Mother's laughter sounded, but malevolent, cruel. *"And what does losing your support look like, Etolié?"*

Dira kept her feet silent upon the stone, soon hidden beneath the kitchen window. Etolié had stayed the night—a second birthday gift.

"Don't be fucking stupid. You need me for this war."

"Your aid is appreciated," came Mother's cold voice, *"but you hold no right to criticize my methods."*

"My methods don't involve burning entire villages to the ground."

"No, instead your method is to sell a whole kingdom to Casvir."

That name again . . . Dira held her breath, committing it all to memory. Burning villages? What villages?

"And I hate myself every fucking day, but all you're doing is proving why keeping it out of your hands was the greater good."

"Then leave, Etolié. Go work for Casvir."

Etolié hesitated. *"I don't know how to respond to that."*

"You'll respond with the admittance that you're not better than me. You won't work for Casvir because Casvir murdered Khastra, and you and I are both slaves for love."

Etolié spoke softly, contrite. Dira strained to listen. *". . . burned a village down for love?"*

"In a better world, my love for Dira would mean to build it anew instead of burn it. Alas, I do not have that luxury."

Etolié spoke too quietly to decipher.

"Dira will never find out."

Again, Etolié muttered. Dira reeled at the implications. Secrets filled these walls. When would they finally burst?

"Do you think I do these things because I want to? Do you think I am not ashamed every damn day? I sought to bury my past. Instead, I unearthed it for her. Do not pretend you are better than me."

"Ayla—"

"You need to leave."

When no response came, Dira darted from her hiding space, as softly as she could manage. Water could wait.

Back in the grove, Demitri lazily rolled over. *You look paler. Go rest.*

"Mother and Etolié were fighting. I have to hide that I was listening."

Well, I won't tell.

"You can't."

That's the joke, stupid. You need to learn to hide better.

"I'm good at being quiet."

Lady Ayla listens by going into shadows. Can you do that?

Of course she knew Mother could walk in shadow. But listen from it? "How do I learn to shadow walk?"

I've overheard Lady Ayla talk to mom about it a few times. She said you have to find the cracks between worlds and slip inside.

Dira frowned, the idea odd. "And the cracks are in shadows?"

That's right. Mom couldn't ever do it. I think she managed to find the cracks once though. Remember how you can focus really hard and heal plants?

Dira nodded.

Just do that, but concentrate on darkness instead.

She dared not let hope flutter, but Dira sprinted to the manor, Demitri in tow, seeking the darkest space she could.

Current era . . .

On the evening before their liaison with Executor Faeborn, Casvir brought troubling news: *"According to our spies, there is no Tierzuroth."*

No answers, and no bodies found at the scene. Flowridia simply felt empty.

In the morning, Flowridia stepped through a portal in Nox'Kartha and appeared on a beach across the sea, hardly an hour before sunset.

Bless the scent of salty air. It set her immediately at ease, even as moist sand sought to cling to her boots. Casvir stood nigh, along with his guards, and emerging from a thick jungle beyond was Executor Faeborn.

Flowridia wore a glove to cover her injured hand, lest it spark questions she refused to provide answers for. She wore fine fabrics, designed to downplay the subtle changes pregnancy did to her body. Hardly a bump but unquestionable swelling in her hips and breasts. Five months along, and her hips ached to sit, stand, walk, sleep—anything and everything.

Executor Faeborn wore their own finery, the crown on their head bearing a pattern of stars. Their envoy carried no weapons. Casvir's skeleton guards were equally unarmed, though Flowridia knew they held the upper hand.

Rage filled her to meet their gaze, resisting the urge to touch her fragile womb. How they had learned of the pregnancy, she could not begin to guess. But the flight of rumors was no surprise to her anymore, and her only regret was Ayla's absence.

Not that anyone would believe it was Ayla's baby anyway.

Neither ruler bowed, though a polite acknowledgement did show in Faeborn's smile. "Greetings, Imperator Casvir. I wish to set the tone with an apology. This meeting is long overdue."

"I concur, Executor. But the return of my ward has apparently swayed you."

So like Casvir, to turn the conversation away from himself. Etolié had made mention of his social ineptitude, and while Flowridia did not quite agree, she could not unsee those subtle signs.

Executor Faeborn's impassive countenance softened by subtle degrees. "I don't think it is out of the question to be relieved to learn of her presence in your kingdom, given last I knew, she had disappeared after the massacre at the masquerade. Rumors swirled that you, Imperator Casvir, were the culprit, but I am nothing without my integrity. I have spent the better part of this year disputing those rumors and have told everyone what I witnessed—that it was a party led by The Coming Dawn."

"You are quick to defend my character," Casvir said.

"I have no reason to lie, though I fear a lapse in that same integrity is what brings me here today." Their focus fell to Flowridia. "Greetings, Lady Flowridia. I am curious regarding many things, but I will withhold my personal interests for the sake of diplomacy. However, I hope you will forgive my inquiry, given I fear it may be hurtful: What of your wife? Did she survive the same massacre?"

Faeborn had been the least infuriating of the executors at the summit, having the sense to at least keep any negative opinions to themself. But this same person had ordered an attempt on her life. Flowridia kept her clenched fists behind her back. "She is well. I hope you'll indulge a question of my own: why did you send that assassin?"

Faeborn frowned. "I beg your pardon?"

Her anger rose. "Are you confused because he failed?"

"I'm confused because I've sent no assassins. The war has been secondary in my mind since Tierzuroth was decimated. Surely you heard."

"We have, but the assassin was a Whispering Elf."

"And it must have been on someone else's orders," Faeborn said, a subtle sharpness to their tone. "Lady Flowridia, I am deeply sorry that there was an attempt on your life, but I truly had nothing to do with it. I am here for peace talks, and from a practical standpoint, murdering the imperator's ward would undermine that goal."

The denial was not unexpected, but Flowridia had not anticipated Faeborn to be a skilled performer. "Then why did you agree to meet if I came here?"

"Because I know you to be reasonable. Ayla Darkleaf said you had a kind heart. And while I am incredibly wary of your changes in allegiance, I am a desperate person. When you were Empress Consort of Solvira, you helmed the welcoming of the Theocracy of

Sol Kareena's refugees. Half my country became refugees overnight. There is no fight in us anymore. Goddess Ku'Shya has defeated us, and we are no longer safe in our homeland."

Nothing they said was unreasonable, and Flowridia so hated how it pulled at the strings in her heart. Furthermore, she could commiserate with their fear of Ku'Shya. The demon goddess was a frightful enemy to have. "Why would Goddess Ku'Shya destroy you?"

"We are asking the same question, I assure you. I fear it was our alliance with the God of Order, toward whom she holds a grudge. The God of Order assured us we would be protected, but he has disappeared. Surely you know our beloved Goddess of Chaos has returned, but she has vanished as well. Despite my people's prayers, we are an open wound. We are starving, picked off by feral animals in the jungle."

It was too simple; too convenient. If Faeborn spoke true, some piece was missing. "Why us, though? Why not approach your allies?"

And there it was—the first flicker of anxiety across Faeborn's face. "We elves are barely aligned." Clear hesitation showed in their breath, yet they said nothing more.

"Yet Velen'Kye is housing refugees from the north?"

"Precisely why they lack the resources to help us."

Flowridia said nothing, instead assembling what pieces she had in her head.

"Surrender can be negotiated," Casvir said. "Where is General Khastra?"

Their flickering smile showed the second chink in their armor. "She is not a piece I am in a position to negotiate."

"I will accept the Whispering Elves' surrender upon her return."

"The Bringer of War is not under my jurisdiction, Imperator."

The truth slammed Flowridia like a blow to the stomach. "That's why Ku'Shya destroyed Tierzuroth. Because of Khastra."

Faeborn's hesitation showed in a twitch in their eye, the sudden sheen of sweat on their brow. "It was a contributing factor."

"Khastra is back with her mother, isn't she. You don't have her at all. And your allies are angry that you lost her."

A glance to Casvir showed a darkened countenance. There was weight to her claim.

"Lady Flowridia, we are discussing matters that would damn my people to verify," Faeborn said, their tone as taut as harp strings.

"Be that as it may," Casvir said, "my terms have not changed."

"And with all possible respect, I fear Goddess Ku'Shya far more than I fear you, and there is not a citizen among the Whispering Elves who would disagree."

"If protection from the Goddess of War is part of your terms for surrender, it can be negotiated."

"Imperator, I have no say in the Bringer of War's fate. That is simply fact."

"Then it was your mistake to give her up."

Resignation fell upon Faeborn's face, though bitterness stained their words. "Imperator Casvir, you are a man with a reputation, but your reign is shorter than an elven lifespan. Goddess Ku'Shya is older than the Convergence of Planes, and with the death of Sol Kareena, there is no contest to her place as the most powerful of the New Gods. My mistake was trusting the God of Order to keep his word and protect us while I lied to Goddess Ku'Shya that we did not have her. We were only spared bloodshed because I returned her before the news reached Goddess Ku'Shya. It does not curtail the cost of her revenge. Do not make the mistake of assuming she would not do far worse to you. Cut your losses. Leave the Bringer of War in Goddess Ku'Shya's possession. I do not say that as an executor. I say that as a person with a soul, who does not want to see your innocent populace slaughtered. I will send machines to fight the dead, and perhaps seasoned soldiers to a fight they have accepted might be their doom, but I do not condone genocide."

They looked to Flowridia, whose rage had quelled, leaving only emptiness. "Lady Flowridia, I am, again, deeply sorry someone sought to take your life. They were not one of mine. And while I accept the futility of my plea, I am not too proud to ask one final time. My people need help. If you have any sway, I am willing to offer my brightest minds for your schools, my finest inventors for your employment, even shed my mantle of executor and work in Nox'Kartha's court. Our children are dying in the jungle. Please."

It would be bold, indeed, to send an assassin to slay a pregnant woman and plea for the children's sake in one breath. Flowridia thought of the life in her womb, how vibrant and bold it would someday be . . .

"Nothing they're asking for is unreasonable," she said softly, turning to Casvir. "I know you're angry about Khastra, but your terms for citizenship have always been a pledge of godhood. If the Whispering Elves will agree to that, would you accept it? I suspect Faeborn would accept a harsher punishment, but they have a point. They have bright minds to offer your populace. All they ask is what you already provide."

Casvir gave no indication of his heart on his face, but his words were crystal clear. "Any citizen of yours who will pledge their allegiance to me will be accepted into my country. Any who will not will be left to die. My plans for you, executor, will be determined, and will be put into writing before you are allowed to join them. Those are my terms."

"That is acceptable," Faeborn said, palpable relief in the words. "I will have the message delivered. Time is of the essence, however."

"I will return in two days to this same beach. Bring any who will pledge."

"Of course."

"As a gesture of goodwill, you will pledge now. Right here."

Words were nothing, meant nothing until sealed with signatures signed in blood. But all the shackles of pride left Faeborn as they fell to one knee and gave allegiance to the enemy.

Just one more step toward Casvir's supremacy over the realm, and Flowridia's gut clenched to see her part in it. Today, she saved lives. But if Faeborn knew the darkness Casvir would bring, would they throw themselves in Ku'Shya's maw instead?

Flowridia left with a curt farewell, her mind too loud to listen to Faeborn's gratitude. When Casvir summoned his portal, she walked wordlessly through, numb above all else.

They appeared in his office. Her stomach ached from more than simply the meeting, trapped in the ails of pregnancy.

But when she tried to leave, Casvir said, "I am impressed."

She met his gaze, the silent question conveyed.

"I did not expect to be disappointed, but you were clever in your assessment. You did not allow your anger to control you. And your argument for providing aid was practical enough to sway me."

Pride did fill her at the words, his approval unexpected. "Thank you."

His reply was held hostage in the silence, his gaze uncharacteristically soft. "You are a capable person, even without your magic. I hope you have not forgotten."

To deny it came innately, yet to actually speak it . . . She curtailed her response, contemplative instead. "I've felt so lost since Demitri's death. My focus was on healing, and now on this baby. I . . . I don't want to say I've forgotten, but I've felt useless more often than not."

"You survived in the woods without magic," Casvir replied, paternal warmth in his words. "I will not pretend to understand the extent of what Mereen stole from you, but I can say you are strong for growing past it. Do not discount what I just witnessed. As many elven lives as will pledge to me are lives you have saved. That is a different sort of magic."

Flowridia managed to nod, torn between pride and existential despair for what it meant. Each step forward would take miles to undo, but it did not change that there was no one who built her up quite like him. "Thank you."

"You were instrumental in protecting the refugees in Solvira. Would you be willing to helm the integration of the Whispering Elves?"

Yes, her bleeding heart said, or perhaps it was desperation, trapped in the golden chains of sickness. Or was it practicality? She did have Solvira's template to work with. Even now, she felt pride at her own success. "I would—"

But Ayla . . .

". . . like to think about it."

"Understandable, but I need an answer quickly. I am meeting with Faeborn in two days. There is much to plan in the meantime. I will find you tonight."

There were no windows in Casvir's office, but instinct said it was still early. Just a few hours more, and her fate—and that of the elves—would be sealed. "Of course. But . . . what about Khastra?"

"You were equally clever in deducing that from their responses."

"But what will you do?"

"I have not decided."

He said nothing more of it, simply bid her farewell as she left, her response half-hearted as she declined his offer of an escort. She could save these people; she already *had* saved these people, but the thought of abandoning the task now made her ill. Had she not done the same in Solvira? Saved the refugees, only to skip away and leave them to Nox'Kartha's mercy? Etolié had once done the same—freeing slaves in Moratham, saving lives, only to abandon them to Solvira's whim, who eventually insisted Etolié do the work herself.

But Ayla had said . . . Ayla had *begged* . . .

She set her hand on her stomach as she walked to the medical ward, wondering idly if Etolié had returned. Was the news of Khastra's presence in Ku'Shya's Realm actually good? Etolié would know. Perhaps hope was not lost for Khastra to return.

She found only Ayla in the medical suite.

Ayla set aside her book—*Blood and Battlefields: A History of the Solviran Monarchy.* She flaunted a precious smile as she skipped to Flowridia's side, embracing her tightly. "Did you get your revenge? Is Faeborn a wet stain on the ground?"

"Faeborn didn't send the assassin," Flowridia said, the truth of it finally settling. But if not them . . . who?

Ayla frowned. "Tell me everything."

Ayla escorted her to the couch as she began her tale, withholding nothing—until the end. "Casvir, he—"

Her words stopped abruptly, stolen by slight fluttering against her hand. Her joy surged. Flowridia looked to her stomach, gasping to feel the motion again.

"Flowra, are you all right?"

Gently, Flowridia took Ayla's hand and set it against her womb. "The baby's moving."

But Flowridia felt nothing inside her, nor did Ayla seem nearly so enthralled. "As would be expected. You are approximately twenty-two weeks along."

Flowridia willed the baby to move again, to let Ayla feel this same magic...but it had quelled. She shoved away her disappointment. "Next time, perhaps."

"Such interesting developments," Ayla mused, though Flowridia questioned if the segue were so deliberately sharp. "Faeborn will tell the world they fear Ku'Shya more than they fear Soliel. I cannot say they're wrong, but I wonder how the world will respond."

"If Casvir takes proper care of the refugees, it'll show the world he's reasonable."

"He will. He treats all citizens the same."

Flowridia cursed her hollow stomach, cursed this anxiety she felt toward her wife. "Casvir is impressed with how I managed the refugees from the Theocracy. He asked me to helm integrating the elven refugees."

All amusement drained from Ayla's face. "You see what this is, right?"

"He really does have faith in me. He's not trying to be manipulative."

"But you told him no, right?"

"I told him I would think about it," Flowridia muttered, wondering when it had become so wrong to want. "If I follow the same path as Solvira, it'll only be a few weeks of work. Less, even, given it'll only be one group. Ayla . . . I want to do this. I want to do something other than stay caged in this suite. I finally have an opportunity to make myself useful."

"Even though I explicitly asked you—"

"Has it occurred to you that you're being unfair?!" Though she tried to bite back the sharp words, they came from deep inside, highlighting a bitter and poignant truth. "You're paranoid. Worse, you're being controlling. I don't want to go against you, but can you please try to see my point of view? Every part of me hurts. I haven't had magic in almost a year. I'm in constant pain and for as much as I've worked to heal, I'm languishing in so many ways. Finally, I have this opportunity to make a difference, despite my limitations, yet you would guilt me into giving it up? I'm not going to stay in Nox'Kartha, and your obsession with this . . . this *idea* that I would shows that you don't trust me. This baby will be born, and then we're walking away. What more can I give you than my word?"

Ayla did not blink. Instead, she rose from the couch, evading Flowridia's touch with ease. Her stare never faltered, trapping Flowridia like knives against the wall. Yet her words came small, as fragile as a candle's flame. "I have made a fool of myself enough in the past by refusing to trust you. But I . . . I do. It's Casvir I don't trust, but you're right. I am sorry, Flowra."

"We're leaving, Ayla," Flowridia said, rising despite her aching hips. "Please, trust me in that."

When offered, Ayla fell tentatively into Flowridia's embrace. "I love you, Flowra."

"I love you too."

They held to the other, the strings that bound them weathered but strong, and Flowridia prayed it would be enough.

Officially, Etolié was not allowed to have leaves of absence given Flowridia's current physical state.

But when she had informed—yes, *informed*—Casvir that she would be attending Sol Kareena's funeral, he was surprisingly receptive. Intrigued, even.

"You will report everything you see."

She would not, but she could spin a good yarn.

As it was, Etolié felt ill as she sat beside her mother inside a temple in Vanir Sol. Silence reigned. Etolié swore she heard the faint undulations of her own wings against the air. This temple was built of white stone, with no roof, so the light might freely permeate the space. It spread out as an amphitheater of sorts, circular seating all facing an altar in the center of the room. Hundreds of angels and Celestials filled the space, their misty eyes settling upon the closed coffin in the center.

In the era before the Convergence, though angels had lived long lives, they did pass on to the Unknown. And after the Convergence, all the angels who had lived through it had passed away with time—except for the ones who had become gods, blessed and cursed with true immortality. Funeral rites were rusty, but Celestials did pass on at rare times.

As far as Etolié knew, the last funeral for an angel had been . . . Neoma's.

And how ironic and heartbreaking, for the next to be one of the other few remaining relics of Old Vanir, in the era before the Convergence. Even Etolié's own mother had no memory of the time before the Convergence in Celestière. She had been born on that fateful, apocalyptic day, hailed as a symbol of hope to a decimated populace.

Eionei was among those relics, and so of course he led the rites. His voice wavered. He held no foundation at all, simply let his tears flow as he bid farewell to an old and dear friend. Upon an altar before the casket, three candles burned—one for each sun that had once cast their light upon Celestière. The Triple Suns were long extinguished, destroyed in the Convergence, but a few alive remembered—Eionei among them. First, he had lit each candle with a song written for the fallen Sun Goddess. Now, as he spoke of Sol Kareena's childhood, he extinguished the first candle. The second burned as he spoke of her accomplishments—and there were many.

Etolié realized she might've had the only clear eyes in the room, numb at the influx of emotion around her. Of course her mother wept, both for the loss of a complicated friendship and for the child who would never see his mother again.

Soliel was still at Momma's house, watched over by a nanny.

Etolié had been confused at first. Refusing to give the little boy that final closure, even if he wouldn't understand, was cruel. And yet . . .

Celestière was no monarchy, but some already whispered that Soliel could grow into Vanir Sol's throne. One remained to contest that, and a few in the know feared it could come to blood.

Seated in the front row, granted a place of honor for his status as Sol Kareena's nephew, was Morathma.

Etolié had never met the man or seen him in person. Artwork rarely depicted him, but Etolié knew through song that he was a mutilated man, burned in the early years of the mortal realm by Neoma's Silver Fire. But imagination didn't fill in the brutal truth: that his wings of light had been melted into the other, that there was no part of him that wasn't a scar. There was not a speck of hair upon his body that she could see, the rough texture of his skin apparent even through the amber glow burning beneath. Blasphemers called him "The Snake God." Once, Solvira had burned a wooden snake statue to celebrate Neoma's victory in the Festival of Flame.

She'd imagined their meeting before, usually with it devolving into a series of swears on her part, perhaps decapitation. It was a damn good thing she was too numb to function, but looking at him definitely kindled some truly rancid emotions.

Speaking as the empress, it seemed about fucking time to revive the Festival of Flame.

When Etolié zoned back in, she realized the second candle had been extinguished. Eionei spoke of legacy now, struggling with composure all the while.

Soon, the final candle was snuffed.

Eionei opened the casket, heartbreak appearing anew on his shattered features. He knelt, then collapsed, his weeping filling the quiet space. Something sharp pierced Etolié's stony defenses to see it, clenching her fists to ward away tears. Eionei was a laughing god, unflappable . . .

Staella moved to stand, but Alystra appeared first at his side, coaxing him to rise with gentle whispers. Those in the first row rose to pay their final respects, including Morathma, who was not a friend here, no, but he was a relic. He was Sol Kareena's nephew. Family was always complicated.

What a strange void in life, funerals. Grudges could be set aside; family and lovers could reunite for this one blip in time and cry as one despite their feuds. Tomorrow, Alystra would hate Eionei. Tomorrow, Morathma would be banned from Vanir Sol.

Today . . . Etolié followed when Staella rose, receptive when she held her hand. So many mourners sat ahead of them, but Etolié trusted Momma to know what was right. She illusioned her sixth handkerchief since the start and offered it forward, managing a small smile at her momma's gracious nod.

Sol Kareena's body was dressed to hide her injuries. But a scarf around her neck did not change that the God of Order had decapitated her—his own mother. Once, she had radiated gold, yet her wings were extinguished, her body greyed without their light. She appeared as though sleeping, though there was no gentleness in her demeanor, no familiar smile welcoming Etolié into her palace as a child.

And no tearful acceptance when Etolié had told her she would rather be banished than tell Celestière the truth about her father's murder. Simply nothing at all.

Etolié was fifty years old, but once she had been fourteen. Once, she had been a child weeping in her aunt's arms for a final time. And, *gods*, it wasn't fucking fair. It wasn't fair to do to a child, wasn't fair that it severed the tenuous family bonds between Sol Kareena and Staella, wasn't fair that Etolié had grown up too quickly in the first place . . .

It wasn't fair that as soon as the tentative strings of forgiveness had been tied . . . Sol Kareena's life had been extinguished.

Tomorrow, Etolié would scream. Today, her tears prickled in her eyes, streaming down her face. At her first sob, Staella squeezed her hand. Etolié held her, shoving away the discomfort of touch for her momma's comfort. But the world didn't vanish in her momma's embrace. In Celestière, the gods mourned; in Sha'Demoni, Khastra's future lay uncertain; in the mortal realm, a God sought to destroy them all.

Today, Celestière wept, but tomorrow . . . a vast unknown.

Etolié soon let Momma lead her away, toward the wall where Eionei wept in Alystra's arms. Alystra was not a relic of Old Vanir— the youngest of the New Gods, aside from Ilune. Her tears flowed softly, caught between her own heartbreak and keeping Eionei from collapsing anew. At Staella's appearance, Alystra let her take over, sparing a moment to wipe her own tears. Her red glow was dim as she forced a smile. "Your mom says you don't like hugs." Instead, she took Etolié's hand, squeezing as fresh cries shook her.

Etolié watched through blurry vision as other deities paid their respects, bidding farewell to their beloved leader. Not always popular, no, but beloved, her authority unquestioned even when she herself was questioned.

Etolié's sorrow faded again into numbness, though her tears never dried.

Eventually, Eionei rose, joining Alystra in holding her hand. "I love you, Starshine," he managed with trembling lips.

"I love you too, Gramps." Etolié let them go, and Alystra escorted Eionei away.

Momma faced her, her face swollen though her tears had dried. "When Neoma died, Celestière froze, too shocked to even mourn at first. So many didn't believe it. But here . . . our memories are longer than mortals. I don't know that we ever stopped mourning Neoma, yet now, we mourn her sister—" Staella's voice broke, breath catching as she warded away fresh tears. "Death is no longer a part of our existence. We don't know how to move on."

Etolié's attention flickered to an approaching beacon of amber light. "Momma . . ."

Rather than figure out how the hell to inform Staella that a certain snake was slithering, Etolié's tone apparently held warning enough. Staella's entire demeanor shifted, a practiced vacancy stealing even her sorrow. "I know what you want to do, but say nothing."

Staella turned to stand between Etolié and the approaching Morathma, the latter towering above her sweet momma. "Tragic times," Morathma said, his deep voice oddly soothing for a man with none of his original skin.

"Indeed," Staella replied, and while she was not quite cold, Etolié couldn't say she was welcoming either. "I'm sorry for your loss. Kareena's death is a blow to us all, but her ties to you are through blood."

"And your ties are through marriage. We have both lost family this day. But you have not lost everyone." To Etolié's aggrievement, his attention fell to her. "You must be Etolié."

Etolié had lost track of her facial expression, surely looking horrified to face this asshole—the same asshole she had spent ten years of her life undermining and freeing slaves from. Momma had said to say nothing, which was turning into a shockingly easy order to obey, given her entire repertoire of words had vanished from her head.

"Morathma, look at me."

He obeyed, though Etolié's gaze followed. Now, Staella did radiate ice, her gentle demeanor becoming stone. "This is a funeral," she whispered. "It's a place to be polite to people we can't stand for the common good because ruining a funeral may be the second highest of social faux pas—behind spousal rape, of course. But it's not an invitation to talk to my baby. Walk away before I ruin your aunt's funeral."

Etolié illusioned a neutral face to hide her shock, hands flying to cover her mouth lest she squeak—or clap. Hardly a twitch to Morathma's eye, though Etolié questioned how much facial mobility he had, given his scars. Still, the chill between them ran both ways as he offered a polite nod and left.

Once alone, Etolié dropped the illusion. "Holy shit, you murdered him."

"I don't besmirch him coming to this event," Staella said, her anger wafting, "but he has some audacity talking to my child."

"He sounds like the kind of man who's gotten pretty far in life through audacity."

Staella's smile held no joy at all. "You're not wrong, Starshine. As it is, my heart is now both broken *and* bitter, so unless you have business to attend to, I would like to leave."

The reminder held weight. Etolié had nearly forgotten where they were.

There sat the casket, the mourners still attending. Etolié spotted a glimpse of golden hair and felt emotion choke her. "I'd like to go."

Staella took her hand and led her away. Through Vanir Sol, Etolié cried anew.

"I gotta start wrapping this up, Beefcake. Funerals are only so long."

Etolié lay secure in her favorite demon's arms, cursing that the world must turn. Time passed differently in Sha'Demoni, and Khastra's face had filled out, no longer resembling death's door. Still lither than Etolié had always known, but Khastra had managed to walk from her bed all the way to the entrance to her mother's cave and back today, supervised by the Goddess of War herself.

With Khastra's healing came uncertainty of the future, but for now, strong arms crushed Etolié in a precisely perfect way. They'd done nothing more intimate than swap a few impassioned kisses. Khastra even wore clothing this time, which made her an oddity among her family. While Etolié would rank naked cuddling above even the finest of booze, with or without sex, her presence was more than enough. Khastra kissed her cheek, her temple, her hair, and finally her ear.

"I'd truly never seen a murder both so quick and so painful," Etolié said, regaling the tale of the funeral. "And I'd definitely never seen my sweet mother so damn scary. This tops the time I accidentally joked about dead aborted babies in front of her."

Even Khastra cringed at that. "Why would you possibly jest about that in front of Staella?"

"Because I'm stupid and got carried away. But the devastation I felt was still nothing compared to how he was surely feeling. Not that he could show it. His skin seems a little . . . stiff. You ever met him?"

"Yes. Our first meeting was much longer ago than you would think. He was not yet a god, but he and your mother came to my mother to forge an alliance and left unsuccessful. My mother did not like him, but she became fond of yours. I was there." Khastra gave a nervous chuckle. "I should not say how young I was, but I was, at least, younger than your mother."

Etolié shrugged, unflappable while in Khastra's strong embrace. "The family dynamics are weird, Beefcake. I'm trying to just embrace that. I might even ask you about dating my sister someday."

Khastra's nerves clearly didn't settle, her smile less enthused. "For honor's sake, I will answer any questions you have, when the time comes."

And to Etolié's surprise . . . she didn't feel too awkward as one bubbled up. "I know you don't still love her, but . . . did you?"

"Of course I did. I am incapable of not falling in love with my partners, as you have often teased."

"Did she love you?"

At that, Khastra became quiet, contemplative as she stared onto a blank space on her blanket. "Perhaps. Perhaps not. Forgive my jaded perspective, but I am not convinced she is capable of love without selfish intentions. I had pledged myself to Solvira and to her, and in my moments of doubt, there was nowhere to go, and in my moments of certainty, I still often bit my tongue. We were as brutal and effective a team as you would imagine—the Bringer of War and the God of Death—but it was only after the war, after she was put in her prison, that I realized how far from myself I had fallen. I was not proud of who I was or the things I had done. I had never been a hero, but I hated to think I had become a villain in the history books. So I disappeared from Solvira for a century and lived in Sha'Demoni instead, while I healed my mind and heart."

Etolié had expected a single word answer, perhaps a small diatribe—not to gain a taste of Khastra's once-broken heart. She brought a hand up to cup her demon's cheek. "You've always been a hero to me."

Khastra chuckled, some light returning to those glowing eyes. "It is simply a fact that you have always brought out the best in me. I was not much of a hero in Staelash, but I think I was a hero to you."

"You're still my hero, you fucking sap."

Yet something dimmed in Khastra's gaze once more. "To fight for Casvir is heroic to you?"

Much to Etolié's chagrin, this was a damn fine segue . . . Ku'Shya's request weighed heavily upon her. "Casvir has your brain in a vice. It's not the same. That said . . . Beefcake, you don't have to go back."

Khastra frowned. "It is as you said—he has my brain in a vice. He will break it if I delay too long. The fact that he has not only means he is holding to hope of my return."

"Your mom seems to think there're ways to free you."

Fuck, the sudden darkness in Khastra's gaze didn't bode well. "I was unaware you two had spoken."

"Before you accuse me of conspiring—no. We had one conversation, and she asked me if I would talk to you about letting her help you get away from Casvir. She also brought up that malice isn't in the repertoire of emotions demons evolved to have, so while I don't fucking know what that means in the end, she's not going to betray you."

Resignation colored Khastra's sigh. "No, she is not. It is not Demoni way."

"I think the most important thing is what you want. Do you want to go back to Nox'Kartha?"

To her surprise, Khastra shrugged. "My apathy has only grown during my captivity. Perhaps I am jaded because of it. It was not a comfortable experience."

"'Not a comfortable experience'—Beefcake, you were chained up in sensory deprivation hell for ten fucking months. Has it occurred to you that you're traumatized?"

Khastra's chuckle set the whole world at ease, despite the bitter subject. "Death would have been preferable, yes. Alas, I am still here."

Just as quickly, Etolié's ease plummeted. She pulled away from Khastra's embrace, trembling as she stroked a soft line down the half-demon's cheek. Gods, her next words might break her, but it had to be said. Khastra had already met her earned end. "Is that what you want? To . . . to move on?"

Khastra's smile remained, yet her glowing eyes seemed to dim. "It is not so simple as that. I am sorry to worry you. It was not my intention."

Etolié resisted when Khastra sought to pull her back down atop her warm body. Her warmth was not natural, for her undeath was cursed by a brutal blending of science and magic. "What if you were alive? Would you feel like this?"

Khastra quieted. Her thumb stroked soft lines across Etolié's back, a perfect comfort even in the chasm of time. "No. I was unhappy in Staelash, but I was not . . . restless. My days, no matter how mundane, had meaning."

"And what if you were dead but free from Casvir?" Etolié pulled back to touch her beautiful face, to trace the etched lines of her smile, those ancient laughter lines. "You'd have the whole world to yourself. No wars, unless you want them."

Khastra's hand covered Etolié's own, engulfing it fully. "Is that what you would ask of me? Or is that what my mother asked of you?"

"Your mom just asked me to talk to you. She says she has the means to free you, but . . ." Emotion choked Etolié, her own tears finally threatening to rise and fall. "Of course I want you here, ya big lug. But not if it's killing you to stay."

This was not a ledge Khastra needed to be talked away from. Khastra had fallen years ago, stabbed through the spine by a demon god. Khastra had earned her peace, only to be ripped back.

Khastra, the sun to her orbiting moon. If she extinguished, what became of Etolié?

"I will consider it," Khastra replied. "But you must know that while my mother holds no malice, neither does she hold altruism. There is a cost to every bargain."

"If it makes any difference, she said she'd have to fight you to get the hammer back. So it wouldn't be that."

"She has mentioned it, yes."

Yet something else discomforting swirled about in Etolié's head, her interactions with the Goddess of War . . . perhaps unnervingly pleasant. "Am I stupid to think your mom isn't all that bad? She's kinda charming in her amoral way. And I know you have your issues, but she's shown she loves you. According to Sora, she never stopped harassing Executor Faeborn about you. She destroyed an entire city over you." *And let them all live*, but those were words Etolié did not say, though they made her contemplative.

There were times Etolié's heart ached to consider her relationship with her own mother, but nothing compared to the warmth she felt to think how far they'd come, that she'd spoken healing words: *"I forgive you."*

"Do you know why I left my mother's court?" Khastra asked.

"You led a slave rebellion and stole your mom's hammer. My momma put a constellation in the sky over it. Of course I know that story."

"Yes, and I led that rebellion because the cruelty she was exhibiting was unbearable to me. I have never quite seen myself as an elf, but it does not change that they are half the blood in my veins, and to watch her work them to death and torture and eat them became too much."

The added details did paint a far more gruesome tale. "But that was thousands of years ago. She doesn't have slaves anymore . . . right?"

Khastra shook her head, resignation in the gesture. "She stopped shortly after the rebellion, yes. But it was not because she learned a grand lesson. It was in deference to me."

"I don't want to push, but this proves my point, doesn't it? Your mom wants to help you. And look . . . if you want to go—" Etolié choked on the word, cursing her sudden rise in tears. But for Khastra to feel so lost . . . Was it only because of the torturous prison, or did this run deeper? "If you want to go, you've earned that, but if you think you might find a second chance without Casvir, she would help you." Despite herself, mist filled her vision. "Is this about that 'villain in the history books' thing? Is that what you think you are now?"

Khastra gulped, her jaw becoming stiff. "My legacy could have been to have perished in a fight against Izthuni and an Old God, but it is far too late for that now. They will not remember. They will only remember that I inflicted death upon the very people I once fought my own mother to save."

"I hate to risk sounding manipulative," Etolié said, forcing a smile, "but breaking free could give you a chance to rewrite that. You might even be happy again."

"It is a lovely dream. I will consider it. Truly."

When Khastra wouldn't meet her gaze, Etolié gently coaxed her, setting a hand on her chin. "For what it's worth, I . . ."

I want you to stay, but she didn't say it.

". . . I want you to be happy."

She meant it, but it paled to how desperately she yearned.

Khastra kissed her silently, her own longing conveyed. "It has been longer than you intended. You should go back to Nox'Kartha."

"I don't want to leave you like this."

When Khastra sat up, Etolié shuffled back, meeting her embrace with desperation. "I am asking for time to think. But I swear, this is not the last time. You will see me again."

Oh, her heart ached. But didn't it always? Though safe, for now, Khastra was a world away. "I love you, Khastra."

"I love you so much, Etolié."

Khastra kissed her before loosening her embrace, and though it tore her soul in twain, Etolié managed the fortitude to leave her behind.

Etolié wasn't familiar enough with any particular part of Nox'Kartha to risk teleporting herself there, so Solvira it was. The underground library was reminiscent enough to the one in Staelash for her to envision its sights, smells, and the sound of an angry Skalmite clicking at her to eat.

The world shifted, and Etolié stood on wooden floorboards.

The space held purposeful clutter, organized chaos at its finest. She knew where everything was, as did Zoldar, and no one else actually mattered.

Speaking of, her insectoid friend skittered down from one of the massive shelves, aggressively signing upon landing.

"Casvir's here? Where?"

Zoldar gave a few fast clicks. *Upstairs, somewhere. Murishani is here too.*

"I don't have any hickeys, right?"

Zoldar, forever longsuffering, inspected her neck with bulbous crystal eyes, and quickly signed, *No.*

Bless him. He never asked questions. Etolié put on a robe and actually brushed her hair—damn Murishani and his Silver Fire—then illusioned a fancier ensemble to cover it and hurried up the stairs.

A servant pointed her toward the parlor, and while the question remained as to why they were having a meeting in *her* house, at least she hadn't gotten the dreaded, *"Hi, knock knock!"*

It was her own damn house, so knocking was optional. She pushed the double doors open as dramatically as her waifish frame could muster, hands on her hips as her least favorite dictator and his yappy dog quieted. "Hello, boys. I'm guessing you're here for me."

Casvir wore armor, and there was nothing clever to say about that at this point. Murishani stood at her entrance and bowed, just as he was trained. "Well, good evening, Empress Etolié of Solvira, Daughter of Stars, Savior of Slaves, and former Magister of Staelash."

"You forgot one." She didn't say *bitch*. Bitch was implied.

Murishani's smirk could have stabbed a kitten. "Granddaughter of Eionei."

"Thank you." She sighed and bowed as low as she needed to be beneath Casvir's head—which thankfully, even sitting, wasn't too low. "If he's gonna be good, so am I. What's going on? We don't normally meet here."

"Empress Etolié, have a seat," Casvir said, his monotone somewhere between *your girlfriend is a prisoner of war,* and *I intend to kick your ass in this sing-off.* "There is news pertinent to both you and Viceroy Murishani, and given the boundaries set around Flowridia, I elected to meet here."

Murishani's eye sure twitched a lot more lately, and never so violently as when that flowery bastard was mentioned.

"Per your preference, I will tell you the important part first. General Khastra has been found."

That this was news was frankly so insane that Etolié nearly forgot to be surprised. As it was, she prayed her delay was taken as shock. Due to fuckface and his Silver Fire, there would be no illusionary acting this day. Instead, Etolié drove her nails into her palm while dwelling on the memory of Khastra's crispy body, and managed to summon tears. "What?"

"My meeting with Executor Faeborn took an unexpected turn. They gave the general to Goddess Ku'Shya to evade her wrath, which is infuriating but workable. They and a subset of their citizens have offered surrender, and I will be accepting them in two days' time."

Thankfully, Etolié only had to pretend to not know half of that. "Wait, what happened with Executor Faeborn?"

Casvir elaborated, though utilitarian the explanation remained. Etolié spent half the explanation thinking about her final goodbye to Lara in order to shed more tears.

"But how this pertains to you," Casvir continued, "is a part of Lady Flowridia's written proposal involves the possibility of Solvira accepting a subset of skilled refugees to assist in the rebuilding of the palace. Is this feasible?"

"Zoldar keeps my notes, but I would say most likely."

"Aside from that, while your connection to General Khastra is pertinent, it is your relationship to her family that may be most valuable. You are friendly with The Coming Dawn. Are you friendly with Goddess Ku'Shya?"

"Uh . . . yes, kinda?"

"Good. Then you will speak to her."

No need to ask what about. Etolié spared a moment to wipe her eyes as she contemplated what non-suspicious thing to say next. "Are you sure?"

"Why would I not be? I would presume you have personal investment in her return."

Because under any other series of circumstances, the risk of antagonizing Ku'Shya further was a death sentence for Khastra, given there would be no use in keeping her spirit in her body if there was no hope in getting her back, but Etolié's common sense began tingling, so she forced a smile regardless. "Just checking. I'll need time to, uh, set up the meeting."

"Will you need assistance? I can provide an emissary."

"No, my momma can help. She's Ku'Shya's best friend, apparently. I also think her only." Oh, Etolié was just dropping facts today. Better to keep things impersonal.

"I expect an update before the end of the week."

That timeline made her want to puke. "With all the funeral business, Celestière is more than a little bit in crisis, and, uh, Sha'Demoni isn't much better. It's a big deal when a god dies. Can I have . . . two?"

As always, Casvir was a closed book encased in stone and buried six feet underground. "At the most."

And Etolié would do her damnedest to get the fucking ritual done before then. "Absolutely, Imperator First and Last."

"Excellent. Now, Viceroy Murishani, will you tell her your news?"

"Oh, it's nothing *too* important," Murishani said, drawling his words to suggest his news was, indeed, very important. "Just this."

And that bastard opened a box in the table to reveal the fucking Light Orb. "What the actual fuck?"

"Your friend Sora stopped by with her rude ghost friend." He snapped the box shut. "They wanted to see you, but you were out. They've gone to Moratham to try and win over the Jewel of the Desert."

"This is a safe space. I encourage scaly slander."

"Fine, fine. Off to win over the reptilian rapist. Are you happy?"

"Medicine to my soul. You said 'rude' ghost friend? Did she do a crazy?"

"I would say more 'threatening.'"

Etolié, having been on the receiving end of 'threatening,' gave a curt nod. "Got it. Well, I wouldn't have been much help, given my whole thing was…is…undermining the crispy man's slave network. Speaking of." Etolié had damn near forgotten. "I won't lie. I was going to keep this boring—because it by and large was, aside from me crying like a goddamn baby. But my momma committed a whole verbal murder, and I think everyone needs to join in insulting my least favorite crispy nugget." She looked to Murishani. "Take notes. I expect you to use your rumor powers for good."

Etolié told the tale. Casvir might've even smiled, just a tiny bit.

Beyond the walls of Haven, flanked by Etolié and Casvir, Flowridia stood upon a platform and faced a sea of desperate elven faces. Though their features were far different than the Theocracy refugees, Flowridia recognized that same heartache, the same yearning for a home that no longer existed. Mothers and fathers and children—too many children—all looking hungry and afraid; strangers in the enemy's land, now seeking salvation.

There was little comfort to give in the face of such dire circumstances. Flowridia summoned her courage and continued her pragmatic welcome to the newly acquired citizens.

"…Housing construction is ongoing, aided by a few De'Sindai sorcerers. However, temporary accommodations have been erected on the outskirts of Haven. Food will be provided, of course. In the next few days, postings for apprenticeships and skilled workers will be distributed, though anyone is welcome to apply elsewhere should they have specific specialties. Conversely, the university will be opening for enrollment in the next week. You are encouraged to apply there instead, should that suit your goals.

"However, Empress Etolié of Solvira, Daughter of Goddess Staella, has generously opened her gates to any refugees who are so inclined as well, whether it be due to the climate preference or job opportunities. Instructions on how to apply will be coming soon."

All of that was practical, but there was more to be said. Flowridia had reviewed her notes and practiced her speech a hundred times at least, and here her empathy showed. "In the meantime, I wish to acknowledge the heartbreak I know each and every one of you must be feeling. It is no small matter, losing your ancestral home. I weep for you, truly. I hope you can find your peace. The Temple of Staella is always open for those who wish to unburden their hearts. You need not be a worshipper to find comfort among the priestesses. It is my commitment to you that you will be cared for just as any other citizen under Imperator Casvir's protection, and should any issues arise, there will be De'Sindai messengers stationed among you who will bring concerns straight to me. I am Lady Flowridia Darkleaf, and I am here to serve you."

For a few more months, at least. Though those were not words to speak aloud.

The applause came scattered, steadily gaining life when Executor Faeborn joined from their place beyond the podium. Flowridia would not say she reveled in it, but a certain pride filled her—pride she had not felt since before she lost her magic, months ago.

When she stepped back, servants filed out to deliver specific edits, offering directions to various sectors of the city and housing assignments. Casvir remained quietly stoic, though his approval showed in his calm aura. Etolié, however, clasped her on the back. "I hate to say you did good, but I'm impressed."

Flowridia managed a small smile, surprised at the endorsement. "Thank you, though I don't know that I did anything special."

"The plan didn't have to be original. It had to be concocted at fucking lightning speed, which you did. I must begrudgingly admit my respect."

Casvir's shadow loomed. "You did well."

Flowridia blushed, fighting the urge to resist their praise. "I'm just doing what I can."

"Executor Faeborn has accepted a position as an advisor, with the promise of protection from any retaliation from their former allies."

Flowridia lowered her voice, sparing a glance for the disgraced executor in quiet conversation with a recruiter. "Is it wise to allow them into your inner circle so quickly?"

"No, and so they will be kept from knowing any valuable secrets. Viceroy Murishani has already agreed to helm more subtle tests of their loyalty, feeding false information and so on. But that will take place in Solvira."

Flowridia nodded, still a little uncomfortable at any mention of the, quite literal, Silver Fire bastard. "Thank you," she said simply. Murishani could rot in the remains of his murdered pride for all she cared.

When they left, that sensation of accomplishment glowed quietly within her, rising to overcome even her exhausted body. No, she had no magic, no true power at all. Her back ached from the walk through the city, her hips protested each step through the halls, and all the while fatigue followed like a fog around her head . .
.

But she had done something remarkable. That beautiful truth led her all the way to the palace.

When she returned to her medical suite, the prison walls fell around her once more, extinguishing the fire in her soul.

Ayla sat as a statue on the sofa, intently focused on her book. "How did your speech go?"

She sounded more polite than interested. "It went well," Flowridia said, uncertain of this sudden bitterness inside her. But Ayla was here, indifferent to her success . . . She couldn't have even swallowed her pride to watch from the shadows. "What are you reading?"

Though she kept her finger between the pages, Ayla responded by shutting the tome and holding up the cover. *Uncommon Phylacteries*, it said.

Intrigue filled Flowridia. "Have you learned anything?"

"Nothing new. At least this one explains what sort of creative boxes liches have used to house their hearts. Anything can be infused with the necessary dark matter."

"Knowing Casvir, it'll be something so innocuous we would never take a second glance."

Ayla gave a curt nod, returning to her book.

Flowridia could not dismiss the feeling of being snubbed. When she sat beside her, Ayla kept still. "Anything else?"

Only Ayla's eyes shifted, glancing to meet her gaze. "No."

Definitely snubbed. Flowridia gently pushed the book down, revealing Ayla's impassive visage. "Ayla, what's wrong?"

At the query, Ayla set the book aside, tense as she spoke. "I think it's best we drop this."

Flowridia frowned, given they hadn't even started. "I don't. Tell me."

"Do you care about the phylactery or not?"

"Of course I care—"

"Yet all you have done since reproposing finding it is skip off to help Casvir and Nox'Kartha." Condemnation filled Ayla's stare, her silver eyes unblinking. "We don't have to do this, but I would like you to decide."

"I already told you—"

"Flowra, my sweet, infuriating love, you are doing the thing where you have a hope yet lay a path entirely contrary to leading to it. I *want* to walk beside you, but you've sent me on a quest and then ignored it. If you want to find it, you have to help me."

Flowridia's pride bristled, though only just. "I fail to see how what I'm doing is contrary."

"You're helping him. By proxy of where your bleeding heart has led you, you are *helping* him win this war."

"I'm helping save lives," Flowridia spat back, unwilling to face Ayla's words, seeking only to shove them away. "I've given Casvir a handful more citizens. What difference does that make compared to what he already has? You don't have to help me, but you don't have to attack me either."

And there it was, the subtle slip in Ayla's self-control. For a small moment, the predator twitched her eye. "I did not attack you. You asked me how I felt, and I answered."

A thrill shot through Flowridia, fury melding with heat. "I asked because you were oozing disdain."

Ayla rose, saying nothing as she grabbed her book and left for the door.

"Where are you going?"

"I am leaving, lest I be accused of attacking you again."

Though her aching body hindered her, Flowridia managed to rise as well. "You would leave your pregnant wife all alone?"

Ayla stilled at the door, her glare causing Flowridia's boiling blood to sing. "I shall watch from the shadows."

"Gods, you are insufferable!"

Ayla's eyebrows rose high enough to risk flying from her face. She spoke through gritted teeth. "And you, my dearest, darling wife, beloved of my heart, are pregnant, as you yourself just said. Ask the doctor for tea to help with those hormones, hmm?"

"How dare—"

But Ayla slipped into the shadow of the doorframe, disappearing from sight.

Not sound, though. Ayla would only go so far. "Ayla, it's not my fault you've decided to shut yourself in and refuse to grow!"

She met only silence.

"Gods forbid I try to make a damned difference in the world! Gods forbid I do anything other than languish in this room, selfishly wrapped up in my own damn woes! I'm hurting, so I'm trying to help! But you can't even *pretend* to support me when I've finally found some way to feel good about myself. All you've done is hide and wait for this baby to be born so you can run away, but life is happening *now*! You're acting as though this baby is the beginning, but nothing ever ended! I don't want to sit in this room and wait! I don't want to hide from the world anymore!"

The final word echoed against the walls. Flowridia seethed, finding no peace in the silence—

But the fire within her rose anew when Ayla reappeared from the shadows, fury in her gaze and trembling lip. "I am not hiding," Ayla said, her voice eerily calm. "In addition to doing what *you* asked me to do, I am preparing. I am facing a potential future where my wife is dead from the whim of the very tyrant she works to appease. As it is, you have me in a bind because if I find the phylactery tomorrow, I can't stab it. I have to wait until Demitri is back under your stewardship, lest this entire quest be lost. And so I am still facing that awful future where I lose my wife to a parasitic monster I was forced to create—"

"And how were you forced, Ayla?!" Flowridia touched her womb, shoving aside the offense at the word *monster*. "You did this willingly!"

"Need I remind you why you sold the baby in the first place? I do, in fact, feel forced—because what fucking alternative was I given?"

Damn that shame. It never fully faded. "I thought we were past this."

"I don't want a baby. I have told you before, I don't want a baby. And sometimes, I worry that you are caught up in a fantasy that I *do* want a baby!" Ayla bit back her raised voice, fists clenched as she steeled her control.

"That's an assumption," Flowridia spat, and before her very eyes, Ayla's steel became pure ice.

"Hand me a baby, Flowra. Trust *me* to raise it in love. Would you?"

"That's not . . . Ayla, I would trust you, but—"

"Shall I relay to you the many ways I've murdered infants?"

"That's not necessary."

"Oh, but I think it is." No life in Ayla's gaze. No kindness; no light. "I think it's entirely necessary for you to acknowledge the fact that I starved little infants and skinned them alive—"

"Ayla, stop it." Flowridia set a protective hand upon her stomach, panic rising with no outlet.

"Say it," Ayla whispered. "Say my crimes, and in the same breath say I am in any way fit to be a mother."

Flowridia's rage simmered as she forced the hateful words. "You murdered babies. You starved them and you skinned them alive. And . . ." The bitterest truth didn't matter though, did it? Flowridia swallowed furious tears. "And it doesn't matter whether or not you're fit to be a mother, because this isn't your baby. This baby is owned by Casvir."

Ayla deflated somewhat; her acrimony tempered. "Then what purpose is there in killing Casvir?"

"The purpose is to save the realms."

"No, it isn't." Ayla's lip trembled. "I know you. You have done a spectacular job at lying to yourself once more. But I don't believe the reality of any of this has truly set in. Have you looked at yourself in the mirror lately?"

Flowridia bristled, uncertain of how to feel about the remark. "I . . . well, yes."

"Then you know your appearance is worrying."

On instinct, Flowridia brought a hand to her cheeks, remiss to admit they were sharper than what she recognized. "I am well aware of my condition. I do live in this damn body."

"You are so strong, my love, but so fragile. In a matter of weeks, that . . . that *thing* will grow teeth, and if you don't perish from being burned alive, it'll tear you open from within. As it grows, your condition will become increasingly precarious, and there is a very large part of me that wishes to beg for you to—"

Again, Ayla bit back her words, but even faced with her misty eyes, Flowridia's rage boiled anew.

"Beg for me to what, Ayla?" Flowridia seethed, gratified to watch Ayla nearly crumble.

"It doesn't—"

"I want to hear you say it."

"It's killing you," Ayla said, and the first of her tears fell. "But to abort it means to either give up Demitri or wait for you to heal enough to try again without the Silver Fire—and then we are back where we started, with me standing aside while some man fucks my wife until she conceives. How am I supposed to feel but helpless?"

"Yet you'd beg for it anyway?"

"Because I *don't want you dead*!" Ayla wrenched herself around, hiding her weeping in the crux of her elbow. Heaving sobs wracked her figure, and with it, a semblance of pity filled Flowridia, her anger finally easing away.

When she took Ayla in her arms, Ayla immediately clung to her dress, nails threatening to tear her skin as she cried. Flowridia struggled to find her own breath, struck to wonder . . .

Oh gods, had she caused this?

Her grip tightened, Ayla's tears lacerating her heart. "I love you," Flowridia whispered, and Ayla's reply was to bruise her aching body from the desperation of her embrace, as though willing her to *stay*.

"I'm not stupid, Flowra. I know you want to keep it. But don't you see why we can't?"

Faced so boldly with reflection, Flowridia averted her gaze. "I know I can't."

"It's killing you. I know what Demitri means to you, but it is *killing you*, Flowra."

Flowridia swallowed a lump in her throat as she kissed Ayla's hair, her forehead, holding her with all her limited strength. "If I'm in my deathbed, cut it out," she said, voice shattering on the final word. "I'll accept a new familiar. We'll find the phylactery together. But I'm not ready to give up yet. I'm not ready to give up on Demitri. Not when there's even a sliver of hope."

Against her dress, Ayla nodded.

"Come to bed," Flowridia whispered, and Ayla obeyed when she beckoned, revealing a face shiny from tears.

Flowridia pulled her beneath the sheets, uncaring that they both still wore their shoes. Wrapped in the fortress of blankets, she held her heaving wife.

"I never wish to hurt you," Ayla said between sobs. "Without you, I would have nothing. I would be nothing."

"That's not true."

"But it is, Flowra." Ayla hid her face in Flowridia's dress, her final words a whisper. "And how tragic is that?"

She fell into sobs once more. Flowridia held her through the night.

CHAPTER 18

Dira's next birthday came and went, and still she could not breach the shadows. Every night, she would sit in darkness and narrow her focus, only to find nothing to grasp.

Of course asking Mother was suspicious, useless really, but desperation drove her.

On a cold winter night, Mother tucked her into bed. "I swear, every time I return from a trip, you've grown so much," Mother said.

By her feet, Narella and Nilly, her sweet little cats, cuddled contentedly. Demitri lounged beside the fireplace, basking in its warmth. When Mother stroked her growing locs from her face, Dira leaned into the touch. "You never leave through the gates."

"That is true."

"How do you travel by shadow?" Mother's face suggested she had said too much. "W-When I asked Demitri, he said that's what you were doing. You can go to the demonic realm and travel faster that way."

"Demitri and I may need to have a talk."

In his corner, Demitri stirred. *Don't go blaming me.*

"He didn't say anything else," Dira said. "He just answered my question. But how did you learn? Is it magic?"

"Not magic, my darling. Nor is it something you need worry yourself with."

Oh, the rejection stung. It always did. "But why can't I even know how you learned? I'm not asking you to teach me."

Mother patted her head in a much too patronizing way. "My little lamb, I was in a much darker place at your age than you are. My reasons for learning were for survival. So it is nothing you should trouble yourself with."

Dira sat up as Mother stood, ruining the careful placement of blankets. "So you were a kid when you learned?"

Mother's lips pursed. "Yes, I was young. Much younger than you."

"And you were in danger?"

Mother stopped in her tracks, displeasure in her tense stance. "Yes, but I would rather not speak of it. And you would rather not hear it."

Mother? In danger? The thought was too strange to consider, just as strange as it was to consider Mother as a child. "Was it from monsters?"

"Yes. Can we drop it—"

"The same monsters you want to protect me from?"

With frightful slowness, Mother turned around. Her composure held, but Dira slunk back into bed. "Darling, if I could go back in time, I would have never stepped a foot in that damn demon realm. There are monsters there you cannot even conceive of. No, they are not the same that hunt for you, and it would be best to keep it that way. And to be quite clear, I don't think a younger me could have entered the realm from this continent, because the world is far more stable in Ku'Shya's Realm. The shadows are not so dark. And let that be your warning. Ku'Shya and her ilk are no friends of ours, so do not even dabble in this, all right?"

Dira nodded, though she did not mean it.

Mother sighed, anger seeping out to leave an exhausted shell. "You know I am only trying to keep you safe, right?"

Dira nodded once again, though fought to hide her disappointment.

"When you are older, I will tell you whatever you want to know. But cherish your youth and innocence, my love. There are monsters out there who would steal all that away, given the chance. So let me handle the cruel world."

"All right," Dira whispered.

When Mother returned to her bedside, she set a soft kiss on Dira's brow. "I promise that someday I will tell you all. I love you, my Dira. There is nothing in this realm more important than you."

Dira reached out from the blankets to hold Mother's hand. "I love you too."

Mother lingered a few moments. Dira felt only guilt for her loving gaze. Her resolve shook. For a year, she had been trying this. Could she really give up now?

When the door clicked at Mother's departure, Dira dared to sit up, amused when her cats rose and stretched. "Demitri?" she whispered.

Demitri's grump wafted over her. *What do you want, traitor?*

"I barely told Mother anything."

Just tell me what you want.

"Mother said it wasn't dark enough in this half of Sha'Demoni to get in very easily. What if I found pure darkness?"

I accept the logic. What if you tried outside? Or the cellar?

"I'll get caught in the cellar, but the trees outside are awfully dark." Dira went to the window, admiring the fluffy blanket of snow. "I'm not supposed to go to the woods, but what if you were there to protect me? No bears will come if you're there."

I'll do it. But you'd better tell Lady Ayla it was under duress.

"We won't get caught."

A hopeful assumption, but Dira had only gotten this far due to hope.

Sneaking Demitri out of the house took time, his steps far less silent than hers. But no one came, light from the parlor room revealing where Mother likely was.

Outside, the winter chill cut through Dira's nightgown. Regret filled her for forgetting a coat, but she had gotten this far—and had at least remembered shoes. In silence, they crossed the grove behind the manor, only to reach the back wall.

A problem struck them both. *I can't climb.*

Dira's hope sank. The front gate would attract attention. "We can try the trees here."

Demitri followed as she went back into the dark grove, the dense trees thick enough to block even the faint starlight. No moon tonight. Surely a sign to move forward. The breeze cut her skin like knives.

She cleared a patch of snow away, revealing frosty, dead grass. Demitri curled around her when she took a meditative pose, protecting her from the wind.

Between Demitri's shadow and the thick trees, darkness rose to frightful degrees. Dira shut her eyes.

Mother had been a frightened child, trying to escape unknown danger. Mother had found darkness enough to see the cracks in the worlds and slip through. Now, Dira sought that same desperation inside her, the yearning for freedom rising to overtake her.

Even so, she breathed.

And then, in the blank slate behind her eyes, she swore she felt . . . something.

Warmth.

"Dira, what are you doing?"

Mother's silhouette wrenched her focus back. Dira was too shocked to speak, too shocked to even accept when Mother offered a hand.

"Dira, get up."

Dira stood without her aid, quick enough for her head to spin.

"Answer my question. What are you doing?"

She could lie. She had to lie. But what lie to give? "I couldn't sleep."

"So you came to meditate in the snow?"

Dira nodded.

Mother set the back of her fingers on Dira's cheek. "Darling, you'll catch a chill." Still terse. Still skeptical, but Mother said nothing more of it. Instead, she took Dira's hand and led her back to the manor. "At least you had the sense to bring Demitri. There are all sorts of dangers in the dark."

Demitri did follow, though leisurely. *Too bad. Next time for sure.*

His tone was less than inspiring, but he didn't know what she'd felt.

There was another world, and she had so nearly touched it.

Current era . . .

No, it was not particularly professional to leave just because Flowers and Ayla were having 'a moment' as Etolié had decided to call it—she wasn't going to admit to overhearing Ayla sobbing—but she'd be sitting around twiddling her thumbs otherwise.

Sha'Demoni time worked differently, anyway. It was fine.

Besides, the more often she drew in her focus to teleport into the ancient cave across the sea in a whole other realm, it decreased the chances of her splicing herself or others later. And while it seemed rude not to knock, it was far less daunting to appear in Khastra's designated room than the throne room where Ku'Shya lurked.

It wasn't that Etolié was afraid of Ku'Shya herself. She was afraid of puking in front of her.

Instead, Etolié sparkled into existence, biting back screams as her body reassembled a world and ocean away. Her stomach lurched, but blessedly didn't expel, so instead she forced a smile as she took in the red walls around her, the impossibly high ceilings, and Khastra seated at a mortal desk so very out of place in the alien world.

Khastra beamed at her appearance, rising from what appeared to be a makeshift work station for a collection of rough gemstones, sure to be cut and polished beneath her expert eye.

Etolié bounded forward, overjoyed to fall into her arms— stronger with each visit. "Look at you and your fancy stones. Anything for me?"

Khastra's light chuckle filled the space. "Admittedly, I am struggling to finish anything. I have only been tinkering." She set a cut stone into Etolié's hands, the amethyst still bearing rough edges. "Tell me of the world."

"Eh, the vibes were rancid in Nox'Kartha. I'm allergic to strong emotions, and anything that makes Ayla Darkleaf fall into a pit of despair isn't something I want to get too close to."

"Admittedly, I do not care about her feelings."

"Neither do I, but I care that she's having them." When they parted, Etolié grinned simply to face her, Khastra's presence still surreal and sacred. "Though regarding good ol' Cassie, he knows you're here now. In fact, he's asked me to orchestrate negotiations with your mother to hand you back over."

"My mother would never agree."

"Duh. But it does put a timeline in place. I can only put him off for so long. I think he'll crack if I push it more than a few weeks."

Khastra's resignation suggested she well and truly understood the implications. "Regarding that, there is something I should say." It wasn't that Khastra's expression fell, but some hesitation filled her gaze as she led Etolié to the bed, even as her smile remained sincere. "I have considered your words and my mother's intentions. I . . . I will say yes. I will allow her to help."

Etolié couldn't quite name the swelling inside her—in part because she didn't know how she was supposed to feel. "This . . . this is good, right? You're going to let her cast her spells and sever your connection to Casvir?"

"It will be her witches casting, but yes."

Yet Etolié remained suspended, her emotions refusing to settle. "How do you feel about it?"

"There is a strong element of danger, Etolié. It is possible the spell will fail. Imperator Casvir may sense the shift in power and let me go before it is complete, or seize his power in some other way. I cannot say, only that necromancers are not something to underestimate."

No jest in Khastra's stare. She remained utterly unreadable. Etolié felt sick but managed to nod. "And something tells me you wouldn't be the same if he pulled something like that."

"Difficult to say. If he did so, he would have only my spirit and not my body."

"So he'd have your soul. Great. Fantastic. I hate it."

Yet Khastra remained unnervingly calm, jovial even, beneath her serenity. "That is not something to fear. Not yet. I am surprised the imperator has held on for this long. But it is also possible the spell will fail and I will be destroyed. Perhaps only my body. Perhaps my spirit. The power is volatile, my mother says, but to accept this aid could help me to find meaning again," Khastra continued. "Perhaps I am exhausted from endless wars and suffering and stagnation. Despite my reservations, and there are many, I do want to do this."

One blink, and Etolié's world became mist. "I want you to be happy, Khastra. And if the only way to have a chance at finding your purpose again is to do this stupid, risky ritual, we're gonna fucking do it."

Khastra cupped her cheek, wiping tears from her eyes with her calloused thumb. "Thank you. And have faith in my mother. She does not wield idle power nor have idle servants. The risk is there, but not so high as you think."

Etolié remained skeptical, but she forced herself to nod.

"There is a smaller worry I hold," Khastra continued, "that the spell will keep me properly dead, and I will lose my blood powers. I know you would still love me if I cannot make love, but it is something to prepare for."

Khastra might be cold. She might have no blood to race, no passion to chase. And Khastra was correct—for Etolié, sex was the cherry on top of a sundae, but a cherry did not a sundae make. "A small price to pay."

Some relief fell upon Khastra's countenance. "Speaking of, my mother has named no price for aid—not yet. I am . . . wary."

"I thought we'd established that your mom wasn't the malicious type."

"And you are quick to trust her. This confuses me."

"Aren't demons inherently trustworthy?"

"Demons spin deals in their favor—always. But . . ." Khastra swallowed her words. In all their years, all their trials of friendship and love, Etolié had never seen Khastra so . . . apprehensive. "That is not what I wished to discuss, however. I am contemplative."

Khastra's eyes were beautifully blue, their pupilless glow at times indiscernible. "The ritual may fail. That is simply truth. But if I return to Nox'Kartha, I would not be with you. I would be thrown back into a war I do not care for. I am tired, but I have been tired for centuries, Etolié. I told you of Ilune and the Civil War and the damage it all did to my soul. But truth be told, even after hiding away for a century, I did not feel truly alive again until the day I first saw you, when you marched in and screamed at Emperor Malakh." Etolié mirrored her smile, some light returning to her elegant face. "I have told you before that the meaning of life is to love. I measure my years in love. Were I living, I would be eleven years away from my ten thousandth birthday. And that is only by mortal years. It is unfathomable, even to me."

Khastra gently took her hand, bringing it softly to her lips. A kiss fell upon Etolié's palm, the curtailed passion leaving her blushing. Khastra released her, then withdrew something small from her pocket. "I promise what I will say next was not contingent on your answers here. But I am setting my affairs in order, because I do not know the future anymore. There is little left for me, but I have contemplated regrets. I have contemplated my selfish wants. There is something I have never mentioned because of your station in Solvira. You are an empress, and that is a title that means something to this world. But I have been considering what remains undone in my life, and what I would regret in the Beyond, should that be my final rest." With a deftness Etolié had not known the demon capable of, Khastra slipped something metallic into her grasp. "Say no. It would be the better part. But there would be no greater regret than to leave this world without telling you that you are my light."

In her heart, Etolié already knew. Still, she gasped when Khastra removed her hand—and revealed a wedding band.

Surely crafted by the half-demon herself, for it was perfect: a gold band inlaid with precious amethyst stones and diamonds that spun when she flicked it. No, no, she should not accept this. *Empress of Solvira* was a title with rules, and Etolié had sold her soul to a higher god to protect her kingdom.

At the same time . . . being the empress meant she made the rules. "Well, as the superior reigning monarch of Solvira, I'm hereby decreeing that marriage to the empress doesn't make anyone a fucking consort. So no titles or money for you. How's that for a deal-breaker?"

Khastra laughed, her tears falling fast. Etolié too—she laughed and wept as she slipped the ring onto her finger, receptive to Khastra's salty kiss. "I've made quite a name for myself doing stupid shit," Etolié said amid her weeping, "and yes, accepting a marriage proposal from the literal heir to this half of Sha'Demoni is pretty fucking high on that list. But goddammit, after all the shit I've done for this realm, I deserve to be selfish. We'll sort out the details after the ritual. I would love nothing more than to be number twelve."

Khastra withdrew at the odd statement, confusion mingled with her joy. "Twelve?"

"Seven husbands, four wives—that's eleven. I asked you once if you'd make it twelve, because twelve is an objectively better number. So yes. I'm twelve. Marry me, bitch."

Each kiss was filled with laughter. When Khastra escalated her touch, drawing Etolié into bed, pulling their bodies flush together, Etolié rejoiced at the attention. Their laughter faded to brewing passion, and Etolié's clothing disappeared when she dismissed her spell. She set Khastra's hands on her breasts, reveling when she squeezed, gasping at the teasing on her nipples. Oh, she was sensitive, parched for touch, for lust, heat welling between her legs as Khastra kissed her neck.

"You're sure you're feeling up to this?" Etolié asked, humming with each press of Khastra's lips.

Khastra spoke as a prayer, a whisper. "I want you."

A thrill shot through Etolié, settling warm and wanting between her thighs. "Then take off your clothes, Beefcake. I wanna trace your tattoos while you fuck me."

Amusement cut through even Khastra's clear lust, pulling back as she slipped out of her tunic with ease—an impressive feat, given those horns. With her reduced muscle mass, her tits were larger than usual, and Etolié drifted off as she wondered if watching them bounce would be even more engrossing than lighting up her tattoos.

But then Khastra took off her trousers, revealing tail and ass, and Etolié remembered her favorite body part. "Look at those thighs—getting bigger every day."

Khastra chuckled as she returned to bed, immediately pulling Etolié into her lap to straddle her. Where they touched, her demon's tattoos illuminated like constellations, the sensation of magic splendid against her skin. Etolié grasped Khastra's breasts, giddy at how they bounced in her hands. "I know they won't be this big forever, but they're so much fun."

Khastra's laughter remained, ceasing only when Etolié pursed her lips around one glowing—yes, glowing—nipple, resisting her own chuckle when she poked the opposite one, leaving a single shining light.

Advantages of having a giant girlfriend included the length of her arms. When Khastra's hand grazed her ass, Etolié whined to soon feel skilled fingers stroke along the wet folds of her cunt. "So wet already," Khastra teased.

The nipple left Etolié's mouth with a *pop*. "Khastra, it's been a long year. Just fuck me."

Etolié gasped when Khastra's other hand scooped beneath her ass, lifting her so their faces were level. The flex of her arm brought memories of kinder times, but any thoughts of sentiment faded when Khastra's free hand resumed teasing her vulva. Etolié set her arms around Khastra's neck and kissed those beautiful lips, only to gasp and cry at the sudden push inside her, but it wasn't enough.

"Two fingers, Beefcake. Not one—" She bit her lip at the sudden intrusion of pain. Gods, it had been so long, and Khastra's fingers weren't exactly small.

Khastra's glowing eyes held passion—and concern. "Etolié—"

"Don't. I want this. I want you. Now move."

Slowly at first—it was Khastra's signature in gentle times like this. Etolié's body ached for pain and want, but she resisted the urge to beg for more. Khastra was here. She was real. She was *inside* of her after a long year of waiting and wondering and weeping . . .

Suspended in Khastra's arms, Etolié trembled as she slid a hand to cup Khastra's cheek, unable to deviate from those glowing eyes, even as her own watered. "Keep it slow. I want you to stay here as long as we have."

Khastra nodded, each gentle thrust inside sealing their souls as one. All the world became distant, save for the burning of her blood, each deep motion within, and Khastra's unwavering gaze. Etolié could not speak, only release her gasping breaths—for to speak might scare this moment away. In Khastra's arms, she was untouchable. Beneath her gaze, she was beautiful.

This was love. Boundless and pure.

What was once pain soon became torture—not because she ached but because she needed *more*. "Khastra," she whispered, shattering the silence of the spell. "I . . ."

"You want more?"

Etolié nodded, then cried as Khastra complied, friction leaving her boneless. Her head fell to Khastra's shoulder, helpless as her demon fucked her, stretched her, each methodical pang against her clit sending shockwaves through her blood. Her teeth bit Khastra's skin, her demon's ensuing cry leaving her head light. Her nails dug into Khastra's back, no gentleness in how she scraped along her tattooed skin. But she craved stability amid this storm, gripping tight and *screaming* as Khastra ripped the orgasm from her soul.

She came to as a trembling, sweaty heap, the aftermath of pleasure leaving her tingly. Khastra's motions were slow now, the presence of her gentle fingers inside welling all manner of sensations, dusty from disuse. When Etolié lifted her head, Khastra moved to withdraw. "Wait," Etolié managed, voice sore and rough. "Just . . . Unless you're tired—"

"Shh . . ." Khastra cooed, her own gaze watery and filled with lust. Without removing her fingers, Khastra tenderly laid her back onto the bed. "I am being selfish, remember? We will make love as long as you want."

"And you," Etolié added, weak when Khastra grinned.

Etolié gave a light gasp when Khastra resumed her gentle thrusts, her exhausted body fully ready for more. "When it is my turn, we fuck."

She couldn't even laugh at Khastra's inability to say the word 'fuck' properly. If brains were eggs, hers were scrambled. "I love it when you're feeling spicy."

Khastra hummed as she leaned down to kiss the side of Etolié's breast. "Touch yourself. And tell me how you want to fuck me."

Hindered by her dazed mind, Etolié managed approximately seven words, all of which were forgotten the moment they left her mouth.

For the fifth time, Flowridia read over her response to the day's updates regarding the Whispering Elf refugees, seeking flaws, seeking wistful thinking . . .

"A coin for your thoughts, Darling?"

Ayla's voice pulled Flowridia from her study, setting her mind back into her medical suite. Ayla lounged on the nearby couch, a drawing pad in her hands, but her gaze was for Flowridia alone.

Flowridia set aside her quill and parchment. "I'm thinking this would be a lot easier if I still had my magic."

"How so?"

"Because providing food for a massive influx of people is trivial when you can make a field of wheat grow overnight. Nox'Kartha has ample amounts of food, but it's still something to consider. Casvir insists it's fine, but it's frustrating."

"If Casvir says it's fine, then all is well, my sweet summer blossom. You are capable with or without magic."

Flowridia bit back a bitter retort, questioning how to even begin to articulate how spectacularly Ayla had missed the point. Her mind didn't hold a candle to the powers she had lost. "I need to deliver this." Resigned, Flowridia blew on the parchment a final time and rolled it up, mindful of her balance as she rose. Her hand ached less today, but the subtle tingling up through her wrist grated on her patience. Even wrapped, it was aggravating.

To her surprise, Ayla rose as well. "I would like to escort you."

"I thought you wanted nothing to do with this."

"Walking my wife down the hallway when there was a recent attempt on her life is a far different thing than helping my most annoying enemy." Ayla appeared at her side, offering a hand. "And with Etolié in Celestière, I am taking no chances."

Flowridia smiled, warmed by the protective gesture. Though a dilemma rose when she set the rolled-up paper into her injured hand, the light weight nothing even to the damaged nerves—but a sudden sharp surge contracted her hand. Flowridia gasped as it dropped, doubling over the cramping appendage.

"Flowra, sit. Let me help—"

Flowridia waved her off, though she was unable to fight when Ayla took the afflicted appendage and began a tender massage. Flowridia sat at Ayla's continued insistence and held back tears, unwilling to admit to the pain, even if it were as plain as day. Gods, she hated this weakness, hated for Ayla to see her so vulnerable, but the cramping did ease . . . even as Flowridia choked back a sob.

When her hand was finally coaxed open, Ayla continued the tender gestures. "May I unwrap it?"

Flowridia looked away, giving no answer at all—unwilling to admit her relief when Ayla took it as permission anyway. Hideous, those scars, the missing fingers, the mutilated mockery of a hand, but finally Ayla had *taken* something instead of acting as a sycophant.

Ayla's motions did not cease, her touch the perfect balance of pressure—not deep enough to wound Flowridia, nor light enough to aggravate the nerves. "Does it still tingle?"

Flowridia nodded. "Constantly."

Ayla remained silent. When Flowridia forced herself to look, Ayla's gaze held a glassy sheen. "At this point, it may never stop. It has been long enough that the damaged nerves would have healed, were they capable. Surgical intervention might help, but it would be too risky in your current state."

With the decree of the somber verdict, Flowridia felt she'd been given a death sentence. "If I cut it off now, it would regrow when I'm a vampire, right?" Though bitter, there was no jest in the words; pain was pain.

"That much trauma to your body at this stage of your pregnancy would have a high likelihood of leading to a miscarriage. It . . . it is risky. But there are spells to—"

But Flowridia sharply shook her head. "The baby might absorb any spells, remember?"

Ayla gave a grave nod. "There is pain management we could pursue—"

Flowridia yanked her hand back, cursing the return of the faint pins and needles. Ayla's touch had actually been working. "As soon as the baby is born, it won't be an issue anymore. I can last until then."

"Darling, you cannot even grip paper."

"And soon, I'll be able to rip trees from their roots. I can last."

When Ayla gently sought her hand, Flowridia stood instead—though stumbled at the swirl of dizziness coursing through her body, head spinning as she set her good hand to her knees.

Ayla's stance was small, small enough to irritate Flowridia's already addled mind. "You have nothing to prove, my love. There is no shame in accepting help."

So why did shame creep hot and cloying inside her anyway? Flowridia shoved those tender feelings away and began rewrapping her mutilated hand. "I don't need help," she said, determined to swallow the hated truth—that Ayla had just saved her from several minutes of debilitating pain. "And I don't need you babying me."

"That was not my intention."

"So stop doing it."

Ayla shrunk. "I'm sorry. I haven't meant to overstep."

Dammit all. Flowridia could barely articulate her bitter feelings, much less understand them herself. "It doesn't matter. You can overstep."

Ayla said nothing, simply watched with wary eyes, a stranger's eyes. "May I still escort you?"

Flowridia finished her wrapping, fury rising with no source. "You insisted mere minutes ago."

"Yes, but not if it's aggravating you," Ayla replied, as tentative as dew dangling upon a leaf.

"You'll only follow from the shadows if I say no."

Oh, damn that watery sheen in Ayla's gaze. Her jaw stiffened to match. "I would hope to try and convince you to have someone escort you, but if you want to make . . ." Ayla's words faded, her hands idly scratching the other. Not enough to break the skin, but Flowridia felt tension, nevertheless. "I would hope you'd have some thought toward self-preservation, given everything, but you can make your own decisions. I won't impose."

Every grudge inside Flowridia simmered. "What if I want you to insist?"

"What do you mean?"

"What if I want you to impose? What if I want you to protect me?"

Ayla seemed taken aback, and Flowridia *felt* something at that spark of offense. Ayla said, "When have I ever stopped—"

"What if I begged you to stop asking me for permission for every little thing and take what you want?!" Flowridia bit back her words, though her fury rose ever higher. "What if," she continued, forcing her tone to quiet, "I wished you were a little more assertive in your day to day. You used to be."

Nothing in Ayla's stance changed, yet Flowridia felt her own rising rage and found it splendid. "When have I ever tried to control you?"

The question nearly sparked laughter. Oh, she loved it when Ayla pushed back. Flowridia's fury remained, but something else rose to join it—something just as hot. "Well, you used to turn control into an art form during sex. Not that I've seen that side of you in months."

"I . . ." Ayla stammered, apparently lost for words. "You're pregnant. You're in pain. I don't want to add to that."

"Oh, I *dare* you to hurt me more than my body already does." The words were bitter, but that bitterness wasn't for Ayla, no. Not this time. "I know I'm fragile, but if I fall on my knees and beg, will you just pretend for a night that I'm not? Can we pretend like things are normal? We can withhold ropes and blood until I'm feeling better, but all I want is for you to force me against the wall and fuck me until you're satisfied. I want to pretend like things are . . . are *normal.*"

Ayla said nothing, nor did she move when Flowridia came forward. Gods, this tension was sublime, and Flowridia dared to touch the woman she loved, that fury in Ayla's gaze the familiarity she had craved. When she cupped Ayla's cheek, her wife did not move, neither did she respond when Flowridia pressed their lips together, willing that passion to ignite.

Instead, Ayla stepped back. "I thought you had a meeting with Casvir."

"He can wait—" The knock on the door set her fury ablaze. "Unless someone's dying, go away!"

"Someone is dying," came a familiar voice. It seemed Casvir had come to her instead.

Flowridia looked back to her supplicant wife, cursing how quickly she withered. "I can tell him to leave."

"This is important."

"You're more important."

"Flowra, I am not in the mood."

Were Casvir not standing on the other side of the door, Flowridia might've screamed. Instead, she sat on the bed, staring daggers when Ayla marched to one of the couches, hiding her face behind a book.

Flowridia forced her voice to steady. "Come in, then."

Casvir did, and if he sensed the toxic mood, he gave no indication. "I have received troubling news that may affect our new refugees. Do you have a moment to speak?"

At her affirmation, he came to her bedside, pulling up a chair to join her. "I have yet to go investigate for myself, but my spies have informed me that there was an attack on Meskheta—the Ember Elf capital city. Apparently there is evidence that Ku'Shya's servants were the perpetrators, and given the destruction of Tierzuroth, it is not unreasonable to assume we may be about to witness a repeat."

"But why?" Flowridia asked. "Meskheta is nowhere near *Daemenacht*. Does Ku'Shya have the power to do any true damage?"

"Ku'Shya was not present, and the motive is currently unknown. My advisors have suggested withholding asking Executor Faeborn for information for now, in case they are involved in any subterfuge that might harm Nox'Kartha. Be that as it may, I wonder if the Ember Elves would accept the same offer of sanctuary."

"I'm not certain if we have the resources to take so many more at once, to be quite honest."

Casvir's silence held no peace, only contemplation. "Perhaps something more decisive, then."

"What do you mean by—?"

The door burst open—and there were very few audacious enough to ignore a *Please Knock* sign. Thankfully, it was only Etolié. The Celestial held a beaming smile, glowing both literally and figuratively, her light cutting through even the discomforting fog lingering in the room. "Oh, hello everyone," she said in a singsong voice. "Am I interrupting? I can go get drunk in the library."

By all accounts, this was an imposter Etolié, but given Ayla hadn't reacted, Flowridia was at a loss for any other explanation. Casvir reacted accordingly. "Where were you?"

"I took a break for personal reasons."

"You are not paid to take any breaks. You are not to leave Flowridia's bedside unless necessary."

"And it was necessary, sir. Your protégé and her emotional support vampire were having a moment, and I'm allergic to strong emotions."

"And did this 'break' involve coordinating negotiations with Ku'Shya?"

Etolié's smile seemed sincere enough, but Flowridia had oft suspected she illusioned her face when she was hiding something. "Things are moving slowly, of course, but I finally got my momma to reach out to Ku'Shya. I'm waiting for her reply."

"I see."

But what was Etolié negotiating with Ku'Shya for? Surely not to do with this latest attack. "What accommodations are in place for Solvira to accept refugees?" Flowridia asked.

"I pay people to know those kinds of details. I can fetch them if you want."

"We may be getting many more refugees than anticipated," Flowridia continued, unsure of how to feel at all. Yet she held her tongue, realizing the wiser part would be to say nothing at all. "I would like you to fetch those people, yes. As soon as possible."

Etolié glared as though slapped. "Sure thing, your majesty. Unfortunately, you aren't my boss." She turned to Casvir. "What do you say, boss?"

"If Flowridia deems it wise, you should listen."

Etolié waved them off as she left—

And in that wave, Flowridia noticed a glint on her finger.

When the door shut, Flowridia spoke softly. "What is she negotiating with Ku'Shya for?"

"The return of General Khastra."

The logic was so nearly sound, but while Casvir anticipated betrayal at every turn, his misunderstanding of the boundless nature of love led him to miss when it was right under his nose. "I see. Does she know about the attack on the Ember Elves?"

"I have not informed her yet."

The gears slowly spun in Flowridia's head. "Don't tell her. It might color her view of the negotiation."

Casvir raised an eyebrow. "That seems like a stretch."

"Is it? And here I thought you had personal experience regarding what Etolié does when faced with the destruction of entire cities."

Casvir's good humor faded. "You bring up a good point, but your sarcasm is not appreciated."

"I apologize," Flowridia said, though forcibly bit back the urge for rebellion. "My point is simply that Etolié is a wild card, and if you want that card to keep playing in your favor, hold off for now."

Etolié was assuredly a wild card, potentially working with Ku'Shya already, but if Etolié slipped up and revealed if she knew anything of the Ember Elves herself, well, there was solid evidence of treason. In theory, Etolié wouldn't be so stupid. Yet Etolié waved around an engagement ring.

Flowridia would ask Etolié herself, when the time was right.

"I thought you were skeptical of accepting new refugees," Casvir said.

"I am, but I wanted the news kept from Etolié. What do you mean by 'decisive'?"

"Per my reports, the Ember Elves have holed themselves up in Meskheta for protection from Ku'Shya. The entire countryside has been evacuated. They have resources to hold up in their stronghold for years to come, and perhaps it would be better to take advantage of that."

A sudden chill swept across her. "Do I want to understand what that means?"

"Are you as offended as Empress Etolié by the destruction of entire cities?"

She felt no better. "Perhaps I am." She offered him the rolled-up parchment with her good hand. "This is where we currently stand," Flowridia said, appeased when he accepted it. "Let me know what needs to change in light of this development."

"Currently nothing. I will deliver this to my advisors in the meantime." Casvir stood, though paused before the doorframe. "Are you well?"

"Of course I'm not."

"Empress Etolié alluded to you and Ayla having a dispute."

Flowridia forced back a sneer. "That happens sometimes. It's nothing worth discussing."

"My door is open if you need to."

He turned to leave, but Flowridia found herself clinging to those fatherly words. "I just want things to be normal again."

He stilled. "Explain."

Flowridia's gut clenched. To speak the truth left her no lighter. "I need this baby to be born so Ayla and I can run away and pick up where we left off. I don't want to assume her feelings—" *Nor speak about them to you*, but she didn't say that. "—but things between us were finally mending before we created this baby. Now I'm hurting physically, and she's hurting emotionally, and I don't feel like we know how to communicate anymore. Things were perfect, Casvir. We were so happy in our home in the woods, but now I feel like I don't know how to reach her. I feel—" Gods, she hated to say the final piece, but say it she must, lest she drown. ". . . I feel like she's pulling away, but instead of holding on, all I'm doing is pushing."

Casvir appeared thoughtful, his aura as kind as the man she had traveled with in the woods, far away from kingdoms and politics and grabs for power. Somewhere within Casvir was kindness, and for all her grudges against him, she would never deny him that. "This is but a small moment, both in your life and in your marriage.

Small moments can define our whole lives if we let them, but they are simply that—small. This will end. Hope is far from lost."

Flowridia nodded, the lurking fear of Etolié's own predictions still leaving her cold. But surviving was the only path. Death was something she had already chosen, and it would be on her own terms. "Thank you. I needed to be reminded of that."

"I fear that I have been neglectful in my care of you," Casvir replied. "I will make it my priority to visit for social engagements and not only when there is business to discuss. I know you are uncomfortable in your current state. I wish to help."

Flowridia managed to smile. "You're already doing so much."

"My aid in your health is practical, but you are still my friend."

"Thank you. I would enjoy a friendly visit."

What a rare and odd thing, to see him smile. Casvir left.

Only then did Flowridia recall that Ayla hadn't actually left.

She tried to rise, yet was struck by a frightful wave of dizziness. She clung to the bedpost, willing her head to settle, but a quick glance to the couch revealed her worst fear.

Ayla was not here.

After a long and taxing meeting with Etolié's paid 'experts,' wherein Flowridia danced around the subject of potentially *more* refugees, she was soon left with Etolié alone.

She lay on the couch, desperate for any sensation but the bed. The Celestial played with her left-hand forefinger as she sat opposite Flowridia. Visually, her finger had nothing on it. Most wouldn't even notice the repetitive action. But Flowridia couldn't deny the glint of light she had spotted earlier that day, and by all accounts, Etolié was spinning empty air on a naked finger.

Terribly unsubtle, at least to those who were looking.

"So where's Darkleaf?" Etolié asked.

Flowridia resisted the urge to grimace. "I wish I knew."

"Well, she can't exactly go off and die, so the worst-case scenarios aren't as bad as they could be."

"I don't think I need to tell you how unhelpful that statement was. I could say the exact same thing about Khastra."

Etolié shrugged.

"How's Khastra doing, by the way?"

"She's fine—" Etolié's mouth snapped shut. After a beat, she muttered, "*Bitch*," and nothing more.

Triumph filled Flowridia. "Well, I would have nothing to say to anyone on the matter anyway, except that I love that new ring of yours."

Etolié glanced frantically between her definitely-not-illusioned hand and Flowridia.

"I saw it earlier," Flowridia continued. "I don't need to know anything, except whether or not whatever you're up to will impede on my duties aiding the refugees."

Etolié's confusion faded into a glare. "I would never do anything to hurt innocent people."

"That's all I needed to hear."

And Etolié said nothing more.

Flowridia resumed her count of the stones on the ceiling, boredom the greatest pain of all.

She knew not how much time had passed, but she did know that Ayla finally appeared. Not because she saw her, but because Etolié jumped. "Fucking Morathma's Whore Mother—could you not?! You can't keep popping out of fucking fireplaces, Darkleaf!"

Flowridia's relief surged as she faced Ayla by the aforementioned fireplace, her demeanor obtuse as she stepped from the shadow. Flowridia tried to rise, though the extra weight in her stomach and exhausted limbs made that a titanic feat. Thankfully, Ayla helped to steady her. "Thank you."

"You're welcome," Ayla said, far more subdued than Flowridia recognized.

"So, should I leave before the energy gets weird in here?" Etolié said. "I literally need no excuse to get drunk with the nurses."

Ayla remained unreadable. "You should go, yes."

"Scream if you need me."

Etolié left.

Ayla looked prepared to speak, but Flowridia could keep silent no longer. "Ayla, I'm sorry. I don't know what you heard, but if I overstepped any bounds or said anything cruel . . . I'm just so sorry."

Ayla gently shook her head. "No, you spoke your truth. I'm not angry. To be honest, I appreciate it, in an odd way. And I hate to attribute any gratitude to Casvir, but he is right. This is not forever."

And though relief flooded Flowridia in waves, she remained suspended. "No, it's not."

"How are you feeling?"

"Predictably bad, but no more than usual."

Ayla stood and offered her hand. "Would you come with me?"

Flowridia accepted, the expanding bubble in her chest not quite ready to deflate or burst. Ayla looked so . . . somber.

She followed fearlessly when Ayla led her to a shadow, the familiar landscape of Sha'Demoni enveloping them. Flowridia shivered, the muted world casting a chill across her skin. The world shifted in hues of grey, as though blurred behind fog.

Wordlessly, Ayla led them through the winding halls, the trip proving to be short. They quickly reappeared in what Flowridia realized was Ayla's old bedroom.

Yet it had been shuffled around, all furniture shoved against the walls, leaving a sizable space in the center. An endless array of candles lit the scene, casting romantic light upon the room, and upon the futon, scattered rose petals filled the space with a captivating scent and softened Flowridia's worried heart.

"This is beautiful," Flowridia said, breathless as she took tentative steps forward.

Behind her, Ayla encircled her in an embrace. "I have been thinking upon our argument and your words to Casvir. The truth is that I am not ready to give you what you want in bed, but I think my more recent fears have been causing me to neglect you entirely. I am so sorry you see me as pulling away. I don't feel like you're pushing me, if that is any comfort."

It was, though Flowridia hadn't known how dearly she needed to hear it. Emotion choked her; she gripped Ayla's arm tight, even as her wife softly released her.

Ayla stepped toward a set of drawers littered with trinkets she had once stolen from Flowridia herself and a few candles. There, in the center, was a small box. When she lifted the lid, a gentle melody played, bearing the levity of a lullaby.

Ayla returned gracefully to her side, the subtle shift to her stance creating far more confident steps. She swept into a bow, then offered her hand.

Charmed, Flowridia accepted, following along as Ayla directed her maimed hand to her own waist, setting Flowridia's wrist upon it instead, and led with the other, sweeping Flowridia into a leisurely two-step. Oh, how beautifully the candlelight reflected off her love's alabaster skin, casting her in warm hues, a glimpse of how she had appeared in life. Ayla laughed when she twirled and helped Flowridia to do so as well. How precious it was, her wife's laugh.

In those moments, Ayla was free.

The rush was short-lived, for not even Flowridia's joy could overpower the debilitating fatigue constantly shadowing her. When she faltered, Ayla held her tight, swaying in time to the music's tender flow.

It broke her, this delicate moment of peace. Her tears fell softly, silently. "I love you."

"I love you, Flowra."

Ayla leaned back to kiss her; the salty taste of her lips perfect beyond compare. Ayla kissed her as she led Flowridia to the bed of rose petals, kissed her as she gently—oh, so gently—removed her gown, and left no patch of skin untouched.

Basking in the glow of love, Flowridia, too, became free.

CHAPTER 19

Thirteen years after the end of the world . . .

Yet for months afterward, Dira felt nothing again. No warmth. No other world.

Fed up with failure, she eventually stopped trying.

One lonely evening, when sleep eluded her, Dira crept through the dark home, seeking to evade Sora's notice. Mother was not home, so it was only Sora she could play this game with.

As she sipped from the pitcher of blood in the cellar, disappointment filled her. Would this be her entire life? Entertaining herself by sneaking through a house she was perfectly allowed to sneak through? She knew every squeaky floorboard and unstable tile, could dance her way through silent halls and make not a sound. Even outside, she could creep as silent as night, but what was the use?

Dejected, Dira returned to the upper floor, not even bothering to avoid the creaky steps.

Yet . . . She stilled as she approached Sora's door, for a faint glimmer of light shone through the seam. Was it candlelight? Something about it didn't seem right.

Curious, Dira kept on her toes as she approached, suddenly keen to whispers dancing in the silent night, indecipherable as they were. She stopped as near as she dared, straining to listen.

". . . have to be more careful . . ."

Dira came nearer, holding her breath as she set her ear to the door.

Someone else whispered, but far too quietly for Dira to understand. Sora's words were slightly less muffled, but perhaps that was only because she would know her aunt anywhere.

"There's every reason to be careful. Celestière is in crisis, and what if Morathma is desperate enough to silence you through me? Or Dira?"

A pause. More faint whispering. Dira did not even dare to breathe. Mother didn't allow strangers in the house. The only visitor was Etolié, but she would recognize Etolié's golden glow beyond the door's seams, right? This wasn't Etolié. This light shifted in hue, sometimes silver, sometimes gold, sometimes melding into a coppery sheen.

"When the war is over?" Sora said. *"I don't know. My first duty is always to Dira and Ayla, but I can't throw away my friendship with Etolié either, and you know that's what it would do."*

Among the unintelligible sounds, Dira heard, *"There is no end to my atonement, is there?"* She pressed closer, straining to hear more from this new whisper.

"Some crimes are beyond atonement. And until you humble yourself enough to admit that, she'll never forgive you."

Silence settled. Dira focused, fearing she missed something, until . . .

"Yet you've stayed with me," the stranger said. *"Why?"*

"I could ask you the same."

"I believe I asked first."

A pause; the softest whisper. *"Because against all sanity, you're the one."*

A strange sound pulled a frown to Dira's lips. Some sort of smacking, like a mouth after a good meal, a sigh of pure joy—

"Wait," came Sora's voice.

Dira froze.

"Ayla is gone, but Dira's room is nearby. I should check on her first. She likes to wander at night."

The doorknob turned.

The light expanded as the door opened. The shadow of the door grew large. Dira did not think, simply reacted. She dove into the shadow's recesses, seeking to disappear—

Only for humidity and light to choke her.

She hit the earth with a thud, the moist ground quickly seeping through her nightgown. Dira gasped as she scrambled to stand, shocked to see an alien world.

The plant-like growths held warm shades. No greens, but yellows and oranges in a range of hues. Though it had been a warm night, the humidity immediately coated her skin like a film. She did not easily sweat—she could, but not as easily as Sora—yet she'd be drenched in minutes if she stayed, if not from her own sweat than from the very air.

Then, her panic returned. Oh gods, oh gods—how did she get home?

She huddled against the tree-like thing, covering her head to find darkness once more. She sought her home, the trees, darkness instead of light—

And fell.

Dira gasped as she blinked and saw her home once more.

Sora's door was shut. Sora herself stared at her from the other end of the hall.

Dira stood as casually as she was able, praying the darkness obscured her dirtied nightgown. "I was just heading back to bed."

Sora blinked, hesitating a second too long. "Were you there the whole time?"

Dira shook her head.

"Go to bed."

"Yes, Auntie."

Dira skirted past Sora on nimble feet, seeking to avoid touching her.

Only once alone did it all settle in.

Sha'Demoni. She had fallen in. She had *returned*. And—

Sora . . .

Dira quickly changed, etching the conversation to memory.

Sometimes, secrets were the way of the world. Mother kept them. Now, Sora too.

Current era . . .

'Tomorrow' quickly became 'two weeks.'

Sora politely asked to see the Speaker every morning.

Every morning he came, and he said the same bullshit: "*Morathma is in Celestière.*"

"Every day, Soliel gets closer to finding us," Sora muttered, grumbling as she stared at the ceiling from Chaos' bed. "Every day, my sister is more and more pregnant. Every day, there are other gods we could have gone to first."

"We should discuss how to reach Onias at some point," Chaos replied, splayed beside her. Boredom slurred her words. Even the undead had a limit to how exhausted they could be. "I can go underwater, but we will have to find a spell for you."

"I suspect water breathing is a fairly simple request among witches."

"I would agree."

Sora groaned, counting the minutes to their next meal—because what else was there to look forward to? "At what point does someone die from boredom?"

"I went ten thousand years once, but I was already dead. At least I had Demitri."

"Oh, at least?" Chaos replied to herself. "Sora, I know you love Mom. Can you imagine being trapped underground with her? For ten thousand years? After the first two or three thousand, having your soul eaten sounds like a vacation."

"And I miss being able to yank your tail, asshole," Chaos grumbled.

"You know what you used to call Dira and I? Dira-mitri. Because we were so inseparable." Chaos, who was Demitri, laughed, though it devolved into a sigh. "You're a fucking prophet. Fuck you, Sora."

Sora managed to smile. "Do I still get to call you Dira-mitri?"

"Not in front of strangers."

"How aware *are* you?"

"Always, though sometimes I stop paying attention."

"And sometimes he does not shut up," came Dira, for the inflection was different, the words more formal. They were utterly different entities, forced to share one form. "Worse is when we argue. You have seen the results of that. I . . . *we* become erratic."

"That's not the worst. The worst is when you get cozy with sunshine boy."

It was too much, and Sora groaned as she rolled off the bed.

"I'm surprised you haven't asked, Sora," the voice that was Demitri continued. "You're too nosy to overlook it."

"It's almost as though I'm not a pervert." Sora trudged to the window, bracing herself for the heat emanating beyond. Beyond, citizens went about their day, most likely preparing for the holy day tomorrow. "I don't want to know."

Though she feared it might reignite the issue, Sora grimaced as one query did bother her. "Demitri, you knew who Soliel was all along though, right? Why didn't you say anything?"

"Lady Ayla said I couldn't. Said we don't talk about the future. Until I got absorbed. Then Dira heard everything."

"It was distressing, to say the least," Chaos whispered to herself.

The knock sounded for dinner, interrupting their moment.

Sora could find many things to insult the Morathans for, but their cooking wasn't one of them. When she answered the door, an agreeable older woman kindly smiled and brought a large tray carrying meat, cheese-covered potatoes, and some sort of gelatinous dessert. "Anything else you need?"

"I need to see Morathma," Sora said, as she did each time someone asked. Already, she served herself a plate from the platter, stomach growling for greasy potatoes. "But I don't think you have the power to make that happen."

"I'm so sorry, no. But Morathma works in mysterious ways. I'm sure there's a reason for this waiting."

"Of course," Sora said, unsurprised when the woman proceeded to leave. Chaos sat upon the bed, looking less forlorn. Sora said, "Clearly, we're being dismissed. Is there anything we can do to convince them that this is important? Any magic you could do?"

Chaos gave a regretful shake of her head. "There is no magic I could perform that they would respect here, or not outright run away in fear from. My talents are many, but they circulate around two cores—Silver Fire and necromancy."

"I understand why Morathma would hate Silver Fire, but why necromancy? He isn't . . . *wasn't* aligned with Sol Kareena." The reminder of her goddess' death stirred tension in her throat, but now was not the time for tears; Sora was so damn tired of tears.

Chaos stared outside into the sunny day, a foreign sneer upon her face. This was not Demitri's familiar glower, but Dira's. "Ilune."

Sora waited for further explanation, sidling up to Chaos when she received none. A gorgeous day, even the heat from the window enticing after so long cooped indoors. "Just . . . Ilune?"

"My apologies. It is an old and complicated grudge. I didn't know to resent her until long after I had been sent into the past with Soliel. To put it simply, Ilune spent thousands of years antagonizing Morathma, but never overtly enough to cause actual conflict between Solvira and Moratham."

"You knew Ilune?"

"She plays a significant role in the life of my future self."

A bit daunting in theory, though Sora knew so little of the God of Death. Certainly not enough to comment.

Chaos continued. "Ilune is often said to be the origin of necromancy in this world, and it is true that all necromancers in the time of the New Gods appeared after her or because of her. But necromancy was a prominent magic during mine and Soliel's reigns. And with all due respect to Ilune, she is the root of its corruption. Necromancy was never meant to spark fear or be about control. Necromancy is a kindness and the highest of responsibilities. One of my main duties as Goddess was to escort the dead to their final rest, or even to ease the passing of one from life to death. At times, I would entreat the dead for wisdom, and other times shepherd willing spirits back to the mortal realm. The Beyond is a beautiful place, Sora. It is not an ending but an epilogue, and necromancers are the ones granted the honor of sharing the stories of those who have passed. It's a high calling, keeping watch over the dead. And it vexes me how far necromancers have fallen from their higher calling. Violating the dead by exploiting their bodies and spirits for violence is a sacrilege.

"And there are others to blame. With respect to my origins, vampires should not exist. A dead creature that must feed on life to survive? A disgrace to the order of the world. It is not their fault for existing, but Izthuni has much to answer for, for creating such a curse."

Chaos gave a bitter smile. "For all his wickedness," she continued, "Casvir at least does a few things right. Using the mindless dead to toil the fields and do menial labor isn't something I actually condemn. It isn't what I would have done, but it follows the spirit of the law. Neoma created Ilune, which follows the way of the world: Silver Fire and necromancy are not opposites, no, but companions. Creation and death are meant to exist in unison, a never-ending cycle. Neoma treated the Silver Fire with the respect it deserved, whereas Ilune gave in to her selfish instincts and corrupted necromancy at its core."

Tension lay in Chaos' grip on the bedsheets, the flecks of sunlight harmless against her fingertips. Sora was reminded unwillingly of Mereen reaching for the sun, cursed to burn should she come too close, and shoved the memory away. Mereen was Sora's past, but she was not Dira's—and thank the Light for that. How offended her grandmother would be to think there was a half-elf, half-vampire even remotely adjacent to their family tree. Sora nearly smiled. "I'd never thought of necromancy like that."

But Flowridia had, she realized. Her sister had once been altruistic regarding the so-called 'evil' magic, until she had been corrupted as well.

"Few have. It is what it is."

Chaos said nothing more. Sora resumed eating.

When she had eaten her fill, Sora trudged back to the window, the sunset over Andiamen a magnificent sight. Shades of orange and pink melded into deep purples, the colors unlike anything she had seen before.

Leelan sat dormant next to the glass. For two weeks, Leelan hadn't moved from the window. Did he crave the sunlight? Did he sense his fallen goddess? There was so much left unknown.

Sora watched the sun slowly set, missing the fresh air and energy of people. So many churches dotted the city beyond, and there in the distance was the sole Temple of Staella, the final vestiges of sunlight glinting off its steeple. The stars would rise, and the world would sleep, protected by their Goddess Mother.

A thought struck Sora then. "People pray to Staella through dreams, right?"

From the bed, Chaos replied, "In Solvira, they do."

"What about here?"

"No. Any kind of drug or mind-altering agent is banned here."

Sora frowned, the implications upsetting. "Is it so Staella can't talk to them?"

"How else would Morathma keep control of his side of the narrative? Take away the means for his people to hear the words of Goddess Staella."

"So what do they do in the temple?"

"Mostly sit in the chapel and try to feel her spirit. There is also a prayer roll you can submit names to. The priestesses pray for the individuals on the roll for Staella to bless them. They don't worship there."

Sora surveyed the distance from the window to the earth, mentally calculating how many bedsheets she would need to climb out the window. "If the priestesses pray . . . don't they have Spore?"

"You don't have to have Spore to pray to Staella."

Sora frowned, feeling quite lied to. "You don't?"

"You need Spore if you want her to answer. Though she can also visit in dreams, if she so chooses."

Sora immediately knelt, though just as quickly questioned how to approach this. "We need to reach Etolié and explain what's going on. If I explain the situation to Goddess Staella, she might relay it to Etolié, right?"

"That seems plausible," Chaos replied, and she sat up, intrigue on her pretty features. "But what would Etolié do?"

"I don't know, but what we're doing isn't working. We don't have time." From memory, Sora created the sign of a four-point star with her pointer fingers and thumbs, then shut her eyes and whispered. "Goddess Staella, please hear my prayer . . ."

Etolié had lived through many a terror-filled moment—murdering her sperm-donor, hiding underground while the City of Light was destroyed, facing The Endless Night more times than was reasonable—yet for all her years spent in an anxiety-fueled existence, never had she struggled so much to breathe than when she walked into the underground amphitheater in Sha'Demoni.

Ku'Shya dominated the scene by size alone. Yet, as impressive as her massive figure was, the decorations immediately caused Etolié's head to buzz, despite the concentration of booze in her blood. Glowing runes spanned the walls, bearing resemblance to the ones tattooed onto Khastra's body. Countless De'Sindai witches bustled about—some drawing on the walls, some sprinkling some sort of dust around the perimeter of the room, others simply muttering to themselves as they studied various scrolls. A cauldron sat in the center, large enough for the Bringer of War to bathe in, but it was simply Khastra who stood beside it.

The half-demon was deep in conversation with her mother, swapping rapid Demoni. Kah'Sheen peered from around Ku'Shya's leg. "Hello, Etolié!"

"There's a lot going on here, Sheen Bean."

"Yes, yes. The witches are making their preparations. Almost done. You are here to watch, yes?"

Etolié nodded, though her heart skipped a beat at Ku'Shya's sudden bellowing. "Ah, yes—Etolié!" Ku'Shya need only take a step to be beside them, unlike Khastra who had to jog to keep up. "We are nearing completion. My witches are working hard."

Etolié tried to speak, only to be swept up into strong arms, laughing until Khastra planted a firm kiss upon her lips. "It is wonderful to see you."

"With any luck, I'll be seeing a helluva lot more of you soon."

"Etolié!" Ku'Shya's booming proclamation stole the moment, but Etolié couldn't be angry, given Ku'Shya was the reason they were here. "I am told you are controlling my Khastra through song, yes?"

Between the accent and the odd verbiage, Etolié blinked three entire times before the meaning fell into place. "Yes, I can calm the Bringer of War through magic singing."

"Yes, yes—it is possible my Khastra will transform during the spell process, and you will sing to keep her calm, yes?"

Bless the fates. That was a trivial task. "Of course." She didn't mention that sometimes taking off her clothes, while less effective, was faster and might buy her the time to get her spell going. However, while showing your tits to your supposed mother-in-law was its own trauma, she suspected she'd be forgiven, given the cause.

Trivial, yes, but the firm embrace around her highlighted the stakes. Though urgency filled her, Etolié gripped her favorite demon's forearms, savoring the sensation of magic beneath her fingertips. All would be well, but Etolié wore a ring now. "You better fucking make it through," Etolié whispered, for only them to hear, "or we aren't sealing the 'contract,' got it?"

Khastra's chuckle warmed her whole body. "Unless you want to do it now."

"We can't do it now. You're too stubborn to die if you have unfinished business, so come finish me off when you're done."

Again came Khastra's laughter, and Etolié savored the sound and the vibration against her body. Khastra's calloused fingers brushed across Etolié's arms as they parted, the sensation leaving her spinning.

"The ritual is two parts," Khastra explained. "First to sever my connection to Casvir, and then to bind my spirit to my body. The spellwork is . . . gruesome, but my mother has reassured me there will be no murder."

"Admittedly a relief." And a surprise, but Etolié would take whatever concessions she could get.

"Khastra!" Ku'Shya's cry shattered their moment. "It is time. Into the cauldron."

Before Etolié could beat her to it, Khastra swept her into an impassioned kiss. Magic surged between them, their touch igniting the tattoos across her body, and when they parted, it was far too soon.

Yet for all their intensity, Khastra's words were simply light. "I love you, Etolié. Whatever comes next, you will always have my heart."

"Mechanical pieces and all," Etolié teased, her own emotion rising. "I love you, Khastra."

Khastra approached the cauldron, stopping at the side to remove her clothing. Naked and glorious, she allowed herself to be lifted by her demonic progenitor, disappearing into the cauldron's depths.

A shadow sat beside Etolié, Kah'Sheen's presence reassuring and marginally humorous with her long legs tucked under her body. When she offered a hand, Etolié squeezed it tight.

Ku'Shya lifted what appeared to be a gargantuan metal stake, carved with more of those magical runes. Her Demoni words meant nothing to Etolié, but Kah'Sheen's grip tightened.

Nothing could have prepared Etolié for the sudden flash of metal in Ku'Shya's grip—nor the horrendous *crack* when she jammed the stake through her exoskeleton, right in the center of her torso. Etolié stared, utterly stunned, as a torrent of red splattered the cauldron and Khastra inside. But Kah'Sheen didn't even flinch, so despite the gory results, Ku'Shya presumably wasn't about to die.

The scent of blood only rose when each witch cut a deep line across one wrist, kneeling so the blood could drip upon the lines drawn upon the floor. Deep red spread along the runes, the amount far more than the witches had spilled, or even the demon goddess.

All light vanished, save for the spreading blood, which emanated an ominous glow. Etolié supposed she wasn't in danger, but it didn't change her ill-hidden horror at the scene. Demoni chanting echoed across the walls. An explosion of bubbling blood erupted from the cauldron. Etolié screamed, only for Kah'Sheen's hand to cover her mouth and press her against her side, silently willing her to *hush*.

Bestial roaring came from the cauldron as the Bringer of War emerged, covered in blood, her tattoos glowing brighter than Etolié had ever seen. She did not seek to escape, simply beat upon the cauldron's edge, her cries conveying pain.

But Kah'Sheen did not remove her hand, and so Etolié did not sing, simply watched in horror at the blue glow bursting from the half-demon's body, the clear image of Khastra's mirror shining within. That was her soul, her spirit, severed and . . .

. . . thrust back with a burst of light. The cauldron shattered; thick sheets of iron ripped apart like paper. The Bringer of War knelt hunched in its center, breathing heavy—but *breathing*, and therein lay the miracle.

Silence settled. The glow upon the walls faded, bringing the return of ambient light. Ku'Shya's wound dripped like a leaking pipe, her expression unreadable, though her four eyes never deviated from the heaving woman in the center. When Kah'Sheen's hold loosened, Etolié pulled out of her grip, running to the blood-soaked Bringer of War.

A mere step away, she matched eyes with that glowing gaze. Utterly monstrous ... yet the pain in her eyes faded into recognition. When she reached out a hand, large enough to engulf Etolié's entire torso, Etolié gave no care to the blood and held her finger tight, her suspension finally breaking when the Bringer of War pulled her into a gentle embrace. Blood soaked her hair, her illusionary clothes, coated her skin—but all Etolié could feel was relief.

Demoni words came from Ku'Shya, her tension thinly curtailed. The monster who was part of Khastra replied in turn. Strange, to witness the Bringer of War so docile, perhaps too exhausted to misbehave.

Ku'Shya left without her usual gusto, clutching the horrific wound on her stomach, half the De'Sindai trailing after her.

Only then did Etolié's tears strike, weeping into her demon's firm embrace. "You're all right. Oh, Khastra, you ..."

How she loved the Bringer of War's voice. *"Etolié..."*

Nearby, Kah'Sheen lingered. Around them, the remaining witches began cleaning the bloodstained space. The Bringer of War's embrace loosened, the beginning of her transformation shown in her shrinking.

Soon, it was only Khastra—who Etolié kissed with all her might, uncaring of the blood, of the ritual, of all the horror around them. All was well, and for once, the future seemed bright—

Starshine ...

"Momma?" Etolié lurched back at the voice.

Khastra stared, confused. "I beg your pardon?"

Etolié held up a hand, waving away her touch. Her tears threatened to overwhelm her, but this was a secret nobody needed to know—not even Staella. Not yet. She set a hand to her temple, willing her mind to focus on the sudden task at hand.

Momma?

Sorry for the bother—

Not a bother.

I received the strangest message from your friend, Sora. It might be easiest to explain in person. Can I bring you here for a moment?

Sora could drown in Onias' Hell for all Etolié cared in the moment. *Can it wait ... an hour?*

Of course. Just tell me when you're ready.

Etolié lowered her hand, the world returning—and with it the reality of sitting in a bloody heap beside her favorite demon. "Celestière shit. Apparently Sora talked to Momma. Nothing important—"

But when she tried to steal Khastra's lips, the half-demon gently held her back. "If this is—"

"Beefcake, I very nearly risked watching you die all over again, so you can shut the fuck up about honor and shit. Let me enjoy this."

Khastra's laughter brought light.

CHAPTER 20

Dira did not try to reach Sha'Demoni again for months, shaken by the experience.

"Do you have any maps of Sha'Demoni?" she asked Sora one day.

Her aunt stilled in preparing dinner, the aroma of spiced meat sweeter than even the scent of blood in Dira's glass. "There are some in the library, I would guess. Why?"

Dira hid her guilt behind her cup. "Mother won't let me leave this place, but I can at least learn a little bit about the world, right?"

Sora's skepticism remained, but she didn't ask.

Dira gathered maps from both worlds—Sha'Demoni and the elven continent Zauleen—and drew maps of her own comparing the two. How did one navigate between the two? How did Mother never get lost?

There were patterns to find, but was it enough? Dira drew maps and burned them, lest she leave a trail of her . . . plan? What was her plan? Had there ever been one?

What was the point?

Every day, the manor became more claustrophobic.

Perhaps there was no point at all.

She resisted throwing the books into the fire as well one night, instead stowing them back beneath her bed, as always. She left her bedroom, her cats, and the sleeping Demitri behind, wandering instead to the kitchen. No effort was made to quiet her feet. What was the point?

To her surprise, Mother was there. Dira stilled in the doorframe. "I didn't know you were home. Hello."

Given the basket of newly acquired fruit and bread and wrapped meats on the counter, Mother's whirlwind in the kitchen made sense. She smiled, though some sorrow lingered in her eyes. "I'm gone for three days, and all I get is a 'hello'?"

When she opened her arms, Dira met her in an embrace, conflicted over her softening heart. Dira squeezed her tight, sudden emotion welling in her throat. When had she outgrown Mother? Barely so, but the difference was stark.

Apparently Mother noticed as well, for pride showed in her smile when they parted. Her hand came up to the top of Dira's head, settling upon her hair. "Goodness, look at you. Growing so quickly. You might end up as tall as your aunt at this rate."

Mother returned to her domestic duties, wrapping the fresh bread in clean cloth.

"How was your trip?" Dira asked.

Mother shrugged. "Exhausting."

That was as descriptive as she ever was.

"How is the world?"

"Also exhausting."

Dira swallowed frustration. Mother either feigned obliviousness or simply was. "Is it ever not exhausting?"

"Not in my lifetime, to be quite honest."

"Perhaps you've just lived an exhausting life."

Mother's quiet scoff led to a shrug. "An exhausting life and death, yes."

"I don't actually know anything about your life."

The question lay unspoken. Mother's silence only fueled her frustration—but then Mother spoke. "I grew up across the sea in a country that no longer exists, away from the Sun Elves. Which isn't to say there were not any, but it was a predominantly human country."

Dira perked up, dampening her enthusiasm all the same. Mother was . . . speaking? Freely? "Were you happy there?"

"No. It was not a pleasant experience. I have told you I was an orphan, and orphan lives are rarely easy. Although, your other mom was also raised in an orphanage and only had positive things to say."

"I thought she knew her mom."

"She did, but she did not grow up with her—and that is definitely for the best."

"You haven't told me much about my grandmother either."

Mother's grimace precluded a familiar phrase. "Perhaps a story for another time. She was not a kind person."

Another time meant 'never,' if experience was any indication. "I don't see why learning my own family history would put me in danger."

"History is overrated."

"Sora always says those who don't know history are doomed to repeat it."

"That's in regards to the world, my lamb. I do not believe you are in any danger of repeating mine or your mother's histories."

Dira swallowed bitterness. Gods, she had been so close.

Nearly four decades ago, Etolié had taken her first step across the Morathan border, uncertain of her cause—only that she had rage with no outlet and a bone to pick with momma's exes.

Eionei had warned her away from treading too far south. *A thousand miles of desert isn't exactly a walk in the park, Starshine.*

Etolié had never seen Andiamen and was remiss to admit it was aesthetically shiny and pretty to look at. As it was, she had little time to admire the gleaming towers. Already, people were staring, likely because of the wings and because she had simply . . . appeared.

She marched forward, head high, fully accepting this would go terribly wrong, but leaving her friend to flounder wasn't an option, and she supposed she could help that batshit Goddess too.

As it was, the reception was more enthusiastic than expected.

Children stared, some following the wispy motions of her wings, but their mothers gasped. A few even wept. Men paused in their business, but while Etolié was used to men's eyes, this wasn't quite the same as ogling. But surely there were other winged Celestials here. Surely she couldn't be so foreign.

Her answer came as a bold child ran to her—a little girl who couldn't be more than six. "Mother Staella!" she cried, and she hugged Etolié around the knees.

Well, if this wasn't a brilliant turn of events. Etolié raised her pitch, rounded her vowels as Momma did, and prayed this didn't blow up in her face. Goddess Momma forgive her—she had promised to never do this again, but the greater good called.

She patted the child on the head. "Oh, you sweet little, uh, thing!"

A woman ran to grab the child, but slowed as she approached, eyes watering with her gasp. "Goddess Mother, you . . . you've returned!"

"For a little while," Etolié said, realizing this was going to cause some serious rumors to fly. "It's been some time since I've stopped by. Can you point me toward the castle?"

"It would be an honor to escort you."

"Yes, please." Etolié took the grabby child's hand and held that instead, following the enthused mother.

More and more followed as they went. Children fought to stand beside her, and Etolié cringed when a few tugged at her tender wings. All around, prayers and praise sounded, soon segueing into song, and Etolié illusioned a beaming smile even as she slowly died inside.

Unfortunately, it was not a short way, and by the time Etolié faced steps to a gleaming castle, she had gathered a whole army of an envoy, the song sounding throughout the entire city. When an old, well-decorated man emerged from the castle, he joined in the singing throng, and when they continued on with an eighth verse, Etolié contemplated self-immolation.

But thank Alystra's Ass—the singing concluded with an overly long final note. The people cheered as Etolié broke free from the grabbing hands of children and approached who she assumed was the Speaker.

"Goddess Mother," the Speaker said, breathless as his own tears began to fall. "I did not think I'd live to see your second coming, yet . . ." He fell to his knees as he grasped her hand, which might've been sweet if Etolié weren't radiating static.

Well, she had dug her grave this deep. Might as well lie in it. "I come on official Celestière business. I have heard rumors that there is an Old God in your establishment and wished to see her for myself."

"Of course, Goddess Mother."

"And if you wouldn't mind arranging a meeting with Morathma, I would be most appreciative."

"I . . ." His hesitation melted into warmth. "I'm certain his work in Vanir Sol can wait. I will send prayers immediately notifying him of your presence. Come with me, please."

"Oh, I meant with . . ." Deeper and deeper, she dug this damn hole. "Yes, that sounds wonderful."

She followed, of course accepting his hand as he escorted her, all while praying as loud as she could. *Momma, I fucked up. They think I'm you.*

They crossed the threshold into the castle, but Etolié felt too much like puking to admire the fine art. She felt no peace at all to hear Staella's voice in her head. *In hindsight, I see how this happened.*

I know you said—

There's a difference between mistaken identities and actual identity theft, Starshine. Don't worry.

Momma, I asked if I could see Morathma and they said yes.

Silence. And then . . . *Well, if it's any consolation, he won't think you're me.*

You see how this is a problem, right?

Get your friends that audience, Starshine. If he won't bend, call me again.

Etolié owed Momma a plant, or perhaps several.

She was led to a grand throne room, the crystal chandelier on the wall larger than her bedroom in Solvira. Windows scattered the room with sunshine, glittering against the white stone paving the floor. The throne was suited for a god, and every guard and servant they passed wept and touched her hands, her skirt, her wings. Etolié wanted to vomit. "Wait here," the Speaker said. "Blessed Mother, even Staella, Father Morathma will be notified immediately."

When the Speaker left, the guards lingering at the outskirts came to greet her, some too emotional to speak. "Is this truly your return, Goddess Mother?" one asked amid his sobs.

"We'll see how it goes with Morathma, now won't we? Can one of you check if anyone's gone to fetch the Goddess of Chaos—"

"Goddess Mother!"

Etolié and the rest stood alert at the Speaker's return, warmth in his elderly smile.

"Father Morathma has agreed to bless us with his presence. Goddess Mother, it is an honor to facilitate this reunion."

And that's when he began to glow. Etolié studied the window, wondering if she had the fortitude to fly through the glass as an escape if it all fell apart. Nothing she hadn't done before.

But the Speaker stretched and grew as Morathma slipped inside his body like a glove, wings bursting from his back—though melted and deformed. Morathma's scars didn't appear quite so starkly with the Speaker as his host, their figures melding to appear as one. But he unquestionably changed, his entire demeanor becoming . . . brusque.

Morathma did not sit, instead lording his massive size above her as he crossed his arms, taller than even the Bringer of War. He spoke in terse Celestial, and judging by the continued awe on her fellow's faces, they hadn't a clue what he said. "Well, well. Goddess Staella herself blesses my kingdom."

Etolié matched his curt tone, also speaking in her mother tongue. "Listen, I didn't tell them. They assumed."

"Yet, you led them on. Their hearts will be broken upon your exit. So tell me why I should not proclaim you an imposter and banish you from my kingdom."

"Straight to business, aren't ya," Etolié said, resisting the urge to call him some variation of 'crispy.'

"Etolié, you have been a thorn in my side for decades, and I have stood nigh out of respect for your mother, and that alone."

"You stood nigh because of Eionei's deal, ya—" Nope. No rapist jokes. She could save that for when they succeeded. "Anyway, are you aware the Goddess of Chaos is waiting in your guest room?"

"I was not aware."

"Look, if the God of Order breaks the realms apart, you and your collection of child brides—sorry, *young women*—are done for. So will you please meet with her and hear what she has to say?"

To his credit, Morathma politely conveyed the order to a set of servants waiting in the wings, who scurried away. In Celestial, he said, "You are not particularly tactful."

"I have narrowly refrained from several insults, excuse you. This is me being polite. You're the one being emotionally manipulative."

Morathma gave her pause, then stepped back toward his throne, far less aggressive when seated. "Perhaps I have been forward, and I apologize. But consider how it would have looked if I had refused to see you? You say I am manipulative, but look what you've done."

"Buddy, this was an accident. It's not my fault your people didn't question how Goddess Mother could be here in the flesh."

"I am exhausted from your excuses."

And thank Eionei's Asshole she didn't have to come up with a response to that. The doors opened, and mad-flame-ghosty appeared alongside Sora.

Sora gasped, her pace increasing, but before she could speak and fucking ruin it, Etolié put on a broad smile, resumed her Staella impression, and said, "Hello, friend of Chaos. I'm the ever-friendly Goddess Staella. Nice to meet you for the first time." Then, to Chaos herself, Etolié offered a wave. "Oh my goodness, the real Goddess of Chaos. Never thought I'd see the day!"

Chaos stepped forward in a very non-ghost way, her Silver Fire radiant even in the sunlight. "God Morathma, it is an honor to finally meet you."

"I apologize for the wait," Morathma said, the same warmth from the funeral filling his words. He returned the reply in Common, as Chaos had done. "Goddess of Chaos—I will admit, I have been curious to see you return since the rebirth of your counterpart. Rumors spread wide, even to Moratham."

"Then you must know of the God of Order's quest to separate the worlds," Chaos replied. "It is my own quest to stop this madness and save Celestière, but with as many orbs as he has and with my return being so recent, I do not yet have the power to defeat him. I seek pledges from the most powerful of the Celestière gods, and who is more powerful than you, God Morathma?"

Etolié supposed she might not be wrong with that assessment, with Sol Kareena's death. Pity.

Morathma's chuckle held a fatherly chide. "I am resistant to flattery, especially so plainly stated. You want my power."

Thankfully, Chaos did not miss a beat. "For the sake of saving the realms, yes. All of them, including yours. Any supposed flattery is accidental, I assure you. I have lived in many timelines, and that includes your future. You are great now, and your greatness lasts for years to come."

Etolié resisted the urge to gag at the buttering up.

"I do not make bargains on flattery alone," Morathma replied.

"The bargain is that I have the power to save the realms," Chaos said.

"What proof do you have that this is not a poor investment? I cannot revoke my power."

"I would hope my title is proof enough."

"While I cannot say I have met an imposter of the Goddess of Chaos, I have met imposters wielding your power. Show your true face. No tricks. Then, I will consider it."

To Etolié's surprise, the ghost obeyed—and was definitely not a monster anymore.

Etolié had seen her from afar in the abandoned temple, but here she had the chance to actually study this strange hellspawn. Chaos was awfully pretty, her olive skin grey yet boasting rosy cheeks. Youth showed in her face despite the laughter lines and greying temples, but when she smiled, Etolié was smacked with the visual of fangs and the uncanny sensation that she had seen that particular twisting lip before.

Oh, damn. She really was Ayla incarnate.

"I apologize, God Morathma," Chaos said, stepping boldly forward. "I am best known to my people across the sea by Silver Fire, and so it is the form I adopt the most. I meant no disrespect to you. This is my face."

Morathma's curiosity indicated no malice, though Etolié's skin bristled as the time ticked steadily by. "I would not have guessed you to be a half-elf."

"Most would not."

"Nor a dhampir."

"We are a rare species."

Again, he paused to reply, intrigue in the ensuing silence. "And where will you go when this quest is complete?"

"Assuming I survive at all, I do not know."

"You say you know me in your future, and so you must know what is considered status in my kingdom. I will offer my pledge, should you offer your own. Join me in Celestière as my wife. One night with me after our wedding, and then I will pledge. And when you succeed, you will return."

Etolié made no effort to hide her shock, nor did Sora, who appeared to have had her daggers taken even as she skimmed her hand along the sheath at her hip—not that she didn't have at least five more hidden somewhere on her person.

Chaos, however, barely flinched. "I am afraid I would not be able to provide what you're asking for. Due to my mixed undead heritage, I cannot have children."

"There are other ways to achieve the honor of motherhood," Morathma said, and Etolié finally felt her brain had finished its reset. "Those are my terms, Goddess of Chaos. You would be a welcome presence among my other wives."

"I'm flattered, but—"

"There is no but—"

"I'm so *tired!*" Etolié proclaimed, rolling up her illusioned sleeves. "I didn't want to do this, but if you're gonna be a pervert, I'm gonna be an asshole. You want emotional manipulation? I'll show you emotional manipulation, bitch."

Goddess Momma, I need you literally immediately, please.

And thank the Stars, the Moon, whoever the fuck was blessing her this day. *Oh, I've been listening.*

A gentle tap on Etolié's shoulder, and Etolié accepted the invitation, gasping at the odd sensation of another person filling her body. Etolié shut her eyes as her body stretched and pulled—not painful, no, but strange. Warmth emanated from inside her, like a perpetual hug, and then a sweet voice that wasn't hers sounded from her mouth. "Hello, Morathma."

Etolié opened her eyes, noting her own radiant light. All gazed upon her, varying stages of awe on the faces of the servants and guards, and of course Sora and Chaos, the latter of whom gave an impish smile.

Morathma's shock silenced the room. No anger in his features—but wonder. "Staella?"

"What an honor it is to stand here before you, Goddess of Chaos," Staella said, and Etolié bowed when Momma bowed, her body simply a glove. "I, too, have heard of your noble quest. Saving the realms from the cruel God of Order—Moratham is indebted to your service, as is the whole of the mortal realm." Staella went to one knee, meeting Chaos' gaze with a kind smile. "I pledge my power and heart to you, Goddess of Chaos. For the sake of all the realms, my service is yours."

All around her, the servants and guards followed suit, bowing before Chaos and muttering their pledge. When Staella rose, Etolié fought to keep her own mouth shut, lest she praise her momma's genius aloud. "What say you, Morathma? Would you unite with me for this?"

The conflict upon Morathma's countenance was simply sublime, his eyes spelling desperation even as his smile remained false and gentle. He rose and bowed, hesitating only a moment before proclaiming, "I pledge my power and heart to you, Goddess of Chaos."

"Now, come with me," Staella said, beckoning to Sora and Chaos. Though she stood over twice their heights, she knelt to touch their backs. Her voice lowered. "None can portal in, but a few of us can portal out. Where shall we go?"

"Uluron awaits outside Andiamen," Chaos replied.

"And so it shall be."

"Staella . . ." Morathma approached, though hesitated to join them. "Won't you stay? Your people praise your return."

"I thought you preferred me silent," Staella replied. "Trust me, you wouldn't like what I'd tell them."

The world disappeared with Momma's spell.

As relieved as Sora was to escape the oppressive boredom of Moratham, the blast of afternoon heat was quite unwelcome.

Blinded by the sun, Sora immediately covered her eyes, blinking to adjust.

"What a stimulating engagement," she heard Staella say. "It really is lovely to meet you, Goddess Chaos. Is that your preferred name?"

"It's how most know me, yes."

"I don't quite feel comfortable leaving you three here until we find your dragon. Has she been waiting long?"

Sora finally found her bearings, met with the sweeping desert landscape and the distant city. "As long as we've been in Andiamen."

"I will fly up, then. Give me just a moment."

The goddess who was both Staella and Etolié floated up into the air, her shadow steadily shrinking.

Chaos scanned the horizon, her frown foreboding. "I don't know what I expected, but I forgot Morathma's sin is lust."

"Thank the Light Etolié was there to throw a fit," Sora teased, grateful to see Chaos smile once more.

"Thank the Light, indeed. Demitri would never have allowed it."

"No, I wouldn't have," Chaos replied to herself. "Soliel killed our baby, but Morathma also killed his babies. *And* he's creepy. He's a worse option."

"Does Etolié get to know about you, uh, Demitri?"

Chaos ceased her study of the horizon, her attention on Sora alone. "No. It's too much."

A shadow appeared above—but it was not Uluron. Staella had returned, but it was Etolié's voice. "So . . . I think I found her. She's not that far."

Chaos had no breath to lose, yet her voice came stilted, empty. "What's wrong?"

In response, Staella took her hand, as well as Sora's own, and led them along.

Not even a minute's walk, and Sora's gut clenched at what lay before them.

Bones and shards littered the desert, as though blasted and torn apart. A rib larger than Sora, a claw as big as her head—and a skull fragment bearing vacant eyes.

A howl tore from Chaos' throat, haunting, inhuman. She collapsed before the skull fragment, wailing as she clutched it with her small body.

Tears prickled in Sora's eyes, the cruel reality slowly descending. There was no orb here—not anymore. There was no Uluron. The gentle giant . . . gone.

Amid Chaos' screams, Staella made tepid steps toward her, kneeling as she offered a tender touch. Chaos wept into her arms, still clutching the skull, even as the jagged edges sliced her skin. Sora understood, though she knew she couldn't fathom the depths of her pain. Uluron was a daughter. A Daughter of Chaos.

A daughter . . . slain by her father. By Soliel.

The God of Order had five orbs.

Minutes passed in tense quiet, the only sound Chaos' sobs. They did not quiet, but broken words appeared among them, spoken by the goddess herself: *"My baby. My Ulu . . ."*

"I know, I know," Staella soothed, and she clutched Chaos tight. Her own tears flowed. "I am so sorry."

"How could he do this? How could Soliel . . . to Ulu. To Valeuron. All of my babies . . . All of them are gone."

"Will you tell me about her? Or any of them?"

Sora made her own tentative steps forward, cautious as she knelt beside them and set her hand on Chaos' shoulder. Dira was broken; Demitri was unpredictable.

"When the world became too much to rule alone, Soliel and I created the orbs and dragons in tandem. The orbs were both a tool and a birthright." Chaos trembled as she withdrew her pouch from her belt. She opened it, revealing the metal shards her spirit clung to. Realization struck Sora—where she had seen those pieces before. "I had no need for a crown, but this was a gift passed down in my bloodline. I broke it into pieces and removed its six gems. One for each child. I molded them from clay and used the Silver Fire to create their souls. I loved them as though I'd birthed them.

"Valeuron was always an old soul," Chaos continued, gazing upon one shattered piece. The crusted remains of green stone were stuck to the inset. "Wise and fair."

She withdrew another, filled with remnants of orange and red. "Mulgora was my performer. She loved to make you laugh."

And another, this one bearing hints of blue and yellow. "Rulira was headstrong and courageous. A bit like you, Sora. Nothing stopped her."

Sora choked at the statement, her misted eyes finally expelling their tears.

Chaos lifted the next, glittering in blue and white. "Yaleris, my soft and sensitive one. A gentle soul filled with empathy and love."

The next, Chaos clutched tight, fist trembling as a fresh sob interrupted her speech. "Solanis was his father's shadow. He melted at any praise. He was a healer, just as his powers would suggest."

Finally, Chaos set the sixth prong upon the skull, shards of onyx stone glittering within. "Ulu . . ." Chaos set her head against it and wept anew, her wails akin to a woman broken apart.

Somewhere in the realm, a titan wielded five orbs. And though all should tremble, Sora felt no urgency—not yet. Not now. The world became quiet, nothing but the sweltering sun and the cries of an ailing mother.

In Solvira, Etolié had heard Momma's kind voice: *"Be patient with her, Starshine. There is no pain like losing a child."*

And then Momma had left for Celestière.

Etolié teetered, the sudden rush of blood to her head from the void of power leaving her faint. Sora steadied Etolié as she leaned against her shoulder, groaning. "That never gets easier."

"Do you need a minute?"

Etolié's wings spread, causing her to levitate from the ground. "We don't have a minute. Soliel has five fucking orbs."

Beside them, Chaos remained slumped. No tears on her face; she could not cry in her possessed body. But residual anguish lingered in the crease of her eyes, the tremble in her lip. "She's right," Chaos said, no emotion at all. "We have to keep moving."

At Etolié's beckoning, the guards let them through the gates leading to her mansion, though they kept a wary eye upon the distraught Goddess. Etolié didn't bother to explain, simply let Sora pull her levitating body along. A nap sounded nice, perhaps a glass of fine wine, but Sol Kareena was dead. Uluron was dead. And so many more would come next, should they falter.

"Tell Murishani to get his ass over here," she said to the guard at her front door. "Emergency red alert. Tell him it's about the God of Order."

When they entered, Etolié directed them to the library. She could have a meeting in bed.

She didn't speak until the scarves engulfed her, melting into the pile of warmth and safety. "Well, you did it. You got all the Celestière gods to pledge. Not to sound callous, but what's next?"

"It's not enough," came Chaos' muted voice. Etolié peeked up from her pile, noting how she had become a small ball on the floor. She curled up like a puppy, fetal in pose, with Sora beside her, hand stroking those thick locs. "I made a promise to Sora, that when we found you again I would tell the truth about how to stop Casvir."

"Stop Casvir from . . ?"

Judging by the look the duo shared, there was more Etolié didn't know than she thought.

"Sorry," Chaos remarked. "I assumed you knew already."

"Knew fucking what?"

And that was when Etolié learned what Soliel had meant about the 'oncoming darkness' all those months ago.

Somehow . . . despite the gravity of Chaos' words, nothing about it really struck her as odd. "Yeah. That's what Casvir would do, that piece of shit."

"You took that well."

"I'm not saying it's a good thing. It's just not surprising. But you said . . ." Etolié frowned, unsettled at the unlocked memory. ". . . so what does killing yourself have to do with stopping Casvir—"

"Hi, knock knock—!"

"Gods-*dammit, Murishani!*"

Murishani flinched as he peered around the staircase, looking like he'd eaten a rotten grape. "I beg your pardon. You invited me."

Right. "I'm on the verge of actually getting some damn answers, but the important part is Soliel now has five orbs and the one here is in serious jeopardy."

"I would recommend moving it, then. He would have felt it before I put it in the box."

"Do that. Take it to Nox'Kartha. I want it out of here—now."

Murishani furrowed his brow as he surveyed the ensemble of guests, perhaps only just realizing her company. "Oh, the rude Goddess is back. You want it delivered *personally*, you say?"

"Stop with your bullshit. Give it to Zorlaeus."

"I would like a 'please.'"

"You will get your 'please' when there isn't an apocalyptic God trying to destroy the realms."

"Fine, fine. Enjoy your existential despair." He left, presumably. Fortunately Zoldar, ever-lurking, followed after to shut the door.

"Anyway," Etolié said, forcing a pleasant smile, "why do you want me to kill a fucking baby?"

Chaos sat up, exhausted as she nodded. "It's my fault that Casvir marches. I told Sora I would leave the choice to you. Once you knew the truth."

It's not that Etolié hadn't contemplated infanticide before, for this exact same purpose even. But it really fucking sucked that this was the exact baby she'd vowed to protect. "All right. Fine. I'm ready to listen."

Chaos shut her eyes, then offered her hands to each of them. "Someday, you'll even agree that it is my fault. I want to show you."

With equal trepidation, Etolié and Sora accepted her outstretched hands. All the world became darkness.

Etolié blinked and stared upon an arid wasteland, evidence of burned terrain all around. The very ground was scorched, ash swirling in the air. Distant fire seared the horizon, casting the night in ominous light.

Beside her, Sora stood equally stunned by the scene. When she took a step forward, her foot made no mark upon the ashy ground, but the figures ahead certainly did. Etolié knew them—Gods of Order and Chaos in the making, but youths comparatively. Chaos was hardly a woman at all, that or stuck in perpetual youth due to her dhampirism, but Soliel wasn't a day past twenty, though his face had hardened from strife.

Young Chaos wept with the same intensity of the woman who had lost her dragon daughter hours ago, clutching a dark pile of ash. Blood saturated the earth in various spots, but there were no bodies, no dead—simply Chaos and Soliel, the latter of whom knelt with his arm around her small body.

"Dira . . . We have to go."

But when he moved to rise, Chaos—*Dira*—did not follow. When he gently grabbed her arm, she wrenched it away, screaming into the ground.

"There's nothing protecting you now," he pled, his face coated in grime and smoke. "With her death, the bargain is over. We have to leave before Casvir—"

"*Don't pretend like you care!*" Dira screamed, her tears streaming bloodied marks down her face. "You wanted her dead all along!"

"Of course I care. I know what she meant to you—"

"Just *get out!*"

Soliel rose, pain in his strides as he tore himself away from her.

Dira clutched the shifting ashes, trembling as she withdrew a flask. Though she tried to make a funnel, her hands shook too violently to make their mark. The ashes fell away, coating the flask instead of filling it. Again and again, she grabbed the ashes, increasingly frantic with each failure.

Distant light startled Etolié in its familiarity—and for good reason. Her own doppelganger approached the weeping Dira, her wings a beacon upon the desolate landscape.

Future Etolié stood before Dira, who ignored her in favor of her futile quest. "Kid, we have to go."

"No."

"Casvir will come."

"And his dead will eat me. I don't care."

Future Etolié sighed and withdrew a wide-brimmed flask from her extraplanar space—Etolié recognized that gesture—and offered it instead. "It's dry. Gather what you can."

Dira quivered as she accepted it, her tears saturating the ash even as she grabbed it.

"We'll have a memorial," Future Etolié continued. "Whatever her crimes, she was an incredible force. No one can dispute that."

"She knew who I was," Dira whispered. "She said my name, and then . . ." She clutched a fist filled with ashes to her heart, a fresh sob tearing from her throat. "She wasn't a monster."

"Dira—"

"I could have saved her!"

"No, you couldn't have."

"This is all my fault!"

"You did what you had to do—"

"*I did this to her*!" Dira fell again into weeping, choking on her own cries.

Future Etolié scanned the horizon, then knelt beside the fallen Dira. "You're right. You fucking killed her. So what are you going to do now?"

Dira said nothing, merely cried.

"We're in a war, Dira. I know it hurts like fucking hell, but you have to keep going. Casvir's forces are on their way, and if you stay here, Ayla died for nothing. She wouldn't want you to give up. She'd want you to mourn and then rise again to kick Casvir's ass."

Amid her sobs, Dira frantically shook her head. "You hated her too. Of course you'd say that."

"Are you fucking kidding me?! No, I couldn't stand her, but it doesn't mean she wasn't one of the only fucking people left in this world I could rely on. What do you want me to say—that she wasn't a fucking monster?! She was, but I didn't want her dead! Just because I don't see her as anything less than a saint doesn't mean I wanted this to happen. That's your problem, Dira. You refuse to see her as she was, which was a deeply flawed fucking psychopath who was also our greatest hope. Yes, she could have done it. Ayla Darkleaf could have defeated Casvir. I'd bet my wings on it. But she's gone." Future Etolié choked on that final word, her eyes misting. "She's fucking gone," she continued, sorrowful now. "It's on us, all right? So come with me, please. I can't lose you too."

When Dira didn't immediately move, Etolié grabbed a fistful of ash and helped to funnel it into the flask. Together, they filled it to the brim, and when Etolié capped it, Dira held it to her heart. "You can keep that," Future Etolié said, then she offered a hand.

But Dira did not move just yet, instead trembling as her final few tears slid down to land in the ashes. When Dira accepted the hand to rise, the first hint of something . . . green sprouted from where her tears had fallen.

The scene faded as the first growth revealed petals of crystal blue, a moonlily blossoming amid the tragedy. They sat in Etolié's library instead.

Sora wiped her eyes on her sleeve, uncharacteristically weepy. Etolié felt . . . numb.

"Ayla can only be killed by someone she loves," Sora said, which was news to Etolié. "Did anyone tell you that?"

Chaos also cried, though silently so. She shook her head. "You were already dead. You weren't around to tell me. All I've known is that it was the end for her."

"Why, though?" Etolié asked. "If those are the parameters, why the fuck would you have had to kill her?"

"I'm told you know about Staff Seraph deDieula?"

The first pang of emotion struck Etolié's stomach, whereas Sora's face fell into her hands. "Oh."

"It's my fault Casvir was able to take her," Chaos said. "I was a child who didn't understand the game the world was playing. I'm the reason she lost her hold on the war against him. I'm the reason she died a monster. I'm the reason we lost the war. It's as you said—she could have stopped him."

"Hold the fuck up." Etolié sat up, swallowing her own brimming emotions. "Bullshit. That's what you got from that speech? That was a tough love speech, not a damn condemnation. I don't know what you did, but I do know that Casvir is a fucking brutal bastard, and you don't know whether he would have gotten his hands on her eventually anyway. The only way to stop Casvir is to destroy his fucking phylactery—not murder your past self.

"I don't know if I'm the person you need to hear this from," Etolié continued, and all she could think of was a broken fourteen-year-old Celestial child, forever scrubbing her hands of blood, "but it wasn't your fault. Casvir killed your mother. Not you."

Chaos' face fell into her hands, her cries echoing that of her past self.

Sora embraced Chaos. Etolié held her hand, surprised to feel empathy for this Goddess at all, surprised to know she'd someday be shattered over the death of The Endless Night, who had died for loving a child she didn't want.

"Tonight, we cry," Etolié said. "You fucking need it. Tomorrow, we find you more pledges. Morathma might be the most powerful god in Celestière now, but he's not the most powerful New God. I have an in with a certain Goddess of War, but first, there's a Temple to Izthuni in Nox'Kartha. You can have his pledge by nightfall."

Chaos nodded amid her cries, and Etolié didn't understand, only knew that it was truth.

Ayla loved her daughter, Dira, and that was the oddest revelation of all.

Part Four

SHA'DEMONI

CHAPTER 21

Fifteen years after the end of the world . . .

Etolié's presence was a gift, and not only because she often brought them for Dira.

Hidden on the other side of the door, Dira set her ear to the seam of Mother's bedroom and caught whispers of conversation.

"There is a rebellion in Sune," came Mother's voice, though Dira knew not what it meant. *"Of course it would be the humans. Ornery bastards, all of them."*

"Well, they all remember having their homes destroyed by a particular evil vampire tyrant—"

"I am destroying nothing."

Beneath Dira's mattress was a notebook detailing every conversation she had ever overheard between them.

She knew there was a war beyond the estate's walls. She knew Mother led some sort of charge. She knew there was a monster across the sea.

She also knew better than to ask.

"But there is something else . . . upsetting," Mother continued. *"Do you want to guess who leads the rebellion, Starspawn?"*

"I don't. Just fucking tell me."

"A certain cousin of yours. Perhaps you remember."

"Fuck."

Etolié's cousin led a rebellion in a town called Sune, filled with human refugees. Dira recited it over and over in her mind. Definitely one for her notes.

"My spies say he has quickly gained popularity by wielding his mother's name. Even the elves are receptive, though they are more hesitant to taunt their ancestral foe. I fear to assassinate him would make him a martyr at this point, and that is the last thing I need. They already have their goddess to inspire them. They don't need the son to join that legacy."

"I mean . . . would killing him stop . . . everything?"

Of course Etolié's cousin would have a godly mother—Etolié's mother was a goddess.

"Perhaps. Or perhaps it would make it so much worse. I am in the business of killing Casvir. Not Soliel. Though I suppose if he drops dead some other way, we would know that the world is saved—or damned. Who can say?"

Casvir was the monster across the sea. Which meant the other was the name of the rebel leader—Soliel. Mother wanted him dead, but she could not do it herself. Dira recited it in her head, resolving to remember—

"Dira!"

Dira froze. Sora had mastered the art of the 'whisper yell.' Though stiff, Dira glanced back, cold to see Sora looking so . . . panicked.

Sora quickly beckoned. *"Get over here!"*

More whisper yelling. On silent feet, Dira followed along, cursing this turn in luck. Sora slept early. She should not have been here at all, but though Dira was fifteen, her aunt took her hand like a child and led her upstairs.

Once out of earshot, Sora actually whispered—which, ironically, was louder. "What did you hear?"

"Only that—"

"Shh!" Sora held a finger to her lips. "No, you didn't."

Dira frowned, for that . . . that was not in character at all. "But I did hear—"

"No. You heard nothing. Understood?"

Implication dripped from that final word. Dira glared, for this was Sora, her aunt, her companion, her teacher . . . but this was not the woman she knew. "Why?"

"Because there are things I wish you knew, but not like this. I need you to trust me. I need you to just let this all go." Sora forced a smile, pain etched onto her familiar features. "So what did you hear?"

"Nothing," Dira said, though there was no foundation to the lie. Instead, her blood burned. Humiliation filled her for reasons she could not quite name.

"Good. Keep it that way. Now go to bed."

Sora walked away, yet the pressure within Dira burst.

"Why don't you trust me!"

Sora whirled around, staring as though struck by a bullet. "Of course I trust—"

"No, you don't! Not you, not Mother, not Etolié—no one! I'm not fucking stupid! I know Mother's an executor—whatever that means. I know there's a monster she's trying to fight. I know there's a war and a rebellion and that the troops aren't being manufactured as quickly as Mother wants, and that Etolié's a spy, and the monster is a necromancer named Casvir, and that Etolié's cousin is somehow involved, and—"

"Dira, will you *shut up!*"

Dira's mouth snapped shut, shocked at Sora's outburst. Never had Sora yelled. Never had Sora told her to lie.

"There's a whole world out there and a whole lot of shit you don't know. Ayla and I see eye to eye on virtually nothing—except you. I agree that you need more freedom to wander, but when she says the world isn't safe, she's not lying." Sora's lip trembled, a mirror to Dira's own. "Look, I'll speak to your mother. I don't share her sentiments about keeping you in the dark on everything, but I need you to go to bed and let me handle this."

Dira refused to cry, but shame rose to choke her. She ran to her bedroom, leaving Sora far behind.

But she did not go to bed.

Dira locked the door and lit her candle, the flame silver at first spark before fading to orange. She withdrew her notebook, secret and safe beneath her mattress, and quickly scribbled all she'd heard—and all that Sora had said.

As she stared at the words, Dira's offense only rose. There *was* a world out there, and Mother was lying to keep it a secret. Perhaps it was dangerous, yes. But why didn't Mother trust her? Why didn't Sora fight for her until pushed into a corner?

With her anger seeped . . . determination. All these years she had held herself back from exploring, even with Sha'Demoni at her fingertips. But now . . .

Dira slipped the notebook back into its private place, then danced over to her bookshelf, withdrawing a book of maps. Sora had taught her the different countries of the world and their history—though apparently not recent history—and turned to the maps of Falar'Sol.

Sune was due north. Hardly a journey at all. Certainly not if she traveled through Sha'Demoni.

Sora had taught her to fight, even when Mother disapproved. Etolié had taught her to wield her Silver Fire, as both a weapon and to absorb magic. But Dira had never had a real opponent—not yet.

Within her bedside table were daggers—some stolen, others gifted. She took her favorite by the hilt, power flowing through her at its weight. Mother had gifted it to her at six years old, stating that it was an art piece and not a blade for combat unless the need was dire. And what need was more dire than to gain the trust of that same mother?

She hadn't dared go back to Sha'Demoni, but the path was so clear . . .

Mother had wanted Soliel dead. So be it.

Current era . . .

"Where is Empress Etolié?" Casvir asked the next morning.

No greeting. Just a question. Flowridia paused before taking another bite of toast in bed, realizing he actually seemed agitated.

From the couch, Ayla peeked from behind her embroidery. Flowridia set down her bread, wary at the opener. "I haven't seen her since yesterday."

"I am concerned—but whether it is for her well-being or how long to condemn her to my dungeon, I am not yet certain."

Flowridia balked at the statement. "What happened?"

"I hold no more connection to General Khastra. She is no longer under my influence, and I have not seen the empress since. I do not know if she was involved or if it is merely a coincidence that she has been out of Nox'Kartha since."

Flowridia's gut twisted, those condemning suspicions threatening to become so much more. "I think waiting to see what she comes forward with is the best path, for now. If she's guilty, she may accidentally reveal herself."

And if the Celestial had any sense at all, she had foreseen this issue.

"Additionally," Casvir said, "my spies have intercepted a troubling letter from Executor Bluefield of the Ember Elves to their Iron Elf counterpart. The details may be upsetting to you."

"If you brought it up, I assume you want my thoughts. I'm stable enough."

"Ku'Shya's forces returned to Meskheta. The executor describes the incident as though Ku'Shya herself was there, but it is possible the message is being misinterpreted, given that is, in theory, impossible. However, whether it be by force or otherwise, it is implied that Ku'Shya took a bounty of elven children."

Flowridia lost her breath. "What?"

"I do not know for what purpose, but the executor warns that the same might happen in Velen'Kye. I am troubled by the news. I do not know what it means, and so I cannot anticipate if this will turn the war in our favor or lead to something worse."

Flowridia's stomach grew ill. "And there's nothing we can do to help?"

"Even if we were inclined to help our enemies, I cannot help when I do not even know the purpose. But given the timing of General Khastra's apparent disappearance, I fear to ignore the details would be foolish."

"I have nothing to say," Flowridia replied, sick to consider all those children. Were they dead? Held captive? What did this all mean? "But I'll think on it."

"Unfortunately, there are other pressing matters to discuss, and they do pertain to you. There is unrest among the refugees and my more established citizens. A De'Sindai couple was attacked at the outskirts of the Whispering Elf's established district. The man's body was mutilated. Carved from his back was a symbol my experts have yet to identify, but it is believed to be Demoni in origin. The same was done to his partner, left for dead, but she managed to survive and crawl her way to safety. Though her condition remains critical, she has confirmed my fear. This was done by an elven attacker."

Deeply upsetting, yet the mystery was more so. "Why would a Whispering Elf dedicate a murder to a demon?"

"I do not know enough about their culture to say."

A muted voice spoke up, Ayla's remark terse. "While it is rare, it is not unheard of for there to be witches dedicated to Ku'Shya among the Whispering Elves. Given the method, it may have been part of a blood ritual."

"For what purpose?" Flowridia asked.

"You would have to ask the attacker."

"Demons are attracted to violence, right? Ayla, you could find out who . . ."

Her words trailed away at Ayla's glare.

Yet the mistake had been made, and Casvir's intrigue turned upon Ayla. "I would pay you."

"I decline."

"I could punish you."

"I don't work for you."

"And so you stay in my house upon my goodwill alone." Casvir's intrigue faded, leaving a blank slate. "My loyalty to your wife is personal as well as practical. You are here because it is decent of me by proxy of that loyalty. However, your 'marriage' is not legally binding in any country. Consider the price of disobedience."

Horror struck Flowridia, to realize he was right. Legally, she had married Empress Alauriel, who was deceased.

Ayla set the embroidery aside, her smile false and vicious. Flowridia was remiss to say . . . she had missed that wicked grin. "Casvir—"

"You will address me by my title."

"Imperator Casvir, First and Last of His Name, Tyrant of Nox'Kartha, and Marshall of the Deathless Army—I have been polite and innocuous for nearly a year, and only now do you hold it against me? When my wife is helpless to leave if you choose to banish me? Flowra is insistent that you don't play games, but the timing is indeed suspicious."

"It was your mistake to not anticipate being asked for payment. Be grateful this is a minor thing."

"I would love to not be here. Alas, because of *your* bargain with *my* wife, legally binding or not, I am forced to tolerate your company."

"Ayla Darkleaf, you will do this for me."

Ayla cooed the word, sensuous and cruel. "No."

Casvir rose, far too aggressive to be innocent. Ayla matched it, fearless despite her small stature.

Panic filled Flowridia as she shoved her breakfast aside, imprisoned in blankets and her own ailing body. "Wait! Both of you, stop!" Her feet managed to reach the ground, and she stumbled to stand between them. "Casvir, please don't do this. If you need a practical reason to keep Ayla here, it's that she's invaluable to my health and well-being."

"She is replaceable."

Appall filled Flowridia at his callous demeanor, her anger spiking with it. "I'm in far too much pain to put up with your audacity. Ayla *is* my wife for all spiritual purposes, and I will not let you shit all over that." When she turned to Ayla, there lay only tension upon her sharp features. Flowridia took her hand, coaxing their gazes to meet. "If you say no, I will respect it. But this is not a favor to him—this is for me. My name is the one attached to this, and it will save me considerable pain if the perpetrator is found quickly."

Resignation sank Ayla's features. "For you."

"Please don't if you're . . ."

But Ayla released her hand, graceful as she walked toward the shadows. "I shall return soon."

She vanished, leaving neither peace nor tension.

Amid the uncertainty, Casvir tipped the precarious scales. "I forget the hold you have on her. Impressive handling."

Flowridia's rage set her veins aflame. "*Handling*?! What the hell does that mean?"

Casvir's frown was so rarely seen—today, it was a reward. "You will control yourself."

"Ayla's not an animal! She doesn't need a fucking handler!"

"I would say she is volatile enough to warrant one, but perhaps I should say the same for you lately."

Flowridia had never felt the urge to slap someone before and cursed his height. She settled on jabbing her finger at his armor instead. "Antagonize me all you like, but leave Ayla alone."

With uncanny restraint, Casvir's clawed hand wrapped around her forearm and pulled her away. Ice encased his volcanic voice. "Touch me again, and I will forget you are pregnant. I grant you a long leash. Do not provoke me to shorten it."

Flowridia chilled at his tone, a warning churning her gut. "If you lay a hand on me, I'll never speak to you again."

He released her, though the threat remained. "Grant me the same respect. I acknowledge that you are pregnant and in pain, but you will quickly lose sympathy from your loved ones if you do not lose this attitude." Casvir marched to the door, his motions more deliberate, far more controlled than typical. He did not slam the door, though tension lingered at his departure.

Flowridia stumbled back into bed, resisting the urge to scream. Unthinking, she drove her fists into the pillow—only to cry out when a jolt of pain ripped through her injured hand, shooting up her forearm. She clutched it protectively to her chest, biting back further cries lest he hear her and return.

Gently, she coaxed her fingers to straighten, swallowing tears as the pain lingered, slowly ebbing with each controlled exhale. When her pain finally quelled, she found her anger had gone with it.

Flowridia continued the practiced motions, clenching and unclenching, exercising her belabored fist. He had some gall, insulting Ayla so cruelly . . .

She gasped at the sudden presence beside her, relief flooding her to see Ayla.

"What happened?" Ayla asked, quickly sitting beside her. With care, she took Flowridia's afflicted hand, her touch sending static across her skin.

"I bumped it. It's fine."

Ayla's lips were but a butterfly upon a petal, but the kiss to her fingers warmed Flowridia's heart all the same. "Thank you for standing up for me," Ayla said. "I despise how powerless he makes me feel."

"He was completely out of line."

"And I am grateful to still be your wife, at least spiritually." Sorrow marred Ayla's smile, her soothing touch upon Flowridia's hand never ceasing. "I think we are all stressed. When this is done, you and I would benefit from a long vacation. And that includes Demitri, but forgive me when I send him away at night to bask in you alone. Is it strange to say that I . . . that I've missed you?"

Such vulnerability in Ayla's blessed gaze. Flowridia cupped her cheek with her uninjured hand. "I hadn't considered the sentiment in that way before, but . . . no. It's not strange. I miss you too."

Was that the source of this emptiness? When had this chasm formed between them? Ayla was Ayla, yet ever since the Mountains of Kaas, Ayla was . . . not.

Ayla kissed her palm. "I'm trying to hope." When Ayla released her, there came the relinquishing of peace—a peace Flowridia hadn't realized returned in her presence. But the noise of the world returned, the muted throbbing in her hand a constant irritant, her tired, aching body . . .

"We could dance again," Flowridia whispered, for the memory softened even her bitter heart.

How soft, Ayla's smile, and though strange to describe her wife in such terms, Flowridia found relief in it, nevertheless. "Yes. Tonight?"

"Tonight."

They kissed, and therein lay the very heart of hope.

Yet when they parted, chagrin marred Ayla's perfect visage. "I hate to ruin this, but I found your perpetrator. It was not difficult. The shadows are particularly fearful of Ku'Shya's magic."

The weight of Flowridia's quest returned full force. "This needs to be dealt with quickly. If there's one, there may be more, but not if I make an example of the one."

"What do you need from me?" Ayla spoke so softly, so muted.

"Nothing," Flowridia said. "Not if it hurts you."

"Everything is hurting you, my love. If I can help that burden, please let me. I . . . I want to support you. In this."

Contemplative, Flowridia considered the cost should word spread. Distrust for the refugees, disdain for the De'Sindai, the threat of retaliation—this would snowball if she did not cut off the head—and perhaps that solution was literal. "I need an envoy of guards to escort me. And I need the perpetrator in chains. Will you bring her to me?"

"Of course. But you don't want Casvir involved?"

Flowridia shook her head. "He delegated this power to me. I'm going to use it."

"I did not expect to awaken to news of bloodshed by the Whispering Elves."

Flowridia stood upon a makeshift platform surrounded by skeletal guards, facing a crowd of weary people. Beside her, Ayla had illusioned herself to appear De'Sindai, not wishing to place her name behind this quest. But held in chains, as promised, an elven woman knelt before the crowd, head forced down by Ayla's claws.

"And I'm appalled that any one of you would be ungrateful enough to disrespect my kindness in this way," Flowridia continued, projecting her voice as well as she could without magic. "This witch murdered one of Imperator Casvir's citizens last night, mutilated a second, and sought to use them in a ritual. In Nox'Kartha, we do not tolerate any disruption to the peace."

Flowridia shoved the woman, though Ayla's strength was far superior. The woman fell forward, forced to remain when Ayla's foot pressed down upon her lower back. "It is an eye for an eye in this kingdom," Flowridia cried, and she withdrew a knife from one of the guard's hips, "and I pray this is the only example you need to witness for that lesson to sink in."

Flowridia knelt, then cut a line down the back of the witch's dress, taking no care to avoid lacerating her skin. The woman's whimpers became pleas for mercy, but Flowridia hardly heard them, simply envisioned her as a palette. The guard's tabard bore Nox'Kartha's symbol, and Flowridia copied its template. First a circle, blood rising from the imperfect lines. The woman shrieked, an exultant song. Within the circle—a coin—Flowridia inscribed a messy skull, her artistic skills lacking, but her conviction more than enough. Gods, it was a release, the scent of blood enriching to her soul, the woman's screams euphoric.

It ended far too soon, the kingdom's symbol as utilitarian as its tyrant, and so a few embellishments swirled along the edges, each slice of skin sending Flowridia's mind back to that cold dungeon floor, reliving the screams, the terror, the agony and pain. But she was the executioner now; she wielded the knife, the power as rapturous as it was healing—

"*Flowra.*"

Hardly a whisper, yet Flowridia awoke to the call. Ayla's illusion held no expression at all.

With some chagrin, Flowridia positioned the knife to the base of the shrieking witch's skull—and drove it through. Her cries cut off, leaving dead silence.

Ayla helped her to rise, blood staining her fanciful gown. Flowridia gazed upon pallid faces, tears, some horror, and felt that thrill anew. "This is Nox'Karthan justice," she said, shoving the corpse with her foot. "Do not make me return."

The guards grabbed the fallen witch. With Ayla's hand to lead her, Flowridia stepped down from the platform, surrounded by her envoy as she made the journey to the palace. "It certainly left an impression," Flowridia said, her cheeks sore from smiling.

Ayla remained muted. "Indeed."

Once, Ayla would have reveled in that display of rage, she would have kissed her, groped her, fucked her while coated in blood—

"I would say a good impression," Flowridia pressed, seeking any reaction at all.

"The witch deserved to die for her crime."

Utterly aloof, her love remained, and Flowridia swallowed her rising discomfort, choosing silence instead.

Though she ached from the walk, she belligerently made it, too discomfited to ask Ayla to take them through the shadows. She attracted attention, splattered in blood, and held her head high despite it. Even up the steep hill leading to the castle's entrance, though the gates could not come quickly enough.

"There she is. *Flowers!*" Etolié's golden wings were a beacon, but Flowridia gasped to see Sora swiftly approaching, her sister breaking into a run to greet her. As a rule, Etolié didn't run, simply marched to greet them. "We scoured the whole damn castle— *Why are you covered in blood?!*"

Flowridia cringed at Sora's ensuing horror. "None of it's mine. Everything is all right."

Even so, Sora surveyed her stained dress. "That's not a small amount of blood."

"I'll change. Then you can hug me—" Flowridia gasped when Sora swept her into a hug, nevertheless. A month apart, and Flowridia hadn't realized how accustomed she'd become to having a sister to love. She returned the gesture, clinging as tight as her exhausted self was able. "*Just a few days,*" she teased, then gasped when Sora rubbed her fist over her hair.

"There was a world-saving detour."

"So I heard." When they parted, Flowridia gave her most apologetic smile to Etolié, who grimaced as she stared at the splatters of blood. "I promise, it's nothing."

"Sure." The Celestial *huffed* and offered a hand. "I'm not hugging you."

Flowridia accepted it, squeezing tight. "I wasn't sure when you'd be back."

"I had to go save your sister from dying of boredom in Moratham. We aren't here for long, but Sora wanted to stop by."

Flowridia's hope fell. "Where are you going?"

Sora glanced about. "Do the guards actually hear and report things?"

"Yes," Etolié answered.

"Can we speak in private, then?"

"The garden is relatively secluded," Flowridia said. "Or we can visit Demitri."

"Demitri would be a perfect someone to visit," Sora replied, and to Flowridia's surprise, she addressed the now-undisguised Ayla. "You too, if you don't mind."

Ayla made no attempt to feign a good mood. "I mind immensely."

"It's about Izthuni."

"All the more reason for me to be uninvolved."

Flowridia's blood ran cold at the name, relieved that Ayla rejected it. For as much as Izthuni plagued her, he was a far greater source of anguish to Ayla.

"I understand," Sora replied, the unspoken remorse taut between them. "But let's say I had to speak to him. Do you have any advice?"

"My advice is 'don't,' but I would assume that isn't an option. Bring a light to his temple, and not one you can easily extinguish. Holy light would be seen as a threat, so consider buying a spell."

Sora pointed at Etolié. "Wings?"

"Oh, you're bringing her?" Ayla cringed. "Yes, that would work, but be careful bringing the child of an angelic goddess to that temple. Izthuni has no grudge with Staella that I know of, but tread lightly."

"Thank you," Sora said. "We also brought Dir— Chaos."

"You have her?" Flowridia said, the thought far too surreal. "Where?"

Sora and Etolié shared a look. "There're people in this castle she didn't wanna risk running into," the Celestial said. "I'm not actually sure what you know."

Flowridia lowered her voice, now wary of the guards. "Do you mean Casvir?"

"Seems we have a whole lot to discuss, Flowers."

Flowridia gently took Ayla's hand, ambivalent as she whispered, "Are you certain you don't want to come?"

To her dismay, Ayla slipped from her grip just as lightly. "I'm not in any mindset for that. I shall find you when I'm ready."

Flowridia tensed to watch her leave, her festering emotions rising to choke her. But she squashed them back down, uncertain of what it meant—only that there were others who needed her now. "I should change."

"Unnecessary," Etolié said, "unless you're worried about attention."

Nothing really mattered, and Flowridia's hips ached enough from walking through Haven. She joined them instead, leading the way to Demitri's cage.

"You've been holding on to that apocalyptic nonsense for two years?!"

Etolié had never heard such bullshit before.

To the backdrop of the comatose Demitri, Flowers had whispered a frightful tale—straight from the God of Order himself, apparently, regarding the end of the world.

"I haven't exactly been friendly with you lately," the flowery idiot said, though slightly more imposing than normal, given the inordinate amount of blood on her skirt. She sat as a blight in the grass, the vine-covered stone surrounding them unable to balance her lack of charm.

"This transcends 'friendliness,' you dumb cunt—"

"You didn't tell me about the conversations you had with Lara about cycles—"

"Can you both stop?" Sora said, and all Etolié could do was roll her eyes. "From what I've overheard, Soliel is explicitly trying to change the narrative, and not just by separating the worlds."

"Has it ever occurred to either of you," Flowers muttered, "that if this is a repeating cycle, Soliel is doomed to fail every time?"

Somehow it hadn't. Not in so many words.

"I don't mean to say we shouldn't be extremely worried," Flowers continued. "One wrong move on our part, and Soliel succeeds—at least, in theory. He fails in every cycle, but Chaos and Order also fail to stop Casvir in every cycle. And Soliel has said explicitly that he would give up his quest if he found Casvir's phylactery. As important as it is to stop Soliel, the way to break the cycle is to find the way to stop Casvir."

"This hurts my head," muttered Sora, who apparently thought about time too linearly.

Not Etolié. "That all makes sense. But what if we had this exact same conversation in the last timeline and failed anyway? Do we have to be unpredictable? What if we were unpredictable in the last timeline?" Etolié groaned. "Never mind, my head hurts now too."

Flowers became silent, that devious brain of hers practically spouting steam as she glared at the ground. A flowery idiot, no moral core to speak of—Flowers was pure chaos, which meant she might be onto something . . .

Etolié sighed at the obvious connection. Of course she was the mother of Chaos.

"The only way to deviate from the path knowingly is to convince either Soliel or Chaos to tell you a way to do so, or for one of them to do it themself," Flowridia said. "Because they know the future. They'll know if something changed."

Etolié hung her head. "And who says we haven't had this conversation in the past—"

"You have to at least try."

"There's a second risk," Sora said. "Deviating from the timeline might also change Chaos and Order. It might break the cycle in a worse way."

"Dammit." Etolié rolled onto the ground, too tired to use any muscles. "Lara once said there had to be some sort of key that was missing."

"I suspect the key was the phylactery," Flowers replied.

"Dammit again."

"I highly suspect it's in this castle," Flowridia whispered, which was not a twist Etolié expected. "Ayla and I have been on the hunt for it for years now."

That was worth sitting up for. Etolié forced herself to rise. "It occurs to me now that you're something akin to friends with Casvir, yet you're sitting here plotting his death with us—turns out, even longer than we have."

"I have my reasons, one of them being the greater good."

"You're not exactly a greater good type, Flowers." Etolié scooted closer, suspicions bubbling in her stomach. "I don't buy it."

Flowridia's countenance lost all amusement. "To get out of my bargain."

"What bargain?" Sora asked, but Etolié waved the question away.

"Ask me later. You'll be equally pissed—" Etolié choked as an obvious truth struck her—that the baby Flowers had sold was the fucking Goddess of Chaos. She couldn't withhold her sudden bout of nervous giggling, praying no one asked for specifics. "But, Flowers, that ship has sailed, or . . . is sailing actively, as it were. So why now?"

"Habit," Flowridia spat, but it was far too quick of an answer.

"You are entirely full of shit—"

"Is it not enough that I'm helping you?"

Etolié evaluated that, her *hum* segueing into a, "No, because you're a twisty, two-faced bitch, currently covered in mysterious blood, and it wouldn't surprise me one fucking bit if you turned around and told Casvir everything we were just discussing. I don't think you'll do that today, but I literally can't guess your mind aside from knowing intrinsically that you never think more than one step ahead. So it does matter, actually, because I want to know if I'll be thrown into prison for treason, but we can set it aside for now."

Before Sora could open her fat mouth, Etolié shot her a glare, daring her to disagree.

As it was, Flowers seemed oddly unbothered, her smile cruel and curt. "I look forward to it."

Etolié held up a hand, suddenly keen to heavy, metallic footsteps. "I believe we have imperator company."

Panic flashed through Flowers' eyes. "He thinks you betrayed him over Khastra," she muttered through gritted teeth. "Be *very* careful."

Etolié's gut clenched. "What?"

Imperator First and Last did, indeed, walk in a few seconds later. "Flowridia, we need to speak. Now."

He nearly sounded like an angry dad, if that angry dad were seven feet tall and capable of ripping her head off with his bare hands. Flowridia rose with a stiff jaw, pausing to smile at Sora. "Good luck to you."

"I'm excited for the baby," Sora replied, no question of that truth.

Flowridia left in silence. Casvir lingered, his imposing gaze set upon Etolié. "Where have you been?"

"Moratham, actually. World-ending shit."

"Can anyone confirm that those were your whereabouts?"

Yes, Etolié was in trouble, but an uncomfortable stirring in her stomach suggested she was not in the kind of trouble she'd predicted. "Morathma himself could vouch for me, as could my momma, and Sora, and the Goddess of Chaos."

"I see."

Casvir left, following the trail Flowers had left behind. "I don't envy Flowers," Etolié whispered, "but I'd sell my left tit to be a fly on the wall."

Sora remained wary, looking prepared to dart. "Do you think she's in danger?"

"Danger? No. In for a verbal slaughter? No doubt." Etolié rose, mentally preparing for more time on the road. "Let's go, before I have no excuse not to meet with him."

But Sora did not immediately follow, instead lingering to stare at the prone Demitri. "I know I shouldn't blame myself, but . . ."

Etolié patted her on the shoulder, failing to not sound calloused. "Welcome to the club of misplaced guilt. I've got twenty years on you."

They left as a unit, the weight of their quest returning.

Onward, to Izthuni.

"You will sit, and you will say nothing," Casvir had said.

And she didn't.

"You had no right—"

"That is not how justice is served in this country—"

"Her death was warranted, but not in that manner. We are not barbaric in this country—"

"I am stripping you of your responsibilities. You are not to leave the castle grounds without my express permission—"

"Be grateful you are not under room arrest—"

Flowridia left Casvir's office with a face streaked with furious tears. He hadn't yelled. Not even once. His capacity to remain deathly quiet was far more brutal.

Flowridia trudged away, head aching from dehydration, her body sore from walking, from the baby, her hand radiating static whenever she cared to notice. But the greatest wound was her pride.

Still covered in blood, she did not shy away from any she passed. Emotionally, she was utterly numb, but her hips burned from walking, her back cramped from bending, exhaustion her constant shadow, her strength sapped by small degrees, the walls slowly closing in . . .

She touched her womb, her bump a fragile, blessed thing. A reward for her suffering—

But no. It was not hers to keep.

Fresh tears welled in her eyes, that horrible truth heavy today. Demitri was her reward; Demitri was the prize she sought now. Demitri and freedom.

And Lara's freedom. But that was not something to speak aloud.

She thought of Ayla, who hated this baby—and oh *gods*, the anguish that filled her to dwell on it. How cruel life was, to provide the means for Flowridia to have a baby of her own after all . . .

Passing De'Sindai servants reminded her that she was a mess, their lingering stares filled with horror. Her dress was in shambles. Flecks of blood covered her neck and hands. But she couldn't stomach the thought of nurses panicking over her bloodied form, nor stand their grabbing hands. Instead, she trudged toward Ayla's washroom, uncaring that no one would hear her scream if she fell.

Flowridia brought her hand down along the hidden space, leaving a glowing line. The wall parted, revealing a foggy picture, and when she stepped through, a chill engulfed her.

Ayla had been gifted a gorgeous personal washroom, the stone tub carved with the illusion of vines and roses. Flowridia had not seen it in years, surprised for how it had fallen into disarray. A layer of dust covered the robes hung in a space in the wall, grimy mirrors showed her exhausted form, but toward the far wall, her stomach twisted to see ashen footprints on the floor—fresher than anything else.

A bath could wait. Flowridia repeated the ritual of before, bidding the wall to part. A staircase lay revealed, leading steeply downward.

So strange, to simply hear nothing.

The eerie silence enveloped her, maddening to her anxious mind. Ayla was here somewhere. Likely hiding in her morbid cathedral, though Flowridia feared the prevailing wonder of *why*. She kept a hand to the wall, following each right turn as it came, trusting that the only danger here was what grew inside her.

If she did collapse . . . would Ayla hear her scream?

Her wounded hand came to touch her womb, gently, lest she trigger the sensitive nerves. It still tingled, a maddening undercurrent.

The faint scent of ash filled her nostrils, stagnant but unmistakable. Familiar landmarks 'decorated' the walls—a smear of blood, an embedded skull—long forgotten. Flowridia felt nothing at all as she stared upon them, for they were merely stains. Though the path remained a maze, it was designed to have only one destination, and after a few turns, Flowridia gasped to find her quarry.

The stone arch remained to welcome her: *"The Light will burn away all your fears."* But beyond it, she faced a graveyard.

A sea of ash, charred stone, and shriveled leather bits. Her steps disrupted soot long settled, sending it swirling like an eerie flurry of snow. Gone were the macabre decorations, the garland of entrails, the sewn patches of humanoid leather—all ash. All destroyed. At the front, where the statue of Sol Kareena had once stood, nothing but black remained, little flecks of string and leather within. Flowridia covered her mouth with a handkerchief, lest she breathe poison, nearly dashing away until she saw fresh footprints in the soot.

Shock slowed her as she absorbed the destruction. Who could have done this? Years and years of Ayla's work—burned. This was not recent either. Had Casvir destroyed the cathedral when they'd fled all those years ago? Its loss left her empty, for though horrendous, it had meant something to Ayla. It had been beautiful to her mad mind.

The footsteps led to the laboratory behind the cathedral, where she heard familiar whimpering.

Flowridia peeked inside, and there stood Ayla, hunched as she frantically wiped tears from her eyes. Yet this room was just as ruined, all the research, the paper, the books—all burned. The dress forms held no form anymore, merely charred figures, the projects in motion all destroyed. No bodies, no poisons—simply scorched instruments of torture. Shards of glass littered the floor, and Flowridia tiptoed with care toward her weeping wife.

"Ayla . . . who did this? Do you know?"

Flowridia felt no danger, for the damage was old. But Ayla trembled as she soothed herself, merely a step away. "Nothing to worry about."

"Who did this?"

Ayla remained silent as she surveyed the decimated scene. Radiant waves of shame wafted from her form. Ayla appeared so small as she hugged herself. "Me."

The word jarred Flowridia into silence.

"On the night we first returned to Nox'Kartha," Ayla whispered, "I burned it."

Flowridia's gaze fell upon the remains of the bookshelf, little more than ashes and charred wood. "You . . . why?"

Ayla scratched idly at her arms. "I don't want it anymore."

Gods, what was the meaning of Ayla's shame? Flowridia felt she faced a stranger. "Why didn't you tell me?"

"Darling, you have had far more important things to worry about than me."

Flowridia clenched a fist behind her back, the words striking a match within her. "I want to understand you," Flowridia said, fighting to keep her voice from seething, "but I can't if you keep withholding secrets from me."

Ayla stood like a mouse before its feline captor, a hitch in her breath—yet she did not breathe, the motion merely a conduit to stabilize whatever turbulent emotions churned beneath her surface. "I am not trying to be secretive. I have said nothing because there is nothing to say. I don't understand. I don't know what I want. I don't . . ." Her voice fell, hardly audible at all. "I don't know who I am anymore. What I do know is this was not a temple to my legacy. It was a temple to the hatred Izthuni instilled into me."

Flowridia softened her stance, fearing her beloved would flee. "Then why did you come here?"

"I often do, to be alone." Fresh tears welled in Ayla's eyes, though she flinched and stanched them with her sleeves. "Sometimes I think of who you were years ago, when we first met. A bit of a fool, yes, but you radiated the sort of light a creature of darkness craves. You rebuked me when I called you innocent, but you *were*, Flowra. You were." In Ayla's pause laid hesitation. Still, she would not meet Flowridia's eye. "Have I corrupted you so fully?"

"What? I . . . I'm confused."

Yet Ayla was silent.

"I have done nothing blindly," Flowridia continued, tepid as she set a hand on Ayla's waist. Her wife remained cold, freezing at the touch. "Even when I knew who you were, I forged ahead to bring you back to me because I loved you. And I still love you. So what is this about? I don't understand."

"Neither do I."

"But you're unhappy."

More hollow air than words made up Ayla's reply. "I suppose I am."

"Why? Talk to me, please."

"There is nothing to say." Yet it was too quick, Ayla's words brusque and final.

Flowridia's anxiety faded into ice. "Are you nostalgic for my younger self? What about her? She was weak."

"That's a cruel thing to say," Ayla whispered.

"I beg your pardon?"

"You were vulnerable, yes, but not weak. Never weak. You survived unspeakable abuse yet remained a gentle soul. And you are, you still are, but I am frightened of what I saw today. I am terrified for you, because I know with utter precision where this path leads. And not only the torture. I see how Casvir's shadow is engulfing you, leading you along. I want to support you. I know you've finally found meaning, but he wants you to stay."

"We have discussed this, Ayla," Flowridia said, her patience wearing thin. "Of course he does, but that doesn't mean I will. You'll be happy to know he's taken away my responsibilities after what I did. Congratulations. You win."

"I am not happy."

"Then what do you want?!" Flowridia cried, Ayla's groveling no reward at all. Where was the monster? Where was the predator she feared and loved?

"I want to leave." Ayla's tears finally fell. "I know we can't yet, so I am surviving. But everywhere I go, I'm reminded of everything I hate most about myself—and this damn cathedral is both my greatest crime and the only safe place."

The words were strange; she faced a stranger wearing her wife's face. "Will you please explain?"

"My entire life has been a lie, Flowra. My legacy is the cruelest of jests. If there were justice in this realm, I would have lived a short and beautiful life with Sarai, but instead I was deceived by a monster—and no matter what I do, I see it everywhere. I don't know what's changed except that I know the truth, but the result is that I flinch to think of my past life. I can look back and see precisely where and how he molded me to be his perfect monster, but it does not change that it is my name that has become synonymous with monstrosity. The blood is on my hands. And Flowra, my darling, I love you with all my heart and soul, but the price of loving you is the hundreds of thousands who died by my hand."

And Ayla wept. She cried into her hands, sinking steadily to her knees despite the grime and glass and shattered things.

A shard of glass cracked beneath Flowridia's boot, a mirror to her fracturing sanity. "I have always loved you as you are."

Ayla did not move, pitiful as she sobbed.

"I love you for *you*. Whatever part Izthuni had in it, that legacy belongs to *you*. You are the Scourge of the Sun Elves. You are The Endless Night. You are the monster who fills shelves of history books. I fell in love with that monster, so there is no need for shame, my love."

"You experienced a taste of my methods, darling," Ayla whispered, her blubbering only burning Flowridia's blood, "yet you would condone it?"

"I've forgiven you. I never even blamed you. Mereen twisted your mind. None of it was you, so there's no need to be ashamed."

"But I am," Ayla mouthed, hardly a sound at all.

Gods, it enraged her. "Ayla, I married The Endless Night. I married you knowing your darkest moments. What I didn't marry was the pathetic mess that's shadowed me since we left Kaas!" Flowridia clenched her fists, daring to speak the root of it all. "I suppose I, too, am nostalgic for the woman you were."

Thank the gods that Ayla rose, though she remained a hunched, pitiful creature. Even standing, she stood so small. "You have always praised my growth."

"This isn't growth," Flowridia spat. "I don't know what to call it, but I don't like it."

"I don't know what you want me to say. I am speaking my truth—"

"And I am trying to speak mine!" Flowridia screamed, enraged to see this stranger. Ayla stumbled back against the wall. She shrunk, but she wasn't small enough. "You don't need Izthuni. You don't need his legacy. Of course you're angry—so slit his throat and take his throne! Burn his kingdom to the ground! Anything except rolling over and crying! You want to know how he wins? By falling apart without him."

Ayla managed pitiful words. "I am so tired. I just want to let it go—" She stopped when Flowridia marched forward. Vacancy filled those fearful eyes.

"You always tell me I'm walking a path contrary to my goals— but fucking *look at yourself now*!" Flowridia's anger echoed off the charred walls; Ayla said nothing at all. "You are The Endless Night! By gods, the blood you've spilled could fill oceans! You can't walk away from what you've done! And so damn yourself. Have no regrets. Let go of Izthuni. I'll be immortal soon, and we can make a new legacy. Can you imagine?"

Gods, the euphoria brewed anew. Was this her destiny all along? What would it mean, to be a monster like Ayla?

"No."

The word shattered the silence. "What?"

"If that's what you want," Ayla whispered, and it was so regretfully clear—the moment her heart split in twain, "do it alone."

Hardly a blink in time, Flowridia remembered nothing; she felt nothing but rage. She grabbed a shard of glass from the scorched desk. *"After everything I've done for you—!"*

And a mere whisper from Ayla's face, near enough to reflect the fear in her eyes, the shard stopped its swing.

Flowridia swore she burst from deep water, the plunge leaving her icy cold. "Oh gods . . ." Her hand slackened. The shard fragmented as it hit the stone. Blood welled from her palm, though numb she was. "Ayla . . ."

Ayla was not a stranger, no. She cowered against the wall, yes, staring vacantly from shock; her perfect face, not broken, so nearly broken. Ayla was indomitable, yes. Unkillable, yet she stood helplessly before a monster.

She did not see Ayla. What did it mean, to face a mirror?

Flowridia stumbled back, gasping as she slipped on the shards. Her elbow slammed against the desk, narrowly catching her fall. A heaving breath shook her body. Tears welled in her eyes.

Oh gods, what had she done?

She saw nothing, heard nothing, merely felt the sudden absence of cold. Ayla was no longer there.

Flowridia crumbled to the floor, and through blurred vision saw Ayla lingering in the doorframe beyond. Her wife—her precious, beloved wife—wept as she clutched herself, nails tearing deep lines through her sleeves.

Flowridia could not speak, simply bowed her head from shame and sobbed. What did it mean, to plunge someone into the very anguish she had once drowned in?

When she looked up again, Ayla was gone.

Flowridia stared at her bloodied palm, sensation returning, throbbing with the drum of her heart. Each droplet soaked the ashes; the blood of countless victims stained this place, but Flowridia was not a victim. Upon the floor, splintered glass reflected her image, but though she did not see herself, her image was not a stranger.

What did it mean, to finally wear her mother's face?

CHAPTER 22

Current era . . .

"Etolié, would you care to explain what you meant by 'bargain'?"

Haven was beautiful, but Sora had no time to admire its fountains and statues. Instead, as they made their way to the religious district of town, she stared expectantly at Etolié, unsurprised by the Celestial's sudden constipated grimace.

"I assume you mean Flowers' bargain?" Etolié asked. At Sora's affirming nod, the Celestial stared quite obviously at Chaos.

The Deity appeared as a half-elf dhampir, attracting no attention at all among the varied populace. Around her neck, she wore her anchor as a necklace. "I know about it," she said, though subdued.

All Chaos had said and done had been subdued after Uluron's death.

With that, Etolié gave a pained groan. "Flowers sold a baby."

Sora's stomach dropped. "She what?"

"She sold her firstborn in exchange for Lara's soul so that Casvir wouldn't keep her as an undead slave for all eternity. Happy?"

No, but the qualifier certainly helped make sense of it. Sora stared at nothing, lost as she followed her companions in silence. Flowridia had sold her baby to Casvir? The baby who was the Goddess of Chaos?

... Sora's *niece*?

"How do we get her out of it?" Sora asked, but Etolié burst into laughter.

"You wanna break a contract with Casvir? Good fucking luck."

"We can't just let . . ." She gestured fitfully to Chaos. "You know."

"Oh, I fucking know."

Sora hadn't felt the need to strangle Flowridia in years, good cause or not, but a gentle hand on her shoulder shadowed her rage. Chaos gave a sorrowful smile. "It will be all right."

Chaos would know, but Sora still couldn't shake it—not even when their destination appeared.

The Temple of Izthuni was all circles, with black stone and swirling spirals thinner than rock should have allowed. It was built into a wall permanently in shadow, its door as round as the building itself. Though unique in its way, only a small engraving of The Lurker's symbol hid among the seals in the door—a dagger imbued by a swirl of magic, coiling like a snake. Sora shied from its energy, each step filling her with dread.

"The fact that any idiot off the street could just walk in here and get eaten is upsetting," Etolié said, her grimace suggesting she felt the same growing blight. "So how do vampires feel toward dhampirs?"

Silver Fire swept around Chaos' form, coating her in potent magic. "Poorly."

"So, avoid mentioning the shared heritage? Got it."

Sora took the leap to roll open the door, unprepared for the mass of darkness. Still, she ushered them inside, her dread peaking as the door shut.

Etolié's golden glow melded with Chaos' silver, revealing a stone path into the darkness ahead. Yet the light did not cast as far as it should, ending in an opaque fog—or reflecting off the many eyes ahead.

"Your power is strange," came a voice from the void. A man emerged, far too pristine to be merely human. The dark hue of his skin might have matched Sora's were he not touched by the grey blight of vampirism. A few others followed, their predatory gazes all falling upon Chaos. "We were told the Silver Fire was extinguished."

Chaos spoke boldly, even as Sora kept her hand on her wrist sheath. "I am the Goddess of Chaos, reborn upon this realm. I seek an audience with God Izthuni."

The vampires glanced among themselves. More eyes flashed in the darkness. "With this Celestial? With this mortal? Surely you do not need both. Perhaps the half-elf can keep us company."

Sora bit back a retort, instead staring the man down as the predator he was. All beasts were different. This was one to face boldly.

"She is a stronger force than you give her credit for," Chaos replied. "My quest pertains to saving the three realms, and time is of the essence. I have no quarrel with you, so please let me pass."

"The Celestial is familiar," another said, a De'Sindai woman with eyes as fiery as the sunset. "Not many walk this realm with wings. Who is your godly progenitor?"

Unlike Chaos, Etolié made no attempt at politeness. "Someone who would be rightly pissed off if I went missing."

A third spoke—another human man. "I recognize her face. She is the empress of Solvira. This is the Daughter of Staella."

"The second and potentially more important part is that I'm romantically entangled with the Bringer of War, so let's keep things peaceful, shall we?"

They flinched at the title. Khastra's name apparently bore weight. "It is Izthuni you will have to convince to remain peaceful," the third replied. "It is rare he does not consume mortal trespassers."

As the only mortal, Sora refused to blink even as the vampires dispersed into the darkness. She trekked forward in silence, clinging to the knowledge that she lived to see the future with Dira.

. . . Unless something changed. But surely all was as it should be, right?

The oppressive darkness crept closer, the light from Etolié and Chaos shrinking with each step. "I'm not the only one with a twisty stomach, right?" Etolié whispered, and Sora curtly shook her head.

Her anxiety rose, and she resolved to track down a Spore vender in Haven at any cost.

Their footsteps ceased echoing. Even their breathing cut off, diffusing as though beneath the waves. Sora studied the darkness, felt a creeping rise of ice against her skin. The hair rose on her neck. "Something is here."

A monstrous laugh emanated from all around. Sora remained in her companions' pool of light, yet swore the darkness neared, seeking to devour.

The voice held depths oceans deep. *"Daughter of Stars—did they not tell you it was unwise for the child of a goddess to tread into my domain?"*

"No," Etolié replied, like a liar. "I'm also not the most impressive one here, so please state your threats in the proper order."

Again came that bone-shaking laughter. *"And the heir to the Theocracy of my fallen nemesis? A surprise, Sora Makosa, sister to Flowridia."*

"We have our reasons for being here," Sora said, but felt the words were flat.

"But a being of Silver Fire? I am . . . intrigued."

From the darkness emerged a putrid beast, bearing a vague resemblance to The Endless Night, yet not. No eyes; no face at all, aside from its endless maw, lined in rows of teeth. It could have consumed Sora, eaten her alive, but more horrifying was how it hung oddly from its neck, attached to a six-legged spindly monstrosity. Izthuni moved in eerie motions, far too graceful, unnatural, as it rose, balanced on four legs instead. *"Rumors spread, but tell me your name."*

"I am the Old Goddess of this realm, known to you as Chaos," the Deity replied, no tremble to her voice. "It is an honor to stand before you, Lurker. I seek pledges from the New Gods of this world so I might gain my full power and defeat my counterpart. The God of Order seeks to separate the realms, which would destroy your world. I will defeat him, but I need all the help I can gather. He has five orbs now. We have every reason to fear."

Izthuni's horrendous laughter rattled Sora's bones. Her knife provided comfort, but she was not foolish enough to think it would save her.

"Ah, but that is not Demoni Law. I will give you your pledge, but the favor must be returned."

"You wish for my pledge?" Chaos asked.

"Something of equal value." And though he bore no eyes, no face, Sora felt that consuming energy fall upon her, the urge to flee unbearable. *"I know your company, Sora Makosa. There is a certain knife in the possession of Ayla Darkleaf. Bring it to me, and my pledge will be given."*

Fear rose to choke her. Sora swallowed it, nevertheless. "I'm afraid that's impossible. Ayla destroyed it."

And Sora was fully confident in that truth, until Etolié's eye twitched.

"That is highly unfortunate. And while I do not feel its power, I have no patience for liars. Revise your answer, and I shall spare you for lying."

"I . . ." Sora glanced to Chaos, to Etolié, the latter of whom began to giggle.

Etolié only laughed when she was particularly nervous. "She's telling the truth, as far as she knows. The knife is currently, uh, preoccupied, but I can pull a few strings and see if I can get it to you in the next one to three months. What is time, anyway?"

The silence held no peace. Again, Sora felt the threat rise against her skin, her gut screaming in warning. *"I hold the power to close your path home. Perhaps I shall keep Sora while you fetch my prize."*

"God Izthuni," Chaos said, her voice bearing hints of strain, "there is no need for threats. Is there any other gift I can offer you? Information, perhaps? A promise for my aid when my power is restored?"

"I have no need for empty promises from Gods. My terms are set."

"But the world cannot wait—"

"Well, well—what a grubby party here to grovel."

Sora wrenched around at the new voice, startled to see Ayla Darkleaf herself approaching from the darkness. Yet she was not the Ayla Sora had come to recognize in the passing months, subdued and often silent. This woman walked with grace, wore spite in the twist in her grin and a dress suited for dancing and death. Her hair was brushed and styled. Perhaps she even wore a bit of dark liner around her eyes. The smallest of them all, yet she stood taller than even the demon god.

"The prodigal daughter herself." Satisfaction tinged Izthuni's ominous tone. *"Surely this is no coincidence."*

"I was aware they were coming." Ayla stood at the cusp of darkness, undaunted as she placed herself between the demon and their group. "They were unaware I was, however. I suspected you would attempt to muddle this negotiation."

"And so you overheard what I desire."

"I did. You shall have it when I am done with it."

"When? Upon your death?" Gods, he was a giddy soul, his laughter ever present. *"Do not toy with me."*

Sora had no time to contemplate whatever implications were shared with the threat of returning that cursed blade. Chaos' face hid behind a curtain of flame, yet the glow of her eyes did not waver from Ayla, even once.

"Upon the birth of my child—or had you not heard?"

Izthuni could not be deciphered, yet Sora could not shake his rise in intrigue. *"Rumors, yes . . . But I had not believed them."*

"I would be far happier to abandon you to your fate," Ayla said, unnervingly calm, her false demeanor shielding ice, "given how painful I can only imagine oblivion to be, but I find no sense in leaving a broken world for my family. You won't find the knife without me. That is a fact. But it shall be hand-delivered upon my child's birth—and my wife's rebirth, if you follow my meaning."

Sora's stomach dropped, dread rising anew at the statement. Flowridia . . . Her own sister . . .

"Your addendum is more tempting than the Daughter of Stars'—but you are a woman of deception. Prove to me that you are sincere and pledge your fealty to this Goddess first."

A strange request, and judging by Ayla's frown, she thought so as well. But she took fluid steps away from the frightful demon god, then showed herself to Chaos. Ayla surveyed her, curiosity in how she peered into the flame. "And so you are Chaos," she whispered. "I expected you taller."

"I am taller than both my parents," Chaos replied, "so I at least exceeded my own expectations."

Amusement twisted Ayla's smile. "I like my Goddesses with a sense of humor." She bowed her head and muttered, "Goddess Chaos, I pledge my life and death to thee."

To Izthuni, she gestured, raising an expectant eyebrow.

"And what do I get should you betray me?"

"I will soon have a helpless infant. Surely you can be creative."

"Helpless, assuredly. But you have grown a heart?"

"My wife has always had a heart, and her happiness is of the utmost importance to me. I am impatient. Make the connection yourself."

Again, Sora gritted her teeth at the implications and spared a glance to Chaos, given she was the subject of trade. But her flame revealed nothing, a perfect mask.

"Goddess of Chaos . . ."

Chaos faced him, though her orbit had shifted, Ayla's bright star capturing her instead.

"I pledge my power and fealty to thee."

"Thank you," Chaos said. "This will be remembered."

"Take care that Ayla Darkleaf keeps her promise, lest I kill a few more than she implied."

With the same fluidity as his entrance, Izthuni slunk into the darkness.

"It's a good thing I'm not wearing pants, because I'd need to change them," Etolié said, her nervous giggling returning. "I didn't expect you, Darkleaf."

"Few do." To Chaos, Ayla said, "I hold little stake in the end of the world, aside from my wife's continued health. But as this proved, you need me—much more than you need her." She pointed to Etolié, who stiffened in appall.

"Bitch, I oughta—"

"And what will Onias ask for? I presume that is your next destination. What secrets would he ask of you to allow you to leave? Your love affair with Khastra holds weight, yes, but he will ask you about Ku'Shya. Are you willing to answer?"

Etolié glared, but she did not bite back. "What do you want?"

"I want you to return to Flowra—where you are supposed to be. I will take your place and escort them through Sha'Demoni instead."

"Wait, why?" Sora blurted, this break in character frankly hurting her head. "What if something happens to her while you're gone?"

"Then Etolié will be far more effective at saving her than I."

Suspicions rose with no foundation or name. Ayla was not altruistic. "What do you actually get out of this?"

"What matters is *she* gets Onias' pledge."

"That's not—"

"Do not make me rip your tongue out again."

Sora seethed, but Ayla's ire matched. Tension rose, until Etolié said, "Again?"

"Sora can tell you all about it when we return," Ayla replied. "Though I am arguing with the wrong person, given you are the weakest link. What say you, Goddess of Chaos?"

Though every part of her bristled, Sora breathed out her frustration. Whatever her turmoil surrounding Ayla, Chaos matched it tenfold.

And surely only Sora noticed the warmth in Chaos' voice, her grandeur fading in Ayla's bright aura. A Goddess of ancient times, having lived thousands upon thousands of years—yet no matter how far a child wandered, their mother's shadow never truly faded.

For better or worse.

"I would love for you to join us."

A wraith emerged from the scorched hellscape, nothing to define her but blood, ash, and tears.

Flowridia wandered through the castle's halls, uncaring that she tracked soot upon the carpet, too blinded from falling tears to mind the stares of the hooded servants and guards.

Alas, mortals were prone to empathy. A De'Sindai dared to stop. "Lady Flowridia, is . . . is something wrong?"

As polite a way as possible to suggest she was a mess. She could have laughed were her soul not a morass. But when she met his eye, her misted vision recognized him. "Hello, Zorlaeus. I think you already know."

"Can I escort you anywhere? If Lady Ayla is near, I can . . ."

His words faded at her sob, the name deafening her to all else. "I don't know where she is. But if you see her, tell her . . ." Her voice broke anew, memories assaulting her of Ayla cowering against the wall, weeping on the ground, watching from the doorway . . .

She gasped a heaving breath. "Just make certain she's all right."

Zorlaeus offered his arm. "Imperator Casvir, then? Or the medical ward?"

"I won't ask you to take me to Casvir."

"I can set aside my fear for this."

No, she did not want to face Casvir, but her guilt rose to choke her. *". . . lose all sympathy from . . ."*

Oh, gods, what had she done?

Flowridia accepted his arm, knowing he was a spy, knowing he would report her swollen face and ruined clothes to Murishani and brighten his day. But she clung to him and his kindness, weeping even as they came upon the large door to Casvir's office. When Zorlaeus knocked, there came a muted, *"Enter."*

Zorlaeus kept a bowed head as he opened the door, releasing Flowridia as she stumbled inside.

Casvir's frown remained, though his eyes did travel up and down her ash-covered dress, finally landing upon her tear-streaked face. "Explain."

The door shut. Flowridia choked back her sob but did not sit in her usual seat—instead sinking to her knees as a supplicant. She faced the floor, unworthy of his gaze. "I'm sorry." She gasped her next breath, fighting her tears. "I shouldn't have acted without your permission. I shouldn't have yelled at you this morning. I . . . I don't even recognize myself anymore."

Except she did, she did. And nothing had ever frightened her more.

"I need help," she continued, fighting the break in her voice. "And I'm not worthy to ask that of you—not after everything you've done and already do. But my mind is sick, and I'm terrified." A weight fell beside her. When she glanced up, Casvir knelt near enough to be a comfort. Gods, it tore her apart to find kindness in his countenance, but the bare and painful truth remained that despite all he had done, he cared.

He loved her in every innocent way. And what did it mean, for so brutal a man to comfort a delicate thing? "I cannot stay angry with you," he said. "Your apology is accepted, though I would like to know what happened to your dress this time."

"Did you know Ayla's labyrinth was burned?"

"I did, though I do not know how. I can only assume it was you or her."

"It was her. I . . . I shouldn't say too much about it. But it's nothing but ashes, Casvir. I found her there and we . . . I nearly . . ." She clenched her fist, forcing her tears to abate. "I said horrible things. Perhaps unforgivable. I don't know what to do."

"What do you want to do?"

"I want to beg for her forgiveness, but I don't know how to even begin."

"You have been lashing out. Have you stopped seeing the priestess?"

Flowridia nodded, uncertain of when the meetings had faded.

"To quote a simple adage," he continued, "'hurt people hurt people.' While you heal, you must keep yourself tempered."

Before Flowridia could manage a blubbering nod, beyond the door sounded an irreverent, *"Look who's back, bitches—"*

Which cut off as soon as the door opened, revealing Etolié's startled self. "Oh. Shit. Sorry."

Casvir did not bother to grant her the respect of his attention. "Empress Etolié, would you contact Flowridia's head physician and request she bring a priestess of Staella to the castle?"

"Right away, Tyrant Deathless."

"Etolié," Flowridia said, voice wavering, "where is Sora?"

"Sora is with our special friend and your wife. Did you know Ayla was . . . ?"

The statement shook her—for though startling, something in it rang true. "No."

"I'm gonna put that tidbit in a box and go find the doctor."

Etolié left. Flowridia ceased trying to subdue her weeping, anguish rising to know this awful truth. Ayla had . . . left.

"I do not know what she means," Casvir said, "but it appears it means something to you."

Flowridia nodded. "It means I don't know when Ayla will be back."

"Perhaps space will benefit her. Perhaps you, too."

"May I say the worst thing?"

"Always."

Though it shattered her resolve to even think on it, Flowridia pulled memories from their exchange, daring to speak it into truth. "Ayla has changed. And so have I, but I fear we . . ." She gasped, reeling to admit the worst of it. ". . . What if we're growing apart?"

"Explain."

"You've said yourself she's grown. It's true, and it was once so rewarding to see her take those steps to better herself, for me. But lately . . . I don't know when, but I feel like I don't know her at all."

And though she didn't repeat those awful insults, didn't echo the very cruelty she'd thrown at her beloved, she heard them anew, this time unclouded by rage. The bare and bitter question remained—did she mean them even in the light?

"Do you think it stems from Mereen's torture?" Casvir asked. "I have no insight into Ayla's own healing journey, but trauma can warp even the most stubborn of minds."

It barely touched the surface, but that was not Flowridia's truth to tell. "Part of it, I'm sure. But that's not the end of it. I've changed too, as I said. And it makes me wonder . . . when? I look back on the girl I was when I saw Ayla at that ball years ago, and I don't know her at all. When I try to think back on the journey I've taken, I can't help but dwell on who I . . ."

She couldn't admit it. Couldn't speak the name. Her greatest fear had been shown in that broken mirror—for though Odessa's face had always lurked in mirrors, never like this.

". . . on everyone who had to die to get me here."

Gods . . . there were so many.

"Would you like to speak to any of them?"

Flowridia shook her head, fearful of opening the floodgate. "I don't want you bringing anyone back for my sake."

"Not me. I have other means."

The bait had been laid. She pounced. "Tell me."

"It is rarely used due to the power it consumes, but there is a magical device I acquired some centuries ago that allows the user to call back spirits for a limited time. It has been named the Soul Speaker. Unlike traditional necromancy, the spirits are not forced, nor would they have to fight to resist. It is a gentle invitation."

The idea seemed so . . . soft. "And they're simply back?"

"No. The time you have with them varies depending on how ancient the spirit is and how much they dither deciding to come. It is usually mere minutes, and the device requires a day and a night to recharge. But perhaps that is all the time you need. Would this interest you?"

Gods, it could only hurt. But the temptation remained. What would it mean to ask Odessa face to face . . . why?

Flowridia nodded.

"I must insist you clean up and rest first. Consider if it is worth unearthing the past. If so, I will take you tomorrow."

Flowridia wiped the tears from her eyes, and when Casvir rose, she accepted his hand to follow.

"There is a callous truth to consider," Casvir continued. "People grow apart. Ayla was the first woman you ever loved, and you were a child when you met her. Humans often love for a lifetime, but you seek immortality—and there is not an immortal or long-lived race upon this realm who loves only one person in their lifetime."

The words left her hollow.

"But that is a conversation to have with her. Not me."

She said nothing as she followed, though her mind screamed to unravel it all. Ayla wanted to run . . .

Flowridia set a hand on her womb, gasping to feel a gentle fluttering within. It should have sent her heart soaring, but instead shed light on the truth she had been denying all along, a looming regret she had been shoving away.

Flowridia . . . wanted to stay.

CHAPTER 23

Fifteen years after the end of the world . . .

The moment she emerged from Sha'Demoni's confines, Dira forgot all her training in stealth.

Sune was . . . so very beautiful.

Or perhaps it was not, for Dira had no concept of what made a town beautiful. But she loved the way her boots tapped upon the cobblestone road, loved the flickering lanterns in nearby windows, loved the smell of damp air and food wafting from the homes she passed. Laughter sounded from buildings, emitted from small groups of humans walking at the opposite side of the road. Dira kept her hood up, but oh, how exquisite it would be to join them, to laugh, to find friends who were not her caretakers. Perhaps if she could prove herself. Perhaps Mother would open up her world.

Sune was also larger than anticipated. But surely one man could not be difficult to find. He was Etolié's cousin, which meant he had wings too, right?

Sora had taught her many things, and keeping many knives on her person was one of them. Though Dira's favorite dagger was kept at her hip, she had slipped sheaths into her shoes and sleeves, prepared for whatever tricks this *Soliel* might have. He was a Celestial, so surely some sort of magic.

"Halt!"

Dira's heart skipped, so jarred to be addressed. She turned to the approaching set of men, both of whom had swords at their hips. It occurred to her that she had never seen a human in the flesh, only pictures, and while they shared similarities to Etolié . . . they were so plain, comparatively.

"My apologies for startling you, my lady," the same man said, "but it is policy for all travelers to present their papers to Captain Rolam, day or night. I would be happy to escort you."

What . . . What was this human custom? "Papers, uh, sir?"

"Yes, from your local magistrate."

He spoke as though that answered everything. "I must have forgotten them."

The man frowned, and Dira did not miss how his hand fell upon his sword's hilt. "Remove your hood, my lady. Let me take a look at you."

Panic filled her, yet when she opened her mouth to protest, she again stared upon that sword. If she started a fight now, she might not find Soliel. With shaking hands, she lowered her hood. "I'm looking for someone. Perhaps you could help—"

Yet her words vanished when the men brandished their swords—and scrambled back. "Monster!" one yelled. "Look at its fangs!"

Was . . . Was that so strange? Dira held up pacifying hands. "I am no monster—"

"Sound the alarm!" the other man cried, but neither charged her, only stumbled over each other to get away. "A vampire has invaded Sune! Call the priests!"

"Call for the son of Sol Kareena!"

Amid their cries, uproar sounded from within the buildings. Footsteps scrambled. Shutters banged shut. Dira clutched her robe, uncertain of this rising apprehension, yet all her resolve faded away, leaving only fear. "I'm not a vampire," she said, but she could summon no power behind it. It went unheard.

Her shadow grew, illuminated by something akin to the sun. And then, a cry: *"Son of Sol Kareena, save us!"*

Who else glowed with golden light? Dira's fear remained, but perhaps . . . her moment had come.

She turned, and there he stood—a resplendent man, though barely grown, his armor worn leather, his shield battered, but his stance made it magnificent. He bore no wings, yet he emanated beautiful light, strongest around his head, as a halo, accentuated by his golden hair. As tattered as his armor was, his sword was sleek and polished, yet showed subtle signs of use—it was loved, and its wielder had seen battle. He was built like an ox, far larger than she, yet his eyes were soft, softer than tilled earth and just as deep

Yet he faltered, confusion falling upon his regrettably handsome face. "You're not a vampire—"

Dira charged. Dagger readied, she sought his neck, and ducked beneath his sword, twirling to dodge his shield. Oh, what fun, what exhilaration filled her to dance with her weapons in hand. Dira sought his arm instead, surprised at his speed as he evaded. Over and over, she danced around his stances, her blade meeting shield, meeting armor, meeting sword—like fighting a brick wall.

But even brick would chip away eventually.

"I won't hurt you if you—"

Dira cut off his pretty words—for his voice was pure silk, pure poison—when her dagger slashed near his face, then narrowly dodged his blade. Oh, he was *fun*—a pity his death was foretold.

Again, her dagger met shield—but then a hand caught her wrist, a mere blink before his sword clattered to the floor.

Dira yelped when Soliel pulled her against his chest, his mass easily engulfing hers. He held her arm away, his grip akin to chains. "Drop your weapon, and I'll release you."

She had others. Dira obeyed, and with the clanging of metal on stone, his hold fell away.

She darted, uncertain of the surging heat against her cheeks as she met his gaze, though she cringed when his boot covered her blade. She loved that dagger.

"I didn't mean to make you feel threatened—assuming that's why you attacked me." Soliel held her eye as he set his shield down, leaving himself unarmed. "There's been a mistake, my lady. I apologize on behalf of the men who called me. They can't sense undeath like I can—and you're certainly not that."

Curiosity furrowed his brow. Gods, he was entrancing to watch.

"I hope it's not rude to ask," Soliel continued, his hesitation truly adorable, "but are you mortal?"

And Dira realized in that moment . . . she did not actually know. "I think so."

"You think?" Oh, his laughter—pure honey, and she starved for its sweetness. "I suppose I wonder the same thing about myself. If I may say, you are exceptionally talented with your knife."

Dira bit her lip, her mind alight at the compliment. "Thank you."

"What does bring a woman of your talents to our humble town?"

Woman . . . Amusing words, given he was barely a man. "Well, I forgot my papers, which is why I was stopped."

"Forgive me, but something tells me you might not have them at all." Yet his smile was kind, despite the clear accusation. "I can allow you through, though I would need your name. And if you're inclined . . ." Curse that shy smile—Dira melted to see it. "Perhaps we might share a drink and a story. I would pay."

Perhaps she was the honey instead—and he the unwitting fly. Everything about this was perfect, for if not by force, she could slit his throat by subterfuge instead.

And . . . well, it would be lovely to hear a few more lines from his soothing voice. "Yes, I would like that."

"My name is Soliel," he offered, and she pretended not to know him, to not know his cousin, his quest, his name upon her mother's tongue . . . "What do I call you?"

Common sense said to keep her mouth shut, but that same sense whispered that her name was not actually her true name . . . not technically. "Dira."

"It is wonderful to meet you." He stooped down to collect her knife, then offered it, hilt first.

She stared at it, debating the merit of seizing it and cutting off his hand. "You're very trusting."

When she took it, he chuckled, rekindling the warmth in her heart. "I choose to believe the best of people." He bent again to grab his sword and shield, his gaze upon the floor. How easy it would be to drive her blade through the back of his neck; how simple to spill his blood here and now, regain that wanted trust . . .

But . . . why? What would his death accomplish? "May I ask you something first?"

Soliel returned the sword to its sheath. "Of course, Dira."

"There is a war, isn't there?"

He stared at her as though she had sprouted wings. "Yes."

"Sorry, I've been traveling for . . . for a long time." She held her question in her mouth, tasted its bitter shell. To speak might mean to crack it . . . and discover what lay inside. "What do you know about . . . the executor?"

His expression did not change. "You will have to be more specific. There are many of them."

Dira thought back to her notes, to every conversation she had heard, every piece of knowledge Mother had kept locked away . . . "The one fighting the monster—Casvir."

Recognition flooded his face, though his confusion did not clear. "Grand Executor Darkleaf?"

"Yes, that one!" she said, but her enthusiasm must have been too much—for his expression became dark.

His hand caressed the hilt of his sword. "There are history books to answer that. The Endless Night is no secret. What precisely do you wish to know?"

He emanated fear, but . . . that made sense, she supposed. Mother wanted him dead, even if Dira had no idea as to why—not someone so beautiful, so radiant, so kind. But . . .

The question fell so smoothly from her tongue: "What is The Endless Night?"

Immediately, he withdrew his sword, holding it aloft. "You can't be a spy. You're far too unsubtle. So what are you?"

Oh gods, of course he didn't trust her. Dira returned her dagger to her hip, presenting empty hands. "I'm Dira."

"Do you work for Ayla Darkleaf?"

"No."

"I want to believe you."

The unspoken message rang loud in the night, the streets empty save for them. "I can explain over that drink . . ."

The words faded away, for the world became . . . colder.

Clawed hands appeared from pure darkness, gripping Dira with merciless might. Her scream cut off when one smothered her mouth—but she knew that cold grip.

Soliel cried, "Dira!"

But the world shifted, the dark mortal realm disappearing—replaced by the warm hues of Sha'Demoni and its eternal day.

Dark words caressed her ear, cool and far too calm. "Come home, my Darling Dira. We will speak there."

Current era . . .

"Forgive me if this is naïve," Sora asked in the midst of a barren, monochromatic wasteland, "but you seemed adamant that Onias will ask for secrets. What does that mean?"

Sora might've been daunted by the dismissive glare Ayla graced her with from the corner of her eye—but whatever her lingering distrust in Chaos, Ayla wasn't the sort to act out in front of an Old God. Chaos followed quietly beside them. And she finally, *finally* had Spore. Her mind had settled into a pleasant lull, the cloying scent comforting and familiar. She took another puff of her pipe, savoring each blessed sensation. Otherwise, she felt oddly unequipped. Ayla had insisted they would not need a potion for water-breathing. Instead, she had given Sora a mirror.

"What do you know of Onias?" Ayla asked.

"Not much."

"He is many things, most importantly the God of Knowledge who hungers for secrets. Knowledge is power, and Onias expands with each truth that falls into his infinite abyss. He is too large to leave his lair, but his prey inevitably comes to him, bringing knowledge or anecdotes in exchange for insight or sacrificing themselves for a peaceful oblivion. Onias' Hell is a very real place."

The terrain held a film of fog, and Sora swore glowing eyes stared in the distance, watching their every step. So different than the demonic world across the sea. "Why would anyone sacrifice themselves?"

"To gaze upon Onias' eye is the ultimate suicide. Not a true death, but total madness. A complete separation from your mind. You lose yourself and float in a state of nothing for the remainder of your days, eventually consumed."

The idea was unsettling. "Again, why would anyone do that?"

"Consider it a blessing to not understand."

Months ago, Sora had discovered a grimy journal in a haunted place, had read brutal words regaled by elegant script, the longing to burn and become nothing . . .

Sora would not claim to understand, but Ayla assuredly did.

"My point," Ayla continued, "is that he will ask for information. Sometimes, he will accept unique gifts or items he has never seen before. Other times, he accepts memories, but to give them means to lose them forever. The heartbroken sometimes offer their sorrow to him to forget their pain. So consider, Sora, what you will give him, lest you be unable to leave."

Were there any memories Sora would be willing to lose? Of course she held pain, but to release it forever . . . Would that not change her? Would it mean she unlearned those lessons? Either way, she had knowledge to offer, painful as it was. "What if I told him my account of Sol Kareena's death? Would I lose it forever?"

To her relief, Ayla gave an approving nod. "That is certainly unique. I think he would accept it, and no—if you are merely relaying the account, that does not mean it is lost."

In Sora's tunic, as silent as sin, Leelan remained but a shell yet lived. "Could I ask him something while I'm there?"

"So long as you can pay the price, why not?" Ayla's curiosity turned upon Chaos, her studious stare akin to a wolf surveying its meal—ironic as that quietly was. "What about you? What would you offer for a pledge?"

"I come from the future." Even behind her silver flame, Sora recognized that mischievous smile. "I could tell him what happens next winter, and he would be impressed."

Ayla chuckled darkly. "And what does happen next winter?"

"It is a difficult one for Nox'Kartha. I would prefer to leave it at that. Truthfully . . ." Chaos never quite lost her smile, no matter how somber the subject. Sora did not know what was Demitri, what was Dira, but her energy fluttered like butterfly wings. How seamlessly she spoke to Ayla; how desperate she became for approval. ". . . while I would be most inclined to let him ask, I have a fallback."

"Hold to that. We are nearing the shore."

Sora recalled the grey shoreline seen from Ku'Shya's Realm, how the vibrant, otherworldly hues had faded to monochrome. Here, the fluid landscape gained substance, no longer mist. Instead, the sand shifted beneath her feet, though filled in even as she lifted her boot. Not a single wave, a serene sea of black glass, and Sora wondered if she would be driven mad from the stark silence. Even her steps gave no sound. Instead, she whispered to preserve her sanity. "What about you, Ayla?"

"What about me?" the vampire snapped. Her voice did not echo, no, but its volume violated the stillness.

"What will you offer?"

"Whatever I decide in the moment."

Given Sora still questioned her motives, she simply prayed that 'whatever' didn't end up being Sora herself. Did Onias accept mortal sacrifices? It seemed pedantic to ask.

They continued walking along the shore. When Sora lapsed behind, she realized any question of Chaos' parentage would disappear to simply watch them walk in unison. Both held grace, held power in their strides, but it was the finer details that revealed the truth—the particular sway of their hips, the elegant pivots in their steps. Had Ayla taught her daughter to dance? Surely, for they were perfect partners, cut from the same cloth.

"I know I have said it before, but thank you for escorting us," Chaos said, her bright voice more akin to Flowridia—yet those parallels remained, nevertheless. "There are few who know Sha'Demoni better than you."

Derision stained Ayla's words. "You speak like you know me."

"Who in this world does not know The Endless Night? You are a legend in every timeline."

Perhaps Sora was keen to notice, given her innate wariness of this monster's presence, but Ayla's grace faltered, stiffness marring her control. "I suppose my reputation precedes me."

"Assuredly, but perhaps not in the way you mean. You have a role to play in the world to come."

Ayla stopped dead in her tracks, flinching as though struck. "Your flattery confuses me."

"Not my intention," Chaos said, and though she stood a head taller, there was no question of her supplicant form.

Ayla raised a scathing eyebrow. "Your counterpart said I would kill myself to avoid my fate." She resumed her steps. In the far distance, a silhouette marred the horizon.

Chaos became unreadable, sinking into the sand instead. When she spoke, she all but spat shards of ice. "Did he?"

"Among other things—the likes of which make me wonder why you would have any positive investment in my well-being at all."

"Would you accept an alternative perspective?"

Judging by the subtle flexing in Ayla's hands, Sora feared she grew irritated. "Perhaps when we are done with Onias."

Lest Chaos' earnest pestering lose them a guide, Sora said, "What's that up ahead?"

"The dock." Ayla sped up, her tiny feet hardly leaving an imprint at all. "Were we sane individuals, we would ask the ferryman for a ride across the sea. But this is hardly a sane quest." She glanced to Sora, her silver eyes a perfect complement to the landscape. "Unless a leviathan surfaces, this beach is the safest place in Sha'Demoni."

"A what?"

"Are you absolutely certain you wish to come?"

While Ayla's concern wasn't personal, it did at least affirm that Sora likely wasn't in any danger from her sister-in-law. "Please explain what a leviathan is first."

"A child of Onias. If we're lucky, we won't see one. Now, answer."

"Of course I'm coming."

Ayla shook her head, a sigh escaping her despite her undead state. "Your sense of loyalty makes no damn sense to me. I won't stop you, but for the sake of Flowra's continued happiness, you will keep quiet unless spoken to and do nothing to endanger yourself. Understood?"

Unease filled Sora, but she nodded.

A long dock jutted into the sea, leading to a simple raft and a mysterious, cloaked figure bearing a long oar. So this was the ferryman. Though he held a humanoid shape, tentacles poured from his black robe. In the shadow of his hood, numerous glowing eyes studied her in return. He spoke heavily accented words, guttural and harsh—and Sora was sent back to the heat basin of Ku'Shya's throne room, for the language was the very same.

Ayla replied in the same tongue, the words unnatural, nauseating to hear from her elegant voice. Whatever her reply, the ferryman slowly turned to Chaos, her Silver Fire radiant even in the dank atmosphere. Again came Demoni words, and one name sounded louder than them all: *Onias*.

"Demoni is a language I have not spoken in years," Chaos replied, "so I will not insult you by bastardizing your mother tongue." Beside her, Ayla interpreted. "But I understand you. I am Chaos, and no doubt your master has heard of the threat my counterpart holds for your world. I seek his pledge. I offer knowledge of the future in return."

The ferryman stared, the subtle blinking of his many eyes twisting Sora's stomach. He turned in fluid motions, a creature of both sea and land, and raised his oar to the sky—

When he slammed it down, the whole ocean *echoed.*

Sora gasped when the waves rose before the dock, parting in a perfect line. Farther it spread, a narrow path forming through the very sea. The walls of the ocean reached astronomical heights, and Sora reeled at the shapes swimming within those walls. Small things, mostly—but a dark shadow peered with more tentacles than Sora could count.

"This is our path," Ayla announced. "Tread lightly."

She jumped from the dock to the muddy floor, the dark sand cushioning her descent. Chaos offered Sora her hand, then pulled her into a tight embrace before jumping down. The licking sensation of silver flame covered her—not painful, no, but stimulating. Though Sora's stomach lurched, she hardly felt their landing. Her feet gently touched the ocean floor, whatever magic Chaos held saving her a twisted ankle. "Thank you."

Chaos did not release her hand as they traversed between the gargantuan ocean walls, the path bearing no visible end.

"Have you done this before?" Sora whispered.

Chaos nodded. "That doesn't mean it gets any less daunting, however."

Strange, to feel fire engulfing her hand and not burn. Chaos gripped tight, keeping distance between them and Ayla. The shadows in the ocean walls darkened, the occasional shifting of a massive tentacle causing Sora's blood to race. Every instinct within her screamed to run, haunted by the knowledge that death was assured if the walls crashed down.

"I cannot believe he said that," Chaos whispered.

Sora thought of the ferryman first, questioning her notion of Demoni gender, but the obvious truth struck her moments later. "I get the sense Soliel doesn't like her."

Ayla sauntered fearlessly ahead, unintimidated by the surging walls of water. Deeper, the ocean floor descended. The sky was nearly a memory. "Oh, he despises her," Chaos said. "And I won't besmirch his reasons. I only wish I knew how to save her. If not by my death, then what?"

Flowridia had spoken of hypotheticals, of ways to break the vicious cycle. Only Chaos and Order would know how. Was the key truly Ayla? Would her life save the worlds? "The only ones who can truly make an impact on the future are you and Soliel. You're the ones who know the future. No matter what I do, it'll be what fate designed, but you can break the cycle. If not by your death then *what?*"

"Casvir's," Chaos replied, no hesitation at all. "But I have lost hope of finding his phylactery, Sora. I am not convinced it exists at all. Soliel, Demitri, and I scoured the realms for centuries, and we never made any ground."

"But you think Ayla would have found it?"

"At the very least, she would have bought us more time. I think you underestimate the power she attained in her quest to destroy him. Power enough to grant me a familiar. She became Grand Executor of all the elven kingdoms. She could have held him off for years more, burning his troops, spying from the shadows—and yes, perhaps finding the phylactery. He could not kill her—" Though fire shrouded her face, Chaos failed to hide her anguish. ". . . instead, he could enslave her. And I do blame myself, Sora. And not only because I had to stab a knife through her heart. I was a stupid child who delivered her right into Casvir's grasp."

Chaos' steps stilled; her composure barely held. Ahead, Ayla turned, a statue on the horizon. But Sora could pay her no mind, instead stopping in her tracks and forcing Chaos' glowing gaze to meet her own. "How?"

"I beg your pardon?"

"Tell me how you delivered her right into Casvir's grasp, and I'll stop it."

Chaos shook her head. "You cannot."

"Does your other half agree?"

"He's contemplating it—"

"Care to explain?" Ayla stood with crossed arms a ways ahead, her fierce expression indecipherable.

Sora released Chaos, instead bracing herself for conflict. "She's having a difficult time."

To her surprise, Ayla merely shrugged. "We are in no hurry. Time is slower in the mortal realm, and these walls will not collapse until we breach Onias' Realm."

Again, Sora's suspicions rose to irritate her. "You're awfully nonchalant."

"Life is pain. I simply hide it better than she does."

Sora frowned. "Why are you here?"

"Taking you to Onias is not good enough?"

"You've never cared about the end of the world."

"Because Nox'Kartha is suffocating. Is that enough?"

"You haven't left Flowridia's side in months, but you volunteered—nay, *insisted*."

"And I would still be there, if she wanted me."

All the fight left Sora, startled by the statement. "What do you mean?"

"Ask her," Ayla spat, but her words cut off. Tension laced her tone. "Or perhaps ask Onias. I certainly intend to have a few words."

Sora could not place this new apprehension. Her talents were in observation, not interpretation. But her gut screamed that all was not well.

"You will call me selfish," Chaos whispered, "but I always told myself, in the time before, that if I could stop Casvir, at least she would not have died in vain. More than anything, I want to save her."

"Soon, we'll have space to breathe and speculate," Sora replied, and somewhere deep inside . . . she understood. "We'll find a way, I promise."

Chaos' grief remained, even as a sneer appeared. "Bet you could stop it. Lock little Dira up. In the basement. In the cellar. Never let her leave the house. Or kill Soliel. That'll do it. Kill him dead."

"I'll think about it. But please don't make a commotion in front of Ayla."

Chaos, now Dira once more, kept a hold of Sora's hand as they walked, led like a forlorn duckling. So far from the egotistical Deity

Sora had nearly left behind; this woman was contrite, broken. Losing Uluron shattered her. Not for the first time, Sora felt that maternal instinct rise anew, the connection of family strong despite rocky beginnings.

All the while, the sensation remained of being watched.

Their path ended at a hole veering into the ground. Nothing of interest at all; nothing but a cave in the middle of the sea, but even Sora felt waves of radiant power emanating from within. Peering down, the faint shimmer of water rippled in the darkness. "How do we get down?"

"We jump," Ayla said. "The water will catch you."

"Need I remind you that I can't breathe underwater?"

"You will be fine," Chaos muttered. "There is an enchantment in his realm. Otherwise, no mortals aside from merfolk could enter. I entered as a mortal in my time—or, mortal enough."

Nothing made sense, but they had come this far. Sora took her first step downward, taking care not to slip on the slick stone. Chaos followed, Ayla as well.

The ocean crashed above them. Sora cried out at the deafening roar. The dark water collapsed, the serene sea now cacophonous and wild.

But water did not breach their small pocket of air. Though her blood raced, Sora tentatively reached out to touch the unnatural film of water blockading their exit, skimming across it like the surface of a pond.

The question remained of how they would leave, but others had before. Chaos herself had come to this place, so surely she wouldn't die in a foreign world beneath the sea . . .

From a pocket in her dress, Ayla withdrew a small mirror. "Keep yours ready."

Sora obeyed, Chaos too.

The sharp descent led to a pool of water. Ayla held up a hand and went first, ducking to submerge her head. A stream of bubbles surfaced, then she herself. "I can confirm that the enchantment is intact. You will be able to breathe."

And though every instinct within her screamed, Sora walked into the pool, surprised how easily her feet moved, unhindered by the water at all. Neither cold nor warm, the water matched the stagnant air, and when Sora drew a breath, panic filled her—

As well as air.

"I don't like this one bit," she said, shocked to hear herself so clearly.

"Good." Ayla beckoned them forward. "It will keep you alert."

Did Sora imagine her tension? Gods, everything about this sent her soul reeling.

Chaos' fire lit the path, unhindered by the crushing depths. The cave expanded, massive and ringed, as though carved by an insect.

Though slippery, the floor held. The silence became unbearable, yet to break it meant to disrupt the taut energy of this space.

Ayla had said Onias had grown too large to leave, yet these caves would accommodate even Ku'Shya's massive bulk. What eldritch abomination would they be facing? Sora knew so little of Onias, only that approaching any demonic god meant subsuming yourself to their laws.

There was no mercy in Demoni Law.

As the minutes passed, the sensation of magic and dread rose higher. Ahead, a massive wall of darkness expanded, greater than even Chaos' power could breach. No guards, no speaker, but Onias' name was enough to deter all but the bravest or most foolhardy—or desperate.

The path continued through the darkness, but the walls parted, revealing a gargantuan amphitheater. Larger than castles, larger than Neolan—Sora could not see the edges. Like the plank of a ship, the stone path jutted forward, leaving them exposed to whatever horror they would face. Chaos' fire was but a spark, yet gentle light glowed far below, a star beneath the sea.

The first tentacle rose along the walls, wider than roads, wider than entire ships. Shifting shadows in the darkness revealed countless others, slinking along the wall like monstrous serpents. One came far too near. Sora withdrew a dagger before Chaos shoved her forward—behind them, the appendage slipped into the hole they had emerged from, blockading the path.

Yet that light remained, oddly comforting despite Sora's rising terror. Alluring even, and she approached the end of the jutting rock, her companions close behind.

Gazing down, the ocean of tentacles undulated like worms, a mass with no source. Humanoid bodies swirled in a slow whirlpool around it, gently orbiting like comatose planetoids. Golden light shone from within the mass, its source covered by the writhing appendages, but as Sora peered forward, seeking the origin, a firm hand on her tunic wrenched her back.

"Are you stupid?" Ayla whispered, and she held up the mirror, using it to peer into the void.

Aw yes, the madness. Sora copied her stance, the mirror's reflection revealing . . . horror.

The tentacles parted a mere moment, revealing the great void that was Onias' eye. A glowing sun for the bodies to orbit, no pupil or iris—pure light. No beginning or end to his gaze, his body, his presence. Onias simply was.

A great rumbling shook the amphitheater, deeper than this cavern in the sea. Sora's very bones shook, yet within the sound were words: *"Goddess of Chaos, I have been waiting."*

"Great God Onias," Chaos said, the echo of her words bearing power, "it is incredible, standing in your presence. You must know my quest, then."

"Yes."

"Then you understand the urgency as well. Tell me the price of your pledge. Whatever knowledge you want of the future will be yours."

"Patience. There is no time here."

Within the light of Onias' eye, more tentacles rose, their ends vanishing into the darkness. Any moment now, and they would consume Sora's small party.

If Sora lived to complete Chaos' quest, she swore to never stand before a god again.

"Sora Makosa, whispers have said you are the envoy. Your righteous nature precedes you."

Sora's stomach twisted to think he knew anything about her at all.

"Ayla Darkleaf . . . you are the enigma."

"And you are not the first who's called me that," Ayla replied.

"The lion does not protect the lamb, nor does the woman who burned half the world seek to save it."

"How can I burn a world someone else has destroyed?"

"I cannot be lied to. But your agenda is not the most pressing. Goddess of Chaos, my price is a question that has vexed me for many a millennium. What has no beginning can have no end, yet even I am not immune to death. Tell me: what is my end?"

Beneath her mask of Silver Fire, Chaos became mortal anew, slumping to reveal the exhausted woman behind her title. "It must never be repeated."

"There is none to hear it but the void."

"There is a growing darkness that will consume the mortal realm," Chaos began, and behind her façade of indifference, Ayla stared from the corner of her eye, "but it will not stop there. All the demon gods will fall. Izthuni is the first, his undeath a weakness to this rising force. Ku'Shya is the last, even her might in battle a wall eventually breached. But between them . . . it is you. I watched the endless waves of undead eat you alive. They had no minds to lose, and for every one you destroyed, a hundred came to replace them. They, too, had no beginning or end. It is a noble death, a sacrifice in the quest to save us all. You are mourned and remembered for eternity."

Her final echo led to silence. Sora could not tear her gaze away from the tentacled mass, the bodies below, the light luring her like prey to an angler fish.

And then . . . *"Goddess of Chaos, I pledge myself to thee. My power is yours."*

Sora lost her footing, relief flooding her as she fell to her knees. Perhaps she might see the sun again, instead of losing her mind to this false and intoxicating star.

"Sora Makosa, you are a person who clings to noble causes, and that is reason enough for you to accompany this Goddess. But is there anything more you seek?"

She hesitated to bargain with the entity, but a weight remained against her chest, hardly breathing yet refusing to die. "I do have a question. May I offer you my payment first?"

"Yes."

"I was there when Sol Kareena was murdered. Would you like to know my story?"

"Yes."

Sora relayed the tale in muted tones, the death and its horror fresh in her mind. Running for her life, the terror of Soliel as he became a monster . . .

"What do you seek?"

With utmost care, Sora withdrew the comatose bird from her tunic. "I'm told that when gods die, their power remains in their priests and priestesses through their familiars, but while I still have my magic, my familiar has been ill. He won't move or chirp or react. Can you tell me what's wrong?"

"This familiar was with you when Sol Kareena passed."

"Yes."

"Show it to me."

Though hesitant, Sora held Leelan before the void, visible to the god's great eye. She shut her own, fearful of insanity, each passing second welling fresh terror within her.

"That is not a power I have felt in eons."

Sora stepped back, finally able to breathe as she held Leelan to her cheek.

"There is a secret among the gods, withheld from mortals as the angels fail to understand it themselves. Whispers have reached me that Neoma's death separated her from her granted power, for that power cannot leave this realm. Where it has gone, even I cannot say. But if those whispers are true, Sol Kareena's spirit has moved on while her power remains somewhere in the lands of the living, transferred into whatever vessel she could reach—and while I am fallible, your familiar may be the vessel."

Sora stared into Leelan's vacant eyes, seeking any sign at all of that impossible theory. Was his coma a symptom of an influx of power? What did it even mean?

"Be cautious. Even allies would seek to steal this power—or destroy it."

"What do I do to help him?"

"That was not your question."

Sora had to sit, mind reeling from the demon's words. Idly, she stroked the ailing bird, fearing his pain.

"Ayla Darkleaf, my curiosity is piqued."

"I would prefer to speak alone."

Sora frowned, suspicions confirmed. Ayla had an agenda. Onias had said himself she would not care to save the world.

"You came as one; you shall leave the same way."

Brash, for Ayla to sneer at a demon god, but perhaps Ayla had dealt with enough to no longer fear them. "Then I shall leave and return."

"No."

Ayla tore her gaze from the mirror, landing on Sora instead. Amid her rage, anguish twisted her sharp features. "If what I say leaves this cavern, I won't hesitate to slit your throat."

"I won't breathe a word," Sora replied, and though she kept her gaze to Leelan, she listened, curiosity her driving force.

"What will you offer?"

"Hear my question first."

"Dangerous, but you know the risk of being unable to pay."

Chaos' comforting presence joined Sora on the ground. The Goddess had no qualms about watching the mother she yearned for, even as Ayla's breath hitched.

"God Onias, you have spoken of my nature, but that is precisely what I would . . . *erase.*"

Sora's stomach dropped.

"Recent revelations have revealed that my life and legacy are lies. And I have been tormented for months by that weight—by the knowledge that I was molded to be a monster from my birth, and by the guilt of understanding what harm I've done. I tried to burn the world, as you said, but I . . ." Ayla's voice broke, her fight for control slipping from her grasp. "Gods, I feel it. And I can't run from it. My name is synonymous with fear and hatred. My legacy is a cage from which I cannot escape.

"In the midst of all that, my wife is dying—a wife who cannot stand the person I've become in my depression. She sold our child to save the soul of a woman I hate. She has caged herself and me in this bargain, because to ask her to take it back now means for her to give up the life of her familiar."

And so there was the other side of Flowridia's bargain, Sora realized—a wife left brokenhearted. A woman who would someday love that same child enough to be slain by her hand.

"Onias, I am trapped. My wife may die, and I shall have nothing but my name and my broken heart. If by any miracle she lives, she loves The Endless Night, but I want to scream and never hear that name again. The cruelest irony is that I made her what she is now, and she, in turn, made me. But I'm not someone she can love anymore, and I fear it would ruin me to love her too."

Ayla stilled, voice trembling amid quiet tears. "I'm drowning. I cannot face this ending. I love her with all my heart, but the price was the blood of hundreds of thousands. Of course I deserve to lose her. I deserve to burn in holy light for eternity or face oblivion in your Hell. And so I ask—nay, *beg* for guidance, for hope, for . . . a path. I don't know, but I . . ." Her sobs overtook her, shaking her to her core.

Sora dared to study her, this woman she despised, who had ended Sora's life all those years ago. This woman was the Fireborn legacy, the reason they became hunters of the dead. This woman had burned her own people, had sought to destroy them in a slow, agonizing genocide. This woman was a monster.

Yet Sora's heart broke.

"You were molded. Tell me. That is the price of aid."

And Ayla, stripped of pride, a raw, open wound, told the tale of a child corrupted by Izthuni, ravaged and abused by the very institution Sora had once sought to join, groomed and raped by a predator celebrated by history, yet for all the horrors, the bitter end was the most poignant piece—Sarai Fireborn, deceived into creating a monster.

Ayla wept. And Sora, despite all that harbored hatred, cried her own silent tears. By the Light—Ayla hadn't had a chance, had she? And of course, it negated nothing. It did not bring back the lives she'd taken. Ayla was the very core of monstrosity.

A monster . . . now pleading for that chance.

Onias' words shook the very walls, the floor, inescapable in this cavern in the depths. *"All your life, you have been shackled. You seek an escape."*

Sora's unease rose. A whisper of *danger* bid her to stand, keenly aware of Ayla's stance and her trembling hold on the mirror. She set Leelan into Chaos' hands, who could not cry but shook to suppress her sobs.

"Of course you feel shame; it is the price of sin. The blood you have spilled could fill oceans. Once it brought you pride, but it never brought you peace."

As silent as the predators she had studied, Sora crept forward. Her boots made not a sound.

"I know I don't deserve peace," Ayla whispered.

"Nothing is deserved in this life. Neither peace nor forgiveness."

A step away from Ayla, Sora stilled. This was not The Endless Night. This weeping creature held far more resemblance to the monster in the dungeon beneath Kaas—an enslaved wretch. Instead of the staff, her shackles were guilt and her own cursed legacy.

But who would believe in Ayla Darkleaf? Not even Flowridia, if her words were true.

"For some, atonement can be found in death, should the cause be great enough. But you do not seek atonement, do you? You came to be told to succumb."

"God Onias, I . . ." Ayla's voice broke.

"You wish to throw your sins away and run. You crave oblivion, but oblivion will not bring you peace. To be nothing is not peace. It is silence."

"I don't want to run. I don't want peace." The mirror fell from Ayla's hands, plunging into the abyss below. "I want to be free."

Ayla would not accidentally falter. When her knees failed her, she did not panic; merely became limp in her free-fall to oblivion.

Sora pounced, wrenching Ayla back by the collar of her dress. Ayla slammed into the ground. Shock cut through her torrent of tears. When she rose, Sora bombarded her with her own body—and though Sora's strength was nothing to this monster, Ayla remained still in the embrace.

By the Light, she was small, the top of her head barely reaching Sora's armpit. When Ayla shifted, Sora's grip tightened, expecting any moment to plunge off the edge with her. Ayla was capable. It would hardly be a strain.

"I forgive you," Sora whispered, and with those words came the release of a pain years old. "I know it's just a small thing, but please don't go—" Sora suppressed a sob as thin arms wrapped around her.

"There is no fate, Ayla Darkleaf. There is only the path you forge. You will never erase your sins, but someday you may free yourself of their burden. In your darkest moments, consider: how much more powerful is it to live with those sins and seek that impossible redemption, nevertheless?"

Ayla said nothing, merely wept in Sora's embrace. But where there was once anguish, rose catharsis.

"When you find peace, you will know you have found your way."

Around them, the tentacles covering the distant walls steadily fell. Their exit cleared, the threat finally ebbing.

Chaos waited beside the open cave, her anguish hidden by Silver Flame. But her voice conveyed it, her words trembling and soft. "Forget what Soliel said. You are the forger of your own fate. To tell you your future would take it away—and there is so much left for you to live for."

When she offered a hand, Ayla held it in her own.

With her arm around Ayla, Sora led her family from Onias' Hell.

CHAPTER 24

Fifteen years after the end of the world . . .

Dira walked through a vibrant realm, any semblance of nighttime forgotten in this world of endless day, all the while avoiding Mother's eye.

Mother was often quiet, but silence was another feeling entirely.

When they appeared at the Fireborn Estate, the moon hung high in the sky, its silver light revealing the overgrown fountains and topiaries. Light shone from within the home, but Mother stilled beside a fountain, stiffness in her stance. She released a small gasp.

Mother . . . didn't breathe.

Dira hung back, helpless when the first of Mother's tears fell—her indomitable mother, a fearsome creature of the night, utterly broken before her.

Sora had said she'd be angry. This was somehow so much worse.

When Dira came near, guilt rising every second, Mother stole her into an embrace, her grip desperate, nearly painful. The dam of her tears broke, and Mother wept against her shoulder. Dira, too, felt wetness prickle in her eyes. "Mother, I'm sorry."

Mother said nothing, merely stained Dira's shirt with her tears. And so Dira held her, suspended between guilt and anticipation. What would come of this? Mother was heartbroken. This . . . This was not what she wanted.

When Mother did pull away, she did not remove her touch, simply gripped Dira's shoulders instead. "What were you thinking, my Dira?" Gods, she tried to sound angry—but there was no foundation beneath it.

A tear slipped from Dira's eye. "I was trying to help you."

"Help me?"

"I wanted to prove that I could." Dira suppressed a sob, her lip trembling instead. "I overheard you tell Etolié you wanted someone named Soliel dead, but you couldn't do it yourself—so I went to do it."

"Dira, no, no." Mother gasped as she pulled her back into her arms, clinging tighter than before. "You must never kill. My innocent little girl—you mustn't lose that."

"Then what's the use of me learning to fight?"

"I don't want you to fight, but there are practicalities to knowing self-defense. I pray you never have to use it." Moonlight reflected from Mother's teary face when she released her, this time collapsing onto the fountain's lip. "Sora said you have been listening for some time. I went to find you after, but you . . ." Mother's face fell into her hands, fresh sobs shaking her small form—and Mother, though petite, was never small. "You are not very subtle, my love. You ripped a map from your book and left it wide open."

Dira managed a smile amid her own falling tears.

"Is this the first time you've left the estate?"

"Yes."

"But not your first time in Sha'Demoni."

It was not a question. "No, but I've never gone far."

"Did someone teach you?"

"No," Dira said, though it was a lie. But implicating Demitri wasn't worth the truth. "I simply remembered what you said, about finding the cracks between the worlds. It . . . it made sense to me."

The whistling wind highlighted Mother's lapse into silence, her tears falling softly now. When Dira sat beside her, Mother set an arm around her.

"You're not angry?" Dira asked.

"I am furious, Dira." But there was no substance to it, merely tragedy. "But not nearly so much as I am at myself. I . . . I don't understand why you would rebel, but here we sit. Explain, my darling. I beg of you. I thought I had done enough, yet . . ." Fresh sobs wracked Mother's form.

Dira hugged herself, sheltered by Mother's arm. Mere hours ago, this had all made sense. But now, she had faced the man her mother wanted killed and faltered herself, had gotten a taste of the world beyond—but here her mother wept, and there was no one more important. "I want to understand the world. I-I want to see it. I want to make friends. I love our home, and I love you and Sora, but I know you're keeping secrets from me, and it feels like you don't trust me enough to tell me."

"It is not a matter of trust," Mother said, her broken words so tentative, so frail. "It is a matter of protecting you. I have never lied to you—there are monsters in the outside world even I fear, and all I have done is to protect you from them."

"I didn't see any monsters," Dira whispered, yet Mother's grip became tight, her claws threatening to break skin.

And then . . . she released. Mother's arm fell away. "There is nothing more precious than innocence, my lamb. Once it is taken, it cannot be restored. To be protected from the cruelties of the world is all I have ever sought for you because it was not a luxury I was given. I don't speak much of myself—and perhaps that has been an error. But at the same time . . . the first time I held you in my arms, I knew, like I knew the very markings on my soul, that I would do anything in this world to shelter you, even if it meant keeping elements of my own life in the dark." Hesitation stilled her tongue. Mother wiped her eyes, her tears finally quelling. "What you don't know is I did not hold you until you were one year old."

The words were strange. They . . . they did not make sense. "But you're my mother. I'm your flesh and blood—a-at least, I thought."

"You are. You are mine by blood and name and birthright. You are half my body and my whole heart. But I have said before there was magic in your conception. I have said your mom died upon your birth. And when she did, I ran away."

Dira's stomach dropped.

"But while that admittance is overdue," Mother continued, a vacancy to her tone, "it is only a fraction of what I will share with you today. Because there are things I must keep secret, my love, but I suppose it is a disservice to hide what does directly affect you. And that is the circumstances of your conception—because the cruel and brutal truth is that you were not conceived because of love. I loved your mom, yes, but you were made to fulfill a bargain. We were never meant to keep you."

Dira felt nothing, simply waited with breathless wonder.

"I do all I can to speak glowingly of your mom, and I fear I shall tarnish that shine." Grief settled upon Mother's countenance, though her voice remained firm. "I married her for love. She changed the very trajectory of my life and saved it. But your mom was shortsighted. She was selfish. In a desperate bid to save the soul of someone I would prefer to never hear the name of again, she sold you, her firstborn. You were not even a thought, but she sold you to appease a monster.

"That monster is named Casvir, and he is the imperator of the distant kingdom of Nox'Kartha. You lived in his home for your first year of life, but Etolié conspired to free you—and enlisted me to fake your death. You were meant to live in her mother's home in Celestière, but . . . it is as I said—when I held you for the first time, my very soul shifted. You and I sat alone in the wasteland of Sha'Demoni across the sea where you fell asleep in my arms, and I loved you, my Dira. I saw Flowra's face in your sleepy visage, but that was not the love I experienced in that quiet moment, no. You became the very center of the world, and while I would have burned the world for her. . . I would have built it anew for you.

"And that is what I am trying to do, my Dira. I am trying to create a world where you can be safe to live and thrive. Imperator Casvir believes you to be dead, but the blood he would spill to take you back would fill oceans, if he knew you were mine. As long as he walks this realm, you must stay here. This is the burden I accepted when I took you home that first night—and no matter how heavy, I will bear it until the task is done. I love you, Dira Darling. And I hope . . . I hope you understand."

Dira said nothing at all, the words settling gently in her soul. Of course Mother loved her, yet now that warmth washed over her, manifesting in Dira's own quiet tears.

Yet one errant grain of sand remained to scratch her 'til she bled—why did Soliel speak of Mother with such fear?

"I love you too," Dira finally said, yet that annoyance itched inside her. "M-May I ask one more thing?"

"You may."

"I did find Soliel."

"I saw. And whatever I must offer for you to forget him, I will give."

He had entranced her, but Dira would say nothing of that—not of the beautiful boy and his light. "He called you something. The Endless Night. What does that mean?"

Mother became . . . cold.

When she took Dira's hand, there was no sweetness in the gesture, no seeking of comfort. Instead, she clasped it fitfully, ice in her gaze. Dira could not run—yet the urge rose, as instinctive as breathing. "Forget that name as well," Mother said, cool and calloused. "It means nothing now."

Mother stood—too quickly, too terse—still grasping Dira's hand. "Come inside. You don't deserve a cake, but we shall bake one anyway."

Current era . . .

Under Etolié's watchful eye, Flowridia cleansed herself of blood and ash.

First, Etolié healed her bloody hand, allowing Flowridia the means to scrub her skin raw. She washed her hair, her face, removed any trace of tears. Yet the grime coating her soul remained, no matter how many times she lathered the soap across her aching body.

"You've got some, uh, big feelings there, Flowers."

Flowridia had no qualms over nudity—at least, not in front of Etolié, whose only exception to her asexuality was a massive, muscular, demonic monster. Besides, pregnancy meant she had been poked and prodded by nurses in every state of undress. There was nothing left to hide. So even when the suds ebbed, there came no instinct to shy away. "I'm not ready to talk."

Not even to the priestess, though Casvir insisted.

In her medical suite, Flowridia lounged in bed, her hips throbbing from the walk. The Priestess of Staella was the same she had spoken to after the horrors of Kaas—a pretty Celestial matron, elegance in her smile and kindness in the turn of her lips.

"And that's all right," the priestess said. "You don't have to talk yet. Healing has a mysterious timeline. It's not a linear experience."

Too numb to cry, Flowridia muttered defeated words. "I thought everything was fine."

"If you don't mind me saying it, Imperator Casvir did make mention of anger issues. It's not unreasonable to say you might've suppressed that pain and now are lashing out."

"Being pregnant hasn't helped." Bitterness filled her, the joy of conception a distant memory now. "I feel trapped by weakness, by pain, and of course by my hand . . ." Her words faded when a gentle fluttering touched within her stomach. Flowridia gasped and set her hand upon her womb, then beckoned for the priestess to join her, wishing to share the miracle with someone, anyone.

Yet the priestess' smile merely reminded Flowridia of what she would lose. "Magical, isn't it? I have three little ones of my own. To be honest, I never enjoyed being pregnant, but moments like that kept my spirit up until their births. If you don't mind me asking, have you chosen a name?"

The words were salt upon Flowridia's deep gashes. "I'm not supposed to keep it. It's a long story, but the baby is promised to someone else." Her arms fell protectively around her womb. "I thought I was fine with that. I've finally admitted that I'm not."

"My dear, I'm so sorry. Is there no way to change that?"

Outside, Demitri lay comatose in a cage, a stranger in his own mind. "Not without great sacrifice."

"How does your wife feel about it?"

The question was innocent, no unsaid accusation—though there should have been. Rumors surely flew of Lady Flowridia, pregnant with the imperator's baby. It was how Murishani would have spun it, just to irk her. Leaving it at Casvir's doorstep wouldn't help. "Ayla doesn't have the same attachment to children that I do. She sees it as the means to an end."

"It seems a lot has happened since we last met."

So earnest, the priestess was, and Flowridia's walls finally cracked. "My marriage may be over, but I'm not ready to face it. Can we not talk today?"

"I do have to stay for an hour, per Imperator Casvir's orders. Tell me about your plants instead—the ones on the windowsill."

Flowridia did manage to smile, speaking softly of the potted plants under her care.

The priestess did eventually say her farewell. "I will return in two days. But if I may leave you with this—consider those plants. No matter how much pain you feel, no matter how sick you've become, they still thrive under your care. You are not helpless. You can still bring healing to others."

The priestess left, and Flowridia supposed there was wisdom in that. Yet she wondered . . . when had she ceased to be a healer of people?

Etolié brought a small pile of books, as well as a folder filled with dusty, ancient parchment. "I managed to sweet-talk the golems into showing me the records department. Those are castle maps, Flowers."

Whatever her depression, Flowridia certainly felt a spark of something as she skimmed the ancient drawings, showing the castle layer by layer. "This is incredible."

"I didn't spend therapy locking myself in my library just to learn nothing."

Flowridia handled the pages with care, uncertain of what she sought, only praying she would know it when she saw it. The pages were numbered, notes scribbled here and there to distinguish different rooms' purposes. The handwriting was not Casvir's, but perhaps it would lead to something.

Casvir's phylactery was somewhere among these pages. She knew it like she knew her own breath.

A quiet knock sounded. Flowridia set the folder beneath the covers. "Come in."

A human-looking gentleman peeked his head inside, his uniform reminiscent of a healer. Flowridia did not know him, but his smile suggested he knew her. "Lady Flowridia, I'm Healer Vibal from Staraeus. Imperator Casvir has asked me to evaluate your condition."

"Nice to meet you."

"Staraeus?" Etolié asked. "That's not far from Ilunnes. You're from the same backwater nowhere as Flowers."

"A delightful coincidence."

Etolié floated up from the chair to the bed, leaving the seat for Vibal. He set his satchel upon the bedside table and withdrew a few potions and instruments Flowridia did not recognize. "If you'll let me touch your forehead . . ."

He tested her temperature, her pulse, even shone a light in her eyes 'to check her head,' or so he explained.

"I spent quite a bit of time down south as well," Etolié said, "during my uppity slave-freeing years. Did you ever travel to Vaile?"

"I did not."

"How about Oron?"

"Unfortunately, also no."

"Ilunnes?"

Exasperation stiffened his smile. "Yes, once or twice." He uncorked one of the potions in his arsenal, a faint, fruity aroma filling the space.

"How about that lake, huh? It glitters at sunrise."

Flowridia certainly didn't remember a lake in her hometown, but Etolié's raised brow was reminiscent of their time together in Staelash—when the Celestial implored her to *fucking play along, or so help me.*

"Truly nothing like it," the man said, clearly dismissive. "Drink this, please."

"Flowers, did you ever go camping by the lake?"

Flowridia frowned at the question, because of course she hadn't gone camping on a lake that didn't exist. When the man offered the vial, she accepted and said, "It was a summer pastime. The best way to see that glittering sunrise."

"I only saw it once," Vibal said, which of course was impossible, because there was no lake in Ilunnes. "But it certainly stuck with me. Now if you wouldn't mind drinking—"

Flowridia feigned a dry heave. She shoved the potion into Etolié's grasp, then ran as fast as her sore body would take her to the nurse's lounge next door.

A utilitarian room, leading to a nicer bedroom for the head physician, but bless fate—the physician herself sat at her desk. Flowridia made a loud show of heaving beside the shut door, holding a finger to the physician as she did. Finally, she whispered, "Is there supposed to be a doctor from Staraeus here?"

The physician shook her head.

"Call for the guards immediately. And Casvir."

The woman rushed to obey, her cry of *"Guards! Guards!"* echoing through the hallway.

Amid the ensuing chaos, Flowridia sunk to the ground, a cold numbness engulfing her. A tussle ensued in the room beyond, as well as obscenities courtesy of Etolié herself. Flowridia scooted herself beneath a table, uncertain of her own mental state, only that she clenched her fist to stanch her threatened tears.

Etolié was the first to find her, actively seething as she knelt beside the table. "Casvir's gonna get the potion tested, but it's not a far stretch to say it was another assassin."

Flowridia nodded, willing her mind to stay blank.

"I doubt you noticed, but his accent? Nothing like yours, you little bumpkin."

Again, Flowridia nodded, her welling tears spiraling her into turmoil.

"You have every right to scream, Flowers. It's healthy, actually—"

And Flowridia did, a primal scream tearing from her throat. Etolié shooed away the rushing nurses, but Flowridia didn't hear her words—simply wailed first into the air, and then into the pillow Etolié shoved into her face.

But try as she might, even when her voice became ragged, even when pain seized her vocal cords, even when she became more animal than woman, it was but a whisper to the screaming in her mind.

Flowers did finally sleep. The idiot surely needed it.

Flowers was dying. That much was clear to anyone with half a brain. She just wasn't dying fast enough for anyone to worry— except Etolié, against her will, and perhaps Ayla, who was clearly going through something. Etolié could heal all manner of physical ailments, even the occasional curse, but the life force being drained out of your body by a parasite? Not even Momma could reverse that.

Static radiated from Etolié's skin as she watched the woman sleep from her place on the couch, the internal debate causing her to be restless. Khastra was in Sha'Demoni. The ritual had presumably worked. So what did that mean? Where did they go from here? So many questions, but Etolié couldn't leave until no suspicion would be had—

There came a soft knock. Casvir entered and spared a silent glance for Flowridia, then looked to Etolié. "Come to my office. There is a private matter to discuss."

And important enough to whisk Etolié from his ward's bedside. Etolié rose, Flowers' warning in the garden causing her mind to race for excuses. Of course he would have felt the change, but did he know what it meant?

"How go your attempts to arrange a meeting with Goddess Ku'Shya?" Casvir asked.

Was this the test? Etolié prayed her lie was sound. "I hate to admit defeat, but it might be time to send that emissary. Ku'Shya made it clear to my momma that she wouldn't be mixing business and friendship." Etolié illusioned a wet sheen around her eyes, then sniffed for good measure. "Sorry. I just . . . I'm worried."

"I see."

Etolié kept up the ruse of dabbing her eyes until they reached Casvir's private office. Neither spoke until the door to his office shut. Casvir did not bother to sit at his desk, simply loomed above her. Etolié responded by levitating up to his height. "You have unique insights into magic," Casvir began.

"This is true."

"What do you know of blood magic?"

Etolié couldn't say if she'd studied for this quiz or not. "That it's demonic?"

Casvir pressed on with his questions like a battering ram. "What is the relevance of carving demonic sigils out of a victim's skin?"

Etolié winced at the mere thought. "Ew, first of all. But . . . I know there's power in having a physical symbol of your chosen deity for particular rituals, demon or angel."

"What if there were multiple symbols?"

"I feel like there's a story here I should know."

"This morning there was an incident involving a witch carving a demonic symbol in two separate victims' backs. The witch's corpse was questioned but only repeated the same explanation over and over—that she followed orders with no clear cause. Another victim was discovered well after the time of her disposal."

Given it was so much more convenient to just have a wooden carving, there must've been some relevance to flesh or blood. "That's extremely disgusting, but I'll add it to my list of things to research."

"I am consulting experts. I only wished to know if you had insight."

Etolié would still be researching. "What was the symbol?"

"We do not know."

"Can I see it?"

For all Casvir's stoicism, he was oddly easy to read today. Behind his aloof aura, he glared. "Fine. Follow me."

Shocked, Etolié nearly forgot her legs as Casvir marched into the hall. She stumbled to keep up, his relentless pace akin to moving into battle. Casvir wasn't nearly as tall as Khastra, but Khastra had always politely slowed to match Etolié's usual moseying. Not so with him, and Etolié fought to hide the fact that she was nearly jogging when he withdrew a ring of keys from a crevice in his armor. The door he unlocked was as utilitarian as the rest down the hall, but when he motioned inside, Etolié was met with cold.

Gone was the grandiose main hallway. Instead, Etolié walked into a stone prison, dimly lit by crystal sconces. "I see where you focused your decorating budget," she muttered, but Casvir ignored her, instead marching past without a word.

They had taken two turns before Etolié thought to count steps—or even pay attention, for that matter—but despite Casvir's novel of flaws, he wouldn't leave her here to die with twenty-three years left on her contract. Five more turns, through several dark corridors, and finally they entered a morgue.

The stench of noxious chemicals burned her nose, and Etolié grimaced at the two De'Sindai corpses on their separate tables, each lying prone. Both were stripped naked, the causes of death unclear, but gaping wounds had been carved into their backs.

"The work is rough," Casvir said, lingering by the doorframe. "But it is clear that the same symbol was attempted both times."

Etolié illusioned a mask to protect her nose and mouth as she approached, grateful that they showed no signs of rot. Artistry had been attempted, albeit clumsily. A circle had been carved from both, but the details were murky. Indeed, the carvings matched, or attempted to, but while the various lines did appear to copy Demoni characters, Etolié suspected even fluent speakers would struggle to make sense of it. "Any idea what it says?"

"No. All we know is that what little we can decipher of the patterns does not match current Demoni conventions. We are seeking experts in ancient Demoni, but those are difficult to come by in this realm."

Etolié illusioned a drawing pad and pen, then attempted to find some meaning in the patterns. But aside from the circle, it was just a bunch of lines. "Dammit." Etolié dropped her supplies, which sparkled out of existence. "I truly don't know. I've never had a good grasp on Demoni."

"That is unfortunate." Casvir stared a few seconds too long for comfort, that level of eye contact making Etolié itch. "Shall we leave then?"

Etolié glared at the open wounds, wracking her brain for any recognition. Nothing. "You said there were three victims. Where is the third?"

"She survived, but she knows nothing."

Was there relevance in that too? Etolié felt so lost. "We might as well leave."

"Follow me." He paused, then added, "Do not tell Flowridia."

He said nothing more, simply walked away. Etolié would decide later if that were an order or suggestion.

"The potion held an extract of Avor Weed, which is most commonly used to induce labor when a mother is overdue, or abortions if she is early on."

Casvir delivered the news clinically as Etolié sat nigh. Flowridia felt nothing, simply looked to the morning sun through the window.

"There was no other poison. Other than the risk of premature birth, this was not a threat on your life. Only the child's."

While one assassination attempt should not be dismissed, two presented a clear danger—and a frightful pattern. "I assume you don't know who hired him?"

"He has said all he claims to know—that his employer was a woman keen to hide her identity. The first assassin revealed something similar."

"You were able to question him?"

"It was difficult, given he could not write as well as speak, but there are methods. In the meantime, any new doctors will be personally introduced to you by me from now until you're well again. You will also not leave this room without an escort, nor be left alone without a guard at the door. Am I clear?"

Flowridia nodded, too exhausted to argue. She would lose anyway.

"There is a separate matter to discuss, and that is your interest in the Soul Speaker."

In all the stress, Flowridia had forgotten entirely. "I would like to see it."

It was foolish, but Flowridia sought to understand this broken path she'd taken. Casvir helped her to rise, but she dismissed his aid to walk.

In the hall, Casvir soon took a turn she had not traversed before, leading to a door so plain she would have overlooked it left on her own. He held it open, and she entered a domain eerily alike to the main area, yet utterly sparse. No decoration. More of a dungeon. Flowridia felt the shift in energy as they traversed toward the dark, for the light had dimmed as well. The hidden recesses of the castle seemed limitless, both in their depth and their depravity.

Flowridia stayed near enough to risk tripping over his armor, lest she be lost in this new labyrinth. The eerie silence was far worse than sound. Their footsteps echoed far too long. She ingrained the turns to memory, however, and noted the number on the door when Casvir finally stopped. Dust wafted from the doorframe as he pushed, the old wood creaking as she entered.

Inside was a plain stone chamber, no windows or second door. A small box sat in the center, decorated in sigils she could not make out in the limited light.

Casvir touched a crystal on the wall, and the room filled with soft, white light. "It is a simple process. First, you must offer a small sacrifice of blood, though it does not have to be your own. Place a drop on the top and visualize your target. Speak their name and wait. If the box ceases to glow, you will know they rejected your invitation."

Flowridia took tentative steps forward, apprehensive at what could come. "I really can call anyone?"

"Anyone who could be called by traditional necromancy, though bear in mind the inherent cruelty of disrupting their afterlife. This is not something to use without cause."

Nearer now, the runes upon the box were nothing Flowridia recognized. The simple design surely deceived the power it held. Casvir wouldn't hoard something without merit. "Where did you get this?"

"This was an offering from a small settlement of De'Sindai in Zauleen, one of the rare remaining few on that continent. It is elven in origin, said to belong to ancient priestesses of the Goddess of Chaos." Casvir offered a dagger. "Shall I leave you alone? I will stand outside."

"Yes. Thank you."

Casvir left, and Flowridia was left with daunting silence once more.

The echoing refrain of Odessa's death paled to her usual nightmares, though it did not mean she wasn't filled with disgust to recall her vomiting blood and her ominous final words: *"I feel nothing."* But Odessa's true omen was her life and its legacy, and Flowridia felt faint as she contemplated what she must do.

But did she want to meet Odessa? Assuredly not. Her heart knew precisely who her soul craved to meet again, at least one final time. There were others, yes, but one brought her to tears to think of his cruel end. Surely he hated her, yet he had loved her until the end . . .

But no. She was here to speak to Mother. Flowridia pierced the calloused flesh of her finger and touched the box, grasping the image of Odessa in her mind. But she failed to speak the name, her turbulent emotions rising to choke her. The spell had been set, awaiting her word, and Flowridia, panicking, sought for any name to replace it—

"Thalmus," she whispered, and the box glowed a ghostly blue.

A large part of her hoped he would not come. It was cruel, as Casvir had said, and Thalmus deserved to rest.

Oh gods, this was a mistake. But before she could run to the door and ask how to reverse it, a figment rose from the cracks in the box.

It had been a few years, yet he was precisely as her memory might've painted him—but with no bruising or injury. He was not a cursed ghost, doomed to linger and retain whatever appearance he had at his death. The longer she looked, the more she realized how much younger he was, lacking the workworn lines of his face, his hardened skin. Though his exterior remained rough, this was a man in his prime, bearing no scars. Perfect, in the way Ayla was perfect, yet nothing unnatural about it.

Thalmus' dark eyes sparkled as he smiled. "Hello, Flower Girl."

His voice sent her back in time, the name reminiscent of an era where her life had been simple, peaceful, charmed. Tears welled in her eyes, for against all odds, there was love here. "Hi, Thalmus. I'm surprised you came."

"Why?"

"You despise anything to do with death magic."

"I can't imagine you would call for me without a good cause."

She nearly laughed; it came as a scoffing, pained sound instead. "I don't know about that. I . . ." Her words trailed away, her heart aching at the familiarity of his presence. She missed his woodsy smell, the crackling of fire that forever permeated his workshop, but his voice and smile were enough. "I don't entirely know what to say, except that I'm . . ."

Dying. But she did not say that. "Thalmus, I'm pregnant."

His smile softened. "Is this good news?"

A condemning question, but she knew he meant it with love. "Yes. It was planned."

"Then that's wonderful. Congratulations."

Flowridia's hand fell to her stomach, the firm weight within a comfort despite her failing health. "I met you at the lowest moment in my life." She swallowed the forming lump in her throat. "Until now. I only have a limited amount of time to speak to you, but I'm desperate to make sense of it. You were the first to tell me I was on a dark path, and you'll be disappointed to know I never strayed. Though perhaps that's not a stretch, after what I did to you. I had no choice, but . . ."

His eyes misted, though ghosts could not truly cry. "Perhaps not in the moment. But surely you understand how that's where that same dark path led."

The words rang true, for it would be her legacy: a woman who skipped down a gilded path to hell, and somehow never saw it coming. "I don't know how to turn back." Or if she wanted to, but she did not say those words.

Yet it highlighted a painful truth: that fear had brought her here. Not resolve.

"I don't think that's a question I can answer either."

"Then answer me a different one," she pled, for any second now, he could fade. "The world stole everything from you, yet you are the kindest man who ever walked it. How?"

Thalmus became thoughtful, his attention on some far off place. "Acceptance," he finally said. "Justice is a man-made concept—or demonic, depending on your origin. Fairness is not a guarantee in life. Some of us are born into wealth; others into shackles. And some die just the same. My life became my own when

I stopped waiting for someone else to save it. My daughter's death gave me that push, but mourning her is what helped me to heal. I accepted what I could not control and made the best of it."

Sweet Kedira—named for the sun. "Have you seen her?"

"She was the first one I found." Such softness in his countenance. Flowridia cried to see it. "Flowra, I have always worried for you. I always will. Acceptance led me to meeting you, and while I was not your father, you were a daughter to me." He frowned, looking down at the box. "I feel disconnected."

"I suspect it's about to release you." Flowridia stood, nowhere near able to face him, but despite the foolishness of it, she embraced his ghostly form, shoving aside the prickly sensation of cold. He held no substance, but he remained real. "There's no restitution I can give you. I . . . I'm sorry, Thalmus."

That cold covered her back. "The greatest gift you can give me is to raise your child in love."

Though the touch was merely surface, a chill sank into her bones. "I love you."

"And I love you, Flower Girl."

His light faded. Flowridia felt nothing, her arms falling around herself instead.

Comfort came as a gentle push inside her. Flowridia set her hand upon her womb, tears filling her eyes in tandem with inspiration so strong, it was nearly akin to knowledge.

To her beloved spark, never meant to be hers, she whispered, "Hello, sweet Kedira. Or perhaps Thalmus. We shall simply have to wait and see."

Her contract said nothing about names. Perhaps one legacy could live on.

CHAPTER 25

Current era . . .

"Flowers! Look who's back!"

Etolié's announcement was unnecessary, given Flowridia was immediately swept into Sora's hug. Casvir loomed behind, her escort back to her medical suite. Her sister's strong arms were a blessing after the vacant embrace from a ghost, though she did smell strongly of seawater. "How did it go?"

"We succeeded." Sora pulled back, her joy marred by . . . something. Flowridia feared it was her own haggard appearance. Lately, she looked as awful as she felt. "Onias pledged. We're here to ask Etolié . . ." Only then did Sora seem to notice Casvir, straightening her stance before giving a deep bow. "M-My apologies. Greetings, Imperator Casvir."

"Your quest is fascinating," Casvir replied, though his tone did not reflect that. "Where is the Goddess of Chaos? I would be intrigued to meet with her."

"She chose to remain in the city."

"Extend to her my formal invitation. Perhaps I could be convinced to pledge."

"I will inform her, Imperator."

Casvir left. Flowridia's breath caught, one mystery remaining. "Where's Ayla?"

Sora gestured toward the couches—and there she sat. She held neither a smile nor malice; Ayla's expression and heart remained well-guarded.

Flowridia longed to run to her, her yearning rising even to drown her guilt. Instead, she held Sora's gaze as she asked, "What were you saying about Etolié?"

"We only have one god left to face," Sora replied, "and Etolié is the best hope we have to convince Ku'Shya."

"I'll make it clear that we gotta be quick," Etolié said. "If you die while I'm gone, Casvir will make soup out of my entrails."

"So Ayla will be watching over me?" Flowridia asked.

"I would assume—"

"No, actually." Sora hesitated to speak the rest, and whatever Etolié's comedic confusion, Flowridia's heart threatened to split in twain. "She's invaluable. Greater good, you know?"

Flowridia didn't know, only that this made no sense. She nodded. Ayla remained indecipherable.

Etolié's incredulity broke the tension. "I mean, she might be a liability given she fucking murdered Ku'Shya's daughter."

"She's going to disguise herself," Sora replied.

"I'm going to just assume you have a stellar reason for that and leave while I pray to Momma for help, given how goddamn rancid the energy here is. Whatever it is, I don't want to know."

Etolié skipped drunkenly into the nurse's station.

When Flowridia tried to step toward the couches, Sora became a wall between them. "I don't know if she's ready for you."

Flowridia bristled at the remark, resisting the urge to shove her aside—or try, rather. "She's my wife."

"And I won't pretend to know precisely what happened between you two, but it's been a rough journey for her."

Nothing in it made any sense. "Since when would you defend her?"

"We've set our pasts aside . . ."

Sora's words faded to the dark presence beside her. "We can speak," Ayla said, nothing to read at all in her countenance.

Flowridia flinched as Sora left, swearing she faced a stranger. But her anger quelled to be left alone with the woman she loved— who she had wounded irrevocably. Yet, what was there to say? An apology was hollow when the wounds were so raw. Flowridia still sifted through the scattered pieces, but Ayla was here now, ready or not.

"Etolié told me there was an attempt on your life last night," Ayla said, muted and hollow. "I am sorry I wasn't there."

"Etolié's the one who saved my life again." Flowridia said nothing more. Her greatest anguish would be for Ayla to have hoped he succeeded. "You've made amends with Sora?"

"I suppose I have."

"That's wonderful." Flowridia forced her smile, waiting for the floor to drop. "I don't know how much time we have—"

"I doubt much."

Gods, all she had done was cry these past few days. Flowridia swallowed back the tears prickling her eyes, forcing herself to calm. "I won't give my apology yet, because I'm still searching to understand why this happened. But I'm trying. I've started speaking to the priestess again. What I said to you was awful, and I'm working to make sure I never treat you like that again. So if you can give me a chance . . ." Her words disappeared as she suppressed a sob. She would not cry in front of Ayla, no. She would not compel Ayla to comfort her today.

Ayla's own tears welled, stubbornly refusing to fall. "We can speak when I get back."

Flowridia nodded, unease making her nauseous.

Of course, Etolié burst back in then. "All right, I've got Momma ready to—" Etolié clamped her mouth shut, forever more intuitive than she let on. "Do you two need some time?"

"We have discussed what we need to for now," Ayla replied, her graceful turn evading any hope Flowridia had of touching her. "Come along, Starspawn. Sora is waiting."

Ayla left. Etolié lingered at the door. "It won't be long. I've instructed one of the nurses to keep you company." She glanced out the door, her hesitation rising. "Are you all right?"

"Go save the world, Etolié," Flowridia whispered.

Etolié's regret slowed her exit, but leave she did.

Flowridia shuffled to the bed, her prison and comfort both. Beneath the sheets, she buried her ailing self and wondered how assured her ending truly was.

Soliel had spoken all along of her death. The writing was on the wall, had been for months. Somehow, it was not her deepest fear anymore.

. . . And she was to simply lie here and take it?

Emboldened, she burst from the cocoon of covers. "Nurse!"

A woman rushed inside, worry on her features. "What's wrong?"

"What is the state of the garden?"

"As well as it can be so early in spring."

"Can you fetch me a rose? It must be quick."

"I will try my best, Lady Flowridia—"

"But a pink one." Flowridia sifted through her knowledge of flowers, all she had learned of the language they spoke. "It must be pink. I need a few other flowers too, actually. I'll write them down."

Flowridia cautiously stood, head spinning even as the nurse came to steady her. She gripped the bedpost, breathing through the vertigo, then went to her desk and withdrew a fresh sheet of parchment and the inkwell.

Ayla would return soon. Flowridia vowed to be ready.

Call me when you need me again, Starshine.
Thank the powers that be for Momma.

For simplicity, Etolié had requested she and her party be placed in the mortal realm, but that didn't make her headache any easier as she stared into the portal to *Daemenacht.* Gozrith Jungle had been a cursed place since the Convergence, populated until just a few weeks ago by the belligerent Whispering Elves, and the cause was clear—a gaping, nausea-inducing hole between planes. It consumed all light, this portal of pure shadow, and Etolié gave up all dignity and puked at the feet of the Goddess of Chaos.

Chaos burned with silver flame. Wonder filled her words. "Our quest for the demonic pledges is nearly complete. I can hardly believe it."

"What comes next?" Sora asked.

"We protect the final orb and await my first breath upon the mortal realm."

Etolié groaned as she spat lingering bile onto the lush jungle floor. "You can just say 'born' like the rest of us."

She regretted the words, however, hoping Chaos' silence wasn't an omen. 'Born' implied a smooth exit from the womb. Sora didn't know how dire Flowers' condition was, nor did she need to so close to the end.

And of course, Ayla didn't say anything. The woman radiated gloom, and Etolié feared there was trouble in paradise. "How long will that be?"

"Difficult to say," Chaos replied, which wasn't quite a lie. "But soon."

"Is it something you can feel?"

"In a way. I received a surge of power at my conception, which is an uncomfortable realization given what it means about my parents, but I digress. My power has slowly grown since, but if Soliel's experience mirrors mine, I'll have the power to regenerate my body once I'm born, instead of wearing this puppet."

"And then we pray the power is enough?" Ayla's smile held no joy, merely resignation. "Where is the final orb?"

"Well, these two geniuses gave it to Murishani," Etolié said. "Which . . . was actually a good plan. I told him to take it to Nox'Kartha, so I would assume with Casvir."

"Not the most creative solution."

"I'm open to alternatives."

"We can discuss it once we've won." Ayla shut her eyes, focus rising as her form shifted, a glamour forming over her undead self. She resembled no one, just an elf on an adventure with a Goddess. "No sense in wasting time."

Ayla stepped first through the ominous portal. Chaos next, then Sora. Etolié braced her stomach, unenthused about puking for a second time.

. . . Yet she met a gentle landing, hardly a leap at all.

Etolié recognized the terrain of Ku'Shya's Realm, the vibrant, warm hues contrasting to a purple sky. No celestial bodies, but oppressive heat, and already beads of sweat pooled from her pores. They faced a massive canyon, yet behind, the portal had vanished. "I've never seen her front door."

"It's quite the sight," Sora replied, and she beckoned them onward. "Last time I saw her was the time Mereen, um, stole the staff, so please help me not get eaten."

"You could just wait outside."

"I've come this far."

Etolié rolled her eyes and practically spat the spell. Sora also gained a glamour, appearing as boring as Ayla. "Don't be stupid."

They went on their way, soon standing before Goddess Ku'Shya, imposing on her throne of bones.

Really, Etolié was the last to judge her strange nest, even if the bones were excessive. And while Ku'Shya could not quite smile, a shift did occur in her draconic countenance. "Etolié! I am not expecting guests. Not Silver Fire guests."

Kah'Sheen sat nearby, her joy conveyed by revealing her many sharp teeth.

"Well, Mother, I have some exciting ones." Etolié gave a dramatic flourish toward Chaos, who kept a regal stance. "Perhaps you've heard. This is the Goddess of Chaos."

"Yes, yes—she is in the city holding my Khastra hostage."

Oh. Right. "Well, that wasn't her idea. In fact, she wants to stop the one who did think of it. I'll let her explain."

Chaos' figure expanded. Not enough to match the great War Goddess but nearer enough to face her. "Goddess Ku'Shya, I'm honored to stand in your presence. I will be brief, lest I waste your time—it is my quest to stop the God of Order from separating the worlds. He wields five orbs, but if I can gain the pledges of the New Gods, I may still hold the power to stop him when the time comes. I gathered the favor of all the angelic gods, and your noble rivals— Izthuni and Onias. If you pledge your power to me, I swear it will be used in the quest to save Sha'Demoni from destruction."

Ku'Shya did not immediately speak, her many eyes falling upon Etolié instead. "You are speaking for this . . . Old Goddess?"

"She's the real deal, signed and certified."

"If there is any favor I can provide in exchange for your pledge," Chaos said, "I am willing to discuss."

Again, Ku'Shya contemplated her answer. Behind her, those crystal weapons glittered before Chaos' silver light. "What are you doing to stop the God of Order?"

Etolié's nerves rose at the sudden shift of energy in the room, Chaos' stance becoming more . . . casual. "I'm gonna rip his fucking face off."

Ah, so she was choosing violence. Etolié glanced to the illusioned Sora, who looked fully prepared to tackle the twenty-foot-tall Goddess.

Yet from the massive demon goddess came... laughter. A horrible bray, far more akin to a donkey than a mortal, but unquestionable in its amusement. "I am wondering myself why no one else is thinking of removing his head. His face is good enough."

"I would get to his head, but I'd unwind his entrails," Chaos continued, to which Etolié's jaw dropped. "Strangle him first, then behead him."

Ku'Shya positively heaved with laughter, discussions of violence apparently the pinnacle of humor. "It is funny to imagine strangling a God. I am liking you, Goddess of Chaos. You have my favor. You have my assistance, if you are calling." Ku'Shya crossed her arm across her exoskeletal torso, bowing as low as her arachnoid form could manage. "I am pledging my power to you, Goddess of Chaos. Slay the God of Order in my name."

"Goddess Ku'Shya, that is the least I can do. Thank you."

Etolié supposed she should have felt triumph, given it was technically a wondrous moment. "Thanks, Demon Mother. I need to take these three back to Nox'Kartha, but afterward, could I come back to—"

Kah'Sheen skittered forward, overly enthused. "Etolié, I can escort them."

"Across the sea?" Etolié would have fought, but given Kah'Sheen's insistent nod... perhaps Khastra had something important to say. "Sure, I'd appreciate that."

"What is it you are wanting?" Ku'Shya asked, and while not unwelcome, her genuine confusion left Etolié unsettled.

"Let's wave my friends off first. Bye, friends!"

Was it suspicious? Assuredly, but none of them would interrogate her with the gargantuan demon goddess in their presence. Sora would be safe with Kah'Sheen, and so Etolié let her illusion fade once Ku'Shya had turned aside.

Once gone, Etolié spoke softly. "My visit was cut a bit short last time. I was hoping to visit Khastra."

"I see. That is unfortunate. She is not here."

The idea was... so very strange, because while Etolié had spent quite some time trekking through Sha'Demoni some months ago, somehow imagining Khastra with a purpose in the land she was fucking born in was difficult. "Oh. Where is she?"

"It is her business. But I am telling her you are coming, yes?"

"If you wouldn't mind. Or, could I wait for her?"

"You can wait. But I am not knowing for how long."

Nothing in it was suspicious. There was no reason to be concerned because Khastra was a grown woman with a new chance at freedom—undead but belonging to her own self—so of course she would go out and visit the world, and of course she didn't owe Etolié her whereabouts, especially when they didn't currently live in the same realm, so why, oh *why* did Etolié's gut twist and churn?

Ku'Shya's stare was not purposefully imposing, but the lingering silence set Etolié ill at ease. "Actually . . ." Etolié's common sense started tingling, the twisting in her gut making her ill. She wasn't sure why she was giggling, but she sure couldn't fucking stop. But Ku'Shya stared expectantly, and who was a better expert than an ancient demon? "Have you ever seen something like this before?" Bless her fifty years of experience. Etolié conjured a perfect re-creation of what she'd seen carved from the two De'Sindai backs, albeit as simply dark lines in the air.

To her surprise . . . Ku'Shya laughed. "You are so funny, Etolié. Like your mother. But you are not inheriting her art skills, it seems."

Why . . . Why was this funny? Etolié studied her apparently piss-poor re-creation, seeking any accidental phallic imagery—or whatever made demons laugh—when Ku'Shya resumed her path, apparently finding the question too funny to answer.

"Not to, uh, ruin the joke by asking you to explain it, but why is that funny?"

Ku'Shya stopped once more, her monstrous face indecipherable. "Because it means Khastra. Bringer of War."

Etolié surely hoped that demons sucked at interpreting Celestial faces as much as she sucked at interpreting theirs—she had no time to illusion away her shock. "Oh. Right. Silly me, forgetting my own wife."

Khastra? What . . . What did that mean?

"You know what, Mother," Etolié said. "I forgot I left something in the oven. I actually have to go back."

"Oh. Next time then."

Ku'Shya seemed jovial enough. If she realized Etolié had fallen into an existential crisis, she gave no indication. Nor did it seem her question was suspicious—thank Goddess Momma for that.

"Can I see Khastra's room first though? I'd like to leave her a message. Then I can see myself out."

"You may. You are knowing the path, yes?"

She did, and at the affirmation saw herself off, relieved to be away from the Goddess of War. Ku'Shya was not a danger, but Etolié didn't trust her own tongue anymore.

The symbol was . . . *meant* . . . Khastra?

Khastra's room remained the same, even showed small signs of living. Uncut gems on her workshop table, the bed imperfectly made, trousers left on the floor . . .

Etolié quickly riffled through the desk drawers, soon finding parchment. She illusioned a quill, then scrawled a quick message in Solviran:

To my favorite Beefcake,

I have a dilemma. Let me know when we can meet.

"I am thinking it is you, Sora. Etolié is saying you are with Goddess Chaos."

Thus was Kah'Sheen's whisper as they hiked out of the massive canyon.

Relief filled Sora. "We weren't sure how your mother felt about me."

"Very bad. It is wise to make a disguise." Her daunting gaze fell upon the illusioned Ayla, hesitation in her girlish tone. "And you are . . . Endless Night."

Only then did Sora recall that the last time Ayla had seen Kah'Sheen they had been in battle in the Mountains of Kaas. Ayla's disguised form stilled, then faded away, revealing a bristling woman. "Yet you came anyway?"

"I am having reasons. You are lucky you are here with Goddess Chaos. Mother is not smelling you, but I am smelling you now. Silver Fire and vampire."

A sardonic smile twisted Ayla's lip. "Of course. Your sister could smell it too."

Kah'Sheen gave a nervous glance to the cave, quickly ushering them along. Her voice lowered. "You are seeking pledges from gods, yes?"

"Yes," Sora said, a swelling of pride filling her chest. "And I actually feel like we have a chance now. We've done it. We have the pledge of every god, both demon and angel.

Kah'Sheen's many hands grasped each other. "But is it . . . every angel?"

Sora nodded, uncertain of Kah'Sheen's hesitation.

Hardly audible, Kah'Sheen uttered a single, damning word. ". . . No."

Something devious fell upon Ayla's countenance. "Oh, Kah'Sheen, I do hope you aren't teasing."

Kah'Sheen shook her head, immutable guilt in the gesture. "I am doing this for Sha'Demoni. Mother is not needing to know."

"But you know." Such glee in Ayla's chuckle. "You *know*."

"Of course you know," Chaos muttered, her own wicked chuckle joining the throng.

Sora raised a hand. "Know what?"

"The location of the God of Death's prison," Chaos said. "She's going to take us to Ilune."

Shock snapped Sora's mouth shut.

"Very bad idea," Kah'Sheen muttered. "But I will take you now."

"B-But—" Sora's mind raced past a hundred thousand things, managing to land on the precise memory she sought. "You said only Sol Kareena and Ku'Shya knew."

"Yes! And I am lying. Are you never lying? I am not supposed to be knowing, but I am young when the prison is built, and Mother is not lowering her voice in my presence to speak of it. She is even taking me there for the final inspections."

Sora released a steadying breath. If Sora had learned nothing else in the last few weeks, it was that Ilune's legacy was . . . *complicated*. "She's been there a thousand years. Would she care enough about the world?"

"I do not know. But if the worlds are separated, even she is dead." Kah'Sheen frowned. "Well, not dead. She is a lich. But if the worlds are separated and her phylactery is destroyed, then she is dead."

"I am greatly in favor of trying," Ayla said, though held up a finger when Kah'Sheen whirled around. "I have nothing to gain by spreading the news. Her prison shall remain a secret."

"Agreed," Sora said, though her unease remained. "Take us to the God of Death."

PART FIVE
DEATH

CHAPTER 26

Fifteen years after the end of the world . . .

In the shade, Dira lethargically bid the flowers to grow and entangle her.

She sighed as they tangled around her body, creating a cocoon of sorts—or perhaps a coffin.

Fitting, given she was going to die here, having never seen the world.

Why so dramatic?

She cleared the mask of flowers from her face, staring into the golden eyes of Demitri. "Nothing really matters, does it? I'll never prove to Mother than I'm old enough to see the world."

Probably not.

"It's just not fair!" Dira tore flowers from their stems as she wrenched herself free of her floral prison, seething anew. When she stood, she hadn't a hope of facing Demitri eye to eye. The wolf forever towered over her.

The flower trick was neat.

"It's the only thing I can do. I'm useless."

The Silver Fire isn't useless.

Frustration welled as she tried and failed to summon a spark. It fizzled and died in her hand. "I'm useless though."

Everyone is useless at first. You should've seen Mom when she first started raising the dead. Somehow, his eyes narrowed. *Stupid fox.*

Dira perked up, the acknowledgment of her other parent treasured and rare. "What fox?"

She raised a fox cub, but only one. It was stupid. Stupid Ana.

"But Mom raised it?"

Yes, and it had no brains at all. Apparently it had a soul. That's what stupid-head Casvir said. But what does he know. I think it was more like a plant.

Disregarding the childish insult, Dira withheld a gasp at that surely forbidden slip. She forced her voice to remain nonchalant. "What else did Casvir say?"

Not much. He was just proud of Mom for trying.

"But he was a 'stupid-head'?"

He smelled gross. Most undead do. Not Lady Ayla though. She smells like battle.

"Battle?"

Yes, like charging into battle. That's what she smells like.

Again, Dira eased in as cautiously as she was able. "Casvir is undead?"

Demitri couldn't glower. But dammit all—she felt it as acutely as the sweat on her skin. *I think I said too many things.*

"Says who?" Dira asked, but she feared she already knew.

Lady Ayla.

Fury seared through Dira's blood. She stood, lest she burn Demitri alive. "You want to know what fucking sucks? The fact that Mother controls every damn piece of my life!"

I don't think that's true—

"Even you! You're just here to control me too!"

Not control. Just watch and protect.

"What if I don't need any protection!? If this 'Casvir' was friends with mom, was he really so awful?"

Well, he's the reason mom is dead, so I would say yes.

"'Lady Ayla' says he's the reason I was even born," Dira replied, mockery in the words. "To fulfill some stupid bargain. Perhaps I should thank him for living!"

You're being stupid, and you know it.

"Do I!? *I don't know anything!* Who is Casvir, really? What is this war?! Who is Soliel, and why does Mother—"

Wait, do you know Soliel?

"YOU KNOW SOLIEL?!" Dira screamed into her arm, furious as angry tears prickled in her eyes.

I thought he was dead.

"CLEARLY NOT!" Gods, Demitri's reactions boiled her blood, his nonchalance utterly infuriating. "Do you know what The Endless Night is?"

Lady Ayla said I had to say no—

"Are you fucking kidding me!?" At Dira's cry, there came a blast of blight.

Pain and weakness flooded her. From her body expelled a fog of purple. Grass shriveled; trees wilted; birds ceased their song as even the sky darkened. Only Demitri remained untouched, watching curiously as the fog rolled harmlessly over him, dissipating into the air.

Dira stumbled back, screaming. Desiccated grass stabbed her bare feet, providing no cushion as she fell to her knees. "What was that?!"

A distant voice called. "Dira!"

"I'm here!" Dira cried, her tears falling fast as Sora tore from the manor's walls. She ran fearlessly into the blight, immediately helping Dira up.

Sora went about inspecting her head. "What happened?"

Dira's lip trembled as she plodded through her story, quick as it was. As she spoke, Sora studied the withered remains of plants. "And you've never done anything like this before?"

Dira shook her head.

"I'd wondered when your necromancy would manifest," Sora replied. "It seems drama runs in your bloodline."

Dira hugged her tight, clinging lest she wither away too. "Did my mom ever do something like this?"

"She learned to control it, but yes. I never saw it personally, but she mentioned it once or twice."

I saw it.

Dira's attention darted to her wolf companion, lounging without a care in the world upon the blight. "Really?"

Well, the aftermath. She screamed and killed a lot of trees. Mom was scary when she was mad.

"Is that why I can do it too? Because you were mom's familiar?"

That seems logical.

"Looks like Demitri has something to say about it," Sora said, approval in the words. She released her, then coaxed her to sit.

"What if I hurt someone though? I didn't mean to do it."

"You'll have to learn to control it. You had to learn to control the Silver Fire, right?"

Dira nodded, managing to coax a bit of flame to cover her hand. "Mother and Etolié taught me. Is there anyone who could teach me necromancy?"

Judging by Sora's sudden forced composure, Dira had certainly stumbled onto something. "Um. Perhaps. You'd have to ask your mother."

"You always say that."

"This time, I actually mean it."

Current era . . .

"You're, uh, really planning a spectacle, aren't ya. Need help tying that thing?"

Flowridia wouldn't have called it a spectacle. Had she her magic, perhaps. Instead, she wrapped the finishing touches on a bouquet—or tried to, that is. Servants had been sent to the market to fetch her preferred pieces. Other witches held magic to enhance plants, even through the cold winter.

A few pink roses for love, for happiness, for gratitude. Flowridia plucked a few petals from a spare to scatter onto the bedside table. Presentation was half the present, sometimes.

Lilies could be purity or death, but moonlilies had always held a special place in Flowridia's heart for their color. Ayla now had silver eyes, but that cherished blue still remained in her memory. One for a centerpiece, the largest in the bunch.

But the bulk of it, a whole dozen, were tulips, pure white. Ayla deserved a field, but this was all she could do. A plea for forgiveness, a second chance.

Flowridia tied the ribbon for the third time, willing the bow to stay symmetrical. Her maimed hand was acting well enough today. At least she could use her thumb for stability. "No, I'm fine."

Etolié plopped on the corner of the bed, her hesitation painfully clear. "Look at you, doing something nice for someone you love."

No question that Etolié was trying to lead to something, that something surely to do with, as Etolié would call it, the 'rancid' energy between her and her love. Deterring her would hopefully be simple. "You haven't mentioned Khastra in a while."

"That's because your perceptive ass knows too much as it is."

Content enough with her bow, Flowridia set the bouquet into a designated vase and placed it in the center of the pink rose petals. Simple, yes, at least compared to others she'd assembled, but poignant.

"So what's going on with you and Ayla?"

Flowridia bristled at the question. "Who's the perceptive ass now?"

"Excuse me, I never said you were the only one. If I can help—"

"You can't."

Etolié held up defensive hands. "Whatever you say."

"Why do you even care?" Flowridia spat. "You hate Ayla. I suspect you still hate me. So what does our marriage matter to you?"

"Tone down the bite, Flowers. Fact is, I get hives from witnessing other people argue, and I don't know what the fuck I walked in on between you two, but it was nasty."

"Things were said that shouldn't have been said. Can I leave it at that?"

"You can leave it wherever the fuck you want."

Though anger itched beneath her skin, a different pressure rose deeper still, threatening to burst. Flowridia managed calmer words. "Hypothetically, would you marry Khastra?"

"Hypothetically, I would."

And though Etolié was an actress, though her tone gave nothing away, Flowridia was not an actress—not today. "Did you get married?"

"No." Etolié returned to the stacks of documents, though muttered a soft, "It's just been discussed in a positive fashion."

"Congratulations, for whatever it's worth." Gods, Flowridia hated to even come near the subject, but Casvir's words remained haunting. Immortals never wed for life, yet was Etolié not among them? "Do you think you'll be with her forever?"

No hesitation. "Yes. Well . . . assuming she wants me around, but I'm not going anywhere. She's one of the few things I believe in in this fucked up world. I'm no oracle, but I am a stubborn bitch. Left up to me, it's forever or death."

Something different rose to suffocate that brewing rage, a new sort of infuriating heat. Yet she feared to name it, lest it puncture more holes in this sinking ship. "Have you ever doubted?"

"I mean, she pisses me off sometimes. You can take the lady out of Sha'Demoni, but you can't take Sha'Demoni out of the lady, and Demoni Law is full of shit sometimes. But doubted? Before we were officially together, perhaps, but after? Fuck, no."

Flowridia had been drowning in doubts in the beginning, tormented, for lack of a better word, by Ayla's games. But there had been a switch, wherein Ayla had sobbed an apology, revealed her heart, and begged Flowridia to send her away . . .

Flowridia had not. And Ayla's tearful reply had been the crux for change: *"I will live every day of my eternal life proving myself."*

Perhaps that was their true beginning.

And so jealousy permeated her bitter form, because Flowridia, forever discontent, drowned in that sea of doubt anew.

Etolié's hand waved in front of her face, sending her back into the present. "You all right, Flowers? You got all misty-eyed."

So she had. Flowridia dabbed her eyes with her sleeves. "Ayla's different."

"Different how?"

Ayla had insisted Flowridia not breathe a word to Casvir, but Etolié had never been mentioned. "I hardly know how to describe it, but . . ." Flowridia tried to lay back onto the bed, only to gasp as something pinched in her back. With care, she shifted to lean against the headboard instead. "I need to ramble, so please keep your comments to yourself until I'm done. The woman I married wasn't . . . this. Not this shell. Ayla was full of pride and joy. She had a life she loved to live for better or worse, and while I had to turn away from the screams in our basement, we were happy. She leaned on me, and I on her. She let me carry her heart, and I freely gave her mine. But now . . ." She swallowed her threatened tears. "You mustn't repeat this."

Etolié offered an affirming nod.

"She lost so much of herself in the Mountains of Kaas. The moments where we are happy are so beautiful, but more often than not, she's a stranger now. I'm trying to help her, but she's keeping secrets from me. I'm trying to love her, but she's not the same. She thinks she wants to bury The Endless Night, and I told her she can't. We can't escape who we are."

And to hear herself say it . . . again, came the image of Mother's face in the mirror, her own cursed reflection mocking her.

"I married a monster," Flowridia continued. "You don't need to tell me that. So what does it mean if I say I miss that monster? I miss the Ayla Darkleaf who was confident and alluring and even frightening at times. Our life wasn't perfect, but it was damn near, and now she's pulling away. I just . . . I don't understand."

Etolié said nothing, simply bit her lip. Flowridia realized she was waiting. "I'm done. You can speak."

"Flowers . . ." Etolié cringed, visibly mulling over whatever hurtful thing she tried to curtail. ". . . that sounds like depression."

"Well, if Ayla would accept help, we could fix it. I've done my part."

"Have you, though?" Etolié kept her grimace. "I don't mean to suggest that you talking to the priestess again is a failure, no. But you've been kinda screamy lately. Has it occurred to you that trauma isn't always simple?"

Flowridia sighed, remiss to admit Etolié was right. "I can give her time."

"See, that's not really the core of the issue though, is it. Flowers, we all change. Me, you, even Zoldar—we're not who we were when we met. But you've changed a little more than most. From spineless bookkeeper to 'sometimes mysteriously covered in blood.' And Ayla still fucking loves you. Bitch has her flaws, but she's devoted. So what will you do if Ayla is never the same again?"

Memories of the burned cathedral danced through her head, the vicious words she'd said . . . For all her regrets, she couldn't deny that she'd meant every word.

"I should give her a chance at least," Flowridia whispered, far more a whimper than words. "Even if we were doomed from the start."

"While I won't disagree, I suspect we aren't actually coming from the same premise."

Flowridia winced at the memory of Casvir's sentiment. "Immortals never love for life."

"The fuck? You're going to say that to the daughter of Staella? Neoma had one lover her entire life, who she kept for thousands of years. That bitch was committed. I'm not saying it's common, but that's some defeatist bullshit."

The reminder was rather sweet, but Flowridia could find no solace this day, even in truth. "It doesn't help that..." Curse her tears; all she did lately was scream and cry. "I hurt, Etolié. I hurt all the time. There are moments late at night where I wonder if it would be easier to just be dead. I'm trapped in this broken body, and every day I weaken more and more, feeling like the walls are closing in around me, and I..." Flowridia withheld a sob, for admitting the truth ached as badly as her pain. "I know there's an end, but... what if I really do die?"

To Flowridia's shock, there came a gentle touch on her arm. "I'm doing my damnedest to stop that," Etolié said.

Flowridia leaned against her unexpected friend. "I know. And I'm so grateful. I'm sorry I'm such a bitch."

"I can take a little bit of bitching, as long as you can take it back."

Flowridia managed to smile, even as she lifted her enfeebled hand and flinched when sparks of static shot up her arm when she flexed the remaining digits. "I've never actually asked if there's anything you can do about this."

Etolié shook her head. "I don't know how to heal things that are already healed."

Flowridia swallowed grief as she set her hand on her stomach. "What if I told you I want this baby? What if I told you that I'm the stupidest fucking person to walk this realm, thinking I could sell a soul and be at peace with it?"

"To be honest, I'd say you finally learned something for once in your goddamn life."

Despite the brutality of the remark, Flowridia gave a pitiful laugh. "And all it took was for me to destroy my marriage. But I have to do right by Lara. I have to get Demitri back."

"I mean, if you and Ayla do split up, I would bet big buckets of gold Casvir would be thrilled to have you stay and raise the baby."

A cruel irony, for all Ayla had feared might come to pass after all. Flowridia could stay, yes...

"You're pretty set on your marriage being over. Did something happen?"

Flowridia's head became light at the question. She struggled to breathe. "I can't say we had an argument. More that I screamed at her and she took every blow."

"I mean..." Etolié shrugged. "I've done similar things, and Khastra still loves me. Though in my defense, I'm thinking of the time she didn't tell me she wasn't quite dead, or the time she murdered the archbishop at Marielle's wedding—things like that."

Through her tears, Flowridia could do little more than stare. "Khastra murdered the archbishop?"

"Well, fuck me. Keep your mouth shut. My point is that couples fight, and it isn't the end of the world."

"Etolié, I don't think what you're describing is entirely healthy either."

Etolié had truly never appeared more murderous. "Yeah, well . . ." To Flowridia's surprise, Etolié shook her head. "Forget it. I'm not supposed to talk about it with you anyway."

"Talk about what?"

A knock sounded. Flowridia quickly blotted her eyes, gaze averted as she bid the visitor to enter.

Casvir stepped inside, difficult to read on the best of days, but something in his countenance seemed . . . tense. "Empress Etolié, I shall tell you the ending first, which is that casualties were minimal, and your friend, Zoldar, is safe. But there was an attack on your district in Solvira."

Etolié stood, poised to fight. "What? Who?"

"The God of Order."

All color left the Celestial's face. "The orb."

"My suspicion as well. But the orb remains safe."

"Thank fuck. Murishani did something right—" She stilled, intrigue raising her brow. "Is Murishani all right?"

"He is well."

"Damn. Oh, well. Go on."

"There is little else to report, except that he vanished when he did not find his quarry. I suspect he will come here next."

"That was my guess too. Where is the orb?"

"Safe, as I said." He turned to Flowridia. "This pertains to you because Murishani's home was destroyed in the attack. He has been confined to his quarters in the lower levels, but he is in the castle for the moment. Arrangements are being made, but you should be warned."

No, that was not comforting. But nothing about her was comfortable at the moment. "I understand. Thank you for telling me."

"Empress Etolié, your home sustained less damage. I have sent a party to assess the wreckage and report on necessary repairs. Is there anything that needs to be removed in the meantime?"

"Just Zoldar."

"He will be sent somewhere safe." To Flowridia, he said, "Forgive me, but you are clearly distressed. May I be of assistance?"

Urgency swelled in Flowridia's gut, but Etolié was here, and there were secrets Etolié simply didn't need to know. "The other day, we went to . . . I want to go back. Can you escort me?"

"That is fine. Though my warning still applies."

It was not something to abuse, no. Still, she forced her aching body to stand, content to leave the confused Etolié behind. "I understand."

Casvir walked to match her sluggish pace, each step setting undo pressure on her feet. Her head spun, though not enough to be worrisome. Even so, she kept near the wall, lest she fall.

"Would you benefit from a wheelchair?"

He asked so nonchalantly, yet the statement wounded her bruised pride. "I don't want to say yes."

"It is not a weakness to accept one's limitations."

Each day, she lost something new. "Fine, then. But not right now."

It took time, but soon enough they came across the nondescript door in the wall, entered the vacant hall, and finally the door leading to the Soul Speaker.

Casvir offered a knife. "I will wait here," he said, and Flowridia entered alone.

Cowardice had deterred her from her quest before. But Flowridia steeled herself, accepting a new sort of fear. As much as Odessa frightened her, it held not a candle to that face in the mirror.

Odessa was dead. Yet her legacy lived on in the tears Flowridia now evoked from others.

Flowridia nicked her finger with the knife, then placed the bloody appendage on the box, visualizing her hated target in her head—though the image melded cruelly with her own, a mirror in so many ways. "Odessa," she muttered, and the box glowed blue.

The light shifted. Flowridia scooted back as the spirit made no delay. There, floating above her, Odessa stared curiously around the room. "Well, this is unexpected."

"I'm surprised you answered," Flowridia said, for her heart already pounded just to hear her voice, breath becoming faint.

Odessa's scathing gaze fell upon her. Yet she lacked the gruesome reminders of her death, no knife in her throat, no blood on her dress. Precisely the same in all other ways, but at least a more peaceful appearance. "Then why did you call?"

What was an afterlife for someone with no god? Would anyone take someone so wicked? Or did she wander aimlessly in that vacant hell, lost and alone? "I can't believe I'm saying this, but I need . . . wisdom. A warning, perhaps."

With a mere flick of her eyebrow, Odessa became docile once more. "Go on."

"I'm pregnant," Flowridia said, and Odessa floated down to join her on the floor, though far away enough to keep her blood pressure from rising too high. "You don't seem surprised."

"I was only surprised when the rumors swirled about it because I knew there was no way your wife would let some man fuck you. It doesn't suit her character. So which is it, Flower Child? Did you leave her, or did you find a spell?"

Flowridia stiffened at the callous words. "We found a spell."

"Huh. Dhampir half-elf—that's a unique combination. It explains why you look two degrees from death, sweetheart."

Flowridia set a protective hand upon her womb, determined to not let this meeting go to waste. "I know it's cruel, but I have nothing to lose. I'm terrified of becoming you. You have nothing to lose by answering me, so if you please—what went wrong?"

Gods, Odessa's chuckle held all the malevolence of life, setting Flowridia's nerves on edge. Yet when it faded, there shone not a shadow of teasing, only pure, cold sobriety. "You know my history."

"I do."

"I've told you of my first daughter."

"You've mentioned having one."

"She was not my first pregnancy."

The lingering silence held a warning, yet Flowridia knew not what to make of it.

"Steel yourself. It's a gruesome tale," Odessa continued. Though incorporeal, her stare held enough substance to sear a hole through Flowridia's head. "I was raped by Prince Azrael of Solvira. I absorbed Rulan's spirit and destroyed him and his party. But fate is cruel. I never told you I fell pregnant because of it. I never told anyone. A horrible affair—Silver Fire pregnancies are notoriously dangerous . . ." Her gaze narrowed. "Ayla has Silver Fire."

Flowridia said nothing, merely nodded.

"I never became quite as ravaged as you, but I did suffer. My powers grew, as did the life in my womb, even as my own life drained away. I fell into labor prematurely, and at seven and a half months, my body expelled it. A tiny, fragile little thing. It cried, full of life despite being so early. I soothed it. I fed it from my breast. I felt nothing except panic, but then it showed me its eyes—stark silver. I saw only its father.

"All that rage returned. I slit its stomach and let it wail until it bled out."

At the cusp of consciousness, there remained the lingering scream of Flowridia's brother barely born, murdered mere minutes after coming into the world. Her breath seized at the awful words, for they seemed more biting than ever before. "Are you trying to torment me?"

"Assuredly, but there is a lesson. My answer to you is *rage*."

The word echoed like an omen in her head.

"Rage is what blinds us in those twisted, defining moments," Odessa continued. "Anger is a tool to wield, but rage must be leashed, if not caged."

Behind Flowridia's eyelids waited the image of Ayla cowering against the wall—yet her memory could not even call it Ayla, merely a faceless shadow.

Merely an *it*.

"I have been in the mist long enough to contemplate my sins, and I know they are many. Though I would argue they don't hold a candle to your wife's." Odessa's grin returned, her impish nature manifesting. "What did you do to make yourself afraid of becoming me?"

"Nothing."

"Liar."

"It doesn't matter."

Odessa laughed, and *gods*, it chilled Flowridia's blood. "Cycles repeat, Flower Child. I doubt you'll be an old hag in the swamp, but we're so alike, you and me. The best thing I ever did for you was drop you on a doorstep. Imagine how much more fucked up you'd be if I hadn't. I can selfishly hope my grandchild survives to adulthood for the sake of preserving my genetic line, but I'll keep an eye out for it in the mist when you inevitably snap."

Offense rose to blind Flowridia. "How dare you."

"Or you'll beat her into a spineless little wraith like yourself. One or the other."

Flowridia tried to stand, her own body betraying her as she teetered back. "I will never treat my child like you treated me."

"You say that, but tell me this, Flower Child—who are you abusing now?"

The question stunned her into silence, faint at the unspoken answer.

"That's what I thought—" Odessa glanced at the box. "Seems my time in this world is short. Call for me any time."

"I hope you go mad from loneliness, you bitch."

Odessa's cackle echoed far after she disappeared.

Again came the memory of Ayla backed against the wall. Helpless, though indomitable; vulnerable, though indestructible.

Flowridia's tears came fast, sobbing alone in the dim light. When Ayla returned, she would grovel and plea, but *gods*—who was to say it was over?

Was this who she was now? A creature of *rage*?

A knock interrupted her tears. Casvir entered, concern upon his countenance. "Flowridia, are you all right?"

She managed a nod, though could not move. When he sat beside her, she wept into her hands. "I made a mistake."

"You see now why this can be a curse."

He didn't know. He could not know. He despised Ayla, but he would rightfully hate what Flowridia was becoming.

Who she had become.

"Do you need to talk?"

She shook her head.

"Would you like me to help you back?"

When she nodded, he stood and offered a hand. She let him escort her away, the pit of her stomach as deep as the floor.

For hours, Kah'Sheen led them through the thick jungles of Sha'Demoni, insistent on evading any chance of running into anyone else. *"If they see me, they are telling Mother. If they are telling Mother, I am dead."*

Sora was noticing a pattern in Kah'Sheen's treatment of her mother.

They walked until even the lush, alien plants became a rarity, leaving only rich, red stone. Farther still, until Sora gazed once more upon the black sea. In the far distance, she swore she saw the ferryman's silhouette upon the horizon, wondering what deep magic he truly wielded, when Kah'Sheen offered one of her many hands. Sora accepted along with the rest of them, and then the world shifted.

A blast of cold assaulted Sora. Night had fallen. They faced an icy sea, tumultuous winds churning the waves. "Where are we?"

"At the southernmost tip of Saphaira."

Saphaira, home of the Ember Elves. And though their land was known for arid heat, tundra could be desert too. Sora rubbed her arms, warding off the need to shiver. When Chaos illusioned a blanket, Sora grasped it tight.

"We must make the journey through the mortal realm," Kah'Sheen said. "Sora, you are the most normal. You are going into town to purchase a boat, yes?"

Warm light shone in the distance, perhaps a half hour's walk. Yet whipping wind slapped her face, the elements their greatest foe. "You want us to sail in this?"

"It is the only path."

"I'm also a half-elf. I don't think—"

"I will go," Ayla said, her skimpy costume utterly insane for the weather, but her vampirism was the greatest protection of all. "Save Sora the risk of freezing to death in this storm. Wait here."

She twirled into Kah'Sheen's shadow, vanishing from view.

Kah'Sheen, too, rubbed her hands along her arms, her wispy figure unsuited for the snow. "We sail into the sea. There is a rock leading deep underground."

Chaos summoned a second blanket, large enough for even Kah'Sheen's substantial height. The half-demon accepted it graciously. "I don't know how to sail," the Goddess said.

"Unfortunately, I do," Sora muttered, for her papa had taught her many things. "Please save me when we capsize."

"I will do my best."

Sora liked this quest much more when she'd thought it was complete.

Ayla soon returned, carrying a comically large boat above her head. "Well?"

Though she had lost feeling in her toes, Sora managed a quip. "It doesn't have a sail."

"You think a sail can combat this weather? I was intending to steer it myself."

Vampiric strength did have advantages. "Better than nothing."

"I can help," Chaos said, that earnest tone returning. "If you can direct me, I can use the Silver Fire to propel us. If my body gets frostbite, I can fix it or get a new one."

"That would certainly make it easier." Ayla swayed as she carried the boat to the frigid beach, the wind a test even to her strength. Sora remained a safe distance behind, not wishing to be crushed if Ayla toppled. "You two will need to cuddle," Ayla said.

"I am also needing to direct you," Kah'Sheen replied, centering herself in the boat. It wasn't a particularly small vessel, but Kah'Sheen's arachnid leg span took up most of the space, even with her legs tucked beneath her. Sora managed to squeeze beside her, far more secure when a lithe arm snaked around her. "You are heading south. If the clouds are clearing, the constellation of Mermaid's Triumph will point the way. We will follow her tail."

Sora braced herself when Ayla and Chaos gave the boat a shove. Surely this was suicide, the waves only growing with the racing wind, but the boat breached the water nevertheless. Her stomach lurched as it sought to return to the beach, but Chaos remained in the water like a shark, her small figure managing to push them forward. She sank. Ayla held Chaos' arms as she climbed back into the boat, and from below the waves came brilliant, silver light.

For better or worse, the energy propelled them into the abyss. Sora wondered if she'd ever be immune to fear, given the stupidity of her decisions lately. Helpless, she hid her face behind the blanket, grateful for Kah'Sheen's emanating warmth.

Occasionally, Kah'Sheen shouted above the storm. Ayla answered, though Sora could not decipher it. When she peeked out, she was met with only a dark sky and darker ocean, though Chaos' flame cast sparkles along the water behind them.

"Look!" came Kah'Sheen's cry. "The clouds are moving. You can check, yes?"

Sora peeked from her warm cocoon, the glittering stars a wonder amid the frigid storm. Exactly as described: a mermaid's tail led the way. The boat shifted course by small degrees, the message relayed.

For comfort, Sora set a hand against Leelan's lump in her tunic. If only for him, she prayed they lived. He deserved better than to freeze to death in the Onian Sea.

She had hardly had time to consider Onias' words, the whole world spiraling beyond her control. Could Leelan be saved at all? What did anyone do with the vessel of a goddess' power?

For hours, she had only her thoughts for company, useless in this horrible storm. She swore her lips were frozen, fingers and feet numb. Kah'Sheen fared little better, her spiderous legs as cold as stone.

"There! You see? That rock!"

Sora peered out, breath catching. 'Rock' was an exaggeration. Nothing more than a small island in the middle of nowhere. Still, hope kept her warm in those final, agonizing minutes.

Together with Chaos, Ayla directed the boat onto the rock, pulling it securely forward once Kah'Sheen and Sora disembarked. Slick stone threatened to steal her footing, but she fared better than Chaos, who fell to her knees on the small island.

"I didn't think I was capable of exhaustion," the Goddess said. "Give me moment."

Ayla, too, worked to stretch her wrists—which had frozen solid. Horror filled Sora, though she dared to approach. "Do you need help?"

Ayla shook her head, though her hands seemed unwilling to budge. "Look away if you're squeamish."

"Why—"

Ayla bit her forearm and *yanked*, severing bone and flesh.

It was somehow worse the second time, Ayla's stumpy limbs leaving Sora slack-jawed. But her purpose revealed itself. From the mangled appendages grew something new. First bone, then sinew, and finally skin, wrapping pristinely around her newly formed arms.

"Don't you feel pain?" Sora asked, shaken as Ayla flexed her new hands.

"Pain is obsolete."

Sora had nothing to say to that.

Ayla returned to the Goddess' side, offering a hand to help her rise. "Well, that was one of the more unpleasant things I've done, but I am grateful it's halfway over."

"Oh, joy," Chaos muttered, but she managed to find her bearings. "We should secure the boat. If it's swept away, it will be a long swim home."

Sora left them to that, using Kah'Sheen as a barrier from the wind. "We must find the cave," Kah'Sheen said when they returned. "Should be in the center. Not hiding."

Amid the rocks, a jutting hole led into the ground, large enough to accommodate Ku'Shya. Sora sensed magic. Perhaps that was why it wasn't flooded. Ancient steps had worn away, leaving a frightfully smooth descent. Kah'Sheen, with her many limbs, led the way with only some hesitation, slow but steady. Chaos offered Sora a hand, the duo supporting each other as they made the precarious climb.

Only Ayla seemed unbothered, her steps as easy as solid ground. "Can you not float?"

"Yes, but I don't have the strength to support her without a counterweight."

Ayla rolled her eyes as she took Sora's other hand, her dead flesh as cold as Sora's. "Take care of yourself," Ayla said. "If Sora falls, I can catch her."

Chaos obeyed, rising as easily as Etolié and her wings. Despite their height difference, Ayla did a fine job keeping her steady, easily shifting to balance whenever Sora tried to slip.

"I'm not used to feeling this inept," Sora muttered.

"Give yourself a thousand years or so. You will be as nimble as me."

Nothing cutting. Nothing sarcastic. Nothing more than a friendly remark. They'd not spoken of their experience in Onias' Hell—Sora took Ayla's threats of death quite seriously—but what a strange turn life had taken. "Perhaps I should learn to dance," Sora replied. "It might help."

"Can you not already? I think you would be surprised how easily your fighting stances translate to dance. You would have no trouble."

Sora chuckled, the conversation so surreal. "I suppose you would know."

"You might call it my signature."

Their idle conversation continued, its innocence as baffling as it was comforting. Forgiveness had been extended, accepted . . . Generations of hatred had culminated into this: helping each other to balance in a slippery tunnel, their laughter easy and true. Some void had been filled, some ancient scar finally healing, and Sora wondered what her ancestors would think, whether they would see this as betrayal, an insult—or perhaps as the softest ending of all.

Here she was, the last Fireborn, though a Fireborn no more, extending a hand in the monster's most desperate hour. Whatever the ramifications, Sora felt peace.

All was well, until the stone no longer sloped. Chaos' flame lit the scene, revealing . . . nothing. The path ended at a wall. No carvings. Not even a spell. Sora felt nothing except the icy air. "Do we have to break through?"

"No, no," Kah'Sheen said. "We are not there yet. Now, we step into Celestière. The barrier is thin here."

"She's in Celestière?"

"Angels cannot be in the mortal realm." Kah'Sheen took their hands once more. "Focus with me. We are all falling through."

Sora had no idea what that meant. Instead, she prayed to be led with the rest—

Her stomach churned as the world shifted. The chill subsided. When Sora opened her eyes, they stood in a world of white mist.

"Stay close," Kah'Sheen continued. "If you are lost, you are not found. I will lead."

"How much longer?" Sora asked.

"Halfway there."

Sora simply prayed they braved no more icy seas. She trudged along, rubbing feeling back into her limbs.

"*Psst.* Flowers. Are you awake?"

Flowridia blinked into consciousness, confused momentarily to see Etolié peeking at her bedside. The sun had fully risen. Later and later, Flowridia slept, missing the sunrise more often than not.

"Look, I'm kind of losing my mind about something. Can we talk?" Without waiting for a reply, Etolié sat fully on the bed, her wings undulating disconcertingly close to Flowridia's face. "Do you know anything about murdered De'Sindai?"

Stiffness slowed Flowridia's motions as she tried to sit up—so much so, that she grimaced and sank back down into the sheets. Gods, her hips burned when she tried to move. "Are you talking about the elven witch?"

"I might be. Not trying to be facetious—I don't know her race. Seems statistically improbable, though."

"Ayla said there are sometimes Whispering Elf witches pledged to Ku'Shya. What are you getting on about?"

Etolié's shrug held no conspiracy, despite her next words. "Casvir said I wasn't supposed to tell you—you specifically. But the other day, Casvir showed me some De'Sindai who had been murdered, and they had a symbol carved out of their backs, and . . ."

Again, Flowridia tried to sit up. Etolié did an admirably decent job pretending not to notice her struggle, until Flowridia winced when a sharp pain cramped her spine. "Do you need help, Flowers?"

Defeated, Flowridia removed her good hand from the sheets. Etolié eased her into sitting, the unexpected rock in these turbulent seas. "I know what you're talking about. I killed the witch. That's what got me fired from helping the refugees."

"Gross. Anyway, uh . . . Casvir didn't know what the symbol was."

Flowridia frowned at the implications. "But you did?"

"Not at the time. But I do now." Etolié's distress radiated, her fidgeting hands constantly spinning the ring she wore. "You can't say anything."

"I'm not even supposed to know, apparently. I'll keep it from Casvir."

"The symbol means Bringer of War. It's Khastra."

Taken aback, Flowridia was fully awake now. "What does that even mean?"

"I don't know what it means, Flowers. I don't know what the fuck kind of spell they were planning to perform, but it involves Khastra. It might mean nothing because of reasons I shouldn't tell your treacherous ass but involve a spell that's already done and complete, but it might also mean . . . . I don't know."

"It was done by a refugee. I would guess it's some sort of retaliation against Ku'Shya."

"By using Khastra? Then I should warn Ku'Shya, right?"

Even as she said it, Etolié didn't sound convinced. Flowridia's own hesitation remained. "Or you don't do that, because if you're wrong, it could backfire spectacularly."

"How so?"

"I don't know. It's just a feeling."

Etolié nodded gravely. "Yeah, I have a feeling too."

"Just a feeling?"

"It's not a good feeling, but I don't know what else to say about it."

And that was that—until a knock hushed them both into silence. "Come in."

Casvir entered, followed by a few servants carrying an odd sort of invention. "Good morning," Casvir said. "My insistence that you have an escort remains, but this will help you keep some independence."

For a moment, Flowridia forgot her ailments, enamored by the magical device presented to her.

The spellwork was not complicated, but it was quite sophisticated—a floating seat, controlled by touch. Nearly a chair, but it had no legs. Instead, a base that ended in a point beneath, emanating a soft glow. When Casvir helped her to sit, Flowridia smiled as it dipped like a boat, finding the padded chair blissfully comfortable after so long seated in bed.

A ball of sorts was embedded into the right arm. "This controls the spell," Casvir explained, and when Flowridia maneuvered it, the chair gently floated forward. "It can also be pushed, but I know your independence is ideal for your continued mental health."

Lack of independence was hardly a drop in the bucket of her strife, but though the chair was a little slower than walking, there was joy even in making a lap around the room.

She stopped the chair before Casvir, amused to barely face his hips at her lower height. "Thank you. Truly. This is more than generous."

"I am happy to provide it. You have always flourished in the outdoors, so I hope you will take the opportunity to enjoy the sun as often as you can."

It was unbearably sweet. She thanked him with a hug.

Etolié joined Flowridia on a trip to the gardens outside, the early spring blossoms filling her empty soul with light. Guards were stationed nearby, far enough to give them a semblance of privacy, but Flowridia remained haunted by the reminder their presence brought—that someone, somewhere, wished her dead.

"I think the greatest issue," Flowridia said, "is that there is realistically no end of people who want me dead—or the baby, given the most prevalent rumor is that it's Casvir's."

It wounded her to be unable to kneel beside the new growths, but at least she could caress the trees as she passed. Within, she yearned to feel them as she had before, back when the life in them had sung with the magic inside her.

Someday, perhaps. But someday felt more and more impossible each day.

"Let's make a list," came Etolié's sardonic reply. "All of Solvira. Most of the elves. Anyone in Nox'Kartha who thinks you're a throne-hopping hoe. My demon mother-in-law. Izthuni. Hell, throw Murishani onto the list—he was a little too happy you got fat."

"I think he'd be more than happy to add my soul to his collection. He has a habit of doing that."

Yet Etolié frowned, a blight in the sunny day. "Our most recent assassin was sent by a 'woman keen to hide her identity.'"

"Yes, but that means nothing. Disguise spells are a dime a dozen."

Still, Etolié's smile was entirely pained. "And the first assassin was a Whispering Elf," Flowridia said.

"Yes, but Executor Faeborn had nothing to do with it."

Flowridia stopped her chair in front of Etolié. "What are you thinking?"

"I'm thinking I need to have a stern conversation with someone who isn't you."

Flowridia pushed the chair forward, bumping Etolié's thigh with her knees, causing the Celestial to stumble back. "Is this some misguided attempt to protect me?"

Etolié responded by levitating. "Bitch, I will push your chair into the lake. It's not. It's shit I have to speak lightly about, but if my theory is true, you're safe at least until Ayla comes back."

The name spiked Flowridia's blood pressure. "Are you insinuating that Ayla tried to have my child murdered?"

"No! Oh, for fuck's sake—if Ayla were going to do it, she'd do something way cleverer than anything we've already seen. Whoever wants your kid dead doesn't behave like they have personal access to your food, water, and sleeping body. Give your wife more credit than that. It's definitely not her."

"You understand why I'm frustrated by this conversation, right?"

"I do, but I need you to shut the fuck up because we're about to have company."

With some mobility struggle, Flowridia managed to turn her chair around—and there approached Marielle, with Zorlaeus trailing like a puppy close behind. "Flowridia! I was told I'd find you here!"

Blessedly, her expected hug was far gentler than her last, the chair a deterrent for suffocating Flowridia with her cleavage. "Hello, Marielle."

"And Etolié!" Marielle seemed lost, her offered hug disappearing as quickly as she had raised her arms—given Etolié simply folded hers and glared. "It's been so long. How are you?"

"I was enjoying the fresh air." It was not coincidence that she spoke in past tense. Her expression softened to greet Zorlaeus, however. "Hi, Zorlaeus. Lovely day, wasn't—isn't it?"

"It's a beautiful afternoon," Zorlaeus affirmed.

"Oh my goodness, look at you in that awful chair!" Marielle gave a dramatic grimace as she inspected Flowridia's new device—if she were offering comfort, she was doing the worst possible job. "I'm so sorry your health keeps taking these turns. But things will look up once the baby comes, right? How much longer is that?"

"We're not quite sure," Flowridia replied, her struggle to keep her composure a losing battle. "Half-elf pregnancies are known for their mysterious timelines. It could be next week. It could be a month or two. Perhaps even longer."

"Well, you're glowing, and that's what matters! Where is Ayla on this fine day?"

"Why do you give a shit?" Etolié asked, uncharacteristically monotone.

Marielle made a small frown. "Because Ayla is my friend's wife."

"Ayla is currently assisting with saving the world," Flowridia replied, her patience running threadbare. "You can let Murishani know that too."

To Marielle's credit, though her acting skills were questionable, she had the good sense to look marginally offended. "I don't actually work for him, you know."

"I never said you did. I just said you can let him know." Flowridia forced her smile to stay, even as her words remained terse. "Let him know I'm in terrible spirits. It'll make his day. Let him know I'm constantly in pain somewhere and exhausted and pushing everyone I love away from me. A pity for him that I'm not quite 'fat' anymore, but perhaps those will make up for that slight on my part, hmm?"

Marielle's countenance held all the guilt of a child caught with their hand in a cookie jar—and behind her, Zorlaeus simply looked at the ground. "I can see that you're angry—"

"As Etolié said, it was a lovely day. But then Staelash's resident bully and her loyal cuckold decided to ruin my day."

Beside her, Etolié made a noise akin to a donkey trying not to wheeze, but Flowridia merely glared as Marielle muttered a half-hearted, "*Have a nice day,*" and trudged away. Some part of her felt a modicum of guilt for the jab at Zorlaeus, but she was far too exhausted to apologize, content to watch as he followed her away.

Finally, Etolié snickered. "Fuck, I feel so awful. That was fine art though, Flowers."

"It's the least she deserves." Though Flowridia seethed, she managed to squash it down. Etolié deserved plenty of things, but not to be screamed at. "Is she the one you were thinking of?"

"Marielle? No way. Bitch doesn't have enough brain cells to plot a proper assassination."

"But you're not going to—"

"Look, I don't *know, Flowers.*" Etolié's dramatic sigh somehow deflated Flowridia's own frustration. "So shut the fuck up before I say something I shouldn't."

Flowridia navigated forward with her chair, uncertain if she should feel patronized or not. "It's strange that Ayla *isn't* back yet though, right? Could something have happened in Sha'Demoni?"

"Given the group consists of a daughter of Ku'Shya, The Endless Night, and the Goddess of Chaos, I literally can't fathom what could have happened. Am I worried? Yes, but I've been having a silent panic attack since being crowned empress, so no point in worrying more than we have to—yet."

No, Flowridia was not appeased. Not in the slightest. But Etolié wouldn't budge, and she already skirted the edges of what was acceptable rage, so Flowridia directed her chair back toward the castle. "I'm restless. Did you say you wanted to assist in finding . . . the thing?"

"There is truly no better use of my time, Flowers."

Together, they returned to the castle, thoughts of murder on Flowridia's mind.

CHAPTER 27

By evening, Flowridia was merely numb. No space for guilt or worry over her love's failure to return.

A candle lit her bedside table. Flowridia's gaze shifted between the flame and the bouquet behind it, its poignant message forgotten in the echoing torment of Odessa's words: *"Or you'll beat her into a spineless little wraith like yourself—"*

At least Mother had never denied her crimes. Never justified them. Never lied to herself that all was well.

Though her heart and soul were muted, her body was assuredly not. Her hips burned from the previous day's walking, her back cramped from carrying the small weight in her stomach, and all the while her hand tingled, the incessant sensation a hum whenever she cared to pay attention to it. Like blinking, it was easy to forget it was there until she was all at once acutely aware—except eyes never seared in pain in the moments she forgot her disability.

Above all, she was so very, very exhausted.

On the couches, Etolié's wings served to better light the scene than any fireplace or candle, the Celestial's feigned obliviousness to Flowridia's dour mood appreciated. Flowridia was done talking. Perhaps she would be better off never opening her mouth again.

"Who are you abusing now?"

Abuse didn't have to be physical to leave scars. Flowridia knew that too well.

A knock at the door roused her from her stupor. Flowridia could not have risen if she tried but managed to catch Etolié's eye and nod.

"Come in," the Celestial said dully.

To Flowridia's shock, Executor Faeborn let themself in.

The elf looked far humbler than in their last meeting, wearing not the robes of an executor but simpler attire cut to hide their figure. Etolié's wings caused their skin to nigh illuminate, their pale flesh not suited for golden light. "Lady Flowridia, I apologize for intruding. Might I have a moment of your time? I would not ask if it were not important."

Flowridia frowned, trapped in the dilemma of showing weakness when she failed to sit or showing weakness by refusing to. Thankfully, Etolié appeared at her side to steady her, helping her to rise even as her back screamed in protest. "Of course. You may pull up a chair if you'd like."

Faeborn shook their head. "I should not stay long. I doubt Imperator Casvir will be pleased with what I'm about to tell you. Might we speak without your attendant?"

Thoughts of assassination attempts rose discomfortingly in Flowridia's head, but that paled to the laughable nature of what the elf had just said. Flowridia managed to smirk at Etolié. "She won't talk. Right, attendant?"

Etolié took no bait, instead playing her part well. "I'm here for Lady Flowridia."

Faeborn did not look appeased, but instead said, "First, I am sorry to hear that your health has taken a turn. I was disheartened to hear you had stepped down from your role in assisting refugees, but I understand. Pregnancies can be precarious."

Flowridia kept a neutral countenance at that. "At least the baby will be coming sooner rather than later."

She hoped.

"You have a compassionate heart, which is why I've come," they said, their confident stance betrayed by their fingers fidgeting with their trousers. "It's because of you that my people have a place in this kingdom. No question Imperator Casvir would have left us to die or worse. I know this because of what he has decided to do in Meskheta. Do you know?"

"I only know there were rumors that Ku'Shya's people had made an appearance."

"Ku'Shya did what?" Etolié asked, breaking her attendant persona.

Faeborn seemed lost on how to proceed, likely not used to such unruly 'servants.' Flowridia shook her head. "Ask me later. Go on."

"I attended a meeting with Imperator Casvir today," Faeborn replied, "wherein he asked for my input on Ku'Shya's actions. I told him that I feared we are witnessing further retaliation from her for what the Four Kingdoms did to her daughter. I won't pretend to understand the details of Demoni Law, but I do know it demands all crimes be rectified."

Flowridia recalled all too well, once captured to be a sacrifice to pay for what Ayla had done . . .

"The Ember Elves have turned their capital into a fortress, hunkering down for some unknown cause. Casvir intends to release a disease into Meskheta and destroy them all."

"What?" Etolié balked.

For her part, Flowridia simply stared, dissecting the grim statement. "A disease?"

"I don't know the details, only that he mentioned it to one of his generals, but I was there. I know what I heard. I wished to implore you to make him reconsider. This is not warfare—this is genocide."

Etolié geared up to speak, her fury palpable, but Flowridia held up her good hand, calculating the task ahead. "Would Ku'Shya consider it an insult if Casvir took her victory away from her?"

"Perhaps. It would depend on what she wants from them."

"Pleading to Casvir about what's right or wrong is futile, I've learned. We have to appeal to whatever serves him best in the long-term. He's patient. Frankly, a plague seems out of character. His goal isn't genocide—"

"Except when it is," Etolié muttered.

"Yes, but Casvir has no personal grudge with the Ember Elves." Flowridia matched Etolié's eyes, praying her silent message of *shut up and ask me later* was conveyed. "Casvir wants pledges of godhood. Killing the Ember Elves en mass doesn't accomplish that. It sounds like he wants this war over, and finding out why might help us stop it. I'll need to come up with a way to have found out about this without it coming from you, but I will do what I can. I swear."

Unless it was already too late, but Flowridia shoved thoughts of defeat away.

"Thank you. I should go before it's suspicious, but please know I won't forget this aid."

Faeborn left. Beside Flowridia, Etolié's jaw had set. "So instead of slaughtered in a night, Casvir is attempting a slower death. Just great."

"This doesn't seem like him." Flowridia stared once more into the candle, seeking meaning in its flame. "There has to be a gamble we don't know about."

"Care to explain what happened with Ku'Shya in Meskheta?"

"The very short version of the story is that Ku'Shya's servants attacked. We don't know why, only that the outlying people have gathered in Meskheta for protection."

Etolié's forced smile revealed nothing. "When?"

"A few days ago—at least, that's when Casvir told me."

Etolié said nothing, merely kept her grimace.

"What are you thinking?" Flowridia asked.

"I don't know what to think, Flowers. That's what fucking scares me. But Casvir's motives are changing, you said?"

"That's the only way it all makes sense to me." Flowridia scooted to the edge of the bed, suddenly distrusting of her legs. "Could you find someone to fetch him? I want to speak to him alone. Tell him I . . . that I want to talk to him about a project."

"It's probably best I don't see him right now. I'm not super great at keeping my mouth shut when I'm on the verge of ripping some dick's head off." Etolié left the bed, heading for the nurse's station.

Without the angelic light of Etolié's wings, only the candle remained. Flickering shadows reminded Flowridia of who was lost, the fear she'd once felt for the dark now the only hope she held for her love to return. Oh, where was Ayla? Should she worry that her party had yet to return?

Apologies fixed so little. In the silence, Flowridia was reminded once more of her hand, its incessant tingling of severed nerves driving her mad. She touched the mutilated scar where her pointer finger had once been, the sensation not quite painful, but cold and radiant. Wherever she traced, that prickling followed—to her palm, to the scar of her amputated pinky finger, and finally to the ghost of her ring finger, its loss simply one of many casualties in the Mountains of Kaas. Her wedding ring had been lost amid the ashes.

There was nowhere to place it anyway.

Flowridia shifted from tracing with the gentle pad of her finger to her nail, the spark of pain a warning. She braced herself as she pressed the nail into the vicious scar, pain shooting through her hand, up her forearm. She squeaked but did not cry; tears prickled in her eyes, but she would not cry. She squeezed her eyes shut, forcing herself to feel. A whimper escaped her lips, but that was weakness. She dug until her hand burned, until the skin split, until the first welling of blood assuaged her anguish.

Flowridia gasped, shaking as she brought the maimed appendage protectively to her chest. Hardly a sliver, the barest bead of blood. Proof that she lived, that this damn body had not fallen completely apart. The pain lingered, yet waned with every pounding throb of her heart.

There was a time to fall completely apart, but not when there was a knock at the door. "Flowridia?"

Flowridia knew that baritone voice well. "Come in."

Casvir appeared, a slight furrowing in his brow as he surveyed the scene. "Where is Empress Etolié?"

"I sent her away. I wanted to speak without her."

Casvir was deliberate in every motion, even as he took the chair from Flowridia's desk and set it near the bed. "I was told you had a project to discuss."

"Yes. I know you stripped me of my responsibilities, but I thought of a few ways we might potentially be able to accept Ember Elf refugees." She lied, of course, but was saved from her internal scramble by the brisk shake of his head.

"Actions have already been taken that would negate any help we could have provided. Though I am pleased you have been keeping your mind busy."

Dammit—he would change the subject if she let him. "What sort of actions?"

"You already declined to know the details, and they are irrelevant to your current responsibilities anyway."

"I understand," Flowridia said, though her own heartbeat might deafen her. "I just know that your goal is pledges of godhood, and accepting refugees is a sure way to achieve them."

"The Ember Elves would never. They are too proud."

"We would've said the same thing about the Whispering Elves."

"Then you are naïve to different elven customs. The Four Kingdoms are not a monolith. Executor Faeborn informed me that Ember Elves are more skeptical of outsiders than any of the rest. Their borders are closed to all outside influence. Even foreign elves are viewed with suspicion. A human would be captured on sight. They are worth decimating quickly, to make an example."

And there was the gamble—perhaps to scare the Iron Elves and what remained of the Highland. "What about Ku'Shya?"

"What about her?"

"We don't know what she's after from them. Do you want to risk angering her?"

Casvir was a closed book, but even Flowridia sensed the veiled suspicion behind the words. "I have no use for gods, nor do I worry about their affairs. If Goddess Ku'Shya wants me to stop, she may tell me herself."

Flowridia couldn't say if he was mad or audacious, but given his disregard to risking Ku'Shya's wrath in the past, perhaps both. "I see."

"Be that as it may, decisive action has already been taken."

The words said so little, yet Flowridia's stomach sank. "My apologies then. I didn't mean to waste your time."

"You have not. I am pleased that you thought to tell me. It is good to see you taking action."

Defeat stung bitterly, and she prayed he misinterpreted it. Executor Faeborn had risked everything to plead to her, and instead she would deliver a death sentence. "I'm doing what I can."

"I know. May I be of help to you?"

The question was laughable—by all accounts he had paved this path to her own personal hell, but it was she who had tread willingly. But tonight, she had no will for the nagging grudges between them. Her quest to find his phylactery continued. But alone, the candlelight was reminiscent of campfires in the woods. Once, she had been entrenched in grief, yet had found a friend in those dark times, who read history books, who made wry jests, who sang to fill silent moments. A mentor who taught her to fight, taught her of magic, had taught her how to grieve and how to find her strength.

Perhaps that was the bitter truth. For there was Imperator Casvir, the ruthless tyrant she despised, who crafted draconian bargains and held knives to the throats of those she loved to get his way. A ruthless man who aspired to be a god, relentless enough in his ego to someday succeed.

But in rare moments, there appeared her friend in the woods.

With realization came heartbreak. There was no rage without hurt, and Imperator Casvir had hurt her deeply over the years. No one could demoralize her so swiftly, nor build her up so high. It hurt to trust him.

Tears stung her eyes. How she yearned for the woods. "Can we just talk? About nothing?"

"What sort of nothing?"

From her bedside table, Flowridia plucked a leaf from the bouquet and offered it forward. "I don't care. I just be-*leaf* it's been too long."

Rare warmth showed in his visage, his smile dusty from disuse. "I be-*leaf* you are correct. But we must decide what topic to *branch* into."

"Am I really qua-*leaf*-ied to decide that?"

"It is a *tree*-mendous responsibility, but you have always been capable."

Laughter sparked between them, and what a priceless gift that was. For a precious time, Flowridia forgot her ailments and woes, uplifted by a man who did not wear his crown, nor wield his titles.

Away from the throne, he was simply Casvir.

On instinct, Sora counted her steps through the consuming mist.

Two hundred on the dot before Kah'Sheen turned, though of course the half-demon would have to take significantly less. Alas, the next number was not quite so smooth—three hundred and seven—nor the next—five hundred and eighteen.

But when Sora feared she'd go mad from endless white, a landmark appeared.

A smooth statue, bearing perfect geometric lines. Sora ran ahead, curious at the mysterious breach in monotony. No other sign of land. Simply a shined slab of rock. Nearer, she saw it sat upon a rectangular stone, mimicking a grave.

Her companions' presence filled the space as Sora studied the deliberate symbols carved into the rock. "What is this?"

"This is it," Kah'Sheen muttered, yet her four eyes narrowed as she surveyed the land. "That is Celestial writing. I cannot read it."

Chaos came to the forefront. "It's faded, but . . ." In rhythm, she recited odd words:

Death awaits, my mourning son
Embrace that which you fear
Together, sing to greet each row
But cut the cord when bare

"What is that meaning?" Kah'Sheen asked.

All remained silent, the strange words too deliberate to mean nothing and yet . . . "It must be a riddle," Sora said. "Who would leave a riddle at the end of the road?"

"Sol Kareena and Mother are the only ones to know the location, but it does not mean they are not asking for help with protections."

"Eionei is the sort to dabble in riddles and mischief," Chaos replied. "Perhaps we should have brought Etolié."

Kah'Sheen frantically shook her head. "I am not bringing Etolié on purpose. I am not knowing how she feels about Ilune."

Truthfully, Sora didn't either, which meant the Celestial likely felt little to nothing at all.

"*Death awaits*," Ayla muttered. "That can only mean Ilune, given the context. But who is the son? Was Ilune's first child a boy? Was he particularly sad?"

When even Chaos shrugged, Sora realized none of them had studied Solvira's history. "I doubt it's that simple, anyway."

Chaos brought her hand to the stone, skimming the smooth surface. "I do not feel a spell, which means I cannot absorb it."

"So we must be answering," Kah'Sheen said. "Is anyone having any rope? We are making it threadbare?"

"What counts as a rope?" Ayla mused. "Could I cut the hem from my dress? That cannot be right. We must be overthinking this."

They spoke among themselves, speculating which *son* held the key to opening Ilune's prison, but Sora could not shake the third line: *Together, sing to greet each row* . . .

Flowridia had once sung it herself while busying herself in the winter garden. *"Rows and rows of roses* . . .

"Each row," Sora said. "Rows is plural. Could it mean *roses*?"

Ayla's sigh held pain. "My gods, this is a pun. The Song to Greet Roses is a prayer to Goddess Alystra, which of course a god like Eionei would include in his riddle. Apparently the key to solving this is to think like Flowra."

Mourning son, mourning son, mourning su—

"Morning sun." Sora summoned a spark of light in her hand. "Sunrise. It must be in reference to Sol Kareena. Perhaps a priest or priestess? Holy light?"

"*Embrace that . . . witch*," Chaos said. "Perhaps a priestess and witch must sing the prayer to Alystra, potentially while hugging."

"I think they'd prefer a witch to Ku'Shya, given who put her here, but it doesn't specify."

"This cannot be so stupid," Ayla interrupted.

"This was set by Eionei," Sora replied. "It really can be this stupid. But consider the deeper meaning—it means both agents of Celestière and Sha'Demoni have to agree the time is right to open the prison."

"Be that as it may, we don't have a witch with us."

With some hesitation, Chaos raised her hand. "It's not particularly well known, but I'm a witch."

"Convenient."

"Does anyone know the prayer to greet Alystra?" Sora asked.

Ayla made no attempt to hide her contempt. "I know at least the beginning. I'm not the best singer, so bear with me."

Sora knew little of singing aside from belting hymns with her father as a child, but Ayla's voice was actually quite lovely, if breathy here and there.

Kiss the roses; kiss each thorn
Beauty is worth pain
None are worthy; none could bear
To speak Alystra's name

"*Cut the cord when bare*—it means a music *chord*. We stop singing at 'bear,'" Sora said, all those months in the garden with her sister paying out in strange and wonderful ways. She held out her arms to Chaos. "It's insane, but I say we try."

Chaos returned the hug, the warmth of her magical fire stimulating against Sora's skin, even through her clothing. They sang with Ayla's direction, repeating the words until the final line.

And waited.

When the final echo of 'bear' vanished from the vacant landscape, a loud *crack* sounded from the gravestone. The center split in twain. A perfect line; the two halves swung up like cellar doors, revealing a staircase into pure darkness.

"We've done it," Sora whispered, yet horror seeped in with the words. "By the Light, we're really doing this."

Tension tempered Kah'Sheen's words. "I am preferring to stay. I will wait here and make certain you are not trapped forever."

Of course Ayla did not fear the darkness. She practically danced down the stairs, pausing at the cusp of light. "Come along."

Sora considered her many sins in life, her pile potentially higher than most despite her best efforts, and decided that this skirted far too near among the worst. The greater good called, but hadn't Mereen called their plot the greater good?

Sora still paid the penance for those awful sins.

"Sora?"

Though her features remained obscured by flame, Chaos' question was clear.

They had come so far, yet Sora hesitated at the plunge. "We're certain about this, right?"

Chaos extended a hand. "All will be well. Ilune is no threat to you."

That was assuredly not Sora's worry, but she accepted the aid nevertheless, letting Chaos lead her down the first steep steps.

Surely spells preserved the staircase, the cut stone clean enough to be new. Sora counted fifty steps before the path leveled, ambient emerald light glowing in the distance. No sound except their steps, and each was as silent as a mouse.

A sharp turn revealed a change in the stone. The solid grey became a coating of glowing green. Maldectine, surely, but Sora had never seen it in such quantity. This hall was worth more than the riches of Solvira, Nox'Kartha, and Moratham combined. Sora braced herself for the muted sensation, the world ineffably quieter when she entered the maldectine-laden hallway.

Ayla gave no hesitation either, no lapse in her step. But Chaos lingered at the outskirts, for when she reached forward, her flame diminished, revealing olive skin.

"Can you cross and still keep your body?" Sora asked.

Chaos nodded. "But I cannot cast any magic."

"We'll convince the God of Death some other way." But as soon as the words left Sora's mouth, she realized . . . Ayla watched. "Can you change your appearance?"

"Not without—"

Ayla spoke. "What's wrong?"

Perhaps all would be well. Perhaps Ayla would not recognize the daughter she would someday love. A fool's hope, but what choice did they have? "Dir— Chaos, it's all right." Sora offered a hand. "What's the worst that can happen?"

Ayla watched, but Chaos took the hand and stepped boldly forward. Her fire dispersed, leaving Dira—beautiful Dira, with eyes that stared like a nervous doe and lips prepared to spew fire. Her heterochromatic stare fell upon Ayla, who gave no indication of anything odd at all.

Until . . . she grinned. A wicked chuckle escaped her lips, leaving Sora's blood cold. "Forgive me, but this is the greatest jest the universe could play. For thousands of years, the elves have worshipped a half-elf? Simply marvelous."

Chaos gave an impish smile, though refrained from revealing her teeth. "Bold of you to assume the irony ends there."

"You have done nothing but surprise me," Ayla replied.

So lax the mood became, that Sora forgot to be tense at all—until they rounded a final corner.

For there, a monster lay.

The walls, the roof, the ceiling—all maldectine, but the faint glow of green was not the only light. For there, languishing upon the floor, an angel lay in shackles, attached by her wrists to chains leading to the walls. She was naked, her body luminous in muted gold, but her massive wings shone brightly in dual hues—silver and gold. They hung limply, as wide as the walls. Long tresses of black lay splayed across the floor, matted and dull, and the woman's head rolled to face them, her silver gaze empty and all-consuming both.

Ilune. The God of Death.

She did not smile, but her dusty voice seemed reminiscent of an old harp—well out of tune, but holding beauty, nevertheless. "I know you."

She had not specified which person, but Sora saw equal confusion upon each face.

"But not the . . ." Ilune shut her tired eyes, a soft groan sounding as her head lolled back to face the ceiling.

"Which of us do you know?" Sora dared to ask, fearful of prodding this sleeping giant, imprisoned or not.

"Endless Night." Each breath held pain, as though passing through gravel. "It is rare that I admire anyone, rarer still to feel threatened, but you are why I created my staff."

Ayla revealed nothing, save for the slight clenching of fists behind her back. "So I have heard."

Ilune's chuckle set Sora's nerves on edge, the goddess' frayed sanity showing its edges. "You're a pleasant change from my typical array of visitors, though it's rare I hallucinate someone I don't know."

"We're not hallucinations," Sora said.

"Precisely what a hallucination would say." Ilune's shackles clinked as she rose to sit, her wings floating up from the cold ground. She had no qualms about her nudity, luxury in each pained motion—a shadow of her former grandeur. "I will indulge. Why are you here?"

"The realm has changed since you last walked it," Chaos said, her curtailed tone so unbearably mortal. She conveyed no grandeur as she had for Morathma, for Sol Kareena, for any demonic gods. Today, she played a different role. "The ancient God of Order has returned, and he seeks the six Convergence Orbs so that he can separate the three realms. I am Goddess Chaos, and I intend to stop him. I have gone to all the gods of Celestière and Sha'Demoni to ask for their pledges of power—except for you."

Ilune's smile cracked the porcelain façade of helplessness, the fractures revealing a goddess once charming and beautiful. "Oh, this is a new story. I like that. Tell me more."

"There is little more to say. I come to humbly ask for your pledge."

Ilune's gaze lost its dusty sheen, sharpening as she studied the Goddess of Chaos. "You don't look much like the artwork."

"The maldectine prevents me from summoning Silver Fire."

"You and me both." Ilune turned her attention to Sora, who froze at the stirring of cold invading her blood. All the world became silent to her stare: charming and beautiful, yes, but with crimes worthy of eternal imprisonment. "Who are you?"

"Sora Makosa. I'm a friend of Chaos."

"Is that more impressive than claiming a royal name in the Theocracy? You underplay your worth." Ilune hummed, intrigue falling upon her lovely face. Sora's breath ceased beneath her gaze, shackled by silver eyes. So much of Staella in her full lips and luxurious figure, but Staella was a sheep to Ilune's wolfish smile. Even dirtied from a thousand years in chains, she remained beguiling. "What strange hallucinations. Come to torment me for my crimes?"

"I don't know how to convince you that you haven't lost your mind," Sora said, "but if it *is* all in your head, what do you have to lose by pledging?"

"What is there to lose at all?" Ilune gestured to her glowing prison, the skin around her wrists rubbed raw, streaks of ancient blood staining her arms. "Destroying Celestière would send me spinning into the void, and that might be preferable to this."

"If you have any empathy left in your heart for those you left behind—"

Ilune's musical laughter filled the space, the dust steadily clearing from her voice. "So you have come to torture me. Say more. I welcome it."

Surely not hopeless, but Sora was at a loss.

"I would not claim to be a friend of Chaos," Ayla said, calculation upon her sharp face, "but if torment is the price of a pledge, I would gladly deliver."

Ilune's laughter resumed, dancing at the plunge of unhinged. "From you? Tempting, to actually feel something, but I am far too fond of my looks to let you carve me to bits. Let me keep what remains of my dignity, won't you?" Her chains clinked as she rose, though her gait remained unsteady, her legs surely weakened from centuries of disuse. She could barely rest her arms, so taut her bonds remained, yet more of her raw, abused flesh appeared beneath her shackles, the metal fused to the skin in places. "The only price for my pledge I can conceive of is my freedom, but you won't pay—not with a zealot to my dearest auntie keeping watch."

Sora supposed she should have felt threatened, yet Ilune remained a shadow, a god spoken of only in whispers, forgotten yet not.

"I could ask how you've even managed to come here, but I am not curious enough to make that my price. Isolation has made me apathetic and perhaps a little callous, so forgive me for laughing at your audacity. The greater good means nothing to me. Who is even left to love me? I've murdered them all or broken their hearts."

Chaos did not match Ilune in height, nor hold her same grandeur. In her mortal façade, she approached, fearless before the God of Death. "Your mother loves you."

And there it was: the crack in Ilune's armor of ego. "I thought I was a god of lies."

"Soon, my mortal form will be reborn with the birth of my past self. I have lived the future. Staella was an ally in my quest to defeat the coming darkness—and so were you. There is hope for reconciliation between you, but that hope vanishes forever if Celestière is destroyed."

Ice filled Ilune's gaze. "I have no reason to believe you."

"Neoma's death is not so simple as most of the world believes. You died that day too."

Ilune's fists clenched, wrists straining in their shackles. "I was already dead."

"The Silver Fire's explosion killed you both," Chaos continued, a plea in the words, "and Staella knows this. She knows there is more to you than hatred."

"She is a fool."

"Every mother is, when it comes to loving their child."

Silence settled. Ilune turned away, shackles shifting. Long enough to allow her to sit and stand, but short enough to prevent her from strangling herself.

Chaos stood just beyond the reach of the God of Death, heartbreak in her whispered words. "I killed my mother too. And not a day has passed where I was not haunted by that bitter truth. Like you, I blindly carved a path I could not hope to see the end of, and while my punishment was not to be chained underground, guilt is stronger than any physical shackle. I would give anything to change it, but sometimes fate steals what we love the most. And we are, tragically, the forgers of our own fate." She offered a hand, bridging the space between. "Touch me, please. I am not a figment. I want to save you, and I want to save Staella."

Muted, the God of Death did not face her, no—but her hand met Chaos', nevertheless. At the moment of touch, anguish fell upon Ilune's features. When she squeezed, Chaos did not falter, did not move an inch. "I pledge to thee, ancient Goddess of Chaos," Ilune whispered. "What little power I claim is yours."

"Thank you—"

But Ilune snatched her hand back. "Get out."

Despite her clear reluctance, Chaos stepped away. "Your pledge will not be wasted. The world won't know to thank you, but I will."

When Chaos turned, anguish rested upon her pretty face, though she could not cry. "Our quest is complete. Ilune should be left to rest."

To rot, but Sora did not say it, cursed to feel empathy for this murderous woman. Was it a moral lapse to feel compassion for monsters? Or was it growth? Perhaps she had more in common with her sister than she thought.

"Always lovely to meet a fan," Ayla said. Were she emotionally compromised, she did not show it.

Sora walked ahead, silent all the while.

It was Kah'Sheen who broke the silence, once they'd reached the surface. "Well? Is it working? Is Ilune giving her pledge?"

"She did," Chaos said numbly.

Kah'Sheen clapped, her own small applause with her four arms. "Then it is complete! No more secret gods."

A small *hum* sounded from Ayla. "How do we close this?"

The doors to the prison remained wide open. Sora shoved against one of the massive stone doors, finding it barely budged. "Are there any more puns in the inscription?"

Ayla traversed a few steps down, inspecting the underside of the doors. "There may be something here. Give me a moment." Chaos moved to join her, but Ayla waved her away. "Stay there, lest I accidentally shut myself in for eternity—"

The words were prophetic. The doors shut above her.

Sora banged on the sealed doors, finding no seam or lines. *"Ayla!"*

Nothing.

"Dammit. Help me remember the song."

It took a few tries, but Kah'Sheen proved to be the one with the memory for lyrics. Chaos and Sora managed to sing the doors open again, revealing an impatient Ayla, tapping her shoe. "Exactly as I said." Ayla emerged, and with one shove, the first of the doors fell with a thunderous *bang*. "Look at me—overcomplicating everything."

She shoved the second. The God of Death's prison shone pristine, as though never breached at all.

"Halfway there," Chaos said, her sigh long-suffering. "Hopefully the storm has quelled. I don't quite know how much time has passed in the mortal realm."

Urgency surged through Sora. "We should hurry. Flowridia is due soon."

The mists surrounded them once more, and Sora felt no peace.

CHAPTER 28

Fifteen years after the end of the world . . .

Such uncanny abilities the Silver Fire provided. Dira always sensed when Mother was near, drawn to her magic as kin.

How strange, to awaken and feel it but . . . different. Stronger. New.

Dira quickly dressed, then roused Demitri. "Do you smell anything weird?"

Demitri made a show of sniffing the air. *There's someone here.*

Tepid, Dira crept out the door and to the balcony wrapping around the second floor.

Whoever this new guest was, she made no attempt to hide. Already, foreign laughter filled the massive entry room, and when Dira peered down from the balcony, she caught a glimpse of glowing wings.

"And where is the darling girl anyway?"

"She's on her way down, if my senses are accurate."

The second voice was Mother. Dira's hesitation faded away. There was no danger here, and so she headed for the stairs, with Demitri as her shadow.

As she descended, the winged woman came into view, like Etolié yet not. Though she seemed Celestial, her wings held a magnificence that Etolié's lacked, expanding across the room in shades of silver and gold, the light melding as copper where it touched. Her black hair held luxury, her body flawless and dressed to enhance it, but most engrossing were her silver gaze and smile, instantly holding Dira hostage.

She was beautiful, yes, but . . . terrifying.

"Good morning, Dira," Mother said, a slip of a woman compared to this statuesque goddess. "I hope we haven't alarmed you. I was told you required a tutor in necromancy. Kindly pay your respects to Ilune, the God of Death."

Dira stood transfixed at the statement. This was a real god? An angel? "I thought angels couldn't be in the mortal realm."

"And you are correct," Ilune said, her voice musical and bright. "My body is in Celestière as we speak. However, not all of us require living vessels, which is a talent I'd be happy to teach you, too." She approached with superlative confidence, her smile revealing perfect white teeth. She floated up to meet Dira on the stairs, then offered a hand. "A pleasure to meet you, Kedira Darkleaf."

Dira accepted her hand, shaken at how cold and clammy the touch was. "Everyone calls me Dira."

"Dira it is then. You're a beautiful girl. You look a lot like your aunt, if I may be so bold."

Dira perked up. "You know Aunt Sora?"

"As well as anyone can know her. But I hear you had a little incident yesterday."

Though sheepish to give the details, Dira grimaced through the explanation. "I got angry and destroyed part of the grove with necromancy."

"That's what your dear Mother said. I would be more than happy to help discipline those instincts."

The pressing question remained of how Mother had managed to enlist a *god,* but Dira bit her tongue. No one would tell her anyway. "Thank you, um, God Ilune."

The door to the kitchen swung open, revealing Sora in a worn nightshirt, hair mussed and mouth full as she held a plate of steaming bacon. She stopped and stared at the assembly of people.

As Sora struggled to swallow, Ilune floated gracefully down, mischief in her grin. "Well, well—the elusive Sora Makosa. Delightful to see you."

She smells horrible.

Dira's heart skipped at Demitri's voice. For a being so large, the wolf so easily blended in.

The woman is very dead. Double dead, somehow.

"It's nice to see you," Sora finally managed, clearly uncomfortable as she none-too-subtly wiped bacon grease from her fingers onto her worn nightshirt. "You seem busy."

"I am always busy. Celestière seeks to cannibalize itself, but that will happen whether I am there to sow discord against Morathma or not. But today I owe my friend a favor." Intensity sharpened Ilune's gaze, even as the melding of gold and silver light prickled at Dira's memory. "Perhaps you might take a walk with me when I'm done. Just for a short while."

Perhaps necromancy could wait. The two clearly needed privacy. Sora gave a small nod. "I'll be ready."

Dira looked not at them—it seemed so rude to stare—but at Mother, only to notice something strange.

Confusion.

Conspiracy turned the gears in her mind, because Sora kept secrets, kept them for others, kept them behind doors to which Dira had no key.

Except now.

But before Dira could think through her epiphany, Ilune returned her attention to her.

"Come down, won't you? I won't bite. Let's see about aiding this necrotic power of yours."

Current era . . .

"I counted seventy-two floors."

Flowers cringed. "I counted seventy-five."

Together with Flowers, Etolié had made something of a mess on her bed, scattered papers of loosely organized castle plans making up the bulk of it. "Well, fuck me."

"It was likely my doing. I'm the one whose head is chronically spinning."

"Sounds uncomfortable. I'll give it another look, though."

Etolié began her count, pretending she didn't notice Flowers fall back into existential despair. She did that often—for good reason—but history showed she'd tell on herself eventually.

"My goodness," Flowers said with a sudden wince, but then she froze, a small gasp leaving her lips.

"You all right? You went all misty-eyed again."

Flowridia grabbed Etolié's hand and set it on her stomach. Seconds passed, and Etolié felt pressure from inside Flowers' stomach, a small poke from within. She gave a begrudging smile. "Fine, that's fucking cute. Spunky little girl, you got there."

"It's perfect," Flowridia whispered, but then she frowned. "You said 'girl'."

Shit. Fuck. Etolié hid her panic behind a smiling face, then settled on blaming her favorite scapegoat—the scientific method. "Well, if there's any science involved in the making of this little half-blood, it's a girl."

"I hadn't considered that." Flowridia hugged her stomach, those tears threatening to fall from her eyes. She fell quiet, tension in her slump.

"Flowers?"

Flowridia sniffed back tears, and while Etolié intellectually tried very hard to not care about her feelings, empathy was a far bigger bitch than Flowers.

Starshine . . .

"Hold on," Etolié muttered, holding up a finger. In her head, she prayed to Goddess Momma. *Hi, Momma. What's going on?*

Well . . .

Etolié's eye twitched, because she knew that tone—the tone Staella used when she had some nasty little secret she really didn't want to tell.

Staella finally continued. *Is everything well in the mortal realm?*

Given there's an apocalyptic Old God trying to separate the worlds, you'll have to be more specific.

You don't happen to know what your friends are up to, do you?

Ominous little statement, that. *I brought them to Ku'Shya's Realm to get her pledge. They were successful.*

You know what, I'm going to speak to Ku'Shya.

Momma, what's going on?

But Etolié didn't get an answer.

"Are you all right?" Flowers asked. "You went on quite the facial journey."

"I know your mother was a piece of shit so you won't understand that this is meant affectionately, but my momma is terrible at delivering news. Especially bad news."

"What's the bad news?"

"I don't know, but she asked if all was well and then where my 'friends' were."

Starshine?

"One moment." Etolié shut her eyes, settling back into prayer mode. *Star Momma?*

Did you escort your friends back home?

No, Kah'Sheen was supposed to take them back. Etolié's stomach dropped, uncertain of what she'd just realized—only that it was bad. *Are they all right? Did something happen?*

No, no. Just trying to explain a funny conundrum. Can you come home for a moment, sweetheart?

"Um . . ." Etolié winced as she surveyed Flowers, who looked more corpse-like by the minute, torn between duty and her damn nosy self. "Flowers, my momma wants me to go up to Celestière. Will you die in the next ten minutes?"

Flowridia shrugged. "You should go though."

Etolié groaned and tore herself from the realm, shooting her body and soul through the planes, her whole being stripped and built anew—

She landed in the desert meadow and vomited on an unfortunate patch of prickly pears. But there was no time to recover. Etolié spat the last bits of bile from her mouth as she ran to Momma's house. "I'm here!"

The door rolled open, revealing Momma. She held a babbling Soliel, oblivious to whatever panic had the rest in a stir. "Before you come in, I need to make certain that it's you. What's the name I always call you?"

Taken aback, Etolié nearly fumbled her answer. "Uh . . . is this a trick question? It's Starshine."

Staella's smile became tense. "When you were a baby, how did you entertain yourself?"

"I sprayed illusionary glitter all over the house?"

"What's the name of your favorite horse?"

This had gone on long enough. "I fucking hate horses."

Staella's stance finally relaxed. "All right. Come in."

Though baffled, Etolié obeyed, then froze at the mess she beheld.

It wasn't to say Staella's house was ever clean. But the trail of clutter seeped out from the kitchen, pots and kettles strewn across the front living space. Etolié ran to the kitchen, only to behold a whirlwind. "What the fuck?! Momma, were you robbed?"

"I don't think anything's missing. I'm a little disoriented though."

Etolié followed the mess, realizing it had all fallen from a cupboard beside Momma's iron stove. "Then what happened—?"

But Etolié's words dried up when she saw what rested peacefully in the back. Tucked deliberately away, a purple teapot with a shoddy, child's paint job radiated pure fucking evil. Etolié knelt and cautiously withdrew the cursed object, noting her momma's sudden look of horror. "You were supposed to get rid of this."

Staella set Soliel down, ushering him into the ruined kitchen. "I said I would take care of it. Not get rid of it."

"Well, it's still cursed, so may-fucking-haps the Breaker of Curses should get on that." When Staella offered to take it, Etolié held it out of reach.

"I think we should focus on the problem at hand, Starshine," Staella said, reaching again for the teapot—which Etolié continued to keep away. And while Etolié prided herself on her expert reading of body language, Momma's sudden shift into anger left her reeling. "Please be careful with that."

Startled, when Staella reached a final time, Etolié let her steal it, suspicious when her momma cradled it like a baby. "That was in the exploding cupboard."

"This isn't the focus of our problem, *Starshine*."

"Did it possibly cause the explosion, *Momma*?"

To add further suspicion, Staella ripped a small line in the air with her finger—not unlike Casvir—and stuffed the teapot inside, before closing it with a wave. "Will you please listen?"

Etolié nodded, though half her attention was kept with Soliel, who had begun banging on a stray pot with a spoon.

Staella lowered her voice, as though even the walls could hear. "I was in the garden with Soliel. Something . . . strange happened. I felt something shift in my meadow. The energy, it . . . it was wrong. And then I heard a commotion inside my house. When I ran inside, it was already like this."

Still, something was suspicious. Momma wasn't a liar, but she could withhold the truth. "You didn't call for help?"

"I called for you."

"Only after you investigated the mess. What if someone had broken in?"

"Who could possibly?"

"*I don't know, Momma. Who*?" Etolié bit back her terse words, frustrated by a great many things. "What did the teapot do?"

Momma's hesitation spoke volumes. "You weren't supposed to see the teapot."

"Is it a portal? Does it summon evil things?"

"No and no . . . but also not entirely no on either."

Everything was wrong, and Etolié's gut screamed with no cause. "Momma, what did you do?"

"Well, something fell out of my cupboard, and given Ku'Shya's tantrum in Sha'Demoni right now, I have a hunch as to, uh, what. I just wonder if, perhaps, your friends had anything to do with it, given the nature of their quest."

Etolié blinked, surely unprepared.

Pain showed in Momma's wince. "I need you to promise me you won't breathe a word about the teapot."

"*Is it really that important?!*"

Thankfully, Momma did have a spine, so while she cringed at the yell, she didn't fold or falter. "Yes."

"I fucking swear. Now for the love of god—"

"Ilune."

The name brought Etolié's thoughts to a stuttering stop. "What."

"I felt Ilune in my house, Starshine. She escaped from prison."

Truthfully, Etolié had little foundation to stand on for how to feel about this. "Wait, what does that have to do with the teapot—" Etolié gasped, hands flying to cover her mouth. Through muffled fingers, Etolié said, "It's her phylactery."

Staella shrugged in a way to definitely confirm without confirming.

"For a thousand years, you . . ." Etolié stared down her diabolical Momma, whose layers never ceased to end. "It was in the back of your fucking closet."

"Technically, it was in the kitchen just now."

Etolié said nothing, simply felt the world spin.

"I don't know what she's going to do," Staella said, voice lowering once more. "Ku'Shya is having an understandable meltdown. But I need to know—did your friends go find Ilune and get her pledge?"

"Literally, I don't know. Doesn't no one know where she is except Ku'Shya?"

"Ku'Shya and Sol Kareena, or so I thought too."

As Etolié's mind wrapped around this strange new world, again, she realized she had no idea what to feel at all. "Am I in danger?"

"I don't know."

"Is Khastra?"

"Etolié, it's been a thousand years in your world. More or less for Ilune, depending on where her prison was. Either way, I don't know where her mind is at. I doubt she even knows you exist."

Etolié nodded, the pressing reality of time starting to tick in her head. "Are you going to be safe?"

"I suspect if she wanted me dead, she would have done it already. But I already called for Eionei, just in case. And Ku'Shya was quite insistent that I could stay with her."

Etolié offered her hand, grounded by small degrees when Staella squeezed it. "I'll interrogate my friends. Can you send me back to Nox'Kartha? You're much better at it."

Staella smiled and obeyed.

Etolié's steps spun as she appeared back in Flowridia's medical suite, shoved back into reality by the presence of guests.

Sora sat on the bed beside Flowers, releasing her from a quick hug. Kah'Sheen was here—highly suspicious—and Ayla lurked uncomfortably behind Sora, trying very hard not to stare at the bouquet on the table.

Kah'Sheen noticed her first, her glee radiant. "Etolié! Small one is saying you are going to see your—"

"You three!" Etolié sputtered rather than spoke, too appalled to even find her accusations. "Or four—depending on WHEREVER THE FUCK CHAOS IS."

Sora whirled into standing, her stance defensive as she stood between the resident Darkleafs. "Excuse me?"

Etolié clamped down her virulent feelings, surely turning red as she forced calm words. "Where the fuck were you?"

"We are taking a detour," Kah'Sheen said, putting it fucking lightly. "They are wanting to see more of Sha'Demoni."

"Oh, you're gonna fucking lie—*got it*!" Again, Etolié stomped down those nasty feelings, their audacity reaching new heights. "God of Death, huh?"

Only Ayla kept a neutral face. Sora couldn't lie worth shit. Even Kah'Sheen looked nervous.

"I get it," Etolié continued, cursing her sudden awkward giggle. "Greater good and all. Gotta get those pledges. But freeing her? What the actual fuck?"

Sora's expression turned to horror. "What? We didn't—"

"THEN WHY IS SHE FREE?!"

Whatever Sora's bullshit reply, it was interrupted by a knock at the door. A pretty Celestial woman peeked her head inside, her smile perfectly diplomatic. "Hello, I..." She surveyed the tense scene. "...I can come back later."

"Yeah, fucking do that," Etolié said, waving her away, her rage surging anew as the door shut. "How did you even find her?!"

Sora's eyes diverted to Kah'Sheen, who looked increasingly suspicious.

Etolié gritted her teeth. "You know what? I won't ask. But you'd better go home and lay low, Sheen Bean. Or beg for mercy. Depends on whether your mother suspects you."

"Mother is hopefully too angry to notice I am missing. But if not, it is nice knowing all of you."

Etolié simmered as Kah'Sheen vanished into a shadow. "Start explaining."

"I have no idea," Sora said, her expression too stupid to be insincere. "We did see Ilune, but we locked everything back up. I have no idea how this could have happened."

"What about you, Darkleaf?"

Ayla raised a scathing eyebrow. "Are you accusing me?"

"I'm trying to figure out who to accuse. You seem awfully quiet."

"It wasn't me. What use would I have?"

"Chaos, then?! Is this some bullshit future thing?"

Sora held up her hands, bidding Etolié to chill the fuck out—which she would not do. "I can ask her. She hasn't said anything about Ilune, but it's the only lead we have left."

"Did you leave something behind?"

Sora shook her head. "I swear, Etolié. I know it looks suspicious, but we left everything as it was, including Ilune."

Only then did Etolié notice Flowers staring oddly at Ayla, and not in the 'marriage in crisis' way. She filed that away for later. "Go ask Chaos right fucking now. I don't even know what this means, but my momma is concerned, and Ku'Shya's pissed, and that should worry us all."

"I'll go." Sora glanced to Ayla. "Are you coming or staying?"

Everything about that friendly question was wrong as well, but Etolié simply accepted that her whole life was a lie. As it was, Ayla glanced from the door to the bouquet and finally back to Sora. "I will stay."

Sora left. Ayla softly said, "Etolié, would you mind leaving—"

The door swung back open. The Celestial woman peeked her head inside. "Is now a better time?"

"Depends on what it's about," Etolié said. Something about her aura prickled against her senses, some familiarity she couldn't quite place. "Do I know you?"

"I'm new here." The woman stepped inside, her black hair lush and flowing free, her alabaster skin nearly vampiric. She dressed as a physician might, and in her hands was a wooden box. "Flowridia Darkleaf, right? I'm Doctor Lily Enaline, a specialist in, uh, *alternative* medicine, you might say."

Etolié's gaze narrowed. "So where's the imperator?"

"I beg your pardon?"

"Imperator Casvir introduces all new physicians personally."

"Oh! Of course." The woman laughed, musical and light. Etolié's hackles raised. "He said something about that, yes. But he was caught up in imperator things. I didn't quite understand it. I'm a doctor, not a monarch."

When she tried to step forward, Etolié blocked her path, surprised to match her gaze. "You need to go."

Mischief twisted the woman's smile, which absolutely did not help her case. "And who are you to tell me that?"

She was either stupid or especially diabolical. Etolié rustled her wings, about as obvious a hint as she could fucking give. "You don't fucking know me?"

"Well, you're clearly Celestial with those wings. I'm guessing Eionei's lineage? You have his face."

Everything about the woman was deceit. "Ma'am, I'm about two seconds away from lighting you on fire."

"No, no," came a dark voice from beyond. Ayla appeared in Etolié's peripheral. "Let's see what she has to offer."

"Darkleaf, you weren't there for the last assassination attempt."

But Ayla placed herself between the so-called 'Doctor Enaline' and Etolié, allowing her to approach her frail wife.

"Flowridia, you poor, brave thing," the 'doctor' said. "It's rare for a mortal to carry a child with Silver Fire. I was sought out specifically for my expertise."

Etolié's eye twitched, but Ayla stepped to block her path. "What the fuck are you doing?" Etolié seethed.

Ayla didn't speak, merely glared.

"I see," Flowridia said, yet she did not look at the doctor, but at Ayla.

"Now, don't be alarmed. I promise they're harmless." The woman opened the box.

No amount of preface could have prepared Etolié for whatever . . . the fuck . . .

Three . . . pustules? Nasty, fleshy mounds pulsed in the box, roughly the size of Etolié's closed fist. Discoloration marred them, bruised and streaked with veins.

This was beyond even Ayla's bullshit. "What the fuck are those?" Etolié asked.

The woman offered an impish smile. "Cysts. They'll feed on the magic the baby is releasing and siphon it back, thus sparing poor

Flowridia the pain of being eaten alive. It's something the Solviraes did for centuries, did you know?"

"No."

Doctor Enaline looked back to Flowridia. "Forgive me, but would you mind lifting your dress? They need to attach to your stomach—"

"This is too much," Etolié said, but Ayla held her back once more. "What the fuck is your problem?"

Ayla's sudden grip on her wrists threatened to break bone. "She was sought out specifically for her expertise, wasn't she?"

Etolié said nothing, simply fought to stay calm as the doctor helped Flowridia remove the sheets and lift her nightgown. The cysts attached with little suckers on their bottoms. Flowridia cringed but did not scream. "Keep them on at all times unless you're bathing," the doctor said. "You can remove them for an hour without consequence. They should last you until the baby's birth, at which point dispose of them by burning. Outside though. They'll stink up your room."

When they set Flowridia's nightgown back, the three little bumps poked up like mushrooms. "Thank you," Flowridia said warily.

"My pleasure." The doctor shut her box, standing primly. "Such a gorgeous day. Make certain you go enjoy the sun once you've got a bit more color back in those cheeks. Should only take a few hours. But if anything goes wrong, I think your wife knows how to alert me." The doctor smiled at Ayla, the shared understanding making Etolié ill. "Right?"

"Of course," Ayla replied, far too serene with this apparent doctor and her creepy, body horror medicine.

Doctor Enaline met no resistance as she left, but the moment the door clicked, Etolié shoved out of Ayla's grip. *"Fucking talk, or so help me."*

"All the pieces are here. It's not my fault you're too bullheaded to put them together."

"That's hedging if I ever fucking heard it."

"Etolié . . ." Flowers spoke so quietly from her bed, though she had lifted her skirt again, poking at the strange pustules. ". . . I have my own theory, given I'm keen to know when my wife is lying."

"You're awfully nonchalant about living acne sucking on you, it's true—" *Lying,* she had said. Etolié stared down Ayla Darkleaf, who somehow didn't falter despite their impressive size disparity.

The woman had felt . . . uncannily familiar.

"What use would you have, indeed," Etolié echoed, seething as the truth assembled into a damning puzzle. "It would certainly be unfortunate if Ku'Shya found out who fucking freed the God of Death."

"And it would be equally unfortunate if Ku'Shya found out Kah'Sheen brought us to her doorstep. Your point?"

Etolié supposed she had none. She glanced to the door, where not seconds ago one of the most feared deities in Celestière had just walked away.

She said nothing at all—simply darted from the room.

As far as she knew, Ilune hadn't inherited momma's portal talents, which meant the God of Death had fucking walked through the doors like an asshole. Etolié sprinted for the staircase, resolving to commit a felony if she became sweaty over this.

Servants parted for her passing. Hooded figures floated aside. Etolié illusioned her most audacious gown, crown and all, determined to intimidate this bitch if it killed her.

Which . . . it might, but that was a tiny fear compared to her resolve to . . .

Well, Etolié didn't actually know her goal.

Her wings kept her from tripping down the stairs as she took them three at a time. At the first floor, she finally spotted the 'doctor' and her leisurely strides—as though she weren't a fucking trespasser in the home of the most dangerous man in the realm. *Hey, doc!*

The doctor that was Ilune stilled, unbothered as she smiled. "What can I do for you?"

Etolié stopped far closer than was polite for a standard conversation. This was a very evil god with whom she happened to share half her blood. They matched height. Etolié stared into those damned silver eyes and refused to fucking blink. "Explain, bitch, before I call Ku'Shya."

Not a skip in her banter. "Explain why you're naked first."

. . . Fucking Silver Fire. Etolié glared as she covered her magically exposed tits. "Illusion magic. I hate clothes. You were saying?"

"A deal was made with the devil. Who the devil was is up to interpretation in this case, but I think you can guess the terms. She slit my throat, and I appeared at my phylactery. Happy?"

No, but if Etolié were entirely fucking honest, she didn't even know why she was here. "Where are you going?"

Ilune's mask had not slipped, utterly unfazed by Etolié's interrogation. She remained serene and pleasant, that smile still a fucking lie. "Truthfully, I intend to sit in a tavern and eavesdrop. I have quite a bit to catch up on. This kingdom didn't exist before my imprisonment, so what else has changed in the realms?"

"And after that?"

"You seem like you're digging for something." Ilune's wink showed hints of malevolence. For a mere moment, the illusion slipped, revealing expansive wings. "You know who I am, so who are you? Clearly self-important, given you threatened to inform

Ku'Shya, but are you full of hot air, or should I actually feel afraid? Bear in mind, I could rip the bones from your body without so much as a thought, so choose your answer wisely."

In moments like this, Etolié wondered if she was just an idiot with inspirationally good luck. But Etolié had spent fifty years being tormented by the existence of this bitch and all she represented. Catharsis was a worthy thing to die for. "I'm Empress Etolié of Solvira, Daughter of Stars, Granddaughter of Eionei, Savior of Slaves, and Former Magister of Staelash."

And whatever Ilune had been expecting . . . it clearly wasn't that. The woman stepped back, brow furrowed as she looked Etolié up and down, studious as she glanced to Etolié's hair and finally her eyes. She lost all airs, confusion in her slack jaw. "Daughter of Stars?"

"Staella herself."

Whatever else Etolié might've threatened Ilune with was lost in the God of Death's immediate burst of radiant . . . joy? Ilune's gasp led to utter glee as she screamed, and Etolié was engulfed in an itchy, albeit friendly, hug. Too stunned to speak, Etolié froze, and not just from the unnerving coldness of her skin. "Look at you!" the God of Death exclaimed as she pulled away. "Oh, you're stunning! I always wanted a sister, but . . ." She waved at her eyes, as though warding away invisible tears. "This body can't cry, but I just might try anyway."

Etolié stuttered to find her words, wondering when she'd left the real world and entered this bizarro dimension. "I'm so confused."

"Me too, but this is the best day of my life. Freedom and a sister? I don't know what you must think of me, but I assure you— you've become the most important person in my whole world, and I would die to defend you."

Etolié could do little more than blink.

"You'll come with me to that tavern, right?" Ilune continued, pleading as she took Etolié's hand. "I have so many questions, and not a single person in the realm to answer them. I don't know who's alive or dead. I don't even know what year it is, to be honest."

"I . . ." Everything about this was suspicious—or should be. Etolié found she couldn't read this woman at all. "I don't know—"

"Please, just an hour of your time. I can only imagine what they've told you about me, and while it's all true, every nasty thing, it doesn't mean I'm not sincere in my wish to befriend you. It's not a trick. I'm not going to hurt you, I swear it. But I'm a little desperate and likely more out of my mind than I realize due to isolation. So there is my ulterior motive if that reassures you, but it has no bearing whatsoever on my proclamation of love."

Well, they were definitely related. Ilune was a rambler too. "Are you always this forward?"

Ilune's smile faded by small degrees. "Yes."

It wasn't that her better judgement said 'no.' It was that her better judgement said Khastra would have an aneurism, Ku'Shya as well, and potentially Momma too. And while Etolié had no intention of alienating the most important people in her life, this might be her only chance to deduce whether Momma was in danger. "Let me put on a real dress first. Meet me at the front gates."

Ilune's joy returned. "Of course. I'll be waiting."

Etolié wouldn't say she was put off, but she was certainly unbalanced as she watched the God of Death leave, her composure returning as she resumed the appearance of a woman who was supposed to be here.

When Etolié stepped away, she focused on a silent prayer. *Goddess Momma . . .*

. . . Staella didn't need to know yet.

Starshine?

Just checking in.

Things are well. There's been no sign of Ilune.

That's good. I'll leave you to that.

After a brief goodbye, Etolié contemplated whether this was her dumbest or finest hour. Either way, befriending the unhinged woman she begrudgingly called 'sister' was better for everyone.

Family was complicated. Etolié had accepted that. Perhaps she and Sora could commiserate over evil half-sisters.

All the air left with Etolié. Flowridia felt suspended as her mind settled into this strange reality. "You freed the God of Death for me."

Ayla's gaze fell upon her, some softness there. "Are you surprised?"

Flowridia's heart became warm. "No."

Yet Ayla remained distant, despite the calming mood. "I do hope Etolié doesn't actually tell Ku'Shya, though I have done enough for her to hate me already. I suppose it doesn't matter."

Flowridia held out a hand, bidding Ayla to join. Instead, Ayla's grip fell around herself, her stance becoming small. "Flowra—"

"These are for you," Flowridia said, gesturing to the bouquet. "I wish it was more, but there's only so much I can do in this state. But I made it especially for you."

Ayla came to sniff the bouquet, cupping one of the roses in her hand. "It's beautiful."

"Shall I explain the meaning?"

"White tulips to ask forgiveness," Ayla replied, and she plucked one out, holding it to her chest. "Moonlilies for sentiment, I would guess. Or as a jest, given I'm dead."

Flowridia smiled. "Something like that."

"Roses for love?"

"Yes, but no. Red roses mean passion. Pink is friendlier. It's . . . contentment. A comfortable love. I don't mean to say I don't feel passion for you, but it's meant to say I'm happy. Happy with you."

She prayed she did not lie. But it was as Etolié had said—had she even tried at all?

Ayla set the tulip on the bedside table, her touch lingering on the soft petals. "Is this your apology?"

"It comes with words, but yes. It's not as grand as I wish, but I'm trying to . . . accept. Accept my own limitations." Flowridia spared a glance for her ruined hand. It did not hurt today. "Ayla, I'm so sorry. I don't understand what you're going through, and when you tried to tell me, I . . ." She swallowed her tears, so exhausted from crying. "I treated you with unfathomable cruelty. It will never happen again. I want to be a safe place for you, and I promise I will work to gain that trust again."

Ayla shut her eyes, hands trembling as she fidgeted with her lefthand finger. It wore no ring. She had lost it in Kaas. "You are not sorry. You don't know what to be sorry for."

"I don't understand."

"I can name, to the very digit, how many years it has been since anyone yelled at me the way you did." No emotion at all; Ayla confessed in pure monotone. "I had just turned eight. I was sick. I had thrown up the mealy gruel given to us at the cathedral—and been screamed at as I sobbed, covered in my own filth. I was called all sorts of names, told I was ungrateful, disgusting, useless. The priest hit me across my face before holding my head in my own refuse, nearly drowning me. So you can imagine how devastated I was to have my own wife unearth that point of torture in my life."

Flowridia's breath hitched at the words. Gods, Ayla had been so small, hardly a wraith as she'd wept on the floor. "Any apology I can give is shallow, I know—"

"You *still don't know*!" Ayla spun to hide her sudden sob, gripping her hair so tight, her knuckles threatened to burst from her skin. "I-I . . .'"

Ayla blotted her tears with her sleeve, yet they fell nevertheless. Flowridia sat suspended on the bed, fearing she did not have the strength to embrace her love, though it paled to the fear of harming her wife more.

And so she stayed still, heart aching as Ayla took a stumbling step toward her. She fell to her knees, pressing her face into Flowridia's skirt, clinging to the fabric.

Flowridia remained still, lest she scare this weeping figure away. "Ayla . . ."

Ayla met her gaze, though hers was shined with tears. "Gods, I am a slave to you, whether we admit it or not. Look at me—weeping at your feet after you utterly destroyed me."

Flowridia said nothing, simply blinked back tears.

"Can we speak of this divide between us?" Ayla asked. "How long have we been lying?"

Yes, a chasm had been carved between them, and to speak of it revealed its depths. But it had not been dug through lies. Flowridia forced out the bitter truth. "I don't believe we've ever lied. But I do believe we bite our tongues when we fear we'll hurt the other."

Ayla hid her face in Flowridia's nightgown, the fabric drenched by her endless tears. "Darling, my truth is that I meant to throw myself into Onias' Hell from grief. Your sister is the only reason I am crying at your feet. And *gods*, I am agonized to admit it. I don't want you to hurt, I don't . . ."

In the span of silence, Flowridia's heart and composure shattered.

"My truth is that I was seeking any hope to live, but you severed the few strings I had grasped. My truth is that I would rather have oblivion than face the future, but then I would be a coward as well as a monster. My truth is that I don't know what I want or where I am going. Onias said to find the path to peace, but my greatest fear is that I cannot walk that path with you."

Ayla's words fell prey to her sobs, and all the while Flowridia wept her own silent tears. Yet now panic rose, her hands desperately falling to Ayla's skin, her dress. "Ayla, please . . . don't—"

"I don't know what I am doing. But tell me your truth. You cannot hurt me worse than you already have."

Despite her anguish, Flowridia breathed away the cloud of fear, for here Ayla lay weeping at her feet once more. Now was the time for redemption, and she sought what words could fix this, what lies she could spin to keep Ayla here . . .

. . . And that's what they would be. Lies.

Gods, it hurt to carve those lies away and allow the truth to trickle like a stream, like blood. But Flowridia allowed the pain to flow and spoke just as bitterly. "My truth is that my regrets have been the sharpest knives used against me, and I'm trying my hardest to let them go. I don't know where I'm going either, but . . ." Her voice caught. She breathed it away. ". . . But I fear we're both spinning. I fear we're both lost. And I fear that we don't know how wide this chasm between us actually is."

She ran her thumb across Ayla's neck, seeking comfort in her cold skin. "My truth is that I fear being weak, but look at me now. I'm weaker than ever before, and perhaps it's even more than I thought. My truth is that I'm at peace with monstrosity, or thought I was, at least. I've certainly adopted it.

"But I think the most pressing fear I hold," Flowridia continued, numbing with each phrase, "is that we're growing—growing apart. My fear is that it was always naïve to think we'd love for all our lives. My fear is that we were little more than children when this journey began—yes, even you. You were so young when you were murdered. And look at you. Ayla, you're incredible, truly. Gods, it takes courage to change, but I'm terrified that I can't be the one to help you—"

Her words choked, that numbness bleeding into cold. Every part not filled with grief screamed to fight.

"Is there any hope for us at all?" Flowridia managed to whisper, for Ayla was here, and she knew precisely what emptiness it was to have her gone. Once, she had murdered, she had betrayed all she loved just for the chance to have her back.

And now . . .

"Do you want there to be?" A plea lay in Ayla's tearful gaze, the question revealing the cracks in their foundation.

Something else Ayla had said had highlighted the very root of it all, Flowridia realized. Though the words burned in her throat, her own returned plea of *yes*, she let them fester, and instead spoke what she prayed were not knives. "You told me once that you would be nothing without me, and the fact that you believe that . . . it breaks my heart. Perhaps this isn't about what I want. Perhaps it's . . ."

The words could not be unspoken. But love was not a cage. Countless times, Ayla had professed her want to be free.

"It's about what you need. And only you can decide that."

Ayla no longer met her eye, staring into the nothing beyond. When she rose, she hugged herself, tension in the grip of her hands. Ayla had always been too willing to tear herself apart.

Once, Flowridia had held her hand down the path to self-love. Somewhere, sometime . . . Flowridia feared that same grip now held her back. "I love you, Ayla. Even if that's not enough, I need you to know."

Oh, how beautiful Ayla's gaze, those silver eyes finally meeting her own. Her tension abated, some burden released. "Whatever else comes, you have saved me in every real way. Flowra, my darling . . . I love you so." And Ayla smiled, though it balanced beauty and sorrow in tandem. "I will consider your words."

And despite the peace in Ayla's gaze, Flowridia could not speak, simply felt her dreams fall like sand through her fingers.

From the bedside table, Ayla plucked a tulip from the vase and held it gently to her heart. She kissed it sweetly on its petals . . . then offered it forward.

She asked forgiveness. Flowridia understood.

Their skin brushed as she accepted the flower, that dwindling comfort the last to go.

It was the cruelest of ironies, for Flowridia to see the woman she'd lost in Ayla's departure. A creature of grace, of pride, of poise—all of it showed in her stance as she vanished in a shadow, leaving silence in her wake.

Flowridia had offered a choice. But it was no choice at all, was it?

She crushed the tulip in her hand, her wails unheard. All the world was silent.

Casvir's image loomed above the central square in Haven, a gargantuan statue surveying his domain, rising in the center of a large fountain. As designated, Chaos sat upon its edge, but instead of watching the spray of water or the life passing her by, she held her pouch, fingering the broken prongs. Sora wove through the bustling citizens to reach her.

Though she smiled, something in Sora's face must have suggested panic. "Is everything all right?" the Goddess asked.

Sora lowered her voice. "Ilune escaped her prison."

To Sora's dismay, Chaos seemed unfazed. "Huh. So that is when this happened."

"What do you mean?"

"Ilune was always free in my time. My mother did it."

It was far too much. Sora withdrew her pipe and Spore. "And we shouldn't worry?"

"It has no bearing on our quest to stop Soliel."

That was not the answer Sora wanted, but she supposed it would have to do. "Good luck being so nonchalant in front of Etolié." Sora took her first puff from her pipe, relaxed from the smell alone. "What now?"

"We wait. We rest. We protect the final orb. Etolié suggested it was here, right?"

Sora nodded. "So that's it? We've truly done it?" Despite the magnitude of the question, Sora felt as though she stood on a trapdoor.

"We've done all we can for now."

Sora reached gently into her pouch and withdrew the lethargic Leelan, all the memories of Onias' Realm flooding her. If Onias spoke true, Leelan housed the power of one of the most powerful New Gods. And if he perished . . . assuming he did perish . . . what then? Urgency filled Sora, within her rising the desperate urge to act—but how?

Chaos became quiet as she focused again on the prongs of what was once a crown. She twisted one in her fingers, her agitation quiet but clear. What else could she feel but heartbreak? All her children were gone, and so nearly her mother as well.

When her rage toward Chaos had faded away, Sora could not say. Sol Kareena was dead, the world never bleaker. But Sora had already forgiven one remorseful monster.

She saw no monster here, nor a Goddess. Chaos was her niece, an ageless dhampir, a lost little girl.

Sora stroked her finger across Leelan's feathers, providing whatever comfort she could before setting him carefully into her lap. The motion felt odd as she pressed nearer to Chaos, tentative as she set an arm around her shoulders. Chill rose from beneath the Goddess' clothes, but Sora paid it no mind. When Chaos turned into her, Sora set her other arm around her, heart aching when Chaos set her head against her shoulder.

"Do you want to talk?" Sora asked.

Though curled against her, Chaos clutched a prong to her chest. She couldn't cry in this dead body, but still she trembled. "It would not help. My Ulu is dead. With any luck, I will be too. Once Soliel is dead, I promised to kill myself, remember?"

It felt like a lifetime ago. Now . . . it broke Sora's heart to hear it. But by all accounts, Chaos deserved to move on. She had lived an unbearably long time, only to linger for ten thousand more years in death. "When you go, will you see Uluron again?"

"I will see all my children, Sora. Solanis, Rulira, Mulgora, Valeuron, Yaleris, and Uluron—I will see them and love them as myself, free of godly troubles and mortal woes, and no Demitri whispering in my head."

"What happens to him if you go?"

"He comes too. But we will finally, *finally* be apart. My family can be whole someday. I only hope . . ." Oh, that wicked smile, increasingly forced; Sora's heart ached. "There is hope for me, but what of Ayla? Once again, I am condemning her to death by my own actions. Etolié did not explicitly comment on the matter, but she made it clear where she stood regarding my own death. If I keep my promise, I am truly lost."

"Did we not take a step toward saving her already?" The moment in Onias' cave remained a tender memory, an open, raw wound. But raw meant things could heal.

"You did. All I did was watch my mother nearly die a second time. I'm coping with that."

Gods, and who wouldn't be? Cloying dread filled Sora to imagine what could have been . . . had she not followed her instincts . . .

Ice gripped Sora's heart—the same ice that had encircled her the night her own mother had passed. "I told you I would help you save Ayla, and I meant that."

"Then let me die," Chaos whispered, a plea in her moonlit eyes. "Flowridia has to lose the baby. If there's no Dira to love, then there's no Dira to kill her."

Sora gently shook her head, the tragic truth crystal clear. "Ayla wants to be a better person for all the right reasons, and I think . . ." By the Light, the words were strange. "I-I think you underestimate what kind of healing that really is. She died because she loved you, but taking that away isn't saving her. Love is what will save her."

"Love is literally what killed her."

"Casvir killed her." Sora lowered her voice, recalling the bustling city around them. "You blame yourself because you think you could have prevented it, but you were just a kid in that vision, Dira. I won't pretend to understand everything that brought you there, but you were a child."

Chaos' words came choked. "I was not a child. I was nineteen."

"If you were human, yes, but you're a half-elf. You were a child. I would know." Sora forced her voice to steady, far more fired up than Chaos needed to hear right now. "I know I asked you this in Onias' Realm but . . . is there anything you could tell me now that I could take with me into the future? I know it goes against your rules, but to know my fate is to take it away, right? Perhaps to know hers and yours would do that same thing."

To Sora's relief, Chaos did not immediately rebuke her, instead falling into contemplation. "You cannot stop it. It happens so quickly. Gods, I was so naïve. I did not know what greater game the world was playing. You say that love saved her, but love is what drove her to become every evil thing she once tried to reject. All for me, to protect me, but I didn't understand that."

Sora considered the vision, considered Ayla in Onias' hellish realm, considered the remorseful woman seated before her . . . and hurt to know the answer. "You were never going to be safe until Casvir was gone, so the way to save Ayla is to kill him."

"And so we are right back to where we started. I failed that in my last life, and I shall fail it in this one. Whatever the means to find his phylactery, it's well beyond Soliel, Demitri, and me. Killing myself is at least the most practical solution. You can call me self-loathing if you want, but perhaps I'm actually selfless. If killing yourself were the key to saving the world, you would do it. I know you. So why stop me?"

"Because if what you just said is true, you were the reason Ayla rose up to fight him at all," Sora replied, the truth so glaringly apparent now. "She wants to let go of her grudges. She said so herself, that she's tired. So of course it's cruel to give her a reason to keep one, but if we're going to really consider that 'practical' solution of yours, there's my practical response."

"I cannot kill Casvir." Chaos pulled away from Sora, out of her embrace, and held herself instead. "That is the end of it."

Sora gave Dira her space, though ached to see how alike her anguish was to Flowridia's in her darker moments—pitiful and hunched, fighting tears. "Perhaps you can't save your mother either."

Shock filled Chaos' face. Sora pressed on. "Perhaps neither were ever meant to be your responsibility," Sora said. In Chaos' hands, the shattered crown was a damning marker of heritage—for her bloodline was not merely The Endless Night. "Perhaps both are too much responsibility for any one person."

"Who else, Sora?"

"I don't know. Is saving Ayla a single action or many? Days ago, it was me. Perhaps next it will be you, but will that be the end of it? There are others who love her. Saving someone is about more than a physical action. What's to stop Ayla from returning to Onias? Love, Dira. But in this case, Ayla has to love herself. And she's trying. All we can do is be there and love her too."

Something in the words gave Chaos pause, sorrow in her contemplation. "She was always ashamed of who she was. She hid every part of herself from me. In the end, I went to find the truth for myself—and here we are, Sora. Tens of thousands of years later, and I am still just as lost."

Sora set a tentative hand onto Chaos' shoulder, uncertain if she should comment on this slip or not. Such vulnerability was so unlike her.

"What are you asking of me?" Chaos whispered.

"I'm asking you to understand that none of this was your fault. You were a little girl cruelly tasked to carry the whole world, but you deserved none of that."

Chaos shut her eyes, no peace in her silence.

"Etolié and I," Sora continued, "have discussed how neither of us can actually change the course of fate. But you can. You've lived the future, so you know how to change it."

"I told you how to change it."

Resignation filled Sora. Perhaps she was not so inspiring as she'd hoped. "Then do it. Kill your past self. I won't help you, but I can't stop you. I just beg you to at least consider what you're taking away from the person you're trying to save."

"I am," Chaos whispered.

"Then what about what Demitri said about not killing Casvir— just subduing him. What about that? He's not wrong."

No surprise when Chaos' stance shifted, becoming stiff. Demitri's curt tone came from Chaos' mouth. "It would take more planning than we have time for. At least right now."

Sora removed her hand from Chaos' shoulder. She had the wolf's attention, and while he was often Dira's tormentor, could he help? Who knew her better? "What do you think about saving Ayla?"

"I think killing baby Soliel would do just as much good as killing Dira. We should do that instead."

Not a simple solution to execute, given the toddler was in the care of the Goddess of Stars. While Staella was not a formidable combatant, the thought of disappointing her was its own death sentence.

One final query; a fool's hope, but Sora had a few to spare. "Is there anything I can do?"

She expected snark, perhaps an insult. Instead, Chaos became hunched, vacancy in her visage. "You did enough when you saved Lady Ayla."

All her focus had been for Dira, but of course Demitri would be affected by Ayla's near suicide. "Thank you. And . . . I'll keep doing whatever I can."

"You do help. You take care of what Lady Ayla loves most. Dira."

His words were uncommonly kind, and Sora felt that same kindness well inside her. "Do you need anything? A hug?"

Chaos' glare held no bite. Merely exhaustion. "Not from you."

The answer was so obvious. "Let's go visit Flowridia."

When Chaos jerked, confusion shone in her frown. "What?"

Dira spoke so often of Ayla—never Flowridia. Sora prayed it meant nothing; surely it meant everything, but Dira would say nothing of it. But perhaps Demitri might. Sora stood and offered her hand. "Come with me. I want to see my sister, and I'm not leaving you behind. Can I trust Dira?"

Chaos' stare never wavered. "Probably. But you're stupid. Everyone would know who we are."

"You don't have to possess this body," Sora said. "What if you found something different? Something . . . cuddlier?" A thought struck her, something impossible and . . . wild. "Could you possess the current Demitri's body?"

"I don't know. But it would be suspicious anyway."

"Something else then. We can find you another rabbit. Don't you want to see your mom?"

She feared she'd be rejected, Chaos' stubborn nature reminiscent of both her mothers. But Demitri hadn't seen Flowridia in thousands upon thousands of years . . . Presumably Dira as well. Perhaps it might trigger something.

Besides, Dira had been different, tempered by seeing Ayla once again. Perhaps . . . Perhaps there could be trust there.

To her surprise, Sora received a bittersweet smile. "Can it be a dog instead?"

A bit of searching, and a bit of poking around in oddities shops, but they did find enough of a dog skeleton for Chaos to deem it appropriate. Off to a graveyard, where they hid Chaos' current form in a mausoleum.

When the ghost withdrew, Chaos casted no illusion—a woman with skeletal scars, half her skull exposed. "I'll be limited to what this dog's body can provide," she said as Dira. "I'll be able to speak, but not through the dog, if that makes sense."

"I think I follow," Sora said, and she watched curiously as Chaos' spirit slipped into the bones, vanishing even as they began to glow.

Like the humanoid body she had stolen, the dog gained a form. Muscle and sinew wrapped around the clean bones, fur sprouted from flesh, and despite the macabre origin, Chaos was . . . a rather adorable dog. Nothing like a wolf, no, but golden fur and a wagging tail revealed a friendly figure—and those eyes remained the same. One silver; one gold.

Not too large, though Sora would have struggled to carry this new form. "How do you feel, Demitri?"

Chaos—Demitri—responded by giving a small *bark*.

They moved unhindered through the town and castle, the skeletal guards thankfully having no qualms about dogs, it seemed. Through hallways and staircases, Sora had too much time to stew yet felt only peace.

At Flowridia's door, she knocked. "Flowridia?"

Sora heard nothing. She tentatively peeked inside.

A lump showed beneath Flowridia's sheets, shaking as Sora neared. Quiet cries sounded from beneath, and when Sora gently moved the blankets aside, it revealed a shattered figure, face swollen and streaked with tears.

Sora kicked off her boots before climbing in beside her, uncertain of what to do when Flowridia wrapped around her like an anemone. "I brought a friend."

Demitri set his head on the edge of the bed. Flowridia reached for his soft, golden head, gasping when he licked her hand. With Sora's aid, she sat up as Demitri climbed onto the bed, practically shoving himself into her arms.

And Flowridia, soft-hearted for all creatures, wrapped her arms around him and sobbed.

Sora struggled to speak, swallowing her own rising tears as Demitri did his best to embrace her, his whine somewhere between joy and heartbreak.

Minutes passed. Sora scratched tender lines along her sister's back, lost amid her tears. Neither spoke; Demitri's fur was drenched with her sorrow. When he licked her face, Flowridia gave a broken smile, making no move to stop him.

"Ayla and I, we . . ." Flowridia choked as she forced the words. "We . . ."

She said nothing more. She did not need to. This omen had been spoken in Onias' Realm.

Sora joined in the embrace.

CHAPTER 29

Current era . . .

"Empress of Solvira, you said? Is my lineage really so useless that you had to take the throne?"

Ilune laughed to curtail the criticism, but she wasn't exactly wrong, nor did she make any attempt to show any subtlety at all in the extremely busy tavern. The one saving grace was the anonymity of crowds, and with Etolié's wings illusioned away, there was little to suspect about either of them.

Etolié ignored the drink brought by the bartender, preferring the comfort of her much stronger, illusioned brew. Ilune, however, downed her second tankard without even a blink—which meant she was either suicidal, or possessing a body meant she had an undead constitution.

"Explain how the fuck you're here, first. Are you being hosted?"

"This is a dead body hosting me. I can morph it to be whatever I want."

Yes, it was gross, but Etolié consensually fucked her very much dead fiancée and thus had no space for judgement. "And you possessed a convenient corpse available in Nox'Kartha, which is how you got here so fast. Got it. Can you teleport?"

"Alas, I didn't inherit that piece of our mom's powers. My true self is in Celestière, and I lack the capacity to move it particularly fast."

Etolié took another long sip, bracing herself for a bit of uncomfortable trivia. "We have a lot of ground to cover, so take notes. Your legitimate lineage is dead due to a lot of finger-pointing, but I guess ultimately the God of Order. I did, however, have to stake claim over a reprehensible Solviraes bastard under Casvir's thumb whose tears sustain my life force."

To her credit, Ilune seemed oddly unfazed, even shrugging as she waved down the bartender for another drink. "Unfortunate."

"Trust me, I hate every minute of it. Feel free to usurp me any time—" She hid her sudden choking behind her drink, realizing the sheer stupidity of what she had just said.

Ilune's laughter gave no indicator of her feelings. "Good to know."

Typically, Etolié would resort to illusioning facial expressions at this point, but Ilune's Silver Fire put a damper on that. Instead, she accepted that she'd just have to look constipated as she forced her smile. "It actually might be funny to do that to Casvir."

Ilune gleefully sipped the offered tankard. "I keep hearing that name. Tell me more."

And Etolié did, muttering blasphemes amid the loyal crowd of citizens. From their first meeting to her current station as 'political prop.'

"And he's a necromancer, you said?"

Etolié nodded.

"Perhaps with a little sorcery, he could be a decent progenitor for my new lineage."

And it was a damn fine thing Etolié hadn't quite put her drink to her lips, given the amount of phlegm that escaped in her scoff. "Don't even joke about that. Also, he's a lich. As are you, it should be noted."

"As I said, it might take a little extra sorcery. Liches aren't like normal undead, and let us not forget I have the Silver Fire. I don't have to be the one who carries the baby. But all right. As my sister, I shall allow you one veto. And if you really wish to waste it on your employer, so be it."

"I don't like that you called him that."

"It was the politest word I could think of. But restarting my lineage is one of my top priorities, so prepare your sanity for that."

Truthfully, having a little niece or nephew to dote on sounded delightful, but Ilune's segue ruined everything. "Where is Ku'Shya at nowadays? Any living children?"

As much as Etolié was begrudgingly enjoying this awkward encounter, here lay one of their two deal-breaking subjects. Again, she braced herself. "So, about Khastra."

The name brought confirmation that Ilune was also not illusioning any of her expressions, despite her ability to do so. Her effortless languor stiffened, that impish smile of hers stale. "You know her?"

"Yes, and she doesn't like you, so stay away." But to stop here was what cowards would do, and Etolié vomited the rest. "Also, she's with me now, in a romantic and sexual fashion, so . . ." Godsdammit, how did you end something like this? ". . . family reunions might be a little awkward."

"They would have been awkward anyway," Ilune replied, her sip from her tankard just a little overlong.

"Is this a 'lance the boil' kind of situation, or should we tiptoe around it until we die?"

"Which part of it? Khastra despises me and rightfully so, but anything to do with family is a little touchy, now isn't it? I suppose with Khastra the honest truth is, with all possible respect, that she was devoted to me, as well as in love—and I think I loved her as much as I was capable of loving anyone that way, but you'll come to see that I am far more a user of people than I am capable of sincere affection. I used her. I exploited her love for me and asked her to betray her family and commit heinous crimes in my name. She finally saw me for what I was and had the Bringer of War let me know very well what she thought of it. But yes—family reunions. That was the same incident where I tried to have our mutual mom killed, and . . ." Something shifted beneath her aura of cool, the crack in Ilune's indomitable presence. ". . . well, blessedly, Khastra didn't listen that day. In fact, she never listened to me ever again." Beyond, the sun had shifted. Ilune shifted with it, content to avoid the sunlight. "It's been an hour. You can go, if you want."

In general, people said this to politely end a conversation without saying they wanted to leave, but Ilune gripped her tankard just a little too tight, that easy nonchalance having never quite returned.

"Look, I don't hate you," Etolié said, because against all odds, she didn't want to go. "Which is weird, because I spent far too many years of my life being resentful of you, or resentful that I wasn't you. We don't have to talk about momma if you don't want to, but I won't judge you if you need to."

Ilune set her tankard down, calm despite the tremor in her voice. "My one mercy in that prison was the knowledge that I would never have to face her again."

"She kept your creepy teapot safe."

Etolié kept perfect eye contact as she sipped from her own illusioned tankard, content to watch the many stages of grief flash across her sister's face. "I did fall out of her kitchen cupboard."

"Yes, but my actual point is that she does love you, though I suspect you two need to have many long and tearful discussions."

But Ilune shook her head. "What I took from her isn't something I can ever accept forgiveness for, no matter how sincerely she'd give it."

Etolié had little to say to that, despite the innate desire to fix her sister's bad mood. But no, no—matricide was worth feeling guilty over. "I know I'm a piss poor consolation prize compared to Neoma, but I'm here for you."

No, Ilune couldn't cry, but her possessed corpse body sure could mimic it. Grief twisted her features, and Etolié sucked up her disdain for hugs as she slid from her chair and wrapped her sister into a tight embrace.

Ilune reciprocated, desperation in how she clutched the fabric of Etolié's not-illusioned dress. Though she had no tears, her words held a sob. "Don't say that. You're perfect."

Fucking hell, now Etolié teared up. Just when she thought her crusty heart had reached its capacity, it never failed to grow.

And Ilune, for better or worse, was a new piece of it.

Thank gods for the anonymity of crowds. No one spared them a glance, and when Ilune did finally loosen her hold, there showed sincerity once more. "I'm not ready to talk about Neoma. But I'd be charmed to know your story."

"I'm not always an inspiring story."

"No one is, yet we're all still judged by our worse sins. You know mine. I certainly won't judge you for yours."

The world still turned, and Etolié wondered if it was selfish to hide away in a tavern with the one person everyone she loved would condemn—or if, perhaps, she'd earned this one, small sin.

She could spare a few hours. Etolié settled back into her seat.

When darkness settled in the bounds of Flowridia's room, no sunlight left to fill it, Sora's breathing became steady and slow.

A comforting presence, yes. Flowridia wasn't used to silence.

Sora's dog was suspiciously cold, but he certainly had a soul. Flowridia's tears saturated his fur, and all the while he remained in her arms, receptive to her gentle pets.

But even canine companionship did little to soothe her shattered heart.

Flowridia had no more tears left, and despite the tense ache in her head from dehydration, she felt stronger than she had in weeks. When she sat up, her vision remained steady. When she rose, her legs did not wobble.

The dog followed as she stepped carefully to her vanity mirror. She lit a candle, but even beyond the saturation of warm light, a bit of color had returned to her cheeks. The cysts popped up awkwardly from beneath her gown, but they were a small price to pay for returned mobility.

Ayla had freed the God of Death for her. And Ayla was . . .

Flowridia sat on the vanity's chair and slumped across the desk. Too exhausted to cry; her mind simply spun in circles. More than likely, Ayla watched from the shadows. Flowridia traced the natural divots of the wood with her finger, numb above all else. Beside her, Sora's dog wagged its tail stiffly, like a pendulum. Dogs were highly expressive by nature, but this one's face remained blank despite his otherwise pleasant body language—not unlike a wolf. And such odd heterochromia—silver and gold.

However, the dog was clearly dead, so expecting standard dog traits of it was foolish. Once Sora awoke, Flowridia would ask about that.

Ayla was . . . hurting.

Ayla had nearly ended it all. Ayla had nearly thrown herself into Onias' Realm. Ayla had mysteriously made amends with Sora, but Ayla remained in stasis, nevertheless.

"Ayla, if you're watching . . ." Flowridia's whisper faded, her breath hitching. Yet she forced the final words, though cursed her trembling lip. ". . . just be safe."

As she stood, there came a faint light from the seams of her bedside table drawer.

Flowridia opened the drawer, startled to see her mirror glowing. Its other half was lost; Sora slept hardly a touch away. Wary, Flowridia stepped toward the window, then touched the mirror's surface.

There appeared a face she felt no emotion to see—for pure numbness filled her, along with shock.

The God of Order spoke. "Good evening, Flowridia. Are you alone?"

Panic filled her. She glanced to Sora, then to the dog, who emanated a faint growl. "Alone enough. How are we speaking?"

"Your sister dropped the mirror's other half in Neoma's Valley. It was not a far leap to assume you held the other end. But before I tell you my purpose, I wish to ask—have I ever harmed you?"

A strange query. "You've threatened me more than a few times."

"Have I ever acted?"

She shook her head.

"And have I ever helped you?"

She nodded, remiss to admit he had even saved her life.

"Please trust that I am trying to help you again," Soliel said, the scene behind him dark, yet occasional light scattered beyond. "This is no trap. This has no bearing on my quest for the orbs, I swear it. But I am begging you to leave this castle and come with me."

Taken aback, Flowridia struggled to even speak. "What?"

"You are in grave danger."

"As you've alluded to many times, yes."

"The future be damned—come with me. I can save your life."

Logic said to throw the mirror and scream for Etolié, but intrigue kept her rooted. "Ayla already found a way to save me from death. So far, I'm feeling much better."

"You don't die from the pregnancy."

The words sank like a stone.

"Flowridia, all I want is a better future for the ones who survive. I have had a change of heart. Come with me, please. Bring Ayla if you must, but for the sake of the future this might yet save, I beg you to trust me."

His sincerity bruised her worst of all. "How do I die?"

"I don't know. But I will tell you everything I do know if you will only let me protect you."

"You've told me all along that you know my death. Tell me the truth, or I'm staying here."

"I haven't lied. All of us—Dira, Etolié, Ilune, *everyone*—thought your infant consumed your soul, but your soul was never freed when Dira was killed by the Convergence. I don't know your fate, Lady Flowridia, and that terrifies me. So come with me."

The wrongness of it prickled the hair on the back of Flowridia's neck, yet she saw only desperation in Soliel's weary countenance. "Why now?"

"Because I will soon be—"

The dog's growling surged, his snarl fierce enough to startle her. Sora shot into wakefulness, drawing a knife from who knew where.

On instinct, Flowridia tapped the mirror. Soliel's face disappeared.

"What happened?" Sora said, her stare shifting between Flowridia and the dog.

"Nothing. I must have startled him." Flowridia sat on the bed, casually slipping the mirror in her blouse, away from Sora's keen gaze. The dog seemed to have calmed. When Flowridia cautiously offered a hand, he gave it a small kiss.

With the apparent danger gone, Sora finally rubbed the sleep from her eyes, slumping forward. "By the Light, I feel like I haven't slept in a month."

Flowridia's mind remained far away, upon Soliel and his impossible offer. Suspicion and intrigue battled within her. This man had murdered Lara, yet he had also saved her life. Had he lied? Had he *ever* lied? But, no. Soliel would stoop to any depths for the final orb—now was the time for lies. "You just completed an incredible journey," Flowridia muttered,. "You've earned your rest."

Sora sniffed her tunic. "I smell like it too. Sorry."

"You smell like the ocean. There are far worse things."

Flowridia kept her attention to the dog as Sora shifted to sit beside where she stood. "Do you want to talk about . . . whatever happened?"

The reminder twisted Flowridia's stomach anew, bringing a wash of grief. "Ayla said you saved her life in Onias' Realm. How literal was that?"

Sora's grimace stole the final remnants of sleep from her face. "I'm under threat of death to not repeat anything I heard."

"Then don't repeat it. Just say what you can."

"Then, yes. It's entirely literal."

The statement rang like a discordant chord in Flowridia's head. "I see."

That same sorrow reflected in Sora's countenance. "I assume you know about . . . a-about her life? Before The Endless Night?"

Flowridia nodded.

"She never really had a life at all, did she?"

Flowridia swallowed tears at the statement, the memory of a tear-stained night in Solvira's castle, where Ayla had spilled every dark secret in her heart, playing anew behind each blink. "No. She didn't."

Moisture shone in Sora's own gaze. "I told her that I forgive her. That's what saved her—though tackling her to stop her from jumping into the void might've had something to do with it as well."

Flowridia's scoffing laugh led to a sob, for with it came guilt unparalleled for words said in anger in a cathedral underground. The Endless Night truly was put to rest, the fires of that rage quelled by the descendant of those who lit it.

But who was Ayla now? Who was Ayla without the monster?

"I don't know what happened between you two," Sora continued, "but she's deeply hurt."

"What happened was Kaas, Sora," Flowridia said. "What happened was Mereen breaking us both down into nothing—and here we are, desperate to build ourselves anew, only to find we're stark shadows of our former selves. What happened is Ayla throwing away the very monstrous traits I embraced to be able to truly love her. What happened is—" Flowridia swallowed back tears, each word a fresh laceration upon her heart. "What happened is me. It's my fault. I've become everything I feared I would. Despite everything I aspired for, I've become my mother instead." A few tears escaped, and when Sora's hand fell upon her back, Flowridia leaned into the touch.

"I . . . really hope that what I'm about to say doesn't backfire horrifically," Sora began, and through Flowridia's blurred vision, she saw Sora staring far away. "Odessa killed my father, the man who meant everything to me. She was awful to you. I won't pretend to know the extent of it, but she alluded to it herself. And so it haunts me, that . . ." Sora's breath hitched, though her threatened tears did not yet fall. ". . . that despite every evil thing she was, she was my friend. She was always kind and welcoming to me, and even berated me for accepting the bare minimum of decency from others. She made every effort to make certain I felt accepted and—" Gods, to watch Sora bite back a sob . . . Flowridia's own tears fell ever faster. ". . . a-and loved. I miss her. Isn't that fucked up? I miss the woman who murdered my father, though I don't believe she ever knew."

Sora remained quiet a moment, the conversation utterly surreal. "Sometimes I think about who Odessa must have been before the Solviraes took everything away, because there was once a kind soul inside of her. There was once a woman burdened with magic she had to keep hidden, who loved a man named Elyas—and who watched him and her familiar be murdered. It doesn't dismiss all the horrific things she did. I-I'm not trying to apologize for her crimes. But beneath the legend of the witch in the Abyssal Swamp was a woman who was funny and kind and befriended those who needed it.

"That's always been you, Flowridia. I won't pretend to understand your damn puns, but you were born with wit. You've always been kind, and you have an uncanny way of worming your way into people's hearts. For the Light's sake, you're friends with Imperator Casvir. You stole the heart of Ayla Darkleaf. You love the unlovable, and while I won't say it always leads you to the best of places, love is still love. To be honest, I really admire that about you."

Flowridia failed to hold in her sob, the words puncturing the pressure in her chest. Here catharsis lay, found in the tears staining her sister's shirt.

And finally, there fell a few of Sora's tears, her shuddering sob barely controlled. "I understand your fear. My final words to Mereen were a vow to never become like her. And like Odessa, there was someone good there once, someone who had everything taken away from her by a monster. But they both let that grief consume them. Cycles repeat, and they became monsters themselves.

"Odessa took my father from me. Mereen took my mom. They were my everything. And I shudder at how easily I could have become just as consumed by rage and grief as Mereen. It cost me everything to break that cycle. I lost my Fireborn family, I lost my entire sense of self, and I nearly lost my life, but I don't regret a damn thing. I gained so much more than I gave up—including you.

"I'm not trying to talk about myself. I just mean to say that Odessa took your innocence. Mereen took Demitri and might've taken Ayla too. And because you're like Odessa, it means you could let that loss change you the same way. But you can break that cycle. It might cost you everything, but you don't even know what incredible things you'll find instead."

What was there to even say? Flowridia had no words, simply wept into Sora's shoulder, her grief parting for something new and bright.

Sora pulled her into a hug, no words passing between them as they cried. Here they were, bound by blood, and Flowridia had never considered the extent of her sister's own journey to absolution, to end the cycle of hatred and pain with a monster . . . who had also been consumed by sorrow and rage.

And what would it cost Ayla to change?

Everything.

"How do you even begin?" Flowridia whispered.

"If I were to pinpoint my first deliberate step away from Mereen's legacy, it's when I tried to save you from the dungeon in Kaas. There was no turning back after that. But . . . I think it truly started when I accepted that I cared about Odessa. Accepting that even someone so monstrous had a soul inside her was entirely dissonant to my worldview. Mereen passed her black and white sense of justice down her family line, and that was the first time I'd truly questioned it."

Flowridia thought of Thalmus and his wisdom, his acceptance of his life's trials . . . and the peace that had followed. A quiet life in Staelash, using his inner strength to aid the populace around him, and of course his kindness toward a broken girl and her wolf.

"I think only you can know what course you have to take," Sora continued, "but I'm always here for you."

"I'll think on it," Flowridia said, and while she did not quite feel hope, she felt acceptance after all.

A knock sounded. When no one entered, Flowridia said, "Just a moment," and wiped her tears, helped Sora to wipe her own, and hugged her as tight as Flowridia could bear without squishing the strange cysts on her stomach. "Thank you. I know we haven't always seen eye to eye, but you've really come through for me. When I say I don't deserve you . . . I really mean that."

"My—*our*—papa said once that family is who you choose," Sora whispered, her scent familiar and sweet. "It doesn't have to always make sense, and it's not about what you deserve. Sometimes it's just what sisters do."

When they parted, Flowridia wondered again . . . what it meant to lose everything and gain so much more. Because that was Sora— who had lost the family she'd known and found Flowridia instead.

Sora helped Flowridia to rise and went to grab her chair, but Flowridia waved her off, feeling much stronger than before. When she answered the door, one of Casvir's hooded servants floated nigh. "Lady Flowridia, Imperator Casvir requests the presence of Empress Etolié in the war room."

"Etolié isn't here," Flowridia replied, aware of Sora's shadow behind her.

"That is unfortunate. Imperator Casvir pressed upon its urgency."

"I know where she is," Sora said. "I couldn't name the tavern, but I saw her enter. Tell him I'll go to Haven and fetch her as fast as I can."

"It would be appreciated." The figure bowed and floated away, its eerie motions leaving Flowridia uneasy.

"Will you be all right alone?" Sora asked.

Flowridia nodded. "Are you taking the dog?"

Sora glanced back, as though the dog could read her glance—or perhaps it could. Flowridia had no expectations of a mysterious undead dog. "I think he wants to stay."

"Are you going to explain where you found a dead dog?"

Amusement filled Flowridia to watch Sora's minor panic—because yes, it was suspicious, but Sora had no ill will, and Flowridia was content to find anything to laugh over. "When I get back."

"Stay safe," Flowridia said, and she prayed the universe didn't test that plea.

"So Emperor Malakh has the audacity to track me down, haul me to Neolan, and demand I assist in rehabilitating the refugees I freed from slavery—which sounds like sunshine and daisies, but what he actually meant was place me in charge of territory in northern Solvira. He tried to make me queen." Etolié balked at the word. "I compromised for magister."

Well past sunset, the gentle dizziness of drunkenness had actually begun to affect her. Her and Ilune's blended laughter had filled the rowdy space for hours, invisible among the other patrons. "At least I got to meet my best friends in the entire realm. Khastra, of course, and the man I bullied into being king."

Ilune's own musical laughter rarely faded, even when the stories were more serious. "Bullied?"

"Clarence was the empress' brother, and he'd practically been running the show before I got there anyway. *He* was going to be magister, but fuck no."

"I'm shocked Khastra consented to being a part of that, no offense."

"Is it weird if I say she only went along with it because she fell madly in love with me instantly?"

"As long as we're being lighthearted about it, I'll say no and keep laughing."

Etolié shrugged, before refilling her stein with mere thought once more. "It's the trauma. If you're nice to me, I'll adopt you for life."

"Well, we will have to see what the trauma of being locked underground for however the hell many years has done to me. Perhaps I'll even be nice."

Etolié waved off the words, though a little clumsily in her tipsy stupor. Alcohol rarely affected her in any normal way, but concentrated efforts at least got her buzzed. "I think you're nice."

And just when things might've gotten mushy, Etolié caught a glimpse of familiar blonde locs cutting through the crowd. "Fuck. Real world, incoming."

"Should I disguise myself?"

"More than you already are? You're fine. Sora has no reason to suspect." Biting the bullet, Etolié waved her arm at the searching figure, finally making eye contact. "If Flowers were dying, Ayla would have come, which means it's not important."

Sora finally appeared at the table, no Chaos in sight, but Etolié supposed she was a grown Goddess who could make her own decisions. "Etolié—"

"Anonymity is akin to godliness."

The half-elf grimaced, biting back whatever long-suffering retort she might've conjured. Instead, Sora smiled awkwardly at Ilune, and Etolié's twisting gut suggested she might've spoken too soon. "Hello."

If there was one thing Ilune couldn't hide, it was that mischievous smirk gracing her visage, one that both flirted and threatened all at once. "Sora, right?"

"Correct, uh, my lady."

Ilune's laughter was nothing like the raucous joy they'd shared just minutes ago—far more charming and controlled. "My lady?"

"Empress Anonymous likely wants your identity secret as well."

Ilune's returned chuckle was far more flirtatious this round. "Perhaps that's wise. May I ask something? Your surname is unique, as I mentioned in the cave, and you're the older sister. Does that mean you're the heir?"

Etolié couldn't decide if she felt put off by . . . whatever she was witnessing, but Sora simply looked confused. "It would, but that kingdom is no more."

"No more? No, merely occupied. Someone else is keeping that throne warm for you—or cold, given his lack of blood flow, but you see my point."

. . . Why, oh, *why* was Ilune biting her lip?

"How interesting," Ilune continued, that impish grin returning. "To what do we owe the pleasure?"

Sora tore her attention away from Ilune, probably not high enough to deal with whatever shit this was. "If we're using shit aliases, Imperator First and Last needs you, and it's apparently important enough to need me to come all the way here to fetch you."

Etolié's stomach dropped. "Wait, no. Casvir can fucking deal."

"You tell him that."

Damn soul contracts and damn Flowers and the baby, too. But if Ilune's falling countenance was any indication, the disappointment was mutual. "I suspect this isn't something I can join you for."

"If you want to come to the castle, we just need to make sure you're away from the viceroy, unless you're willing to explain away the wings. But my house in Solvira was, uh, blown up a little, so I can't have you stay there—yet."

Ilune's expression was kind. "Don't worry about me. It would be wise of me to move my angelic body somewhere safer anyway. Clean up a little. Collect myself. Figure out my new purpose in life."

"But I'll see you again, right?"

"You will."

When Etolié stood, Ilune followed, stealing her into another firm embrace. There would be a time and place for the 'hugs make me itch' conversation, but today, Ilune was a puzzle piece she had never known she missed.

There really was something special about this sisterly business.

But the moment they parted, Ilune resumed that odd persona about Sora, batting her eyelashes just so. "Delightful to see you again, Sora. I must say, at the risk of being forward, you're far prettier not stained by that damn maldectine glow."

Thirty plus years of political bullshit hadn't prepared Etolié for this. She tried desperately to gauge Sora's reaction, but her panicked brain heard static instead.

As it was, Sora seemed to also be thinking in static. ". . . Thank you. You— You look prettier not in chains."

Ilune gave a dramatic sigh—surely for show, given corpse bodies didn't breathe. "I'd say you'd look prettier in them, but that *would* be forward. Instead, I'll simply say that I dearly hope to see you again."

When Ilune offered a hand, Sora set her own in it like a puppet, her motions awkward and stilted—and visibly gulped when Ilune brought it to her lips and kissed it. "Farewell, Sora."

Ilune escorted herself out of the tavern, leaving Etolié's heart warm and her stomach a vat of bubbling stew. "Well, that wasn't how *our* meeting went."

Sora stared at her hand as though bitten by a spider.

"How do you feel?" Etolié pressed, hoping that Sora might help her decide how to feel as well.

Sora sounded exceptionally pained. "I don't know."

"I might be the only person in the realm who won't think that's a bullshit answer. Let's take a weeklong carriage ride and sort it out, hmm?" As much as remaining anonymous was important, the tavern continued its riotous party around them, paying them no mind at all. "Where's our resident Goddess?"

Only then did Sora put her hand down, though still sounded dazed. "Um, she's in a dog body right now."

Etolié blinked, but supposed it could be weirder. She had been a rabbit once, after all. "That's not a 'where,' but thank you for clarifying."

"She's in the castle. With Flowridia."

Despite the noise of the tavern, Etolié heard the precise moment her sanity fractured. "I'm sorry, you left the matricidal Goddess with *who now*?!"

Thank fuck, that finally blasted Sora out of her stupor. "She said she wasn't going to."

"That's nice, but I have a theory about those assassination attempts—"

"What assassination attempts—"

"Fuck, I don't have time for this—WALK HOME."

Fury pulled her focus fast, and Etolié perfectly crystallized the image of Flowridia's medical ward, the couches, fireplace, the bedding—

And ripped herself to shreds—but when she opened her eyes, she was standing in the ward itself.

Alone.

CHAPTER 30

Fifteen years after the end of the world . . .

Sora kept secrets. Now, Dira had one too.

By evening, Ilune had left. Dira found Sora in her aunt's bedroom.

"So how does Mother know a god?"

Surprise colored Sora's features. She set a hand on her chest. "You startled me."

Further evidence of Sora's compromised state. Dira suppressed a smile. "How does she know Ilune?"

Sora sat on the bed, looking pensive as she gathered the anticipated rejection. "Your mother released her from prison shortly before your birth."

Dira fought to hide her own shock. That was . . . uncommonly honest. "Oh. Why?"

"Because your mother thought she had the means to save your birth mom's life. But don't hold that against Ilune. We didn't know it was too late."

This was supposed to be a much more delicious moment, revealing her hidden cards. Dira shoved aside the grief that came with any mention of her mom. "So, you're in love with Ilune."

Sora frowned. "I'm not in love with Ilune."

"Then why have you been sneaking her into the manor?"

Cards on the table. Sora became very still, her calm demeanor failing to hide the panic in her eyes. "What are you talking about?"

"Actually, I have a better question." Dira plopped beside Sora on the mattress, fighting the urge to grin. "Who is Soliel?"

"I told you—"

"I'll tell Mother."

Sora stared as though slapped.

Dira made a show of checking her nails, no longer hiding her triumph. "Tell me a secret, and I'll keep yours."

The seconds ticked by. Sora did not breathe, her voice terse when it finally came. "I'm not the one keeping secrets from you, Dira, and I'm powerless against the person who is. I love your mother like a sister, and she's said the same, but that doesn't stop her from threatening to kick me out of the estate every time I've begged her to be honest with you. I swear to you, I'm trying."

This victory was starting to feel much less satisfying. "Well, then how do you know Ilune?"

"Ilune is Etolié's half-sister. Did you know that?"

Dira shook her head, the thought a revelation.

"Then you likely don't know that Etolié had someone else in her life that she considered a sister. You know about Khastra, right?"

"That's Etolié's fiancée who passed away."

"Khastra had a younger sister. Etolié loved that sister like her own. But she . . . Kah'Sheen was her name. She's dead. And Etolié blames Ilune."

The words settled, somber and soft. "But why would Ilune kill her?"

Sora's gaze became distant as she looked upon the past. "Ilune is reckless. Kah'Sheen wasn't her target, but it didn't matter. It's why Etolié never wanted her to meet you. If she knew I was involved with Ilune, much less sneaking her into the house, it wouldn't end well. Etolié is too valuable an ally to risk alienating—which she would do to herself, because I know your mother well enough to know she'd take my side."

Gods, there really was a whole world she knew nothing about. Dira set her hand on Sora's forearm. "So you are in love with Ilune?"

"It's complicated. I don't trust her." Tears prickled in Sora's eyes, causing Dira's breath to hitch. "Etolié isn't wrong. Ilune is bullheaded and reckless and arrogant, and I wish I didn't care. I wish we'd never met. My heart hurts for Etolié—the day Kah'Sheen died, she lost Ilune too. So, no. I don't . . . I shouldn't. I can't."

But she did.

Dira wrapped her arms around Sora. "I won't tell Mother."

"Thank you."

"I'm sorry I tried to blackmail you."

Melancholy colored Sora's smile. "I'm always on your side. I hope you know that."

Foreign guilt choked her. She swallowed it down. "And I kind of feel like I'm the reason you can't be with Ilune."

"Not at all."

"But you could be in Celestière with her."

Sora set her hand atop Dira's, vehemence in her teary gaze. "You are the most important thing in the realms to me, Dira. If I had a kid of my own, I would be damn lucky for them to be as wonderful as you."

Dira shifted awkwardly, well aware that her next words were equal parts manipulative . . . and true. "I'm basically your kid."

Whatever she expected, it was not for Sora to stiffen and brace against tears. "Oh, don't say that. You'll make me cry more."

"It's true though. It doesn't mean Mother means any less to me. I just mean that even though I never had Mom . . . I had a mom."

Sora gave firm hugs, and today she had no apprehension about crushing Dira in her arms. Dira clung tight to her embrace.

"Being your mom is the best gift life's ever given me."

"Even though I blackmailed you?"

"Even though you blackmailed me."

Current era . . .

Cheering ensued at Etolié's sudden disappearance, the drunk patrons perhaps assuming her stunt was a party trick, but Sora simply stared at where she'd left, utterly off balance.

No one had bothered to tell her about any damn assassination attempts. "Goddammit, Etolié," she muttered, squashing her innate rise of panic. Where the hell had she gone?

Quick as she could, Sora ducked under and around drunken patrons, considering it a victory to escape without getting any ale spilled on her clothes. When she stepped into the cool night air, the city itself was far quieter, the hour late, and there, in the distance, was a wandering God of Death, ignorant to Sora's distant presence.

Ilune had no clear destination, simply stopping to gaze inside closed shop windows, an elegance to her steps that immediately drew Sora's eye, though she just as quickly averted her gaze.

Sora burned where Ilune's lips had touched her hand, uncertain of this . . . *something* smoldering inside her. Everything about Ilune was suspect, her history the least of Sora's worries at the moment. Sora placed a hand to the small lump in her tunic, to a bird apparently cursed to hold the power of a goddess no longer of this world, or any.

Ilune had slain a goddess once.

And Ilune controlled death.

Onias had said to trust no one. Chaos had said Ilune was not a danger to her.

Flowridia might be in danger . . . But what if Ilune could help? Dammit all, if Ilune wandered away, Sora would never see her again. And while everything about Ilune ran contrary to Sora's beliefs about the world, she had befriended such people before. If she could befriend the likes of Odessa and Ayla Darkleaf, she could hold a civil conversation with Ilune, strange flirtation aside.

Swallowing back every bit of common sense she had, Sora walked briskly toward the incognito goddess, praying this would be the last time.

Before she had to awkwardly come up with a hail that wasn't Ilune's name or title, Ilune herself turned at her approach, her curiosity escalating into intrigue. "Well, well. This is far sooner than expected."

There was something about that smirk of hers. Sora struggled to look away. Whatever Ilune's intentions for her, they couldn't be noble—or simple. "I want to talk to you about something. A few somethings."

"Anything."

Sora glanced around the mostly empty street, then lowered her voice. "Do you know who my sister is?"

"I was her doctor, Sora."

She said it with such disappointment. Sora cursed how it ruffled her own feathers. "I have reason to believe she's going to die."

"You have good reasons to think so. She'll be fine now."

It was simple. Too simple. "But you could help if she worsens, right?"

"I've already made a bargain for her life—and her death, should the worst happen. Don't you worry."

Ilune was so confident, yet Sora felt no peace. She shoved it aside—for now. "Something else, then. Before we came to ask for your pledge, Onias was one of the gods we visited. I gave him my account of Sol Kareena's death in exchange for understanding what happened to my familiar after. My bird is comatose. Not dead, but certainly not the way he was. Onias said it was because he became the vessel for Sol Kareena's godly power after she passed, and I wanted to know if you had any idea how to help him."

Confusion looked so wrong on Ilune's features, the lines on her face not meant for it. "I only understood about half of what you said. Would you elaborate? What's this about vessels?"

Sora's stomach twisted. Onias had said it wasn't common knowledge, but . . . surely the one who had slain Neoma knew. "When gods die, their power remains. It doesn't move on with them. Did you not know?"

Ilune shook her head. "That fascinating tidbit aside, would you let me see your bird?"

Sora was regretting a great many things, and offering Leelan to this woman would have been the pinnacle. "He's back at the castle."

"Liar," Ilune cooed, that malevolent grin returning. "He's in your tunic. I can feel him. I do only need to see, though. I won't make you hand him over."

Something was so wrong in all of this, but Sora gently scooped Leelan from his designated napping space. Of course he gave no reaction, not even in the face of this objectively evil woman.

At the end of the day though . . . Sora simply wanted to understand.

Ilune's scrutiny went on for a few daunting seconds, then she shifted onto one hip, her pose surely not accidentally seductive. "With all the affection I can muster, I must say you're a little naïve. I wouldn't need to touch him to steal that delicious power away. Silver Fire is dangerous, so keep him safe and secret from any of my lineage. Understood?"

Though futile, Sora did draw Leelan nearer as she nodded.

"However, if I did that, the burst would be short-lived. Powerful, but short-lived. The Silver Fire absorbs magical energy, but I would not be absorbing her actual holy powers. Your familiar would be destroyed, and once I used that power to fuel my Silver Fire, it would be gone forever, and what sort of legacy is that for my dearly departed auntie?"

"Do you have any idea what I can do to help him?"

Ilune's grimace did nothing to mar her pretty face. "I suppose I could try to gently siphon the power out of him, but that still might kill him. And all killing him would do is lead to the dissolving of your powers—not ideal. If there *is* any way to gently transfer the power into another vessel, that might give him a chance, though I must admit to only speculating. Given he's your familiar, you could absorb him, though who knows what would happen with that." That intrigue returned, her silver gaze utterly magnetic. "Now you have me curious."

Yet the statement made Sora's blood run cold. "Absorbing your familiar leads to insanity."

"More or less. Some familiars are more invasive than others. But it's not so bad being a little insane. Being heir to the Theocracy means you surely have that sense of honor instilled as deep as your soul, so perhaps it would survive a little splicing. Consider: if given the choice between absorbing your bird or watching your bird waste away and die, which would it be?"

The question left Sora ill. "Do you think he's going to die?"

"Now, I *would* have to touch him for that. As a necromancer, asking me to check how close a poor soul is to death's door is something I'm quite capable of. But do you trust me?" Something in Ilune's ensuing wink left Sora rooted, some unnamable thing adjacent to fear rising to shackle her.

It was not fear, though, which is why she refused to name it.

"You said yourself you're a God of Lies," Sora replied, trying to juxtapose this flirtatious tease to the monster in the underground. They were one and the same, and Sora would be a fool to forget it. "I don't, unless we make a bargain."

"Oh?" Ilune's quirked eyebrow left Sora bristling. "Perhaps not so naïve after all. What will you offer?"

"What do you want?"

Nothing in Ilune's expression changed, yet Sora felt like little more than meat set on a slab at the butcher's shop. "Not the best negotiator, are you? I *highly* suggest that you make a proposal, lest I take advantage of you."

Sora was not a good negotiator, no. She was not a politician of any sort, utterly wrung about by this . . . person. Be that as it may, Ilune was too transparent to be sincere. "And why wouldn't you want that? Why not take advantage of my naïveté or steal my familiar? You're being extremely reasonable, to be honest, and it's confusing."

"Perhaps I want you to like me."

In moments like this, Sora wished she had spent more time studying Solvira's history and not strictly Sol Kareena's texts. She knew next to nothing of Ilune and her temperament, but this woman shared blood with Etolié, and Etolié would speak such a line just as flippantly, yet still mean every word. "All right. That's what I'll offer—my friendship."

Ilune stared as though Sora had spoken a particularly wry jest. "Are you serious?"

"Unless you were lying, God of Lies. I will offer you friendship and everything that comes with it, most notably loyalty and my promise that I'll like you."

Sora stood tall despite Ilune's ensuing chuckle, uncertain of what to think when the God of Death set a hand on her chest. "Well, if that isn't both the stupidest and sweetest thing I've ever been offered. Thankfully for the both of us, what you want is so trivial that I'm going to say yes." Ilune presented a hand, but before Sora could grip it, she took it gracefully back. "One question, and perhaps an addendum: is friendship a boundary or is it . . . a gateway?"

Sora stiffened at the remark, her body far too keen to recall the sensation of Ilune's lips on her hand. "Why are you so interested in me?"

"Does it not behoove me to foster positive political relationships with the monarchs in my presence?"

"That doesn't mean propositioning them."

"Perhaps you are naïve." Darkly, she chuckled, and Sora hated how it caused her blood to warm. "My motives in no way harm you, so I shall keep my cards to myself for now. If you want my help, you'll have to accept that. But answer the question, won't you? Let me set my expectations properly."

Dammit all. Sora wasn't the one who should be negotiating with a flirtatious, self-serving god, even over something apparently so 'trivial.' Ilune might only add it as an addendum if Sora tried to shut it down completely. Instead, she prayed her next words were right . . . or right enough. "Friendship is whatever it leads to."

Sora was coming to hate that smirk, hate how it burned her cheeks. "Sora Makosa, I accept."

Sora took her cold hand and felt no relief—not until all that mischief faded from Ilune's countenance, as her gaze settled upon Leelan. When Ilune beckoned, Sora set the bird in her hands, the chill of brushing against her hand bringing reminders of Ayla, though Ayla brought no intrigue, not like this.

Ilune set the bird against her breast, a flash of purple passing through her eyes as she caressed his soft feathers. "He's in ill health, and his condition does worsen. Whatever this nonsense about vessels, I doubt a living creature was ever meant to house the power of a goddess like Sol Kareena. I can't say with perfect precision, but I would be surprised if he lasted more than three days. Perhaps less. There is your timeline. Do with that what you will."

Sora's heart sank as she accepted the familiar back, then cursed her trembling lip. How she loved Leelan and his morning chirps, his innocent companionship, how he always knew when she needed affection and love . . .

And from a practical standpoint, she would lose her powers too.

"Three days," she muttered, unable to hide her anguish.

Ilune's sigh interrupted her mourning. "I do wish I could help you more, but necromancy and Silver Fire aren't what you need. If you become desperate, I can try to siphon the power out, but I truly do fear that would kill him."

"I'll figure out something." Sora stroked Leelan's feathers, praying the time truly wasn't so limited. "Thank you."

Sora wasn't certain what to brace for when Ilune came forward, but it definitely wasn't for a butterfly kiss upon her cheek, the spark of cold paling to the blush it pooled to her skin.

Ilune's impish smile was nearly kind, her lips near enough to smell the saccharine magic in her breath. "If you tell me to stop, that'll be the last time."

Sora said nothing, too stunned to speak.

Such pleasure in Ilune's temptress sigh. "If you need my help siphoning the magic out of him," Ilune whispered, "or your sister worsens and there's no one else who can call for me, crush this into dust and say my name." And there in Sora's hand, she slipped something soft. A flower? "I will hear your prayer and come as quickly as I'm able."

Sora managed a nod, unable to breathe as Ilune stepped away, torn between reeling and . . . confusion. In her hand, she found a crumpled lily.

And there it came—the return of that cruel and mischievous smirk. "Anything else I can do for you, Sora?"

"No," Sora replied, perhaps too curtly to the woman to whom she had bargained friendship. But Ilune was dangerous; best to keep that in mind.

"In that case, you have a good night, friend."

Ilune wandered away, leaving Sora tethered in place until the final vestiges of her silhouette disappeared into the night.

Flowridia still didn't know what to make of the dog, only that it watched her in earnest. Dogs mirrored human smiles, yet this one's expression remained vacant. Perhaps it had not grown up among humans.

Well, Sora had agreed to explain. In the meantime, her curiosity overcame her, and she tapped the mirror once more.

It glowed . . . and glowed . . .

And faded.

Damn Soliel. Damn every action he had taken, both good and wicked, damn him for taking the lives of people she loved and saving them at different turns, and damn him most of all for luring her in time and time again with his shifting loyalties and whispers of what would come.

She slipped it in her gown's pocket and sat beside the dog, idly stroking his fur. Soft, but the cold undertones beneath brought memories of Demitri in his cage outdoors, causing her heart to sink.

"You're a sweet pup," Flowridia whispered, managing to smile when he licked her hand.

She was, for once . . . all alone. A rare gift, yet loneliness threatened to steal her anew, for the future had become a daunting thing, assuming she lived to see it.

Animals had always been her confidantes—first Aura, then Demitri, and even Ana had known her heart. "I don't know the cost of breaking free from this cycle I'm spiraling down. All I know is I've become the very thing I feared all along."

The dog pushed his head against her hand, perhaps sensing her melancholy.

"My mother was a nightmare I couldn't wake from. Not until she literally killed a piece of my soul through Aura, and I reacted by throwing a knife at her head. Had I known it would be that easy, perhaps I might've done it sooner." She gave a humorless scoff. "Or not. All I wanted was to be loved. Is it terrible that a part of me is jealous that Sora could be her friend? I'm not resentful, just . . . hurt that there was a heart inside her all along. She just couldn't bring herself to love me."

Her free hand fell upon her womb. Denial had been a fog around her, a shield. She saw, she felt . . . so clearly now. "I can't fathom not loving my daughter."

Yet the words shed light upon a distant hope—that if she were like Odessa, as Sora had said, that Flowridia still had a heart inside her too.

"My mother murdered her first baby when it was mere hours old," Flowridia continued, the story lingering in her memory like a toxic fog. She wrapped her arms around the dog, trusting by now that he wasn't one to snap and bite. "Murdered it out of rage for what its father had done. But if rage is the root of my problems, is talking to the priestess enough to put me on a better path?"

No, and the truth descended with the gentleness of a dove— that rage was a symptom. And the root of it all, the root of Odessa's pain, of Thalmus', even Ayla's, even her own . . . was loss.

It was as Sora said—monsters had taken everything away from them.

"Is it possible to cry but have never mourned?" Flowridia asked, the sudden choking in her throat verifying the truth in it. "Is that what it means . . . to accept?"

Is that what it meant . . . to let go?

Flowridia turned her face into the dog's fur, the ache within her deep but not foreign, no. Perhaps what Mereen had taken away could not be restored. Months of fighting, months of healing, months of resentment brewing for what Ayla was not . . .

Yes, The Endless Night was dead and gone. She had found finality in that. But though she had cried countless tears for Ayla, sought to patch the walls of their marriage home and save it from the winds and rains . . .

The very foundation had shattered.

For all her anguish, there was peace in the realization. There was . . . acceptance.

"Perhaps Mereen succeeded in killing us after all," she whispered to her canine companion. "Perhaps I've been trying to save a relationship between two people who no longer exist. But mourning doesn't mean that there can't be hope, right?"

She was met with silence from the dog, yet she realized Ayla had asked the very same query before: *Do you want there to be?*

Flowridia had no tears left to cry, and while she had some clarity, she had no path.

She prayed her next words were heard. "Ayla, are you there?"

Silence.

Flowridia stood, still shaken to not feel lightheaded every time she rose, and approached the door, then realized she had a shadow. "You should stay here."

The dog gave no reaction. Not when Flowridia pointed, snapped, or even beckoned him back to the bed. "Baby boy, you can't come with me. What if Sora comes back and you aren't here?"

But the dog simply whined and would not be deterred. Flowridia didn't have the strength to shove him back when he slipped out the door with her. Perhaps it was safer anyway. She wasn't supposed to be alone, technically. The dog meant she wasn't.

Ayla could be anywhere, but the most likely place was a forsaken graveyard underground.

The hour was not late, so Flowridia kept her head down when anyone passed, unwilling to answer any questions about her condition. Yes, she was a few degrees further from death than usual, but her heart was a bloody smear on the floor.

"Lady Flowridia, do you need an escort?"

Flowridia stilled at the soft-spoken voice, bracing herself for a discomforting interaction, no matter how well-meaning. She matched eyes with Zorlaeus. "I have one." When she gestured to the dog, he wagged his tail, apparently happy to be noticed.

Zorlaeus seemed to accept this, offering a polite nod before turning to leave.

But guilt clenched Flowridia's stomach, for reasons beyond her crumbling marriage. "I'm sorry for what I said the other day. In the garden. It was uncalled for."

Zorlaeus paused, his solemn expression suggesting he thought much deeper upon it than he would ever say. "It is what it is."

It seemed her marriage was not the only one failing. Flowridia continued on her way.

The somber journey brought shame, each step welling memories of cruelty unmatched. To the washroom, the labyrinth, her loyal canine shadow following all the while, unfazed by the smears of blood or lingering bone residue.

In a cathedral of smoke and fire, there Ayla sat where there had once been a pew, a supplicant in deep contemplation.

She glanced up at Flowridia's appearance, no lingering tears upon her face. When she silently beckoned, Flowridia sat near enough to touch, though not near enough for their bodies to brush together. The dog settled contentedly on her other side.

Flowridia's whisper sounded like ghosts within the walls, unnatural amid the eerie quiet. "What are you thinking?"

The barest hint of a smile sounded in Ayla's words. "Truthfully, I am wondering why you have . . . *that*."

And how glorious it felt, to smile after such anguish. Flowridia glanced at the strange shadow trailing her. "He belongs to Sora. I have questions too."

Ayla's gaze lingered upon the dog for a few seconds more, then drifted to the ceiling and the charred walls, reticence falling upon it. Silence settled upon them.

"I think, sometimes, about the Ayla I stood across the altar in Solvira with," Flowridia whispered. "I think about myself—no longer a child, but not quite grown. Gods, we were at the top of the world. But even after we lost everything in Solvira, I had you. It still felt like I held the whole world, just to love you. For all the lies we'd built around us, our relationship never was one of them."

Ayla remained silent, but something akin to a smile pulled faintly upon her lips.

"But those aren't the faces in the mirror anymore," Flowridia continued. "Ayla and Flowridia Darkleaf died in the Mountains of Kaas."

Any joy in Ayla's visage faded.

It should have hurt to speak the truth. Instead, each word left her lighter and lighter. "I don't believe there's a marriage left to save. There might be a marriage we could build, but what we had is gone, isn't it?"

Ayla gave a gentle nod.

Bitterness sneered Flowridia's lip. "Well, according to Casvir's logic, there was nothing to lose anyway. We were technically never married."

"Don't even jest," Ayla whispered. "It was the happiest era of my life."

Whatever words Flowridia could have conjured choked in her throat, for Ayla's sentiment was poignant . . . and so perfectly illustrated precisely what had been stolen.

Flowridia felt a hand softly touch her back, hidden by the shade of her hair. There was love here. It had never left; the one thing Mereen couldn't touch, despite her plot to exploit it. And love was many things, but there was one beautiful, bittersweet thing love could never be—a cage.

"May I ask for one thing?" Flowridia said, praying it was not selfish, praying she could be granted this small mercy. "For months, I've been terrified of you disappearing in the night. If you decide it's time to go, will you please say goodbye?"

Gentle fingers parted the curtain of Flowridia's thick curls, revealing Ayla's misted eyes. Her wordless nod smothered whatever embers had belligerently burned in the ruins of what once was.

Nothing but darkness remained—and love.

Always love.

CHAPTER 31

Fifteen years after the end of the world . . .

Dira kept her focus sharp, directing the mouse like a puppet on a string, each eerie motion stomach-churning . . . and invigorating.

She directed the creature in a dance she knew well, taught by Mother in her younger years. The mouse twirled on its toes in an uncanny display, its little paws perfectly set to mimic graceful hands.

The test came when she grasped its partner, necrotic smoke swirling around its form, breathing false life into the corpse. Sweat pooled upon Dira's brow as the second mouse rose, twirling on light feet.

But something in the minute articulations of its hands . . . the moment the mice touched, Dira's concentration broke. They collapsed—and so did she.

Dira flopped back against Demitri's warm fur, her watchful guardian on this cloudy day. "Dammit."

Why 'dammit'? I thought that was neat.

Dira did manage a tired smile at that, Demitri's encouragement admittedly appreciated. "I've never been bad at magic."

I'm very sorry that the single thing in all your life you're bad at is the rarest magic in the realm.

Alternatively, his sarcasm pissed her off like no one else could. "Fine."

It hasn't even been two weeks. Ilune said it would take time.

"And I have all the time in the world, apparently," Dira grumbled, sneering as she forced herself to focus on her mice once again. As the first one rose, her anger rose with it. "What's the point though? No matter how good I get, Mother will never trust me."

The mouse collapsed. Dira pounded her fist against the grass. "Dammit!"

Speaking of . . .

Dira looked up, no less appeased upon seeing Mother approach from the manor. Mother's pleasant expression was frustratingly inscrutable—though most likely she had heard the expletive. Dira stood.

"No need to stop on my behalf," Mother said. "Dira Darling, how goes your magic?"

"It's fine."

"Might I see?"

But Dira couldn't summon her focus, wouldn't even try. Instead, she glared at Mother. "No."

Mother's smile remained unreadable. "All right. You do not have to show me."

"I just don't see the point anymore."

"The point of what, my lamb?"

"Any of this. What am I practicing for? Not the war."

Mother frowned. Dira's vindication rose.

"You won't let me leave this place," Dira continued, "so clearly it's not to protect myself."

Dira waited for a reply. Mother did not elaborate. "So what's it for? To fight Casvir? I know there's a war, Mother!"

"Someone's nosy today—"

"If you'd actually fucking talk to me, perhaps I wouldn't be so nosy!" At the final word, Dira's power burst, ripping from her body in a painful ricochet. She doubled over, uncaring of the blight permeating the land, her fury only rising.

"You have to learn to control—"

"*What's the point if you won't even let me leave this place!?*" Dira screamed, blind to all but Mother and the blight. "Who am I controlling it for!?"

"Dira, this is incredibly unbecoming—"

"Why do you even care?! You treat me like a child—"

"Because you're acting like one—"

"—but I'm not! I'm not a child! But you keep all these damn secrets, and nobody tells me anything, and you control every part of my life and my training and my learning. You treat me like a fucking prisoner, and I'M TIRED!"

Dira heaved deep breaths. Upon her skin, purple smoke seeped ominously, the grassy space around her a memory, replaced with death. Infuriating above all was Mother's calm demeanor. She glared, but she did not bend. "Are you finished?"

Dira cried out in rage, screaming at a brick wall. "Are you just going to keep me here forever?!"

"I will keep you here until it is safe."

"Safe from what?! From 'monsters'? Perhaps you're the fucking monster, Mother—"

"Dira, will you *SHUT UP!*"

Dira reeled at the sharp sting of the words, her entire body freezing.

Mother flexed her hands, lip trembling as she stared directly into Dira's eyes, down to her soul. The world silenced. The hairs on the back of her neck rose in warning. "We will revisit this conversation when we are calm."

Tears welled in Dira's eyes. She found she couldn't speak at all. Mother left on silent feet.

Dira sank down to her knees, shock fading to a soul-crushing ache. Gods, it was hopeless. That truth sank like a stone. It really, truly was hopeless.

You really struck a nerve, wow.

Her tears flowed faster. Hopeless, the temptation to disappear into Sha'Demoni's wilds rose higher than the walls to the manor—which could no longer keep her. She was a prisoner, but . . . now she held her own key.

Mother wouldn't talk. But there was someone who might.

Demitri poked her with his nose, interrupting her melancholy. *Are you all right?*

"I'm fine," Dira said, lest she reveal her cards too soon.

Mother would never crack. Sora wished to speak but wouldn't. Couldn't. Etolié was far away.

But Soliel . . . he would have plenty to say.

Current era . . .

The first thing Etolié did was bang on the nurse's door. "Hello!?"

A healer popped her head out. "Is everything all right?"

"Where's the patient?"

The nurse's shock was answer enough.

"If we don't find her, we're all fucked. And if you see a suspicious dog, burn it."

Etolié left the nurse to do whatever nurses did when their patients vanished and ran into the hallway instead, uncertain of how to even begin. Did she rally the guards for this? Did Casvir need to know or was this her job anyway?

Etolié sucked up her pride and tried a simpler, albeit more drastic method. "Ayla!"

When no depressed vampire responded to the call, Etolié knew it didn't mean nothing. Beyond that, she wasn't sure.

"Etolié?"

Ah, Zorlaeus, her second most reliable friend. The fluffy-haired De'Sindai approached with his usual lack of confidence—the man would have horrible back pain if he kept this up. "Figures you'd respond to the call of a sociopath."

Zorlaeus nodded. "Self-preservation."

"Have you seen Flowers?"

To her relief, he perked up. "Yes. Not too long ago. I passed her in the hallway."

"Was there a dog?"

"Yes, actually. She said it was her escort."

Only then did Etolié start giggling, her nerves bursting at the seams. "You don't happen to know where they were going, right?"

"No. I can take you to where I passed her, though."

"Yeah, do that. Please."

She followed as he led. "Is something wrong?" he asked.

"Everything's wrong, Zorlaeus, but most of it is shit that can't get into your boss' slimy ears, so I'll spare you the burden of hearing it."

Zorlaeus whispered, "That's the wisest course."

"But what I can tell you is I'm mighty concerned about those assassination attempts on our dumb wilting Flowers' life—and this isn't unrelated, so pick up the pace."

Zorlaeus obeyed, both of them speed walking. "Given the proximity, she might've been heading for Ayla's bedroom, or potentially her washroom."

"Seems a long way to walk for a bathroom."

However, Zorlaeus stilled in front of what anyone with a lick of magical sense would see as a fake wall. Etolié's headache prickled at its proximity. When he knelt, he righted himself holding . . . yellow fur. "The dog was here."

Headache or not, Etolié nearly forgot the urgency of their quest when Zorlaeus followed an invisible line with his finger upon the wall—leading the wall to part and reveal a foggy entrance, blurred by magic. "So is it a portal or an illusion?" Etolié asked.

"Given it leads underground, I've always suspected a portal."

Etolié followed at Zorlaeus' lead, pleasantly surprised when she didn't puke upon entering the austere washroom. "This reeks of Darkleaf influence. But there's no Flowers."

Zorlaeus didn't respond, instead staring intently at the floor as he made small steps forward. "There are paw prints in the dust, see?"

There surely were.

"They went underground."

At this point, Etolié accepted she was just along for the ride and followed when Zorlaeus parted the far wall, revealing a staircase leading down. "I suspect this one is just an illusion," he said, though even his lowered voice echoed down the stone path ahead.

"Flowridia's been here before, if Murishani's bragging is anything to trust, so it's possible. It's . . . a little much, though."

"My life is a little much, Fluffy, and this secluded secret underground chamber looks like an excellent place to commit a flowery murder."

Though pain colored his grimace, he nodded and led her downstairs, soon appearing in a vast stone hallway. "Just keep your hand on the wall," Zorlaeus said. "We'll get there eventually."

"There? There's a destination? How do you even know about this?"

Zorlaeus' pained expression looked increasingly constipated. "Well, Ayla and I used to be something akin to friends. At least in her mind."

"Is that why there was weird energy when you used to visit Staelash together?"

He nodded, all while doing a stellar job at trying to hide his nervous breaths. "She was jealous of Marielle. Perhaps that was obvious. She and I never had a sexual relationship, but she was possessive."

"I can see that."

"I made the mistake of following mysterious crying in the hallway one day. I didn't realize who she was when I found her."

"So you were nice to her and she turned you into a pet."

"That feels like the correct word, yes. I don't think she knows how to have friends—or at least, didn't then. She showed affection through threats."

"That's a little bit relatable, but I won't think too hard on that one."

"She used to say things like, 'Lae— *Zorlaeus*, I'll hang you up by your armpits if you don't join me for poker'—little threats like that."

"Did you just almost call yourself the bad name?" Etolié teased, though that constipated look settled back onto Zorlaeus' features. "It's so infantilizing. I see why you hate it." As though 'Fluffy' wasn't, but Etolié hadn't sensed any disturbances in the wind over it yet.

Now he was stewing—watching Zorlaeus' face was a master class in analyzing facial expressions. "It's not quite that. Murishani started calling me that years ago, when I first became employed by the palace. I think making fun of my new name was a power trip for him."

"Did you witness a murder or something?"

"I beg your pardon?"

"Why did you change your name?"

He stared as though she'd spoken Demoni. "Well, I wasn't always— Do you really not know?"

"Sometimes I blink and miss things."

A charming smile tugged shyly at his lips—a rare sight. "It's really not a secret. I chose the name Zorlaeus when I realized I was a boy."

Etolié had to pause to parse through that and all she'd seen and heard from the man, genuinely trying to decide if she were a dunce. "Oh. Neat. But why the fuck do you still work for Murishani?"

"I don't really have a choice at this point. My family won't take me back, and, well, Murishani has given me everything, which means he can take it away."

The machinations of Murishani's evil mind weren't entirely unknowable, but sometimes Etolié was reminded with stark clarity that he was far more insidious than anyone could ever truly fathom. "You speak a lot more freely down here. Is it because we can't be overheard?"

"At worse, we'll be overheard by Ayla. Murishani thought this place was gross. He won't go down here."

Etolié didn't see much of anything disgusting going on, but perhaps Murishani just hated beige walls. "I'm going to make a few assumptions, and you're going to tell me if I'm wrong."

Zorlaeus nodded, stilling in his tracks.

"You're one of Murishani's most valuable employees, despite not having a malicious bone in your body."

Zorlaeus shrugged. "I know I'm valuable, at least."

"He pushed for you to court Marielle. That's why he kept sending you on diplomacy missions to Staelash, even though you aren't a diplomat."

Zorlaeus' grimace spoke a novel's worth. "Yes, but let me explain. It was only after she and I met that he started meddling. My love for her was and is sincere."

It made far too much sense. "And then you became the king of Staelash, which eventually fell to Nox'Karthan rule, again, despite not having a malicious bone in your body. But you knew."

"Murishani is careful in how he feeds us information. By the time I knew his full intentions for Staelash, it was too late."

Etolié's gaze narrowed, the next leap a little more personal— and volatile. "Murishani literally has your balls in a vice, both in meddling with your marriage and in controlling your medical care."

The defeat in Zorlaeus' features was no less than heartbreaking. "Murishani has a way of charming us into placing our shackles on ourselves, but only he holds the key. Honestly, no matter how low your opinion of him is, that's still leagues too high."

"Look, just say the fucking word, and I'll smuggle you to Celestière. It's a little bit in crisis right now, but that doesn't mean we can't get you a nice cottage away from all this bullshit in Vanir. Alystra would make sure you're taken care of."

Zorlaeus shook his head. "I can't abandon Marielle with him."

"Oh, fuck that huss— Sorry." Etolié pursed her lips as she considered less inflammatory language for the reigning hussy. "Not to overstep, but she hasn't exactly been treating you fairly either."

"It's complicated, and I know that sounds like an excuse, but all I can say is . . . she deserves a little more credit than she gets."

How to politely insult a man's wife . . . Etolié took a deep breath of stale air. "I'll take your word for it."

"I promise, you can trust her. But don't tell anyone else that."

That was . . . different. When Zorlaeus resumed walking, Etolié followed without much thought to the path, simply tried to make that outlandish statement make any sort of sense in her head.

Eventually she said, "My offer doesn't expire. Let me know if you ever need an escape. Her too, I guess."

"I will. It won't be quite yet, but I can't speak for the future."

"Well, that's ridiculously ominous."

"It should be. Just . . . be careful. I genuinely don't know of any plans involving you, but I doubt he'd tell us anyway. Murishani's most dangerous talent is getting people to underestimate what he's capable of. Dismissing him as an idiot is a fatal mistake."

"Intellectually, I know that, but I appreciate the reminder. In fact, remind me of that at least weekly. Anything else ominous I should know?"

Zorlaeus rapidly shook his head. "Keep doing what you're doing. I'm handling the rest."

It occurred to Etolié, then, that Zorlaeus also was someone to very easily dismiss and underestimate—this same man who had served under Murishani for years.

And perhaps . . . Marielle . . . too . . .

Etolié wasn't ready to digest that, nor did she have to with the sudden scent of stagnant smoke assaulting her. "Fuck, is something burning?"

Zorlaeus' frown suggested this wasn't part of the plan. "Is it?"

There was a sign up ahead, the mantra one of Sol Kee's, and when they turned Etolié balked at the ruins before them.

Whatever this had been was . . . large. Now it was ash—piles and piles of it. Etolié couldn't breathe without getting a mouthful of soot, so of course her gasp upon seeing Flowers led her to a coughing fit. "Damn you—" *Cough.* "—you motherfucker—" *Cough, cough.* "Where have you— You!?"

As prophesied, that damn dog was nigh, though thankfully not committing matricide—yet. Flowers and Ayla were cuddling, the soot in the air stuck to the residue of tears upon their faces, but that wasn't any of Etolié's business.

Instead, she marched up to the dog who was Chaos, irate when it had the audacity to stand and wag its tail at her. "Don't be fucking cute with me. Flowers, are you hurt? Dead?"

Flowers, alive and breathing, shook her head. "How did you find this place?"

Etolié pointed to the obvious factor of Zorlaeus in the doorway. "Assume Fluffy knows everything. If you're not dead and Ayla's supervising, I'll take the dog and go. The fewer questions I ask, the longer I'll live."

"Can you explain the dog?"

"Nope." She looked directly to the canine Chaos. "I can and will illusion a muzzle and leash, so let's do this peacefully, all right?"

The Chaos dog whined, then returned to Flowers and Ayla, leaving a mess of ashy footprints on them as it tried to perform something akin to a hug. "Oh, you're very enthusiastic," Flowers muttered, her chuckle sincere even as Ayla batted the dog away. "And a lot smarter than anyone's telling."

Ayla looked to Zorlaeus, making no effort to look friendly. "I would not have guessed you still knew the path, Lae Lae."

"Hey now, bitch." Etolié stepped forward. "We don't use that kind of language in my house."

Ayla's frown deviated to Etolié. "Disregarding that this is far more my house than anyone else's, I don't know what you are referring to."

"The name. He doesn't like it."

Ayla's frown fell to Zorlaeus, though softer now. "All right."

"Etolié, it's all right," Zorlaeus said. "Like I said, Murishani pushed everyone to use it. She didn't know." Zorlaeus came nearer to where Ayla knelt, her pitiful form at odds to everything Etolié had ever seen from the prideful woman. "Are you all right?"

Whatever Ayla's depression, it didn't change her talent for scathing looks. "Zorlaeus, you must know how stupid you sound."

"Fair enough—"

"No, no—I . . ." Her grimace faded. "I apologize. I am not all right. And . . . I am sincerely sorry. For everything."

Etolié had to look away, the cloying sensation of other people's emotions having already exceeded her tolerated dose for the day. "It's all right," she heard Zorlaeus say, grateful when his next words were directed at Flowers instead. "You have more color in your cheeks today. I hope you're feeling better."

"As well as anyone can be six months pregnant."

Zorlaeus returned to Etolié's side, at which point Etolié snapped at the hidden Goddess—who thankfully did join her. "I don't get paid enough for this," she said. "Let's go."

"If your shoes are illusioned, you need to float through the next room," Flowers said. "There's glass everywhere."

How dare she be thoughtful. "Thanks."

Flowers hadn't exaggerated. Etolié floated over a truly precarious mess, the glass shards and the knives leaving a lot of questions unanswered.

Zorlaeus was wearing proper shoes and even kindly scooped up the Chaos dog and carried it across. "Can you explain the dog?"

"No. Can you explain where the hell we're at?"

"This was Ayla's, uh, workspace."

Upon further study of the ruined lot, as Zorlaeus navigated around the piles of charred wood and shattered glass, Etolié noticed scalpels, the burned edges of books, and potentially a few immolated corpses as well, but she chose to not look too closely. "I have more questions."

"I don't know why it looks like this."

Etolié put the development into a box and soon stalked up a new staircase—and due to the bullshit of interplanar travel, appeared back in the washroom.

However, as soon as they appeared back in the hallway, a hooded figure immediately rushed to meet them—which was an off-putting visual, given its floating robes remained serene despite its speed. "Empress Etolié, you are requested by Imperator Casvir to attend a meeting in the war chamber immediately."

Right. Fuck. "I have to return a dog first."

"It is urgent."

"The dog is urgent."

"I must warn you that the imperator is quite irate—"

"Fine." Etolié's common sense was tingling. Forced to ignore it, she cursed the universe instead. "Zorlaeus, take the dog. Bring it to Sora."

"Um, all right—"

Etolié grumbled as she marched away, refusing to keep up with the hooded figure. This wasn't a cause worth getting sweaty over. Casvir could keep his fucking panties on.

Flowridia didn't know quite how it started, only that when Etolié and Zorlaeus took the strange dog away, Ayla kissed her softly on the cheek, sighed when Flowridia returned with a sweet kiss upon her lips . . .

Oh, the silent, permissive breath Flowridia held, lingering a whisper away from Ayla's divine mouth. To speak would ruin the spell, might scare this ghost of her wife away, but Ayla parted her mouth and allowed their tongues to mingle, sweet and slow.

Flowridia tentatively breached the skin beneath Ayla's gown, savoring the smoothness of her calf, her thigh, the embers of want fanned by Ayla's precious sigh: *"Oh, Flowra."*

Flowridia kissed her neck, trailed down to Ayla's collarbone, longing for the days her magic could leave marks upon her beloved's skin. Bright, blessed days spent in an innocence they hadn't known they'd shared, naïvely thinking they'd already faced the world and its ills . . .

They were different people now. Ayla and Flowridia, but not.

Flowridia swallowed tears at the thought, focusing instead on the beauty of Ayla's skin, how magnificent she looked as she sat back and slipped her dress and underclothes away, revealing her sensuous form. A lifetime ago, Ayla was the first woman to kiss her, to present the temptation of her body, to spark desire deep inside her, and make her feel brave.

And what had she called Flowridia to lure her into bed? The words held a sting now, for she did not feel *devastatingly beautiful* anymore.

Now, Flowridia shied as she removed her nightgown, mindful of her damaged hand, the reveal of the cysts on her swollen womb comical in a way. But there was no humor in the scars across her chest and stomach. No matter how far she ran, she could not escape their meaning, and Ayla could not escape the memories.

It showed in the twitch in her smile, in her eyes. Ayla loved her, yes. Ayla still found her beautiful, perhaps devastatingly so, but Ayla couldn't celebrate her body quite so freely anymore.

Damn Mereen for planting knives in their marriage bed.

But it was rude to stare when one kissed, and so Flowridia shut her eyes at the meeting of their lips, the apprehension of frightening her precocious stranger away returning. Yet bliss came in the touch of their skin, their embrace bringing both comfort and lust. Those cysts were an obstacle to navigate around, but after some giggling they found their stride laying on their sides, kissing to the echoing chorus of joy ringing across the cathedral ruins.

Flowridia touched her beloved's body with no shame, savoring the weight of her breasts. She only had one hand to use, yes, but it didn't mean she couldn't leave Ayla as a puddle of desire. When her lips romanced Ayla's breasts instead, her hand skimmed tenderly across Ayla's taut stomach, down to the sacred space between her legs.

And soon, within the ashes howled ghosts of a love that was gone—but not forgotten. Oh, Flowridia loved her so, each thrust joining them closer, their union harkening to a peaceful past. The world became far away, time passing only in the growing ache in Flowridia's arm and Ayla's falling tears. Flowridia left her breast and held her gaze a blessed moment, the affirmation of love never stronger.

Strong enough, even, for Flowridia to imagine she hadn't lost her after all. So strange, the suspension of time in the cathedral ruins.

Strange and bittersweet.

Ayla cried out at her climax, pulling Flowridia to her mouth to smother it. They kissed as she trembled, as she wept against Flowridia's body, and when her spirit returned to its mortal bonds, Ayla did not let go.

Flowridia's body burned from arousal, her breathing labored, but Ayla froze as a statue around her. "What are you thinking about?" Flowridia whispered, and it joined the echoing across the cathedral walls.

Ayla's grip tightened, but Flowridia wouldn't tell her it was hard enough to bruise. Gods, she simply wanted her here, the reality that there would be a final time they embraced slamming her like the blunt end of a spear.

Her breath hitched. She steeled her tears, willed them to slow, but when Ayla met her gaze, she shattered.

Ayla did not need to speak to affirm that her mind dwelled in similar domains. They wept in the forsaken hall, their weeping fading when their lips met once more, drowning their grief in distraction. Flowridia's yearning only grew, screaming when Ayla touched her wet, tender folds—

And when Ayla moved inside her, all the world became silent, save for the beating of her heart and a whisper she might've imagined: *"Darling, Darling, I love you so."*

With orgasm came hazy thoughts and the heaviness of exertion. Flowridia wondered if she slept; only knew for certain she came to with the weight of her dearest wife beside her. Ayla stroked tender lines upon her skin, her gaze soft as it followed her finger across Flowridia's body.

This was assuredly the Ayla she knew—studious and devoted in all her dealings. Embers of her wife remained somewhere in the ashes, the reminder bittersweet.

It would be blasphemy to interrupt so sacred a moment, and so Flowridia kept still, writing the affection to memory.

Yet Ayla's touch slowed as it neared her womb. To her surprise, Ayla cracked a smile. "A little crass, isn't it? To think we technically have company."

Flowridia laughed, her tears still fresh, her body and heart raw, but Ayla joined in the joyful throng, and gods, it felt so beautiful.

When it waned, Ayla gently touched her stomach once more. "What will you do when it's born? Will you stay?"

Oh, the question broke Flowridia's heart, forcibly shoving the world back into their private domain. "I haven't thought about it much, but . . . I suppose I will. I don't have anywhere else to go, and . . ." All those regrets, the ones she'd vowed to never feel again . . . One in particular whispered cruelly in her ear. ". . . she'll need an advocate to protect her from the monster who owns her soul. Ironic, that it would be the monster who sold it, but perhaps it's a step toward redemption."

"Is that what you seek? Redemption?"

The question gave Flowridia pause. "I seek to run as far away as I can from following the path of my mother. I don't care about redemption. I just never want to treat my daughter the way my mother treated me."

My daughter. She had never said it aloud, had she.

"Daughter?" Ayla's gaze held genuine intrigue, and Flowridia prayed the moment lingered. This small moment . . . where perhaps the façade of family could be hers.

"Etolié said if there's any science involved in her conception, she will be a girl. It feels right."

Ayla became very still, unreadable in the ensuing silence.

Gods, her throat choked at that. Flowridia swallowed her rising grief and forced a subject change. "When I turn into a vampire, will I want to eat her?"

"A dhampir? No." Life returned to Ayla's animated features, forced or not. "Dhampirs live in a somewhat suspended state, caught between life and death. Her blood wouldn't nourish you."

The reminder that she would subsist off of blood remained disconcerting. But at least she would walk in the sun. "But she'll grow up like other children, right?"

"Yes. Her lifespan is more affected by her elven blood than by dhampirism."

Flowridia set her maimed hand gently upon her womb, avoiding the unnerving cysts. "If this is too much, let me know. But I've thought of names."

"I care about you, and so I can care about names."

Despite the affirmation, Ayla's tone became muted. Flowridia forced her reply, nevertheless. "If Etolié's wrong and it's a boy, I'd like to call him Thalmus. And if she's right, I want to name her for his daughter, Kedira." It stung, the bittersweet memory, her own unworthiness rising. But Thalmus still loved her. He had said so himself.

To her surprise, Ayla's eye . . . twitched. Every part the diplomat, she spoke just as politely. "Beautiful names. Both of them."

"I'm much more offended about you lying than I am if you hate the names."

"I just said they were beautiful."

"Can you please explain yourself? Is it because of Thalmus?"

Ayla's forced niceties faded by small degrees. "No, I take no issue with naming a child after those who've passed. They are perfectly nice Morathan names."

Flowridia frowned. "Do you want them to be elven names?"

"No, and you can name the child whatever you want."

"Ayla, this is more investment than you've ever shown in this child before, so you have to see why it's suspicious."

With Ayla's grimace came a sigh. "They are names very specific to the half-giants who live in Moratham—as slaves. And given you already sold this child as essentially a slave to Casvir, it is a little off-putting, is it not?"

Flowridia's frown deepened. "I didn't realize that."

"I don't wish to deter you, but I want you to make an informed decision."

Heart sinking, Flowridia nodded. "There are others I've loved who have died. I . . . I can reconsider. Perhaps Lunestra, or even my father."

"That is entirely up to you, darling."

Hesitation stilled Flowridia's tongue, the question perhaps too personal, too much. "Is there anyone you would name the child after?"

To her relief, Ayla looked thoughtful. "The only loved one I have who's passed is Sarai, and it's still a tender name for me. So, no."

And for all the deaths that haunted Flowridia's heart, at least she had loved ones in the Beyond. Against all odds, she still had loved ones in the mortal realm too.

Ayla had almost no one. And she would walk away from the only one left in this life just to save her own.

In this suspension of time, Flowridia simply memorized the sensation of Ayla's hand in hers, praying it wouldn't be the last, knowing it was numbered, nevertheless. "What about you? What are you looking for?"

Ayla was silent a moment, thoughtful as she rubbed her thumb against Flowridia's hand. Fresh tears welled in her eyes. "I want to not be Ayla Darkleaf anymore. I want to not be The Endless Night. I want to be me—whoever she is. I don't know if it's possible. I certainly don't deserve it. But if I don't try, I'll be back in Onias' Realm."

Flowridia squeezed her hand. "I think it was you who told me we deserve nothing. I know it won't be easy, but don't hold yourself back because you think you're unworthy."

Ayla gave a scoffing laugh, no joy in it at all. "Darling, with all due respect, I believe I told you that in reference to wearing a family heirloom. I murdered most of a country."

"There's no right answer. But don't let guilt stop you from doing what you think is right."

How tragic, the glistening in Ayla's eyes. A single tear fell. "Forgive me, but it stings a bit that you would be so supportive now. It rings a bit hollow."

Flowridia's own guilt welled. "The last time we were here, I . . . I saw my mother in the mirror shards. I have to make a change, otherwise I'll see that fear I saw in your eyes in . . . hers. I'm making peace with the fact that things will never be the same. I just want you to be happy, even if it's not at my side."

Ayla nodded, yet her demeanor became colder still.

"You've always been powerful, Ayla." Flowridia gripped her hand tight, determined to keep her here a moment longer. "It's not too late to use that power for something good."

Slowly, Ayla released her hand and wrapped her arms around Flowridia instead, mindful of the cysts. Flowridia's own tears welled, the finality of the moment breaking what pieces remained of her heart—

There inside her womb came a fluttering motion.

Though bittersweet, a smile came unbidden to Flowridia's face, yet beside her, Ayla had once again become still, her reticent gaze upon Flowridia's womb.

Flowridia prayed her next action was right, her tender touch on Ayla's hand meeting no resistance as the baby kicked once more.

Wonder befell Ayla, breathless despite needing no breath. "Darling, I . . ." Yet her words trailed away, settling among the ashes around them.

"What is it?"

Ayla's thumb stroked her swollen womb, soft against the pressure inside. Yet her bewilderment remained, despite the tender mood. "How strange, to think she's a part of me. A part of you."

Flowridia pulled her close, a longing inside her finally appeased. Here at the end of the world . . . the fractured family she had yearned for could be a little more whole. "We made her."

Dread filled Ayla's stare. "Oh, gods—we made Her."

Flowridia stiffened. "Y-Yes."

Ayla pulled back, eyes dancing from Flowridia's womb to her gaze. "Ilune was kept in a prison of maldectine, and so in that chamber I bore witness to the Goddess of Chaos' face. And she was uncommonly beautiful, which isn't something I typically ever think of half-elves, no offense to your sister—"

Flowridia frowned. "Half-elf?"

"—and her fangs—oh gods."

"Fangs?"

"And she told Ilune . . ." Ayla stared as though she'd seen a ghost. "Oh, Flowra."

"Ayla?"

"You said 'daughter,' and I . . . She couldn't be, but she *is*. It makes so much sense."

"Ayla, will you please just speak your mind?"

So unlike her love to be so flustered. Ayla clenched her fists, settling whatever nerves had come alight inside her. "Darling, darling . . . Your baby is the Goddess of Chaos."

It wasn't that Etolié expected a warm reception in the war chamber, but the sudden engulfing silence was certainly daunting. Her own memories of the chamber were pure mortification, especially to see all the carefully placed figurines on the massive table in the center, but she'd done stupider things. Faces she recognized but just as many she didn't sat in the adjoining seats along the wall. Mostly De'Sindai, but a few looked oddly dead.

Every eye in the room looked to her, no echo of speech dissipating. Casvir stood from his seat, and given the swirl of dust rising with him, that chair wasn't often used.

Oh fuck—had they actually been waiting for her?

Etolié forced a smile, her nonchalance just as strained. "Greetings, comrades."

Casvir stared relentlessly upon her. Even the table, easily as long as Khastra was tall, wasn't enough space between them. "Empress Etolié, I will not mince words. Criomin has been destroyed."

Etolié reeled at the statement. "Didn't you already destroy the Highland Elves?"

"My troops were occupying it, and now they are gone. Half a day later, and my troops in Katchith were decimated as well. Half my army in Zauleen is gone, and witnesses say Goddess Ku'Shya is responsible."

Unease rose within her, though she could not name it. "She did the same to Tierzuroth."

She hadn't even noticed Executor Faeborn seated among the generals—not until they stood. At Casvir's nod, they said, "Empress Etolié, it is not the same. In Tierzuroth, the damage was done from Sha'Demoni's plane. She cast a shadow of herself. She is limited in that way, but so close to *Daemenacht*, she maintains power enough. According to the imperator's spies, Ku'Shya appeared in the flesh."

"That isn't possible," Etolié muttered, for gods simply couldn't, not without a host, and no one could host Ku'Shya except— "Fuck."

"So we have come to the same conclusion," Casvir said. "You were not previously informed because, respectfully, you were suspicious. But this is not her first reported appearance in the realm."

Casvir told a tale of horror. The more he spoke, the more Etolié's head spun. "Why the fuck would she take children?!"

"We do not know, but it would be an unwise detail to overlook."

"Ku'Shya follows Demoni Law stricter than anyone else. How does kidnapping . . ?"

Eye for an eye. The elves had stolen Ku'Shya's child. But was there anything more to it? Etolié felt ill.

"The sea is our greatest ally," Casvir said, "given Ku'Shya cannot easily cross it, nor could any supposed host cross it quickly. However, we do not know her motivations for these first attacks."

Oh, fuck—there she went giggling again, her nerves far too frayed for this bullshit. "Permission to speak freely?"

"To a degree, given our company."

"I think you have bigger problems right now than propriety, *Cassie.*" Etolié's hands shook. Even her breath came labored. "I just want to know how the fuck you didn't see this coming?"

"Excuse me?"

A threat lay in the words, but Etolié was far too angry to give a shit about self-preservation. Could he really be so obtuse to not see how he'd pushed Ku'Shya to the brink? "Are you fucking kidding me?! If we're lucky, Ku'Shya will stop at kicking you out of Zauleen. In fact, you'd better start fucking *praying* this is the end. I don't know what the fuck Khastra's thinking, letting Ku'Shya use her as a host—"

Oh gods. The spell. Did . . . Did Khastra even have a choice? Had Ku'Shya betrayed them after all?

"You know what?" Etolié continued. "I have to go. Hopefully I return with answers."

No one stopped her. In the hallway, Etolié took her prayer pose. *Momma?*

A small span of silence, then gentle words. *Is everything all right, Starshine?*

Etolié braced herself for heartache. *I don't have time to elaborate, but what are the chances Ku'Shya would ever keep one of her children as a slave?*

Though there again came quiet, Etolié felt a foreign confusion infiltrate her mind. *That would be very out of character.*

Etolié knew so little, certainly not enough to know if that were reassuring or damning. *Not even Khastra?*

Especially not Khastra. Is everything all right?

I don't know. But I can't explain now.

And though guilt swamped her, Etolié couldn't summon the emotional energy for a goodbye. Instead, she crystallized the image of the horrible scar in the world with ease, and with only a small lurch in her stomach, appeared in humid, shadowed daylight across the sea.

Of course it was stupid, open invitation or not. Etolié feared she had been the fool all along. But she marched through the entrance of *Daemenacht* with deliberate steps, praying it was not a gallows march.

She had to understand. Staying diplomatic would be the most difficult, given Etolié had no idea what she was about to walk into, much less the emotions it would evoke.

She was unsurprised to find no Ku'Shya upon the throne, but the demonic guards paid her little mind. She approached one, forever cursing herself for not learning Demoni. "I'm looking for Khastra. Got that? *Khastra.*"

The demon repeated it in its guttural tongue, the name translating smoothly, and held up an appendage—the universal sign to *wait here*—and left.

Etolié still wore a real dress, the fabric stifling, especially in the humid atmosphere. She tugged on her collar, sure to go mad if she remained this damp, but dropping her clothes here in the throne room seemed like a poor way to start what would likely be a delicate interaction.

The demon returned alone. It struggled with speech, its mannerisms less decipherable than Zoldar's, but Etolié prided herself in understanding alien body language.

And then it said, in a stilted blend of Demoni and Celestial. "No Khastra. Kah'Sheen here. See Kah'Sheen?"

That would work just fine. "Yes, Kah'Sheen." Etolié gave an exaggerated nod, but was stopped from following, forced to wait once more as it left.

Etolié's anxiety only grew in the passing seconds—because of course Khastra wasn't here, off apparently destroying undead armies instead.

When Kah'Sheen appeared, she lacked her typical radiant cheer, her friendly demeanor oddly forced. "Hello, Etolié! Uh, you are seeking Khastra?"

Etolié's breath hitched. "Where are they?"

"Uh, I am not knowing precisely—"

"I know what they did to the Highland Elf capitol and Katchith. I need to know where they're going next."

"Etolié, you cannot!" Kah'Sheen lost all pretense of calm, clear panic falling upon her as she knelt on her many legs to be nearer. "You are knowing Bringer of War is dangerous. It is worse. Mother and Bringer of War together is worse. You must stay away."

"I need to know what they're doing."

"And report to the imperator? Khastra is wanting you far away from this. She is not wanting you hurt."

And finally, after writhing in a cesspool of ineffable emotions, one rose above all else—*bitterness*. Etolié set her jaw, resisting the urge to scream. "Is Ku'Shya coming to Haven?"

Oh gods, there rose the memory of the City of Light, decimated in part by the Bringer of War's power. Etolié knew how it felt to stare down her monstrous other half in the throes of bloodlust; that night in Haven . . . all those people—

"I am not sitting in the war meeting."

"I don't believe that for a *fucking second*!" Etolié bit back her vitriol, swallowing anger and that bitterness both. "You've always known shit you shouldn't."

Kah'Sheen's grimace spoke the truth enough. "I am not sitting in the war meeting, but I am overhearing it, yes. But it is only putting you in danger to know."

"Khastra doesn't get to decide what puts me in danger."

"*I* am deciding. You are my sister. I love you too much. I cannot let you betray Mother and Khastra." Kah'Sheen's yellow eyes changed, their glow obscured by liquid. Of course Kah'Sheen could cry, but Etolié was torn between empathy and fascination to witness the first tear fall from one of her four eyes. "Mother will not let you live if you do."

Dammit, Etolié was weak to sisterly affection. "I love you too, Sheen Bean," Etolié said, every piece of her torn apart. "But I can't let Haven be destroyed." Of course Ku'Shya would come to Haven. Kah'Sheen didn't have to admit it overtly. Once, Etolié had made a devil's bargain for Solvira, saving them from genocide—at the cost of selling them to Casvir instead. And oh, Etolié cursed fate, cursed Khastra, Ku'Shya, Casvir . . . and most of all, herself. "I can't let thousands of innocent people die."

Defeat showed in Kah'Sheen's stance. "Etolié, please—"

Rumbling sounded from within the cave.

"Mother is back," Kah'Sheen whispered. "You must go."

Yet Etolié remained suspended in time, absently wiping her tears as she stared at one of the massive throne room exits. "What about Khastra?"

"Khastra is hosting Mother, so she is coming from the mortal realm. But you must leave, or Mother will suspect."

A distant, guttural cry echoed across the walls. "Etolié?"

"Too late for that," Etolié whispered, uncertain of what to say regarding the protective grip on her shoulders. Kah'Sheen towered above her, her forced smile revealing shark-like teeth.

Ku'Shya herself appeared from the gargantuan cave path, her jolly laughter downright menacing. "Ah, Etolié. Guards are telling me you have come for Khastra, yes? She is coming. What is your purpose here?"

"I missed her last time, y-you know? Just wanted to say hi."

"Timing is good then! You are always uplifting Khastra's spirit." Her many eyes glanced up. "Khastra!" Whatever else she said was in harsh Demoni, but when Etolié followed her gaze, she understood.

It was not quite Khastra, no, but the Bringer of War, flanked by a demonic entourage. Nearly three times Etolié's height, blood splattered the half-demon's armor and body, her glowing gaze utterly bestial as she responded in turn.

But recognition shown in her blue eyes when they landed upon Etolié, who had seen enough of the Bringer of War to know when there was trouble afoot.

Kah'Sheen did not release her, even when the Bringer of War stood at arm's length. In her monstrous form, Khastra towered above even Kah'Sheen, the slight growl in the back of her throat surely a challenge—a challenge Kah'Sheen returned, crossing her second set of arms around Etolié, hunching protectively over her.

Etolié felt no fear. She felt nothing at all, her emotions caught behind her held breath. "It's all right, Kah'Sheen." In tandem with Kah'Sheen's waning hold, Etolié offered a hand to the Bringer of War, who engulfed it in her impossibly oversized one. "I've missed you, ya big lug."

There was no lie, even if peace was as fraught as a taut string held above a candle's flame.

Ku'Shya grumbled something in Demoni once more. The Bringer of War said nothing as she led Etolié away.

For her part, Etolié regretted being so lax in her study of the ancient language during Khastra's absence, but one word was clear, ominous from Ku'Shya's grand tongue: *"Etolié."*

The knowledge—for it was surely knowledge—that her value was only as high as Khastra placed her had never felt so cold upon her skin. Ku'Shya said she was welcome here, but Ku'Shya wouldn't let her leave this cave given even the smallest provocation.

Her life meant everything to Khastra, but she was nothing here without her.

Once out of sight of Ku'Shya and Kah'Sheen, Etolié gently tugged her monstrous intended's hand, willing the beast to stop. She did, and Etolié didn't dare to let herself feel, just swallowed her revulsion for the blood and grime on the Bringer of War's armor and floated into her arms, breath hitching to feel that beloved pressure around her. The Bringer of War carried her onward, affection in the rumbling sigh within her chest.

Oh gods, why was this a gallows march?

Etolié's lip trembled, though she did not feel—except for the enveloping embrace; except the errant reminder of sticky blood upon her skin; except the fragile beauty of this moment, where Etolié could cling to sweet denial.

How many years had she spent in denial? Over Khastra, over herself . . . Etolié was an expert at lying to herself. The temptation remained. She could do so again.

She could remain in this perfect embrace and leave the mortal realm behind forever.

They entered Khastra's private space. Etolié's grip tightened around her beloved's neck. The Bringer of War made no move to remove her.

"Etolié," she whispered, a deep rumble from her chest.

Etolié clung on as the Bringer of War's body shrunk, her musculature deflating—though not by much. Khastra could still carry her with ease, though she brought her second hand to cradle her as the transformation completed.

"What did Kah'Sheen tell you?"

The silence held no peace. Etolié kept her face hidden in the crook of Khastra's neck. "Nothing."

Khastra's grip had never been a cage, yet Etolié feared what would happen if she tried to escape.

Etolié braced herself, forcing the unspoken truth into the open. "She didn't have to." She pulled back enough to face her demon, but though her embrace remained soft, Khastra had become stone.

"How much did she not tell you?"

"I'm not fucking lying, Beefcake. Casvir told me what you did in Criomin."

Khastra stared upon the far wall, refusing to meet Etolié's gaze.

"Will you please just say something?"

Khastra swallowed, though the tension in her throat muscles remained. "I did not want you involved in this."

A crack split the dam in Etolié's heart. Bitterness was first to seep out. "Was this the plan all along?"

"For my mother, perhaps. She told me nothing until I was free from Casvir's power."

Etolié's jaw set. All the while, she clung to her beloved demon. "And those children? Did you help with that too?"

A chill swept up Etolié's spine at Khastra's reply. Never had she sounded so cold. "They are unharmed and will remain so."

"But why?"

"It is best you know nothing—"

"Why, so I can't return and report to Casvir? You know, you always said allowing Ku'Shya to possess you was the worst possible plan. That she might not let you go."

"We have come to an agreement."

"So you've agreed to let her destroy Haven?"

When Khastra said nothing, Etolié bit back a scream.

She pulled from Khastra's embrace. When Etolié's feet touched the ground, she stumbled back, struggling to find her breath at all. "And the witches cutting your name into victims' backs? Is that related?"

Khastra said nothing.

"Khastra . . . why?!"

The question echoed across the walls. Khastra bowed her head. "Casvir has committed a horrible crime against me and by extension, against my mother, and she will take what she is owed. Furthermore, Casvir is a threat to all the worlds—you have told me as much. He cannot be killed, but to destroy his country means to take away the source of his power. So my mother and I will march with the army to Haven—"

"You can't do—!" Etolié's words stopped all at once, struck at the intricacy of Khastra's words. "Army? Demons can't go into the mortal realm."

"As I said, it is best you do not know."

"What army, Khastra?!"

"You have the pieces. Consider."

"I'm not here to put fucking puzzles together—"

Oh, fuck. The children.

Etolié took a wary step back. "Your mom is blackmailing the elves."

"She took her earned restitution and has offered them the means to have their children returned to them."

"But the elven army can't cross the sea—" The sigils. "They were going to summon all of you. The witches carved your name into the backs of their victims. That *was* magic."

Again, Khastra said nothing.

Gods, Etolié hated every fucking bit of this. "What about the Theocracy of Sol Kareena? You can't do this again! I saw what it did to you. You were forced to destroy them, but you could stop this!"

Gods, Etolié hated Khastra's bitter smile, hardly recognized it at all. "I know with precision what damage the Theocracy's destruction did to Sol Kareena, and it would do as much to Casvir. At least it is for a righteous cause—"

"Righteous?! What the fuck kind of justification is that?!"

"The greater good says that to defeat Casvir now will save the lives of billions later."

"You sound just like the fucking God of Order."

"The God of Order also understands sacrificing for the greater good. However, my mother is keen to murder him too. The God of Order will be dead, Haven will be destroyed, and with it a mass of Casvir's power. He will be put into prison."

"Prison?"

"Ilune's prison is vacant. It is designed for liches. My mother would prefer it not go to waste."

Khastra stood as firm as castle walls, unyielding, unmoving. Etolié's lip trembled, her tears falling freely now. "Khastra, this isn't like you."

A sheen appeared upon Khastra's luminous eyes. "You have known me in some of the most peaceful years of my life. What a splendid time it was. But what do you think 'Bringer of War' means? Do you think the Theocracy's destruction is the first time I committed a genocide? Do you think it is my worst sin? Etolié, this is what I was born for. It is who I have always been."

Etolié frantically shook her head, desperate to purge those horrible words. "No. No, no—you defied your mother and freed the elven slaves. That's your legacy here."

"A legacy I have not undone."

"I held you while you sobbed on the steps of the destroyed cathedral! I felt your pain. You can't lie to me and say you felt nothing."

"I felt everything. I was a slave who—"

"Who was doing exactly what you were always meant to do if this is the bullshit you're really gonna cling to." Etolié's fury rose, but nothing—not bitterness, not rage, not shock—nothing surpassed her anguish. "Thousands of innocent people will die, Khastra. Thousands of families, just like the people in the Theocracy. Moms and dads and children—they won't even be turned into fucking undead monsters. They'll just be dead."

"Innocents are always a casualty in war—"

"And you're the fucking Bringer of War, sure." Etolié swore she faced a stranger. This wasn't Khastra. This wasn't the gentle woman who had stood by her side for twenty-four years in Staelash, who had pledged to die in her name. "Oh, this is what you were born for—that's some rancid bullshit right there. You're whoever the fuck you want to be."

"What I am is someone who understands what sacrifices must be made for the greater good. Respectfully, it is not a concept you could ever grasp, so it is futile to argue this."

And while Khastra wasn't fucking wrong, Etolié felt the creeping cold of insult sweep over her anyway. "Yeah, bitch. I only sold my damned soul to Casvir to save Solvira. I hate every fucking minute of it, but at least I can sleep cozy knowing that the blood of thousands isn't on my hands."

"No, instead you made that monster stronger. Have you considered that?"

Not in so many words, but Etolié said nothing.

"You do not bargain with men like him. You destroy them. I tried once. This time, I will not fail." Khastra's jaw set, yet her next words came soft. "And whatever I must do to convince you to stay here, I would do."

Etolié reeled back. "What?"

"There will be no mercy for anyone in Nox'Kartha, so stay away, I implore you."

Yet Khastra did not fall to her knees. She didn't plea. She simply shed a tear.

"You know I won't," Etolié said.

"I know." Such finality in the words. Khastra remained stoic, even as more tears fell down her elegant face. "You would not be Empress Etolié of Solvira, the woman I love, if you did."

Etolié took a step back, wary of this stranger, of this woman she loved.

"So you will warn him?" Khastra asked.

Etolié stilled, her unease fading . . . to resolve. "What's the point in saving the world if there's no one left to love it? That's the problem with you and with Soliel—you're murdering the very people you're trying to save. You're fighting fire with fire, and the whole world will burn if that's your creed. Of course you'll win—"

Khastra wouldn't win.

All the air left Etolié's lungs at once. Her world spun as her wings spread wide for balance. Khastra appeared by her side, whispering gentle words, but Etolié heard nothing.

Khastra was still dead. Casvir had Staff Seraph deDieula. He could cast Ku'Shya out.

Untold damage would ensue, yes. The elven army would come, and Haven would never be the same. But the staff had stopped even Izthuni in his tracks. It would be child's play to stop only a goddess' puppet.

And she could say nothing.

"Etolié?"

Etolié gasped at Khastra's whisper, realizing her demon was close, so close, kneeling to be beneath her.

"Are you all right?"

There she was—the woman Etolié so dearly, desperately loved.

But instead of collapse into Khastra's arms, though gods she wanted nothing more, Etolié steeled her jaw. Her tears fell freely, for this would be their finale. There would be no wedding—not standing on opposite sides of this war. Not when Khastra led the charge of genocide.

And not when Casvir destroyed her once and for all.

"Run away with me," Etolié pled. "I'll hide you in Celestière or Solvira or wherever you would feel safe. I've got twenty-three more years on my soul contract with Casvir, but that's nothing compared to eternity. We don't need wars or gods or politics. We used to be all the other had, and it could be like that again. We don't need titles. We just need each other."

Etolié's gaze misted as Khastra cupped her cheek. Her calloused thumb brushed precious lines across it. "Etolié, you could never leave the world behind forever. You are a hero. You make sacrifices because that is what heroes do. You will never do what is easy, because you will only do what is right even when the world does not understand. People like you inspire people like me."

Etolié set her hand upon Khastra's, cherishing the touch. "You've been a hero before. You could be a hero again."

"Moments of heroism do not create a hero. I am a villain to most of history."

"Then let me inspire you again." When Khastra's hand tried to fall, Etolié clung tight and forced it to stay. "If your mom is so keen to help, let's murder the shit out of Soliel and go from there. What do you say?"

The weight became too much. Khastra's hand fell away. The half-demon knelt properly now, gaze cast toward the floor. "I have made an oath to my mother. I could not break it even if I wished to. I am sorry, Etolié."

How soft, Etolié's heartbreak. How vicious, to look down upon the woman she so desperately loved, who had lifted her up in the darkest times of her life, who had offered unconditional love to her broken soul, who had done nothing but love, love, love . . .

It would be so easy to stay. But heroes made sacrifices. That's what Khastra had said.

On her left hand, she twisted her engagement ring. "You know I'm going to warn Casvir. Are you going to force me to stay?"

Gods, the selfish part of her prayed for Khastra to say yes.

How precious, the innocent love in Khastra's eyes. "No. And no matter what, I love you, Etolié. Whatever comes of the war, my heart is forever yours."

Despite the pretty words, Etolié felt only bitterness. She offered a hand; Khastra accepted. Etolié brought it up to kiss each digit, for beneath her pain was love, love, love . . .

She slipped her ring into her demon's hand. "Goodbye, Khastra."

Nothing could have prepared her for the shock on Khastra's beautiful face—nor for the moment Khastra's heart split in twain.

Etolié's tears came fast. As quick as she was able, lest she fall back into Khastra's arms, she grasped the vision of home with all her might, willing her power to flow—

And collapsed into a sobbing heap in her suite in Solvira, screaming into her bedding.

PART SIX

WAR

CHAPTER 32

Fifteen years after the end of the world . . .

"Dira? Love?"

The words accompanied a tentative knock on her bedroom door.

Dira half sat from her bed, her nightgown precariously drawn around proper clothing beneath. She had not dressed for battle, no. But something pretty would surely soften Soliel to her cause. And truth be told . . . she would give anything for Soliel to think she was beautiful.

When Mother opened the door, she held both a closed basket and a wilted stance. "May I come in?"

Dira nodded, uncertain at Mother's demeanor.

When Mother came near, she sat at the foot of the bed, keeping her supplicant pose. Tension rose in the silence, until the first of Mother's tears streamed down her face. "I'm sorry."

"No, it's—"

"Do not try to console me. I lost control. I cannot deny the fear in your eyes, and you do not deserve to be afraid of your own mother. A monster I truly am, if I have descended so low. I'm sorry, my love. I swear upon your dear mom's grave that it will never happen again." Mother trembled as she set the basket between them, then slid it gently toward her. "I know this won't fix it, but it might give you a reason to smile."

Whatever swirl of emotion Dira floated in, she hadn't expected to hurt. She opened the basket, surprised to face a trio of doe-eyed kittens all cuddled together.

Despite the thoughtfulness of the gesture . . . Dira's anger rose. "Thanks," she said simply, making no move to pet them.

The silence lingered. Finally, Mother shattered it, tears staining her tone. "Please say something."

Dira's lip trembled, rage and hurt battling for dominance. "You don't trust me."

"Of course I trust you, my darling."

"But you're still hiding things from me!" Dira cursed her own outburst, remiss at Mother's flinch. Oh, why did she flinch? Who was this woman? This stranger? This monster? "You can't just lock me up like a bird in a cage. I feel like I'm suffocating."

Mother said nothing. She needn't, instead the subtle shift of her posture, the twist of her lip, the vacancy in her eyes sent ice through Dira's blood. Oh gods—it was Mother's voice, Mother's face, but not this tone, not this coldness she wielded so precisely. "A caged bird has no concept of the predators lurking beyond its gilded walls."

A warning rang in Dira's ears; the sort Sora taught her to fear; the sort when monsters lurked in dark woods. "There's a war going on," she whispered, but this was Mother, who loved her, who had yelled . . . "What's so horrible to explain about that?"

But Mother rose, eerily calm as she approached the door.

Dira wished to scream, to rage, but not so much as she wished to weep in Mother's arms. "Why is the world so afraid of you?!"

Mother's hand rested lightly on the doorframe. Silence settled. When she turned, there was naught but acrimony upon her tear-stained visage. "If you knew, you would never dare to yell at me like this. So keep it that way. Rage at me. Hate me if you wish. Call me selfish. Perhaps I am, but I would rather have a daughter who hates me than a daughter who fears to even whisper my name. Perhaps if it were in my past, but alas—I have rekindled every evil thing about me, and all for you, my lamb. All to keep you safe. If you have any trust in me at all, you will let this go."

"So . . . they're right to fear you?"

Mother opened the door.

"I wouldn't fear you!"

"You would, sweet lamb. I saw the proof today."

Dira longed to run to her, to beg at her feet, but beneath her nightgown, she wore beautiful clothes. "I wouldn't! I . . . I *couldn't*. I love you."

Mother's tension rose, but when she looked back, the lamp's light reflected unshed tears. "I love you, Dira. But I will speak no more of this."

"Mother—"

Mother shut the door behind her.

Furious, Dira ripped the covers from her bed and tore the nightgown away. Perhaps she didn't trust Mother. Mother certainly didn't trust her. Dira grabbed her knives, her map, and she leapt from the window, willing the shadows to take her—

And phased into a world of day and ran through perilous plants and trees.

Current era . . .

Despite her heavy heart, Sora hurried back to the palace.

Whatever Etolié's plan, she couldn't actually harm Chaos, but she had made alarming comments about assassins in relation to her own half-sister. The exhaustion of travel weighed down Sora's legs, but not so much as the precious weight of her bird in her hands—Leelan, who stared unseeing at the world, living but as cold as death.

Ilune had said he had a few days. Ilune had also said a few other unnerving things, but Sora shoved that aside. Duty called.

The skeleton guards paid her no heed. Sora entered the palace proper, wondering when comfort had become so oppressive.

So much to do, so little time or direction. Her stomach grumbled, and her clothing still stank of the icy ocean. Chaos had bid her to rest and recover, but the thought was inconceivable. Sora headed upstairs to her old quarters, finding she was too stressed to be hungry.

It felt like a lifetime ago that she had last entered her private space. Near Flowridia and Ayla's quarters—empty, she specifically checked—her own was sparse and impersonal. A window, a door leading to a private washroom, a bed with white sheets—her clothing could be stuffed into a pack at a moment's notice, and it would be as though she'd never been here.

It felt normal, natural. Her room in Staelash had held a few more personal possessions, but she had never quite allowed herself to settle, had she?

When Sora shut the door, the outside world vanished. She bathed quickly, her mind replaying that cursed conversation with Ilune, and scrubbed just a little harder against her cheek, tainted by the memory of that cold touch.

Dammit all, and damn Ilune too. The God of Death put on a foppish front, but she was still the monster in the underground prison, shackled by chains and grief.

Sora dunked her head. Her hair clung to the smell of salt and fish.

The arduous task of drying her hair lay ahead, but Sora emerged wrapped in towels, feeling a little lighter. Leelan sat perfectly still in the center of her bed, not even twitching at her approach. Sora knelt beside the bed, staring into his black eyes. "I want to help you, but I'm running out of time—"

A knock interrupted her words. "Sora?"

Sora knew that voice. "Just a moment."

She quickly shuffled into cleaner clothes, grateful to no longer feel dried sweat and salt, and wrapped her hair with care. When she answered the door, she was unsurprised to see Zorlaeus. However, shock filled her to see Chaos, the dog, wagging her tail beside him.

"Thank goodness," Zorlaeus said. "Etolié said to bring you this dog."

Apparently Etolié's anger had been assuaged. Sora managed to smile at Chaos' entrance, endeared when the dog pressed his head against her hand, asking to be petted. "Is Flowridia all right?"

"Last I saw her, yes, and that wasn't too long ago." His voice lowered as he looked fitfully side to side, and then he asked, "Are she and Lady Ayla all right?"

"No, not even a little bit." Dammit, was that not something to say to him? Sora's past interactions with Zorlaeus had been minimal but positive. Etolié liked him, but he was married to Marielle. "Don't spread that around though."

Zorlaeus nodded. "I understand."

Sora took a breath to bid him farewell, only for Etolié to come barreling down the hallway.

"Woah, woah—thought you were allergic to exercise . . ." Sora's words faded as Etolié slowed, the obvious evidence of tears and her swollen eyes marring a pretty face. "What happened?"

Etolié took a heaving breath, nearly a sob. "You have to pack up and leave. Both of you. Stat. Pronto. Immediately."

"What's going on?"

"I don't have time. I just . . . I need to find Casvir . . ." Etolié faltered, suddenly pale as she leaned against the doorframe. "Fuck, this is bad. Oh, gods." Fresh tears welled in Etolié's eyes, the unflappable Celestial defeated. "We're fucked, kids. We . . . we have to evacuate Haven."

Sora reeled at the statement. "What?"

Etolié heaved a pained breath, her tears falling fast. "I . . . Fuck, I hate this."

Zorlaeus spoke up. "Let's get you to Casvir. Can you tell us anything on the way?"

But Etolié trembled too violently to speak, much less walk. Sora took her arm and gently led her to the ground. "Head between your knees. If you pass out, you can't tell Casvir anything. I need you to breathe, all right?"

A passing De'Sindai servant stilled at the interaction. "I'm so sorry to put this on you," Zorlaeus said, "but we need Imperator Casvir here as quickly as possible. Tell him Empress Etolié needs help." Zorlaeus knelt beside them as the servant hurried away. "You said we have to evacuate. How many days do we have? Just hold up your fingers."

Etolié shook as she shrugged.

Chaos came tentatively forward, then began licking one of Etolié's hands.

"This would be really creepy if it weren't so grounding," Etolié managed to blubber out, making no move to take her hand away. "I-I'm gonna be sick though."

Given how often Etolié vomited, Sora left her side to grab the empty wastebasket from her room. The Celestial dry heaved into the bucket.

"It's going to be all right, Etolié."

Etolié responded by puking.

Sora never reveled in Casvir's presence, but at least those armored footsteps meant answers. Zorlaeus immediately bowed his head. Sora followed his lead as Casvir made his entrance.

Chaos snarled.

"I was told you needed me," Casvir said, though then he looked at the growling Deity. "What is that?"

"It's a long story," Sora said, praying his suspicions ended at that.

Etolié was a mess, tears and snot covering her face, vomit on her breath. But his appearance sparked Etolié back to life. She faced Casvir with renewed fire. "Ku'Shya's coming."

Sora said nothing, felt nothing at all.

"You are certain?" Casvir asked, and Sora had never heard such tension from the stoic man before.

"It's a fucking *fact, you bastard!*" Etolié sobbed as she stumbled into standing. Zorlaeus righted her when she swayed. "Khastra is hosting her. You pushed them to this. And I just betrayed the love of my life, and it's *all your FUCKING FAULT!*"

Casvir remained unmoved. "You will calm yourself, you will remember your place, and you will tell me everything."

"Evacuate Haven. You're all fucked."

Casvir walked away like the battering ram he was.

"Wait!" Etolié said, though only those closest could hear the tiny whimper from her throat, see the quiver of her lip.

Casvir paused, though did not grace her with a glance.

"That thing. The thing I can't talk about." Etolié looked near collapse. Sora watched helplessly as the Celestial choked back a sob. "If you don't want thousands of people to die, that's how you stop them."

Casvir did look back at that, understanding in his nod, then marched away.

Etolié lost all strength, even her wings limp as Zorlaeus put her arm around his shoulders. "Sora, can I put her in your bed?"

Sora gestured them in, bringing the wastebasket as Etolié collapsed near Leelan. She set her hand in Etolié's hair and soothed soft lines through it, hoping the gesture wasn't as upsetting as hugs. "What happened with Khastra?"

"It's over," Etolié whimpered. "We're done. And now Casvir will kill her forever."

Oh, Etolié.

"Was I wrong?" Etolié continued. "What if she's right? What if the greater good sometimes does involve killing thousands of people? I just . . . I *can't* . . ." Etolié descended once more into sobs.

Sora took Etolié's hand and squeezed. "Look, I don't know, but now isn't the time for second guessing. Ku'Shya is coming, and we have to act fast."

So much to do, yet their timeline had so drastically shortened. If Soliel didn't destroy the worlds, Ku'Shya would wreak havoc instead. Sora looked to Zorlaeus. "Can you, uh, bring Flowridia here? It's important."

Zorlaeus offered a quick nod and left.

Sora beckoned to Chaos. "Is this what Soliel meant in the cave? Is this the cataclysm?"

To her horror, the dog gave an obvious nod.

"Is this something you could stop?"

The dog looked uncertain as it whined.

"We need to get you a humanoid body."

Flowridia stared unblinking, utterly shocked into silence.

She set her hand on her womb, the impossibility of Ayla's claim laughable—except Ayla was deathly serious.

The statement echoed in her mind: *"Your baby is the Goddess of Chaos."*

Absently, she grabbed her nightgown and fished through the pockets, soon withdrawing her enchanted mirror. "Soliel has the other half of the mirror," Flowridia said, breathless and pained. "He spoke to me not even an hour ago and begged me to go with him so he could protect me from whatever is going to kill me."

Darkness settled in Ayla's gaze. "So he is going to kill your baby."

"He said the baby isn't what kills me. He also said he would answer any questions I had once I went with him. You can come too."

"I would insist," Ayla replied, her skepticism never waning. "What are you going to do?"

Flowridia's very soul tore in twain, for every part of her reeled to imagine placing her life back in his hands, the same hands that had murdered Lara in cold blood. Yet . . .

"If I don't go, I'll die. Is it selfish to want to live? I don't know what the catch is, or if there even is one, but I—"

"We only have his word. We have only *ever* had his word to go on." Ayla cupped her cheek, a plea in the tender gesture. "When I was in Ilune's prison, the Goddess of Chaos revealed to her in no uncertain terms that she had killed her mother."

Flowridia's stomach dropped. "What?"

"She didn't say much of it, only spoke of fate. Perhaps she embellished or lied to manipulate Ilune, but she is a better actress than even me, if so. Either Soliel is lying for some unknown purpose, or he is definitely going to kill your baby."

"But the cysts—I'm feeling much better."

"The cysts can't protect you from a dhampir birth." Calculation sharpened Ayla's visage. "Casvir is adamantly opposed to inducing early labor, but if it saves you, would you consider it?"

Flowridia gave a wary nod. "But is it not too soon?"

"Half-elven pregnancies are fickle. Perhaps it is too soon; perhaps it is due in mere days. We could ask the nurses for help deciding. The baby could also be extracted through surgery, which would of course be traumatic to us both, but I would trust no one but myself."

The idea of surgery made Flowridia's blood run cold, but she forced a nod nevertheless. "Why are you supporting this?"

"Why wouldn't I?"

"Because you don't care about the baby," Flowridia said, though it tore her apart to speak it aloud. "If you're so certain it'll kill me, you should be pushing me to abort it."

"Technically I still am, but with safety precautions."

"Please don't be flippant. I need to understand."

"I don't have to care about the baby to care about you fulfilling your bargain and getting Demitri back." Yet Ayla hesitated, something more lingering on her tongue. Defeat colored her tone. "And because you love her, Flowra. I am making peace with that."

Flowridia knew not what to say. Instead, she drew Ayla into her embrace, uncertain of this ache inside her.

Yet Ayla stiffened. Then Flowridia heard it. Quiet footsteps, followed by—

"Oh my— Lady Ayla, I am so sorry—"

Panicked, Flowridia released Ayla and hid her naked form behind her gown.

Ayla, however, held no such qualms as she glared at the flustered De'Sindai. "Turn around, Lae— Zorlaeus."

Zorlaeus shielded his eyes with his hands. "In my defense, this is far from the worst thing I've walked in on you doing."

"True," Ayla cooed, "but I fail to imagine what could possibly be so critically important that you come all the way down here just to interrupt me and my wife."

Flowridia spoke softly as she slipped into her gown. "All the more reason to think it might actually be important."

"Sora sent me to find you," Zorlaeus said. "But the more pressing news is that Goddess Ku'Shya is coming to destroy Haven."

Flowridia blinked. "What?"

"We don't know when it'll be, but there will be a kingdom-wide call for evacuation."

Flowridia stood, aided by Ayla. "I need to see Casvir. I . . . I can help."

Ayla stiffly put her own clothing back on. "Forgive me, but how?"

"I've been in charge of the elven refugees. What are evacuations except the opposite of that? I'm certain I can help somehow."

"Flowra, it's dangerous. Did you forget what we were only just discussing?"

"And the moment Ku'Shya appears on the horizon, you can rush me away to Solvira—for surgery, if necessary. I highly doubt she's going to be subtle when she arrives."

Zorlaeus looked lost as he stared solely at the ground, perhaps unnerved by Ayla's scrutiny. "How is Ku'Shya able to come?" Ayla asked.

"Etolié says she'll be using Khastra as a host."

"Well, if Khastra comes walking quietly into Haven only to summon her mother there, she could be quite subtle. And she could be here at any moment. Something to consider."

"I don't want to just run away," Flowridia said. "It's what I've always done, and that's precisely what my mother did too, isn't it? She ran away from the world instead of facing it. I know this isn't my fight, but it is the chance to perhaps . . ."

Flowridia's words trailed away, for she hadn't been seeking redemption. But that was the word, wasn't it? Perhaps this was redemption after all. She had let Solvira burn in the aftermath of their reign of terror.

"Just let me speak to Casvir," Flowridia finished. "Please."

"You don't ever need my permission," Ayla said, taking her hand. "Darling, you know Ku'Shya is no one to trifle with, and if her wrath has been kindled so fiercely, this realm is in grave danger. I won't pretend to understand why the Bringer of War would allow this, but when Ku'Shya holds her as a puppet, she'll be helpless. And . . . and so please swear you are not lying, because once she's here, we have to run."

"You have my full permission to kidnap me, no matter where I'm at." Flowridia offered a reassuring smile, though Ayla remained concerned. "We shouldn't delay." She looked to Zorlaeus. "Where is Sora?"

"Last I saw, in her bedroom."

"Tell her I'll be there after I've spoken to Casvir."

CHAPTER 33

In the aftermath of Khastra's death, Etolié had drowned in a grief vaster than she had ever felt before. Nothing—not banishment, not losing Staella, not even the terror of her sperm donor—had sunk her so deep as losing the stability of her dearest friend, her confidante, her demon . . .

Today, Etolié plunged anew into that sorrow, but with crushing guilt to match. She couldn't even stand to think, every motion as muted as trudging through a cloying fog.

But when Sora proposed going all the way to the crypts at the far end of Haven just to retrieve a specific body, Etolié was pulled from her stupor by the sheer impracticality of it.

Etolié lifted her face from Sora's bed, feeling as comatose as the bird beside her. "Was there anything actually special about that body?"

Sora shook her head.

"Then for fuck's sake . . ." She couldn't even articulate her grumbling, just forced herself to rise instead. Etolié floated through the door, not trusting her feet, and waved down a servant who had yet to be burdened by the news of evacuation. Things were quiet still. "You. Hi. I need a corpse. Literally any non-animal corpse."

The De'Sindai servant didn't seem nearly as perplexed as a Solviran servant might've been. This was a city of death, after all. "I'm certain there's something in the dungeons not being used. Should I have someone fetch you one?"

"Yes, but it's priority one importance, world-saving stuff. Bring it here as quickly as magically possible."

The servant nodded and hurried away.

Etolié turned around, noting Sora and Chaos watching in the doorway. "Just because there's a crisis doesn't mean we can't use our fucking brains."

"No need to be a bitch, Etolié," Sora said.

"You're right, but fuck you anyway." Etolié swallowed the sudden lump in her throat. Sora gently took her hand and led her back inside, not unlike a kite.

"What happened with Khastra?"

"It's like I said—I broke it off because she was a bit too complicit with genocide for the greater good or some bullshit, but the joke's on her because I'm a greater gooder too, even if she said I wasn't. And even if I'm wrong, I . . ." Etolié drove her nails into her palms, desperately warding away fresh tears. "I never blamed her for what happened to the Theocracy. It's the worst thing I've ever seen—and you know I've seen some bad shit, Sora—but it wasn't her. It was . . . *him*." Etolié spat the word, unable to even mock him with a pet name. "But she's doing this willingly. She's doing this because she thinks it's right, but murdering thousands of innocent people is never right. I love her so damn much, but what kind of monster would I be to stay engaged to someone who would do that? So now, instead of selling my soul to save a few thousand, I'm breaking my own heart." A tear did fall at that; Etolié cursed it. "I'm so damn tired of being a hero."

Sora squeezed her hand.

"Am I stupid?" Etolié whimpered, and oh gods, the world came crashing down again. Her tears fell fast. "Have I been deluding myself? Is this who she's always been?"

"I don't know," Sora said, and thank what little goodness remained in this miserable world that Sora didn't bullshit. "I will say, I never would have expected this from General Khastra of Staelash. Perhaps death changed her. Or perhaps you changed her, but now she's on a different path. I don't know."

Etolié's throat ached with her sob. "Tell me I did the right thing."

"You stood by your principles, even when it destroyed you. You did the right thing."

Etolié collapsed, weeping once more into her free hand. She couldn't tell Sora about the staff, that final, damning piece. She couldn't tell anyone.

Sora tugged her to the ground, encouraging her to kneel. Etolié's head hit her lap instead.

Starshine?

Etolié gasped, surging into sitting. Though she was a blubbering mess, she resumed the prayer pose, though with her other hand still hugged by Sora's. *Momma?*

I'd ask if you're all right, but the news is a bit urgent. Your, um, sister is here.

Oh shit. *Are you all right?!*

Sorry, not Ilune. Kah'Sheen.

Thank every fucking miserable god.

She has something very important to tell you but doesn't have enough time to go across the sea. Did you know it really isn't all that far of a trip from my house to Daemenacht? She can make it to the Valley of Neoma in amazing time if she hurries—

Momma, you said it was urgent.

Right, sorry. Can I bring you here? Immediately?

Etolié looked to Sora, who looked mightily confused. "Momma needs me."

"We can handle the corpse on our own, don't worry."

Etolié glared at the dog but resumed the prayer pose anyway. *Take me away.*

Etolié didn't even have time to brace herself, her stomach lurching out of her throat as the scenery shifted. Staella's teleportation powers were far more sophisticated than her own, so while Etolié still felt like death as she floated gracelessly through the space between worlds, she didn't feel like peeling her skin off when she landed on Staella's wooden floor.

A bucket was shoved in her face. Etolié gagged, but she had nothing else to give.

"I thought I'd spare the wildflowers," came Staella's teasing voice, soft and feminine both.

Etolié nodded, accepting aid when Staella offered a hand.

"Sweetheart, what happened?"

"I can tell you!" proclaimed a new voice.

Etolié somehow hadn't noticed the oversized half-demon crouched in Staella's kitchen. Kah'Sheen waved, all four of her legs sprawled to fit in the small space, head ducked as she waved.

"Etolié is breaking Khastra's heart," Kah'Sheen said, but Etolié didn't have time to sob again before the half-demon frantically continued. "But, Etolié! Khastra has challenged Mother to—" Kah'Sheen said a Demoni word Etolié had never heard before.

"She challenged her to . . . *Rezoxos*?" Etolié knew she hadn't a hope to say it right, but Kah'Sheen rapidly nodded. "Will you explain what *Rezoxos* is?"

"It is, uh . . . how do you say—a duel! To the death!"

Etolié's mind stopped. Fortunately, Staella spoke what she couldn't. "I'm sorry, what? Why?"

"Because Khastra is not wanting to destroy Haven anymore, but Mother is not agreeing to break their bargain, so Khastra is challenging her to lay claim to all of Mother's kingdom!"

Etolié's jaw fell slack. "Again, why?"

"I am not knowing!" Kah'Sheen's arms flailed about, as though to push her words out even faster. "But I am knowing she is going to die and there is no one who is talking sense into her like Etolié, so I am calling Etolié! You tell her not to do this!"

"Yes, ma'am," Etolié said, though the words were automatic. What . . . what was Khastra doing? She whipped her head toward Staella. "Can you help? Ku'Shya likes you."

"Oh, that's quite the political, uh, *clusterfuck*, you might say." Staella smiled as guiltily as her expletive would suggest. "Khastra has invoked Demoni Law, and there is nothing I will be able to do to sway Ku'Shya from following the law. Our friendship is largely based on me not thinking too hard and keeping my mouth shut, and I will not be able to keep my mouth shut."

"Got it. Can you at least send us there?"

"That's easy. Hold hands."

Etolié took Kah'Sheen's spindly appendage in her own.

"Before you go, listen." Staella gently took their held hands in her own. "I'm no expert in Demoni Law, but if this follows precedent, the only one who can stop this is Khastra herself, if she is willing to revoke the challenge. If you try to directly interfere, you will likely be killed by Ku'Shya. And that would cause me to start a political clusterfuck of my own during a very precarious political time in Celestière, so don't get yourself killed."

Etolié nodded, though made peace with death.

Staella shut her eyes—

And Etolié stumbled into Ku'Shya's throne room, vacant save for Kah'Sheen and a patrolling demon guard. Her stomach hurt, but there was nothing more than bile to swallow.

"*Rezoxos* is not happening here," Kah'Sheen said. "It is faster if I am carrying you to the arena."

"Go for it."

Kah'Sheen scooped her up as she had in the Mountains of Kaas all those months ago and surged forward.

"You wish to aid with the evacuations?"

Standing before the great table in Casvir's war room, Flowridia nodded before an array of generals and other advisors. Executor Faeborn sat among them, apparently trusted enough for this. Ayla stood as a shadow behind her, radiating disdain.

"And your health will allow this?" Casvir so rarely revealed his emotions, which made his confusion nearly humorous.

"I'm feeling much better," Flowridia replied, the proof simply in how she stood tall, though still in her nightgown and robe.

"Then you will be enlisted to work with Empress Etolié and see what accommodations Solvira can offer. Once this meeting is adjourned, the call will go out among my citizens to be ready to leave before sunrise, but those who arrive first at my gates will have priority. See to it that they have a place to go."

"I will do so, Imperator Casvir." Flowridia turned to leave.

"And what about you?"

Taken aback, Flowridia had nothing to say—until she saw where Casvir's stare lay.

Ayla raised a scathing eyebrow. "I am taking care of Flowra during a precarious time in her pregnancy."

"And when Ku'Shya comes?"

"Presumably whisking her away, given she has only agreed to evacuate once the Goddess of War is at your doorstep."

"Your aid in defending my capital would be invaluable," Casvir said. "Name your price."

Ayla's stare never wavered. "Do you really want to have this conversation in front of your friends?"

"These are desperate times, Ayla. I am willing to be generous."

"You won't like what I ask for."

"Say it."

"I want the baby."

Flowridia's breath hitched.

Casvir's glower darkened the whole room. "No."

"Then we have concluded our negotiations. Thank you." Ayla spun gracefully on her heel and set a hand on Flowridia's back, escorting her from the war room.

Once the door shut behind them, Flowridia whispered, "Explain that."

Ayla kept them moving, her tone light, though terse. "Consider the value of the 'package,' Flowra. Of course he was going to say no, but if he had said yes, it would have solved this new dilemma." Her voice dropped to a whisper. "The dilemma of selling a Goddess to Casvir."

Admittedly, Flowridia was still parsing the news and all the unraveling implications. She simply nodded.

"And had he agreed, I suppose I would have helped. Not that I can do much, aside from not die. I am a little stronger than my size would suggest, but Ku'Shya possessing Khastra will likely stand taller than the palace."

Ku'Shya's coming was also a reality Flowridia was still analyzing. "How can Casvir possibly stop her?"

"Most likely, he can't. So let us find Etolié and focus on evacuating."

Warmth blistered in her pocket. Flowridia withdrew her mirror and found it glowing.

Ayla slowed her gait, giving an intrigued *hmm* as she gazed upon the mirror. "I desperately want you to answer. Or if you don't want to, I would happily deliver the verdict."

Flowridia couldn't face him. She handed the mirror to Ayla.

She stood against the wall as Ayla tapped the surface, the glowing fading to Ayla's growing grin. "Well, well," Ayla cooed. "Charming, to see you again. I suppose I never did thank you for your services in the Mountains of Kaas. It's only fair that I do."

"Where is Lady Flowridia?" came Soliel's somber tone.

"Oh, your mother-in-law? She is around here somewhere."

A pause. "So you have pieced it together."

His confirmation made Flowridia's head spin. She set her hand on her womb, torn between wonder and . . . fear.

"We have. Which is how we know you are lying."

"I have never—"

"I heard the Goddess of Chaos—my child, you might say—say it herself: that she killed her own mother."

"You have grossly misunderstood—"

"I have no time for liars, Soliel. We humbly reject. Goodbye."

"Ayla—!"

Ayla tapped the screen. "Shall I crush it for your peace of mind?"

"It seems like a waste," Flowridia whispered as she took the mirror back, for that was all the air she could manage. Ayla had called it *my child*. "Do you think Sora knows?"

"Why don't we ask her? We promised to drop by, did we not?"

Flowridia nodded absently. "Lead the way—"

A great *boom* rocked the castle.

Ayla immediately covered her, though there was no visible threat. Dread filled Flowridia. "Oh, gods. We're too late. Ku'Shya—"

A second *boom* rattled the walls. Commotion rose, including heavy footsteps from behind.

Those present in the war room rushed ahead as Flowridia pressed against the wall—including Casvir, who slowed. "Get her out of here," he said to Ayla, and Flowridia had never heard him sound so tense.

Ayla clutched Flowridia's hand. "To Sha'Demoni, my love."

"Imperator Casvir," a hooded figure said as it floated forward, its serenity laughable on any other occasion. "I am informed that it is not Goddess Ku'Shya at your gates."

Flowridia had assuredly never seen Casvir look so blatantly startled.

"It is the God of Order."

"It does feel nice to use my voice properly again," Chaos said, as the final wrappings of her flesh coated her raw sinew. "Not that Demitri minded. He's grateful, though he'll never admit it."

Alone in her bedroom, Sora had seen worse, but she couldn't say she would ever be comfortable with flesh sculpting. "Do you need clothes?"

Chaos was naked, of course, but it was oddly less disconcerting now that Sora knew they were family. Still, what could only be illusionary cloth soon appeared on her skin, as graceful as her motions as it formed around her. "Yes, please. I am not so focused as Etolié."

"You can borrow anything you like, but we might need to purchase you more clothing in town if we want it to actually fit—"

Far below, an explosion rocked the castle walls.

Sora scooped up Leelan, grabbing a knife from her desk. "What can we possibly do against Ku'Shya?"

Chaos' demeanor had become ice. "That is not Ku'Shya."

There was only one other. "Soliel?" At Chaos' nod, Sora added, "What do we do?"

"That depends on why he's here. Most likely to try and take the orb. But whatever my disdain for Casvir, if he's hidden it, no one will find it."

Sora nodded, though she was only mildly relieved. From her drawer, she all but threw clothing at her Goddess niece. "You need to get out of here. If Soliel sees you, he'll try and take you again."

Chaos sneered as she shrugged into the non-illusioned clothing. "I hate that I agree."

"Let me go alone. I'll find out why he's here. You know I won't get caught."

"Fine."

"Where should I find you?"

"Somewhere near but secure . . ." Incredible, to watch Chaos' entire face change as her jaw shifted, as her stance rolled to become more hunched, more . . . bestial. "Come find me by me."

"What?"

"I need company. I wonder if I'll recognize myself."

"You'll be with Demitri?"

"Yes. Close but not too close. Secure, but you can still go there." Sora jumped when Chaos clutched her arm. "Don't die."

"I won't die."

"You better fucking not. Dira needs you."

And before Sora could ask, Chaos bolted to the window—and jumped.

Sora quickly assembled her weapons, slipping daggers into hidden sheaths, only sparing a moment to agonize over her damp hair. Finally, she made a bed of handkerchiefs to slip into the pouch by her hip, then gently placed Leelan atop it.

Papa had taught Sora to hunt, but Mom had taught and been taught by the best how to be stealthy and quick, how to be so nonchalant that you went unseen, and how to nearly become shadow itself.

Sora stayed light on her feet as she sprinted down the hall. The castle shook. She braced herself against the wall and continued on, nimbly sprinting around frazzled servants. Down flights of stairs, until she reached the bottom floor, slowing to keep her feet silent.

Commotion sounded up ahead. Sora crouched as she approached the throne room. Shock filled her to see the massive doors blown out from within, splinters of wood littering the carpeted floor. What remained held by mere shards.

". . . perhaps we could approach this like civilized people and have a conversation."

Sora recognized Murishani's voice and crept ahead to one of the shattered doors, ignored by the guards stationed around it. Peeking through, Murishani stood at the base of the steps leading toward a throne of bones, hands held in a dramatic welcome, even if his smile was pure poison. Behind him, Casvir loomed before the throne itself, mace and shield readied.

And who stood in the center? Soliel himself. He glowed within his golden armor, his sword in one hand, a helmet in the other. Five orbs spun behind him, their threat painfully clear. "I have not come to negotiate anything."

"I would assume you want the final orb," Murishani replied.

"I have come to take Lady Flowridia to safety."

Sora balked at that.

"If she is brought out," Soliel continued, "I will leave your castle peacefully. Otherwise, I will split it in two."

Murishani glanced to Casvir, rapid words exchanged between them. To Sora's surprise, Casvir himself came forward, taking Murishani's place. "Lady Flowridia will not be part of any negotiations. I cannot speak to her whereabouts. She and Ayla left for the Shadow Realm upon your arrival."

Soliel's face revealed nothing. "I see."

"I would speak to you on another matter, however. There is a dire threat approaching my kingdom, and I wish to contract your aid to stop it."

Sora's heart beat to deafen her, yet still she heard every unsettling word.

"I know what is coming, and I am not here to save you from your own consequences," Soliel replied.

"No, but I have something else you want. Save my kingdom from Goddess Ku'Shya, and you shall have it."

Sora's stomach dropped. Even Murishani looked alarmed. But Soliel remained contemplative as he stared at the floor. "Give me the orb now, and Ku'Shya will be killed when I separate Sha'Demoni from the mortal realm."

"Swear to me my kingdom will not be harmed in the destruction."

"I cannot predict the damage to the mortal realm," Soliel replied, "but once I have stabilized the spell, I will defend your kingdom with my life."

"Do you swear?"

Sora's panic rose. She shoved past the guards.

"I do—"

"No!" Sora barely recognized her own voice as she sprinted, certainly had no idea what she was doing—only that she skidded to a stop before Imperator Casvir, whose gaze burned a hole through her body. "You can't do that."

Casvir spoke calmly. "Guards, remove this woman."

Skeleton guards rushed her. Sora dodged hands and spears, ducking between bony legs as she yelled. "You don't know what you're doing! You can't trust—"

Skeleton hands grabbed her, holding her thrall. She struggled, but they had no muscles to overpower—just pure, wicked magic.

"Lock her underground," Casvir said. "She will be dealt with later."

CHAPTER 34

Fifteen years after the end of the world . . .

The heat was stifling, but Dira didn't mind, the exhilaration of running a glorious thing. This was freedom, though but a taste, but with each taste the sweeter the sensation became.

She supposed she could abandon Soliel. She could abandon Mother too. The world stretched before her—what if she simply disappeared?

But even a world away . . . Dira knew she did not want to stay forever. The cage could remain, but let the door stay open. Let her fly and return. Mother could still protect her, if only they could fly together.

Such were her thoughts until she returned to Sune, met with the town's gentle lights.

She wore no disguise this time, no hood, no cover save for the starry sky above, no moon to light the path. Instead she approached the nearest guards, making no effort to hide her damning fangs. "I beg your pardon, sirs," she said, mindful of their confusion and blades. "But I need to speak to Soliel. Immediately. Tell him the monster, Dira, has returned."

One guard set a hand on the hilt of his sword. "The Son of Sol Kareena is not a dog that will come at your call, nor are you owed his presence."

Dira stiffened her jaw. "The choice is his. Tell him my name, and he can come or not. Please."

Soliel arrived quickly when summoned, gazing as though she were a ghost. "Leave us," he said to the guards, and he kept his own distance. He carried his shield readied, and though his sword remained on his hip, Dira had no doubt he could unsheathe it in a breath. "Last I saw, you were pulled into the shadows."

Though the possibility of his death remained, Dira found his voice too lovely to sever. "That is correct."

"Care to explain?"

"I can offer a trade. An answer for an answer."

Soliel nodded.

"I ran away from home. My mother found me and took me back. She . . . has abilities."

"Is this town in danger because of your presence?" Soliel asked, those soft eyes surveying the scene.

"No one is looking for me, but that is the only answer I will give you for free." She forced a smile, praying it lightened the mood, but Soliel remained somber . . . and skeptical.

"Ask your question then."

The question burst like a popped bubble. "What is The Endless Night?"

Confusion settled upon his handsome features. "You . . . you truly don't know?"

"I'm starting to suspect I'm the only person who doesn't. But it's important that I know."

"The Endless Night was . . . *is* a monster who murdered most of the Sun Elves populace, some thousand years ago. You know of godly possession, right?"

Dira nodded.

"It was Izthuni, the Shadow God, and his hostess, Ayla Darkleaf."

All the world became . . . numb. Dira breathed yet felt no air. "What? That can't be."

"You can ask anyone in town," Soliel replied, his bewilderment fading into something akin to pity. "Anyone in this country. Why is that so impossible?"

Soliel had no reason to lie.

"A-A monster, you say?" Curse her trembling lip. Dira gasped for breath, yet felt only lighter.

"She is terrorizing this country as we speak, though in a different way. She seeks to subjugate the Sun Elves to fight the so-called threat beyond. The rest of the elven kingdoms are already under her control."

Mother was . . . a *monster*.

"That's the purpose of my rebellion," Soliel continued, and somewhere in Dira's peripheral, she saw him set down his shield, saw his stance soften, but knew not what it meant. "We are defending this country against a tyrant who once destroyed entire cities in a night. Who performed demented experiments on its populace. She spilled blood enough to flood these lands once before, and I'll fall on my sword before she does it again."

Dira's head spun. Strong hands steadied her when she swayed, led her to sit on the cobblestone path. She didn't feel her tears, only knew they spilled.

"Dira . . . can you please tell me what you're thinking?"

It could not be true. Mother was stern, but Mother was kind. Mother was cryptic, but Mother loved; Dira had never doubted that love.

"I have rekindled every evil thing about me, and all for you, my lamb."

Her sobs came gently. She felt no shame to cry in front of this stranger; she had no shame left to feel. When a warm touch fell upon her back, Dira leaned into its tenderness.

Upon a dusty, stony path, Soliel answered every question of her heart: of the legacy of The Endless Night, of the war, even Imperator Casvir . . .

"His use of necromancy is reprehensible to some, but his people are well-cared for. His justice is harsh but fair. All of that is more than we can say of Grand Executor Darkleaf . . ."

"First she rose to power among what remained of the Elven Kingdoms, uniting their masses into a single country. There is no justice. There is only the war and her labor camps . . ."

"But when machines were not enough to stop the imperator's forces, she turned to the Sun Elves instead, seeking to enslave their priests and priestesses . . ."

"We have yet to see her in her monstrous form, but the Scourge of the Sun Elves she remains . . ."

Dira said nothing. Nothing at all. She sat against his side, his arm secure around her. Not a cage, no. A blanket.

Hesitation stilled Soliel's words. His thumb caressed a gentle line across her arm, the affection innocent and sweet. Her heart might've soared had she any feeling left at all. "I have my suspicions, but you know Ayla Darkleaf personally, don't you? How?"

All that Mother had worked for, all she had done . . . Every crime and wicked deed, even before Dira's birth . . . But though kept in a cage, Dira was a secret well-kept. To speak it aloud . . . no. "I can't tell you."

And to her surprise, her relief . . . he smiled. "Then it's a secret."

Oh, this beautiful boy. He was so foolish . . . But what kindness shone in his eyes, what light. He could not be much older than her, yet he had accepted the weight of this war.

"Soliel!"

They both turned, though it brought them closer together.

There shone the silhouettes of two men, one of whom waved. "You're late! Kiss your lady and come on!"

Despite the numbness in her soul . . . Dira blushed at the thought.

Instead, Soliel withdrew his arm, regretful as he glanced back at the men. "There is a meeting with . . . well, I should not say, given whatever secret you hold. But it's important."

"For the rebellion?"

"Yes."

Mother had mentioned a benefactor supplying weapons ... Could this be it? Could she ...?

But no, no. After all she had heard ...

"Unless you want to join us." What odd hope shone in his eyes. Foolish boy. Beautiful boy. Gods, what did she want?

"I don't know if you can trust me," Dira whispered, for even she did not. Her very soul split in twain—for Soliel was here, and he spoke the truths she longed to hear, spoke of the world, of the war, of Mother ...

But Mother was ...

"If you wish to stop the tyranny," Soliel said gently, "you could stay and help us. There are things we would have to keep from you until, well, with all due respect, until we do know we can trust you, but whatever help you can give us, we would gladly accept."

Gods, what she would give to be tucked in her bed, shackled by ignorance instead of thrown into the abyss. Innocence was never restored once taken ...

"Don't give me any secrets. I can't keep anything from her. But ... I will at least come listen."

When Soliel rose, he offered his hand, and she let herself be led.

Current era ...

Sora had seven knives, but not a single one could pick a lock that didn't exist.

With no light other than a holy spark in her hand, Sora had inspected her small prison cell up and down, studied the bars, the walls—everything. She had sworn she'd heard the door click when the guards had thrown her in, but now she couldn't even find a door.

Five of the walls were stone. The final was vertical bars—not a door or lock in sight.

Ice could have climbed the walls for how chilly the air was. Periodically, a skeleton guard patrolled past her cell as it shambled down the hallway, its rattling steps the only sound. Sora snuffed out her light as it passed, faced instead with the nightmarish glow of its eyes, invisible until it was the only source of light.

But damn it all. Damn Casvir.

Furious tears welled in her eyes. Sora sat against the back wall of her cell, cursing every part of this. Etolié could have stopped him. Etolié could have screamed and conjured any illusion she wanted.

Flowridia could have reasoned with him, perhaps even convinced him to stop.

But Sora? She had never felt so useless. In the final stretch, she had stumbled. She had faced the end alone and failed.

The world could end at any moment, and Sora would not even know.

She supposed she could stretch her goodwill and pray to Staella, but that assumed Etolié wasn't already back, or that Etolié was even with Staella at all. Still, Sora set her thumbs and forefingers together, wondering how to even begin to explain this horrible twist of fate . . .

But there were other gods to pray to. The makings of what might be a terrible plan formulated in Sora's head, but she had been granted a boon. From a pouch in her satchel, Sora withdrew the gifted lily. A little crumpled and torn, but still bearing an essence Sora shied from, its magic repellent to her own.

She crushed it in her hand, startled when it turned entirely to dust, and blew it into the air. *"Ilune."*

Sora waited, hearing only the scuffling of the skeleton guard. The faint purple glow of its essence appeared in the darkness, its eternal patrol continuing—

All of a sudden, the skeleton lurched.

Sora scrambled into standing as light filled the undead monster. Though it glowed gold, it was not holy, instead intermingled with silver. A strange fog filled its hollow figure, like a formless ghost wearing armor, and from its back burst brilliant wings.

Amid the glow, purple smoke swirled about its limbs, invoking a magic Sora realized she recognized—the very same Chaos performed when sculpting a body of flesh. As the muscles and tendons grew to cover the skeleton form, the glow never dampened, not even when skin created a final barrier from the horror.

Last to appear was her face, beauty in the aftermath of horror, that impish smile the final piece. "Well, well. Who's in the cage now?" Ilune laughed, which unfortunately only served to highlight the fact that she was naked. Ilune could sculpt any body she wanted in this state, and she had created distractingly large breasts, her waves of black hair only serving to frame them.

Sora forced her gaze to latch onto Ilune's face. "Can you help, please?"

When Ilune ran her hand along the cell's bars, each glowed a blinding silver—and shattered, dull and grey. "You can tell me your story while I walk you out."

Ilune offered a hand.

Sora hesitated at the offering, but now was not the time to risk insulting her savior. She accepted, prepared for the clammy touch, but not for how near Ilune's face was, the cloying scent of necromancy both intoxicating and vile.

"Do you know the path?" Ilune asked.

"I made sure to memorize it," Sora replied, resisting the urge to wipe her hand on her trousers. Her heart beat rapidly, but there was a frightful task ahead. It was explainable. "Are you going to put on clothing?"

"I fail to see the use."

"Propriety, perhaps?"

Ilune raised an eyebrow, that smirk never fading. "When you think about it, this body *is* clothing, in a way. Something to peel off and throw away once I'm through with it."

Her logic, though riddled with flirtation, was technically valid, and Sora chose not to comment. Sparking laughter from Ilune, as well as some sort of magical fabric coiling around her like a snake, creating a salacious dress. It covered only what was necessary, but anything that didn't leave her ass fully exposed was a victory.

Sora beckoned for Ilune to follow. "Long story short, I tried to stop Casvir from giving Soliel—uh, the God of Order—the final orb."

"And got thrown into prison for your efforts. I see."

Sora's jaw set, reminded once more of her failure, and nodded.

Footsteps ahead sounded in an organized march. When the first guard rounded the stone corridor's hall, Ilune clenched her fist. It shattered into dust. "Etolié described this 'Casvir' as audacious, to put it politely. I presume this fits his character?"

"Under normal circumstances, I don't think so. But Goddess Ku'Shya is coming to destroy Haven. He wanted the God of Order's help."

Ilune flinched at the demon goddess' name. "Well, with all due respect, I'll be keeping far away from that party. No doubt she'll attempt to make my life uncomfortable."

"You've already done more than I expected," Sora replied. "And I'm grateful, don't get me wrong. But you don't have to stay any longer than you want to."

"Oh, what I want and what I need to do are entirely contrary in this endeavor. I rather like spending time with new friends."

Sora didn't particularly like where Ilune's wink directed her blood.

A small formation of guards faced them next. Ilune destroyed them with a mere flick of her finger. "Either Casvir has a terrible prison system, or you're not considered a threat. I don't believe we've passed anyone else."

It was true. They had only seen empty cells. "Definitely the latter." No need to dive into the intricacies of the Nox'Karthan justice system. Instead, they came upon a staircase, ending in a metal door.

Sora tugged on the handle, finding it barred from the outside. "I might be able to pick the lock."

"No need." With a faint flash of purple, dampened by the radiant light of Ilune's wings, a swirling of bones from the destroyed guards swirled up from the base of the staircase. The bones surrounded the door, some slipping through the faint seams—and crushed it like paper, the crumpling metal screeching like a siren.

Blessedly, no one was on the other side, but Sora cringed at the mess. "Not exactly subtle. No offense."

"I have never been subtle."

Sora chose not to dismantle the implications of that.

They remained in the stone corridors behind the scenes of the castle's main halls, but at least there were no more bars. Sora took the memorized path—two turns, and then a hallway ending in a decorated door. "Thank you. I really appreciate what you've done."

"Oh, don't say goodbye just yet," Ilune said, her teasing tone far from innocent. "Let me get you out of the castle first. No sense in abandoning you now, just for you to be captured by Casvir's little cronies."

Sora nearly smiled; the statement was so reminiscent of Etolié. "Chaos and I have a designated meeting spot outside the castle."

"Lead the way. You'll be safe in my hands until we return you to your Goddess."

It was surely a double entendre, but Sora chose not to comment.

"I just wish I knew what was going on."

Flowridia leaned against the bars of Demitri's cage, her gaze toward the comatose wolf.

Ayla paced, restless in her worry. "He either came for you, or he came seeking the final orb. Either way, we can grab Demitri and run if he becomes a threat."

Demitri slept like the dead he was. Flowridia longed to hold him, to touch his fur and feel warmth. Would he feel warm to undead skin? When she was turned, might things be normal once again? "What if we've made a mistake? Should we have gone with him?"

"The Goddess of Chaos all but confirmed his lie."

Flowridia nodded, though her anxiety only rose. When Ayla knelt before her, she resisted the urge to touch her.

"You are not wrong for being skeptical of his intentions," Ayla continued, "especially given how insistent he was before that your death was assured." Ayla's smile softened. "I think I am the better option to protect you anyway."

Flowridia returned her smile, grasping at this normalcy. "I would trust you above anyone."

Ayla replied by silently slipping through the cage's bars, approaching the still wolf.

Distant footsteps disrupted the grass. From around the corner came light. Flowridia stood as Ayla readied herself to surge forward—but Sora rounded the corner, accompanied by . . . the God of Death?

Sora glanced frantically about, then ran the rest of the distance. "Where is Chaos?"

Ayla swept gracefully out of Demitri's cage. "Why are you with Ilune?"

"It's a long story, but we don't—"

"Since you brought Chaos up, I have a few questions regarding—"

"We don't have time!" Sora cried. Behind her, Ilune stood as nonchalantly as any fugitive god might, her glowing wings idly illuminating the scene. "Casvir gave Soliel the White Orb."

Flowridia balked at the statement, so impossible it was. "What?"

"If Soliel separates the worlds, Ku'Shya will die in Sha'Demoni's destruction."

"And Nox'Kartha might crumble in the fallout—is he insane?!"

"Soliel swore to protect Nox'Kartha."

Oh, the *audacity*—! "I'll speak to him." Flowridia turned to Ayla. "It'll be faster if you take me."

Ayla nodded, though remained inscrutable. "What's done is done, but I will never turn down the opportunity to watch him taken down a peg." When she took Flowridia's hand, they stepped into the Shadow Realm.

The darkness of night swept away, replaced by pervasive shadow. Ayla led her along. Despite the unsettling serenity of the scene, this world might be nothing in minutes. Flowridia's breath hitched to consider it. "Is it right, though?"

Ayla's pace did not slow. "Knowing what we know, it is debatable. Knowing what Casvir knows, it's pure insanity."

Perhaps that was why it unsettled her so. Casvir had never been so reckless.

The palace walls held little substance, but Ayla navigated the wispy halls with ease. Flowridia said nothing, simply seethed at the selfishness of his actions, yet reeled at the prospect of the infinite lives this brutal act might save. He had unknowingly destroyed his own ambitions.

When they emerged before his office, Flowridia had found no peace at all. She threw open the door.

Inside, Casvir sat hunched over his desk, his frown quickly fading. "Flowridia, I actually just sent for you."

Flowridia barged in. "What were you thinking?!"

Casvir's expression darkened. "How did you know?"

"Sora told me what you did. How could you?!"

"If you are committed to throwing a tantrum, kindly shut the door."

Behind her, the door clicked. Ayla appeared by her side. "You have some gall infantilizing me," Flowridia spat. "Is it really a tantrum to be angry when you're the one who sold out the whole world?"

"I do not subscribe to any notions of 'the greater good.' I protect my own. I always have. Soliel's and my plans aligned, and I took advantage of it."

Flowridia studied his demonic visage, stunned by his apathy. "You have no idea what you've just done."

Casvir appeared unimpressed. "Enlighten me."

Gods, to speak the truth would be an avalanche—to reveal he was undermining his own quest for supreme domination, to say he became the greatest evil the worlds would ever know, to say literal Gods rose to try and stop him and he defeated them in every life, starting the cycle anew.

Flowridia clenched her fists, lip trembling as she swallowed angry tears. She turned to leave.

"I wished to tell you," Casvir said, sounding almost pleasant, "that your services in coordinating evacuations are no longer necessary. It is prudent to keep my populace as close together as possible to protect them from the fallout."

Flowridia nodded, too bitter to face him.

"Ayla, I wish to speak to you."

Flowridia did look back for that, in time to witness Ayla's scathing glare.

"Your Silver Fire could be invaluable for protecting Nox'Kartha, in the case of magical backlash," Casvir said, and Flowridia braced herself for conflict.

Ayla didn't even twitch. "I already told you my price."

"And that is not an option. However, consider what else I could grant you, be it a title, land, riches. As I said, I am willing to be generous."

"I will not tether myself to you. I will not accept a title, hold land, or gain riches in your kingdom."

"That is unfortunate," Casvir replied, his glower rare and unsettling. "Consider what I have already given you."

Ayla offered a withering smile. "Goodbye, Casvir."

She took Flowridia's hand as the duo marched out.

Flowridia and Ayla disappeared, and Sora immediately grabbed her knife at the sudden sound of footsteps.

But it was Chaos who turned the corner behind them, horror set upon her features. "I am sorry if I worried you. I heard them talking and hid."

"Did you hear—?"

"Yes." Chaos looked to the sky, searching through the brilliant cosmos. "We are in the calm before the storm. Once Soliel begins the spell, we will know."

"And then it's over? We've lost?"

Chaos shook her head. "It can all still be stopped, but we have no time to delay."

"What do we do?"

Ilune came forward. "Given I have everything to lose if Celestière is destroyed, you have my assistance as well."

"Thank you," Chaos said. "But I do not know. I am but a ghost in a shell. Even with what pledges I've gained, I don't stand a chance against Soliel and his six orbs."

"How long until Flowridia has the baby?" Sora asked, though the question held unfathomable weight.

Chaos' breath hitched. "Soon. Very soon."

Ilune raised a hand. "Pardon me, but what does Flowridia having the baby have anything to do with her?"

"No time for questions," Sora said, "but Chaos is Flowridia's child, but from the future. Once the baby is born, Chaos will have her full powers restored."

"I assume cutting it out isn't an option?"

"I don't know. Half-elf pregnancies are kind of unpredictable."

"True." Ilune made a show of tapping her jaw. "You're a Goddess possessing a dead body, right?"

"That is technically correct," Chaos replied.

"So am I, which isn't something just any god can do, mind you. Generally we New Gods need a living host. However, I'm a necromancer, so I hold a few advantages, such as relatively free reign of the mortal realm. But I digress—can *you* possess a living body? Or perhaps an undead body already housing a soul? I understand better than anyone how vulnerable you are, but with the right host, you could be nigh unstoppable."

Sora's hope rose at Chaos' intrigue. "I don't know," Chaos said, "but it is worth pursuing."

Ilune's smirk held unbridled mischief. "The Endless Night is just an undead god possessing an undead hostess, so why not ask the hostess? Having someone from your own lineage hosting you is ideal anyway."

Despite Chaos' clear hesitation, she gave a fervent nod. "Your logic is sound."

"How much time does Soliel need to begin the ritual?" Sora asked. "Do we even have time to stall for time?"

"There cannot be a 'we' in this. It would be too dangerous."

The rejection struck Sora hard, sudden grief filling her heart. "What do you mean?"

"Soliel has nearly reached the end of his quest. I have no doubt he will resort to whatever desperate measure he can to complete it, including kill you with no hesitation. Sora . . ." Chaos took Sora's hands, her cold touch in stark contrast to the warm gesture. "The best you can do for me now is live to love my younger self."

Oh, this finality scared Sora so. Her touch fell slack as she studied her niece's precious countenance, their shared blood subtly apparent. Here they stood, at the end of the line. Sora wouldn't be the one to walk with her at the end of the world. "Chaos . . . Dira, I know we've had our differences, but—"

She nearly sobbed when Chaos flung herself into her arms. Though time was short, she clung tight for a few precious moments more. The world could wait for this one selfish thing. "In case this is the end," Sora whispered, "I can't express enough what an honor it's been to get to know you."

"I love you, Auntie."

Sora smiled through sudden tears. "I love you too."

Chaos' voice lowered so not even Ilune could hear. "Demitri says he does not love you but that you might not be so bad. His words."

Sora chuckled. "I appreciate that."

Oh, she didn't want to part, but the world still turned and time was short, so short. Such hope shone in Chaos' face, revealing childlike wonder, despite her age. "Whatever happens, this will not be the last time. I will see you again. You will love her just as much."

Beautiful words, bittersweet and true. Sora planted a kiss on Chaos' forehead, torn between heartbreak and pride. "I will. I'll always be here for you."

And though every instinct begged to follow, Sora watched as Chaos ran away.

In the ensuing silence, Sora dabbed at her eyes with her sleeve. 'Stay alive' was her final order, but where was Flowridia? Etolié? Chaos had left, but there were others she could protect—

"I have been thinking about your bird."

The voice and the shifting light reminded Sora of an unsettling truth—that she was far from alone. Ilune stepped into her view, and Sora was once again struck by the sheer magnitude of this god's presence. "What about him?"

Nothing of a jest in Ilune's gentle countenance. The flirtatious woman was utterly sober. "For as little hope as I gave you before, I fear it was still too much. May I see him?"

Sora slipped a hand into her pouch and stroked Leelan's comatose form. "Why?"

The barest hint of a smile turned Ilune's lip. "I'm not going to betray you, Sora. As cute as it's been to tease you, you're Etolié's friend, and I very much want Etolié to like me. Betraying you would undermine that goal." Ilune brought forward a hand.

Though Sora's wariness remained, Ilune had raised a believable—and vulnerable—point. Sora lifted Leelan with care, anxiety rising even as she set the bird into Ilune's grasp.

Ilune remained put, then offered Leelan right back. "He's dying, Sora. And quickly."

Like a punch to the gut, Sora processed the horrible words. A delay, and then she finally took back her dear Leelan, holding him softly to her chest. Swallowing tears, she forced somber words. "Tell me what to do."

"I won't tell you what to do, but I will tell you what would most benefit the world." Despite her solemn pose, despite the tragic message, Ilune's presence held the gravity of the sun. Sora held Leelan, yet watched Ilune with all the might she commanded. "You said Ku'Shya is coming to destroy Haven. The only way to stop her from this realm is to murder Khastra, and that would break Etolié's heart."

Sora nodded, even as she savored this precious touch from Leelan, fearing any breath might be his last.

"Sora . . . It's cruel that fate has set you at this crossroads, but the only two choices I see are that your bird dies in vain or your bird dies for the noblest cause: murdering Ku'Shya in Sha'Demoni. She'll be vulnerable when she meditates. If I absorb his power, I could kill her in one blast and bring an end to a tyranny ten thousand years old."

Sora struggled to breathe, her next influx of air harsh and pained—and fruitless. Her head swam as she brought Leelan up to her cheek, catching a glimpse of black, vacant eyes. "Leelan?" she whispered.

Leelan's glassy gaze stared upon nothing.

"Leelan, you say?" Ilune's words sounded far away. "That's his name?"

Sora nodded, willing her familiar to respond, to hear that joyful chirp again.

"I have granted countless familiars, and I know each and every one means the world to their partner. I know what I'm asking is viciously unfair. And I am asking you to make that sacrifice anyway, in light of his inevitable death."

Despite her grit, Sora blinked and stared behind a veil of misty tears. "Why though? You're not this altruistic, so why would you risk yourself for this?"

"I'm not altruistic at all. There are two wardens to my prison, Sora. One was my fallen auntie. Ku'Shya is the only one left with the ability to lock me back underground, so I have everything to gain if she's gone. But I want Etolié to like me, remember? So I won't just pluck him from your grasp."

Weeks ago, Sora had walked in the ruins of Tierzuroth. She had seen Ku'Shya's wrath for herself. Haven would be the same—but drenched in blood. "I know it's right," Sora whispered, cursing her trembling voice. She swallowed her tears, forcing herself to steady. Now was not the time to cry. "And I'm going to say yes, but it's hard." Sora bit back a sob, shaking as she held Leelan as tight as she dared, her fragile, tender friend.

Ilune's silver light shifted. Sora barely felt her touch on her back. "I know it's callous to mention the more practical loss, that of your magic. But when Ku'Shya falls, I will personally guarantee you receive a familiar from any god you choose."

Sora shook her head, the notion unthinkable. "Sol Kareena was my goddess."

She expected the cold of Ilune's skin, but she never could have anticipated the comfort as Ilune pulled her into an embrace. She expected some crass remark, but Ilune said nothing at all. And the surest truth of all was that Sora never would have expected to find solace in something so innocent—not from Ilune.

But though Sora shuddered against tears, she let her head fall against Ilune's shoulder. "Is there any way I could come with you? I want to be with him as long as I can."

"Well, I don't actually have any practical portal magic. That power skipped a generation, though there is one minor exception. If I abandon my host body, I've found I can bring back whatever I'm holding to my real body in Celestière, and that does include people. What I cannot do is bring people back, so if the worlds truly are separated, you'll be killed along with everything else in Sha'Demoni."

The noble part of Sora whispered to stay, to protect those who remained. But Leelan was dying. He was dying *now*.

Did she not owe him loyalty too?

And . . . if she lived to love Dira in the future, that meant she must survive, right? That meant the cycle continued, at worst. That meant . . .

That meant Dira had never known her with magic at all.

Sora curled around Leelan, in turn curling into Ilune's hold. "Take me with you."

She gasped when Ilune gripped her with new strength. What was once a kind embrace became cold, possessive. "Don't panic," came sensuous words.

All the world vanished. Sora blinked, then saw only white mist.

Flowridia led the march to Ayla's bedroom, where she unceremoniously slammed the door once Ayla had passed. "Forgive me for this comical understatement, but I can't believe the audacity of that man."

Ayla did smile at that, mindful as she summoned a small bit of flame in her hand and lit an exquisite lamp, laden with colored gems. They cast the scene in shades of flickering blue and green. "And forgive me for asking what I pray is not a stupid question—but why do you care?"

"It's not a stupid question." Flowridia went to Ayla's chaise and sat, sore but not nearly so exhausted as she once would have been. "I would argue that Soliel once had me nearly convinced to agree with him. At the very least, I understood why. I think I'm mostly stuck on the fact that Casvir sold out the world to save himself from his own mistakes."

"Are you actually surprised?"

"A little, yes. He can be self-serving, but the risk of swapping probable destruction for different probable destruction and an unfathomable amount of fallout is a bridge too far, even for him."

Ayla softly shook her head as she sat by Flowridia's side, near enough to touch, though she did not. "Darling, this is precisely the sort of calculated risk that preserves his ego. If Nox'Kartha does fall to ruin in the separation of the worlds, what a mighty way to fall. He could rebuild from the ashes, be a hero to the survivors, and resume his quest—as well as he can that is, given he has unknowingly stunted his own expansion. But if he falls to Ku'Shya, this is a foe he could have vanquished but did not. It is a very different sort of defeat." When Ayla did set a hand upon Flowridia's, Flowridia grasped it tight with her other, craving the contact. "The question, instead," Ayla continued, "is what will you do about it?"

Flowridia raised an eyebrow. "I could ask you the same question. Why are we defaulting to my opinion?"

She meant it with no ire, but Ayla was silent a beat too long. Flowridia's anxiety rose, but Ayla finally spoke. "I thought I did not care. The fact that I now do means I am not thinking clearly. I do not trust my own self in this."

Flowridia did not know where to even begin with that. "Can you explain? I'm just trying to understand."

Again, Ayla was slow to speak, staring at the floor as she fidgeted between Flowridia's hands. "Because it was not even half an hour ago that I found out our daughter is the one fighting so desperately to stop him. And I . . ."

Flowridia did not even dare to breathe in the silence, lest she scare those tepid words away.

". . . I should not care. That is the end of it. I *should* not care. It does not change anything. I don't care about her."

A knock silenced the words. Flowridia stared at the door, bewildered until the knock came a second time. "Come in."

The door swung open, and Flowridia's heart . . . shifted.

For there in the doorway stood a woman neither tall nor short, staring with trepidation to match her Godhood. So much could be said of her beauty, those soft, silver eyes bearing the splendor of the moon itself. It was plain to see she was a child of many worlds—her ears ending in a soft point, her olive skin pallid from death yet warm from heritage. From her parted lips peeked fangs, but that was not where she bore her resemblance to Ayla, no. It was the intensity of her stare, the pride in her stance, and the fear in her visage—so much like Ayla when she sought reproach.

And though she showed signs of age, with silver streaks in her locs and faint laughter lines upon her face, Flowridia felt she would know her in any place, with any face, in life or in death.

But it was a mere flash of insecurity. The woman straightened her stance, false confidence filling her—so much like Ayla when she feigned a brave face. "Ayla, could we speak—"

"Oh yes, we could," Ayla spat, and Flowridia stiffened at the aggression in her motions. Ayla rose, standing as a barrier between them. "A few fascinating truths have come to light since our last meeting, and while I reel at the depth of the details I was forced to share in front of you in Onias' Realm, perhaps it was good for you to learn a few nasty truths about your dear old progenitor. I would never insult you by calling myself your mother, given Soliel has more than alluded that we'll someday come to blows, but whatever game you were playing by hiding your identity is over, *daughter*."

Gods, the disdain in the word made Flowridia ill. She struggled with her own words, too startled to speak, yet it was the woman—Chaos—who spoke instead. "There was no game," she whispered. "I am sorry if you felt tricked."

The very air felt taut. Ayla sneered. "What do you want?"

"You know Soliel has all six Convergence Orbs," Chaos said gently, nothing grand about her. Flowridia's heart ached. "But I cannot fight him. Not in my current state. You know who I am, and so you know I have no true power. I am but a ghost possessing a sculpted corpse. But I am also a God, and Gods need not only possess corpses. I wished to ask if you would host me."

At Ayla's balk, Flowridia winced. "All right," Ayla replied. "I will, but you have to answer me one thing."

"If I can, I will."

"Tell me how to save Flowra."

Chaos said nothing though suddenly struggled to meet Ayla's gaze.

"No?" Ayla asked, her step forward bearing menace. "You were so passionate in Ilune's prison about murdering her. So how do I stop you?"

Chaos shut those beautiful eyes, the barest hints of anguish twisting her lips.

"You're not even going to tell me to stab her in the womb? Nothing at all? Is this why we fight, little Goddess? Because after all I did to save her, you slew my wife in cold blood?"

"Ayla, stop," Flowridia said, disgusted as she rose to her feet. She coaxed Ayla to face her, leading with a gentle touch upon her chin. "You don't know any of that."

"I know what she said."

"Yes, but you're making a lot of assumptions beyond it." Flowridia looked once more to Chaos, her yearning only growing, moment by moment. For the first time, their gazes matched, and Flowridia shoved down the urge to rush to her and hold her in her arms. "You can't speak of the future, lest it be taken away."

Chaos gave a small nod.

"I don't know precisely what it was you said in the prison," Flowridia continued, "but I would imagine there was a great deal more you didn't say. Is that true?"

Again, Chaos nodded, and with it the merest quiver of her lip.

Flowridia shoved aside fears of what led to this confirmed truth, clinging instead to the hope that perhaps this pregnancy was not a death sentence after all. "Ayla, I won't ask you to do this, but if you're going to bargain will you please ask her for something else instead?"

"I will do one better," Ayla said, that ice casting a chill across even Flowridia's skin. "I will simply say no."

So subtle, the moment of heartbreak upon Chaos' countenance, but Flowridia's heart shattered to see it. She bit back a bitter retort, instead taking a step forward—only to run into Ayla as she shifted. "Ayla—"

"Now is not the time to let your motherly heart lead. She is not to be trusted."

All the while, Ayla kept her fixed stare upon Chaos. Flowridia set a hand upon Ayla's shoulder and whispered, "I won't fight with you in front of her. But you will let me pass."

Only then did Ayla meet Flowridia's eye, the fury all too familiar—and though Flowridia would be a liar to say it was not satisfying, she said nothing at all when Ayla finally stepped aside.

Flowridia approached Chaos, uncertain of so many things, but danger was not one of them, no. Chaos meant her no harm. "I don't know where Etolié's gone, but you can ask her whenever she returns."

Chaos affirmed with her nod.

Oh, the novels Flowridia wished to speak, to ask this woman, this child of hers, a thousand questions and cherish every word from her mouth. But every bit of Chaos exuded shame, the want to *flee*, and Flowridia cursed the tears in her own eyes as she spoke words to break her heart anew. "Good luck."

She bit back a farewell, hand clenching behind her back as Chaos shut the door—and only then letting her tears flow. She sank to her knees, her sobs coming quickly to consume her.

Ayla's touch did nothing to comfort her. "Darling, will you explain?"

Flowridia bit back a scream, appalled at Ayla's cruelty to a woman she owed no debt, to a woman she had realistically only just met. But her tears flowed hot and furious. Her words held no bite, but they stung nevertheless. "Would you have treated her so vile were she not the child you regret creating?"

"If I knew she murdered my wife? Absolutely."

"You keep using that word," Flowridia spat. "I thought our marriage was done."

"We were also technically never married, remember? But I prefer to not get caught up in semantics."

Flowridia could not face her, grateful for the curtain of her hair as she wiped her eyes. Yet the tears still flowed, like scooping buckets of ocean water from a sinking ship. "I just . . . What did I do?"

"What do you mean?"

"How did I drive her to *murder me*?" Flowridia sobbed into her hands, all those fears washing over her as a tsunami. All that talk of breaking cycles—was it for nothing? Was she damned to be Odessa after all? "When I look at her, all I want to do is hold her in my arms, but there's no love from her. Only shame."

"Flowra, darling, she's not your child—well, she is, but she is a woman who lived in a whole other world."

"Ayla, that's *bullshit*, and you know it! You can't fix this, so don't fucking try."

Ayla said nothing. Instead, her arms came around Flowridia, who wept into her embrace.

Guilt rose, for this was far more than she should ask of Ayla after all she'd done. But weep she did, the overwhelm of Chaos' presence leaving her broken.

She barely recognized when a knock came to the door once again. Some part of her hoped for her daughter's return, but she knew it could not be. She sniffed and forced her words. "Not now."

The knob twisted. On the floor, Flowridia recognized Casvir's silhouette behind her hair.

And what was it he held? Those glowing eyes amid a skull—

The world slowed as Ayla wrenched away from her like a wounded animal, bolting for the flickering shadow of the lamp—only to skid to a stop, as though hitting a wall.

Flowridia's head spun as she stood, but she would recognize that staff in any nightmare—yet this was dreadful reality. "What are you doing?!"

Staff Seraph deDieula's skull stared with purple orbs, yet Casvir's gaze was far colder. "She is earning her keep."

Ayla collapsed to the floor, writhing as she screamed. *"No, no, no—get OUT!"*

And Flowridia no longer stood safely in her lover's old room but in a dark dungeon smelling of metal; of blood; of rot; bombarded by the terror of her wife's shrieks as she ripped her own ears from her skull; as she collapsed on the floor; as she begged for Flowridia's life while Mereen shredded her body over and over and over— *"Darling, darling, close your eyes. You don't need to remember this part—"*

Flowridia did not think; she ran to the staff, sought to yank it from Casvir's grasp—

Only to be held back by the collar of her gown, Casvir's grip inescapable. "You will calm yourself."

"Let her go!" Flowridia could barely see, so fast her tears fell. "Casvir, don't do this! *Please*, don't do this!"

"She will be released once the threat of Goddess Ku'Shya is done. In the meantime, she will assist."

Flowridia fought the grip on her dress, flailing as Casvir dragged her to the chaise and shoved her onto the cushions. "Casvir!"

But instead of responding, Casvir gripped Ayla by her arm and pulled her stiff figure to the door. "This will take more practice."

Flowridia tried to run but stumbled, ramming herself with no strength against his back. She gripped his armor. "Casvir, no!" she pled, but Ayla's cries were far louder. "Please! Please, let her go!"

He did release Ayla, only to peel Flowridia off of his armor instead—and shove her to the ground. Flowridia stared up at him through tearful vision, his silhouette bearing the menace of the demon she once met in the woods. "You are above this," his volcanic voice rumbled.

Oh, his audacity nearly made her laugh. Instead, she gasped another sob. "I'm above pleading for my wife's life?"

"Nothing is at stake." He lifted Ayla once more, who had become comatose.

Flowridia clutched Ayla's other arm as it dangled, only to yelp at the flash of pain ripping up her forearm. She wept as she curled around her maimed hand, watching helplessly as Casvir dragged Ayla away and slammed the door.

Shoving aside the debilitating pain, Flowridia shambled to the door—only to find it locked. *"CASVIR!"*

No reply.

CHAPTER 35

Fifteen years after the end of the world . . .

Soliel led her to a tavern near the town's center, a friendly-looking building with warm light and music emanating from within. He walked in with no aplomb, even as a few patrons waved and the barkeep pointed him to a room in the back. A few looked fearfully to her, but it seemed Soliel's presence was enough to keep them reassured—or at least quiet.

Soliel knocked a particular pattern on the door. An elven woman answered, who looked immediately taken aback at Dira's presence. "Who is this half-elf?"

"She is my friend. She's here to observe, for a little while, at least."

"You're certain you want to bring strangers in when, well, you know who's here."

Soliel spared Dira a glance, her own apprehension rising. "I trust him to know if she's a friend or foe."

The woman let them inside, though her disparaging stare followed.

The room was large, the seating vast, and the volume among the patrons riotous. Everyone drank, most laughed, though some were caught up in heated conversations. A few cheered at Soliel's entrance, clasping him on the back as he passed, and Dira couldn't decide if her twisted stomach was due to hesitation . . . or excitement. This was friendship. This was . . . a party.

Among the crowd, a particular man stood out, if only for his ethereal radiance. Surely not fully human, for humans were never so flawless. His hair was long, blond, and his manner of dress was closer to Mother's than any of the men in this room with his flowing robes and lengthy split at his chest.

Something sparked inside her, some kinship she recognized. Surely he felt it too, for the moment her magic spoke, he met her eye.

His stare lingered. He moved effortlessly through the crowd, not even bothering to end his conversation with the people around him. His smile was splendid, yet it was his eyes that perplexed her—for an illusion spell hid them. She had seen it before, the odd outlines of Etolié's illusions, images she could choose to believe or not. For though this man would hide his eyes behind a mask of green . . . they were silver, like hers.

Soliel waved at the approaching man. "Well met. This is, uh, a guest. She wishes to be kept in the dark on all secret things. Perhaps your name should be one of them."

The beautiful man offered a hand. "What gorgeous company you keep, Soliel. It is a pleasure to make your acquaintance."

Surely this was the benefactor. Why else would Soliel be so secretive? Dira accepted his touch, though was taken aback when he brought her hand to his lips and left a polite kiss. "Likewise."

"I cannot help but comment on your unique heritage—a half-elf *and* a dhampir. A rare combination. Perhaps the rarest combination of all."

He said every word so indulgently, as though savoring a rich cake.

"It is not often I recognize magical kinship," the man continued. "Surely you felt it too."

There was a particular feeling that the Silver Fire cast, known only to those who wielded it. For so long, she had felt it only with Mother, then later Ilune. And now . . . "I did. I didn't know there were many others like, well, us."

"There are a rare few, though perhaps you are the rarest person to walk this earth, once we add that particular talent to your already impressive repertoire." His gaze shifted between them, his smile faltering. "A lovely duo, you make."

Soliel was quick to stammer, "Oh, w-we're not— It isn't like that."

The man set a dramatic hand upon his chest. "My mistake. Though, Soliel, you'll have to forgive me—I'm afraid we shall have to postpone the meeting tonight."

All around, the riotous mood only rose. Dira felt . . . so oddly alone.

"We will?" Soliel asked, his confusion quite apparent.

"For good reason, as you shall soon understand. I think the tides of war will be shifting. But I must take my leave." The man touched his finger to the air and drew a line down, like a seam. It left sparkles in its wake—sparkles that broadened to open . . . something. A portal?

The crowd lurched, as though sickened. Even Soliel held his stomach, but Dira felt nothing but the sweetness of magic.

"I so hate to say hello and farewell so quickly, my lady," the man said, offering his hand one more time. "Truly the greatest pleasure to meet you."

Discomfort rose within her, something in his saccharine tone wrong, so very wrong, but at his beckoning, she accepted his hand—

Only to be shoved through the summoned portal.

Dira screamed as a void in space surrounded her, where she floated among a billion stars. Weightless, she sought Sha'Demoni, the mortal realm—anything.

She landed, collapsing upon cold stone. Stone ceiling. Stone walls. Bars on one side.

The man appeared from the portal he had summoned, the charm in his smile having twisted into malevolence. He brought a hand up to shut the portal—

Only for a third figure to stumble through, a mere blink before it vanished.

Soliel wasted no time in grabbing the mystery man by the shoulders. "What the hell is this?!"

The man gave an impish shrug and vanished, appearing in a blink on the other side of the bars. "So noble. Yet you insisted it wasn't love. Well, if it's not, you'll love what's to come."

Dira could not move, debilitated by the crushing weight of realization. "W-Where are we?"

"You are home, little Kedira Darkleaf," he said, gushing as though she were a small kitten. "Last I saw you, you were but a wailing beast sucking on the nursemaid's teats, but look at you now, an annoyingly pretty mirror of your late mother. Well, besides the blunt ears, the fangs. You got the worst aspects of your other one."

Dira's dread ever-rose. "A-Are you Imperator Casvir?"

The man burst into laughter, both gallant and cruel. "Gods, that is a *jest*. No, no, but grand things come to those who wait—and Casvir has been waiting a terribly long time for you. Soliel, keep her company, would you? Don't have too much fun. I won't be gone long, and Casvir won't want to see his prize so brutally spoiled."

Gods, she felt sick, helpless, his horrible wink as he left leaving her nauseous.

Soliel came beside her, distance kept as horror befell his features. "I-I didn't know. Dira, I swear."

Dira could not speak, could not even scream. She simply fell into weeping upon the cold dungeon floor.

But her despair was cut short by approaching footsteps. Thus returned that horrible man, this time flanked by sentient skeletons bearing swords.

And with them . . .

Imperator Casvir needed no introduction, for no person on this realm held themselves with more esteem, more indomitable might. Demonic in appearance, Dira shied from his glowing red eyes, his sheer mass, his height. His black armor conveyed little grandeur—only spikes.

He said nothing, merely loomed.

"Isn't she splendid, Imperator?" the awful man said, clapping his hands as though presented with a decorated cupcake. "The spitting image of your late protégé."

Amid Casvir's silent scrutiny, Soliel stood, standing as a wall between the men and herself. "Imperator Casvir, explain yourself."

"Now, now, Soliel," the man said, utterly patronizing, "Imperator Casvir has no quarrel with you. Do you really wish to start one?"

"I have a quarrel with him, given his apparent lackey stole my friend."

Friend. Despite the fear in this cold, awful place, a bit of feeling returned to Dira's limbs.

"Oh, you naïve Celestial child—have you ever witnessed darkness so impenetrable that even your light could not cut through? No? Then do not vex Imperator Casvir. Instead, pity the ones who have. Retribution will come soon."

Dira held Casvir's relentless gaze, for Mother had taught her never to bow, never to bend—even if every instinct inside her screamed to *run.*

And then . . . his lip twisted, bearing the faintest shadow of a smile. "Fascinating."

His voice echoed off the walls like distant thunder.

If Soliel were intimidated, he hid it well. "What's so fascinating about kidnapping us?"

Only then did Casvir turn his gaze upon Soliel, towering above by at least a whole head. "You came of your own accord. Would you like to be sent home?"

"I'm not leaving her."

"Then you have chosen your fate."

"So why are we here?"

"I owe no one an explanation. Certainly not a belligerent child. Your parentage warrants minor respect, but you will take care how you speak in my home."

Dira stood despite her numb limbs, trembling as she set a hand against Soliel's back, willing him to stop. "I-Imperator Casvir, I'm confused, and I'm terrified. I haven't meant any harm. I only want to go home. Will you please tell me why I'm here?" Some part of her knew, but let him say it himself; let him lay out her fate.

What weakness did a man like this even have? Dira stared into those glowing eyes, hellfire searing her soul. "I am deciding." He stepped away. "Viceroy Murishani, we shall discuss."

The horrid man—Murishani, it seemed—followed like an over-eager puppy, practically bouncing with misplaced joy. The skeletons departed. Only Soliel remained.

Current era . . .

For as much of Sha'Demoni was untamed, dubiously sentient wilderness, Etolié now realized how much was firmly, violently civilized.

Demons lived in burrows like Ku'Shya's, spreading farther underground than Etolié could even begin to imagine, but their temples were built to touch the sky. Layered like cakes, but square, glittering like cut gems, and Etolié stared like a moth to a flame.

However, for all the roads she and Kah'Sheen crossed, she didn't see a single soul. Not abandoned. Nothing dead. Simply . . . empty.

"Where is everyone?" Etolié asked, illusioning a handkerchief to keep her sweat from dripping into her mouth and eyes. Damn this humidity. It affected even her.

"They are gathering to watch *Rezoxos*. The duel is ending with them praising Mother as the one true goddess or pledging to Khastra."

As neat as that would be, Etolié felt only dread. "Does Khastra even have a chance?"

"Mother is agreeing that Khastra is using *Maz'Khamon*, so . . . no, but she is not dying immediately. That is why you are talking sense into her. She must rescind the challenge."

Etolié was still caught up on the *why*, but at least Khastra was delaying certain doom via Staff Seraph deDieula. However, execution by Ku'Shya was barely better.

A gargantuan, glittering anomaly of architecture appeared in the distance. "We are close," Kah'Sheen said. "It is not forbidden that you are here, but do not draw attention to yourself."

Etolié nodded, that fear ever rising.

The building revealed itself as a square arena. Standing as tall as Casvir's palace, Etolié could barely see the other end, so massive it was. But an arena meant to accommodate someone of Ku'Shya's size could only be monstrous.

Here, the demonic population filed through in an orderly way. Primarily demons with their spindly limbs and too many eyes—or none at all, Etolié noted on a few—but many De'Sindai were gathered among them, though far more heavily demon-blooded than any in Nox'Kartha. Most were Khastra's size or even larger, some bearing bodies like Kah'Sheen and others more humanoid builds. So many colors, for demons came in every shade, but all parted for Kah'Sheen's approach, crossing their right digit across their chests as she passed.

"So you're basically a princess, right?" Etolié whispered, her wings attracting their own attention.

"No, we are not having that title. Only Mother is having power, but I am earning their respect because of my dealings with Endless Night."

"That makes sense."

"But I am also safe because to hurt me means to owe restitution to Mother, and they are not wanting to owe restitution to Mother."

The very thought made Etolié sweat—more than she already was. "That makes even more sense."

Reputation was nice, but having a gargantuan demon goddess mom was the gift that never stopped giving—that was, until you defied her and were stuck fighting in *Rezoxos*.

The splendor of the arena was in its glittering material, but there was little artistry beyond that. Entirely utilitarian, and as Kah'Sheen entered the amphitheater, Etolié could hardly breathe.

The rocky arena floor could have fit the entirety of Staelash, perhaps Haven without the palace. A massive, barred door stood at the farthest end, surely meant to accommodate its goddess.

Only then did Kah'Sheen set her down, tactful enough to not comment on the sticky sheen of sweat Etolié left behind. "Stay very close."

Kah'Sheen led her along the perimeter, far away from the spectators high above in the seats. They approached a guarded door fit for someone perhaps half Ku'Shya's height, and the demons parted for their approach, not even a word passed between them.

Etolié entered a chamber of black stone and mirrors, with glowing gems to light it. Khastra's hammer leaned against a wall. Khastra herself was placed before one of the large mirrors, eyes shut as she sat in a meditative pose.

"Khastra!" Kah'Sheen spat. "Wake up!"

Khastra didn't bother to open her eyes as she replied in Demoni.

Kah'Sheen gave an exasperated scoff. "I am speaking like this so Etolié can listen."

Breathless, Khastra became alert.

"Hey there, ya big lug," Etolié said, forcing a neutral tone. The alternative was collapsing into tears.

Khastra stood, startled to say the least. "What are you doing here?"

"Kah'Sheen brought me. She said you were gonna be stupid."

"Kah'Sheen, I would speak to Etolié alone."

The spidery half-demon left, her mission fulfilled.

Khastra was often difficult to read, those glowing eyes adding a new layer of subtext for Etolié to watch for, but today she was an open book, her shock so plainly intermingled with heartbreak. "I know you, Etolié. It is not safe for you here."

"Kah'Sheen said I was allowed."

"You are, but you are also prone to interfering when you should not. If you disrupt *Rezoxos*, my mother will not spare your life because I like you."

Etolié dared to come forward, uncaring that she was a sweaty mess, but forcibly restrained herself from stealing her—*the* half-demon in her arms. "Then explain to me what the fuck you're doing. You're going to get yourself killed."

Khastra offered a humorless smile. "You have so little faith in me?"

"Never, but Ku'Shya isn't exactly something to discount. Even as the Bringer of War, she's gotta be three times your size."

"Size does not determine talent. Only might. But it matters not. This is something I must do. In truth, it is overdue."

"So why now?"

Shame fell upon Khastra's features, her stare falling to the floor. "Etolié, if I have fallen so far as to become unworthy of you, then I have lost myself."

For all of Etolié's heartbreak, it seemed it still had ways to shatter. "Khastra, that's not true."

"But you are right. After you left, I sat alone to consider what I had become. I remembered the truth—that in the eras of my life where I became war incarnate, I was aching inside. My happiest times were always eras of peace. There is honor in fighting to protect what you love, but I am not my mother. I tried to be once, and you know it ended when I threw myself off the Cliffs of Kaas."

Khastra sank to her knees, a supplicant as she bowed her head. "I am a cynical soul. At times I am empty, and so I have survived by pledging myself to those who are not. You know this. It is why I swore to follow you until my dying breath, and so often I wish it had truly been the end. But I am here, and I face a crossroads that will determine if I throw myself off the cliffs once more. Casvir must be dealt with, but it can be done without destroying Haven. You are right, and you have always inspired me. I have always sought to be worthy of your light, for that is what you spread to even jaded souls like me."

When Khastra offered her hands, Etolié acquiesced, realizing her tears had returned. Only then did Khastra face her. "You have walked away and rightfully so. I expect nothing from you, Etolié. But I am sorry. I was wrong. I forgot myself, and either I shall be destroyed and deny my mother a host for the mortal realm, or I live and take her throne. Either way, I shall have restored a modicum of my honor."

Etolié joined her on the ground, lip trembling as she warded away a sob. "Not to risk sounding manipulative, but I'm taking my rejection back."

"You do not owe me that."

"I don't owe you fucking anything. I just love you." At that, Etolié flung herself into Khastra's arms, the meeting of their lips a rejuvenation of love. Her demon held her tight, kissing as though it were the end of the world.

And perhaps it was. Khastra would soon make a gallows march.

When Etolié pulled back, she stroked Khastra's short locks of hair, willing her to stay a moment longer. "I'm not going to stop you. I hate your stupid honor code sometimes, but you're right."

"When this is done, whatever the outcome, there will be hope among the ashes. I hope you will not abandon my mother as an ally if she is the victor."

"We could still run away."

Khastra smiled as she shook her head. "I would be an enemy to Sha'Demoni forevermore, and that is not something I can accept."

Etolié tucked her head into Khastra's shoulder, praying it would not be the last time she felt those strong arms embracing her.

"I love you, Etolié. Thank you for being my light."

The door opened. A guard spoke quick Demoni words. When Khastra responded in turn, it walked away.

Khastra kissed her hair. "It is time. I hope you leave, but if you stay, do not stop whatever comes."

Khastra made no move to release her. Etolié clung tight. "We're getting married during your victory celebration, right?"

How comforting, Khastra's deep laughter. "It would be too impersonal. But after, yes. Where do you wish to go?"

"If I can boot Marielle out, Staelash would love this."

Khastra's laughter did not fade. "Staelash it will be. Our marriage will create a reckless alliance, but you have often made me reckless."

Etolié kept hold of her hand even as they rose. "I love you, Beefcake. It's going to be all right."

From within her armor, Khastra withdrew a long chain from around her neck. There, at the end, was Etolié's ring. She placed it in Etolié's hand, then closed her fingers around it. "It will."

Etolié floated up for a final kiss, heart pounding with fear, yet swelling with pride all the same. "Now, go be a badass."

Khastra's laughter brought hope.

Of course, Etolié didn't leave.

Instead, she sat in a spectator box with Kah'Sheen at the highest point in the arena, surveying it like a lion might for its pride.

Kah'Sheen fidgeted her fingers. "I am worried."

Etolié forced a smile. "Me too."

The arena was anything but quiet, the raucous cheers of demons and their ilk escalating when the gates on either end lifted.

First emerged Ku'Shya, decorated in gemstone armor crafted to fit her gargantuan figure. Her four trunk-like legs caused the ground to shake, the single hammer she held wielded as casually as a child carrying a doll. In two of her hands, she carried her crystal bow, her final hand unarmed, instead pounding on her chest as she bellowed Demoni words to incite the crowd.

Kah'Sheen leaned in close. "She is proclaiming it will be a feast of blood. It is less clunky in Demoni."

Etolié nodded, her false smile fading.

From the other side came the Bringer of War, her single weapon nearly as tall as she in her monstrous form. At her love's demonic cry, Etolié clapped—only to be stopped by Kah'Sheen. "We do not cheer for the challenger. Neither do we insult them. Cheering for Khastra means to disrespect Ku'Shya. Insulting Khastra means to die if Khastra wins."

Etolié sat on her hands, lest the impulse return. "I didn't realize this was so complicated."

"This is Demoni politics. Nothing simple at all."

Admittedly, Solviran political summits would be far more exciting if the politicians dueled to the death, but now wasn't the time for Etolié to think about death.

A particularly large demon marched onto a platform jutting into the arena. Etolié couldn't have understood it even if she spoke Demoni, for it couldn't match the roaring crowd. But when it held up an appendage, the crowd silenced all at once.

Ku'Shya stepped back, though kept her hammer readied. The Bringer of War appeared relaxed, though surveyed the arena with scrutiny.

The demon kept its appendage raised as it stepped back from the platform.

"This is either ending in seconds or going on until one of them falls from exhaustion," Kah'Sheen whispered.

The demon dropped its appendage, crying out something in the Demoni tongue.

Ku'Shya shot forth like a cannon ball.

Etolié's scream was lost amid the cacophonous crowd. Ku'Shya swept her hammer across the arena's edge, but the Bringer of War was no longer there, instead leaping to evade the massive weapon. From the air, Khastra launched the hammer at Ku'Shya, the weapon soaring—then batted aside by Ku'Shya's own.

Khastra landed on her feet, catching her weapon as it flew back into her grip.

And so it began, a vicious, graceless dance—Ku'Shya, the aggressor, owned the arena, sweeping across it as an ocean wave. But Khastra was no lifeboat in a storm, instead facing the ocean's might without fear. Ku'Shya swung; Khastra dodged. Ku'Shya shot her across the way with her bow; Khastra battered the arrow aside with impossible speed.

Ku'Shya's second arrow missed. It struck the wall.

Etolié's hands were numb, but there was no way she was moving. "What are the chances of us getting hit?"

"Moderate—" Kah'Sheen gasped when Ku'Shya's hammer met its target.

Khastra and her weapon flew in opposite directions, the former smacking against the wall, and then the ground. Quick as a whip, Ku'Shya appeared. The Bringer of War sprinted on all fours to escape. When she held out her hand, her hammer flew into her grip.

Khastra didn't slow. She spun and launched the hammer back—hitting Ku'Shya square in the face.

Etolié withheld a cheer when the goddess stumbled back. "Holy shitballs, this might actually work."

"You are making mighty assumptions, Etolié."

"Who the fuck are you rooting for, anyway?"

"I am not thinking about winners and losers."

A fair point. Kah'Sheen lost either way.

Etolié couldn't relax, even as the minutes ticked by. Both parties visibly heaved each breath—perhaps Kah'Sheen had been prophetic.

Ku'Shya roared when her hammer narrowly missed, sending the crowd into a frenzy. Khastra's weapon landed with a *crack* against Ku'Shya's leg. The goddess spat Demoni words but refused to bend.

What happened in the case of a stalemate? Had it ever happened? Would they truly go until their goddess dropped dead—?

The earth wrenched. The arena shook. The sky . . . brightened.

The combatants ceased their movements, as shaken as the ground. The Bringer of War followed the gaze of every demon to the sky where great beams of light cut across it, glowing in a rainbow of hues. Ku'Shya's sudden cry matched the earthquake's might.

Etolié tore her gaze from the sky, realizing Kah'Sheen had gone pale. "What the fuck is happening?"

"I am not knowing, but Mother is afraid."

Ku'Shya favored her broken limb as she growled at the sky. She spoke to the Bringer of War, who answered in curt tones.

Kah'Sheen gasped. "They are agreeing to pause. This . . . this is never happening before."

Etolié's terror rose to match her confusion. Six beams of light filled the whole sky, each in different hues—

"Wait," Etolié whispered, horror filling her to think . . . no. NO. "It can't be. But . . ."

Soliel only had one more orb to find.

Amid her horror, fury brewed. "I swear to Mom if those fucking imbeciles lost the last orb while I was gone, it won't be Soliel that kills them."

CHAPTER 36

Fifteen years after the end of the world . . .

Time became elusive, the hours fading into days, into years . . . Or perhaps merely minutes. All Dira knew was she soon ran out of tears to cry, instead debilitated by fear as she curled into a ball in the corner. Darkness was comfort. Darkness was safety. Darkness was Mother's enveloping hug.

Try as she might, she could not reach the Shadow Realm. In this cold, dank dungeon, she could not find the path.

Soliel stood by the bars, his voice hoarse from yelling. "Somebody! Anybody!"

He had long given up pleading any specific want, instead simply crying out for attention.

But eventually, even that faded away, and when he met Dira's swollen gaze, she beckoned for his company.

He sat near, though not near enough to touch, not near enough to be a threat. All that strength in his arms, and nowhere to wield it. He felt as helpless as she, she knew, and when she reached for his hand, he held hers tight.

"I didn't know he was the viceroy," Soliel whispered, though the stone walls echoed even the soft words across the dank space. "He was an informant and weapons supplier for the resistance. We didn't know where the weapons were coming from."

"You said Imperator Casvir was a just ruler," Dira whispered.

"I'm questioning everything." Oh, there was comfort in his presence. Even in the pits of fear, Dira could savor that. "He called you . . . Darkleaf," Soliel whispered, but there was no condemnation in the word, no. Despite all the stories of Ayla and her monstrous deeds . . . he simply stated it as fact. "How can she be your mother?"

"I have two," Dira muttered.

"She adopted you?"

Dira finally met his gaze and saw confusion there. "No. She's my blood."

"You did mention magic." Soliel fell silent, his glow the only light in the gloomy space. "Do you know why Imperator Casvir would want you?"

The question choked her, but her eyes already ached from crying. She swallowed the impulse. *My mother said he owns my soul*, but she couldn't stand to say it. She simply shrugged.

"Everything I know tells me she's a monster, but I can't imagine a monster raising someone like you. You love her, don't you?"

Dira nodded.

"Tell me about her. The real Ayla Darkleaf."

"She's my mother." Dira shrugged, thinking it might be enough, but Soliel's query lingered. "I don't even know what else to say. She's everything a mother should be. She loves me, a-and she's kind, she . . ."

Gods, how did you begin to explain fifteen years of love?

"I-I'm realizing she kept a lot of secrets, but she said it was all to protect me. I didn't think it would be . . ." Oh, her heart shattered to think of it all, the cruel stories Soliel had told of The Endless Night still resonating in her head. Dira was all out of tears to cry, but her throat choked, nevertheless. "I don't know what to think, Soliel. I just wish she were here. She can fix this. She can do anything."

"I'll take your word for it. Was it only her and you?"

"No, I have a familiar named Demitri. And my aunt—my other mom's sister—started watching over me when I was five. I think . . . I think that's when Mother started, um, the war."

"Ten years ago? That fits the timeline."

"There are others who come and go, but I shouldn't say who they are."

"What about your other mom?"

Dira's heart sank, the knowledge more a burden today—especially to know . . . her late mom was why she sat in a dungeon at all. "She's dead. I never knew her."

To her surprise, Soliel offered a forlorn smile. "I also have two mothers, one of whom I don't remember. I was brought to the mortal realm as a baby from Celestière to escape the conflict following my birth mother's death. I would have been used as a pawn, I'm told, or perhaps killed. It was decided that the best way to protect me was to place me with a mortal family and let me live a quiet life. My father and step-mother mean everything to me."

Of course his father was mortal, but . . . "How can your father be a mortal?"

"Perhaps you don't know, but some gods can walk the halls of their temples. My father was a priest of Sol Kareena and, as he tells it, he met an odd but beautiful woman in the temple late one night.

She told him he could have any wish she could grant if he would only give her one thing—a child."

Soliel's blush was endearing, even in the cold darkness. "He declined any wishes, but did as she desired. And then nearly forgot about it, and eventually he met my step-mother and married. Needless to say, they were shocked when Eionei himself dropped me off a few years later."

"When did they tell you that you were the son of Sol Kareena?"

"I've always known, but I was told to keep it a secret." His jaw set, bitterness sneering his lip. "Until my family was sent to the work camps. I can't escape my sisters' screams, even now. I managed to escape the guards, and my mother implored me to run. That was three years ago. I decided to use my heritage to rally the Sun Elves against those who took her."

Dira gulped, the subtext painfully clear. "You don't have to avoid using her name."

"Your mother didn't personally take them, but she commanded the ones who did."

"What happens at the work camps?"

"From the few accounts we have, from those who've escaped, they're forced to manufacture machines for her army. Those rare few who still have Sol Kareena's power are forced to fight against the imperator, but that wouldn't be where my family is. They'd be underground with the machines."

Dira felt his tension, her own discomfort brewing, even if it wasn't for her. "I swear, when we get out of here, I'll make Mother free them. She'll do it if I ask."

"You're very kind. But what good does a few freed folk do when there are thousands of others she's taken for her cause?"

"I'll still try. I just . . ." Gods, cognitive dissonance stopped her thoughts in her tracks, the future as murky as it had ever been. ". . . I feel, when we get out, I'll be back with her, and you'll be back with your rebellion. I don't know what happens after that, but I have to do something."

Therein was the most damning truth—that Dira could no longer fall back into innocent bliss. Was this what it meant, when Mother touted that innocence could only be lost?

Dira set her head against his shoulder. "Thank you for staying. You don't even know me, but the fact that you chose to be here . . . I can't thank you enough."

"I feel like it's my fault that you're here in the first place," Soliel said, regret in his subdued tone. "Be that as it may, you're welcome. I would never abandon a lady with that . . . *degenerate*. I should run a sword through Murishani's stomach for talking to you like that."

As grimy as she felt, his reassurance helped by small degrees.

"Besides, I know you well enough. I know you're a dhampir, I know you're incredible with a knife, and I know you're the secret daughter of Grand Executor Darkleaf, which I think is a bit more than most people."

"Which is precisely why you shouldn't be helping me. You should be happy Casvir has her daughter in prison."

Soliel shook his head. "I don't like using hostages, especially innocent ones."

The words sparked fresh fear within her. Dira curled up into his side, seeking warmth and comfort both. "What will they do with me?"

Soliel's hold tightened around her. "I wish I knew."

Current era . . .

Sora felt nothing, saw nothing except for white, endless waves of mist—until tendril-like wings of silver and gold spread wide around her. When she turned, Sora's breath stopped.

Ilune rose from her meditative pose, wearing a dress that revealed a fair bit of her calves, perhaps intended for someone far shorter. But Sora hadn't yet seen the silvery sheen of Ilune's true form, her underground prison staining her green, nor did Ilune bear the scars of shackles and malnutrition, no matted hair or limp wings.

No, this was someone new, her cascading locks of black hair as luxurious as her figure, her wings as magnificent as her godly mother's. Ilune was beautiful as a mortal puppet, but here she held no taint of humanity, flawless in her true, angelic form. Her smile, though sharp, juxtaposed curiously with her silver eyes, brighter than the mists surrounding them.

Never had Sora seen anyone like her. Never had Sora been so stunned to simply *see* someone.

"Oh, stop your staring," Ilune said, breaking the spell. "I know I look ridiculous. I had to steal a dress from my momma, and she's a bit shorter than the average anything. But it was this or meditate naked." That flirtatious wink returned, and Sora knew precisely what jest Ilune was about to make. "I could be naked now if you prefer."

Exactly as expected. "That's all right. We should get going."

Ilune offered a hand. "I'd be insisting on holding your hand no matter who you were, sweet mortal. Can't have you getting lost."

Eionei had insisted on the exact same thing, though of course he'd had intentions as well. Steeling her emotions, Sora set dear Leelan back into her pouch, praying he didn't know it was a gallows march. She accepted Ilune's hand, unprepared both for the stark cold and for Ilune to intertwine their fingers. Damn her blush; Sora forced a neutral face. "Lead on."

Something of victory showed in Ilune's smirk, but she said nothing of it, instead briskly steering them toward what might've been certain doom, as far as Sora knew. "How do you know how to navigate this place?" Sora asked.

"Intuition, though don't let that worry you. I have no talent for portals, but I did at least inherit Staella's innate sense of direction. She's never been lost either."

Sora wasn't actually worried, given she suspected Ilune had no wish to be lost any more than she did. Instead, she reserved her worries for the realms and the grim reality that if Soliel succeeded, she would die along with the angels and demons.

"And one can reach Sha'Demoni through Celestière?" Sora pressed.

"One can, and we gods can fully walk in the other's realm without being pushed out as we are in the mortal realm. But you speak as though you've been to both realms before. We have a bit of a walk. Tell me more about that."

"I've met Ku'Shya before," Sora said, remiss to speak of either occasion. "The first time to take, um . . ."

Shit. Or was this worth cursing for at all?

"Take what, Sora?"

"Uh, your staff. Staff Seraph deDieula."

For the first time in all their meetings, Ilune stared with genuine shock. "Assuming we're alive in an hour, I'll have many questions for you about that one."

"I don't know where it is now, before you ask."

"Pity. But it's not with Ku'Shya, and that's very good to know."

"I obviously went through Celestière to find you, but I went before with Chaos—when we pursued the pledges from the angelic gods."

"I'm shocked you succeeded, to be honest."

"Etolié's the one who convinced them. I'm not much influence."

Ilune raised a mischievous eyebrow. "You accompanied an Old God through three different realms. That's more impressive than you think."

Sora shook her head, reluctant to accept Ilune's words. "I just did what anyone would do for their family."

"You're supremely hilarious, saying that to me of all people. Not everyone is as loyal as you, but from the sound of it, the worlds would be better if they were."

Rather than feel pride, Sora swallowed her guilt at the reminder. "Blind loyalty isn't a virtue. I learned that the hard way."

"Fair enough, though being loyal to no one at all will get you just as few rewards—unless your definition of a reward is a long stay in prison. Alone."

Despite the bitter words, Ilune's aura remained light. Sora, however, was struck once again at the subtle similarities between this angel and Etolié, her sister. So flippant, just when things might've been serious. "Chaos implied that the story of Neoma's death might not be all that history says it is. Is that true?"

Ilune's smile became stale, no joy in those eyes. "I haven't read any history books, Sora. I've been too busy being locked in prison. So, you tell me what they say."

"I don't know much, but I was born in Solvira so I've heard bits and pieces. I know there was a civil war a thousand years ago, I know that it was Neoma and her allies versus you and yours, and I know it ended with Neoma's death."

"At my hands," Ilune said bitterly. "That is an important detail."

"But you didn't mean to, if Chaos is to be believed."

"And what does she know?" Ilune said, and Sora knew that tone—the very same Etolié adopted when you got a little too close to the truth.

"Enough that you agreed with her, in the underground."

When Ilune slowed, Sora didn't rush her, despite the dire circumstances. Somehow, the whole world seemed so far away. "I was angry," Ilune whispered. "I felt Neoma had betrayed me. It is a very long story. Perhaps I shall explain in detail another time. But I never meant for it to get that far. I never meant to widow Staella. Our magics collided in ways magic was never meant to, and we both were destroyed in the explosion, yes. I awoke beside my phylactery and Neoma, she—" Ilune's words ceased. She became iron, cold and harsh. "She never awoke."

How quickly, Ilune's visage returned to mischief, though her eyes remained glass. "But that is the past. We have duties to attend to, now don't we?"

But Sora squeezed Ilune's hand when she tried to move along, bidding her to wait a moment more. "Have you spoken at all to Staella?"

"I'm hardly worthy of that."

"I'm sure Etolié would disagree."

Ilune scoffed. "I've known Etolié for an hour, yet you'd make that judgment?"

"Etolié thinks you're worth believing in, and everything I've seen validates that. You didn't steal Leelan. I don't have to entirely trust your intentions for me to trust you have good intentions for her."

"I spent my entire childhood begging my moms for a sibling, and quite a few thousand of my adult years as well. So I do, in fact, love Etolié and would kill myself to save her. That damn older sisterly instinct hit me harder than *Maz'Khamon*—and I've been on the receiving end of that, so I don't say that lightly."

Sora didn't admit she had no idea what *Maz'Khamon* was, but the sisterly instinct thing was, for better or worse, quite relatable.

"But didn't we bargain for friendship, Sora?" Ilune teased. "And you still don't trust me?"

"I've had plenty of friends I didn't trust."

Ilune laughed, musical and bright. Sora no longer resisted enjoying it, though admitting that was still a leap too far. "I'd be lying if I didn't admit the same. Lovers as well."

Sora expected the wink. She didn't expect her blood to react with heat. The bait was laid once more, and Sora, weak from endless teasing, took a bite. "We're not the same on that front."

Ilune slowed, and though the end of the world was nigh, though they stood in eternal daylight, Sora was utterly absorbed by her gravity. Her breath hitched when Ilune touched her chin. "You're worth winning that trust."

And though Sora struggled to breathe, she laid a challenge, nevertheless. "There's nothing to win. I don't play games, Ilune."

Ilune faced her eye to eye, near enough for Sora to feel her gentle breath on her face. "I love hearing you say my name. Won't you do it again?"

Against her will, Sora shuddered, the request so innocent, so *dangerous*. "I told you I don't play games."

Dammit all—Sora lost her breath entirely at Ilune's sharp stare. The God of Death said nothing.

Sora whimpered, caught between pain and a temptation sweeter than her convictions had ever tasted. "What do you want from me?"

When Ilune drew breath, Sora hoped it was to hear her laugh; there had never been a prettier sound. "My name, *Sora*."

Oh . . . that one was prettier still.

Sora brought her free hand to cup the back of Ilune's neck, entranced by her words and the promise of more. "Ilune—"

Only for an explosion to rock the world, sending her stumbling back.

Within minutes, a nurse came to the door with a key and strict orders to take Flowridia to her medical suite and nowhere else. "The imperator was insistent," the De'Sindai woman said, but Flowridia pushed past her anyway.

Flowridia lingered in the doorway. "Do you know where Casvir has gone?"

"No, but—"

Flowridia could not quite run, her pitiful attempt easily thwarted when a second nurse joined the first. She did not even grab Flowridia, simply stood to deter her path. "Think of the baby," the new woman said. "It's good that you're walking again, but you mustn't excite yourself too much."

Flowridia failed to shove beyond her, instead collapsing in near defeat against the woman's body. "Casvir!" she cried into the hallway.

"Flowridia—"

"He's taken her! He took Ayla. He . . . He's going to . . ." She didn't know, and somehow that was what drove her to fresh tears.

Rather than be moved, Flowridia sank to her knees in the hallway, betrayal rising to match her anguish. When had Casvir taken the staff? 'Why' and 'how' were unimportant, because of course this was what he'd do. Of course he had found it in the ruins in the Mountains of Kaas. But why wait until now?

Gods, how long had Flowridia been living with this cursed artifact beneath her nose?

The nurse's voice jarred her from her thoughts. "Lady Flowridia, let's get you to bed."

Flowridia didn't fight when she was helped to rise.

"Flowridia?"

The voice spoke so softly, yet it could have quelled a hurricane. Flowridia yanked out of the nurse's grip as she turned around, breath hitching to see . . . *Her*.

Chaos approached tentatively from down the hallway, stilling only when Flowridia stumbled toward her. "What happened?"

She did not even have the time to be ashamed of her tear-stained face or marvel at the strangeness of the moment. Flowridia forced her words to calm. "Casvir, he . . . A-Are you familiar with Staff Seraph deDieula?"

No mistaking the horror flooding Chaos. "I am."

"Casvir took Ayla. I suspect it's something to do with defending the city from Ku'Shya, but I . . ." Flowridia swallowed a sob. "I don't know what to do."

That horror drained, leaving only severity. "I will fix this," Chaos said, but Flowridia frantically shook her head.

"You're a ghost possessing a corpse. You said so yourself. What if he takes control of you too?"

Chaos did not speak, instead fiddling with a small pouch at her hip, reaching in and withdrawing . . .

Flowridia gasped, for she had not seen that ring in over a year. "How do you have that?"

For it was Flowridia's own wedding ring, lost in the ruins of Kaas. But the one Chaos held was dingier than the one she'd loved, battered here and there by time and wear. Not dirty, no, but this was more antique by far than the one she'd exchanged vows with years ago.

"This is from my timeline," Chaos said, affirming Flowridia's suspicions. She slipped it onto her own ring finger, the fit a perfect mirror. "All ghosts have an anchor. This one is mine. But I'm told this once belonged to you."

Once belonged to . . ? Flowridia swallowed her shock at the statement. Perhaps the ghost daughter of hers didn't realize what damning thing she'd just let slip. "Yes, that is my wedding ring."

Chaos was *told* it belonged to her. But why would she not have known from Flowridia herself?

"Then you know it will protect me from the staff," Chaos said, and upon her beautiful face came the barest glimpse of light, the merest glimmer of a smile.

Flowridia's heart soared to see it. Words she'd kept locked up burst like a broken dam. "May I hug you? You can say no, but I . . . I wanted to ask—"

Both words and breath failed when Chaos wrapped her arms around her, holding as tight as she could with her swollen womb between them. Flowridia clung back, unprepared for the flood of warmth washing across her.

There came a small whisper. "Hi, Mom."

It sang to something deeper, but Flowridia couldn't think particularly deeply, simply cherished the child in her arms, uncaring that she was grown, and placed a kiss in her hair.

Too soon, they parted, and Flowridia quickly wiped tears from her eyes. "I don't care that we haven't met yet. I love you so much. I hope it isn't strange to hear."

Chaos shook her head, her own quiet joy apparent. Something different fueled her stance, something . . . childlike. "I love you too, Mom. And I'll save Lady Ayla. Just you wait."

And Chaos ran off like the whirlwind she was, leaving Flowridia elated and . . . unsettled. This child of hers didn't speak with any resentment toward her. Oh, perhaps she over-thought—

The faintest *boom* shook the ground. Flowridia froze, hardly feeling the nurses return to her side. "My lady, it must be Ku'Shya!" one said. "We have to bring you to safety."

The statement was logical, yet it felt wrong. Ku'Shya would never make so graceful an entrance. "Not yet. I need a window."

Ayla's bedroom did not have one. They went to a nearby parlor room instead, where Flowridia marched as quickly as she was able to a balcony.

The night brought fresh air and a chill breeze, but not darkness. Not this night. Instead, six bursts of light coursed across the sky, originating in the fields beyond Haven's gates.

Flowridia's breath cut off. "Oh gods," she managed. "It's Soliel."

Part Seven
ORDER

CHAPTER 37

Fifteen years after the end of the world . . .

Against all odds, Dira slept.

Visions of dreadful demons and dark corridors tormented her in dreams, and when she was awoken by a rough shake to her body, she found she was drenched in sweat.

"I'm sorry," Soliel said, a pillar of stability. "You were screaming in your sleep."

"You did the right thing."

Despite her damp form, he never let her go.

Time stood still in the dark. When distant footsteps echoed from afar, Dira immediately perked up. Soliel stiffened. Light appeared along with a small battalion of armored dead flanked by Murishani.

When Soliel stood, he helped Dira to rise, then stood between her and the bars. "What's going on?"

Glee looked horrifying with Murishani's malevolent smile. "Sweet Kedira has been summoned. Unfortunately, she'll have to wear these." He held up a set of shackles, designed for her wrists and neck. "But if you behave, you'll both walk free within the hour. That's the bargain we reached."

Dira lost her breath. "What bargain?"

Murishani ignored her. "Soliel, I know you think you can strangle me with those burly hands of yours, but trust me when I say I don't need these fine minions to protect me against a child, god-blooded or not. Can you fathom the pain of having your soul ripped from your living body? No? Then do not vex me." When he swiped his hand across the bars, a few glowed silver—and vanished. "If you behave, you can even join us."

Soliel's fists clenched behind his back. "I will behave."

"Good. Now." He beckoned to Dira, his tongue click the sort one gave to a shy dog. "We don't have all day."

Dira trembled as she approached, nearly losing her footing. Behind her, Soliel left the bounds of the bars, flinching when the dead grabbed his broad form. *Click, click* went her wrist shackles, but before he attached the final upon her neck, he parted her thick locs, the skim of his fingers upon her skin leaving her ill. *Click.*

He held the final chain, attached at the neck, and tugged it like a leash. With the snap of his fingers, another portal appeared. "You're encouraged to speak, by the way. The imperator would love to hear you beg."

Soliel was forced to walk at the rear, whereas Dira was paraded through the portal a step behind Murishani. Weightless, she floated. When the ground appeared, she stood in a whole new world.

A throne room, surely, with a ceiling built to touch the stars. She faced Imperator Casvir, who stood before a throne of iron, the look of triumph upon his face stretching skin unused to showing any emotion at all. He held a staff of frightful design, a rod as tall as she topped by a demonic skull.

The skull's gaze bore into her soul, but Casvir did not look at Dira. When she followed his line of sight, Dira lost all feeling.

For there she was—Mother, not a sprint away, wearing a gown as grand as her station would convey, with a train of black lace and pauldrons bearing spikes. She had no envoy, surrounded instead by skeletal guards. They did not touch her. They merely seemed . . . ready.

Before she could speak, Soliel came through the portal—and Murishani gripped her neck like a scruff.

Not pain, no, but something horribly wrong coursed through her body, a violation even something as unwelcome as touching her neck wouldn't convey. Her body glowed silver; his matched. "One wrong move," Murishani whispered, his hot breath making her sick, "and your soul will be stuffed in a box."

Ahead, Mother's stance was stiff, her jaw set even when her gaze seared into Dira. But despite the invitation to speak, Dira could say nothing, fear cutting off her tongue.

"I have upheld my end of the bargain," Casvir said, his deep voice rumbling like an earthquake. "Do your part, Grand Executor Darkleaf."

In a motion so unlike her, Mother fidgeted with her finger—whereupon she wore her wedding ring. "Imperator Casvir, I am prepared to beg if it means you consider what Flowra would have wanted for her child," she said, yet it was as hollow as a drum. "If you have any love remaining in your heart for her and her memory, you will not do this."

Gods, Mother had never sounded so broken. Dira blinked and saw only mist.

"Any affection I held for Flowridia does not dictate how I treat those adjacent to her," Casvir said, his words pure ice. "You will find no mercy here."

Again, Mother spun her ring. "Send her out."

"No."

Mother's gaze returned to Dira, all conviction leaving her sharp countenance. "Darling—"

"Do not stall with idle words."

"You would really risk your prize over idle words?" Mother seethed, yet it held no bite. "I will speak to my daughter, *Imperator*." She transformed once again, all ire fading as Dira became the center of her world. "Dira, my heart, no matter what happens next, I beg of you to stay away from this world. Casvir has promised that you will be free to go home, and I pray that you will. Stay there. Be safe. For you to grow up and flourish means this was all worth it."

Dira managed pitiful words. "M-Mother, I . . . I-I'm sorry."

Oh, nothing could have prepared her for Mother's eyes to glisten, for the first of her tears to etch a line down her pale face. "You are worth this. I love you. I will always love you. Don't forget it."

Dira sobbed her next words. "What's going on?"

"Don't worry, my Dira. But would you tell me you love me?"

"I love you so much."

Mother's breath shuddered, her fight for stability quickly falling apart. "Imperator, *please* send her out."

"No."

A final time, Mother twisted her ring—and this time, pulled it from her finger. It dropped to the ground with a metallic *ping*. "There is no point in this war if it is not to protect her," Mother said, a modicum of that conviction returning. Mother did not hold raw power this day, but a dark rumbling beneath the sea. "Fifteen years of loving her is better than even the spite of knowing you lost her. I pity you, Casvir. You will never understand."

"Love is a weakness," Casvir said. "You are the one to pity."

"Does it irk you, Casvir? That even in your triumph you face a woman with no regrets?"

"I have never valued your opinion enough to care."

"And yet you have let me keep talking. Get on with it, you impotent pig."

"Gladly."

The staff's eyes flashed purple. Mother screamed and doubled over.

Dira gasped, panic rushing over her as Murishani shoved her away. Mother fell to one knee, sobbing even as she stiffened and clung to composure by a thread. She wrapped her arms around herself, yet the protective gesture was anything but as her fingers tore into the flesh of her arms, leaving only shreds of skin.

Terror gripped Dira's heart as Murishani escorted them. To breathe wrong meant to feel him literally tug on her soul. But what was wrong with Mother? What had the staff done? "Mother?"

Behind a curtain of hair, hunched on the ground like a wretch, Mother met her gaze, recognition there. "*Dira,*" she whispered—and then she screamed once more.

"Stop fighting," Casvir said, "or this will not be the worst thing your daughter sees."

Mother stiffened as her tears returned, then slumped lifelessly to the ground.

"What did you do?!" Dira cried, but when she tried to run, Murishani's grip tightened. Chills coursed in waves down her flesh as she pulled. The more she fought, the sicker she became. "You killed her!"

Weakness overcame her. When she lost strength, Murishani's repugnant hands were there to catch her. "That's not something we can do unfortunately," Murishani whispered, his breath making her sicker still. "You'll wish we had, however."

The skull's eyes flashed once more, glowing as dying stars. Mother rose, but it was not graceful. Mother was poised and nimble. This creature that rose was ungainly, like a puppet with uneven strings. It held Mother's face, but its glance to her was happenstance, pure vacancy in those dead eyes.

No recognition. No life.

Current era . . .

Back in the room of black stone and mirrors, sequestered in the walls of the amphitheater, Etolié sat atop a stone half-wall behind Khastra, possessive as she held her demon's head to her stomach, running her fingers through her sweaty, cropped hair. She smelled of dust, of battle, of long days spent in the training grounds in Staelash, and what Etolié would give to live in the simpler time once more. It wasn't enough, but Khastra was here—for now. Khastra was near.

And if Khastra's subtle touch on her leg was any indication, the half-demon felt the same.

Before them, Ku'Shya barked orders in Demoni to demons Etolié didn't know, the echo across the stone walls nearly deafening. Her proximity suffocated even the vast room—vast enough for the gargantuan demon to stand as tall as the ceiling. Kah'Sheen stood nearby, her fidgeting hands radiating anxiety.

So sturdy the walls were, Ku'Shya's pacing did not shake them. Finally, the demon goddess turned to them. "I am seeking confirmation that these suspicions are true. But we must plan."

"Can it still be stopped?" Etolié said, though her disbelief remained.

"I do not know. I am unfamiliar with the specifics of these orbs. Only that the God of Order is not yet dealt with, and it is a disgrace."

Wasn't that the damn truth. Etolié kept her panic thinly veiled, worry for her momma making it difficult to breathe. But if Sha'Demoni stood, surely Celestière did too. "I know who was watching the last orb. I can go home and investigate."

Yet Ku'Shya said nothing, merely stood silently a moment. Demoni words left her lips, and Etolié recognized only the name *Khastra*.

Before her, Khastra stiffened. Her reply held the same stilted candor.

"You wish for me to speak freely in front of Etolié who reports to Casvir?" Etolié had never heard the demon goddess sound incredulous.

"She is not forced to," Khastra said, "and this is a time of crisis."

"Fine. I am saying I will go and destroy him myself, but I must have Khastra to host. What are you thinking, Etolié? Since Khastra is valuing your judgment over mine."

Oh, shit. "All I know," Etolié said, praising her fifty years of diplomatic training, "is that you should be really fucking careful if you go anywhere near Nox'Kartha, because Casvir has defenses I'll literally lose my soul if I talk about."

Far too many eyes fell upon her, even if those eyes belonged to only three entities, amplified by the reflective stone. "Defenses?" Ku'Shya said, that bitterness not yet waning.

"I do think ripping Soliel's head off in the final hour is a good plan, but the last orb was in Nox'Kartha, so I don't know what's happening with that."

Ku'Shya stared a moment. "You are knowing. Who is telling you?"

"Telling me what?"

"The plans for Haven. Is it Khastra?"

Etolié's stomach dropped. "No one told me, uh, Mother. I figured it out. Please, don't be angry with Khastra."

Ku'Shya's facial expressions were limited, but there was no doubt in Etolié's mind that this was the nearest equivalent of a glare the demon was capable of—and it was assuredly effective, given Etolié was starting to feel like meat.

To her horror, Khastra stood up, her loose locks of cropped hair clinging to her sweaty, dirt-stained face. "We can point digits later. We have stopped *Rezoxos* to discuss the God of Order, and we will do just that."

"But what if—" Etolié forcibly stopped her words, cursing her damn loose lips. The damage was done, however, and she *did* have a decent compromise, if she said so herself. "Look, I know the plan, yes. And I endorse parts of it. I am all in favor of throwing Casvir into the lich prison. What I don't endorse is destroying Haven in the process. But—"

"No," Ku'Shya said. "The Law is being fulfilled, even in the face of Sha'Demoni's destruction."

"You were willing to put off *Rezoxos*."

"It will be completed."

"So pause the plans for Haven! It would be better that way. I don't know what kind of preparations Casvir has in place for you, but it'll throw him off if you delay, right?"

The mood shifted. Etolié felt every eye, as scrutinized as meat at the butcher. Her gut clenched as she realized her error.

Ku'Shya's shadow loomed, the limited light creating distant fire of those vengeful, glowing eyes. "Casvir is knowing to prepare?" Ku'Shya said, nearly indecipherable for how fiercely she growled. "How is he knowing to prepare, Etolié?"

Before Etolié could speak, Khastra leapt between them. Her hammer flew into her hand, the meeting crashing like thunder. "You will stand down."

"You have no authority, Khastra. If she is telling Casvir, she is betraying my kingdom."

Fear gripped Etolié at the words, her jovial dealings with Ku'Shya long past. Already, the Bringer of War began her transformation, but Etolié screamed when Ku'Shya's gargantuan hand barreled toward her—

Nimble arms wrenched her away. Before her, the Bringer of War roared as she leapt toward the irate Goddess of War, the very foundation of the amphitheater shaking when her hammer made contact with Ku'Shya's arm.

"We are leaving now," Kah'Sheen said unhelpfully, rushing from the scene on her many legs.

"But—"

"Do not 'but' me, Etolié!"

Etolié stared over Kah'Sheen's shoulder as the clash of titans resumed, deafening roars echoing off the walls. One final glimpse as the Bringer of War was swept aside by Ku'Shya's own weapon—

And all the world shifted as they appeared in an expansive grassland, the mortal realm embracing them.

When Etolié and Kah'Sheen appeared in Flowers' medical suite, assisted by Goddess Momma's power, Etolié hadn't expected to be alone, but she hadn't expected an entourage of shrieking nurses. "It's fine! She's just my friend! Nothing to worry about."

Kah'Sheen was, to be fair, nearly twice Etolié's height and far more spidery than most mortals. However, Etolié didn't have more time to pacify them before Flowers shoved past them. "Etolié—"

"Yeah, what the fuck happened?!"

Flowers' voice lowered, and Etolié had forgotten how unexpectedly scary the kid could sound when truly peeved. "Casvir *sold* the orb to Soliel."

Etolié blinked. "I'm sorry, I must have misheard you, because there's no fucking way—"

"Oh, there's a *fucking* way. Also . . ." The color drained from her face—which was admittedly less sallow than before. Perhaps those cysts were doing their job. ". . . Casvir has Staff Seraph deDieula."

Oh thank fucking GODS, because who was around to hear it? Kah'Sheen, who gasped as all four of her hands covered her mouth. "He is having it?!"

"Damn, who would have guessed?" Etolié said, but internally she cheered.

"He took Ayla with it," Flowers said. "He says she has to earn her keep—"

"Sure, but *why* did he give away the orb?"

"Most likely, his logic is that if the realms are separated, Ku'Shya can't destroy Nox'Kartha because it'll kill her. Soliel promised to defend Nox'Kartha as well as he could, in exchange."

Etolié met Kah'Sheen's gaze. "So?"

"I am getting the staff."

"And I'm going with you—" But Kah'Sheen had already vanished into Etolié's own shadow. "Dammit."

"Etolié . . ." Fear showed in Flowers' pretty face. "I'm not saying you should stop her. But I am saying Casvir has fought her before, and she didn't stand a chance."

"And I'm guessing last time he didn't have an evil necromancer artifact or a particularly immortal vampire at his side. Great. Where's Sora?"

"I don't know. She was with your, um, sister though."

This had officially become the strangest day of Etolié's life—and given it might also be her last, well, at least life was going out with a bang. "I have to go stop Sheen Bean from killing herself, please stand by."

"Etolié, wait—the Goddess of Chaos will be there."

Etolié did pause for that. "Explain?"

"She agreed to save Ayla from the staff. It's . . . a long story."

"Be prepared for chaotic engagements, got it." With that, Etolié ran. She could risk getting sweaty for Kah'Sheen's sake.

Khastra was a world away, most likely fucking dead. But Etolié would be dead before she let Kah'Sheen fall.

But as soon as she appeared in the hallway, there came the thought that she had no clue whatsoever where she was going. "Kah'Sheen?!" she cried, but it was a false hope. No one answered.

Instead, she kept a brisk pace as she cried, "Hello! Hooded figures? I need a cloaked creep, now!"

Blessedly, the aforementioned cloaked creeps had no egos to bruise. One soon appeared, and Etolié simply would never get used to staring into a black abyss of a hood, even as it bowed. "Empress Etolié, you called?"

"Where is Imperator Casvir?"

"He is heading to the throne room as we speak, your majesty. The Goddess of Chaos has come to greet him."

Fan-fucking-tastic. Etolié cracked her knuckles and shut her eyes, clinging tight not to the image of the throne room, but to a dining hall nearby.

Teleportation wasn't fun or easy, but Etolié did manage to keep her stomach together as she pulled herself through space. The distance was hardly a leap at all compared to others she'd made. But risking nausea was better than risking getting sweaty, and Etolié sprinted from the room, ignoring the startled servants cleaning up.

She hadn't expected the doors to the throne room to be thrashed, but at least she had a clear view of the oversized being of Silver Fire standing in the center of the room. However, when Etolié tried to enter, the two skeletal guards standing by stepped into her path. "Excuse me, I'm a monarch. This is a meeting for monarchs."

The guards said nothing, merely stared with blank eyes and drawn swords.

Well, thankfully Casvir—or his castle planner—had a taste for the ostentatious, and so Etolié took a few steps back and floated the fifteen feet or so up to the ceiling, and slipped through the shattered doors.

Of course, subtlety wasn't exactly possible when one was a golden beacon who hadn't bothered to illusion away her wings because she never fucking planned ahead. The moment Etolié entered, Casvir stared straight at her. "Empress Etolié, you were not invited."

Etolié glanced down from her post, nowhere near the ceiling of this new space, and leisurely floated down, all the while studying the scene. Casvir did, indeed, wield the damn fucking staff, its creepy eyes directed far too near to her, and Murishani stood nigh, leering at Casvir's right hand.

And there, lurking beside the throne, Ayla Darkleaf stood eerily still as she stared at the ground, no life in her to speak of.

"I took the liberty of assuming I would be a positive addition to this meeting, given I've already established a friendly relationship to this fine, upstanding Goddess." Etolié's feet touched the ground, and by some miracle, she was not instantly arrested.

"I agree," came Chaos' biting voice, emanating both from the figure in the center and all around. "I would like her to join this meeting."

"Very well," Casvir replied. "She may stay so long as she is not disruptive."

Etolié forced a smile as she took silent steps toward the front of the room, nearer to the damn staff.

Chaos spoke once more. "As I was saying, I appreciate you taking the time to meet with me, given what dire circumstances the world has fallen into."

"It is intriguing to meet another Old God," Casvir replied. "Allow me to hurry this along, given those circumstances. You seek my pledge of godhood."

"No. And I will reject it if you try."

Etolié felt no otherworldly presences. Oh, where was Kah'Sheen? Hopefully going home, for how stupid this plan was.

"You have my attention," Casvir said. "Why have you come?"

"You were desperate enough to give Soliel the orb in exchange for aid against Ku'Shya. I wished to know if you'd be desperate enough to bargain with me."

Casvir's words darkened. "Speak, but take care how you address me in my home. That is your only warning."

"I want Staff Seraph deDieula. Ku'Shya will not so much as step foot into the realm if you hand it to me."

Etolié's stomach dropped. This . . . was not the plan.

For better or worse, Casvir shook his head. "I am confident enough in my victory without sacrificing something so valuable."

"That ring upon your finger, then. I sense great power there."

Etolié glanced toward Casvir's hand—and yes, there was Flowers' wedding ring, though dramatically resized.

The barest twitch of a frown twisted Casvir's lip. "I am skeptical of your intentions."

"As is wise. Will you agree or not?"

Much could be said about Dira, but diplomacy was not her strongest point.

"No. With respect to your station, my agreement with your counterpart supersedes any assistance you might give regarding Ku'Shya. Though I do wonder how brave or foolish you are to have walked in here knowing what artifact I have when you are among the dead."

A smirk could be heard in Chaos' reply. "The staff merely gives the wielder an advantage. A substantial advantage, yes, but it is not a guarantee. Perhaps a wager?"

Intrigue lifted Casvir's brow. "Go on."

"If your staff can control me, you can do with me as you will to win this war. I will not fight its control until Ku'Shya's threat is dealt with."

"And you want the ring if you can resist?"

"Would you part with it?"

Casvir looked to Murishani, who hid his perplexity behind a false grin. The viceroy whispered words Etolié would have sacrificed her left wing to overhear. Casvir said, "We have an agreement. Should you resist the staff's magic, I will give you the ring."

Mischief never left Chaos' tone. "You have one minute. Do your worst."

The staff's gaze flashed, purple smoke emanating from its eyes and mouth. Yet Casvir frowned—genuinely, truly frowned—as whatever magic he had hoped to have happened clearly did not. Chaos remained nonchalant with crossed arms, her flame obscuring her features utterly.

The staff glowed ever brighter. Etolié's head spun at the outpouring of magic, pain creeping up the back of her skull. Beside Casvir, the comatose Ayla . . . twitched.

"I think I'm starting to feel something," Chaos muttered, staring idly at the ceiling. "No doubt you'll break through. Perhaps push a little harder, hm?"

The smoke ceased, the skull's light fading into a dull glow. "What trick have you conjured?"

"That wasn't a minute."

"This was impossible, and you knew it."

"And I think you're being *stupid* for wasting your minute crying like a little pup."

Etolié managed to clamp down her laughter at the blatant show of disrespect, but to her alarm—and intrigue—Murishani did too.

. . . What *had* he told Casvir?

"I warned you to mind your tongue," Casvir said, a hair more curt than normal.

"Then hand me the ring—or keep trying. Are you a necro-boy or a necro-*man*?"

Etolié didn't even know what to make of that, only that she choked on her spit to keep silent.

Chaos' goading worked, the staff's bright gaze returning. Etolié grimaced at the spike in her headache, the emanating darkness engulfing all light—including her own wings. They dimmed in tandem with the torchlight, the smoke swirling to fill the space.

Etolié stepped back, not inclined to have her skin eaten by necrotic magic today, soon floating to avoid the rising blight.

Some invisible force protected Murishani, the smoke billowing harmlessly around him. Soon, only the staff's glow and Chaos' flame lit the room. Casvir's tension could create diamonds, his grip on his staff shaking. Beside him, Ayla twitched once more, then again, again—

Suddenly, four new hands appeared around Casvir's, for he now faced a gargantuan spider demon.

Before Kah'Sheen could yank, she *screamed.*

The gentle smoke became a torrent, swirling around the flailing half-demon. Kah'Sheen's shrieks tore Etolié's heart in twain. Raw flesh appeared wherever the smoke touched, then muscle, then bone.

"Kah'Sheen, let go!" Etolié screamed, but the demon did not, agony in her failing cries. Etolié bolted forward, forgetting her magic, her station, desperate to protect this sister she loved, but where the smoke bit her, she too faltered—

Only to be shoved into the fray by Murishani's cruel hands.

Like fire, the smoke burned her skin. Etolié clung to Kah'Sheen's raw leg, desperate to latch onto any place in this pain, but her mind couldn't focus, she couldn't conjure any image at all, so instead she screamed as loud as she could. *"Momma—!"*

All at once, the scene changed.

Etolié gasped from lingering pain, fighting shock at the state of her arms and legs. Her dress had disappeared, revealing patches of skin eaten away.

But this was not Celestière. This was Sha'Demoni's darkness. Staella hadn't saved them.

For whose arm was around her but Ayla Darkleaf's.

No time to dismantle the insanity of her circumstances. Not when Kah'Sheen collapsed to the ground in a bloodied heap.

Etolié immediately forgot her vampiric savior, instead rushing to kneel before Kah'Sheen. Images of Khastra's burned body bombarded her memory, and this was hardly different—Kah'Sheen, her demon sister, burned alive by necrotic magic. Gods, there was so much blood, so much *bone*, half of Kah'Sheen's face eaten away, revealing a raw skull. Yet with Kah'Sheen's gasp came precious moments of life, her two remaining eyes dim but holding steady to Etolié's gaze. "E-Etolié, I'm sorry—"

"Save your final words," Etolié said, because Khastra had lived on for one reason only—and Etolié was just gonna have to be stupid enough to try it herself. Momma's warning sang in her ear, of not taking on more than she could handle, but this was Kah'Sheen, her Sheen Bean. Etolié didn't have the luxury of time. She grabbed her sister's decimated body, letting the pain slosh over her—

All went white. A distant shriek deafened her, ringing in her ears.

"*Etolié!*"

It sounded . . . so far away.

"*Etolié, look at me!*"

Etolié couldn't look away from the hazy silhouettes. Her eyelids wouldn't seem to obey.

"*Dammit, get away from her—*"

Crushing pressure pounded her chest in a rhythmic pulse. But didn't hurt; nothing hurt. If she focused, Etolié could make out the monochrome haze of Ayla Darkleaf.

"*What are you doing? You are breaking her ribs!*"

"*I'm keeping her heart beating. Now shut up—*"

Pressure forced air into Etolié's lungs, yet she felt nothing.

"*Let her go. Let me hold her.*"

Light. Silver light engulfed her. Awareness struck along with feeling.

Fucking damn shit, she felt *everything*. Etolié shrieked, her whole body on fire and doused with salt.

"*Just breathe.*"

Impossible. Etolié fucking *screamed*. Vision returned as she howled to shred her vocal cords, engulfed in silver, facing the flaming visage of Chaos. Amid her cries, Chaos' soft hand cupped her face, yet where she touched came no pain.

"*Just breathe, Etolié.*"

All at once—gone.

Etolié gasped, ravaged yet whole, even as sweat pooled from every pore and cast a film upon her. Chaos handled her gently, but soon it was Kah'Sheen's arms around her instead. Etolié's tears fell fast, relief and agony flooding her.

"That is very stupid of you, Etolié," came Kah'Sheen's tear-stained words. "Why are you nearly killing yourself for me?"

"Because I love you, shut up."

And that was that. Etolié cried into Kah'Sheen's shoulder for a few moments more, but through misted vision saw that they were not alone.

Near, Ayla had knelt upon the ground, curling in on herself. Before her, with the reticence one gave a feral animal, Chaos lowered herself. Such hesitation, but her touch fell lightly upon Ayla's shoulder, who shuddered but did not flee.

Though debilitated from the memory of pain, Etolié forced herself to rise, followed by Kah'Sheen. "Ayla, you . . . you saved us."

Ayla trembled. Only then did Etolié realize the vampire wept.

"Look, I . . . Thanks."

"Yes," Kah'Sheen said tentatively. "Thank you, Endless Night."

Ayla kept her gaze to the ground.

Wordlessly, Chaos' touch dropped. Instead, she took Ayla's hand, revealing punctured flesh in the vampire's arm where her own nails had driven deep.

And into her palm, she slipped Flowridia's wedding ring—reforged but not broken. "Keep this close," Chaos whispered, and Ayla immediately darted back, stumbling into standing.

Shock filled Ayla, tears falling fast as she put the ring around her thumb. It spun loosely but held. "Why?"

"Oh, he wasn't happy, but Casvir never breaks a bargain."

"That was not what I meant, and you know it."

Etolié held back beside Kah'Sheen, terribly curious about this reunion. Chaos stood to match Ayla, her might disappearing in her shy stance. "I wish I could speak my full truth."

"Then do it," Ayla spat, yet her bitterness barely held.

"Because I love you."

Bless Kah'Sheen—she had the good sense to keep her confusion to herself. Etolié spared her a glance, mouthing a quick *"I'll explain later"* before returning to the drama at hand.

"I love you," Chaos echoed, heartbreak in the words, "and I have missed you more than you can ever imagine." Chaos looked away. "Dammit, I didn't mean to . . . I apologize. None of this means anything to you, I know."

Ayla came forward, near enough to touch, should she dare. "Clearly it means something to you. Go on."

It really was startling, seeing the duo together. Dira mirrored Flowers' face, her eyes, her lips, yet every piece was tied together with the ineffable string that was Ayla. Surely Kah'Sheen saw it; surely anyone with half a brain could see the shared blood.

Chaos couldn't cry, but that didn't stop her from gracing Ayla with a tragic smile. "I have so many regrets about you and me, though not the kind you'll think. The only thing left to say is that I'm sorry. I love you, and I'm sorry."

Ayla kept a soft grip upon herself, her stance conveying only humility. "In a world so impossible as one where you loved me, I can only imagine that . . . in that same world . . . I would forgive you."

Chaos' smile became true, despite her clear attempts to stifle her sobs. "I think you might be right."

Etolié couldn't help but recall a vision of the future, of berating a shattered Dira on a battlefield. Here, the same woman cried again, but this time from catharsis.

Ayla's stance gained confidence, resolve sharpening her features. "It seems only fair that I would help you now."

Chaos shook her head. "You owe me nothing."

"I know. But there will not be a Sha'Demoni to hide in much longer if we do not act." Ayla offered a hand. "I will help you fight Soliel."

"Etolié, something is bothering me."

Etolié walked the halls alongside Kah'Sheen, the heavy calm before the storm leaving her limbs tingling. She knew nothing—of Sora and Ilune in Celestière, of Ayla and Chaos who had left to find the battlefield, of Khastra, who might be fucking dead for all she knew. By Eionei's Asshole, she felt so useless.

Little more to do except, well, her job. Together, they moved to Flowers' medical suite. "Lay it on me, Sheen Bean."

"Endless Night is breaking her marriage contract, yes?"

Etolié stopped dead in her tracks. "What? What are you talking about?"

"In Sha'Demoni, Goddess of Chaos is proclaiming love for Endless Night. I am confused."

Oh, Kah'Sheen. Etolié opened her mouth, only to shut it once again and resume her steps. "Ayla absolutely did not cheat on Flowers with Chaos. I'll explain later." Of course Kah'Sheen would understand familial love, but explaining how the fuck Chaos was Ayla's daughter from the future would take time they didn't have.

Etolié ignored the written request to knock on the door, prepared to barge in as always—only for the door to open from within, and out came the head physician. "Oh, Empress Etolié," the woman said with a bow. The rest of the nurses filtered out behind her. "Thank goodness you're back. We've been called away to Solvira. I would assume Lady Flowridia will be joining soon, right?"

"I would also assume," Etolié said, though somewhat stilted. "On whose orders?"

"Apparently, Imperator Casvir's. We are to help prepare hospital beds for the wounded. You'll stay by her side until she's sent for, won't you?"

Etolié didn't bother to mention that's where she was supposed to be anyway. "Sure thing."

Within the suite, she found Flowers pacing, the spark of hope in the kid's eyes fading fast. "Don't look so heartbroken," Etolié said. "Ayla is free from the staff. She's agreed to help Chaos fight Soliel. They've already left."

Flowers nodded, her watery gaze holding no peace. "So that's that. We wait."

In moments like this, Etolié realized how helpless Flowers must feel. Once a powerful necromancer, now bedbound in the face of the apocalypse. Though . . . she had been pacing. "You seem to be feeling all right."

Flowers nodded, and if Etolié looked closely, she could just see the nasty cyst bumps under her dress.

"Etolié, I must go," Kah'Sheen said. "I am not knowing what is happening with Mother and Khastra, but they must know about Staff Seraph deDieula."

That debilitating anxiety returned. "Yeah, you do that."

Kah'Sheen disappeared into the shadows, and Etolié simply prayed there would be shadows for her to return from.

"What happened with Khastra?" Flowers asked.

Etolié's words burst as a flood, quickly relaying *Rezoxos* and the reveal of her betrayal. "I don't know what I can even do. Kah'Sheen is doing the best thing, telling them about . . ." It seemed the contract still held. The words jumbled in Etolié's mouth. ". . . well, you know. But Khastra might be dead."

"Oh, Etolié." Flowers coaxed her to sit on the bed. Etolié followed, feeling woozy on her feet anyway. "You're right. There's nothing you can do. And I'm so sorry. Trust me, I understand. I don't know what's going to happen with Ayla. I'm still wrapping my head around what *could* happen with Ayla and Chaos."

"It's all so much, fuck." Etolié set her head onto her knees, this sudden dizziness making her ill. "You said Sora was with Ilune?"

"Last I saw. I'm as confused as you."

"Do you know where they went?"

Flowridia shook her head. "I last saw her by Demitri's pen, but I doubt they're still there."

Etolié heaved a sigh against the illusioned fabric of her dress, the horrid feeling of helplessness rising to drown her. Yet despite facing the end of the world, despite the gravity of her possible lost love and of losing her Momma forever, Etolié could only be bothered by one thing. "Ilune flirted with Sora."

Flowridia looked equally taken aback. "What?"

"I don't understand anything anymore, Flowers. After I left you and Ayla, I went after Ilune and revealed who I was, and it turns out she's kind of amazing, the big sister I never knew I needed, yada yada. We found a tavern and drank and swapped stories. That's when Sora showed up."

"When you left to visit your mother, that was about Ilune too, right?"

Fuming, Etolié fell back onto the bed. "Can I say something extremely stupid, but I'll explode if I don't tell someone, and even though I don't trust you worth shit, I know you can't do anything about this?"

"Of course, Etolié."

Etolié lowered her voice, muttering furiously. "My momma had Ilune's phylactery all along."

"That's kind of sweet, actually—"

"It was just in her fucking house! It was in the back of her closet for who the hell knows how many hundreds, if not thousands, of years!" Though already flopped on the bed, Etolié managed to dramatically repeat the act. "And then she apparently stashed it in the kitchen cupboard when I told her to destroy it the first time. It's not there anymore, so you can't use that information anyway. I don't even know where Momma stashed it."

Flowers looked properly appalled. "Just . . . in her house?"

"In her damn house." What else did that level of audacity call for but a drink? Etolié reached into her extradimensional space, withdrew her beloved flask, and popped the lid—

An explosion rocked the castle.

Far more spectacular than the first—Etolié might've fallen had she been standing. Instead, she dropped her flask on her head, cursing the very corporeal metal bashing her forehead. "Gods fucking dammit." She sat up, grimacing at the perfectly good booze soaking into the bed.

Flowers ignored her suffering, darting for the window instead—or darted as well as her pregnant body would allow. Horror filled her. "Etolié . . . come see this."

Etolié hardly felt her limbs, supported by her wings as she joined Flowers by the window.

In the fields beyond Haven, from what had once been peaceful night, had come an array of lights and shadows. One lorded over the rest, impossibly large and wielding glowing, amethyst weapons.

Etolié's stomach dropped. "But . . . why? How? Did Khastra . . . ?"

Lose?

"There's no way Kah'Sheen would have had time to warn her," Flowers said. "We have to do something."

Among the stars, Etolié recognized the silhouettes of flying things. The demonic army had arrived. Heavily demon-blooded De'Sindai, elves in their airships and clockwork machines . . .

Casvir had not evacuated the city. Ku'Shya had come, wearing Etolié's love like a puppet. Yet . . .

"Wait," Etolié muttered, for something wasn't right. "Momma said Ku'Shya would never take Khastra as a slave. And gods can't be hosted by unwilling bodies."

"Well, they can," Flowers said, "but it takes a ritual."

"Can gods possess dead bodies?"

"I believe the body has to be sentient, unless the god is a necromancer."

So Khastra wasn't dead. And Khastra wasn't a slave. Yet Khastra was no longer willing to do this . . . "Then that's actually Khastra. But why? Something isn't right. Or . . . something is very right. I don't know. This doesn't make sense."

"I don't understand, Etolié."

"There's no time to explain, but . . ." Urgency filled her, hurried by fear. "I have to go out there."

"Then go. Don't worry about me."

Etolié, rather petulantly, let her truth out. "Well, irony's a bitch because I actually am a little worried about you. Never thought I'd see the day."

Damn that smile of hers. Flowers was ridiculously endearing when she wasn't backstabbing. "Thank you. Now, go. Do what you have to do."

Etolié didn't know what to do, but time was of the essence. With all her non-athleticism, she climbed carefully through the window and floated down.

CHAPTER 38

Nineteen years after the end of the world . . .

Within days, whispers rose of a new weapon in Casvir's army, capable of decimating entire cities—elven cities—in a blast of silver light and flame. Like a shattered dam, Casvir's forces flooded Zauleen in mere weeks.

For that had been what she was: Ayla Darkleaf, damned for standing against the forces of evil.

What a blur it all was, fighting waves of hell upon the earth. Four years passed as a nightmare.

"Hello, Dira. I'm surprised to see you alone."

Dira stirred as she sat alone by the firelight, jarred from the images of violence echoing in her mind. The fire dimmed in response to the glowing figure, the magnificence of her old mentor never losing its gravitas. "I needed to be alone. I'm surprised you're still here."

Ilune offered a tired smile. "I think, given the circumstances, it is appropriate that I stay a little longer. Celestière can wait. Perhaps I might even find whatever means there is to sway them to send assistance. Alas, they aren't exactly keen to listen to me. Not enough of them, anyway. Morathma doesn't take this threat seriously, and apparently I take it too much so. Celestière is caught in between, because of course they are." Ilune's exhaustion fell out with her sigh. "Is it foolish to ask how you're doing?"

Dira swallowed the rising sting of emotion. "I feel lost."

So many had left her. So many were gone.

Sora. Ripped to shreds by undead forces.

Mother. The finest weapon, forced into Casvir's arsenal.

"Is Etolié around?" Dira asked.

Ilune shook her head. "She is drinking, somewhere. But she did speak to me today, so perhaps there is one spot of hope."

Dira's family was being torn apart, but there was still hope for Ilune's, it seemed.

"You missed quite the meeting," Ilune said. "Your mother was sighted in southern Solvira. Not the best omen for those cities, unfortunately."

Mother. A weapon. Her screams remained a constant in nightmares, often joining Dira's own.

"I've been thinking on everything," Dira replied. "There must be a way to free her from the staff. It was yours first, wasn't it? How do we break the bond?"

Ilune's pleasant smile turned stale. "All my attempts to steal it have been thwarted. He can't use it on me, blessed be, but he is somehow able to teleport and I am not. Without the staff, I haven't a hope to steal his undead. And let us not count the times he has sent his assassin— your *mother*, sorry, to send me back to my phylactery. We are at a stalemate, he and I. And break it? No, Dira. It's possible she could break free herself, but it requires a strong will. Stronger than even she, it seems."

Gods, this hopelessness. To hear her fears confirmed left Dira numb. "So there's nothing to do?"

"I will keep trying, but it has been four years. She is deep under his influence."

"But what if she really is the only one who can stop Casvir? Shouldn't that be our focus?"

"Putting all our hope into one plan is a spectacular way to lose a war."

"What if I tried? She loves me. She loves me more than anything. Could that be enough?"

Ilune's cringe so nearly shattered her world, but her words spoke contrary. "I won't say no. But like I said, it can't be our only plan."

"Then we have to make another plan."

"We're trying."

"But I mean another secret weapon. The only way to truly stop this war is to kill Casvir, but the location of his phylactery is a mystery. What if there is someone who does know?"

"What are you getting at?"

"If not my mother . . . Ilune, you're a necromancer. Could you bring back my birth mom? Flowridia?"

What did Ilune's confusion mean? Surely . . . Surely this was a simple request. "Can you elaborate?"

"I know my mom knew Casvir. He was her mentor. He gave Demitri to her. What if she knows something we don't?"

Ilune remained reserved. "What did they tell you about her death?"

"I was told by Mother that she died when she was pregnant with me." Realization struck, cold seeping through her veins. "She died in childbirth, didn't she."

It explained so much—Mother's reserve, her sorrow, her imploring that her mom had loved her so dearly . . . Mother hadn't wanted her to blame herself—

"No. Not quite." Ilune winced, some battle fought inside her. "What do you know of Silver Fire pregnancies?"

"I know nothing."

"Well, damn your auntie, leaving this to me." Ilune heaved out a breath, pacing as she gathered her thoughts. "Silver Fire pregnancies are notoriously risky for the mother. If the mother has magic, generally all will be well. If not, it is always fatal without intervention, but not in any normal way. Dira, your powers have made you dangerous from the time you were just a fetus. You had random bursts of power, and your mother would have succumbed to that had she not had Etolié at her bedside to heal her. But the highest risk wasn't to her body, but to her soul."

Dira could hardly breathe. "What does that mean?"

"Many with the Silver Fire are capable of grabbing souls. With that comes the ability to absorb them or even destroy them. Gods, I hate to be the informant—"

"I destroyed her soul?"

"I don't know."

Slowly, Dira wrapped her arms around herself, those awful words never quite settling.

"It's possible you absorbed it," Ilune continued, "though typically that can be felt by adept magic users, and I have never sensed another soul inside you. But you are a unique person, and for as much of an enigma vampires are to me, dhampirs are even more so, and perhaps there is something about your biology or soul I don't understand. That said, I don't wish to give you false hope. The fact is that your other mother died alone, and you ripped and tore yourself out of her abdomen sometime after. Wherever her soul is, if it was not destroyed, it's somewhere not even I can touch."

Tears stung her eyes. All the rest of her was numb. "So there's no hope?"

"Most likely not. I'm sorry, Dira."

Dira breathed yet felt nothing, head spinning. She stood, uneasy as she stepped. But she took another and another, mind reeling as she walked along into the dark woods. Owls hooted, foxes wailed a long distance away, all the sounds of night embracing her . .

She walked until she could not see her own feet, until the fire of the encampment was but a distant star. Alone, her tears fell freely, all the layers of her grief unraveling. She . . . she had taken her own mom away? She had taken away the love of Mother's life?

She wrapped her arms around herself, wondering if . . . if she could just reach it, could she touch it? If Flowridia's soul was inside her . . .

"Excuse me."

Dira gasped as she wiped her tears. Into the darkness, she stared, seeking any sign of life, any sound—but heard . . . nothing. The owls had ceased. The foxes stilled. Not even insects buzzed.

"Sorry to startle you. But are you not Dira Darkleaf?"

The voice was small, though depthless. It had no origin, no matter where Dira turned. Unease filled her.

"I cannot imagine the depths of your anguish. Your own Mother, stolen and controlled by a monster."

"What do you know about my mother?"

"No need for fear, Dear Dira. Ayla spoke so fondly of you. What a pleasure to finally meet."

The darkness . . . shifted. But how? There was no fog this night. Dira looked higher to the trees, yet no light cut through them. From her hand sparked Silver Fire, yet it cast no light upon the shadow before her.

Pure darkness, this . . . *figure.* Not humanoid, but something more, something large. Merely corporeal fog.

"You knew my mother?" Dira whispered.

"What do you know of Izthuni, dear child?"

"Only that he was the other half of The Endless Night. Mother never . . . She never told me much."

"But she loves you dearly, does she not?"

"Of course she loves me."

The figure did not move, yet Dira felt a smile. *"I am Izthuni, God of Shadows. Ayla was once my dearest protégé, and what anguish it brings me to see her so cruelly used. But she need not be a slave forever. Listen well, for she can be saved."*

Though fear sank as deep as her bones, this *Izthuni* brought what no one else had—hope. "Tell me."

Current era . . .

Within Sha'Demoni's darkness, Dira walked at her mother's side in silence. Oh, what to say? The end drew nigh; Dira felt it in her soul. But Mother was here for a few moments more. Mother was safe, for now.

You could tell her.

Dira said nothing to the voice in her head. Demitri could shove off today.

Learning the future takes it away.

"I have never known how to react to kindness in the aftermath of my own cruelty," Ayla whispered.

Dira stilled in her steps, her urgency fading to the want to savor this moment alone. The apocalypse loomed, and at the cusp of the cliff face she paused, staring not into the abyss but at the woman who walked these final steps with her. "Consider us even for all the shit I put you through growing up." Dira smiled, hoping it conveyed her teasing.

Regret filled Dira when Ayla finally matched her gaze, that hesitation breaking her heart. "Forgive me," Ayla said. "I am still trying to parse the idea that I was worth loving as a parent. But that is not for me to put on you." Ayla's steps stilled, a gasp coming unbidden as she fought tears. "I am sorry. I should not burden you with this."

"What is 'this,' precisely?"

Ayla's arms came to wrap around herself. "The staff. That damn staff."

Oh, the words struck deep. Gods, she knew all too well. Dira removed her own ring, the one resized, reforged, as ancient as the world itself now. When she took Ayla's hand, she stuck it upon her left-hand forefinger, finding it a much safer fit than Casvir's refitted one on her thumb, even a little oversized. Dira took the one from Casvir, her own fingers far less slim. "You're safe now. Just . . . never remove the ring. Not for anything. Not even for me."

But she would—gods, she would. It would be her fate again if the cycle renewed itself. Here, she had saved Mother. But what of the future? Love would condemn her, just the same.

Ayla gazed upon the ring with bittersweet fondness, her smile reminiscent of happier days. Flowridia . . . *Mom* . . . had revealed so much. A shattered marriage, two broken souls . . . and the resolve from both to change.

Mom wanted to change. What would that have looked like?

Mom is the best. Now you understand.

Dira swallowed unexpected sorrow. Once, she had been told she had consumed Flowridia's soul.

Yet she had perished in the explosion, and her mom's soul had not appeared. Centuries upon centuries upon millennia of guilt . . . now in question. The simplest answer was that she had simply destroyed it instead. Gone for eternity.

But what else could have happened? Could it yet be undone? Sora had asked what could be changed to break the cycle, and what else? But who would it condemn to save her? Who would it save?

It would save me the pain of being up your ass all the time.

But could it even be done?

There were worlds to save, as much as she wished to disappear into her own inner realm—not that she would be alone. She hadn't been alone in so damn long.

Dira offered a hand, warmth filling her when Ayla accepted the gesture. A child again, she walked hand in hand with a mother she had missed with all her heart, choosing to pretend it was not the end, choosing to pretend it would not all fall apart someday—again.

Today, she would stop Soliel. She had to. Tomorrow . . .

The world quaked. Light burst in a ray of six beams expanding across the sky. Instinct rose, and Dira pressed closer to her mother's side, forgetting herself, her station, her powers, instead clinging to a comfort once lost.

"Are we too late?" Ayla said, calmer than Dira by far.

"It is not the end, but we must hurry. We're close enough."

Dira released her, then shook her spirit within the stolen body, loosening its hold. She slipped it away like an old shirt and grimaced at the sudden noise inside her own mind.

You could just let me lead.

Dira ignored him, instead illusioning her fire, lest she need to explain her wolfish face. "I've never done this before. So let us pray it works."

Ayla offered her hand. "Do what you must."

Fine, fine. I'll behave.

At the moment of contact, Dira focused on this new prospective vessel the way she had each dead thing, and found it quite different indeed. For instead of an empty glove, she found an occupant, though one willing to share the space. Dira's ghostly self sank into Ayla's skin, stretching to fill this new form. Yet all around, she could not shake the sensation of proximity, the feeling of Mother's embrace evoking tender memories of youth.

"Well?" she heard herself say? "Did it work? Can you move me?"

Dira focused on stretching these new limbs, finding the motions slightly delayed, like pushing against a current. "It's strange," she said, though it was barely her voice.

"I have plenty of my own experience being possessed by gods," her mother's voice said, wise, dark, and comforting. "I don't feel you quite as closely as I feel Izthuni. Do you hear my thoughts?"

"No."

Good thing too. We'd have some explaining to do.

"Nor do I feel yours," Ayla continued, "but I do feel your power. If you're willing to trust me, I will wield your powers with all the esteem that responsibility deserves."

"I trust you completely."

It felt so freeing to say.

All at once, Dira was simply a traveler in a body of flesh, seeing through Ayla's eyes. "To the battlefield then."

They slipped into a dark space and appeared in distant fields upon the mortal realm.

There was no peace this night, for far away the demonic army marched.

Dira had never known Khastra, never seen her except in art—and while this was not her true form, the gravitas she conveyed in tandem with Ku'Shya couldn't be far from the truth. A portent of doom upon the horizon, her silhouette was not their battle to fight, no.

Before Dira could speak, Ayla summoned Silver Fire and ran.

"Might I verse you in flying?" Dira said, startled at how different her voice had become.

"Educate me," Ayla mused.

Dira took the reins and leapt. At her feet, the fire propelled them forward at lightning speed, a shooting star across the land.

Gravity pulled her forward, ever increasing as they neared the orbs. They flew over a mountain's peak and found Soliel in the valley below.

A newborn star lay in the center, glowing a blinding white. If she stared, Dira could just see six floating orbs within, orbiting as small planetoids.

If they could only reach the center, they could—

Instinct led them to duck and tumble to the ground—narrowly dodging the swing of Soliel's blade to their neck.

Soliel wielded his sword and shield, armored in gold and looking just as grand. "So it has already come to pass? You've come back into the world?"

Dira's lips pulled unbidden into a grin. "No, no." She rose to her feet—not Dira, but Ayla holding the reins. "So much worse," Ayla said. "I am someone with no mercy to show."

With fury unbound, fire burned in Dira's palm—then shot to engulf Soliel. His shield came up. Fire sprayed.

"You have always been somewhat reasonable," Soliel cried behind his shield. "Perhaps—"

Dira's fire ceased abruptly. "Somewhat reasonable? That's hilarious. Perhaps what?"

Strange, that she was stopping. But Mother always had a plan.

Soliel peeked out from behind his shield, his ravaged armor filling Dira with rage. "Perhaps we might discuss—"

In a blink, Mother yanked them into Sha'Demoni. Soliel glowed as pure light a world away. Dira burst forward unbidden, diving for the shadow of his shield.

"—this civilly—"

Blood sprayed with Mother's knife. Soliel's cry cut off, clutching at the dagger in his throat. Dira ran for the beacon of light.

Gravity pulled her forward, gentle but unmistakable. "This won't be comfortable," Dira said, "but we won't be destroyed."

With care, they reached inside as one. Power burst as their fingers caressed the Dark Orb, its companions following in orbit as she pulled it to her body.

"Can we run while we absorb the spell?" Mother asked.

Already Soliel rose, yet he seemed distracted, staring intently at something in his palm.

"I don't see why not," Dira herself replied. Her fire blazed anew. When she leapt, she gained flight.

In the aftermath of the explosion, Celestière became quiet.

Sora was no longer holding Ilune's hand, no longer inches away from making the most foolish decision of her life—and Sora would admit to having made a fair few poor decisions—instead stunned into silence as a split appeared in the sky. Beams of light in a rainbow of hues disrupted the peaceful mist.

"Is this it?" Sora whispered. "Are we too late?"

The eerie calm lingered like the fog around them. The colored lights shone in stark contrast to the world of white. Sora hardly felt when Ilune touched her waist. "No idea."

"We should hurry—"

Sora's breath hitched at the sudden proximity of Ilune's beautiful face, the twist of fingers in her locs. When their lips touched, Sora pulled her against her body, blood pounding from adrenaline, from panic, and now from dynamic release. Oh, the relief that flooded her, their tension shattering at the impassioned touch. Through too many layers of clothes, Sora felt the press of Ilune's body, her breasts, every sculpted curve fitting perfectly against her. At the parting of her lips, Ilune's tongue slipped delicately into her mouth, tasting as sweet as her magic. Sora moaned unbidden, mind blank save for Ilune's mouth, the allure of her sensuous figure, the wonder of what it would be like to touch her—

Temptation had truly never burned so bright, but Sora pulled away, shaken at the magnitude of Ilune's effect on her body. For years, she'd been celibate by choice, and were the world not actively ending, the want to be ravished here and now in the mist by a god was . . . *perfect.*

Did Ilune see right through her? Oh, there was beauty in how Ilune bit her lip and grinned. "In case we die."

Sora nodded, utterly breathless. "Understandable."

The music in Ilune's laughter remained intoxicating, but not so much as the sparkle in her silver eyes. "Like you said, we should hurry."

Though she hardly felt her feet, Sora let herself be led along, their brisk pace increasing. "I don't normally do things like that."

"Kiss?"

"Kiss like *that.*"

"I wouldn't have guessed."

Ilune's mischief had never faded, and Sora had no idea how to take that.

"My mind's a bit addled," Ilune continued. "Can't imagine why. But I think we've come near enough." Sora was drawn in like a dancer, held once more in Ilune's arms as they stopped. What was this euphoria? Ilune hadn't enchanted her—she suspected—so was it perhaps simply . . . desire? "Close your eyes."

Sora obeyed, half-expecting plush lips against her mouth—only to reel back when heat and moisture suddenly permeated down to her bones. She opened her eyes to find they were no longer in Celestière but in Sha'Demoni. The sky had no sun, but here those same lights cut through the pristine sea of purple, beautiful and wrong in every vile way.

"Just a short hike from here," Ilune said. Her arms remained around Sora, for which she was grateful. The truth of the words slammed her back into the present, into this walk to the slaughter.

Sora's joy faded. When Ilune finally released her, Sora withdrew Leelan from her pouch, selfishly wishing he would move—but no. She trembled as she held him to her cheek, already moist from sweat. "Let's go," she whispered.

"You don't have to follow, if you'd rather not."

Sora shook her head. "It's only right that I finish this."

Ilune took her hand, briskly escorting them through the lush landscape. "You say you've been to Ku'Shya's home before?"

"Yes."

"Then you must know of the portal from *Daemenacht*. If the world looks like it's about to end, run for it. It is the only passage home for you."

"What about you?"

"If Celestière ends, I will either be killed or floating for eternity in space with my phylactery—at which point, you shall have to live on without me, somehow. I shall simply be a comet in your life, blasting into your orbit and leaving just as soon."

Ilune's dramatic hand on her chest evoked a small smile from Sora's lips, despite her growing dread. She made a point to roll her eyes as well. "I'm saving all my questions and reservations for when we live."

"When? I like your confidence, Sora. Truly inspiring." Ilune slowed, and Sora quickly saw why: a great canyon spread before them, the steep drop not ten paces away. "We are here. This is the time to say goodbye. It's too dangerous for you to follow."

The purple sky burst with too many colors, streams of light revealing the cruel passage of time. Here and there, the earth shook. The world was ending, and Sora felt that weight. Hers was to end with it.

She brought Leelan up, emotions flaring when she matched his hollow gaze. "Leelan . . ."

Her bird said nothing, did nothing, did not move even a whisper.

"Please, if there's anything inside you . . . give me something."

Sora's eyes grew watery, and this time she didn't hold back. The oppressive heat sunk as deep as her skin. Tears joined her beading sweat. Sora kissed him, and he did nothing. She hugged him close, and he did not sing. "I love you so much."

Leelan was nothing. A vessel with no soul.

Sora offered Leelan forward, shame and guilt clawing to the surface. She faced the red earth as Ilune gently accepted him into her grasp. "I'll only be a liability if I follow you from here," Sora whispered. "Just swear to me it'll be painless."

"It will be a swift and merciful end." Ilune gripped her shoulder. "Should the heat become too much, or should the worlds begin splitting apart, run for the portal. But I pray to not be too long."

Ilune left with that piece of her soul, floating gently down the canyon and out of sight.

Sora sank slowly to the ground, ignoring the skittering plants and the violent colors across the sky. The world was falling apart . . . and all Sora could do was wait and weep. She held up her hand, summoning a small bit of light into her palm. Her final connection to Sol Kareena's power, that legacy dying inside her . . .

It was right. But Sora felt no peace.

A small whisper of logic said she ought to conserve her tears, her sweat beginning to drip, but what did it matter now? Sora could be selfish this one moment and cry—for Leelan, for Sol Kareena, and for herself.

"Sora?"

Through blurred vision, Sora was startled to see Kah'Sheen approaching from the living foliage.

"Why are you here?" the half-demon said, offering a hand, despite her impossibly tall figure.

Sora instinctively accepted it, though stumbled before she caught her footing. "It's a long story. You . . . you should wait out here with me."

"Oh, but I cannot! I am finding Staff Seraph deDieula, and I am warning Mother!"

The statement was equal parts comforting and disconcerting. "Really?"

"Yes, it is with Imperator Casvir, and he is using it to destroy Khastra! But, but—why are you here?!"

Instinct said that admitting she was in some level of cahoots with Ilune was not a way to win affection in Sha'Demoni, but

Kah'Sheen was still an ally. Perhaps even her friend. "The world is about to potentially end. Should you really be going down there?"

Kah'Sheen quickly glanced between Sora and the canyon, her frown out of place for the girlish half-demon. "Yes, obviously. You are being suspicious, but I am having no time. I . . ." She gave an endearing *humph.* "You are delirious from heat exhaustion. Come on."

Sora choked when Kah'Sheen lifted her by the collar of her tunic. "What are you—"

Her stomach lurched when Kah'Sheen swung her off the edge—only to keep a firm hold and climb down the side with perfect, arachnoid balance. Sora's head spun at the speed. She nearly vomited when Kah'Sheen righted herself and bolted down the imposing canyon to her mother's burrow. Sora's world refused to stop tilting—not until Kah'Sheen herself stopped, engaging in terse conversation with the demonic guards at the entrance.

Sora's rear touched the ground when Kah'Sheen released her. She rolled onto her back and sought stability from the sky. Whatever they said was well beyond her comprehension, but soon a familiar, four-eyed face leered above her. "Sora? Are you sick?"

"Haven't decided yet."

"Oh good! You are not fainting. You must come inside for water—but first, change in plans! Are you knowing? Mother is no longer destroying Haven! She is only capturing Casvir instead!"

The statement slammed cognizance back into her head. "What?"

"Khastra is winning *Rezoxos!* She is ruler of Sha'Demoni!"

Sora forced herself to rise, her nausea remaining but for a very different cause. "What?"

"I must hurry to warn Mother about the staff, but Haven is safe! Come inside before you faint."

Horror forced her to speak. "Kah'Sheen!"

But Kah'Sheen was already rushing away, deeper into the cavern.

Sora jumped to her feet. "Kah'Sheen, wait!" She ran, but with only half as many limbs as the half-demon, she had already lost sight of her. *"Kah'Sheen!"*

The name echoed through the gargantuan throne room, but no one responded. The demon guards watched her, but none reacted to Sora's presence, Kah'Sheen having dragged her in apparently enough to appease them.

Dammit all. *"Ilune!"*

A few suspicious looks fell her way at that, but Sora did not stop running, following the path she swore Kah'Sheen had gone.

"Kah'Sheen!"

The name echoed across the stone ceiling. As Sora rounded the corner, the half-demon fidgeted with her many hands, her staring shifting rapidly between the panting Sora and the path ahead. "What?"

"There's something . . . Dammit, I don't have time to explain, but—" Time was measured only in Kah'Sheen's frantic motions. Sora knew she had to speak, had to say something, but . . . Dammit, what did she say?! "Can you send anyone else to deliver that message?"

Kah'Sheen glared as she shouted in terse Demoni. When a pair of spindly demons rounded the corner, Kah'Sheen rapidly delivered her message. The duo disappeared down the tunnels. "It is done. What do you want?"

"If I tell you, you have to promise to leave with me."

"No, but you will still tell me."

"Kah'Sheen—"

Sora's reflexes acted faster than thought. Kah'Sheen's hands darted for Sora's tunic collar, but her knife blocked her, sending Kah'Sheen reeling back with a cut palm. "I'm sorry," Sora said. "I can heal that, but you can't—"

Faster than a blink, Kah'Sheen swooped down to grab her—but feinted instead. Sora blocked the blow. A kick from Kah'Sheen's arachnoid legs sent her to the ground.

Before Sora could roll over, the large half-demon lifted her by her arms, plucking the knife from her hand with one of her many. Sora faced Kah'Sheen head on, having never seen her otherworldly face so close. "Sora Makosa, you are suspicious. I am feeling I might be in danger, so you are telling me now."

Sora didn't bother to struggle, Kah'Sheen's entire spindly body pure lean muscle. "Look, as far as I was aware up until a minute ago, Ku'Shya was coming to destroy Haven. There's a plan set in motion to stop that, but I don't want you caught in the crossfire."

Kah'Sheen's glowing eyes stared as deep as Sora's soul. "You are conspiring to kill Mother?"

"Can you blame me, given the circumstances?"

"No, I cannot. So I am not killing you, but you are stopping this."

Despite the sweltering heat, a chill raised bumps along Sora's skin. "I can try," she said, and winced at Kah'Sheen's sudden hiss. "It's not me! I was waiting outside!"

"I am only mostly convinced you are not delirious." Still, Kah'Sheen did set her on the ground, glaring from new, and literal, heights. "How are we stopping this?"

"You send me alone to where Ku'Shya is meditating."

To Sora's surprise, Kah'Sheen pointed farther down the tunnels. "The path is straight. Take no detours, until it is forcing you. Veer left. You are finding Mother soon."

With no time to question, Sora bolted down the path.

Having had the misfortune of standing before Ku'Shya multiple times, Sora shouldn't have been daunted by the span of the tunnels. Yet she felt no safer than an ant infiltrating a royal's home. She had done this before, but never alone. Her mind flickered briefly to Tazel and Mereen, and most critically to Odessa, running through those halls to escape, helping the witch make the final sprint to freedom.

Sora kept her breathing steady, winded prematurely. The tunnels, though not lethally hot, kept a film of sweat permanently coating her skin. Despite her exhaustion, she forced her magic to surge—and a small spark of holy light burst from her palm.

Leelan still lived.

Kah'Sheen had given no credit to the span of the tunnel. Sora lost count of her steps, her breaths, even the minutes by the time the path split. No sign of Ilune in all her running, but Sora suspected Ilune could be quite subtle when she chose to.

Something to keep in mind, as much as Sora remained intrigued.

Having gone to the left, Sora kept her pace. The light steadily faded as she ran, and soon Sora summoned her light for practical purposes. Darkness did not fully engulf her, but night was not when danger peaked. The most dangerous hour was twilight, and Sora became alert in the dim light.

The path widened. Sora slowed, surprised by the lack of company. No guards, no demons, but a massive shadow slowly gaining substance—and when Sora stepped into a dark amphitheater, she understood.

Ku'Shya sat with her massive legs tucked underneath her, apparently at rest. No light from her many eyes—they remained shut. She breathed, and Sora kept near the wall, knowing anything that *was* watching would notice her any moment now.

She dared to whisper. "Ilune?"

The named echoed across the stone cavern, even across Ku'Shya's exoskeleton. Had Sora beaten Ilune here? Had the God of Death become lost in the maze?

Just the faintest brush against the back of her neck—Sora tried to whirl back, but already her feet dangled off the ground. Who stood on the wall unseen but Kah'Sheen.

Her grip tightened around Sora's neck. Sora dangled, grabbing frantically at Kah'Sheen's hands, seeking to not lose her breath. "Ilune, you are saying?"

Sora could barely breathe, much less speak. Her words came strained. "Kah— Kah'Sheen. You—"

From the walls, skeleton hands burst out. The spray of dust blinded Sora. To the song of Kah'Sheen's sudden scream, Sora fell— only to meet a gentle landing upon something . . . *moving*.

Sora coughed, horrified to see a mass of skeleton hands and arms holding Kah'Sheen captive against the wall, dangling well above Sora's head. More and more emerged. The cavern shook, but for all Kah'Sheen's struggle, nothing broke against the might of the overlapping bones. Her screams were soon muffled by fingers jamming into her mouth. Like a cocoon, they wrapped around her spidery figure, leaving only her four eyes to observe.

"Hush now," came a sensuous voice. "Your pain could be so much more."

Sora tried to rise, and was aided by shifting bones, serving as a cushion.

Ilune emerged from the cavern's entrance, purple light emanating from her eyes, from the very pores of her skin, and escaping as smoke with her smile. "Sora, Sora, *Sora*," Ilune chided, though the last came as purr. "Did she bring you here?"

In one hand, Ilune cradled Leelan. Sora forced herself not to stare. Best not to reveal her cards, though dread filled her at even the thought. "Ilune, the plan has changed. Ku'Shya isn't going to attack Haven. Khastra is apparently the new Goddess of War. Ku'Shya is just a vessel. They're trying to capture Casvir, which, trust me, is the best possible plan. The attack is just a ruse."

Ilune said nothing, merely stared as though awaiting a conclusion.

"So . . . so we should let it go. I know Leelan is going to die, but it can't be like this."

Ilune raised a cold eyebrow. "I won't go back to that prison. Ku'Shya's death means I walk free."

"We could negotiate—"

"Who? Who could sway Ku'Shya on my behalf, Sora?"

Sora sputtered, desperately grabbing at names. "Etolié! Etolié could do it. Or Khastra—"

Ilune laughed, that beautiful, ominous song. "You really don't know your history. Leave this cavern before I force you."

"What about Kah'Sheen?"

In the brief glance Ilune spared the half-demon, Sora jammed the base of her palm into the God of Death's nose. Bone cracked; Ilune stumbled back with a gasp.

Sora stole Leelan and ran.

Pandemonium filled the streets of Haven. Etolié stood in the gates of the palace, facing an onslaught of panic.

Sure, she could fly, but angel wings were only so fast, and the battlefield was so far away . . .

But Soliel had not won yet. There was someone who could help. Etolié took her prayer pose. *Momma?*

A few tense seconds passed. *Starshine? What's going on?*

I need you here. Now. Please.

Just hold tight a moment.

Within Etolié, there came a familiar, gentle invitation. Etolié accepted the call.

Warmth engulfed her, stretching through her limbs as a second presence filled her body. Etolié felt herself grow, felt her body move without her volition, then came a sweet whisper. *Has the worst happened?*

"Yes," Etolié said aloud. "I don't know if it's too late or not."

I know you did your best, Starshine. If this is the end, I love you so much.

Emotion welled within Etolié, leaving her choked.

What do you need from me now?

"First, I need to get through this crowd of very panicked people."

Do you want them to be calmed or do you have a destination? I can easily do either.

Etolié moved her head, disoriented by a few degrees. She stared to the distant horizon, to where Khastra's silhouette shone backlit by the moon. "I need to get out of Haven. I need to get to Khastra."

Oh, Stars. That's Ku'Shya, isn't it?

"I'm not asking you to interfere. But I need to talk to her, somehow."

Getting there is the first step. Let me lead.

Etolié let herself go limp, allowing Momma to take the reins. They floated up—

And vanished.

Etolié blinked and saw white mist. Another blink, and she floated atop the outer walls of Haven, facing the vast fields beyond. A boundless army awaited, an ensemble of very demonic-looking De'Sindai and mechanical weapons, even a few airships in the distant sky. But looming above all that, the silhouette of Ku'Shya and Khastra marched on.

Yet leagues away, nowhere near the oncoming army, was a beacon outshining the moon. Etolié's headache spiked, even so far away. "Momma, I think that's—"

A thunderous *boom* left her screaming and clutching her ears. High above, the sky illuminated in colorful beams of light, expanding, stretching far across the atmosphere. Though night, they blinded the stars, casting a mockery of daytime across the land. But more ominous still was the sudden crackling line extending vertically across the field between the army and Haven, expanding to reveal . . . a portal.

From the portal poured a flood of death. Countless waves of undead emerged to rampage across the terrain, screeching and howling as they rushed toward the demonic army.

Amid the storm appeared a god-to-be, a monster atop a skeletal steed, covered head to toe in spiked black armor. Necrotic lightning danced across the bones of his horse, his armor, his power radiant. His horns were unmistakable, as was Staff Seraph deDieula in his left hand.

"We have to go," Etolié whispered. "Now."

Etolié remained weightless as Staella took them into the sky. The scene shifted—first mist and then the mortal realm, though many hundreds of steps farther than the wall of Haven. Closer now, Etolié could just see the glowing orbs of Khastra's eyes. All . . . four of them? Ku'Shya's eyes, yet they shone blue.

Another blink, and Staella brought them closer still, well ahead of the army of death. Nearer now, Demoni words assaulted her ears as the goddess before them barked orders to her troops.

Yet when she laughed, it was the Bringer of War—frightful, yes, but familiar. Etolié yearned.

One more blink, and demons surrounded her. Frightful winged beings, their gazes narrowing upon her. Before Etolié could panic, Staella dove from the sky, falling faster than the demons could follow. When they hit the ground—

The ground vanished. The world shifted. They appeared deeper still amid the demonic army. The caustic scent of death and rot assaulted her, blood and entrails, necrosis and oil.

All stilled to see them, she a glowing, godly beacon. Those great glowing eyes, that unholy melding of Ku'Shya and Khastra, fixated upon them. Two hammers; one bow; four hands to wield them.

I'll be with you, but I can't be the one talking.

"I know," Etolié said, even as fear flooded her. This approaching goddess stared with all the might of a feral Bringer of War. "It's all right."

I will cast an aura of peace. I love you, Starshine. Good luck.

"I love you, Momma."

Etolié swayed as her Momma's presence eased, a whisper instead of a hug, as her feet touched prickly, yellow grass.

Amid the sea of demons, Etolié swam upstream, feeling their eyes but not their weapons. Those who raised their swords dropped them just as quickly, confusion in their glowing gazes as they watched Etolié and Staella pass. Distant shrieking sounded as undead met demon, but Etolié barely heard it. The sky burned brighter, but Etolié only had eyes for the gargantuan demon. She marched with her head high, soon taking a deep breath, and with a tightened core cried, "*Khastra!*"

And to her horror and supreme delight, the demon slowed and grinned. "*Etolié!*"

Oh, damn that precious tone. It truly was Khastra after all. "What the fuck is going on?!"

The first of the flying dead swarmed the demonic Khastra. She batted them aside with ease, wielding her three weapons with grace. Taller than castles, Khastra launched one hammer across the field—then Etolié shrieked when her gargantuan hand darted for her, lifting her gently enough to preserve even a butterfly. Taller than the late Uluron, Khastra brought Etolié level to her face and spoke as softly as her vast self would allow. "What are you doing?"

"What are *you* doing?!"

"I won." Khastra's grin was wide enough to bridge rivers, her fangs reminiscent of the Bringer of War. Her voice lowered. "We will not touch Haven. We will only lure Casvir out so I may take him and cast him into prison. The army is so we may find the God of Order as well."

Dread spread through Etolié's core, leaving her numb. "But you're meeting Casvir on the battlefield?"

"Yes, and so you must leave. It is not safe."

"Even with the elves?"

"They only know not to cross Haven's walls."

"Khastra, you can't—"

But already Khastra was placing her down behind her, standing as a wall between her and the army of death. "You must go."

"Khastra, no! Casvir has the—" The words cut off involuntarily, the curse jumbling her tongue. Damn Kah'Sheen for leaving so quickly. Damn Etolié for knowing too much. "Khastra, you're in danger! You have to leave!"

But Khastra ignored her, standing stalwart as her thrown weapon flew back into her grip. One step, and her demon was impossibly far away.

Etolié spread her wings and jumped, bursting into the sky like the star she was.

She could not speak. But she could sing. *Momma, would you join me?*

Always, Starshine.

Etolié summoned a breath, and from her throat sounded peace.

Staella quelled storms, some said. Staella calmed monsters. Etolié had done little more than soothe the Bringer of War, but today, their duet descended as a dove upon the battlefield, wordless and tender.

Etolié sang, even as the undead army clashed with the demons. She sang, even as the earth shook, the sky split, and the end drew nigh. The melody sounded all across the battlefield, settling like a fog across the combatants. Soon, the clang of weapons faded. The screeching of death ceased its echo. The world stilled, and even the conjoined monster that was Khastra paused.

Etolié knew so little Demoni, but there was one phrase she had practiced a thousand times in tears upon the floor, muttering it like a prayer to the one goddess she had ever worshiped. The words became her song. *"Khastra, come home—"*

Etolié gasped at the sudden stabbing sensation inside her— painless, yet unquestionably a severance. That feeling only rose, until Staella's presence was ripped away.

Starshine—!

Momma became silent.

The wind rushed, her wings fluttering like falling feathers. Etolié plummeted to the earth as herself.

Thankfully, she did still have wings, which stretched wide to catch her before she shattered every bone in her body. In the dirt, Etolié touched her face, glanced at those wings, and realized—

Momma?

Nothing. No connection at all. Where was Celestière?

Before panic could strike her, the earth trembled at the falling of a great titan. Khastra fell to her knees, shrinking rapidly.

If Staella had been expelled, had Ku'Shya also . . . ?

The demonic part of the army screamed in disarray. Khastra buckled to the ground.

Rising like the leviathans of the deep, Casvir strode forward on his steed.

His mace bashed through every flying creature, crippled any who neared. Clockwork beasts shattered, some to his weapon, others to skeletal hands rising from the earth around him. The mechanical lay still. The mortals rose anew, turning violently on their once-allies.

If he saw Etolié, he did not show it. For in his other hand, instead of his shield, Staff Seraph deDieula flashed as light filled the skull's gaze.

It stared upon Khastra alone.

Etolié shrieked as Khastra rose and contorted, fighting the bonds the staff sought to throw upon her. Khastra roared, and even without the Bringer of War's might, she bellowed as an imposing force.

When she wrenched around, Etolié met vacant eyes. No recognition; not the woman she loved; only an undead monster stripped of all autonomy.

Khastra charged.

Flowridia watched until Etolié's wings were long out of sight. Only then did cold fear grip her.

There was no Ayla here. No means to evacuate should the worst come. Oh, where was Ayla now? She stared upon the horizon, hoping to find any sign of Silver Fire.

Would Ayla be all right? Ayla was nigh unkillable, yes, but Sol Kareena had done a splendid job years back. What if Soliel did the same?

Dammit all. Flowridia felt useless. She was blind to the world here in this castle. Ayla was far away, Etolié had her own quest, and Sora was who the hell knew where with . . . Ilune.

Flowridia's gaze fell away from the window, peculiar thoughts swirling through her head. Ilune's phylactery had been in her mother's house, just under everyone's noses. It was so painfully practical.

Nearly two years ago, in the woods when Soliel had rescued her, he had told her where Casvir's phylactery was not. Not in Sha'Demoni or Celestière, not anywhere Casvir could not place himself, not anywhere Casvir couldn't easily reach . . .

Ilune's phylactery was in the back of her mother's closet. As high regard as Casvir held his mother in, she was long dead, likely in an unknown grave. Same for his father. Casvir had no one to trust—only himself.

So close . . . Surely she was all but standing on top of it.

She had poured over pages and pages of castle maps, the palace its own small city filled with traps, filled with spells, filled with dungeons leagues deep . . . But none of that mattered when compared to a mother's closet. Ilune had entire worlds at her disposal, yet had chosen the most practical approach.

. . . So of course it was in the palace, yes, but not buried underground, not sitting behind layers and layers of spellwork, no traps except the sort Casvir himself could quickly dismantle. Casvir trusted no one. The only guard trusted enough to keep watch of Casvir's phylactery was Casvir himself.

No one would expect an item of such worth to be hidden in a closet. Just as the least likely place for Casvir's phylactery was, well, a closet. Or some equivalent. Somewhere he and only he would keep watch over. Within arm's reach, perhaps. He didn't have a bedroom that she knew of, but . . .

Just under her nose . . .

"It's in his office," she whispered, the words leaving her light.

A dull ache in her back stole her focus. Flowridia winced, a new panic rising. It could be nothing. It could be her body preparing. It could still be weeks away, or at least days. Her hand went to her stomach, her firm womb a warning. "Not yet," Flowridia pled, but even as the pain dissipated, her terror remained.

Surely there were medicines to slow the process. The nurses had been called away, but no one had called for her. Their absence was starkly apparent. But there was not time. Casvir was on the battlefield. This whole saga could end if she could only search Casvir's office.

A knock came. The hair on the back of her neck stood on end. "Enter." She fought to hide her grimace when Marielle entered— alone.

Marielle rushed to her side, refraining from hugging her, at least. "Oh, thank the angels. Are you all right?"

"I'm terrified, obviously."

Next, Marielle ran to the window, stilling as anyone would at the oncoming army in the distance. "The portal to Solvira is still open. Casvir sent me to take you there."

Flowridia glowered, rage spiking. "I'm sorry, what?"

"We need to leave. Solvira is much safer—"

"Evacuations were halted. Besides, Casvir would never send you. You're lying. Why?"

Marielle offered a smile as stressed as the situation warranted. "I'm not lying. Casvir couldn't come himself because he's marching out to meet the army."

"And how do you know that when even I don't know that? Did he just happen to catch you on the way out?"

"Something like that. We really need to go. Now."

Flowridia evaluated her options, the lack of weapons in this room glaringly apparent—unless she considered the cursed dagger in the drawer, but that wasn't the right choice. She did have the mirror. Was there anything it could do? "Absolutely not. You should go. I'll go to the portal when my doctors tell me to."

Not that they were present, but that was yet another thing Flowridia wouldn't draw attention to. Marielle was a fop, but Marielle worked for wicked people.

Marielle came forward. Flowridia fought when she tried to take her good hand. "I'm trying to save your damn life, so will you just—"

The door opened, revealing . . . Etolié?

The Celestial glared at Marielle, though it lacked the fire Flowridia had come to recognize. "You should leave."

To Flowridia's surprise, Marielle obeyed without even a word.

"Shut the door, would you?" Etolié said, her tone more sensuous than Flowridia had ever heard. Marielle cast an anxious look around the room, eyes filled with . . . *fear*.

The door shut. Flowridia came forward. "I thought you were going to the battlefield. What happened?"

Etolié gave an idle shrug. "Give me just a moment. I'm savoring this."

Flowridia frowned, a warning stirring in her gut. "Savoring what?"

Etolié grinned, bearing all the pleasantries of a snake. "The moments before your death. The anticipation is just thrilling, is it not?"

Flowridia slipped her hand into her pocket and tapped the magical mirror, though she did not dare to take her eyes off this impostor. She took a deep breath—and screamed.

And to her alarm, the false Etolié laughed. "Oh, scream away. The whole castle is in hysterics. You think anyone will notice? Your doctors certainly won't. Strange, is it not?"

Flowridia ran for the door leading to the nurses' station, only for the impostor to dart much faster. It grabbed her by the arms. When she fought, the person squeezed her maimed hand, sending white hot pain shooting up her arm. Flowridia screamed, tears prickling in her eyes.

Behind misted vision, the image of Etolié sparkled and vanished—revealing Viceroy Murishani instead. "Oh, how I wish I could be a cat playing with its prey. We'd have *such* fun. Alas, no time. Can't be leaving any evidence. Turns out, if you want a job done right, sometimes you have to get your hands dirty."

Flowridia's tears fell fast, horror leaving her stunned. When she tried to wrench from his arms, he squeezed her hand once again, leaving her sobbing.

He grabbed the collar of her dress, forcing her upright. With his other hand, he caressed her hair. "Such a waste. No doubt Casvir was positively giddy when it was a Silver Fire bastard you made for him. If only you'd let the assassins succeed—I could've given you an even better one."

Flowridia could hardly breathe from terror, her strength waning from pain.

"We could have helped each other, but no. I would have even let Ayla join, but no." Murishani glanced to her swollen womb. "Only six months along. It won't survive long without you."

Silver light engulfed him. He gripped her hair. Dizziness filled her, vision spinning as a blue glow surrounded her. In his hand, he grasped something ethereal.

In her final moments, memories of Murishani luxuriously stroking a severed soul struck her.

"Good night, Flowridia. We'll be spending a long eternity together."

Murishani yanked—

For a brief moment, she floated above her own mortal form, watching her body crumple to the ground. Her sight faded . . . faded . . .

Dark.

CHAPTER 39

Nineteen years after the end of the world . . .

Mother.

A title that haunted Dira on every sleepless night.

"But would you tell me you love me?"

"I love you," Dira whispered to the wind, yet far below a great battle waged—living versus the dead.

"Listen well, for she can be saved."

Now, Dira had a plan.

The sky was red from dawn, from dust, from death, the expansive field before her stained the same. She stood a ways off, high upon a hill surveying it all. The sun cast no shadows, too obscured by clouds and dirt, but the man behind her did, his light creating shadows for her solace.

"Last chance to walk away."

Dira met his gaze, this ox of a man, gentleness and strength balanced in equal measures. When she took his hand, he squeezed. "If there's even a chance to save her, I have to take it."

"And you're certain you trust this . . . god?"

"Together they were The Endless Night. Who else would know better?"

Soliel's lips met her brows, leaving a lingering kiss. "Wait for my signal. I'll lure her out."

"Be careful. And . . . thank you."

There were no lives at risk, save for his. Casvir had sworn to not touch her, but Soliel was only half a god, strong but not immortal.

His smile said it all. He loved her, loved her more than he cursed Ayla Darkleaf, loved her enough to risk his life for Dira's happiness.

For the first time, she would let him.

He said nothing, simply drew his sword and charged.

Soliel surged down the hill like a battering ram, his innate glow growing bolder, brighter, blinding. Dust stirred with his steps. Soon, ash too, the undead caught in his light shrieking as they burned.

His sword glowed with equal glory, slicing through the dead like parchment. And though his shield did not glow, it bashed through Casvir's forces with ease, Soliel's strength unmatched in this sea of death.

Cheers erupted from those living—elves, humans, dwarves, and more, united beneath the banner of stopping the imperator's onslaught. Guilt filled Dira to know the son of Sol Kareena was not there for them, but off to redeem a villain instead.

A villain once oppressive.

A villain who might be their only hope.

Soliel, however, was their savior this day, the nonpareil of the battlefield. Dira kept her eyes peeled on the space around him. Her quarry could hide in shadows, but Soliel was pure light. Mother would be forced to appear if she wished to attack.

And she would unquestionably be sent to stop him.

The living side reclaimed their ground in steady measures, Soliel's presence turning the tides. No sign of Casvir, but that did not mean he wasn't watching. He did not have to even be present to see through his minions.

From the shifting shadow of a ghoul far too near Soliel, the darkness grew.

Dira dove off the hill, into the shadows.

Seamlessly, she emerged into a world of greys, of fog. Dira found her feet and darted toward a collection of light, mortal souls lighting the realm even a world away. Seconds ticked by, but far less in the mortal realm. Dira did not even feel her feet, focused on the brightest light of all and the dark figure leaping for him—

Dira burst through the shadow the figure cast, grabbing and tackling Ayla Darkleaf from midair.

But this was not the mother she'd known, poised and regal, frightful but controlled. This person was a monster, dirtied and matted, nearly naked for her ruined clothing. No dignity in slavery, it seemed, for blood years old caked in layers upon her skin, her face.

But it was Mother. Those eyes were soulless, black, but Mother was trapped behind them. "Mother! It's me. It's Dira!"

Dira heaved as Mother shoved her off—then lurched as a knife nearly slit her throat.

Dira rolled to her feet. She gripped her own knives, all the world fading as she kept within Ayla's gaze. "Mother—"

Metal clanged, knife catching Mother's. "It's—"

Dira gasped as Mother struck again, faster than any training could have prepared her for. Over and over, Mother battered relentlessly to reach her. Dira moved on pure instinct, blocking each blow.

"You must break the bond between Staff and slave," Izthuni had said. *"You must stab her heart with your blade."*

But could she? Doubt flooded her, even as nothing of recognition shone in this monster's eyes. Dira's own began to sting—from dirt or tears, who knew? "It's Dira! You know me! I'm your daughter!"

Gods, it was all so quick. Dira's knives did not relent. Their dance continued, even as Mother slowed.

A flash of silver appeared in Mother's eyes. "Dira?"

With no knife to stop it, Dira's own struck—a mere breath beneath her sternum, angled just so.

And then . . . it all slowed.

Dira heard nothing except the thud of the knife. In Mother's eyes she caught her own reflection, saw herself scream without sound.

When Mother fell, Dira scrambled to collect her. But Mother was unkillable, indomitable, nigh two thousand years of glory and death behind her. Had this broken the spell? Dira held her as a baby, cradling her softly. "Mother!"

Their eyes met. Mother's silver gaze dimmed.

"Mother?!"

Mother's lip twisted—so nearly a smile—and she curled into the embrace, eyes closing.

Dira barely whispered: "Mother?"

Like the battlefield, the sun, and all her dreams, Mother turned to dust in her arms.

Current era . . .

Now it was Dira who glowed like a star, coated in silver flame, preparing to absorb the orbs' power. Gods, it ached, yet it was but a fraction of what Ayla surely felt, the hostess to her spirit. But her mother was strong, and so Dira persevered. The spell was not lost. It could be undone—

Only for that pressure to surmount. Dira burned from within. Not from the orbs, no, but deep inside. Her control waned, the orbs falling as she, too, fell—

And was violently expelled from Ayla's body.

Dira plummeted to the ground.

The transformation happened quickly, a body forming from within her ghostly form. Flesh and blood; muscle and bone; when Dira breathed, oxygen burned her vestal lungs.

Somewhere near, an infant dhampir had done the same.

Looks like we're back.

Before she could shatter this new form, Dira illuminated with silver flame, the stream of fire cushioning her descent. She landed on her feet unharmed, only to realize Ayla had not fared so well.

Ayla's burning body crashed upon the battlefield. Dira bolted toward her, fear rising despite knowing her mother could never truly be hurt—not by this. Ayla's Silver Fire extinguished as she rose. Her neck hung at a crude angle, half her skin scrapped away, but the bones repaired when she wrenched her neck back into place. Her skin steadily sealed, each step forward less graceless. When she matched Dira's gaze, realization flooded her. "You . . . You don't smell dead. But your face, it . . ."

Ayla's voice trailed away. Dira ignored the violence around her, ignored the unspoken query. No time; high above, the orbs had resumed their spell. "I can take over the spell from here. Go help Flow— Mom."

Ayla nodded, her fidgeting revealing her deep anxiety.

"Be careful in Sha'Demoni," Dira implored. "The ties that bind the worlds are severing."

Ayla gave a nod, then vanished into Dira's shadow.

Oh, the looming heartbreak. Dira's lip trembled, but there was naught to do to stop it. It was too late.

Demitri's voice startled her. *Is it though?*

"We don't know how."

"Dira—"

She should have felt Soliel's holy light. Instinct lashed out. It was not Dira who struck Soliel across the face with a bony claw, but Demitri. Dira, a mere puppet on strings; Demitri had as much control as he pleased to wield.

Feels like I can finally fucking breathe.

Soliel raised his hands in peace, but Demitri snarled, Dira's knife narrowly missing the slit between his breastplate and pauldrons. "I heard it," Soliel said. "I know how Flowridia dies."

Demitri's rage surged inside her, even as Dira's breath caught. She continued her onslaught, nimble with the knife and claws. "What did you do?" It was not her voice, but his.

"Nothing." He withdrew something—

Only for it to catch in the swing of her arm and shatter onto the ground—Sora's mirror.

Above Soliel, the pull of the orbs steadily built, threatening to pull Dira into their gravity. The grass bent as though blown by wind, tiny roots upturned and specks of dirt sucked into the void. Dira froze, staring at the shattered glass.

"It was the viceroy," Soliel said solemnly. "I heard it from the mirror. He stole her soul."

With the revelation, thousands of years of guilt and pain shed like skin, leaving her raw and enraged. "I knew I should have ripped off his face when I had the chance."

"It's not too late. She can be saved."

Gods, against all odds, hating Soliel was as easy as loving him. For a precious moment, Dira met his gaze and forgot the world, forgot Demitri, forgot Uluron and the orbs and every cruelty they'd shared. He *meant* it, and therein was the most difficult, hateful thing. This beautiful man and his beautiful promises . . . "Where is he?"

"In the castle in Nox'Kartha. I think he was in her bedroom, but I do not know for certain."

A ruse, surely, but those soft, hazel eyes had never lied. For all his crimes, Soliel did not lie.

A seismic *boom* toppled Dira to the ground. The earth cracked beneath her, splitting in a perfect path toward the orbs. The orbs flashed. The wind howled. Clanging metal nearly crushed her as Soliel fell.

Yet his smile showed triumph. Dira felt the shift in the air like her own pounding heart. The spell—oh, the spell.

The orbs melded into a pool of light, becoming one entity. Now. Now was the time. To rise. To grasp them. To tear them apart, lest they rip the worlds asunder.

Soliel scrambled to rise, but Dira had always been faster. With flame at her feet, she burst toward the light, fire engulfing her entire form.

Now was the time. The spell was not yet complete.

"Dira!" Soliel's cry sounded leagues away.

So close, so close, so close . . . Dira slowed at the cusp of light, seeking to touch its center—

Dira—

"Mitri?" Dira whispered.

What about Mom?

In rare moments, she saw the world as a whole, the forest instead of the trees. Visions of now and what was to be bombarded her memory, nearly striking her down.

Far away, a battle raged, demons and dead things vying for control. Etolié's scream broke through barriers of time and space, echoing throughout the worlds. There she was, the Bringer of War—a being spoken of in reverie, in rage, in remorse—ripped from mortality by Casvir's might, her final battle cry cut short by Staff Seraph deDieula. The world trembled at her final death. The demon-blooded ones ran wild without their leader's temperance. The elves rained fire upon Haven. The walls crumbled. The streets ran rampant with De'Sindai loyal to the Goddess of War.

Haven did not fall, but Haven ran thick with blood.

The vision faded. Dira stood at the cusp of the end of the world once more, gravity tugging her closer, closer. Blinded by the light, Dira reached—

Only for a new vision to bombard her.

Far away, Sora stumbled and fell in the expulsion of the spell. The God of Death stole her precious familiar and resumed her path of murder. But Ku'Shya had already been banished from the mortal realm, no longer vulnerable to Ilune's wrath. An expulsion of power there would be, but it would not be the Goddess of War who fell.

Amid the carnage would lie the corpse of her youngest, Kah'Sheen. Shattering trust, shattering family, shattering Etolié's heart—

Dira teetered as her sight returned, once more reaching toward the root of the spell. Close, so close—

"Dira, stop!"

Dammit, Soliel—

And then she saw the present anew.

Far away, a baby wailed, yet nothing compared to the mother's screams, for they were the very core of Dira's nightmares. Not a mother in body, but a mother in blood, spilling tears enough to drown the world as she cradled the corpse of her wife, coated in warm blood, split from within by a baby sensing its own doom in the casket of its mother's womb.

Soon, soon, Ayla would run. Soon, soon, the baby would feast on blood and milk, spend one year in cold splendor, and then be kidnapped and raised, against all odds, in unconditional love.

It was not instinct but knowledge. In every life Dira lived. Dira was stolen. This was the way of the world.

Dira? What about Mom?

A final time, she saw the future—one she had lived countless times before. Wherein she reached the Convergence Orbs, grasped the spell by the roots, absorbed it, grabbed Soliel and burned as bright as she ever had, bringing an end to this apocalypse for good. Two brilliant stars turned cold in an instant. The Old Gods would be no more in mere seconds. With the spell incomplete, the worlds would shake but the worlds would reattach, stronger for this turmoil, yet more divided than before.

The realms could still be saved. The spell could be undone. All it would take was one little touch—perhaps it would begin the cycle anew, but there was safety in familiarity, safety in knowing Casvir would succeed but not forever, that he and all the rest would be brought back here . . .

She stilled at the cusp. There was no time, yet she paused, willing her mind to stretch once more, to show this future where she followed Demitri's call.

Nothing. A great void.

With her supreme power, Dira felt for ghosts, felt for souls, sought in the void to know if Flowridia still had a spirit to save. Countless times in the future, she had tried and failed, and failed, and failed . . . But her domain was death, the Beyond, the guarding of souls—

This was not yet that future. Flowridia's spirit was somewhere. She called; it whimpered.

Dira's breath caught.

"Dira!"

In a mere breath, Soliel would grab her. Soliel's shadow already covered her. Dira could grasp the spell and end this all. They might not win this cycle, but they would not lose—

Dira? Do something!

The choice was presented: save the worlds and begin the cycle anew, or save the heart of the mother she loved—and what? What else? No visions came to answer. Condemn the worlds for good, no doubt. But Ayla would die again and again and again . . .

A touch of metal on her shoulder. Time no longer ticked. Dira reached for the light.

And against all odds, all premonitions, against every instinct that world had instilled inside her, Dira, in one singular lifetime, said, *"No."*

The visions shattered. Her own history shredded at the seams: a childhood of joy ending in tragedy, a mother reaching for the light plunged back into darkness.

She had never been meant to save Ayla. No one could, except Ayla herself.

But . . . she could save the one who could set her free. Flowridia had been going to set her free.

In a motion that defied fate, defied reason, defied the cycles that dictated time, Dira broke from Soliel's grasp and ran from the light.

Dira embraced her animal side, running on all fours as fire projected them at impossible speeds. Mountains passed in a blink. Trees were but a blur. Oh, the sensation of wind was joy. *Will you be able to find Murishani?* she asked internally.

I'd recognize his perfume all the way from Solvira.

Upon the battlefield, she burned through undead and De'Sindai alike. Limbs shredded. Blood sprayed. Time was of the essence, casualties merely the cost of war.

But there among the fray, she spotted Imperator Casvir wielding that fucking staff.

Just one detour? Please?

Dira didn't have to respond, merely pivoted and ran for the imperator instead. In a blink, she saw Etolié and her wings, screaming as a demonic figure charged at her. No question of her identity, for the famed General Khastra was a figure known throughout history.

She moved in unnatural ways, caught under the influence of the staff. Dira did not slow—

And bashed through Casvir's skeletal horse, shattering its gangly legs.

In the confusion, Casvir toppled to the earth. Dira yanked the staff from his grasp. Though she daren't slow for long, she swung the staff back—and struck the skull across Casvir's face.

That's the highlight of my day so far, came Demitri's voice.

I think we can make it even better.

What do we do with it?

We will figure that out once we've saved mom.

With the staff in hand, Dira steered toward the shadows and disappeared into Sha'Demoni's might.

The landscape shook, the mist swirling about like a blizzard. Dira navigated the storm with ease. The palace was a beacon of light, even now.

Do we have a plan?

"No," she said aloud. "But if we can find him, it'll be obvious enough, I think."

They reached the palace in time. In the recesses of shadow, Dira swam through a monochrome sea, led by Demitri.

Down in the basement.

And down they went, the murky depths void of light and darkness both. Gods, the maze of Sha'Demoni hurt her mind, thousands of years since she had last navigated the dark realm alone. But Demitri's ineffable senses steered them, until she reached a door that pinged in memory, though it was not her memory.

She slipped through the seam of the door like silk. Already she heard him, that pompous fuckface.

His murky cackling was unmistakable, as was the light his foggy form cast. If Dira focused, she could just hear him.

"But what to do, what to do . . . How much torture can a raw soul take anyway?"

How simple it was, to step through the realms.

In his private chamber, Murishani stared first perplexed then fearful as Dira stepped from the void. So little light, except the luminous souls floating about and of course, the burning Silver Flame. "Surprise, bitch," sounded her voice—but it was Demitri.

Similarly, it was also Demitri who punched the bitch right in the mouth.

As Murishani stumbled, Dira swiped the fragile soul from his hand. Even coated in magical fire, she felt its warmth and life. Hardly a weight at all.

Before Murishani could regain his bearings, she stepped back into the realm of shadow, paying no mind to the sudden screaming from beyond. Murishani could throw his tantrum in peace. Dira cradled the soul to her breast. A raw soul, more vulnerable than any ghost, and Dira carried it away, holding it like a newborn child.

Can we kill him?

"Not yet," Dira whispered, for though irrational, she feared to startle the poor soul. "If we go back, he could hurt Mom."

Oh. Not yet then.

The march upstairs was comparatively slow, even in Sha'Demoni's dark corridors. Only when she reached the second floor did she phase out of the shadows, entering vacant halls. Most had fled. She couldn't blame them, for Solvira was but a portal away. "Do we smell them?"

Yes. Keep going.

Demitri led, and soon even Dira smelled the sweet aroma of blood. Wailing echoed down the hall. Dira's heart ached, for it was familiar. The door to the medical ward opened at her touch.

All the world stilled.

A massacre lay before her—a fallen woman, Flowridia Darkleaf, bleeding heavily from a gash across her abdomen. Lifeless, her dull eyes stared upon the bloodstained Ayla, shrieking, weeping. Abandoned on the bed, a newborn screamed, covered in birthing fluids and blood, so much blood.

Dira matched Ayla's teary eyes. "Do you trust me?"

Ayla hesitated, heartbreak apparent as she released her fallen wife. "What are you going to do?"

"She must be willing," Dira replied, for this was an old spell, bastardized by modern necromancers for selfish gain. She knelt, keenly aware of Ayla's eyes upon the soul. "Protect us."

Dira touched the soul to Flowridia's chest. All the world went dark.

"Good night, Flowridia. We'll be spending a long eternity together."
Murishani yanked—

Flowridia awoke within a void of white.

She gasped, fear pulsing like adrenaline through her blood. But there was no Murishani. No labor pains. No pain at all, in fact.

Flowridia held up her once-maimed hand—but it was healed. She flexed it, instinctively dreading the pins and needles, the pain, yet nothing came.

She tugged down the collar of her gown. Her sternum was pristine, no scarring upon her torso or breasts. No memories of Kaas and pain and torture.

Only then did she recognize her wedding dress. Luxurious translucent white embroidered with flowers by Ayla's skilled fingers—this gown had been destroyed in the blast in Solvira years ago, yet here it clad her body, restored to a perfect form. She ran her hands down the embroidery, struck by memories of her wedding. For all the dread leading up to it, what a perfect day it had been.

But, no. She had to focus. What was this place? Flowridia placed a hand upon her womb on instinct, only to gasp and remember it all.

"Kedira," she whispered, and the name echoed all across the vacant land.

"Flowridia?"

Flowridia frantically looked about, yet the word had no origin.

"Flowridia?" The discorporate voice sounded anew, as though searching.

"Hello!" Flowridia lifted the train of her gown as she studied the mist. "I'm here!"

With each blink, the landscape darkened. Flowridia stiffened, unnerved as the light dimmed like a candle slowly suffocated. First to grey, then black—

From the darkness, a skeletal hand grabbed her arm.

Flowridia gasped and whirled about—only to nearly sob.

A monstrous face, yet one she surely knew: Chaos, her daughter, the woman she had hugged mere minutes ago. Or had it been? How much time had passed?

But it was not only her visage, the left side revealing a frightful beast. Half of her skull lay exposed, yet it was inhuman, canine, morphed to fuse with her dhampir half in the center. Where an eye should have been was merely a golden glow, but opposite shone a beautiful silver eye, familiar and not. "This is me," Chaos said, as though interpreting her thoughts. "I cannot hide myself in this plane. But I will explain everything, if you'll only come back."

That bony paw still gripped Flowridia's arm. "Why?"

"Because I'm choosing to save you. I'm going to bring you home—to Ayla."

She spoke as though it explained everything. Yet Flowridia swallowed back sudden tears. "That feels like a mistake."

"Why would you think that?"

"Because you and I both know I'll become someone you'll someday have to kill," Flowridia said, choking at the final word. "You could spare both of us that pain."

"No, no—Flowridia, I never grew up with you."

"But you said you missed me. You knew me—and so I must've been there. Explain yourself."

But Chaos remained silent, regret apparent upon her bestial face. "I wish I could explain, but the sooner we leave, the sooner we return."

"Explain, or you get nothing from me."

Such monstrous features, but why? Flowridia stared into that unnatural gaze, torn between welcoming silver and ominous gold, dread welling in the silence.

Who was this person? If Flowridia were dead . . . this was the Beyond. This person could be any god.

Flowridia yanked her arm back, terror spiking with falling realization. "You're not my daughter."

"Of course I am—"

"What trickery is this?! Are you Izthuni?" Memories of Kaas bombarded her, of staring into Sol Kareena's monstrous image, of being eaten alive—

"I am not Izthuni—"

Flowridia ran.

Through darkness, Flowridia sprinted, unhindered except for her voluminous dress. Could Izthuni kidnap her in the Beyond? Could she be dragged unwillingly into his afterlife? Oh, gods, she had never heard of this aspect of the Beyond, but so many mysteries remained in the world. Why not one final victory for the Lurker?

"Mom, please listen—"

The voice was too close. Rage built—and burst. "Stop it!" she screamed, whirling about, yet she saw nothing. "Don't you dare call me that! I've faced my sins, so don't you dare torture me with my own daughter." Tears filled her eyes, furious and hot. "Just let me go. Give me oblivion if you must, but let me go."

Flowridia stood her ground when motion in the darkness narrowed her focus. Chaos appeared, but kept her distance. "I am begging you to let me explain."

"If you're going to lie, at least keep your lies straight. If my daughter doesn't kill me, then . . ." Flowridia cursed her tears but let them flow, even as Chaos swam behind her misty vision. "Then that means she kills Ayla, but you know Ayla can only be killed by someone she loves. Checkmate, Izthuni. You can't be naïve enough to think Ayla would ever . . ." The words were too bitter to speak, the death of a dream she'd thrown away.

"I will tell you everything, if you promise to listen."

"You can spin lies for miles. We both know that."

"What if I showed you?"

Flowridia stared warily when Chaos came forward, but she did not dart. "Show me how?"

"We can share memories, you and I. I can show you my life; I will see yours, in turn."

Years ago, Flowridia had stood in the presence of a dragon who had offered the very same—and she had seen Valeuron's life through the dragon's eyes. "If you are Izthuni, I can run forever and never escape you in this place, can't I?" Flowridia offered her hand forward. "If you're Chaos, then perhaps I will finally have a few answers."

Though the answer to an age-old mystery struck her then. Why had Valeuron given her the orb? He had seen her life. He said he knew her death.

And so he knew she was the mother of Chaos?

One blink, and Chaos stood far too near, the beauty and terror of her appearance equally matched. Chaos accepted her hand, the bony touch unnerving. "Do you accept this?"

"Yes," Flowridia said, yet forgot what for, instantly.

"Witness the world without you. See what will be lost."

And after a plunge into darkness, shedding her identity and life . . . thus arose her first memory: *"It is not much, but it will suffice for now . . ."*

Etolié stared in incomprehensible confusion as the being who was presumably Chaos disappeared with Staff Seraph deDieula—

Until a monstrous *thud* at her feet plunged her back into terror. Khastra growled as she looked to Etolié, to Casvir, and leapt into standing. Ahead, Casvir resumed his bearings, purple lightning coating his figure as he extended a claw toward Khastra.

On her end, Khastra held out a hand for her gargantuan hammer to swing back into her grip. "Etolié, get out of here."

"But—"

Khastra's sudden buckling stole Etolié's words. Pale knuckles gripped her hammer's shaft. "He is still trying— Now *get out!*"

Already, Casvir's horse charged, a fog of dirt and blood behind it.

Struck by confusion, by fear, and some small bit of trust, Etolié grasped onto the first external location her mind could find.

Consequentially, she landed in the most annoying place in the realm: Flowers' medical suite.

Except . . . It had become a bloodbath.

Flowers lay in a pool of blood on the floor, her gown thrashed, revealing a stomach split open by what looked like animal claws. Chaos knelt above her, eyes shut, still as a statue with her glowing hand upon Flowers' bare sternum. Ayla cradled Flowers' head, her sobs barely contained as she brushed aside bloodied strands of auburn hair with trembling hands.

Yet something wailed from the bed. The motherly instincts Etolié periodically beat into submission rose from the depths at what lay screaming—a very damp and lonely newborn, still attached to her placenta.

Etolié immediately ran to the tiny girl, uncaring of the blood and birthing fluid as she scooped her into her arms. "Can someone please explain what the actual fuck is going on?!"

She shook off a pillowcase as Ayla managed tearful words. "I barely know."

Etolié proceeded to wipe the baby of fluid, desperately soothing her all the while. "I know it's cold and horrible out here, baby girl. It doesn't actually get better."

Chaos's light burst. "Get me a box."

When Ayla didn't immediately move, Etolié wrapped the infant in a fresh pillowcase and pulled open the bottom drawer of the bedside table, revealing the secret evil dagger box. She ripped it open, unceremoniously dropping the dagger onto the table. "Here."

She set it beside Chaos, then forcibly swallowed bile when Chaos ripped open Flowridia's chest through her ribs. The bones shattered like branches. Blood seeped from the open cavity.

Etolié had seen Flowers in many varying levels of exposure, but this was too much. Instinctively, she covered the crying baby's eyes.

Still glowing, Chaos tenderly plucked the heart from Flowers' chest—turns out she did have one all along—cradling it before setting it into the cushioned maldectine box. She shut it with bloodied hands. "Trust in me," she muttered, then set a hand back onto Flowridia's broken sternum.

With agonizing slowness, the bones . . . regrew.

Ayla remained oddly muted all the while, tears flowing soft and free. She stroked her own bloodied hands through Flowers' hair, as though any comfort could possibly be given. But what else did you do when the love of your life lay fallen before you? Etolié supposed she understood.

With the mending of Flowridia's body, those scars returned. Chaos resumed her still stance above her. Etolié grimaced as she illusioned a set of shears and cut the baby's cord. "Let's get you warmed up, all right?"

The baby cried all the while.

"Etolié?"

Chaos' voice cut through even the baby's tears.

"I have a special task for you."

Through Ku'Shya's vast caverns, Sora sprinted.

Her heart beat to deafen her, terror rising as the walls shook, sending her stumbling—

But she did not fall.

The earthquake did not quell. Sora kept her hand to the wall, running on uneasy feet.

"We had a deal, Sora."

The voice emanated from all places.

Yet despite the ice in Ilune's voice, that was not what made Sora's blood run cold.

From the very air, a tear appeared. Not controlled as she'd seen from sorcerers in the past, but jagged, uneven. Hardly a line, but Sora watched it expand from floor to ceiling, where it split through the rock.

"Sora!"

Sora kept her pace, yet when she turned, there appeared Ilune. She flew on vast wings, Silver Fire propelling her forward from her feet.

Another rip appeared in the world of Sha'Demoni, this time in Sora's path. She dodged. If she could reach the portal from *Daemenacht*, she could escape.

Ilune slammed the ground with her landing, blockading her path. "Give me Leelan."

Sora held Leelan protectively to her chest. "We had a deal, but neither of us knew the full story."

Sora stumbled back as jagged bones burst from the ground, nearly impaling her feet.

"The world is unstable. That's what those rips are," Ilune said. "You're running out of time."

"All the more reason to let Ku'Shya stay and help if she's able."

Ilune marched forward. "If you want any hope of escaping, you'll have to give me Leelan."

Images of a ghost blockading her escape from a burning mansion prodded her memory. Sol Kareena was no longer here. Leelan could no longer protect her. Sora let power surge through her anyway. Holy light burst through the pores of her skin, illuminating her like the angel before her. When Ilune grabbed her shoulder, the god gasped and recoiled, slight sizzling rising from her fingers.

Sora wasted no time and surged forward, letting that light shine through. *"Sora—!"*

Sora stumbled at the sudden shaking of the earth. Another earthquake, surely, but it did not cease, instead growing rhythmic—and louder.

"Sora, get out of the way!"

Despite the stakes, the sheer terror in Ilune's voice compelled Sora to obey. She pressed herself into an inlet in the wall—just in time for Goddess Ku'Shya to bombard down the worn path. Demonic words were unleashed in a tirade. When Sora peeked from her alcove, the Goddess of War held Ilune by the wings and bashed her against the wall.

Guilt panged in her stomach. She wanted Ilune gone but not dead. When Ku'Shya sprinted down the hall, Sora mustered her courage and followed, her holy glow fading. Of course the monstrous deity outpaced her, though the earth never ceased to rumble.

Sora reached the throne room, startled by the massive influx of demons into Ku'Shya's burrow. She was ignored, though she froze a moment in shock. Sora steadied herself, recalling training of decades ago, and darted through the crowd of panicked demons, nigh invisible as she flowed through the crowd like water, dodging limbs and bodies.

When she reached the exit, a massive *crack* deafened Sora. Horror filled her as the canyon wall ahead shifted then split in twain. Panic filled the crowd as the crack spread downward. Sora could spare it no mind, darting up the path despite the destruction around her.

The sky appeared, and Sora faltered.

Great rips cut through the purple sky, blasting the air with a silvery flame. A massive bellow sounded above—Ku'Shya, surely. Sora found her bearings as more demons ran past her, into Ku'Shya's cave. The portal was close, so close. If she could only reach—

The earth split anew, this time beneath her feet. Sora screamed as she fell, gripping the edge of the walls with one hand. The precipice did not end, leading only to darkness. Sora's fingers threatened to buckle as she tried to shift Leelan onto her back, lest she fall.

But she was not the only one to fall. A few unfortunate demons shrieked as they dropped into the ravine.

Gargantuan arachnid legs shook the earth as Ku'Shya appeared, plunging three of her massive arms into the ravine to catch those unfortunate souls. The earth shook. Sora's grip failed. She caught air—only to grab Ku'Shya's wrist as she lifted her citizens from the fall.

The Goddess of War did not stop her, simply hurried to drop them to the side before roaring into the sky. In one closed fist, Sora spotted gold and silver light.

When Ku'Shya skittered straight up the cliff walls, Sora resumed her steps. The portal was near, but Ilune was in dire straits.

However, callous as it was, Ilune couldn't be killed—not unless they were all killed when Sha'Demoni and Celestière were destroyed.

Sora narrowly dodged when one such split in the sky tore open mere steps from her path. She dropped to the ground before Silver Fire could consume her—for that was surely what it was. How, was the question, but Sora needed to survive to know the answer.

Once out of the canyon, another split tore the earth in twain. Sora stumbled, lest she tumble in, narrowly skidding to a stop. Ku'Shya cried in frustration as she tossed the limp Ilune far away, then *plunged her four hands into the hard ground,* seeking to stop the parting earth.

Whether through might or magic, Sora didn't know. But it somehow worked, the crack ceasing when it came between her arms.

Another tear split the air, a rush of fire bursting across Ku'Shya's body. The demon did not move. When the fire faded, her exoskeletal figure sizzled. Ku'Shya remained alert as she withdrew her great fists, barking commands as more demons sought sanctuary in her domain. Still, fire blasted the world of Sha'Demoni, tearing it slowly into pieces.

One such tear shredded the sky near her cave.

Sora stared stunned as Ku'Shya leapt toward the outpouring of flame, protecting the cave's entrance with her very body.

Sora gasped as *something* sharp grabbed her boots, horrified to see bones rising from the earth. Holy light burst from her skin, shattering the bones, but when she whirled around, there stood Ilune, battered and bruised, wings crumpled and crushed, but very much standing. "Where were we?" Ilune said, her pleasantries strained.

She stood between Sora and the portal, a mere sprint away. Sora hardly felt her own limbs, had to look to verify Leelan was still in her hand. "You could be helping save these people. You have the power."

"Give me the bird, and I'll consider it."

"Save these people, and I'll give you the bird."

"Dammit, Sora. You can't keep changing—"

Ilune's voice faded as the ground beneath Sora's feet disappeared. She dropped like a stone—then floated in space.

Like sinking in still waters, Sora drifted back, staring at Ilune's horrified countenance through the rip. But surrounding her was a sea of stars, the space between the worlds holding her hostage. When Sora reached forward, Ilune reached back.

Yet Sora fell faster, the world solidifying as her back struck something soft. White mist caressed her, coiling around her body like shackles. She winced as she sat up, the innate knowledge of her location bringing questions—the mists of Celestière.

She scrambled into standing, breathing hurried as she ascertained her surroundings: white fog as far as the eye could see, blinding and nigh corporeal.

The worlds were shredding at their cores, her plummet into this new world confirming that.

In the distance, like a monster rising from the depths, Ilune appeared from the mist. "What an unpleasant fall," Ilune spat. "Now you definitely need my help getting home. So hand me the bird, or—"

Sora bolted away.

The worlds might end, or they might not. Sora was trusting fate to give her that future with Dira. She just had to distract Ilune a few minutes more.

The ground rumbled. Bursting like a tidal wave, a wall of bones blockaded her path.

A voice echoed: *"Do you know what truly lies in the mists, Sora?"*

Sora made a rapid turn, only for another eruption of bones to stop her.

"Do you know how many angels died in the Convergence, never given their final rest?"

Sora gasped when her feet sank. She yanked one out, only to watch in horror as skeletal hands clawed up her leg.

Instinct rose; Sora willed her magic to burst. A shield of holy light consumed her, burning the bones where they touched. "I won't stop you from killing Ku'Shya when the battle is over!"

That sensuous laughter merely filled her with dread now. *"I can't defeat Ku'Shya in a fair fight. Otherwise, she'd have been dead long ago."*

Sora caught a glimpse of gold and silver light and resumed running. When a wall of bones sought to stop her, she covered her eyes and ran straight through. The crunching of bones assaulted her ears, but she burned through, freed for the moment.

Eerie silence settled as Sora bolted into the unknown—only to scream as a burst of bones beneath her feet rapidly consumed her, her magic destroying them just as quickly as more appeared.

Beneath her feet, the bones shifted like swarming insects. Mostly shards, but some recognizable pieces—femurs and parts of skulls. It brought her higher and higher, her cage a tornado of bones. Sora fought to no avail. For all her holy might, Ilune remained a god.

The God of Death floated to match her. Close now, clearly her jaw was broken, her collar bone sat wrong, her spine was not quite straight. Yet her easy smile remained. "Give me the bird."

Sora pressed Leelan to her chest.

Ilune sighed and reached a leisurely hand toward Sora's face, cupping it softly. Sora gasped at the sudden flow of dark magic within her. Her mind was hers, but her body was not, her very bones moving against her will. Her arms moved on their own accord, parting through the torrent of bones like water, reaching for Ilune.

Sora shut her eyes, focusing first on fighting, then touching upon Leelan, time stilling as she swore she finally felt . . . *something.*

Their bond was strong. Perhaps not so strong as a witch would have, but Sora loved Leelan, loved his chirps and his cheeriness, his death a torment she had shoved off feeling for weeks.

But Leelan was not dead. For the first time, she felt his spirit, which burst with life.

"When the time comes, you'll know what to do."

There was one final path to giving Leelan new life. She could give Leelan her own.

With a burst of strength beyond any mortal capability, Sora wrenched her arm back, cutting through Ilune's magic. Compelled by an instinct beyond reason and thought, Sora shoved Leelan into her mouth—and choked.

CHAPTER 40

"Flowridia, awaken—"

When Flowridia awoke, her mind remained groggy, suspended in her dreams.

But it had not been a dream, for though a lifetime had passed in her blink, she matched gazes with the monstrous Goddess of Chaos.

Flowridia gasped. Her head spun, mind reeling yet sharp as she stumbled and fell. Where she landed, it did not ache, but tears burst from her eyes, cries wracking her body.

A presence fell beside her. Flowridia pulled her daughter into an embrace, gripping with all her strength. "I'm sorry. I'm so sorry, Dira."

Dira . . . So beloved a name. It fell perfectly from her tongue.

Tearful words whispered in her ear. "There is nothing to be sorry for."

"I'm sorry for all you must go through."

Truly her heart shattered, to consider that a childhood filled with love must end with pain, so much pain . . .

But oh, amid her sorrow was pride. For Dira, for Demitri . . . and for Ayla, who would love a daughter more than she loved herself, more than she loved Flowridia, more than she had loved any other. A love imperfect and shadowed by shame, but no less true.

"So come back," whispered that tender voice. "Come back and change my future. Change Ayla's."

Flowridia sobbed, remiss to part from the embrace. Instead, she brought her hand to the whole half of Dira's face, enamored by the familiarity she found. "You saw my life. You know all that I've done. Your faith in me is sweet, but I fear I'll fail you both."

Dira sweetly shook her head, bringing her hand to cover Flowridia's. "My mother loved you. And you loved her. That's good enough faith for me."

And Dira had loved Ayla more than any other. Such bittersweetness in the thought, but now was not the time for sorrow. Her hand dropped. Her embrace grew limp. "And if I do go home, what then? We are a broken family."

So much expression in that living half; such sorrow in that silver eye. "Broken, perhaps. But if the individual pieces can be whole again, that's all that matters to me. I know that Mother—that Ayla—was haunted by shame, both for who she had been and for who she became to protect me. And in Onias' Realm, I witnessed shame creeping back far earlier than even the crimes of The Endless Night. Shame from abuse she never fully healed from. And what was I but a torchbearer for that shame? I spent my days haunted by the crime of her death. I want healing. I want that cycle of shame to end. But more than anything, I want her to be all right."

"She loved you, Dira."

"I don't ever doubt that."

"But she never did love herself, did she?" Flowridia's tears flowed softer now, the storm having quelled. Still, that deep agony remained. "She built walls around her true self, lest you see it. That was not your fault. You sweet child, born into war—none of it was your fault."

When mist filled that silver eye, Flowridia knew she'd spoken right. "Perhaps you are right," Dira said.

"There is no 'perhaps.' You were handed a destiny too cruel for any person to fulfill, much less a child. Of course you're haunted. And I . . ." The weight of the words had never felt more poignant—or light. "I will come home. Ayla died to try and spare you that destiny. I will live to make it so. I swear upon every grave I've dug that this is the end. There will be no need for Old Gods anymore." Gods, it hurt, but there was more to say. Flowridia choked back a sob. "All Ayla ever wanted was to be free. Whatever that means, I swear to make it so."

Even if it meant letting her go.

Dira took Flowridia's hand in her two, covered by both flesh and bone. "Pledge to me. Then I can raise you as one of my priestesses."

The thought made her pause. "But what about—"

Demitri. Flowridia's gut clenched. "Where is Demitri? Was he with you as a Goddess?"

"You haven't figured it out?" Dira brought Flowridia's hand up anew, this time setting it upon the skull half of her face. "Mom, don't be stupid."

For all the love she harbored for the little girl who would become God, Flowridia's heart leapt. "You . . . You?!" With joy surged both laughter and tears. When Chaos hugged her this time, it was different than the embrace with her daughter, the touch tighter, familiar. "Dearest Demitri, I . . ."

She wept in Demitri's embrace, her soul nearly whole. He was not hers, but he was here. "So the dog was . . . ?"

"Obviously me. I'm gonna be honest—Dira and I have talked about it, and we've decided we're done. I would like to be your familiar instead."

Flowridia laughed. "What?"

"Dira will be your patron. And I'll get to be your familiar. At least, the younger me can."

Flowridia smiled amid her tears, uncertain of what to make of this sacrifice. "Is Dira certain?"

"Dira says it isn't right to keep you away from me if you're around. And, well, I miss you, Mom. I mean, it won't be *me*, but it'll be me. I think that's all right. Dira's soul and mine were friends, but we never became one. Not like you and me. I think it's because I was already yours."

Such a poignant phrase from her sardonic little boy, but it had only been a year since she had seen him. Thousands upon thousands of years had passed since Demitri had seen her. She clung tighter to him, making no move to part. For the bittersweet truth remained—that this would not be the Demitri she reunited with. It did not negate the precious worth of her mindless wolf in the mortal realm, but her heart ached for Demitri, whose fate was greater than she ever could have envisioned, for her daughter whose fate was to be a Goddess, for the horror such a union of souls brought to those who consumed their familiars . . .

Neither had asked for this. Neither deserved that burden.

When they parted, tears seeped from her child's silver eye. "I didn't know how to cry when I was a wolf."

Flowridia leaned close and kissed his skeletal half above his hollow cheek. "I've missed you so much, Demitri. And I'm so proud—of you and Dira both."

"Can you be a little prouder of me than Dira, though?"

Flowridia laughed, for it was so much like her rude, baby Demitri. "I'm not picking favorites."

"Fine. But Dira's done with the ritual, so as soon as you're ready to pledge, you can come home."

"Ritual?"

"She cut out your heart. It's in a box."

Somehow, that wasn't the most invasive thing to happen to her body today. Flowridia took Chaos' hands, one whole and one a skeletal paw. "I pledge to you, my Demitri and my Dira—my power and my whole heart."

"Close your eyes."

Flowridia did.

She awoke into a world of chaos.

Flowridia gasped for air—yet the sensation was hollow, instinct rather than need.

Her sight blurred, but gentle words coaxed her into the light. "Just focus. Your perilous journey has ended."

Yet it was not the sweetness of that voice that forced her mind to settle. It was the distant cry of a baby, growing louder with each blink, each breath. Her yearning heart sought to soothe it.

Chaos' face steadily swirled into view. Her beautiful smile was all Flowridia had seen in her vision. When Chaos took her hand, Flowridia gripped it with all her might, weak as it was today. "Welcome home."

Flowridia sat up with Chaos' aid, slowly gaining awareness of her surroundings. The stench of blood assaulted her. Her clothing was drenched in it, shredded from hip to collar, revealing her plethora of scars.

She hardly had time to collect herself when a small figure bombarded her. Of course it was Ayla, yet her body was lukewarm instead of a familiar chill.

Still, Ayla's tear-stained face soon came into view, her sobs bearing hope instead of heartbreak. Enraptured, Flowridia kissed her like the world might end, brewing old, nostalgic feelings of joy, of trust, of simpler times when the world was theirs . . .

A baby's cry rattled that world.

Flowridia reeled back, keeping a grip on Ayla's waist even as her eyes fell upon . . . Her.

Crying upon the bed lay the loveliest creature to grace the realms, the very center of the world. When Flowridia beckoned, Chaos presented an infant wrapped in a pillowcase. Oh gods, she was so small, and Flowridia trembled as she accepted the baby into her arms, barely the length of her forearm.

Tears stung her eyes. She pressed the infant against her bare chest, against scars, against a heart unworthy of this bombardment of love. Immediately, the baby quieted, reaching on instinct toward her breast. When Flowridia directed her, she latched, revealing the barest glimpse of tiny, sharp fangs. Flowridia winced at the sudden sting, then gave the faintest gasp at the prickling sensation flowing through her breast. A droplet of red stained the baby's lip; it was not traditional nourishment she sought, but blood.

Never had a more beautiful creature entered the realm. This baby with her tufts of black hair, her eyes grey, but Flowridia knew they would shine like silver someday. Beneath the gore, she held a reddish hue, and precious above all were those tiny ears, rounded yet bearing a point.

The baby stared into her eyes, studying her, *recognizing* her. To think this child knew her, loved her, felt safe in her arms . . . "Hello, Dira," Flowridia whispered, the name causing the first of her tears to fall.

Oh, this sensation of peace was unlike any other. Flowridia basked in it, willing the world to go away . . .

Until a distant *boom* shook her to her core.

Flowridia shielded Dira on instinct, relieved when she remained peaceful against her chest. Her gaze fell to the window, to the storm of lights and fire beyond.

"Flowridia."

Her attention fell to Chaos, whose calm demeanor held edges now. Ayla had scooted just out of reach, looking a little lost. "Time is short," Chaos said, "as you would likely guess. The end of the world is nigh. I pray it is not too late. But there is something that must first be done." She presented a jeweled box Flowridia recognized: the one that had held Izthuni's knife.

Flowridia seethed at the idea, willing to die rather than disturb her feeding child. "Will we have time?"

"It's not what you think." Chaos opened the lid. Within the silken cushion of the box lay a bloody, beating heart.

Flowridia looked to her own chest to scars far too fresh, to the infant pressed against them, as the truth struck her like a blade. "You really did cut out my heart. I'm already dead."

Chaos nodded. "You're a lich."

Despite the vast array of logistical questions, Flowridia's mind dwelled in one place only. "Then how am I feeding her?"

"You're freshly dead, for one thing. You would have blood either way. But liches are capable of some biological function, like eating and intimacy. Your body just needs some incentive to start— like the cry of your child, in this case."

Flowridia realized only then that she had never flinched to hold her precious girl. She spared a glance for her hand. Though gruesome and maimed, it no longer ached.

"Liches bear the scars of life but without their agony," Chaos continued. "That aside, there is one more matter to sort before I go. I expect—" A knock interrupted her, but Chaos smiled. "Right on schedule." Louder, she said, "Come in."

The door opened, and in peeked Etolié. "Well, you're looking better, Flowers." Etolié's words were cut off by her own small gasp. "She's just so teeny tiny," she muttered, her face akin to someone seeing a kitten.

"Etolié," Chaos said, "did you bring him?"

"Oh, sorry." Etolié pushed the door all the way, revealing Demitri on what must've been an illusioned leash. "One wolf, as requested."

Chaos beckoned, then turned to Flowridia. "All you need to do is touch him."

Realization flooded her. Flowridia bit back a sob, reaching as well as she could without disturbing the infant at her breast. Etolié escorted Demitri forward, the wolf's gaze vacant and bored until it fell upon Flowridia. Her heart soared as that golden eye gained light, recognition in his expanding pupil. He came forward as though in a trance, his nose touching her outstretched hand—

Flowridia gasped at the sudden flooding of awareness, the sensation akin to that child in the woods all those years ago, accepting a baby wolf from a demon. The world gained color, gained sensation and sound, and Flowridia felt light at the influx of energy, of power, of *life* . . .

Yet nothing compared to the small voice in her head. *Mom?*

Flowridia screamed, her joy matchless as Demitri came down to her level, uncaring of the blood around her as he licked a sticky line across her face. She hugged him with one arm, weeping into his thick fur, and prayed this dream never ended.

But dreams never so perfectly recreated his animal scent; they never quite captured his childish voice. Demitri was no dream.

Mom, did you make that baby?!

Flowridia laughed, grinning as she presented the infant at her breast. "I did."

Smells a little dead. You smell actually— Oh, no. I smell dead.

"Demitri—"

We're all dead. Are we icky like Casvir?

"Only a little bit," Flowridia said, offering a teasing wink.

Gross. But can I touch the baby?

Flowridia beckoned him closer, charmed as he pressed his nose against Dira's hair. "Her name is Kedira, or 'Dira' for short."

It's cute in a wrinkly way.

Flowridia chuckled as she kissed his nose, surreal at the surge of normalcy. Had her heart ever been so full?

"Flowridia . . ."

Flowridia turned at the voice, thrust unwillingly into the present once more.

Chaos offered a bittersweet smile. "I have to go. But I won't forget your promise."

Flowridia released Demitri and reached for her, coaxing Chaos close. She set a kiss upon her brow, aching at this sudden finality. For this was her child too. A different life but a child of her blood, a child who had never known her. Now, she knew why.

But that would not be this young Dira's fate, nor Demitri's. "I love you."

Chaos smiled with all the mischief and beauty of her dark mother. To Flowridia's surprise, that same mother spoke up.

"What can we do to help?" Ayla's voice held the roughness of tears.

Chaos said, "Difficult to say. But I must fight Soliel and pray it is not too late to reverse the spell."

"Then I will go with you," Ayla replied, though Flowridia's fear brewed at the statement. "Time is of the essence, and I make a spectacular distraction."

"You don't have to do that."

Depthless weight filled Ayla's words, her gaze bearing not love—not quite—but curiosity. "You risked so much for me. I will do as much for you."

Chaos nodded as she rose. "Then I accept. Etolié, are you able to stay and protect Flowridia?"

Etolié made moon eyes at the baby. "I will gladly stay with this small bean."

Ayla rose, but Flowridia reached for her, forlorn when her wife pretended not to see. "Ayla."

At her name, Ayla looked to her hand, followed the line of her arm to her gaze, then gave a somber smile. "There is no one better suited to protect the baby than you, sweet Flowra. So let me do my part and make certain there's a world for you to raise her in."

Flowridia's lip trembled, burdened by visions of a future she could not yet speak of. Perhaps there would be a time to tell Ayla that truth—that in that other life, she loved Dira more than her own self. For now, there was a world to save. "Go. I love you, Ayla."

Ayla's smile flickered with life; her sights set upon baby Dira for the first time in Flowridia's memory. She knelt by their side, first offering a stroke to Demitri's soft neck. "It's wonderful to have you back."

I'm confused by at least seven things, but tell Lady Ayla that I love her too.

"Demitri loves you," Flowridia whispered, breath hitching when Ayla cupped her cheek.

Ayla set a kiss upon her lips, bearing all the softness of those early years together. When they parted, Ayla stilled to face tiny Dira, who released Flowridia's breast to follow with her eyes. Once again, Ayla seemed lost, all confidence fading as she forced a smile. "No time to waste."

When they left through the window, the very air thinned around her. Her lip quivered as she set Dira back to her breast, prepared for the sting.

"Is it weird if I get close right now?"

Flowridia grinned through her tears, grateful for the brevity of Etolié. "Not weird at all."

"I promise I don't care about your tits." Etolié's hands flapped like hummingbird wings as she knelt, her squeal small but enthused. "That is the smallest baby I've ever seen."

Flowridia managed to chuckle. "You can hold her when she's done if you want."

"Yes, please. But first . . ." Etolié turned to Demitri, immediately grabbing his wolfish face and kissing him on the snout. "I've missed you so fucking much, baby boy."

Tell Etolié she's still my favorite.

Flowridia rolled her eyes. "Demitri says you're his favorite."

"Oh, I knew that."

Flowridia stroked Dira's sweet face as she continued feeding, bemused by the drying gore in her hair. "The portal to Solvira is still open. Do you think it would be safer there?"

"Bold of you to assume I have any answers."

"Well, we should get Dira cleaned up first." Flowridia stopped, for with this quiet moment came an influx of memories. "Etolié, Murishani is behind the assassinations."

"Oh. That's the least twisty ending— Wait, how do you know?"

Cold washed over Flowridia. Her embrace on Dira tightened. "He's the one who killed me. If he comes back . . ." What a strange thing, to recall so gently the nature of her returned magic. Flowridia removed one hand from Dira's little body, staring as she breathed out a hint of purple smoke. That same smoke seeped from her fingers, coating her hand like fire.

Her lip curled in a sneer. Vehement, she whispered, "If he comes back, I will eat him."

"Damn, Flowers. You got scary there."

Flowridia closed her fist, snuffing the magic with it. No sense in risking Dira. "I feel I may be more capable than I've ever been before."

There came one final memory. Flowridia lurched. "Oh gods. Etolié, I think I know where the phylactery is."

"Well, shit. Don't stop talking."

"You said Ilune's was in your mom's closet. From what we know of Casvir, wouldn't it be somewhere equally benign? Somewhere no one would ever guess, except those who know him best?"

"As the one who knows him best, what are you getting at?"

With all the caution she could muster, Flowridia rose, astounded by the absence of pain or even lightheadedness. "He's on the battlefield still, right?"

"Yes."

"It's in his office. Let's go."

Though still covered in her own spilled blood, Flowridia quickly changed clothing, managing to find a shirt to both accommodate Dira and mostly preserve her modesty. Time was short, but together she and Etolié cleaned Dira as well as they could, then swaddled her in a small blanket. Dira watched the world with curious eyes, good-natured so long as she was pressed against Flowridia's skin.

"All right, sweet thing," Flowridia whispered. "You're nice and clean."

Etolié wrung her hands. "She's so cute, but I'm about to die of anxiety, so we should really get going."

Damn the world. All Flowridia craved was a quiet space with precious Dira, to kiss her sweet head, to count each eyelash and hold those little fingers between her own.

But with the death of Casvir came freedom. It meant Dira was bound to no one.

New resolve filled her. Dira gazed behind long lashes, her innocence bringing the resolve to act. "To his office."

As fast as she could bear, lest she harm vulnerable Dira, she, Etolié, and Demitri traversed the vacant hallways, the eerie silence interspersed by rumbling far away. Like thunder, except it shook the whole earth, and any glimpse Flowridia caught of the sky filled her with fear.

What if Chaos failed in this life? Saved her future self from this fate, only to damn the worlds instead?

When they reached Casvir's office, Etolié twisted the locked doorknob. It clicked at her magical touch.

Never had she entered this space without Casvir present. A strange sensation of violation washed over her, like stepping into a temple to a god she blasphemed.

But they had no time to waste. "Check the locked drawers in his desk," Flowridia said, then sat and meditated upon the ground, willing her senses to expand . . .

Oh, how glorious, to feel the magical tapestry of the world once more. Beyond, that energy screamed, slowly ripping down its seams. But here in this quiet space, Flowridia felt nothing amiss, only minor spells to hold locks together, to keep the inkwell eternally filled . . .

Save for one space in the wall, where she felt nothing at all.

Suspicious, Flowridia rose and inspected the errant brick. "Etolié, may I have a knife?"

Without even turning, Etolié snapped. A knife appeared in Flowridia's hands. She tapped its blade against the edge. "Can you hold Dira for a moment?"

Quick as a wink, Etolié was at her side with waiting arms, eyes widening as Flowridia carefully set the swaddled newborn into her arms. "I get to be her auntie, right?"

With her baby out of the knife's reach, Flowridia began carving around the brick, finding the mortar oddly loose. "Sure, Etolié."

"I'm gonna think of all the stupidest names for you," Flowridia overheard. "Look at you—no thoughts at all behind those baby eyes."

Flowridia rolled her eyes. The brick loosened. She gripped it with her fingernails and pulled, easing it from its space, and found a hollow alcove.

"Well, fuck me. Flowers, you might be onto something."

Flowridia slipped the knife in, coaxing out what she realized was the leg of a metal box. Close enough, she reached inside and managed to slip it out the rest of the way.

A metallic box of no grandeur. No magical lock, but a practical one. "Etolié, can you—?"

Etolié touched it. The lock popped.

Flowridia opened the lid, gasping at the horror she saw.

For there, within a maldectine encrusted box, was a blackened, leathery, shriveled heart beating as a rhythmic drum.

"By Morathma's Whore Mother, you fucking did it."

Flowridia struggled to breathe.

"Stab the fucker, Flowers. Let's end this."

Flowridia gripped the knife with white knuckles, tears welling unbidden in her eyes. For this was the heart of Casvir, her friend, the one who had believed in her in all her lowest moments. This was Casvir, the tyrant who would destroy infinite worlds in every cycle, who became the god he always aspired to be. Casvir, to whom she had sold a baby to save a friend, who had granted her magic beyond comprehension, who had taken everything from her yet given her so much more. Casvir, who cared for her, who mentored her, who loved her in his quiet sort of way.

Behind her eyelids, Flowridia saw the silhouette of a demon in the woods offering a baby Demitri. She saw his figure illuminated by firelight, listening to her heartbreak. She heard his prophetic words: *"Damn yourself. Have no regrets."*

"Flowers, there's a time and place for hesitation, but it's not when the worlds are about to be literally torn apart."

Flowridia's jaw trembled, Etolié's words pulling her from memories. Behind misty eyes, the desiccated heart endlessly beat. Casvir did not know his crimes in the future. Casvir wouldn't know why she had betrayed him.

Would he know it was her? Or would he simply die and never know the cause? After all he had done for her, she would turn around and betray him.

"Flowers, I know you care about him. But this isn't about you. It doesn't even have to be about the greater good."

After all he had given her, she would use it to destroy his legacy foretold.

"This is about Dira."

Love would be his downfall. Flowridia looked at her sweet Dira, watching the world through innocent eyes.

She lifted the heart from its anti-magical chamber, letting the metal clatter to the carpeted ground. "You deserve this too. Which would you like to hold, Etolié? The knife or the heart?"

"Oh, fuck yes. I'll take the knife."

Flowridia offered the illusioned knife to an empress of stolen lands, to the woman who loved a monster held in eternal slavery by the necromancer tyrant. She held the heart in her cupped hands and shut her eyes.

In darkness, she saw her friend in the woods.

"Do it."

Flowridia forced herself to watch as Etolié stabbed the center of the heart and twisted.

CHAPTER 41

No grand explosion; no screams to welcome the end of the world; nothing but a whimper.

At the twist of the knife, the heart ceased its beating. Nothing more.

The knife flickered from view, the illusion fading. Flowridia stared, tears falling as she brought the heart to her chest, cupping it protectively as finality settled.

Kind of lackluster, don't you think?

Flowridia smiled at Demitri, grateful for his levity.

Is Casvir dead now?

A good question. Flowridia knelt to grab the box, a coffin now as she set the stagnant heart inside and shut the lid. "I don't think he would just collapse dead. But he's vulnerable."

So if Soliel cuts him in half again, he'll actually stay gone?

Flowridia nodded.

Guess we have to let him know.

"Would they know he's vulnerable?"

Etolié shrugged. "This is all very new to me, Flowers."

"Someone has to tell them. They're all on the battlefield, and Soliel and Chaos are wasting time fighting each other when Casvir is right there." Frantic, she withdrew the mirror from her pocket, salvaged from her bloodied dress, and tapped on the glass . . . Yet nothing changed. In fact, she felt no connection at all.

Flowridia's gaze fell back to Dira, watching with those grey eyes from Etolié's arms. Sorrow filled her, along with conviction. "It has to be me. I have to warn them."

"Flowers, I think you have solid immunity to get out of any task you want for the next eighteen years."

"You almost got yourself killed, but I have my magic again. I can protect myself from the undead." When she beckoned, Etolié set Dira back into her arms. The world became right again, watching her peaceful infant explore the world through sight and touch.

Flowridia held her upright against her chest, able to kiss her sweet infant's head. "For Dira. I have to do this. Etolié, you'll watch her right?"

"I will literally die before anything comes between me and her, don't you fucking worry."

Reluctant to part, Flowridia stole what little time she could justify, turning to Demitri instead. "Will you stay and watch Dira?"

Her dearest Demitri; wolves couldn't emote the way dogs could, but a wash of sadness overcame her. *I'm dead now, so they can't hurt me.*

"Demitri—"

I don't want to leave you. Please, Mom?

Flowridia kissed his nose, soul soaring at the familiarity of it. Each second together healed her wounded heart. "Yes. But if you're lost again, I'll replace you. This time, with a bigger wolf."

There's no such thing.

"Do you really want to take that chance?"

Demitri couldn't glare, but he could certainly make imposing eye contact. *I guess I just won't die then.*

Despite the petulant words, Flowridia was far more focused on that missing eye, bits of shattered bone exposed. She touched it curiously, her grasp on her own powers tentative but strong, and when she coaxed, the dead bones on Demitri's face knitted together, restored through dark powers as skin and fur grew to cover it. Finally, his eye reformed. She beheld beautiful golden symmetry.

A Chaos Deity, he would never be.

Oh. Everything isn't so flat now. Thanks, Mom.

"Demitri will be coming with me," Flowridia clarified to the watching Etolié. It cut like a knife, but she set Dira back into Etolié's embrace, breath hitching to hear the first of Dira's confused cries. She forced herself to step away, aching when Dira's cries only escalated. "I promise to not be gone any longer than I have to."

"She'll be fine," Etolié said, and Flowridia found it so strange to trust the Celestial once again. "Go save the world."

Flowridia steeled her heart against the baby's cries and ran.

Demitri followed. *You're silly. Just ride me.*

That was an option, wasn't it? When Demitri crouched, she climbed atop his back like old times and gripped his fur.

I don't actually know where we're going. Or what's going on. Can you please explain?

"We're going to the field beyond Haven," Flowridia said. "I'll explain on the way."

So much to condense in so little time. As they ran through the palace, Flowridia explained Ku'Shya's demonic army and the elves. As they ran through the frantic streets of Haven, she spoke of Casvir upon the battlefield, of Order and Chaos, of Dira and her origins, of

Ayla's part to play. She kept her head ducked, gripping tight as he bolted, the crowd parting for his imposing presence.

That's a lot, Mom.

"I know. But it might be over soon."

They rushed through open gates and into pure pandemonium.

Demitri slowed at the distant clash of demons and dead. Beyond, the gargantuan figures of Soliel and Chaos were a silhouette upon the horizon—but it was not a rising sun, no.

The spell. The orbs. Time was running out.

"Demitri, I need you to wait here," Flowridia said. "Wait at the gates."

But you said—

"I know. I'm not worried about them hurting you. I'm worried about accidentally hurting you myself." She dismounted, stumbling onto uneven terrain, stampeded by nigh infinite undead feet. "Stay by the gate. I love you."

I love you too, Mom.

Flowridia surveyed the scene, the dying flora, the strewn bodies of demons and dismembered undead scattered with increasing frequency. Soliel and Chaos didn't know of Casvir's weakness, too caught up in their own fighting.

She would have to get their attention.

With her exhale came a subtle mist of necrotic energy seeping from her hand, glowing purple through the pores of her skin. Gods, the rightness of feeling the caress of magic once more, what was lost, now found. She fought against euphoria. This was hardly the time to revel.

But as she stepped forward, studying the field of death and demons, an ocean might as well have separated her from her quarry. So thick was the army of the undead that already she caught the attention of those at the outskirts. A few mindless ghouls shambled forward, screeching in her direction.

With a wave of her hand, one toppled. Like thread, she spun the intricate tendrils of magic to her whim, seeking to infest its mind—

Only to flinch as she was cast out. Casvir's power vastly outmatched hers when she tried to seize control.

Fearless, she extended her other hand as another neared. Her instincts surged, but instead of darkness—light.

Burning flesh filled her senses as it shrieked. It collapsed, charred as though set ablaze and extinguished. She was not helpless; she was still a healer.

At her whim, that same power expanded within her, holy light glowing from within. Surely she shone as a star, a sun, but what could touch her now? Death danced at her fingertips, diverting any demon who neared, but her core was pure light.

She strode into the fray.

The dead shrieked as she parted a path through them, a rock breaking waves in the ocean. Any dead who came too near were cast aside by necromancy. The De'Sindai fled at her approach. Power radiated; she walked unharmed within this sea of death.

At her command, old bones rattled deep beneath the earth, churning soil as they rose to join her. They gathered as a whirlpool around her, further shielding her from the battlefield. Gods, it had been so long since she had *felt,* and what a joy it was, magic pulsing through her figure. Her focus fell to balancing the light and dark, her holy magic ravaging any flying gargoyles foolish enough to approach her. Necromancy was pure pleasure; the temperance of light kept her mind alert.

Passively, she sought Casvir, but the imperator must have been far away. Through the sea of demons and undeath, Flowridia swam—

Until a shadow appeared at the cusp of her whirlwind of bones, awestruck at the display. "Well, well," Ayla said, loud enough to cut through the carnage. "Aren't you brilliant, darling?" Flowridia retracted her power, causing the bones to collapse as Ayla neared. "What are you doing here?"

Oh, the gravitas of her wife. The urge to embrace Ayla sang louder than even the euphoria of magic. But Flowridia caught herself. Holy light would burn her. "We found the phylactery. Etolié and I stabbed it. But I have to tell Soliel and Chaos."

The grin across Ayla's face was a shadow of old times, predatory and wild. "Flowra, you are incredible. I can escort you."

Necrotic energy still swirled about Flowridia's hands, coating Ayla to the wrist when they clasped hands. Quiet joy filled her at the touch, and despite the chaos, despite the urgency and death, emotion threatened to unravel her at the gentle stroke of Ayla's thumb.

There was still love here. Always love.

With a mere thought, the bones resumed their storm, swirling around Flowridia and Ayla both. They ran, united at the end of the world.

They came upon a calamitous scene. Gods of Order and Chaos clashed as the titans they were. Vastly larger than Flowridia had ever seen, yet the duo moved without hindrance. Soliel stood as a beacon of light and stability, his golden armor reflecting the rainbow of lights above, enhanced by his inner glow. Each swing of his sword caused a gale, whipping up wind. He had long lost his helmet, revealing the exhaustion of a man mere steps from the finish line.

Swift as lightning, Chaos danced circles around him—and dance was indeed the word. Such grace in her savagery, each tilt of her knives. She dodged with precision, for this was a duet they had performed for eons. He swung; she dodged with the grace of the wind he created.

Neither struck. Too combustible, too refined, each masters of their individual styles. Near Soliel, the blinding light of the orbs had expanded to touch the earth, creating a void, but of light. Chaos sought to breach it, but Soliel stood as the insurmountable mountain defending it.

Flowridia hardly breathed to watch them, engrossed by their magnitude and shaken by the horrors around. But urgency struck when Ayla released her. Flowridia dissipated her shield of death, the clatter of bones a backdrop to her cry. *"Soliel! Chaos!"*

Of course they didn't hear her.

Once again, Flowridia's senses expanded, touching this time upon what lived. Though trampled, the prickly grass clung stubbornly to life.

Not for long. Flowridia cast a necrotic wave upon the plain, gasping at the sudden influx of energy inside her. Gods, it was glorious. Addictive. Dangerous . . .

Flowridia nearly collapsed at the release. The earth rumbled; perhaps from her power, perhaps from the apocalypse, who could say? At her will, the dead grass burst with false life, growing thick and lush beneath her. On instinct, she grabbed Ayla's dress, holding her for stability as they rose into the air like a tornado, carried higher by Flowridia's plants.

She let out a scream. No magic, simply pure sound.

Thank every god—Soliel looked her way.

"Listen!" she cried, and though the battle did not cease, Flowridia felt the shift in attention. "Casvir's phylactery is destroyed! Go kill him!"

In the pause before the storm, Ayla's hands fell upon her waist, providing the stability she craved. Soliel and Chaos shared a glance, the shift in their roles fascinating to see; from perfect foes to partners who had danced this violent death for thousands of years. In precise sync, they darted into the fray, toward the center of the undead horde.

Chaos' size decreased, becoming one with the flow of death as she vanished. Soliel remained a giant, cutting through the waves of death with his golden sword. Light radiated around him. Undead who lingered by his aura burned.

Flowridia watched them as she returned to the more stable earth, compelled foolishly to follow.

Chaos burst into view as a titan, expanding rapidly as she swept aside an entire legion of dead—including Casvir. Far surpassing the Bringer of War in height, perhaps rivaling Ku'Shya herself, Chaos' wicked smile twisted.

The undead horde climbed like ants up her figure, but her flame rose, causing them to drop off one by one. Within the expanse of fire, Chaos' figure shifted, growing hunched and bestial.

Her howl was inhuman. When she rejoined the fray, she bore animalistic fury, shrinking as she wielded both claws and knives.

Ayla reappeared. "We should help them."

Flowridia shook her head, forcing herself to voice her heartbreak. "You can. I won't stop you. But I don't have the heart to finish this."

Ayla released her and shot like an arrow back into the fray.

As though caught in a trance, Flowridia swam through the battlefield, steady as she approached the core of it. Occasionally, she gave an idle swipe of her hand, deterring undead who crawled too close, letting necrotic energy flow through her skin lest she be grabbed by any demons. Already the clash escalated, for Casvir swung his mace with fury, blocking each blow of Soliel's sword with his towershield, though he remained half his size. Waves of necrotic magic emanated from his figure, harmlessly fading to Soliel's light and Chaos' silver flame. Soliel and Chaos were a practiced harmony, the powers that prevented them from managing to harm the other now a brutal weapon combined. Casvir remained the discordant chord, refusing to bend though he gained no ground. The undead swarmed. They burned before they could touch Soliel, this beacon of holy light.

Casvir was not a god, not yet. The might of the Old Gods was swift and furious, their powers lesser without the orbs, but greater than the mere mortals around them by leagues. They came closer and closer, the undead storm steadily quelling . . .

Until Casvir withdrew a weapon Flowridia had seen gifted years ago—a maldectine dagger.

Chaos dove. He plunged it into her chest.

Flowridia screamed, pulled from her trance. She ran as the titan collapsed.

The battle seemed so far away, the violence naught but noise as Flowridia fell to her knees by Chaos' side, returned to her humanoid form. "Dira? Demitri? Please say something!"

Relief filled her when Chaos inhaled a pained breath, but when she went to remove the maldectine blade, the Goddess shook her head. "You cannot heal me."

No. She was a dhampir, harmed by both dark and light.

Tears stung Flowridia's eyes as she cupped Chaos' cheek, touching flesh and bone. "Mom," the Deity whispered, "I'm glad you're here."

When Chaos weakly lifted a bony paw, Flowridia held it in her hand. The world silenced. All that mattered was her dying Demitri and her dying daughter from another world. Gods, she'd barely known them. Now, she never would. "I love you, sweet ones."

"Flowra! Run!"

At Ayla's cry, Flowridia tore her focus away—only to freeze as the battle neared. Soliel and Casvir clashed like battering rams. Ayla darted in and out, dodging their magics and weapons with grace.

The world stilled as Casvir's mace swung near, too near, yet not deliberate enough to be on purpose. Some voice inside her said she was safe, that her heart was in a box far away, but who did not know that?

Casvir, whose red eyes burned beneath his helmet and stared as deep as her soul.

So engrossed, she was, she did not see Soliel's blade swing level to her neck, coming near enough to feel it in the breeze—not until Casvir dropped his mace and rammed his shield against the approaching blade with all his strength, a wall between her and sure decapitation.

Nothing stopped Ayla's dagger from impaling Casvir in the neck. Not a fatal blow for the necromancer king, but in the moment of distraction, Soliel kicked him in the armored chest, sending Casvir stumbling—

And cut straight across his torso.

Not a clean severance, but Casvir fell in pieces barely attached, spine shattered, organs spilling out.

Shock kept Flowridia stagnant, until a faint groan pulled her back. She held that precious paw tight, praying it brought comfort in their final moments. Soliel soon fell at Chaos' side, joined by Ayla who cradled her head. Already Chaos lay motionless.

Utmost tenderness directed Soliel's hand, so contrary to their battle moments ago. He stroked bloodied locs from her face. Chaos barely shifted into the touch.

Soliel whispered, "It's over, Dira. We've done it."

In Chaos' faint smile showed sharp fangs.

She did not move again.

Stunned, Flowridia struggled with tears, even as Ayla's began to flow. Flowridia set a kiss upon the fallen Deity's brow, at the juncture of flesh and bone, lingering as her hair fell across Chaos' face. Her wife trembled as she grabbed Chaos' limp hand.

A distant cough startled them all. Nearby, Casvir languished all alone.

Soliel and Flowridia both rose, but Flowridia held out a hand. "Let me," she whispered, and she ran, urgency rising with finality.

Oh, he was a gruesome sight, organs and black ichor spilling from a split torso, his spine cut clean through. Red eyes shone within his helmet, and when Flowridia knelt beside him, she met no resistance as she removed it.

That same ichor dribbled from his mouth, staining his chin. The wind stirred, sending a chill across her skin, but to her surprise, his gaze softened. When she took his hand, he tightened his grip, though weakly.

Flowridia's vision misted. "Casvir, I'm sorry. I know you don't . . ."

Her words faded at his, "Shh . . ." He coughed, sending flecks of ichor into the air. "Death's door is not the time for grudges."

Always practical, even in the end. Her first tear fell as she nodded.

"Was it you?" he asked, his voice hollow, airy.

"Yes." She gave no apology, already reprimanded once. But she was sorry, if she was being honest. Regretful, not for killing him, but that it had to be done at all. More so to know . . . he *knew*.

And he had saved her anyway.

To her surprise, he offered a dusty smile. Exhaustion shone in his dimming eyes. "How ironic."

Despite herself, she returned the smile. "Why ironic?"

"I decided centuries ago that I would never sire an heir because any child of mine would have the potential to usurp me. Ironic, because you became a daughter to me."

Flowridia knew not whether to laugh or sob. She squeezed his hand, realizing he no longer felt so cold. "I love you, too."

He brought up his other hand, weakly offering some odd object—a few dried leaves, crumpled and torn. All but one blew away in the breeze. He gripped it between his fingers. "I must leaf you now."

She did laugh this time; through tears, she laughed as she took the offering, graced to hear a small chuckle from his lips.

The glow of his red eyes faded. Trillions saved and countless worlds with it—not pain, not rage, but laughter in his final moments. Imperator Casvir was no more.

With him went Flowridia's friend in the woods. Flowridia gently shut his eyelids.

Blinding light burst beyond. Flowridia covered her eyes as she looked to the orbs, realizing that whatever was happening in the core . . . it was only growing. She stood, the air shifting to flow toward the light. She wiped her tears and ran to Ayla and Soliel, horror washing over her.

"Soliel!" she cried, but neither Soliel nor Ayla turned, equally mesmerized by the light. "Soliel, you have to stop this!"

The fallen Chaos lay upon the ground, having paid for Flowridia's life in blood—and perhaps more blood than anticipated. Ayla remained beside her, but Soliel was standing now, a statue of consternation. "I can't," he whispered.

Gods, Flowridia already knew, yet she spoke anyway. "What do you mean?"

His tearful gaze tore from the light, gravity's pull growing ever stronger toward it. "We've passed the point of no return. The spell is too strong."

"So . . ." Flowridia's breath hitched, her dread ever-rising. "Sha'Demoni and Celestière will be destroyed? How many lives is that, Soliel? There has to be *something* we can do!"

"We cannot stop it, Flowridia. Even Dira would have been destroyed had she tried to absorb it now. Perhaps she could've harnessed it into something, twisted the spell . . . but she's dead."

"What does that mean?" Flowridia asked. "Twist the spell?"

"Magic of this caliber cannot simply be destroyed, but it can be redirected. To twist it would be to reverse it."

"Reverse it? You mean like . . ."

Combining the worlds.

Oh, *gods.*

Apparently that same realization befell Soliel, wonder filling his gaze. "The Convergence. Dira had always insisted it wasn't her, but I never thought . . ."

"How could it not be her?"

"An explosion as powerful as the Convergence of Planes would cut through every timeline, every world. It need not happen in every time. Only one. Only this one." He shook his head. "But Dira is dead. Only Silver Fire could grasp this sort of power. This cannot be that timeline."

Flowridia lost her breath. In Ayla's gaze, that understanding lay reflected.

To Flowridia's horror, Ayla rose. "No," Flowridia said. "Ayla, no. You don't have to do this."

Her words vanished at the appearance of a giant hammer hurled through the air, landing square into Soliel's chest. The God flew back, landing half impaled in the earth—and who marched through the flame but Khastra, splattered in blood, her grin a harbinger of death.

"Is he dead, tiny one?"

Flowridia said nothing. Soliel's groan answered instead.

Khastra brought her wrist to her teeth in a familiar gesture, slicing through skin and licking the thick blood. Her vicious chuckle deepened as she transformed.

Fear flowed through Flowridia, but the Bringer of War bombarded past them, retrieving her hammer and grabbing the injured Soliel.

Their battle resumed, the Bringer of War content to bash the limp Soliel against the unforgiving earth, but Flowridia couldn't focus on that. Instead, she turned to Ayla, who remained by her side.

Ayla's silver gaze reflected the colorful light, a rainbow dancing through her eyes. Such determination upon her face. Such peace.

Flowridia took her hand. Not as a prison, but a plea. "Ayla, you don't have to do this."

"Who else, Flowra?" All the world faded as Ayla cupped her cheek, her tearful smile conveying only love. "Darling, even if you survive, what will remain of the world you love? What sort of world will that be to raise your child?"

"Then leave me with something—a finger, your ear, I don't care. Then I can bring you back when you're inevitably destroyed."

Gods, it was love, endless love, upon Ayla's precious countenance. "I tire of violence and dark rituals. I tire of Ayla Darkleaf. Perhaps I want that name to burn in the flames."

"Ayla . . . is this about redemption?"

Despite the dire scene, something small and thoughtful fell upon Ayla's face. "I suppose this is not what Onias said." Flowridia didn't even flinch when Ayla brought a hand to her own face and ripped her ear from her head like paper. An amused smile tugged at her lips as she slipped it into Flowridia's pocket. "Flowra—"

Another blast of light. Flowridia gasped, the pull ever-stronger. Time was short, and Flowridia pulled Ayla into a desperate embrace, sobbing to feel that same energy returned. "I love you."

"I love you, Flowra."

And therein was the crack in the plan, dread filling Flowridia to realize the cruel truth. A blood ritual might not matter at all. When Ayla pulled away, she placed a small something into Flowridia's hand.

Her wedding ring.

Flowridia gasped as she tucked it away, then gripped Ayla's shoulders. "Promise me one thing."

"Anything."

Spells were fickle things, Mother had always complained. The letter of the law and not the spirit. Only love could kill Ayla Darkleaf, which meant . . . "You can't go in there thinking about me. Or Dira. No one you care about."

Ayla appeared taken aback. "What?"

"Swear to me you'll find your spite. Find your rage. It's what made you, and I know you don't want to be Ayla Darkleaf anymore, but swear to me—one final time."

Though curious, Ayla nodded. "I swear."

Flowridia released her, all but ripping her hands away lest she falter. Ayla lingered a moment, her alabaster skin reflecting a rainbow of hues, beauty in every line of her body.

Had this been her fate all along? To shape the very foundation of the worlds?

With a final glance, Ayla ran for the light.

There is no fate, Ayla Darkleaf.

Ayla touched the light and felt . . . everything.

There is only the path you forge.

What was once blind now saw all things.

Thousands upon thousands, infinite worlds all existing upon the same plane, hardly a whisper away for some. Ayla stood tall in the realm between realms, visions of stars and those same distant worlds all around. Each floated in their own unique portal, orbiting like moons to her planetoid. Infinite, yet each shone with crystal clarity.

In her arms, she cradled six orbs of light.

One emanated heat and power, in red and orange.

One was ice and water.

One held the essence of earth, its beauty and horror both.

One crackled with energy, a storm seeking to combust.

And the final two were life and death, light and dark, two halves of the circle of mortality.

Ayla caressed them, awestruck as her body absorbed their infinite essence. For all the pain, this feeling of completion was cathartic. The realm had once spurned her. Now, they were one and the same. Once, she had sought to burn the realm. Now, she burned for it.

Oh, she ached, every cell in her body threatening to burst yet hungry for more, more . . . but not yet, not yet. To act too soon meant failure. Ayla had not absorbed enough. Ayla gazed beyond herself, back to the infinite sea of worlds.

If she willed time to slow, she could study each one, pick it apart, sift through time like pages in a book. Instead, she let them play, watching entire life cycles end and begin in a flash. For it was not linear, no. Ayla eased the spell back, and so time went with it. Children dead; children born; families torn apart and created. Joy and pain in infinite cycles, for this was the way of every world. In one blink, she gazed upon Celestière, saw the voids between its broken pieces. How easy it would be to break through the film and reach inside, touch the world as a titan beyond it, rip and tear, throw any entity into the void . . .

But it was not only Celestière. Amid the expanse of space, foreign worlds filled with foreign entities, foreign people lived and died. They stared upon her in intervals, those who chose to see the space between worlds. Humanoid creatures, angels and demons alike, beings she had no name for. And Ayla felt it all—their happiness and heartbreak, their triumphs and tragedies. Eternity in each blink, each second agony as the power continued to flow into her.

One world called to her. Time to slow. Sha'Demoni, a home of sorts, its broken climate in better repair than others. A world of death and a world of life existing upon the same plane, separated by a watery purgatory—Sha'Demoni's residents panicked in the beginnings of the very disaster Ayla sought to undo. Ayla saw them, each and every demon who cried for deliverance from the sure destruction from the orbs . . .

Amid the thousands of entities, Ayla's focus narrowed upon one.

Izthuni lived up to his title, lurking in darkness underground as he peered upon the lights overhead. The world burned around him, yet he hid like the slippery wretch he was. The film between that world and the Beyond was so thin. All it would take was a simple *pluck.*

Find your rage, Flowra had pled. What was rage to a titan among the cosmos? The orbs' power grew within her. Ayla burned and felt nothing. Here was her chance to *be* nothing and move on.

A mere turn of her head, and there among the boundless worlds was . . . hers. And who watched unseeing amid the strife and fear—but Flowra.

Frozen in time, Flowra reached toward the infinite nothing.

To be nothing is not peace. It is silence.

Another blink, and her realm went the way of the rest of them, time moving backwards in vast intervals. Flowra's life was so short, a mere blink before she was merely a newborn babe, and then further still. Countless lives came and went the same way, death and birth, ends and beginnings.

Including her own. But her life was not so short.

Ayla Darkleaf, Casvir's assassin masquerading as a diplomat.

Ayla Darkleaf, the Scourge of the Sun Elves.

Ayla Darkleaf, The Endless Night, servant of Izthuni.

Ayla Darkleaf, molded and groomed from tender years, weeping in a cold, dark cathedral for deliverance, but no saviors came. Only monsters in disguise.

And who was the first?

Ayla burned but felt *everything.*

With a malevolent grin, she looked away from her own tumbling world, fixating back upon Sha'Demoni, frozen at her will. How simple, to breach the span of worlds, to reach inside and rip Izthuni out from his coward's abode. Out of the chill recesses of Sha'Demoni and into the infinite space between realms.

He struggled between her fiery fingers, a mere ant to her titanic figure. In the darkness of the cosmos, Ayla held the flailing god up to her face and whispered, *"Who am I without you?"*

Wickedness laced her laughter, catharsis within her rage. Ayla opened her mouth, ignorant of the screams of this vermin, and dropped him gleefully upon her tongue. Izthuni's bones shattered beneath her teeth. His flesh burned amid her fire. She savored the bitter taste of victory.

The pain intensified. Time spun faster, faster. This lapse of control—would everything now fall apart?

The orbs shattered, crumbling as glass in her arms. Their power was hers; the spell was hers; it *was her*; it was a fact more than knowledge. Now was the time.

When you find peace, you will know you have found your way.

Ayla . . . smiled.

And Ayla let go.

Flowridia stared into the light even as spots appeared in her vision. But it flashed. It expanded. Death's door approached as blinding light.

She turned to run, only then spotting the Bringer of War shaking the battered body of Soliel like a doll, his power cut short without the orbs. Flowridia knew not if he still breathed, but when the Bringer of War gripped his head, Flowridia hardly had a moment to gasp before—

The Bringer of War ripped his head from his body.

When she dropped the body, it remained still. She bit the skull in twain, shattering bone beneath teeth as she feasted, a vicious chuckle cutting through even the roaring spell.

"Khastra!" Flowridia cried, and she began her sprint to the castle. "Recall your troops! We have to run!"

The Bringer of War stared with those glowing eyes, cold and bestial. Demoni words bellowed from her vast self, but Flowridia couldn't linger to see the results. Instead, she all but stumbled upon a tragic scene.

Chaos' body. Casvir's.

She hadn't a hope to move Casvir, but her motherly instincts surged as she tried and failed to lift Chaos. But surely magic could help. She wrenched the maldectine dagger from Chaos' chest and set it into her belt, only for the explosion to pulse. She tumbled to the ground.

One final look at Chaos, Dira and Demitri, spoiled by her misting vision. Flowridia ripped her gaze away and ran.

The dead crawled away with a swipe of her hand. Demons vanished into the fields beyond. Airships veered away from Haven, smoke emanating as they gained speed. No matter how quickly she ran, the light cast Flowridia's shadow farther and farther.

She stilled, the abyss all consuming.

The light glowed in a rainbow of hues, revealing shapes within. Shifting planets faintly seen, stars and moons and . . . someone. A person. A *woman*. Some instinct gripped her. Flowridia reached for the portal.

A shadow suddenly blocked the light. Flowridia gasped as a massive hand wrapped around her figure with ease, lifting her like a toy. Flowridia met the gaze of the Bringer of War, fear pulsing through her as the monster held her to her chest—and sprinted for Haven's walls.

Flowridia released all control as she set her trust in this demi-deity. They had met on the battlefield before, but in violence, not comradery. Her heart beat to deafen her, but still the spell surged forward, consuming all it touched.

Her stomach lurched. The Bringer of War skidded against dirt and then stone as she came to a stop beneath Haven's gate. Panic gripped her chest to watch the expansion of light. "Will it destroy Haven?"

Whatever the Bringer of War said, her tone was lost in her foreign words. But fear was universal, and her glowing eyes *screamed*.

"Set me down." When the half-demon obeyed, Flowridia frantically said, "You can smell Silver Fire. Is that what this is?"

The Bringer of War spat a guttural, "*Yes.*"

Flowridia glanced back upon Haven, upon the castle housing her sweet baby girl, upon Demitri running toward them, upon homes and the few De'Sindai citizens unfortunate enough to not have taken shelter, upon a city filled with innocents about to forfeit their lives.

Solvira had fallen to Silver Fire. She had let it burn. But what had stopped the explosion in its tracks?

Maldectine deep beneath the earth.

She withdrew the maldectine dagger from her belt, its power contained to only the green stone. She narrowed her focus, recalling lessons in a library long ago with Etolié, expanding and retracting this same power over and over . . .

Flowridia ran back onto the battlefield, seeking to grasp that same energy once more. But still she felt the natural world, screaming as the tapestry of magic shredded. Desperation drove her. The worst outcome was not her own death, though the explosion would likely destroy her phylactery too. It was her daughter's death. It was the citizens of Haven.

She could not fail.

She stopped when the wind became too much, the light leaving spots in her vision as it rapidly approached. She gripped the dagger's hilt and focused, *focused*, weaving through splintered magic, fraying threads, seeking the sensation of nothing.

There.

Flowridia shut her eyes as the world of magic silenced. Around her, that nothingness expanded. But what use was this shield if it was only for her? Sweat dripped from her brow, aching from the sheer strain of focus . . .

Light burned even through her eyelids. Tension screamed throughout her body, but failure meant death. Failure meant there was no Haven.

A scream ripped from her throat. Her shield heaved. It burst.

The impact pushed like a breeze.

The light vanished.

Flowridia opened her eyes and beheld a sea of glass—and behind her, Haven.

Safe.

Sora screamed yet heard nothing except the throbbing beat of her heart. The sensation of Leelan in her mouth melted away, melding into her flesh.

Pain seared through every vein, her thoughts rapid, erratic. She blinked and saw bones, saw Ilune. Her back burned in agony; she arched to match.

The world of white shifted. The ground cushioned her, even as the blinding mists grew . . . more so. Colored lights rapidly approached. Common sense said it meant death.

"Dammit all," she heard. *Damn you, Sora!"*

Ilune burst into flame, her Silver Fire rapidly expanding to create a wall. It collided with the explosion of light.

Sora cowered in the shield of Ilune's figure. Ilune's screams filled the vast void. Where the light touched Silver Fire, the spell absorbed.

Within the figure of flame, Ilune glowed like a beacon. Brighter and brighter, and despite the agony, Sora managed a few rational thoughts. Instinct rose, and Sora with it, for Ilune would not last much longer. Her head spun. It fell into hands not her own, for they were changed, clawed—why clawed?

It was not so much a voice, but instinct. Perhaps her own, perhaps not. *We can stop this.*

Sora pushed Ilune aside, driven by thoughts beyond sanity. In the split moment before the explosion could touch her . . . light within her expanded instead.

Power poured through her, burning every vein, but from her grew a shield of pure light. Glowing in shades of brilliant gold, it spread as wide as sight could see, a wall of magic. It did not absorb, no, nothing like the Silver Fire. Instead, the fire bombarded it and scattered harmlessly aside, though the size of a tsunami. Her shield pulsed but did not break, and Sora lowered her strange hands, staring into the inferno.

Her back felt odd, heavy. Despite it all, peace filled her, dulling the radiant pain inside. Sora breathed, for this shield was not knowledge she should have had, yet now it was as natural as memory.

That voice—or something like a voice—sang again. *You will understand soon, Sora.*

For it sang as birdsong, not as speech.

All at once, the fire dissipated.

Sora fell to her knees, her shield flickering, vanishing. Only then did she see Ilune on the ground, trembling as the silver glow within her slowly faded. She was naked, hints of ashen cloth dirtying her figure. But when Ilune looked up, her smile held hints of a laugh. "I think we've managed to live. Thank you for . . ."

Ilune's words became murky. Sora's vision spun, sending her to the ground. She struggled to rise. Why was her back so heavy?

As her sight faded, she felt the touch of cold hands and heard the singing of birds.

Not outside.

In her head.

In Flowers' medical suite, Etolié stared transfixed upon the approaching explosion.

She was pretty certain she had watched Khastra escape, so there was a limit to her anxiety, but all of her attempts at being calm were undermined by a very flustered infant.

"Mommy's just gotta go save the realm, all right?" Etolié rocked the kid in vain, knowing that of all the terrible things that could be wrong with infants, the most likely cause in this instance was simply the absence of mom. "Or something like that. I'll explain when you're older."

Dira wailed, sparking some mixture of annoyance and empathy from Etolié.

"You might as well get used to me, kid."

The light far beyond flashed. The castle shook. Etolié dropped to the ground, holding Dira beneath her in case the roof collapsed . .

Silence. Well, except for the screaming baby.

Etolié crept up to peek over the windowsill, finding nothing amiss at all.

"Dira, I think it's over. I think we might not die."

Dira apparently didn't get the message, given she just kept crying.

Etolié groaned and stood once more, rising as she gently bounced the newborn. "I get it, kid. The world is loud and confusing. I probably ought to scream a helluva lot more than I currently do."

Dira just cried.

"And moms really do make things better, so I won't even take it personally when you calm the fuck down once Flowers gets back." Against all odds, Etolié did begin to worry at that, peering toward the fancy phylactery box locked on the bedside table—next to the cursed knife.

She really ought to put that thing away.

"I mean, if your mom dies, we have the creepy heart here. It'll be fine."

Worrying about Flowers' safety? Who the fuck was she?

There came a knock.

"It's open!"

The knock sounded again.

"Making me take more steps than necessary," Etolié muttered, grimacing as she trudged toward the door. "This had better be important."

She opened the door—

Murishani leaned against the doorframe, giving his creepy little wave. "Hi. Knock knock."

He swung a dagger.

Sharp pain split Etolié's stomach. She sank to her knees, all her effort focused on not dropping the helpless baby.

Before she could gain her bearings, Murishani struck her in her split stomach with a pointed boot, spraying blood and sending her sprawling. Dira screamed, but Etolié managed to hold her tight—

Everything spun when pain split across her throat.

Etolié watched through blurred vision as Murishani held up a bloody dagger—and a wailing Dira. Her pulse pounded in her ears, deafening her to his words.

Etolié sought Celestière, sought Momma, but of course she felt nothing. Fresh pain spiked across her already slit throat. Just her luck, that the last thing she'd see was his ugly, creepy mug grinning, covered in her blood.

His wicked smile vanished when his gaze shifted to the door. He ran.

The edges of her vision blurred. Etolié tried to pray . . .

But Celestière remained silent.

She rolled over, a puppet on her mind's strings, only to stop at the expulsion of pain and also entrails from her split gut. Oh fuck, oh fuck, oh fuck—Etolié weakly lifted an arm, failing to scoop her intestines back into her stomach. Her vision darkened at the seams. Her pulse pounded in her head, her heartbeat a slowing clock.

A name cut through the fog, though it sounded as though plunged beneath the sea. "*Etolié?!*"

Goddammit. It was Marielle.

Etolié shut her eyes, determined that the last thing she see not be Marielle's stupid powdered face, but her scream pulled Etolié from her resigned fate. "Etolié! Oh, gods . . . Where's Ayla? Where's Flowridia? What about the baby?"

Fuck. She couldn't die just yet.

Though she was certainly running out of alternatives, given how rapidly her vision lost focus. No amount of adrenaline would magically keep her entrails inside.

The dagger.

Shit.

The noise from her own throat was a bubbly garble. Liquid filled her lungs. Etolié coughed, panic filling her when she gasped for air and felt nothing.

She pointed. Glittery sparks shot haphazardly from her fingers, her magic sporadic as her eyesight faded. The sparks landed on the knife—or, she hoped, rather.

"You want the knife?"

Etolié tried to nod, but pain was a helluva drug. Also, she was confident she had been at least partially decapitated. Marielle's face swam in her vision—but what did she bring along with it? That damn cursed knife.

Her strength rapidly faded. Marielle's image was but a pinprick. The clock's ticks slowed . . . slowed . . .

In her final moments of life, Etolié swung her arm out and grabbed Marielle's wrist with a final burst of strength. She plunged it down—

PART EIGHT

IMPERATOR

CHAPTER 42

Flowridia shuffled through the gates of the castle, passing collapsed skeleton guards at each threshold.

Khastra said nothing, their tentative truce exactly that. Her own exhaustion was apparent, though Flowridia would never mention it. Demitri, however, walked confidently, his occasional commentary bringing a tired smile to Flowridia's face. *It's less stinky already. Look at all those bones. Can I take one?*

"Yes, you can take one," Flowridia replied, bittersweet amid her familiar's joy. Demitri gleefully bounded to a fallen skeleton and selected a femur.

Khastra broke her silence. "How is he back? Etolié said he was murdered."

Flowridia fought to curb her enthusiasm, relieved to have any chance at friendly interactions with the half-demon. "The very short version is that the Goddess of Chaos is behind it. I'll gladly tell you the long version if you'd like, just as soon as I've cleaned up and can hold my baby."

"So you did both live. I am impressed. And surprised. It seems you have won, tiny one."

Victory held a potent sting. Behind every blink, Flowridia was assaulted with visions of Ayla before the orbs ripped her apart. Had she listened? Had she died pursuing bitterness instead of love? Flowridia had no more tears left to cry, numb to the whole world, but every flickering shadow from the torchlight drew her eye, every creak upon the floorboards a possible sign of her wife's return.

Casvir was gone, the castle but a hollow shell, and Flowridia reached surreptitiously into her pocket to touch the leaf he had given her. A silly memento, but it meant so much.

And Chaos, her child in another life, her familiar too—gone, but at least Chaos had known of her victory.

Soliel . . . for all his crimes, sorrow filled her to think of his cruel fate. Not his death; that was well deserved. But once he had been a child set on a path no child deserved, handed responsibility surpassing even kings.

She couldn't cry for the Old God, but she could mourn the boy he had once been.

But Demitri was here, the knowledge so surreal, the reminders of his comical self constant as he paraded proudly with his new bone. She touched him idly on his back, savoring the sensation of his thick fur.

"You are escorting me to Etolié, yes?"

Flowridia nodded. For all her heartbreak, her baby was just a few steps away. Her familiar, her dearest Demitri, was here. She lay suspended between anguish and joy, for Ayla's fate remained unknown, Casvir was gone, Chaos was gone . . .

Yes, she should clean up, but first she would see Dira. Flowridia opened the medical suite—

And gazed upon carnage.

Blood stained the bed. Blood splattered the hysterical Marielle. Blood seeped from a brutalized Etolié on the floor.

There was no Dira.

Marielle babbled, but Flowridia charged forward, magic crackling from her fingertips. Marielle didn't fight her touch, but screamed when a potent blast of necrotic magic coated Flowridia's skin. *"WHERE IS MY BABY?!"*

"I don't know!" Marielle screamed when Khastra snatched her collar. Her feet dangled as she fought Khastra's grip, as high as the half-demon was tall.

"Talk," Khastra spat, her rage potent, barely curtailed.

"I heard a commotion and came running and found Etolié lying on the floor covered in blood, but she wasn't dead and she used her magic to direct me to that dagger and stabbed herself! I know it sounds insane, but I swear!"

Dagger?

On high alert, Flowridia's attention darted to the fallen Etolié, slashed across her stomach, her throat, bleeding from cavernous wounds. But there, embedded in her chest, was Izthuni's knife.

Etolié had known she was dying. Had she taken matters into her own hands?

Flowridia yanked the dagger from Etolié's chest, the magic potent and vile. Etolié showed no sign of change, but . . . if this were real, she could hurry this along.

Flowridia summoned all she could and blasted necrotic energy into Etolié's chest.

The Celestial shot up into sitting and vomited a stream of blood.

A slight, *"Oof!"* as Marielle hit the floor, and Khastra was immediately at Etolié's side. "Etolié? Oh, thank the gods."

Again Etolié puked, a pale sheen rapidly overtaking her skin. Her throat wound sealed. "Oh gods, everything *hurts*—" Etolié dry heaved, this time only dribbles of blood escaping her lips.

Flowridia grabbed her shoulders, staring her dead in the eye. "Where is Dira?!"

"Murishani has—"

Flowridia ran from the room.

Demitri followed, frantically sniffing the air. *I have a scent. I'd remember his perfume anywhere.*

"Then *run*! You're faster without me!"

Demitri sprinted, his bestial self leaving her behind.

In the dark recesses of Murishani's domain, Zorlaeus paced.

Marielle should've been back by now. And given her tears when she had failed to save Flowridia's life, Zorlaeus feared what she had done to atone.

All manner of debauchery existed in these halls. Zorlaeus had heard and seen things no man should face. But as he passed one door, he couldn't help but pause upon hearing . . . crying.

A baby crying.

Without much thought, Zorlaeus opened the door, following the sound through a short hallway and into a kitchenette.

Indeed, there was a baby—a tiny girl, perhaps premature, wailing and covered in blood. His breath caught, but not two paces away was Murishani, who grinned far too broadly at Zorlaeus' entrance. "Just in time! Quiet that monster, would you, Lae Lae? It's ruining my ruined day."

Shock kept his motions slow, but a quick glance to the baby revealed no visible wounds. Thank Ku'Shya's might, none of the blood belonged to her.

That was when he noticed a pile of potatoes and onions. Murishani was manically chopping them. "Aren't you going to ask about my woes?"

Zorlaeus gently took the infant in his arms. Six younger siblings and being raised as an eldest 'daughter' had taught him a few techniques for soothing fitful babies, but the poor thing was cold and so very frightened. "What happened to ruin your day, Viceroy?"

Murishani slammed down the knife, causing Zorlaeus to jump. "That cunt is *alive*!"

Well that . . . that was not what Marielle had reported. "Flowridia? A-Are you certain?"

"Of course I'm certain! She was reported on the battlefield, but not before *murdering* Casvir."

Murishani put on no airs. This was not the feigned fop Zorlaeus had catered to for too many years. His voice held an edge, no flamboyancy to his motions. Nothing but rage and erratic chopping. "So you took her child?" Zorlaeus asked.

Murishani's chuckle frayed at the seams, his crazed visage revealing a man far beyond sanity. "I'm going to eat it."

For a man known for hyperbole, Murishani showed no sign of jesting. The boiling pot suddenly made too much sense.

"I'm going to *eat* it, Lae Lae, and sulk as I hand her the fucking crown. We need a necromancer of her caliber. I so *hate* to give her any credit, but what a fine figurehead she'll be. She needs me."

Zorlaeus glanced in horror between the fitful infant and the chopped potatoes. "Forgive me, but has it occurred to you that it might be difficult to be on her good side if you eat her child?"

"There's no Casvir to protect her now. I'll make certain we have the perfect heir to make up for this little mutt's loss, don't you worry."

Oh, so Murishani had completely lost it.

Murishani glanced to the water, nodding at its rolling boil. "Just about there. Once I'm done with this onion, toss it in."

Zorlaeus crept back.

"Lae Lae, what are your thoughts on garlic? Six cloves for the entire pot? Seven?"

Zorlaeus glanced to the door, left slightly ajar. "Add as much as possible."

"You're so right."

There was nothing to grab and throw. No weapon to attack the madman with—not that he would succeed anyway. No, no. There was only one path, and Murishani was halfway through that onion.

Zorlaeus willed the infant to keep quiet as he stole a breath for courage.

Dammit all. Damn Murishani and damn himself for deciding to be a hero this day.

Zorlaeus sprinted out the door.

Instinct pulled Flowridia like a distant scream. There would be one more murder this day; oh, she could *feel* it.

The castle lay nearly vacant as she sprinted toward the underground realm belonging to Murishani.

Far away, she swore she heard a cry: *"Flowridia! Etolié! Anyone!"*

Closer, she heard a familiar snarl.

Spurred by adrenaline, by magic, and by motherly rage, Flowridia raced the final leg toward the underground. Demitri growled at a fearful person holding—

Dira.

"Give her to me!" she screamed, and who turned? Zorlaeus.

He offered the infant with no hesitation. Flowridia immediately hugged Dira to her chest, awash with relief and fear. Covered in blood, but none of it hers. Dira wailed, but Dira was merely afraid.

"You have to run!" Zorlaeus said, still pinned to the wall by Demitri. "Murishani is—"

"Well, well!"

There he was.

From the dark hallway emerged a manic figure, his disheveled hair and blood-soaked robes suggesting a man unhinged. "Zorlaeus, I thought better of you! Turns out you're still the ungrateful, mewling brat I picked up out of the gutter." He grinned at Flowridia. "Welcome back."

Flowridia grabbed Zorlaeus by the arm, cursing as she shoved Dira back into his grasp. "Etolié is in the medical ward. Take Dira there. Fuck this up, and there will be no place you can hide."

Zorlaeus gave a frantic nod and ran.

With Demitri at her side, Flowridia faced the Viceroy of Nox'Kartha, the rage within her potent, depthless. "Your death is long overdue."

"I wouldn't do that if I were you," Murishani cooed. "This poor country—soon to fall into ruin without its imperator. What will gather the grain before the long winter? What will patrol when scavengers come to infiltrate our weak walls? With no necromancer leading this country, these people will starve within months."

Flowridia barely heard him, emboldened by Demitri's growl as she stepped forward.

Light glowed at Murishani's feet, the first hints of Silver Fire rising to coat him. "These people need me. Or will you let them die because of whatever selfish instinct led you to murder their savior? Was your plan to take Casvir's throne? You'll need me even more then. I'll even allow it. You play the figurehead while I dance behind the scenes, keeping Nox'Kartha from falling apart. Nothing I haven't done before."

Purple smoke seeped from Flowridia's skin, escaping with her breath. "You wouldn't be negotiating if you weren't afraid."

"Afraid of you? A little girl? You're nothing more than a pretty face and a loose cunt. Unlike you, however, I don't want Nox'Kartha to fall to ruin."

Just say when, Mom.

They'd failed this tactic once before. But they both were grown now. "Shut him up."

Demitri leapt. Flowridia's power flowed.

Murishani's fire flared at the sudden emergence of necrotic tendrils—but he fell screaming when Demitri landed on him. Flowridia ran to join, waiting for the moment a silver glow surrounded Demitri—

And grabbed Murishani by the throat, coated in her own necrotic power.

Murishani gripped her hand, his power flaring. Purple lightning crackled along her skin, combating the rising fire. His power served as a shield and lance both, but hers washed over him in relentless waves. Push and pull, their powers met as fire and ice, lightning and thunder crashing all at once.

"You're a fool if you think you can keep this country afloat on your own," Murishani spat. "You stupid cunt—you need me. *You need me!*"

Rage twisted his hateful face as her necrotic glow cast monstrous shadows upon his features. He glowed yet absorbed all light. This creature from the depths; this monster who had brought so much grief and pain; this wretch who had lied and cheated, threatened and *murdered* her in the end.

For all his crimes, one enraged her above all. This man had tried to kill her daughter. "Demitri!"

Demitri's jaws snapped around his head. A muted scream, and his skin desiccated. His body withered. His essence flowed into her, fueling the cruel magic in a cycle.

Once dead, there was nothing more to take.

His Silver Fire faded. Flowridia gasped as she stumbled away, dry-heaving at the influx of energy. Demitri continued savaging the body, ripping it apart like the animal he was. Murishani's withered form barely bled, leaving his skin to peel away with the ease of a grape. Flowridia watched until her head spun.

She collapsed to her knees, gasping with each breath. Murishani was dead. Her daughter was safe; she was safe; the castle was . . .

Nigh vacant. So many had run.

The mutilated Murishani had no face. Demitri currently feasted on it, chewing on his flesh like a toy. Flowridia's adrenaline and rage faded . . . into dread.

Nox'Kartha needed a necromancer.

Flowridia looked at her trembling hands, one whole and one maimed. So much blood upon them; blood stained her entire body.

Murishani was right. Casvir was dead, and Nox'Kartha would fall. Their blood would join the rest, inevitable that it would drip from between her fingers.

Flowridia buried her face in those bloodied hands and wept.

The chronic headache plaguing Etolié had abated.

Replacing it, however, was the suspicious urge to lick the blood off Khastra's biceps, and not in a sexy way.

Overpowering all the discomfort from her changing body was Khastra's arms around her, a fortress she longed to hide in and never emerge from. Blood sealed them—Khastra with her gore-splattered armor and Etolié and her shredded, bloody dress. If she didn't pay attention, her fangs scratched the crystal surface. The smell was strong but it was alluring in a fucked up way. What she smelled was already dead, but she'd be lying if she said she hadn't covertly licked a bit from her armor, just to find out how it tasted.

A little spicy, to be honest. Somehow, she knew it was demonic in origin.

All that aside, her interrogation of Marielle continued. "So *you* were the woman keen to hide her identity?" Fucking hell, those fangs were annoying to talk around. Memory said they'd recede when there was no more blood, but now was not the time for baths.

Marielle paused in her rambling tale. "The what?"

"One of the assassins described the person who hired him that way."

Marielle nodded.

"And I shouldn't ask Khastra to punt you out the window . . . why?"

"Because I worked pretty damn hard to coordinate hiring the worst assassins for whatever the situation required, all right?"

Etolié merely blinked.

Marielle set hands upon her shapely hips. "They failed, right?"

"Yes."

"And you were conveniently around to thwart them, right?"

"Also yes."

"And that's only the ones you knew about."

Dammit. It seemed Marielle deserved perhaps a little bit of credit. "So you've been behind the scenes all along trying to protect her?"

Marielle nodded. "I know my behavior's been strange, but the more suspicious I acted, the less all of you would tell me, so the less I had to tell Murishani, and the more I could try to manipulate you into being where you needed to be to keep her safe."

"But how?! You're not that . . ."

Etolié cut off her own callous words, annoyed when Marielle smirked. "Not that what, Etolié? Not that smart? It's a lot easier to get away with things when people underestimate you. That's what

Murishani taught me. Turns out, he's not immune to his own tricks."

Fortunately, Zorlaeus entered then, so Etolié didn't have to admit Marielle was right. A beat later, she realized what he was holding. "Khastra, let me . . ." Khastra released her. Etolié stumbled on limbs much too coordinated and confirmed her hopes. Here was Dira, upset but alive.

Zorlaeus was a bit pale, however. "Etolié, what happened?"

"I'm kind of an undead monster now. I'm not thinking about that yet." When she beckoned, Zorlaeus set the infant into her arms. Whatever else could be said about the baby, she didn't smell appetizing—unlike Zorlaeus and Marielle, who stood a little too close for comfort. "What happened?"

Zorlaeus' explanation, accompanied by the wailing infant, left her speechless.

"Allow me," came a soothing voice, and Khastra gently took the baby from Etolié's arms.

To Etolié's chagrin, Dira quieted within seconds. "How . . . *How*?"

Etolié had seen Khastra with babies before, the sight of the massive half-demon cooing over something so tiny never not adorable. "Do you think dhampirs are more difficult than demon infants?" Khastra said cutely, speaking to Dira. "I have had many babies, Etolié."

To Etolié's alarm, Dira tried to bite Khastra's finger when she brought it near. "She is hungry," Khastra continued. "Do we know if the tiny one is alive?"

As fate would have it, Flowers entered then, accompanied by Demitri.

Defeat rested upon her exhausted features, her demeanor starkly juxtaposed with her words. "Murishani is dead." She looked to Zorlaeus, lip trembling. "Thank you. I owe you her life."

Zorlaeus' smile came shyly. "I just did what any decent person would do."

"It was still incredibly courageous. Thank you." She looked to Marielle, her smile forced but not false. "You were trying to save my life."

Marielle nodded.

"I've treated you unfairly."

"No, you haven't," Marielle interrupted, her smile apologetic. "You treated me exactly how I hoped you would. I couldn't get too close. Otherwise, he'd be too close."

"Why though?"

"Because I've done a lot of horrible things these past few years, and I can blame Murishani all I want, but I'm still the one who went along with him. When he began hinting at his plans for you, something in me just snapped. I'm sure you don't see me that way anymore, but I always considered you to be a friend, and when I realized you were pregnant, I couldn't do it anymore."

Flowers offered a small smile, the clear forgiveness annoying, but perhaps Etolié was just hungry. "Thank you," Flowers said.

"So, uh . . ." Etolié struggled to phrase the issue. "What's eating you, Flowers?" Dammit. Now was not the time to be thinking about eating.

Flowers gasped, sudden tears welling in her eyes. "Can I hold my baby, please?"

Khastra carefully placed the calmed Dira into Flowers' arms. Flowers all but melted into the sweet embrace, holding the baby against bloodstained clothes—a sight which bolstered Etolié's anxiety.

"Can we get you two into a bath before the baby gets exposed to non-baby-friendly diseases?" Etolié asked.

Flowers glanced around and nodded. "We all need baths."

"Wait," Marielle said, hesitation in the word. "Where's Ayla?"

Flowers's tears fell, carving through grime and smoke. "I don't know." She rushed away with Dira, stealing the air with her.

"The tiny one has spoken true," Khastra said. "We would all benefit from reconvening once we have cleaned up." She paused. "Though I would be remiss to let *that* remain unattended."

Etolié followed Khastra's gaze. There, discarded and splattered in blood, lay Staff Seraph deDieula. "Oh, yeah. Snap that shit in two for all I care."

"And unleash the energy it has harnessed? No, better it is returned to my mother's catacombs."

Etolié followed when Khastra moved to rise. Something else drew her eye, and she offered the very cursed and evil dagger. "Care to stash this one too, Beefcake?"

"It creates Izthuni Spawn, you said?"

"I'm living proof—or dead proof, rather."

"Then, yes. It will be locked away and forgotten."

Etolié grimaced as she handed over the bloody dagger, thankfully not tempted by the scent of her own mortal blood. However, Khastra visibly recoiled as she held out the staff. "If I thought I could safely destroy this, I would. But only a Silver Fire wielder could do so."

"Does that mean Ayla is dead?" Marielle interjected. Right, she was still here.

Khastra was quiet a moment, oddly somber at the mention of the name. "I saw her run into the light. She did not emerge. Perhaps the tiny one can provide answers, but there are very few who would survive what I witnessed."

Etolié took Khastra's hand. "I'm getting sticky. Let's get these things out of here and clean up. To Sha'Demoni?"

"Can you feel Sha'Demoni?"

A valid question. Etolié shut her eyes, focusing on faraway worlds. First, Celestière. *Momma?*

A few beats, and then . . . *Starshine!*

The relief in Staella's voice nearly moved Etolié to tears. *We have a lot to talk about, and we'll have to do it later, but you're all alive, right?*

Yes, Starshine. We're all alive.

'We' wasn't accurate in the literal sense, but that was a conversation for another time. *Love you, Momma. We'll talk soon.*

I love you forever, Etolié.

Etolié relaxed her pose. "Well, Celestière is still around, so it's a safe bet for Sha'Demoni too." She took Khastra's hand. "Let's hope we don't splice."

They did not, landing safely in Sha'Demoni's humidity.

Cleansed of blood and birthing fluid, Dira soon was swaddled in a fluffy blanket, well within sight and reach of Flowridia.

Naked, Flowridia stilled before a mirror in Ayla's washroom, coated in blood, in ash, in scars.

Yet now her magic flowed anew. She had manipulated dead things before, had she not? Curious, Flowridia brought her right hand to her scarred chest, coaxing the shined skin to heal.

At the first tingle of molting skin, she stopped.

Flowridia brought up her left hand, maimed and bearing reminders of pain and grief. Yet her lip trembled. Healing was within her grasp, but Ayla had hidden all her scars, every totem of the past. What had that done?

Each scar held memories, first of pain and then survival. Her hand and its three fingers—for so long she had rejected it, grasping at the hope of vampirism and the perfection it brought. Lichdom could bring something different. It was still undeath. Her magic could restore her hand to a perfect form. If she didn't act, Dira would someday ask why her mom was different . . .

. . . and what was so wrong with that? Once, she had been mortal, broken down into nothing, subjected to agonizing months of healing. She flexed it, shaken at the absence of pain.

A reminder. A memory of all she had done to survive; a memory of mortality, lest undeath ever stray her from her soul.

Dira cooed, bringing her back to the present.

In her bath, Flowridia scrubbed herself of grime, unfortunately needing to dunk her whole head and wash her hair as well. Best to get it done with now. This would be her only rest.

All the while, she watched the shadows in Ayla's washroom, seeking figures within them. But Ayla was . . . gone.

The ear in her dress' pocket remained pristine. She knew not what it meant, except that with Murishani's demise, she would be hard-pressed to find more descendants of the Moon Goddess to slay.

To her surprise, the walls parted, her private space infiltrated. Flowridia frowned to see . . . Etolié and Khastra?

Both were clean, though with the absence of blood, Etolié's appearance was all the more disconcerting. Flowridia had never known someone before and after a vampiric transformation, the ethereal beauty of the Celestial ineffably enhanced beyond natural bounds. Her hair held a shine unseen in life, her lips slightly fuller, her sardonic stare sharper. Even her wings radiated more allure, engrossing in ways Flowridia found strange. A demonic curse conjoined with the otherworldly beauty of Etolié's mother's realm, resulting in a creature unlike any other.

"You seem to be dealing with this well," Flowridia said, shocked at how docile she presented.

Etolié shrugged. "Khastra still loves me. Once I can confirm that my momma does too, I don't exactly see the downside. Watch this." Etolié wrapped her arms around Khastra's torso and lifted the half-demon. Khastra said nothing, but her gaze landed somewhere between affection and deep amusement.

"That is quite impressive," Flowridia said.

"You left this." Etolié offered forward a familiar box, currently stained in blood. "I didn't think you'd want your literal heart unattended."

Flowridia set it on the floor beside the tub, ideas already swirling through her mind. Mere steps away was a secret passage leading to the ruins of her love's once-greatest achievement. So few even knew about it, and no one dared to enter.

She could carve out a stone and place it inside. No one would ever know. A fitting place for her broken heart.

Dira's coo brought her back to the present. "Would one of you like to hold Dira while I finish up?"

Flowridia recalled that vampires didn't care for dhampir blood, unbothered when Etolié scooped the baby up. As she resumed cleaning herself, Etolié said, "We wanted to know . . . What are you planning to do now?"

Flowridia sighed, defeated to say it aloud. But she had to, lest she play the part of a coward. "I have to stay."

"Stay?"

"Nox'Kartha needs a necromancer," she said, echoing the cursed words. "Forgive me if this is a sore point, but after everything I did in Solvira, I ran away and left people like you to pick up the pieces. I can't do that again."

For that was what Odessa had done. Hide away from the world instead of face it.

"I'll keep an eye out for it in the mist when you inevitably snap."

Flowridia reeled at the memory of those toxic words, scrubbing herself until she was red and raw.

"That's uncommonly noble of you, Flowers. Or it's one of the most vicious power grabs in history. Could go either way with you."

Flowridia couldn't meet Etolié's eye. "I don't want to rule. I'm fucking terrified, Etolié."

"Well . . . I mean, I still have twenty-three years left of working for the imperator of Nox'Kartha. Stands to reason you should take over that debt."

Flowridia did look at her for that, shocked at the offer. "All of Casvir's contracts are void upon his death, and you know that."

Etolié glared. "Just let me fucking help you. Good intentions still run kingdoms into the ground. You're gonna need Solvira's help. Because you're right. Fucked up as it is, you're the best candidate as Casvir's successor. Some will agree, some won't, and I'll be here to help you know which of the latter will try to stab you in the back."

Were she not bathing, Flowridia might've hugged her.

Once finished, Flowridia wrapped herself in a robe and took Dira back, quickly parting the top to let her daughter feed. Again came that sting, a stream of blood and white liquid nourishing her beloved child.

She lowered herself to the ground. "I know this needs to be discussed, but can it wait? Just for an hour. I . . . I need to be alone with her."

Khastra gently led Etolié away, perhaps empathetic to the plights of a new mother. Alone at last, Flowridia gazed upon her beautiful infant, mesmerized by every breath, every motion—

"Or you'll beat her into a spineless little wraith like yourself—"

Flowridia nearly choked on her own spit, anxiety clawing from within her skin. Her breath shuddered. She cradled Dira with utmost affection, resisting the urge to cry.

Once, Odessa had gazed upon a baby Flowridia, had aided her when she had struggled to breathe at birth, had fed her from her breast . . .

How had she not felt this same boundless love?

Flowridia stroked her gentle infant's scalp, parting wisps of black hair. Odessa had touched locks of auburn, just like her own, and not felt this love.

Had she left Flowridia on a doorstep because she knew she'd snap? Perhaps the thought was more charitable than her mother deserved. How many threats had she screamed? How often had she ripped out chunks of Flowridia's hair? There were far more threats than acts of abuse, but there were far more nights Flowridia had cried herself to sleep than not. How many buckets of blood had she mopped? How many victims had she harvested organs from? How many times had she covered her ears and cowered in the dark as Mother had her way with enchanted victims and slit their throats?

Yet the horrors she'd been forced to commit and witness paled to the withholding of love.

Perhaps there were more suitable homes than hers. Right now, she was a mother, perhaps even a widow. But when she left this room, she would be an imperator. What love could she possibly offer to a child when a whole kingdom needed her aid?

What love could she possibly offer her daughter when her own mother's shadow lurked to consume her?

Gods, she needed wisdom, but where could she turn?

Her breath hitched at the slight hum from tiny Dira's throat. Those beautiful eyes had opened, watching her with untainted trust. When would that trust fade? When she ruined that precious innocence?

Flowridia wept as she basked in Dira's love, her heart never so torn as this.

CHAPTER 43

Sora awoke to warmth.

Her vision blurred, slowly swirling into focus with each blink. Celestière was a world of day, light permeating despite the stone walls surrounding her. With each blink, more details came into view—sigils of sunlight, weapons on the walls. She was on her stomach, cushioned by blankets, but when she tried to rise, a sting cut through her back.

She gasped. There came a shifting of light. "There you are! She's awake!" At the boisterous proclamation, Sora's eyes adjusted to topaz and Eionei's effervescent smile. "Welcome back to the light!" He turned to someone out of sight, beckoning rapidly. A few Celestials entered, each wearing robes with sunlight sigils. "How are you feeling?"

Sora shifted uncomfortably as the Celestials touched her softly on her back, unprepared for the sharp pain. "Sore. What happened?"

"We were hoping you might tell us."

"Why am I in Vanir Sol?"

Eionei's grimace held hesitation leagues long. "The God of Death brought you. I was hoping you might explain that too."

Sora shut her eyes, willing her memory to return. She had been running in the mists, hadn't she? Running from Ilune, then had faced a blast of light, but there was something else . . .

She gasped—then groaned as pain ripped through her core. "Leelan."

She had eaten him.

"Yes, I meant to ask about that too," Eionei said. "You, uh, ate your familiar. That's what it looks like anyway."

Sensations Sora didn't recognize flowed through her, originating from limbs she simply didn't have. She tried to rise, only to tense against the pain. "Dammit."

Eionei came nearer, careful as he waved away the priestess' hands. "Let me help you."

Sora grasped his hands, grateful for the support as she braced her core to rise. Not quite so excruciating now, though the unnaturalness of it didn't escape her. When a priestess brought a mirror, Sora lost her breath.

She was naked from the waist up, save for a wrap around her breasts, revealing a massive pair of golden wings hanging from her back, draping across the bed. Smaller feathers rose up her arms, thin by her hands, thicker by her shoulders. Her hands themselves bore claws and a bird's rough flesh—not unlike Rulan.

Sora brought a claw up to caress those golden feathers. They reflected the fire in a sunset of hues, a stunning display. "I . . . I really did it. But I feel . . . well, sane."

"I won't pretend to know much of anything about this," Eionei said, his touch lingering on her waist. "But the results speak for themselves. You saved us."

Saved them? Sora gazed into the fire, reminded of Ilune and her Silver Fire, the explosion, the shield . . . "No, I—" Ilune had been the one to try. Sora had acted to save Ilune. "Where is Ilune?"

Eionei's expression brightened. "She's been detained, thank the Suns."

"Detained?" Panic filled her, though she struggled to name the source. "How?"

"Well, after she stumbled into Vanir Sol with you, we couldn't exactly let her waltz around. We argued quite a bit, she and I, which gave a few paladins the chance to overpower her. She's in the Temple of the Moon, I believe. You're safe from her, don't worry."

Ilune would do nothing accidentally. So why had she brought Sora here? Sora tried to stand, swaying from the added weight on her back until Eionei and a priestess grabbed her feathered arms. "I want to see her."

"And you can. However . . ." Eionei gave an apologetic grin. "You have quite the crowd waiting for you."

"What?"

"You wielded the power of Sol Kareena to save Vanir Sol. The people have questions."

"Can you please explain what you mean by that?"

Eionei looked taken aback. "The shield you created prevented the blast from overtaking Vanir Sol. Did you really not realize?"

Arguing that it had been an accident would do nothing for her cause—whatever that cause was. Sora ignored the question and took a step without them, though Eionei kept a hold on her forearm, and managed to make her way through the back room of what she realized was a temple.

And once outside, Sora balked at the crowd.

Surely half the city waited, excited chattering erupting through the crowd. "Now, now," Eionei called, releasing her as he held up his hands. "She's as exhausted as you'd imagine."

Despite his placating, Sora got lost listening to the crowd, shocked at how articulately she could make out individual voices:

"How can this be? Has Sol Kareena returned to us?"

"That is the Sora who came with Chaos!"

"Sol Sora? Is the goddess' spirit reborn?"

"Wait!" Sora cried, surprised at the power in her own voice, even more when the crowd silenced at her command. "I . . ." So many eyes were upon her, desperate gazes bearing the shadows of panic and fear. What could Sora even say? Who was she to say anything at all?

In her mind, she felt it—not words, no, but a presence. Warmth. Love. She was not nobody.

"My name is Sora Makosa," she began. "I was the traveling companion of Goddess Chaos, yes. A-And yes, it seems I do now wield the power of Sol Kareena. To summarize a long story, her power was in a vessel, uh, granted to my care. I absorbed it to protect it, and I suppose I saved Vanir Sol too."

The crowd did not stay silent. "Then you must stay!" one Celestial implored.

Sora looked to Eionei amid the crowd's panic. "Vanir Sol has no leader," Eionei whispered. "You could stay."

Cold sank as deep as Sora's bones. "Stay? And rule?"

"You wouldn't be alone, but yes. The power is as important as the influence. If you wield the power of the sun, your powers would do an incredible amount of good for Vanir. No one would contest your claim after what you did."

There lay a plea in his words. Yet Sora's heart waited a world away. "I can't stay here. I can't rule. I have to go home."

"And that's your choice," Eionei said, though something in his expression sank. "But may I ask why?"

"My family needs me. My sister just had a baby. I . . . I need to be in Dira's life."

At the name, Eionei paused. "Was that not the name of the Goddess?"

Sora shut her mouth. But Eionei offered a wry grin. "Secrets are the way of the world," he said. "I can keep one more." He looked to the crowd, bidding them to quiet through gesture alone. "Sora needs time to consider it. In the meantime, she has places to be."

Eionei shielded her as they made their way through the gathering of citizens, though Sora's new wings seemed to have a mind of their own on the matter, reacting instinctively to avoid being touched. "Consider what you'd accomplish if you stayed, however."

Sora balked at the statement. "No."

"You'd have me as your personal friend and advisor."

When the crowd was breached, Sora stopped. Duty said to stay, but whose duty? "This isn't my home, Eionei," Sora said. "I don't know this place or these people. I guess I saved you on a technicality, and I'm happy that I did, but do you really think I have more claim than Morathma? Do you really think I'd do better than Sol Kareena? I have no ties here. These people would accept me until the dust settles and they realize they put a mortal on the throne. I know there are a lot of unknowns right now, but I'm not the answer."

Sora stood tall as she challenged this unfathomably ancient god. Eionei had witnessed the fall of Celestière, had lived through the Convergence, was the first of the New Gods to emerge . . .

And the answer shone brighter than the magic now flowing through her veins. "Why not you?"

Eionei laughed, though it seemed forced. "Don't be ridiculous."

"How am I ridiculous? You just said you'd be my advisor, which you did for Sol Kareena too, didn't you?"

"Well, yes."

"You're the oldest angel in the realm. You were the first New God. There is no one more qualified than you."

With Eionei's foppish grin came his mask, feigning incompetence. "I hardly have the disposition."

"There's more to you than booze and parties. You're compassionate and kind, and you *do* understand the politics of this world—perhaps better than the seasoned politicians. These people love you. They respect you. Morathma would have no choice but to back off if you put your name in the running."

"I would never say aloud that Morathma is more qualified, but—"

"You might not believe in yourself, but I do."

Finally, Eionei dropped the mask, insecurity shining bright. "My legacy is nothing to Neoma's or Kareena's. I'd be a shadow to their might."

"Perhaps Celestière doesn't need might. Perhaps it needs someone who understands how to rebuild."

"Strictly speaking, they'd have understood that too, but . . ." Eionei sighed, wincing as he summoned his words. "I will consider it. Would you be *my* advisor?"

Sora replied by lightly punching his arm, affection in her grin. "Take me to Ilune."

Eionei's chuckle meant all was well.

Their journey came to an end at an austere building borne up by stone pillars and, most notably, sigils of the moon. Surely an old temple to Neoma, and Sora followed Eionei's lead through the pillars into a hall of stone, lit by torches instead of glowing sconces.

They passed a guard wearing Sol Kareena's garb, who nodded at Eionei's passing.

A great chapel of stone met them, bearing no roof to bring in light. Only the torches and angel wings lit the space—Eionei's and Ilune's, the latter of whom knelt in a metal cage.

Sora sensed no spells to speak of, not that they would do any good. Silver Fire absorbed whatever magic it touched. Pristine as always, though with her hands in chains, Ilune's smile conveyed the sensuous splendor Sora had come to expect. Countless armed Celestials stood nigh, armed and prepared for combat.

Sora forcibly stilled her steps, shocked at her own instinct to run to the cage. "As you can see," Eionei said, "she's quite secure."

What a naïve thing to say. Sora didn't mention the horrifying magic she had witnessed in Ku'Shya's cavern. "Might I speak to her alone?"

"I don't think that would be wise."

Sora said nothing, simply crossed the room toward the cage.

At Sora's approach, Ilune rose. "Look at you. The wings suit you, Sora. Might I touch one?"

"Do not let her touch you," one guard said from the wall.

How delightful, Ilune's chuckle. "You know I'd never hurt you."

"I don't know that, but you could have easily killed me or let me die," Sora said. "You didn't, though. Instead, you kept saving my life. Is that why you brought me here?"

That impish facade cracked, just a little. "You needed help."

Even though I betrayed you, but Sora kept it to herself. "This woman saved Vanir Sol," Sora said, loud enough for all to hear it. "She knew where we were and she tried to stop the explosion. I only stepped up when she faltered."

"Sora," came Eionei's pacifying tone, "I don't know if that's the best rumor to be spreading."

"It's not a rumor! She shouldn't be in this cage." She looked to Eionei, whose confusion was balanced by the firm hold on his rapier's hilt. "I've rejected taking Vanir Sol's throne, but if stepping up means Ilune will be freed, I'll proclaim that she's served her sentence."

"You'll be arguing with Ku'Shya," Eionei said.

"I don't care."

"You should care," Ilune said sweetly. "Sora, dear, don't throw this all away for me."

"You're my friend. I made a vow. And I've thrown away much worse for friends." Back to Eionei, she said, "Ilune isn't what you think anymore."

To her chagrin, Eionei burst into laughter. "Not what I think? For you to say that means she's exactly what she's always been—a deceiver. A manipulator."

"I love you too, Uncle Eionei," Ilune muttered.

Through a forced smile, Eionei spoke politely. "Sora, you're young, so your ignorance can be overlooked, but you can't fathom what this woman stole from us. Neoma was our savior in the Convergence. She was a hero who ruled with justice. Ilune murdered her and so many more."

Sora knew that glassy gaze, the very same she'd witnessed in the starry field one night. He wasn't wrong, nor was it her place to plead on Ilune's behalf. "As the apparent wielder of Sol Kareena's power, may I at least speak to Ilune alone?" The guards seemed lost; Eionei too. "I'm not going to free her. I don't have the key. And she won't use my bones to break the lock. I'm safer than all of you, really."

Despite his grimace, Eionei gave a firm nod. "Let's clear out. Sora has earned this much for her service."

When the last of the guards left, Eionei lingered in the doorframe. "I'm confused about the relationship here. You said you were friends?"

"We are," Sora affirmed, even if it was foolish to say. "I can explain the story later. Can you please give us a moment?"

Eionei obeyed, disappearing down the stone hallway.

No doubt someone eavesdropped. Sora leaned in close and whispered, face pressed between the bars. "I'm going to get you out of here. I won't stop fighting."

"Hush," Ilune whispered, her devious smile a mere breath away. "Obviously I'm going to escape. But I wanted to see you."

The words struck a deep chord. Sora met her gaze, mesmerized by her impossible beauty in the ethereal ambiance, both from the torchlight and the angel's glowing wings. "Why? I undermined you. I-I took away your victory against Ku'Shya."

Ilune shrugged. "I don't hold grudges, Sora. As I said, I admire your audacity."

Sora remained skeptical, even as Ilune's shackles suddenly sparked and released. But her mind fell blank when Ilune's gaze glanced down her nearly bare chest, then caressed her face. How remiss Sora was to admit how her blood raced, disappointed when Ilune didn't act. "Where will you go?" Ilune asked.

"Home to my sister. My niece needs me."

Ilune hummed as she caressed Sora's hairline, the reflection of fire in her silver eyes revealing warm amber instead. "What an enigma you are, Sora Makosa. Offered the gift of godhood on a silver platter, only to reject it for domesticity. I admire your sense of duty. I shall miss that about you."

Sora's good mood shattered. "Miss me? You don't have to go. We could hide you in Nox'Kartha. Etolié would love that."

Ilune softly took her hand. "There's something I need to do. I intend to return, but I don't wish to burden Etolié with my presence before it's done."

Sora squeezed her hand. "You're not a burden, especially not to Etolié."

"She barely knows me. You barely know me, for that matter. But I will return." She brought Sora's clawed hand to her lips, leaving a lingering kiss. "And that's a threat. Though . . ." Ilune flashed an impish smile. "You could run away with me. What an adventure we would have."

"Even if I were inclined to say yes, my niece needs me."

"Fair enough. At the very least, I could stop by your bed before I go. It would be our secret."

It didn't sound like the worst way to end this disastrous series of events. Truly, what was one more? But the temptation was merely a whisper to the many questions it evoked. "You're awfully fixated on that."

"You can't say you haven't thought about it."

Sora couldn't, and so she didn't comment. "You implied once that there was a reason for wanting me. Given you're leaving anyway, perhaps if I heard your reason, I'd reconsider."

Realistically, no. She wouldn't—sleeping with someone she was only *mostly* certain wouldn't kill her wasn't going to happen—but victory swelled in her chest at Ilune's contemplative look. "Oh, all right. I shall lay down my cards for your judgment. Given the circumstances, I think you will be flattered."

Sora waited, narrowly avoiding raising a scathing eyebrow.

"I have many wants, Sora. One of them is to restart my bloodline. And given your accomplishments, your titles, and, well, now your fascinating array of powers, what a wonderful candidate you are."

Sora reeled at the statement, even stumbling back and out of Ilune's touch. At least she resisted the urge to yell. "You want me to have your baby?"

"My lich self would struggle to carry my own child to term, but I have Silver Fire. It's quite doable—just like you are." Ilune's wink left Sora burning. "Think on it. Hopefully your niece inspires your own maternal urges. I cannot promise to fall in love, but I would be loyal and true. You would be cherished and adored. That is the least I could do for the mother of my child. You would be the founder of a new lineage of monarchs, a queen at my side in whatever capacity you chose, whether it be to rule or live a quiet life with your family. I am quite generous to those who do good by me. Whatever you asked would be yours, if you do this one thing for me. What do you say?"

The oddest thing of all was that 'no' was not her immediate response. Sora studied Ilune, this strange, enigmatic comet seeking to rip her planet from orbit, and found only mystery unbound.

But what was mystery if not another word for adventure? For now, it was time to rest, but now was not forever. "I say we'll talk about that when you get back from wherever you're going."

Ilune burst into laughter—not maniacal or cruel, purely amused. "Oh, Sora. I do adore you, genuinely." She set the shackles back around her wrists, her grin never fading. "Your niece is fortunate to have you. I wish you nothing but joy."

"So I'll see you again?"

Now came that mischief. "Soon, Sora. And that *is* a threat."

Ilune called her the enigma, but Sora was just as baffled to be drawn to this impish, albeit beautiful, god. "I'll wait for you on one condition."

With lips that dripped implication, Ilune blew a kiss through the bars. "And what condition is that?"

"You'll say goodbye to Etolié before you disappear."

Sora resisted a grin at Ilune's sputtering. "How are those things related?"

"They're not. But those are my terms."

"And how do I know you will keep this bargain, hmm? I don't hold grudges but I'm hardly a fool."

Sora mulled the question over, appalled at where her own rascally mind wandered to. Never had she met someone who made her feel so . . . reckless. Feigning a neutral expression, Sora slipped her fingers under the bottom of the wrap covering her breasts—and promptly lifted it up, flashing the God of Death.

Ilune's gaze sharpened, pupils expanding slightly even as Sora put her top back in place. "You bring up a compelling point. I shall see what I can do. Farewell, Sora." Ilune's groan should not have been so sexually charged, given the context. Still, Sora imagined far too well hearing that voice in the dark.

Perhaps, one day, she would. "Farewell, Ilune."

Sora fought a smile as she walked away.

The funeral was as fancy as Casvir deserved—much to Etolié's chagrin.

The entire kingdom had gathered in Haven, forming a line miles long through the streets. Etolié had personally overseen the dressing of the body, meaning she had held Dira while Flowers set the finishing touches to his casket. He'd been burned something nasty during the explosion, but his armor was in decent enough condition, his bones all in the right places. It was Casvir, just deader than he was before.

A ceremony had been held that morning. Etolié hadn't attended. Now, she stood near the mausoleum that would be his final resting place, waiting for the procession to arrive. Thousands wished to gaze upon the crispy corpse of their former imperator, and Etolié wouldn't begrudge them that.

Truthfully, her greatest source of annoyance was the sunlight through the shady tree. It didn't quite hurt, but it itched in ways sobriety once had. Etolié had yet to successfully drink herself into drunkenness, but it didn't mean she wasn't going to keep trying. Speaking of—Etolié took a sip of her flask then and there, appreciating the taste without the expectation of feeling something.

The issue, of course, was that she'd have to puke it up later, lest it build up and slosh around her stomach. Oh well. Not needing it to mentally survive was a nice change.

Nearby, Demitri sunned himself as Flowers stood regally in the shade, shielding her dhampir baby from the sun. She always held Dira as if terrified she'd vanish, her body tense even if the baby remained comfortable. Motherhood came with anxiety, it seemed. That, or she feared the baby would disappear like its other mother. Etolié could do little except hold the baby when Flowers needed to sign a pile of paperwork.

Today, they mourned Casvir. Tomorrow, she was crowned Imperator Makosa.

Etolié hadn't asked about the relevance of the change in surname. She hadn't asked about Ayla at all. Ayla hadn't resurfaced since her little explodey episode, and Etolié was starting to think she really might be gone for good. Time spent with the Goddess of Chaos had made her a little melancholy at the thought of Ayla truly being gone. She had a soft spot for motherly love, and Dira deserved all that she could get.

Speaking of . . . Etolié set a hand to her temple and whispered, "Momma, I'm so fucking bored."

Momma's chuckle sounded cutely in her head. *Be respectful, Starshine.*

"To this bastard? The one I just had to emancipate Solvira from?"

Be respectful in public, Starshine. You're welcome to come blaspheme here, however. Eionei wants to congratulate you on your victory sometime.

"Does he know about . . . ?"

Oh, the vampire incident? Yes. He had to take a few deep breaths, but I think he took it well. He has much bigger things to be worried about now, anyway.

Aw, yes. God Eionei—the supreme leader of Celestière. Etolié chuckled despite the somber scene. It's what he fucking deserved, in all the best and worst ways. "I'm supposed to visit Khastra after this, but I'll come bother you soon."

What strange times. I do rather like knowing we're in the same timeline now, though it will take getting used to.

After a few hours of conversation, Etolié and Staella had realized something had changed. The time differences between worlds were no more. Celestière and Sha'Demoni both were a little less broken, a little more secure. What a damn strange thing.

"It means Soliel will get to grow up on track with, uh, everyone else."

To you. This was always our normal. But I'm determined to give him the best life I can as Aunt Staella.

With Eionei secure on the throne in Celestière, those vying for its power had disappeared into the shadows—most notably, Morathma had slithered back into his hole. It also meant Etolié resolved to get along with her baby cousin Soliel, who would now be growing up a helluva lot faster.

"You'll do amazing, Momma."

He's Neoma's flesh and blood. I have to do right by her and Kareena both.

"Forgive me if the question is, uh, tender, but what will you do if Ilune stops by to see him?"

A pause. Before Etolié could regret the query, Staella finally spoke. *I'm not sure. I suppose I'll simply have to find out and see.*

"You think she'll come?"

I don't know what to think. But I do hope I haven't seen her for the last time.

Somehow, the topic only caused Etolié's heart to ache. Lest she be mistaken for tearing up at this bastard's funeral, she quickly said, "Talk to me more about Eionei having a hard time. I'm bored as fuck."

After several more hours at least, the damn hearse finally made its way toward her. Drawn by undead horses, the open casket revealed Casvir at rest—or, what was left of him. His general shape had been preserved in the explosion, turned into some sort of bloated mummified version of himself, with shards of armor having melted into his skin. Tucked beneath his arm was the box holding his heart. Held in what remained of his hands was a folded flag of Nox'Kartha, his legacy upon this realm.

A legacy forged from blood and necromancy, wealth and power. Casvir would never be forgotten.

Etolié watched as they passed. Flowers stepped up to the hearse, her protective hold on Dira somehow a shield as she approached the man who was supposed to own her. Flowers cried because she always fucking cried. When she waved them along, she wiped her tears, then kissed her baby girl.

She'd done the right thing for the right cause. Motherly love was a powerful force.

"Hi, Etolié."

Etolié gasped and whirled around, but her shock in no way abated when she saw Sora-fucking-Makosa standing there with goddamn wings.

Etolié stared as she looked her up and down, shock drowning even her relief at seeing Sora alive. "What the actual fuck?"

"It's a long story." Sora offered a very inhuman hand. Etolié took her claw and squeezed—at which point Sora paused. "You have a story too."

"Oh, yeah. I'm kind of a vampire monster now."

Flowers rapidly approached, her surprise a mirror. She fell into Sora's arms, still cradling Dira, her tears still flowing fast. "You absorbed Leelan?"

Is that what the wings meant? Etolié had many questions, but she knew they'd have to wait. When Sora gazed upon Dira, nothing else mattered to her ornery half-elf friend.

Sora accepted the baby with joy, her smile splitting her face. "Flowridia, she's so beautiful."

The baby was pretty damn cute, it was true. But Sora's attention went to Demitri instead, who glared as much as a wolf was capable of. When Sora took a tentative step toward him, the wolf growled. "I know it'll take time," Sora whispered, "but I hope to earn your trust."

Flowers and Demitri shared a look, some silent interaction there, given Flowers' sudden grimace. "He says you can try."

Still, Etolié was feeling impatient. "Can you talk and hold the baby at the same time?"

Sora cradled Dira as she told her tale, and Etolié hung onto every word.

Once the procession ended and Sora's story was told, Flowridia left with her for the castle, leaving Etolié to go off to wherever Etolié went when she wasn't working. Perhaps she needed to process the news about Ilune alone. Flowridia had known about her own sister for barely a year, yet would be lost without her.

Despite the joy of the moment, Sora's return had kindled a hope she hated to entertain. Sora had returned, so would Ayla come too?

Demitri's presence parted the crowd of people as they walked. Though packed, the streets were quiet. Reverence covered the city like a film. Sora spoke softly, ignoring the attention she drew with those incredible wings. "You haven't told your story yet."

Flowridia glanced to Dira. "I'm still processing it."

"Did Ayla leave?"

Flowridia stopped, cursing the fresh rise of tears to her eyes. "I don't know where she is, Sora. She might be dead."

Flowridia had her ear locked safely away, but without the Moon's blood, there was no hope.

Nearby, the great statue of Casvir remained stalwart in the city square. It always would. With muted words, Flowridia sat in its shadow and told the tale of Ayla's sacrifice. By the end, even Sora teared up.

It was uncouth to cry in front of the people who would soon be hers. But this was a day of mourning. No one would begrudge Flowridia her tears. The entire country wept this day.

"I've never been more afraid, Sora," Flowridia continued. "The realms are at peace, but I've never felt so overwhelmed." She looked down to sweet Dira, who had cried half the night, who had refused to nurse and bitten her over and over, who was perfect in every way, but Flowridia had spent the whole night in tears. "How can I possibly raise this baby and lead a country?"

"You won't be alone. You'll have me."

Flowridia spat the hateful question: "Would you take her?"

Demitri perked up, though said nothing. Sora stared as though she'd been slapped. "What? Why would you even ask that?"

"Because for all the wonderful traits you said my mother had, we can't deny that loving her children wasn't exactly one of them. What if I hurt her? What if I hate her?"

"You would never."

"You don't know that." Flowridia choked back a sob, her hold upon Dira equal parts tentative and tight. "You haven't seen me lose my temper."

"You literally wished for my death once, but that's not the point. Have you hurt Dira?"

Flowridia shook her head, horrified at the thought.

"You won't hurt Dira. You *will* break the cycle, Flowridia. You'll be better than Odessa."

"But the stakes are too high. It's not me I'll be hurting if I fail."

Sora pulled a familiar locket from her pocket, opening it to reveal the faces of her mom and papa. Both had long passed, but they lived on in memory. Sora's papa—Flowridia's too—smiled to rival the sun. "I likely idolize my papa more than I should," Sora said. "I know he was torn between duty and heart, and he did his best, but that doesn't mean I wasn't left to live half my younger years without him. Be that as it may, he was my hero. I've told you a few stories, but that doesn't capture the magnitude of his presence. He was an incredible man. He was an amazing papa. He's everything I aspire to be in life. Don't forget, you're half his blood too. You have just as much potential to be as beloved as he was."

Flowridia gently took the locket, knowing it was worth more than gold. Zanoram Makosa, the heir to the fallen Theocracy—the circumstances of Flowridia's conception were tragic to consider, but here she was, holding that torch. "He'd be proud of you," Flowridia whispered.

"He'd be proud that I became a bird woman who absorbed the power of the goddess he pledged his life to?" Sora's smile was broad and kind, a mirror to the man in the picture. "I think he would too. And he'd be proud of you. Sometimes, it's not about the journey. It's about where we end up."

Flowridia looked between Dira and the locket, touched to gaze upon two generations. What would Lunestra have thought of this child? Would she have loved her because she was Flowridia's? Or hated her for her undead blood? "Would Papa have loved Dira even though she's a dhampir?"

Sora released her hand, setting her arm around Flowridia instead. One of her grand wings followed, shielding them from the sun. "Papa always taught to never hate someone based on where they came from. He said to love them based on their choices. He would have loved Dira with all his heart."

Flowridia offered back the locket, managing a small smile. Perhaps . . . Perhaps he was the bridge. Perhaps they shared common struggles, torn between duty and heart.

Fear remained. But for all the dark powers granted by blood, it was matched in equal parts by light.

"Would you ever want to see him again?" Flowridia asked.

"Of course. And I intend to, in the Beyond. Him and Mom both."

"I mean now. Would you want to see him today?"

At Sora's questioning gaze, Flowridia quickly explained Casvir's device hidden in the recesses of the castle, its origin and power both.

Truthfully, she expected a rejection. Necromancy wasn't something Sora endorsed. But to her surprise, Sora looked thoughtful. "You said this was an artifact from the Goddess of Chaos?"

"Dira herself, in the past."

Sora sat back, tepid hope upon her face. "She told me something in Moratham that really stuck with me. About necromancy. The short version is that it's been bastardized in the modern era, a far cry from what it was meant to be. Perhaps . . . Well, you said the device was an invitation?"

Flowridia nodded, intrigued.

Such wonder in Sora's gaze. "Let me think about it. I think the answer will be yes, but I need to process it first."

Flowridia smiled. "Will you tell me the long version of what Chaos said?"

"Sorry to interrupt the tearfest," came a familiar snarky voice. Of course it was Etolié.

Flowridia wiped her eyes. "You clearly had a reason."

"Yes. You see . . ." Etolié's grimace became a groan. "Sora, you inherited the powers of Sol Kareena, right?"

"As far as we've seen, yes," Sora replied, clearly suspicious.

Etolié's slight chuckle set Flowridia ill at ease. "Could we take a walk? Just you and me, Sora."

"You have never sounded more guilty in your entire life."

"Fine, it's not me who wants to talk to you. It's Khastra."

Flowridia perked up. "Is she here?"

"She's the goddamn queen of Sha'Demoni, Flowers. You think she's gonna sully her hooves with Nox'Kartha anymore? Please."

Sora caught her eye. "I'll tell you the story when I get back. Are you going to be all right?"

Flowridia gave a small nod, still mulling it all over. "If not, there's plenty to keep me busy today."

She flinched and laughed when Sora mussed her hair, her meticulously placed crown suddenly loose. But her gaze softened to look at sweet Dira, watching it all with silver eyes. "You're going to be an incredible mom, Flowridia."

Flowridia watched them leave, her hope tentative but true.

"Ilune escaped," Etolié began, whispering when they were out of ear-shot. "I've just been informed."

Sora failed to feign shock. What did it matter anyway? "Am I supposed to act surprised?"

"No. Actually, I'm here on behalf of more anxious parties, specifically the undead Goddess of War."

A good reminder that Etolié might be a neutral party, but Khastra, it seemed, was not. "I don't think Ilune has any intention of seeing Khastra."

"Good luck convincing Beefcake of that. Though from the sound of it, nobody knows what Ilune plans on doing next."

Bitterness stained the words. Sora grabbed Etolié's hand and squeezed. "She's going to come back." Sora had told her everything—everything except the 'proposition.' "It sounds like when she comes back, she wants to come back the right way."

Etolié gripped her hand tight, sudden tension in her words. "I wish she would've at least said goodbye."

Sora kept her bargain to herself, hoping Ilune followed through. "I know."

"I told Khastra everything. She doesn't trust Ilune but she's chosen to trust my judgment. Her words, not mine."

"Does Khastra have some sort of grudge?" Given Etolié's incredulous stare, Sora had said something very stupid. "I know Khastra was against her in the Solviran Civil War—"

"Sora, they literally were a famous power couple from history. Get your head in the game."

That was when Sora knew she'd done the right thing, keeping that proposition to herself. "There aren't any lingering—"

"Feelings? Not on Khastra's end. And there better not be on Ilune's. Can we talk about something else?"

"You did pull me away from Flowridia for a reason."

Rather than release her hand, Etolié took her other one. "Permission to teleport us to Sha'Demoni?"

Nothing made sense anymore. Sora shrugged. "Sure, Etolié."

One blink, and Sora floated. Another, and she stood beneath vermilion walls, facing a mighty figure.

It wasn't a weakness that Khastra had always terrified Sora. It was wise.

But for all the grandeur the half-demon had held in her time in Staelash, for all the might as the general of Nox'Kartha's army, a new glint shone in those pupilless eyes as she sat upon her throne in *Daemenacht*. Sora hadn't seen her in years, now that she considered it. One of her more recent memories was the curse of facing the Bringer of War tearing down the walls in an underground cavern.

And though Khastra did not sit in a pile of bones like her predecessor nor possess her sheer size, this new goddess in Sha'Demoni could still armies with that pupilless stare.

"Sora Makosa, it is good to see you," Khastra said, sincere as far as Sora could tell. "While you may have been hated by my mother, I am willing to wipe the slate, as they say. Any friend of Etolié is welcome here." Even so, Sora's gut twisted at the sudden cruelty in Khastra's grin. "Assuming you do not steal from me too."

"No, uh, your majesty."

Khastra's chuckle did nothing to set Sora's nerves at ease. She rose. Had she gotten taller? "I am not 'your majesty.' How quaint. I am Goddess Khastra, the Bringer of War."

"Stop being a dickhead, Beefcake," Etolié said, her own amusement rudely apparent. "I thought you had a favor to ask."

Sora had wings, but she didn't have audacity. Not like Khastra, whose swagger had only increased with this new title of godhood. "Follow me. I will explain."

Sora obeyed, relieved when Etolié followed at Khastra's side. Their hands met, the tattoos spiraling from Khastra's palm coming alight. For all of Khastra's boldness, Etolié softened her in small and simple ways. Alone, she walked like she owned the world; in Etolié's hand, she walked like Etolié was her world. Sweet, though were Etolié anyone but, well, herself, Sha'Demoni should have feared who whispered in their leader's ear.

But it *was* Etolié. Vampire or not, she had a heart of gold.

They led her beyond the walls of the burrow, toward the canyon and oppressive heat. "I am told you have taken on the power of Sol Kareena," Khastra said.

"That is what they say," Sora replied, actively resisting the urge to sing into the fresh air. The compulsion wasn't constant, but it was new. Leelan was more of a feeling than a voice, but his presence was certainly there.

"My mother is alive. She has agreed to let you heal her."

Sora frowned, taken aback by the words. "It's been days."

"Yes, and she has not succumbed to her wounds. Staella has finally convinced her."

"Forgive me, but can't Goddess Staella heal her?"

It was Etolié who answered. "There's some concern that my momma might not live through that."

Despite the words, Sora was not prepared for the tragedy she faced.

Ku'Shya, the former Goddess of War, lay in the open air within a massive wreath of blooming flowers. She was smaller somehow, perhaps half the size of the mighty goddess, curled on her side like a disposed spider. She had but one leg and two arms, the rest merely stumps. So little of her exoskeleton remained, only charred blotches or pulsing, raw flesh. She followed Sora's movements with one dim eye, the other three burned away. Each labored breath conveyed pain, but breathe she did.

She was not alone. A crowd of demons surrounded her, though kept a respectful distance. Surely to pay their respects, given their reverence. Near Ku'Shya was Kah'Sheen, touching one of the uninjured patches of Ku'Shya's remaining leg, and Goddess Staella, dried tears upon her face. At Sora's approach, she rose. "So it is true," Staella whispered, her gaze upon those feathered wings. "And you still have your mind?"

"So far," Sora replied. "I don't know if I can do what you're asking me to do, but I'll try."

A raspy rumbling came from Ku'Shya, weak Demoni filling the space. Etolié looked as lost as Sora felt, but Khastra, Staella, and Kah'Sheen paid keen attention.

Khastra frowned, replying in turn in the demonic tongue.

At Ku'Shya's next words, Kah'Sheen whispered in frantic Demoni, rushing up to join the rest of them.

"What's going on?" Etolié muttered to Staella.

Staella's lip trembled. "Ku'Shya says she has no wish to be healed. She says to have died defending Sha'Demoni from the same sort of calamity that created it is the greatest ending for her legacy. She is insulted that fate has left her to suffer but wonders if perhaps there was a purpose. She ..." Staella turned to Sora. "She wishes to know what powers you inherited."

"I don't entirely know," Sora said. "I-I accidentally created a shield of light to protect Vanir Sol, but I haven't tried anything else yet."

"That is a unique ability."

Khastra interpreted the words, judging by her gestures. When Ku'Shya spoke, Staella spoke alongside her. "Sol Kareena could resurrect the dead. I suppose you would know that firsthand, Sora. But it required an equivalent sacrifice—" Staella's words choked. Through fresh tears, she asked, "Could you accept Ku'Shya's life and give it to Khastra instead?"

"What?" Sora saw that same shock mirrored upon Etolié, upon Khastra and Kah'Sheen. "I-I don't know. I could . . ."

A strange ringing in her head stole her words. As though in a trance, Sora lifted her hand, a mere puppet as light filled her palm. It was not knowledge, no, but instinct; her magic whispered, and Sora spoke back. "Yes. I could."

Sora did not pull the strings to coax her steps, merely a spirit following along. Before Ku'Shya, she knelt. She heard her own voice, though did not choose the words. "You would give your life for this?"

In elven, Ku'Shya uttered a simple, "Yes."

There came no protests. Khastra seemed suspended in shock. Kah'Sheen openly wept but said nothing. Staella rushed back to Ku'Shya's side, whispering as she wept. Sora could not make out the words, only saw what remained of Ku'Shya's face hold some semblance of peace.

"Staella, my friend," came Ku'Shya's weak words, "my life is for her, for my Khastra. You are understanding." To Khastra, Ku'Shya spoke softly. "It is a supreme honor to be defeated by your hands. You are protecting your sister, yes?"

"Of course," Khastra said, though she spoke as though lost.

Ku'Shya's laughter came as boisterous as ever, though ragged at the edges, conveying her quiet agony. "I am free to go."

Sora felt that rising power anew and set a hand upon Ku'Shya's brow. She shut her eyes. No words; no spell; simply a surge inside her as the life within Ku'Shya flared . . . and passed into her. No pain in the action. Sora opened her eyes and saw a golden glow held safe in her arms, warm and light. Not a soul, but . . . life. Pure light.

Ku'Shya's body settled into the dirt, her death rattle peaceful as she passed on from the world. No one knew where gods went when they died, but demons held death in reverence. Sora knew that much.

Again, words expelled from Sora's lips, ripped by foreign hands. "Khastra, kneel."

Khastra, the new Goddess of War, obeyed. When she bowed her head, the light in Sora's hands flared, seeking its new home.

Sora laid her hands upon Khastra's head, wherein the light dissipated.

Khastra collapsed forward, light bursting from every pore. Kah'Sheen gasped. The demons in the distant crowd followed suit as Khastra burned from within. Etolié fell at her side, fear in her actions as she rolled the limp demon goddess over—only to sob when Khastra heaved a pained breath, as though bursting from deep waters.

Sora stumbled away, leaving Etolié to cry in Khastra's arms. She had . . . raised the dead? She needn't check. She knew, like the moist air in her lungs, like the cloying heat upon her skin, that Khastra breathed with life.

"Are you all right?" came sweet words. Goddess Staella stood nigh.

Sora's hands dropped, a smile twisting her lip. "It seems I have a lot to learn."

Perhaps someday her life would stop being a series of ironic understatements. But not today.

"I'd better head back soon, Beefcake. I have a stupid coronation to attend."

Being a vampire monster had its advantages, notably that Etolié wasn't a sweaty mess despite the horrible humidity. She and Khastra walked hand in hand through Sha'Demoni's wilds. Not alone, no. A small procession of demonic architects followed, listening whenever Khastra spoke the Demoni tongue. A tomb would be erected, a castle worthy of being a final resting place for Ku'Shya's body. Kah'Sheen followed close behind, bruised but overall unscathed after her close encounter with Ilune—a story Etolié had pretended to know nothing about when she'd frantically relayed the tale.

"Unless you need me, that is," Etolié added. "You did just watch your momma die."

Khastra squeezed her hand, even as she surveyed the land like the queen she was. "The sorrow will come, but do not forget I fought her for my life but a few days ago. I am processing the loss and what is to come. In the meantime, you have your duties. I have mine. But you will come to me after, yes?"

How magnificent she was, this new Goddess of War, every part of her enhanced upon earning that glorious title. Her stature, her stance, the glow of her tattoos, but Etolié was most inclined to notice her hair—no longer cropped short but long, lavender locks braided down to her knees. Soliel's defeat at her hands had appeased her apparent 'honor.' Etolié was just happy to have something to tug when feeling impish.

"Well, I may have promised to visit Momma afterward," Etolié said. "She could use the support. You want to come? Eionei will be there, but he'll be nice."

"I would. I will make time for it."

"I was gonna say, you're the Goddess of War now. You can make the demons wait."

Khastra chuckled, releasing the most beautiful sound in the realms. "My title comes with duties, but I do see what you mean."

"I assume you're not coming to the coronation?"

"I am neutral toward the tiny one and will remain so for the time being. Nox'Kartha is no longer of interest to me, and hopefully she is wise enough to keep it that way."

"Yeah, I see the logic."

With her free hand, Etolié spun her engagement ring. "If you don't mind me asking, are we still having our wedding in Staelash? You're kind of a bigger deal now, but they still love you."

"Does it mean Marielle will be there?"

"She did kind of redeem herself, so yes. We owe her that much."

Khastra made a show of mulling it over, ultimately ending in a smile. "Yes, fine. For Staelash."

Etolié levitated, rising to match Khastra's height. "There's no hurry though. I'm immortal now. We can let things settle for a few years."

"You were already immortal, in theory."

"Yes, but now I'm ultra immortal. Flowers explained the terms of the dagger's curse to me. I can only be killed the same way I was killed the first time."

"So you can only be killed by Marielle?"

"I . . ." Fuck. Etolié grimaced. "It could be, but shut up."

Khastra's laughter rang out loud, soothing even that terrible burn.

The one odd change in the hour since Khastra had transfigured into a living being Etolié had noticed so far was her smell—specifically her blood. Stagnant blood was icky, but Khastra's racing and very alive blood? It smelled spicy and so very intriguing. "So are you less immortal now?"

"With the power of my mother's worshippers, I am more immortal than I ever have been before."

"So we're a perfect pair, is what I'm hearing?"

"You? My precious Izthuni-spawn? It will be a scandal." Nevertheless, Khastra took her into her arms, kissing her soundly before the wilds of Sha'Demoni. Against her lips, Khastra whispered, "They would not dare to touch you, my queen."

Well, hot damn. Khastra's blood would never be spicier than that line. "Fun fact, Beefcake, if you wanted to fuck me right here and now, I'd say yes."

To her disappointment, though not shock, Khastra chuckled. "Not in front of Kah'Sheen."

"All right, but you'd better get used to calling me 'my queen.'"

Khastra's lips curled into a rare, teasing smile. She leaned in to kiss Etolié's ear. "*My queen,*" she whispered.

"I can and will unillusion my clothes if you keep doing that."

Khastra didn't lose her good humor as she set Etolié down. "Never change, Etolié. I love you."

Somehow, the perfect ending had been achieved. The realms were saved, Casvir was gone, and Khastra loved her still. "I love you too, Khastra."

Etolié took her hand, radiant amid the glow of peace.

If sleep was so unnecessary for the dead, then why did exhaustion follow Flowridia wherever she went?

The funeral had drained her, preparations for her coronation continued, but finally mortals had gone off to bed, leaving Flowridia with a moment to breathe in the sanctuary of her bedroom.

Her bedroom. Not Ayla's, not the medical ward, nor a guest space. A room for the new imperator and a cradle for her child.

But Dira wept when she wasn't held, and so Flowridia curled up around her in her own bed, wracked with anxieties that would fill an ocean. The core of it was what mattered, notably the simple fact that she had no business running an entire kingdom.

Yet, she was the only one who could. Nox'Kartha needed a necromancer.

Dira stirred, her catnap concluding. Flowridia lifted her before she could start wailing, slowly understanding the pattern of her daughter's mind. "Mom is here, sweet Dira," she whispered, compulsively setting Dira upon her breast.

Casvir had been a highly effective ruler, but their similarities ended with their shared magic. He had ruled justly with a fist of iron, calloused even to those beneath his rule. He had saved thousands of lives, lifted so many from nothing, but all from the shadows, behind mounds of paperwork.

That would never be her. Her short stint in Solvira showcased that.

"How am I supposed to rule a country?" Flowridia asked the void—before remembering she was not alone.

Demitri stirred from his nap, the darkness obscuring his figure. *You've done it before.*

"You mean the country I abandoned after blowing half a city up?"

Yes, but you probably did some good things too.

'Probably.' How very Demitri. "I did, and then I turned a blind eye to a vampire terrorizing her own kingdom."

Real Lara would have never, it's true.

For the first time in years, the name no longer evoked sorrow, but peace. Lara's soul was safe, both due to Casvir's death and the infant in Flowridia's arms. "No, she would not. Her people loved her. They trusted her. And her rule was short, but Etolié says they still speak of her with respect."

By some miracle, the legacy of Alauriel Solviraes, last of the Solviraes line, had been salvaged, with Flowridia's name dragged through the mud instead—which, truthfully, was a fair compromise. But it was not a miracle that had let Lara's soul finally rest. It was penance and pain.

How did she do it?

"What do you mean?"

You asked how you were going to rule a country. Lara ruled a country. I think the progression is logical.

Alauriel Solviraes, kind and good yet respected by all, her wisdom unparalleled, physically unimposing yet could bring a room to silence with merely a word. Was it inborn? Taught? Of all the monarchs to emulate, Lara stood upon a pedestal.

Those were not the shoes Flowridia was expected to fill, but Lara was someone worthy to aspire to. But Lara was gone, that peace bought and paid for, and Flowridia . . .

Held the means to ask.

"I couldn't do that to her," Flowridia whispered, adjusting her dress when Dira finished eating.

Couldn't do what?

"Ask Lara how she did it. I can't bring her back for that."

Forcing her to do something like that would be mean, yes.

The operative word was 'force.' Flowridia, anxious, desperate, pushed to the brink from exhaustion and stress, rose with Dira in her arms. "I'll be back," she said, her steps automatic, pulled along by will alone.

Gods, she shouldn't do this. She should leave Lara be. But Lara could say no.

She had never made the journey without the shadow of the demon in the woods beside her, the absence of Casvir a raw wound. But she remembered the path and traversed it with dry eyes, determined to be strong a few moments longer.

She would not burden Lara with her tears.

The halls became plain, and soon Flowridia came upon her destination. Within the dark room lay the Soul Seeker, awaiting blood.

Flowridia knelt before it, a different sort of temptation rising.

She could ask for Ayla.

If she appeared, it meant she was dead. If not . . .

. . . Or perhaps Flowridia wasn't ready to know.

Flowridia shoved the thought away, withdrawing a knife from her belt instead. A small prick to her finger, and she set it upon the device, picturing the late empress in her mind. "Alauriel Solviraes."

Silence ensued, and Flowridia hoped it remained, hoped Lara did not return, hoped she stayed and clung to her peace. From her arms, Dira stared, mesmerized by the spot of welling blood upon her finger . . .

To her surprise, a blue glow filled the space, and with it emerged a distant ghost. "Hello, Flowridia."

Flowridia stared in awe upon the late empress, shaken at the changes before her. Lara wore simpler clothes than she ever owned in life, her hair flowing and free instead of braided like a waterfall, and no crown to burden her head. There was no hatred here, not like their final meeting in the library far below. Merely curiosity.

"Lara, I—" Flowridia all but hid behind the content Dira in her arms, a shield between Lara and her lingering shame. "I'm surprised you came."

"Perhaps I shouldn't have," Lara replied, "but it's because of you that I am in the Beyond at all, if Casvir spoke true."

Her one good deed, no matter how shortsighted the cost. Flowridia breathed a little easier.

"Is the baby yours?"

Flowridia's smile came unbidden though shy. She came forward, Dira on display. "She is. Created by Silver Fire."

Lara gave a nod, acceptance in the gesture. "Congratulations. But I would guess you didn't call me here to show me your daughter."

"No, I did not. Lara, Casvir is dead. And I am his successor."

Lara tried so hard to hide her appall. Flowridia might've applauded were she not holding an infant. "I see—"

"No matter how unworthy of the title you think I am, I assure you I feel worse, tenfold. But Murishani is dead as well, and Nox'Kartha needs a necromancer to survive. There is no one else but me."

"Only you?"

The question held layers. Flowridia swallowed her sorrow. "Only me, though Etolié has volunteered to keep an eye on me. But you were known far and wide for your wisdom and strength as a ruler, and I wished to know how. For the sake of the thousands of people who will be in my charge, I would humbly ask for a piece of that wisdom."

To her relief, Lara became thoughtful, still, the statuesque beauty she embodied. "In homage to its mother goddesses, Solvira's laws were defined by a balance of justice and mercy. Of course there were tyrants in our history, but the emperors and empresses most celebrated embodied that ideology. You have always lacked a center, Flowridia, and so you have no balance—and not only in the tenets of justice and mercy. Your morality has no roots except, perhaps, in service of Ayla. You must ask yourself what you believe and be unwavering as you move forward.

"Something else to consider," Lara continued, "if you seek to emulate Solvira, is that Goddess Neoma believed those in power owed it to those in their care to serve and protect them at all costs. That was something I took to heart, especially as I gained interest in pledging myself to her wife."

It all felt so familiar, and Flowridia thought back to a letter gifted long ago, destroyed in the explosion in Solvira, from the late Casvir: that justice and fairness were paramount, but that mercy had no place.

Casvir, for all his grandeur, had filled the void of mercy with revenge instead, salting the earth with his expansion.

Balance. "Thank you," Flowridia said, contemplative of this new concept. "I will consider what my center needs to be. A-And truly, I can't thank you enough."

"You are welcome. I do wish for your success, sincerely, both for Nox'Kartha and for you. I gave my life for you, so be someone worth giving a life for."

Flowridia choked up at the words, the weight of Lara's sacrifice having never left her shoulders. "I will. I swear it."

Lara stood straighter, alert. "Whatever ties me here is fading. Before I go, did you succeed? Are the realms safe from the God of Order?"

Flowridia nodded, that anguish returning. "That's why Ayla is gone. She gave it all to seize the orbs and save the realms. We can live in peace now."

For the first time, something true shone upon Lara's face— peace and quiet joy. "Then it was worth it."

Lara faded away, her image misting behind Flowridia's tears.

CHAPTER 44

With all the castle under the stress of finishing a coronation ceremony, Sora sat leisurely in one of the dining halls, content with her plate of bacon.

Tiny Dira was swaddled and wrapped to her chest, fast asleep. Flowridia, poor thing, kept getting called away, but Sora would be lying if she said she didn't love the quiet time alone with her niece.

The wings were cumbersome with the chair, so Sora sat on the edge, still getting used to their occasional involuntary motions. When Dira stirred, Sora set her temple against her infant head, adoring her baby coos.

Astounding, how much Dira resembled her older self, even days old.

Sora had been told of her glorious end. Seated alone, she swallowed tears to think of it anew, the only peace the knowledge that Dira had known, with certainty, that the worlds were saved from Casvir.

Strange, to ache for someone so near. The Goddess of Chaos had fallen, forever holding a foundation in Sora's heart. Here, she held Dira, freed from the horrors of destiny. She would not grow up in the shadows. She would be free to run in the sunlight.

And Ayla . . . was gone?

It did not feel right.

"Fancy seeing you here, snacking. You haven't changed a bit."

Sora chomped on a fresh strip as she raised an eyebrow at the approaching Etolié. "Raising the dead doesn't do it for you?"

"Don't you go getting an ego now. Grandpa sends his regards and his formal 'fuck you.' Leadership already has him growing grey hairs."

"It's been one day."

"I said what I said."

Sora chuckled, though startled when Dira released a particularly loud whimper. She set the bacon aside, wiped her hands on a napkin, and gently rocked her in her wrap. "I love this kid."

"She's pretty cute. Aunthood looks good on you. Where's Flowers?"

"Someone has needed her every five minutes for the last two hours, so rather than keep Dira awake, I'm babysitting."

"Makes sense. Question: how gloomy would it be if I started carrying a parasol outside?"

Sora raised an eyebrow. "Pretty gloomy, Etolié."

"Ah, damn. Sunlight makes me itchy now, but I really don't want to remind people of the former resident vampire." Etolié's expression and tone became flat. "And may she rest in peace, because she's totally definitely dead, no question of that."

Neither of them was convinced, it seemed.

Sora winced at the sudden sour smell hitting her nostrils. "Hold that thought. Dira needs to be changed."

"Yeah, I don't do diapers. Have fun."

With how Dira was swaddled against her body, Sora could avoid touching any part of the baby that was soiled. Dira began fussing, and Sora hurried her steps up to her room, already prepared for inevitable baby accidents.

Fortunately, newborn accidents were fairly benign. Sora quickly changed her, then swaddled her in a fresh blanket, when she noticed an oddity on her bedside table.

A handwritten note on ripped parchment stated two elegant words: *Thank you.*

The writing was familiar, ineffably so. But Sora's breath caught at what lay beneath it. Upon a handkerchief was embroidered a tiny yellow bird, each stitch meticulous, bearing the artistry of a talent many centuries old.

Sora ran her finger along each loving stitch, swallowing her sudden tears. When she brought the handkerchief to her face, Dira watched with curiosity.

"Your mother always was an incredible artist," Sora whispered. Her voice choked at 'mother.'

Such finality in it, yet Sora's hope rose as she tucked the embroidery and the note in her bedside table drawer. Would Ayla return? Was this a gift from the Beyond? Was that even possible?

Whatever her fate, when Sora matched eyes with Dira's inquisitive silver, there was no question she lived on in blood. "She'll live on in stories, too," Sora whispered, adoring how Dira absorbed the words like parched earth to rain. Sora cradled her sweet niece like the treasure she was.

Family was legacy, and Ayla's legacy could be rewritten in her.

Standing before a gilded mirror, Flowridia gazed upon a monarch to be.

Her dress was a melding of armor and finery, gold pauldrons and a decorated breastplate combined with drapings of silk and skirts. Terribly heavy, but not entirely impractical, were she the sort to wield a sword. De'Sindai servants finished the final touch, weaving her inherited crown into her thick curls. Hidden beneath her finery, Flowridia wore her wedding ring on a chain around her neck.

Flowridia saw a stranger, those cheekbones not ones of a child gathering courage for a ball, or even a woman tepid for her wedding day. Imperator Flowridia Makosa was grown, she was a mother, and she was about to accept the mantle of one of the greatest kingdoms in the realm.

A mistake. A jest. Lara had said to find balance, but she had little of that. So much talk of Ayla's monstrosities, but what of her own? Flowridia was a monster, too. She had proclaimed it herself. Was it too late? Was it a legacy she could still erase?

"Is it to your liking, Imperator?"

The attendant's query brought Flowridia back to the present. The crown looked made for her, casting a magnificent aura. Did it rival the might of Casvir? Not at all. Nothing ever would. "It's perfect," Flowridia said, and she dismissed the servants, content to breathe a few moments more before traversing into murky political waters.

Through the mirror, she looked beyond herself at golden wings seated on a bench at the back of the room. Sora always gazed at Dira with pure love, and a small part of Flowridia was envious of the time Sora had been given with the Goddess of Chaos as well. Sora already knew Dira. Flowridia only hoped she could catch up.

"Let's take a look at your mom," Sora cooed, positioning Dira to face her. "Look how fancy she is!"

When Dira reached for her, Flowridia smiled and took her gently, though cursed her armored chest. Dira deserved more than cold metal, but at least Flowridia could offer the warmth of a smile. "Hello, sweet one. You'll be good for Auntie Sora, right?"

"She's incapable of being anything else."

Flowridia's heart swelled, grateful beyond measure for Sora's presence. Soon enough, she would shed this confining armor. She would have her mantle but set it aside for a few blissful hours to live not as an imperator, but as a mother.

When a servant came to say it was time, Flowridia reluctantly returned the baby, only for Dira to release an earsplitting wail. Two tiny fangs revealed themselves in her cry, and Flowridia's heart broke, even as Sora tried in vain to quiet the newborn.

"Let me just . . ." Flowridia took Dira back; a gentle *'shh'* set the child at ease. "Dira . . ."

Yet to stare into her daughter's countenance, to see the golden crown reflected in her silver eyes . . . A truth once feared settled gently into her heart.

Dira watched. Every day, her daughter saw the world with those beautiful, innocent eyes. She studied; she learned; she would emulate the deeds she witnessed.

Far too well, Flowridia knew how it felt to reside in the shadow of a cruel parent. The thought of plunging a child into that same darkness left her cold and anguished. No, Dira deserved to dance in sunlight. And just as her child relied on her to lead her into the light . . . Nox'Kartha was by far the same.

When Flowridia tried to return her, the infant cried once more in Sora's arms. Flowridia's own tears welled to join her. "It's all right, Flowridia," Sora said. "I can calm her."

Flowridia took Dira back, content only once her baby was settled once more against her armor. Those uncoordinated little hands reached for her, and Flowridia knew where she needed to be. "I know you can."

With Dira cradled in her arms, Flowridia followed after the servant, cognizant of Sora's shadow behind her.

She followed a procession out of the palace, to a carriage surrounded by De'Sindai guards. Flowridia took care to shield Dira as she entered the encased carriage. When Sora looked lost, Flowridia beckoned her inside.

It was a squeeze, with the wings, but they made do.

Flowridia watched the city unfold through an open window. Mostly empty; the citizens would be at the coronation.

The ceremony had been hastily planned. Nox'Kartha's vulnerability with no ruler was a terrifying truth, especially in the aftermath of war. The fields were ravaged, the undead rotted beyond the walls, and the people were terrified of a world without Casvir.

So was Flowridia. Casvir—her mentor, her friend, her foe—was gone.

But though gone, his legacy lingered. The great statue in the main sector was only one piece, for every building held his stamp: the fountains of healing, the shops so evenly laid. There were armies less planned than Haven, and Flowridia only hoped she could hold those reins and keep it moving forward.

They would live and die by her actions now. Against her chest, Dira released a small squeal, drawing Flowridia's attention. "Yes, little one?"

Of course Dira did not speak. She could not even smile. Not yet. Yet in those eyes lay trust and love.

It was to the main sector that they traveled. Before the statue of Casvir, a lofty stage had been erected. Rumors of her 'throne hopping' ways had plagued her for years. Best to honor Casvir as well as she could.

It felt right anyway.

Though they stood in Casvir's shadow, Sora became hers, following with all the devotion Flowridia had come to expect. She climbed spiral stairs, scrutinized by the eyes of citizens and guards, until she stood atop a tall platform, gazing upon an ocean of supplicants.

Flowridia had only addressed them through messengers, proclaiming news of Casvir's death and his funeral. They knew her as Casvir's protege, later as the one who aided the Whispering Elf refugees, her influence upon Casvir's royal court short but noteworthy. News of how she had run toward the explosion threatening to destroy the capital city had spread like wildfire. Whispers of her name and titles had emanated far and wide—*a Staelashian Diplomat, Empress Consort of Solvira, lover of The Endless Night* . . .

Imperator.

All these weary faces, exhausted from war, from fear, from sorrow—what hope did they have with the passing of their imperator and savior? Many had come from nothing, saved by the so-called benevolence of Nox'Kartha's fallen hero.

He had earned their respect. He had earned his place in their history books. Flowridia had saved their city, but there was a long climb ahead.

"Greetings, citizens of Nox'Kartha," Flowridia said, the platform echoing her voice to the farthest reaches of the city square. "You may know me by many names, so let me put all questions to rest: I am Flowridia Makosa. And I will not try to convince you that all is well with flowery words. The road ahead is rocky and shrouded, and accepting these reins is not something I intend to do lightly. Imperator Casvir was—"

Her voice caught at the name, the hitch in her breath brief and wrenching.

"Imperator Casvir was one of the greatest men I ever knew."

She forced back tears, clinging instead to the tender body of her daughter.

"Nox'Kartha's promise is hope," she continued, shadowed anew by the demon in the woods. "Imperator Casvir built a country welcoming to all, offering even the most downtrodden the chance to become something more. From freed slaves in Moratham, to the oppressed De'Sindai, to anyone seeking a better life, Imperator Casvir was there, offering hope in the form of Nox'Kartha. Like many of you, he found me at my lowest and lifted me up. In granting me a familiar, he gave me a chance to make something of myself. And like you, he never forced any particular path upon me. He wanted only to see me thrive with what I had. That is the true legacy of Casvir—using his station and his power to uplift those with nothing and give them that chance.

"His legacy lives on in the very roads you stand on, in the magnificent walls that protect this city, in the prosperity found in Nox'Kartha's borders, and in the pride each and every one of you hold toward your country. Nox'Kartha is great because Imperator Casvir was the greatest among us."

A man of unfathomable wickedness and a dear, beloved friend.

Flowridia swallowed tears, managing to hold her voice steady. "If I have any hope to earn your trust and respect, it will be by leading you with just as much integrity and pride. I am not Imperator Casvir, but he was a friend and a mentor to me. I miss him, just as you miss him. To speak on his behalf feels irreverent, but I do know, above all, that this kingdom was his legacy, and he would want it to prosper in celebration of all he accomplished.

"It is not weakness to admit fear," Flowridia continued, grasping what confidence she could. "It is only weakness to let it control you. We all face a future of uncertainty, but I swear to not allow that fear to dictate my own legacy. I swear that I will do all in my power to preserve the legacy he left behind. I swear to you that Nox'Kartha will prosper. We have fallen into an era of darkness, but it needn't remain so. I swear to lead you into the light once more.

"The price of citizenship has always been a pledge of godhood to the imperator, and by necessity, that shall remain. In order to serve you, I must have the power of my predecessor, or at least what fraction can be salvaged. In accepting the mantle of imperator, I accept your pledges of power."

With Dira shielded by her arms, Flowridia stepped to the edge of the platform, calm at the final leap. "What say you, citizens of Nox'Kartha? Will you trust me to lead you into the light?"

There it was, the silence before the breath. Flowridia gazed in wonder as every citizen bowed their head.

With each utterance of loyalty, a dizzying sensation flowed through her. All the world became louder, brighter, in every ineffable way. She swore she floated, swore her skin came alight, but Dira cooed, bringing her back down to earth.

Lara had said to find balance. Justice and mercy. Duty and heart. For whom did she seek to crawl back into the light, but for the little child in her arms? And for whom did she seek to create a new and better world? So many destinies would be forged by her decisions, a kingdom of people now set their trust in her, and for them she could not fail.

If she could raise a kingdom, surely she could raise a daughter too.

Flowridia stood tall as she gazed first upon her daughter and then upon the populace who placed their trust in her. "I am Imperator Flowridia Makosa, and it is my solemn vow to serve you."

Applause erupted as thunder, and Flowridia basked in the storm.

Though Etolié's desire to fall into Khastra's arms reigned above all, there was one small detail to attend to first.

Back to Solvira. Back to overseeing the wreck of her house.

The damage wasn't extensive. Although the roof had been blown to bits, she'd been pleasantly surprised to find her library still intact. And that was where Etolié went now, to visit a friend oft neglected in her adventures.

Zoldar had moved back into the underground library, content among the scrolls and books. But when Etolié entered the space, she was startled to hear . . . words.

"I think you cheated."

What followed were Zoldar's innocent clicks.

"Then explain how we just so happen to have the same hand?"

Etolié levitated to avoid creaking the floorboards, shocked to round the corner and see . . .

Ilune, hunched over a hand of cards, glaring at Zoldar. Her splendid wings filled nearly the entire scene, but Zoldar was undaunted, content to cheat against the God of Death.

They both looked up at her entrance, her gold wings shifting the light. "Your librarian is a sneaky bastard," Ilune said.

"Yeah, I call him that at least once a week."

For his part, Zoldar all but threw his cards in the air, skittering excitedly toward her. He took her hand, enthusiastic as he signed with his other.

"No, you did the right thing," Etolié said, "letting her stay. Mind if I say a few words to her in private?"

Zoldar complied, rapidly climbing the shelf like the insect he was.

Etolié stepped tentatively forward, struggling to find words. "Um . . . Hi there."

Ilune rose, her smile as sweet and anxious as it had been in the Nox'Karthan castle. "Lovely library you have."

"It's all right. You should've seen my old one."

When Ilune embraced her, Etolié held her tight, hoping to ease the inevitable itchy sensation—only for Ilune to reel back and ask, "What happened?!"

"What?"

"Why are you a vampire?"

Oh, yeah. "That's a new thing."

Ilune laughed, even as she pulled Etolié back into a proper hug. "I have time enough for a story, if you'd like to tell it."

"I'm just surprised you're here."

"Sora made a few compelling points. Somehow, I'm not a burden to you. For that matter, do let Sora know I did, in fact, come to say goodbye, would you?"

When the embrace ended, the surreal experience left Etolié feeling light. Ilune was back. She had a sister for a few moments more. "I'll tell her. Where are you going to go?"

"Wherever I must, and now I have the means. Hope you don't mind, but I did a little grave robbing." From apparently thin air, Ilune produced . . . a clear crystal shard.

Etolié reeled at its familiarity. The crystal housed a segment of Murishani's power, specifically the magic that had allowed Casvir to fucking teleport. "That was Casvir's."

"And now it's mine."

"How?"

Ilune's shrug was both infuriating and perfectly in character. "Don't ruin the moment with too many questions. I want to enjoy your company."

Etolié pulled her flask out of its inter-dimensional space, taking a sip before offering it to Ilune. "Can liches drink without puking it up later?"

"We can." Ilune took a sip, unfazed by the taste.

"Lucky bastard. Well, have a seat. You won't believe the week I've had."

"Oh, I think I will." Ilune offered the flask back. "You wouldn't happen to know where my staff is, would you?"

"I'm absolutely not at liberty to say. Sorry, sis."

Ilune remained cheery as she sat at the edge of Etolié's nest. "No chance I could bargain for it?"

"Ask me when you get back."

Ilune's chuckle was so familiar, a testament to their familial bonds. "You're so trusting that I'll return."

Etolié plopped down beside her, flask in hand. "Will you?"

"I certainly hope so."

Etolié shrugged as she took another drink. "You will. I'm too infectious."

"You're incredible. Now, tell me about . . ." Ilune tapped her own canine teeth, mimicking fangs.

"You'll love it. It involves even more evil undead artifacts. Your favorite subject."

Etolié told the story to her glowing audience, cherishing the warmth of sisterhood.

And so the world settled, a sunset upon what promised to be a new and glorious dawn.

Was it irony or fate for the wielder of the Theocracy's crown to now sit on Nox'Kartha's throne? Seated at a vanity mirror, Flowridia unwove the crown from her hair. An artifact of family, and there was much to be said of its worth. But no value was higher than the infant who whimpered from her cradle.

Demitri rolled over, lazily opening one eye to stare at the fitful baby. Flowridia smiled as she rose. "Go back to sleep, Dearest Demitri."

He slept an awful lot for an undead creature. Perhaps it was simply an instinct from life. It never ceased to amuse her, his return surreal and wonderful.

Flowridia lifted her vibrant daughter from her cradle, swearing she'd grown in just the three days she'd been in the realm. So much of Ayla in her features, her black hair and silver eyes, bright and beautiful. Her pink coloring had faded, revealing an olive tint to her skin. Flowridia gently stroked those lovely little half-elf ears and soft cheeks. Every part of Dira was a wonder to behold.

A child of two unique worlds, of life and death, created by magic and love. Tears filled Flowridia's eyes, for Dira was perfect, Demitri was back, yet a kingdom was in anguish with only her to save it. What a world it would have been, the one where she ran away into the woods to raise her child in peace, with Demitri to guard the walls and bring laughter and joy, and Ayla . . .

"Ayla?" she whispered.

So softly, Flowridia could've sworn it was a dream. But Ayla emerged from a shadow by the door.

Flowridia's breath hitched, though she curtailed her pain and relief for the sake of her mellowing baby. But she beckoned from the bed, lip trembling when Ayla obeyed, her touch on her hand confirming the truth—that Ayla was real, she was alive, she was . . . here.

Ayla did not smile, instead studying her with those silver eyes. "I swore to you I would say goodbye before disappearing in the night. And I am here to fulfill that oath."

The words struck a match, burning the final bridge across the chasm between them. Nothing but darkness remained.

And love. Always love.

Flowridia shut her eyes. It did nothing to staunch her tears. Yet they came with no sobbing or gasps . . . or even the impulse to fight. She'd known this all along. "Where will you go?"

Ayla sat beside her on the bed, hands resting gently upon her lap. "I have a few thoughts but no commitments. You, however, have made a weighty one."

Flowridia glanced to her crown upon the vanity. "I can't keep running from my sins, Ayla. I killed Casvir. There are consequences, both good and bad." Oh, sweet Dira. Flowridia idly touched her hair. "It's not what I want, but it's what I must do."

"I know." The finality of the words left a spacious void. "You will be a brilliant and wise imperator. You hold all the potential of your predecessor, and I truly believe you will lead this country with wisdom and grace. You will leave a legacy upon this kingdom greater than even the man who founded it, I have no doubt. This is the zenith of your sacrifices, Flowra. You feared your mother's name, and so instead you've created your own."

Ayla's words were kind and perhaps true, but the unspoken few sang louder than the rest. "And is there no place for you in that legacy?" Flowridia asked.

"The world believes Ayla Darkleaf is dead, and I would like to make it so. Too many know me. I cannot escape that legacy here." Ayla shut her eyes, defeat settling upon her small frame. "I despise introspection. I'm so much happier when I blissfully dance along, but that's the true evil of growth. It hurts down to your core and leaves you raw and different and better. The sad and tragic truth is I am not a whole person. Our crumbling marriage revealed that in the ruins."

Ayla moved to stand, and Flowridia could not stop her, not without setting aside the precious, sleeping weight in her arms. Ayla lingered at the bedpost, and Flowridia swore she had never been a more majestic sight, the very vision of strength and pride and a fierce sort of beauty. Ayla was glorious. She was the world. She was a monster no more.

"May I ask for one thing before you go?" Flowridia said.

Ayla nodded.

"Would you hold her?" Flowridia offered the swaddled infant, trembling as Ayla came to kneel before her in bed. "I can't memorialize moments as you can, not with ink and paper. But hold her, please? I want to remember you and her together in this lifetime."

In silence, Ayla settled before them.

Flowridia placed Dira in Ayla's arms and watched as her wife— her dearest wife—cradled their daughter and stroked the wispy locks of black hair from her face. She smiled, and Flowridia saw it was sincere, despite her trembling lip. "Chaos told me she loved me," Ayla whispered. "She said she missed me. How is it possible that this pure soul could have cared for me?"

Flowridia hesitated, fearing to be manipulative—she refused to be that person anymore—but there was a truth to speak. "When I was in the Beyond, Chaos showed me a vision of her life, and the brightest star in it was you. All she ever wanted was you."

Ayla stared in bewilderment.

"I know it isn't meant to be in this life," Flowridia continued, "but she did love you, Ayla. You gave her everything."

Closer still, Ayla held the sleeping infant in her arms. Then came the first of her tears. "Would you tell me more?"

And so Flowridia told the tale of a world fated to never be, wherein Ayla was *Mother*, where she loved a little girl with all her heart and sought to raise her, shelter her, and protect her from monsters all around. Stories as real and dear as memories, for they were, though not her own. She told the tale of Grand Executor Darkleaf, who dared to stand between Casvir and the world, whose crimes were vast enough to inspire a rebellion, but who did it all for love.

She told of how it all fell apart, how Ayla had willingly chosen a fate worse than death to save her daughter—a daughter who would someday end Ayla's suffering and take her life.

"You loved her," Flowridia whispered, finality settling with the conclusion of the tale, "and so you tried to protect her from monsters, but you considered yourself a monster too. You tried to hide your past, but you should know without a shadow of doubt that there was nothing monstrous about your love for her. And she loved you too, Ayla. She learned of your past anyway and loved you just the same, enough to fulfill Izthuni's curse and slay you."

Ayla's tears fell so softly. When Dira stirred, Ayla held her close until the baby stilled. "I cannot stay," Ayla whispered, but it only barely masked her sob. "But, Gods, I envy her, that other version of me. I envy that I could love."

"You could be her."

"No. My love doesn't have to be monstrous for monstrosity to still shadow her in this life. All the world knows of Ayla Darkleaf—Scourge of the Sun Elves, The Endless Night, all those ghastly titles for a monster in the dark. Nox'Kartha knows my face. It knows I murdered half a country. I hear the whispers behind my back, and it would be the cruelest fate of all for her to hear those whispers too. Crueler, even, than abandoning her."

"You—" Flowridia cut off the words, the pain of them all-consuming. She forced them, nevertheless. "You could take her with you."

"And take her from you? Darling, I would never." Ayla brought sweet Dira close, a mere glimpse of a love transcending time and fate. And though the hourglass of their bond emptied of its final grains of sand, Ayla was *Mother* for a few moments more.

Haunting words of long ago welled in Flowridia's mind, that sometimes life stole what you wanted most through no fault of your own. That your dreams might shatter, all your hopes dashed like waves upon the shore.

So what did you do when life stole what you wanted most?

You moved forward.

"Then go," Flowridia whispered. "The best gift you can give Chaos' memory would be the greatest version of you. You were never given that chance in her life."

The pain in Ayla's countenance faded with those words. Her smile came softly, heralding the light of a new, fragile sunrise. Vehemence weighed Ayla's words. "Raise her in love. Raise her better than we were. If you dare to tell her stories of a particular monster in the dark, reassure her that the monster seeks the light. Perhaps that monster could someday be worthy of her."

"I would hope, if that someday does come, that you would come tell her yourself."

Ayla gasped, fresh tears spilling fast. "I would. I will. Someday."

Ayla brushed a light kiss upon Dira's brow, then returned the infant to Flowridia's arms. Flowridia stood when Ayla did, and she gently laid Dira down into her cradle, sparing glances to Ayla as she willed her to stay for just a moment more.

The infant slept in peace, oblivious to her mothers' broken hearts. Flowridia offered a hand, expecting a tender touch—not to be bombarded by a desperate embrace.

Ayla gripped her like the world might end, a mirror to their parting on Nox'Kartha's plains. Yet Flowridia smiled, even as the dam of her composure burst. Her tears fell freely, finality settling as she gazed upon Ayla Darkleaf. "You were the love of my life," Flowridia whispered. "I have never held, nor will I ever hold, a greater title than that of your wife." From around her neck, she removed the enchanted wedding ring—an emblem forged with love—and slipped it into Ayla's hand. "Go, my love. I shall tell the world I'm a widow. Leave Ayla Darkleaf behind and be free."

Ayla kissed her, tasting of salt and elegy.

Too soon, they parted, though Ayla kept a firm grip on her arm. Her other hand grasped the ring.

"You could stay a little longer," Flowridia whispered. "You could stay until I fall asleep."

She did not need to sleep, not truly. But it was as Ayla had long ago said: that the undead, like anyone else, could shut their eyes and rest.

Ayla gave a nod. "Until you fall asleep."

Flowridia resettled into bed, burying herself in the finely pressed sheets. When cold arms wrapped around her, she curled against the touch. Lips brushed her hair, as well as tears.

Flowridia fell asleep.

Flowridia awoke alone.

But as she resurfaced from the blankets, roused by the cries of her daughter, she spotted something on the bedside table.

Flowridia could not memorialize moments, no. She could not put to canvas what her mind and eyes saw. But drawn on the parchment, though it might as well have been gold, was the image of Ayla and Dira, the latter of whom slept, cradled in her mother's arms. And the former—

Ayla smiled with light and life.

EPILOGUE

In the end, what was legacy?

Odessa's was survival and determination above all.

Casvir's was to lead, to shape the world into something new.

Thalmus' was unconditional love.

A mother and two father figures, the dichotomy of their ideals all leaving marks on Flowridia's life. In the end, each had died by her hand. Who would she be without them?

First, there was the matter of bringing order to the chaotic realm she had inherited, for the grand tapestry of Casvir's legacy was stained by war. Flowridia sought only to end them.

In the days following the Convergence's explosion, the surviving elves were granted amnesty and passage home. "Tell Executor Everglade there will be no more conflict between the elven lands and Nox'Kartha," Flowridia said to the survivors, "so long as there is no conflict from them. I have received assurance from the new Goddess of War that your children will be returned."

The wounded survivors huddled fearfully in her throne room. One forlorn soldier came forward. "Imperator Darkleaf—"

"Makosa."

"Imperator Makosa, forgive me, but what of the plague?"

Another piece of that legacy unfolding. "If Executor Everglade will surrender, I will pour all the funds I can spare into finding a cure."

Casvir's plague, soon called the Imperator's Plague—much to her chagrin—spread to every corner of elven lands, even to those untouched by the violence of war. Ironic that it was the Sun Elves who found an antidote.

When Flowridia wrote to offer aid in funding the distribution of the cure, she received a curt reply:

We are skeptical of the intentions of anyone so closely entangled with The Endless Night, present or not. Nox'Kartha is no friend to Falar'Sol.

So stated the letter from Executor Willowspire of the Sun Elves. When she asked the former Executor Faeborn, now an advisor on her council, they were adamant a response would only do more harm. Some legacies could not be undone. Casvir's shadow still loomed upon the world, and The Endless Night would forever be a scar upon the Sun Elves.

Some legacies could be rewritten, however. Treaties were signed, freeing Solvira from the shadow of Nox'Kartha.

In Nox'Kartha's throne room, Etolié cast a glorious presence, bearing wings of divinity and the subtle intrigue of death. "Guess that means my servitude is over."

Flowridia simply rolled her eyes. "You've already made that joke."

"Dammit."

Flowridia set the signed treaty into Empress Etolié's hands. "For what little it's worth, I'm sorry. I sold Solvira's soul, but you saved it."

"I resold it—under duress, but still. It is what it is. We can be even now." Etolié tucked the parchment into her interdimensional space, where it disappeared as a sparkle. "Guess this means I technically never have to see you again."

Yet, Etolié lingered. "Dira would miss you," Flowridia said.

"I do love my silver sparkling."

"And Sora."

"She's hopeless without me, it's true."

"And me."

With all the drama she'd come to know from Etolié, the Celestial gave an exaggerated groan. "Yes, fine. I'll stay in touch. Once I pawn off the title of *empress*, we'll even negotiate friendship."

"And how are you planning to get rid of that?"

"Ilune's coming back someday, and she'll dispute her claim to the throne over my dead body."

"Etolié, you're already dead."

"Fuck."

All work, no rest. Time passed in a blink, and on the first of Flowridia's birthdays following her undeath, though she did not age, there appeared a single red rose on her bed. Her tears did not cease for hours.

Reparations were given to what remained of the Theocracy, with the promise of aid in rebuilding. Makosa was her family name, bringing the inheritance of a throne, but there was another worthier than her.

"They'll need to remain a colony of Nox'Kartha's a while longer to survive," Flowridia said between writing lines of edicts. "Do you want to take that throne?"

Sora held a sleeping Dira, her clawed, bird-like hands as gentle as Odessa's had been cruel. "I'm not a leader. I don't think I'm who they need."

"It would give them hope to at least know who you are."

Sora thought a moment, then cast a distant smile. "We can do that. I'm ready to tell our father's story."

A nebulous figure in many ways, but Flowridia loved to think their shared father would be proud.

Yet, it sparked a new thought. "All I've done this last year is put out the fires Casvir lit," Flowridia said. "If I want to lead Nox'Kartha into a new age, I have to forge my own path. But what needs done?"

"Are you asking for suggestions?"

Flowridia nodded.

"You're capable of brutality," Sora said, "just like Casvir. And maintaining that iron is important for leadership, but necromancy is only one side of your powers. You're a healer too. Call it putting out fires if you want, but you're healing what's been hurt. What if you did more of that?"

The gears in Flowridia's mind spun rapidly. "Nox'Kartha's health care is the most sophisticated in the realm, but there's nothing that can't be improved. Let me look into that."

And so a new legacy would begin. Yet the past was never far behind, for on Flowridia's next birthday, another rose lay on her bed.

As foretold, Dira followed like a shadow in her mother's light, yet loved the sun and all its glory, though she was often chided for playing too long and letting her sensitive skin blister. With eyes the color of the moon and nearly as large, Dira absorbed her world like a towel to water, and if Flowridia dared to stare too long into her inquisitive gaze, she saw icy flecks of blue within her irises.

She grew so fast; too fast. A blink, and Dira was three years old, spewing small torrents of Silver Fire and proclaiming herself a dragon named Valeuron. A blink, and Dira was four, learning languages in every neighboring tongue: Solviran, Elven, Celestial, even bits of Demoni—well enough, even, to impress the foreign dignitaries who visited. Every day, Flowridia walked with her through the gardens, where Dira insisted on holding her 'special hand,' her other mother's heritage manifesting in her fascination with the scarred appendage. *"Your mother was quite the scientist too, you know,"* Flowridia said one day.

Every mention of Ayla filled Dira with light.

Someday, Ayla's legacy had to be unveiled, but for now, Flowridia watched sweet Dira wander the gardens in ignorant bliss and wondered how anyone—how Casvir, Odessa, Mereen, all the villains in her life—could ever steal such innocence away. Sometimes Flowridia considered the destiny Dira had lost, of a lonely goddess burdened to live countless lives and fail to save the world. And, sometimes, she mourned what had been lost to evade that horrible fate, for as much as Casvir was evil, for as deep as his betrayals cut, he had once been a friend.

"Who is that?" Dira asked one day in the town square.

The statue of Casvir would forever remain as a reminder of Nox'Kartha's origins. Casvir had laid the foundation upon which Flowridia sought her own legacy.

She smiled. "Do you remember when I told you the story about the demon who gave me Demitri?"

Realization filled Dira's gaze. "Was he that huge?!"

Flowridia's laughter filled the scene. "No, my love, though he was very tall."

There were gentle pieces of Casvir's legacy. For now, those could be held in Dira's little hands.

How quickly life changed. Dira was a child, yes, but one morning Dira was too large for Flowridia to easily carry. Dira could nearly stand taller than Flowridia if she balanced on her tiptoes. Dira gained the grace and poise only dance and a court upbringing could give. When she asked to wield a blade, Sora taught her all her progenitors had taught her, but without the metaphorical knives attached.

Legacy rewritten, for Sora's past could be a gift as much as a burden.

When Dira was nine, she asked the first question to make Flowridia pause.

"Where is my other mom? Sora said I had to ask you."

In the dim light of Dira's room, Flowridia found the wound raw and tender still. She stilled in oiling her daughter's hair, gazing behind her in the mirror as she set her chin upon Dira's shoulder. Their faces were similar, yes, for her daughter inherited her innocent eyes and full lips, but her smile held a familiar mischief that chilled her heart. Odessa lived on through blood, but perhaps that smile could be redeemed.

And of course, she was Ayla's, her elven features strong and proud. Flowridia saw it so painfully now: the pale silver of Dira's eyes, her black hair, her slim physique, even the sharper angles of her face. "On the day you were born," Flowridia said, "she passed away."

Of course Dira slumped at that, disappointment filling her precious gaze.

Flowridia wore no wedding ring. She accepted the mantle of her family name. But on the mantelpiece in her own bedroom were nine roses, frozen in undeath, and before her sat a child with fangs and the legacy of a bloodstained name. "But she died a hero because she wanted the world to be safe for her family—for you, Dira."

She did not tell Dira all, but she told her enough to soothe her peppering questions. When Dira's eyelids became too heavy a burden, she asked a final, childish question. "Do you miss her?"

"Of course I miss her. She was my wife."

Was. And never in law. Only in spirit.

Once, she had been Flowridia Darkleaf, vowing to leave a legacy of . . . what? Of darkness? Of revenge? Gods, how childish her dreams had been.

"Then we run away. Not today, but someday. You and me. And Demitri."

"It's a beautiful dream, Flowra."

A dream spoken by two children desperately in love.

When eleven roses were displayed upon Flowridia's mantle, she felt an urgency she had not experienced in over a decade, the reminder of a game long ago, one she had once feared to play. *Twelve roses in a vase . . .*

On the eve of her next birthday, Flowridia placed the vase of roses on the bedside table and then a note on a bed rarely used: *Twelve roses in a vase is all I ask, and then I shall be yours for the night.*

A jest. A childish game. It might make Ayla laugh.

Truly, she expected nothing of it. She returned to her room at midnight to remove her shoes after a particularly cumbersome meeting with her advisory council. Always an onslaught of news to discuss: *a skirmish at the Solviran border, the King of Tholheim has passed, a new Sun Elven executor elected . . .*

Upon the bedside table, she spotted twelve roses. The lights flickered out, drenching her in darkness.

Familiar hands touched her. Her dress did not stay on for long. Flowridia succumbed willingly, joyfully, every kiss upon her naked body pulling tears from her tired eyes.

They kissed in the dark, made love in the shadows, no moon to reflect the light of her lover's eyes. Flowridia needn't see, for her body knew the motions, and the woman in her bed had never feared the night. The darkness caressed them as they caressed each other, every impassioned cry a prayer to goddesses they no longer worshipped.

Flowridia and Ayla Darkleaf were no more yet remained ghosts haunting their own immortal shells.

In the quiet aftermath, Flowridia clung to her ghost. She feared to speak, lest she frighten the specter away, yet in the waning passion of their union, she could not stand the looming silence. "Ayla, I . . ." And to her own surprise . . . she smiled. "I've missed you."

Her tears welled anew at the tender touch along her scalp. From the stillness came the gentle pull of breath so the ghost could speak. "I think of you every day. I hear often of what you have accomplished in Nox'Kartha, and what marvelous work it is. If I may be bold and speak personally . . . have changed. In all the best of ways."

Gods, her voice, a dark enticement Flowridia had nearly forgotten. Yet with it flooded a thousand memories, sweet and profane, tearful and triumphant. In the darkness, there came a faint sheen of light reflecting from Flowridia's lover's eyes. In Flowridia's hitched breath were endless queries yearning to burst from her lungs.

But her ghost's hallowed voice spoke once more. "Political gossip does not generally mention your daughter, however. Is she well?"

"She is. I think, for all my apparently marvelous work, she is the most wondrous by far." Yet she hesitated to say more, startled to realize . . . "Is it time? Are you . . . staying?"

For all her ardent longing, dread rose to choke it. Dira knew of Ayla, but she did not *know* of Ayla.

"I want to say yes. But I . . . I think there is something I must do first."

When Ayla did not speak any more, Flowridia kissed her, tears mingling, their bodies intertwining to match. With passion renewed, Flowridia relinquished the final shackles of the Darkleaf name and loved her as someone new.

"Until you fall asleep . . ."

In the early morning, the specter was gone. It might've all been a dream, save for the ache between her thighs and the faint essence of a lover's smell on her skin. Elsewhere the castle slowly awoke. Dira would be stirring soon, none the wiser to her mother's heartbreak. The sun peeked above the horizon, waiting to be named.

A kingdom sought her guidance, and Flowridia emerged from sheets soiled with tears and sex. She bathed, purging all memories of carnal affairs, even as her own hands mirrored the motions of her beloved on her skin, tender and serene. Yet strange questions haunted her. What if Ayla had stayed? What would Dira have said? What did Dira know?

Dira was young, so young. But not young enough to be shielded anymore. Flowridia's own creeping shame burned, but hiding her own sordid history behind Ayla's was just as dishonorable. Years ago, Flowridia had seen a whole lifetime, lived it through her daughter's eyes. And what had been the great failing of Ayla Darkleaf?

Love. To love so hard she succumbed to fear and kept the world a mystery.

Once clean, Flowridia dressed in a simple gown, for the affairs of the world needed to wait a few hours more. From a private folder hidden in the recesses of her bedside table drawer, she withdrew a beloved work of art—of Ayla and Dira, together for a few precious moments.

She held it to her heart as she contemplated what to even say. So many unknowns and only one certainty.

She could wait no longer.

When her composure became steady, she took the drawing to Dira's bedroom and knocked.

Legacy was found in stories, in legends, in all that was left behind. *Darkleaf* was a name synonymous with death, and Flowridia had once willingly taken it.

For years, she had contemplated that cost. For years, she had contemplated her life, her future, the merit of moving beyond her childhood dream of marrying a monster. Now, she ruled the most powerful empire in the realm, held the natural world in the palm of her hand, her capacity to twist light and dark magics bespeaking finesse unparalleled. This was the fruit of years of patience, of a man who would be God who saw a young girl and offered her the gift of a second chance. The silent question had been asked: *"What will you become?"*

And Flowridia, Imperator Makosa, felt unfinished. Grown, but still growing.

Dira as well. Grown, but still growing. When she had heard those same stories, of witches in swamps, of demons in the woods, of fallen gods returned from the death, or monarchs too pure for this world and others wicked enough to burn it . . .

Dira cried. She became sullen. She had sent Flowridia away.

They had not spoken of it since.

A few months later, Flowridia was interrupted from work. "Imperator Makosa, there is a letter for you."

Flowridia looked up from her piles of paperwork, her desk smaller than her predecessor's but no less used. One of those eerie hooded figures stood nigh, remaining sentient even after Casvir's death and transferring all loyalty to their new monarch. "There are always letters for me."

The figure extended a hand, revealing a fanciful albeit worn envelope, sealed with a symbol that prodded at her memory. "The courier claims it to be from Executor Flamespun of Falar'Sol."

And so that was the symbol. Sun Elven lands.

Curious, Flowridia tore the letter carefully, mindful of the letter opener, and quickly skimmed the text.

Imperator Flowridia Makosa,

We of the Sun Elven court hope this message finds you well . . .
Tensions existed between our mutual predecessors, but it is my hope to look beyond our kingdoms' histories . . .

Flowridia paused, fighting against hope even as the words unveiled themselves.

The hospital in our fair capital of Maagi hosts the most advanced medical science in all of Zauleen. It has been discussed that combining our respective technologies and magics would serve to benefit both kingdoms, and perhaps even kingdoms beyond our borders.

Twelve years, and here was the fruit of her labors, the legacy she had longed for.

Should you agree, I would be honored to host you and yours in our fair city to discuss specifics. I look forward to your reply.
Regards,
Executor Othreis Flamespun

Flowridia stared stunned upon the document, clumsy as she withdrew parchment for a reply, nearly spilling her inkwell. Of course she wrote an enthusiastic *yes,* though tempered to appear professional. The letter she'd received had traveled for months, but this one would reach the executor within the day. "Send for Empress Etolié. Tell her it's urgent."

Though not without some grumbling, Etolié did provide a portal to elven lands, her powers growing vaster by the year.

The correspondence between imperator and executor lasted days, and at the end it was decided that in one week, Imperator Flowridia Makosa and her entourage would be hosted in the fair city of Maagi, a groundbreaking gesture of peace unfathomable to their predecessors.

All was set in motion, until the night before when a tentative knock interrupted her final preparations.

Flowridia stilled in her writing, seated at the desk in her private chambers. Orange hues of sunset cast their light upon Demitri, who perked up from his place on the rug. *It's Dira.*

"Enter."

Dira walked in with false confidence, holding all the gangly fixtures of youth. Barely twelve, still a child, still young enough to cling to her mom instead of yearning to stretch her wings. In her precious hands, she held a strip of parchment.

"Hello, Dira."

Dira stopped before Flowridia's desk and cleared her throat, her tone taking on a formal manner of speech. Sweet Dira—she had observed politics all her life. "Good evening, Mom. May I interrupt you?"

"Always, my love."

"I have assembled a list of reasons why I should accompany you to Maagi tomorrow."

Flowridia straightened her posture, her intrigue matched by amusement. "A list?"

"Yes." Dira looked to her parchment. "One: it would do well in expanding my education of the world."

"I don't disagree."

"Two: it would allow me the chance to practice my elven in an authentic environment."

"I see."

"Three: it's the homeland of my other mother, and I—" Her voice caught; Flowridia resisted the urge to rise, even as Dira composed herself. ". . . It would do me well to connect with my roots."

"What is this really about?"

Dira lowered the parchment, her political training in conflict with the elevated emotions of youth. "What if Ayla's there?"

Startled, Flowridia dropped her pen, splattering ink across the parchment. "Sorry. I . . . I didn't expect that. We haven't spoken about Ayla."

"Well, no. I haven't spoken to you. But Sora and I have talked about it—a lot. And she told me once that Ayla was looking for redemption, even if it would be impossible. So where better to go? She has to be somewhere in Falar'Sol."

"I don't want to discourage you," Flowridia said gently, "but 'has to be' is a very strong statement. We don't know that, dear one. We don't know where she is."

Dira's voice became resolute. "I want to find her. I-I've been thinking on this ever since you told me . . . told me the truth. And whether or not she's there, that seems like the best place to start. I want to look her in the eye. I want to understand.

"I know it's unforgivable," Dira continued, her tremulous voice bearing conviction, nevertheless. "But if she truly has changed, then . . . Well, is it wrong to want to know her?"

Oh, the convictions of childhood. Naïvety and wisdom so perfectly intertwined. How fitting, for Dira to have inherited the capacity to love monsters and seek to understand their hearts. "Of course it's not wrong," Flowridia said. "If Sora will agree to accompany you, you may come to Maagi."

"She helped me write the list. She wants to come too."

"Get some sleep, then. We leave tomorrow evening. It will be daylight there."

But instead of leave, Dira lingered. When Flowridia stood, Dira embraced her and held her tight.

Maagi's beauty was in its elegance, a splendid city of cobblestone roads, green courtyards, and curious people watching from the sidewalks and windows, hoping to catch a glimpse of the mysterious necromancer from across the sea. They didn't know she held the hand of their once-oppressor's daughter. If anything, they barely noticed the girl in favor of Sora, whose magnificent wings stole attention wherever she went—much to her chagrin—and Demitri, who was always an impressive sight.

How wonderful it was, watching Dira's smile brighten with each new sight, whereas Flowridia felt only bittersweet. This was Sora's homeland. This was the origin of half of Dira's blood. This was the land Dira's mother had tried to destroy.

And failed. A monster had come to claim them, and they survived.

"Over there is the hospital itself," Executor Flamespun said, pointing to a building in the distance. "A jewel in our fair city, you shall soon see. You will be given a tour tomorrow. Today's agenda involves meeting with a few members of the administrative staff, as well as the doctor who proposed this entire plan. She has taken a great interest in your accomplishments in Nox'Kartha and apparently twisted the hospital director's arm for days in order to propose this plan to me." The executor lowered his voice conspiratorially. "I'm told she has a, uh, *reputation* for being difficult to work beside, but Doctor Faradelk has sworn to be on her best behavior for you."

Flowridia, who loved wordplay and puns, lost her eloquence. "Who?"

"I beg your pardon. I mean Doctor Laya Faradelk. I forget her fame is limited to Zauleen. She is the executive surgeon at the hospital, and I think you'll be quite impressed. She is a savant if there ever was one; truly, there's nothing she does not specialize in when it comes to the elven body. And forgive me if this is sensitive, but she is the one who cured the Imperator's Plague."

It was not possible, yet . . . "Not sensitive at all. I never knew the hero's name."

"I was invited to sit in on one of her lectures at the university recently, and my goodness, it was too much for me." The executor laughed nervously. "It was on heart valve replacements. Apparently she can keep a heart beating for weeks without a vessel."

Flowridia fought to keep a light expression.

"All for the sake of organ transplants. Organ transplants! Imagine it—or don't, if you're squeamish. Though perhaps not, given your area of magical expertise. You're a healer and a necromancer both."

"I am not particularly squeamish, no." Flowridia forced a pleasant chuckle, even as disbelief rose to fight the odd euphoria of hope.

"Then the two of you will have plenty to discuss. No matter how unpleasant her theses might be, her work is truly incomparable. I cannot speak highly enough of her service to this country. She has saved countless lives."

Flowridia simply could not fight her urge to smile any longer. "I look forward to meeting her."

They soon arrived at the stately building that was the executor's hall. When Executor Flamespun stepped through the stately doors, Sora took Dira's other hand. "We'll go explore the city while you're in your meeting. Perhaps we can meet for lunch."

"Actually, would you stay for a few more minutes?" Flowridia asked, though she released Dira into Sora's care. "Both of you."

Intrigue raised Sora's eyebrow. "Why?"

"I want Dira to meet the doctor."

Flowridia stepped boldly into the beautiful foyer, anticipation keeping her feet light.

Demitri shadowed her, the space large enough to comfortably accommodate even his impressive stature. Nearby, Dira spoke excitedly with Sora, who whispered but responded with the same gusto.

Flowridia kept her focus ahead, forcing her hope to dampen lest it not be true. But even as she wrestled within herself, Demitri began sniffing the air.

Mom, there's something dead here.

Flowridia glanced back at the odd statement. "Should I feel threatened?"

Mom, I think it's Lady Ayla.

And so it was, rounding the corner, casting a presence as wide as the walls of the impressive entryway, surveying the room with a predatory glint in her enthralling silver eyes. Her austere clothing matched the modest style of her elven peers, and her long, silken hair held an elegant bun to match. Strangest of all was the ring upon her finger—Flowridia's own wedding ring: refitted, reforged, and restored.

Breathless, Flowridia managed to tear her gaze away and looked back to Dira instead, as oblivious as Sora was visibly dumbstruck. Flowridia set a gentle finger to her lips and whispered, *"Dira."*

Dira ceased her idle chattering, then stopped abruptly. Precious girl, lacking the control of seasoned politicians; when Sora leaned down to whisper in her ear, Dira's breath hitched; her eyes shined with tears.

When Flowridia turned back around, the doctor's gaze flitted quickly to match Dira's, her aplomb fading to something soft and mild.

But only a moment; her cool composure returned when Executor Flamespun gave a welcoming gesturing. "Imperator Makosa, it is my pleasure to introduce you and yours to Doctor Laya Faradelk."

When the woman—the woman who was Ayla but not—offered a hand, Flowridia accepted, enamored to feel the familiar touch. "Unlike his predecessor," Ayla said, "Executor Flamespun shares my vision of a shared future with Nox'Kartha." Ayla pressed her knuckles politely to her lips, though lingered a whisper too long. Her smile showed the barest hint of fangs. "Imperator Makosa, I think I can entice you to see my vision as well. Consider it a courtship of sorts."

And *oh*, Flowridia had always been weak to that predatory grin.

What was a monster without monstrosities?
Someone who sought that impossible redemption, nevertheless.

The End

Etolié and Ilune will return in
Gods of Life and Death.

Join SD Simper's newsletter at www.sdsimper.com to get updates on
the sequel series to FALLEN GODS.

*In the meantime, keep turning pages for a sneak peek into the life
of Doctor Laya Faradelk.*

Dear Reader,

Thank you so much for reading and supporting Fallen Gods. If you've enjoyed *Chaos Undone*, I humbly ask that you leave a short review on Amazon, Goodreads, and wherever else reviews are allowed. Reviews are the best thanks you can give to a book you love, and they help authors out immeasurably.

If you'd like to hear more from me, you can find me on most major social media platforms as @sdsimper, where I often post writing updates and animal pictures. Additionally, you can join my newsletter at sdsimper.com, where I post sales, book recommendations, and other important things.

If you're starving for more Fallen Gods content or would like to read more about Flowridia, Ayla, Etolié, and the rest, I have a whole backlog on my Patreon, which you can join for as little as $2 per month. It's a friendly place, and I'd love the continuing support. You can find the links for all of that on my website or at the QR Code below:

Again, thank you so much for reading. I couldn't be an author if you weren't a reader <3

-SD Simper

Coming December 2024 . . .

The Strange Case of Doctor Laya Faradelk

When Avaril Wrenfern moves to Maagi with his wife and unborn child to become the new administrator at its most prestigious hospital, he's warned about the eccentricities of its greatest asset: the renowned Laya Faradelk, a doctor whose quirks are tolerated in exchange for her unparalleled ability to save lives and bring funding to the hospital. The young interns adore her, the other doctors despise her, but Wrenfern doesn't know what to make of her—that is, until Wrenfern nearly becomes the next victim of a mysterious series of murders Wrenfern walks down the wrong alleyway on the wrong night and is nearly murdered by a vampire, only to be saved by the mysterious doctor herself, who might be some sort of monster herself. His life is spared when he swears not to talk, but he sure does have a whole lot of questions to ask.

Horror and comedy coalesce in this Fallen Gods novella: only on Patreon! Keep reading for an exclusive sneak peek.

The evening air was cool, the sun having already set, and as Wrenfern set out from the hospital, he tried to shove aside the irritating idea that Faradelk had lied to the police. Such an off-putting concept. Surely her theories would be useful to the authorities. What use was there in withholding information about a victim? Not that he could convince her, but the whole situation itched like a bug bite.

The walk home wasn't long, but as he passed his favorite shortcut, deemed dangerous by Rashel, he lingered. His stomach growled; Wrenfern peered around the vacant street then down the dark alley. It was clearly empty, and a ten second walk meant he was five minutes closer to dinner. He stepped inside.

The busy noises of the city at twilight vanished, leaving Wrenfern with only the slight dripping of water from rooftops and a sudden chill on his skin. But he forged onward, committed to this detour. Even with the knowledge that some sort of serial killer might be on the loose, statistically he was more likely to be struck by lightning than become a victim.

Still, when shuffling from behind interrupted his train of thought, Wrenfern's blood ran cold.

He turned, and in the dark shadow stood a man whose eyes gleamed just a hint too bright in the dim lighting. The man observed the scene with odd posture, skulking to press against the wall. The inner voice called 'self-preservation' screamed in Wrenfern's ear, but the compulsion to be polite unfortunately prevented him from darting away. "Good evening—"

The man leapt. Wrenfern shielded his face as the man tackled him to the ground—and found his breath caught at the terrible visage before him. Behind the man's bloodstained lips grew fangs. His eyes were a colorless void of black. Wrenfern fought to shove him off, but the monster pinned him down with unnatural strength, a horrible grimace twisting his lips as he dove for Wrenfern's neck—

Only to be wrenched away by his hair.

Freed of his bonds, Wrenfern scrambled back against the damp stone, only to face his second terror of the night.

Laya Faradelk gripped the man's neck and head in her arms, her visage unmistakable with those bright eyes—which were illuminate, mind you—and said, "How many of you are there?"

The monster fought, yet whatever his unholy strength, it seemed hers outmatched it. When he didn't respond, Faradelk, shoved him to the ground, stone cracking from the force.

Frozen in terror, Wrenfern watched in horror as fangs elongated in Faradelk's mouth, her own pupils matching the monster's. She held him down with her knee to his sternum and hand to his throat. "*Talk*," she spat.

"I-I don't know," the monster said, his voice choked and pathetic. "I only know the one who made me. I don't know her name."

"Where do I find her?"

"I-I don't know."

"Then I'll use your entrails to spell out a warning for her to leave my city." With that, a sickening snap meant the end of the monster, for Faradelk had ripped its head from its body.

Blood sprayed, though not as much as should have, but Wrenfern highly suspected the man was not among the living. Faradelk spat on the prone body as she rose, then froze when she made eye contact with Wrenfern. She looked to the body, then to her bloodstained dress, her fangs still long and sharp. "Oh. It's you."

Meanwhile, Wrenfern's head spun as he tested his limbs. Was he even capable of running? As it was, he was too numb to rise.

Again, Laya looked to the body, which she proceeded to drag against the alley wall. "You'll be keeping this a secret, won't you?"

Wrenfern nodded.

"Because if you don't," she said, offering a hand—which he did manage to grab, and oh *gods* was it cold, "I do know where you live."

"I don't doubt that," he replied, unable to feel his feet despite the aid.

"And it would be just awful if your pregnant wife were to have an accident, like being thrown down the stairs, decapitated, dismembered, and scattered throughout your house."

Breathless, Wrenfern said simply, "I agree."

"And it would be equally terrible if the baby was ripped from her womb and promptly eaten in front of you—by me, of course. I don't generally eat people, so that's something special I'll do for you. But only if you talk."

All Wrenfern could articulate was a pitiful, "*Uh-huh.*"

"Delightful," Laya cooed. She grinned with all the sincerity of a snake. "You have yourself a wonderful night."

Laya Faradelk stepped boldly away, disappearing at the other end of the alley.

To read The Strange Case of Doctor Laya Faradelk (coming December 2024) and so much more, go to www.patreon.com/sdsimper or follow the QR Code below:

Acknowledgements

In January of 2016, I wrote the first words of what would someday be *The Sting of Victory*, a book that was never supposed to be. Through the encouragement of friends, what began as a short story became a novella, a novel, then two, four, and so on. One million words and eight and a half years later, we come to the end of an era.

What does it take to write a one-million-word epic fantasy/horror/romance series?

A whole army of supporters and friends.

There is no end of my gratitude and love to my beloved Kristen, who held my hand and read every word, who saw the potential in a lost and weary author and loved her with all her heart.

All my love and appreciation to Jaylee, the greatest continuity checker to ever exist.

To LaRae and Ronnie, my forever cheerleaders.

To Shannon, who never failed to cure my writer's block.

To Asher and Andi, who always told me what I needed to hear even when it wasn't what I wanted.

To Anna, who never failed to understand the pain of living and writing.

To Jules, who was there when I needed support the most.

To LJ, who powered through even when I killed his favorites and provided invaluable insight.

To Nicki, who helped with healing and creativity.

To Parker, who gave me the courage to try.

To my amazing proofreaders, to every beta reader and every person I ever bounced ideas off of, and to so many others who have helped in small and large ways.

All my love and gratitude to the amazing artists I've worked with over the years, to Holly, Nan, Cynthia, 2, Marshall, Brenna, and so many more.

A special thanks to Jade Merien and Jerah Moss, whose combined expertise created some of the most kickass fantasy covers to ever exist.

Thank you to all my Patreon supports, to everyone on Discord, and to every person who has sent a few (or many) kind words to my inbox.

I would like to send a special thanks to Mulan, Jasmine, Elsa, Phillip, and Shelyn, who collectively did everything in their power to make sure I never finished. Worst coworkers ever. They're lucky they're furry and cute.

Finally, from the bottom of my heart, thank you, reader. Thank you for reading this far and joining me on this journey. Your support is everything.

With endings comes beginnings. I have so many more stories in me to write, and what I've learned though writing Fallen Gods has given me the foundation and hope to keep moving forward. I know I'll have many more thanks to give when the sequel series is done as well.

Much love,
SD Simper

About the Author

SD Simper is a bestselling horror author, award-winner of fantasy romance, and knows that the secret to writing great villains is living with cats. She and her wife share a home with four cats, a Great Dane, and innumerable bookshelves.

Visit her website at sdsimper.com to see her other works, including *The Fate of Stars,* the story of a mermaid, a human princess, and a love that will shape the future of the world.

www.ingramcontent.com/pod-product-compliance
Lightning Source LLC
Chambersburg PA
CBHW031640200726
48289CB00004BA/970